Brother Kings

Book 1

Of The Warrior Series

By

Sandra J Yearman

 **Seraphim Publishing LLC**

We Will Bring Light To All The Dark Places

Registered trademark-Sandra J Yearman

Seraphim Publishing
438 Water St
Cambridge, WI 53523
sandrajyearman@gmail.com.

Library of Congress Catalog Number: 2014913972

ISBN: 978-0-9841506-9-4

First Edition

About The Author

Sandra J Yearman is a native of Wisconsin, where she currently resides. She graduated from the University of Wisconsin with a Bachelor of Arts degree in Journalism. Sandra was a member of the United States Army Reserves for over twenty years. She retired from the Dane County Sheriff's Office in Madison Wisconsin as a sergeant.

Sandra is a cancer survivor. And it is on this journey that she says she found her voice and began to write. She established Seraphim Publishing LLC in 2008. Sandra has spent decades supporting and working with rescued domestic animals.

Books written by Sandra:

Novels

Brother Kings
The Scroll And The Sword
Song Of The Second Son
The Faces Of The Damned
A Single Lion Roars
Stand Before The Children
Tyrants, Dictators And Kings

Poetry

This book is dedicated to warriors,

Those who serve, protect and sacrifice

Because their honor and integrity will
allow nothing else.

And this book is dedicated to the angels
and the extraordinary people

Who supported me during my battle
with cancer

Contents

7

Introduction

This story takes place on the ancient Continent of Opots, one of seven continents in the mythological World of Nunc. The story starts out with the continent divided into twelve kingdoms, later a thirteenth kingdom is established in the Ice Caves of Mordv by refugees from the Kingdoms of Norkv and Xepoltr.

Kingdom of Wetpr—is the largest and richest kingdom in the Continent of Opots. The Sea of Talmont is the western border, the Phonicha Ocean is the northern border, the Kingdoms of Ryed and Stordt make up the southern border and the eastern border is the Kingdom of Lentz. Wetpr is also the home of the outlaw Kozach Tribe. The capital city of Wetpr is Salar.

Kingdom of Lentz –is a middle sized kingdom that is rich in resources. The eastern border is the shore of the Sea of Grevtd; the western border is comprised of the Kingdom of Wetpr which is northwest and the Kingdom of Stordt which is southwest. The northern border of Lentz is the Phonicha Ocean and the southern border is the Kingdom of Zorta. The Kingdom of Lentz is also the home of the fierce Nordes Tribe and the terrorist Valdore Tribe. The capital city of Lentz is Langer.

Kingdom of Stordt—is the second largest kingdom in the Continent of Opots. Its peoples and resources have been ravaged by the ruthless dictator King Roch. This kingdom is landlocked. The Kingdom of Ryed makes up its western border, the Kingdom of Wetpr its northern border, the Kingdoms of Gandt and Puntd comprise the southern border and the Kingdoms of Lentz and Zorta border Stordt to the east. The capital city of Stordt is Taperia.

Kingdom of Ryed—is a medium size kingdom that lies south of Wetpr, west of Stordt and north of the Kingdom of Ogg. The Mountains of Rihlet border Ryed on the west. This is a long and treacherous mountain range that lies east of the Sea of Talmont. This is a dark kingdom that gives sanctuary to all that is evil. The capital city of Ryed is Teivel.

Kingdom of Zorta—is a small kingdom that lies south of Lentz, east of Stordt and north of the Kingdom of Ganz. The eastern border of Zorta is the Sea of Grevtd, which supplies most of the income for this kingdom. The capital city of Zorta is Charlton.

8

Kingdom of Ganz—is a large kingdom that is rich in resources, including diamond mines. It is bordered on the north by the Kingdoms of Stordt and Zorta, on the west by the Kingdom of Puntd and to the south by both the Safer Mountain Range and the Inlet of the Sea of Grevtd. These two natural barriers separate Ganz from the sinister Kingdom of Marba. The shores of the Sea of Grevtd form the eastern boundary of this kingdom. Port Friada is the largest port city in the continent as well as being the capital of Ganz. It is built where the River Toba meets the Inlet of the Sea of Grevtd.

Kingdom of Marba—is a large kingdom that is home to the murderous Huta Tribe. The Hutas worship demons and are on a mission to rid the world of all who are not like them. The Sea of Grevtd borders Marba on the east. The Rosu Mountain Range forms the southern border of this kingdom. The Inlet of Grevtd and the Safer Mountain Range comprise the northern border. To the west of Marba lie the Kingdoms of Norkv and Xepoltr.

In ancient times these two kingdoms were united into one kingdom named Samona. These ancient people built a tremendous wall between Samona and Marba. The wall runs the length of the kingdoms from the Safer Mountain Range to the Rosu Mountains. This wall is named the Wall of Dorath. There is but one secret opening in the wall that is called the Gate of Isula. The capital city of Marba is Safra.

Kingdom of Xepoltr—is the home of the fierce and isolationist Shettee Tribe. Ancient legends say this race was bred of humans and lions to create a race of powerful warriors. This kingdom lies to the west of Marba, to the south of the Kingdom of Norkv and to the east of the Waste Lands of Manod. The Rosu Mountains form the southern border for this small landlocked kingdom. Xepoltr is located in what was once the southern half of the Kingdom of Samona. The capital city is Vamur.

Kingdom of Norkv—once part of the vast Kingdom of Samona until a civil war tore the peoples apart and toppled the ruling government. The northern half of Samona became the Kingdom of Norkv. After decades of fighting the people sought peace in their new kingdom. A large monastery was built at Avaide and became a religious symbol throughout the Continent of Opots. Peoples from every kingdom did pilgrimages to this monastery that was said to have been blessed by The Great Ruler Himself.

Norkv became a kingdom of farmers and tradesmen. Two main groups populated this small kingdom, humans and Rualas. The tribe of Rualas is unique in all of Opots; legends say these people were once bred of humans and eagles. The members of this tribe look like humans but have wings and are renowned for their beauty and strength.

The Kingdom of Norkv is bordered on the east by the Wall of Dorath and the Kingdom of Marba. The northern border of this small kingdom is the Safer Mountain Range. The Waste Lands of Manod create the western border and the Kingdom of Xepoltr lies to the south. The capital city of Norkv is Shone.

The Waste Lands of Manod—a barren desert that is filled with hot tar pits. To add to the treacherous region quicksand pits lie on the western border of this area, near the shores of the Schenomi Sea. Stories say that no man has ever been able to cross this dangerous region. The Waste Lands of Manod lie to the west of Norkv and Xepoltr. The plains of Mirolt border the Waste Lands to the south and separate the Waste Lands from the Rosu Mountains. The Safer Mountain Range borders the Waste Lands to the north and the Schenomi Sea lies to the west.

Kingdom of Ogg—is a fabled kingdom that once existed on land and now exists on the floor of the Schenomi Sea. The capital city of Ogg is Trapolli.

Kingdom of Gant—is a medium size, landlocked kingdom. This kingdom is poor and sparsely populated. The Kingdom of Stordt borders it on both the north and west. The Kingdom of Puntd forms the eastern border and the Safer Mountain Range borders the south of Gandt. The capital city of Gandt is Tria.

Kingdom of Puntd—a large kingdom that is rich in resources. It lies to the east of Gant, to the south of Stordt and to the west of Ganz. The Safer Mountain Range creates the southern border. The renowned monastery at Malga is located on the southeastern border of the kingdom. The capital city of Puntd is Calix.

Kingdom of New Samona—The Sanuri of Tabrul saved the refugees of the Ruala and Shettee tribes from total annihilation at the hands of the racist Hutas. The remnants of these tribes were brought to the Ice Caves of Mordv to heal. As the tribes learned to peacefully coexist and flourish they created the Kingdom of New Samona.

The Ice Caves of Mordv—are located in the Safer Mountain Range, but the only entrance to this spectacular world is hidden in the face of Mount Petrov. This is a world of caves within caves that are as large as cities in the world below. The caves are rich in animal and plant life; that are sustained by the rivers, pools and waterfalls that lie within the mountains themselves. The caves get their name because of giant crystals that flourish through the caves. These crystals provide, light, warmth and healing energies to all who dwell within the caves.

Chapter I
The Wall of Dorath

Archetenus the Brave gave the order to his men to stand fast. Their horses were snorting and agitated. In the gray dawn, an ominous wall rose in the east, illuminated by the rising sun. The massive structure divided the Kingdoms of Xepoltr and Norkv from the Kingdom of Marba. The Wall of Dorath ran north and south. The Kingdom of Marba lay on the eastern side of the wall.

Mist shrouded the wall, giving rise to billows of thick fog. Horses pounded the ground and moved uneasily. Vicious warriors, the men of Taperia fought their way across the Continent of Opots, destroying all who stood in their path. Warriors, such as these, lived for conquest. Their appetite for mortal battle was satisfied only by the taste of blood and the sight of destruction. These were men unaccustomed to fear, yet the sight of this legendary wall filled them with a sense of impending doom.

Archetenus was gripped with overpowering feelings to flee. Later he would remember this moment and regret his decision to move forward. This wall of fear appeared insurmountable. Dark boulders loomed across the horizon. A twenty foot wall of solid stone except for the metal rods inserted at the top. These rods were approximately twelve feet high and spaced at six foot intervals. A severed head was impaled on the top of each rod. The hideous display extended north and south as far as the eye could see.

The heads were in various stages of decay. The hot sun and predators further desecrated the flesh of the would-be invaders. The stench of the rotting flesh overwhelmed the nostrils of the warriors of Taperia. The message of this grizzly sight was accentuated by the littered carcasses at the base of the wall. Bodies were thrown upon bodies supported by the bones of their predecessors.

Directly before the horsemen, the wall displayed its most recent trophies. Eight heads that once belonged to creatures from the Kingdom of Xepoltr were impaled upon rods. Beastlike countenances, large elongated skulls framed by blood soaked curly manes; their bulging eyes and tongues turning black, directly contrasting their once smooth white skin.

The ears had been severed and taken as prizes. These beasts from Xepoltr were feared as warriors. Their tribe was called Shettees. The legends of the Shettees spread throughout the known world. Some say these fierce warriors were half lion and half man. Others say they were deformed by the darkness that once held them captive.

Legends say that the Wall of Dorath was built by the ancients at the time of the Great Separation. There is only one opening in this great wall; and its secret location has all but been forgotten by time. The Kingdom of Norkv lay directly north of Xepoltr, but at the beginning of time, both of these kingdoms were one. It is said that at the time of the Great Separation, intense fear gripped the hearts of all. The kingdoms each feared the other and they all feared the wrath of The Great Ruler. Those who had once looked upon each other as brothers were now enemies.

The inhabitants of great kingdoms rose up against one another. Brother against brother, family against family. For some kingdoms the word 'peace' no longer existed in their vocabulary. Ending centuries of warfare the Hutas, the inhabitants of Marba, conquered the Shettees. After long months of torture at the hands of the Hutas, the Shettees butchered their captors.

The Shettee revolt was led by Neputa, heir to the throne of Xepoltr. Eighteen months he endured the humiliation and torment that the Hutas imposed upon him and his brethren. Retaliation was brutal. Taken by surprise, the Hutas fought savagely, but they had underestimated the Shettee slaves and were not prepared for such a bloody onslaught.

With nothing to lose the Shettees fought their way to freedom, leaving nothing in their wake. Neputa commanded his army of former slaves, westward through the Kingdom of Marba and to the Gate of Isula, the only passage through the great wall. The location of this gate would forever stay in the mind of Neputa; for many of his warriors were killed at this site as the conquering Hutas forced them to enter the Kingdom of Marba.

With the taste of blood and revenge still sweet on his tongue, Neputas' victory turned to sorrow. For no longer did a home exist for them to return to. The Kingdom of Xepoltr had been decimated. Remnants of beautiful cities lay in ruins, their inhabitants tortured and slaughtered.

Vowing to return his kingdom to its former glory, Neputa commanded his army, to search for Shettee survivors. He divided his troops into two groups; one went north through the Kingdom of Norkv and Neputa led the second group west into the Waste Lands of Manod. Long and hard they searched; through the Plaines of Mirolt to the shores of the Schenomi Sea, past the tar pits of Opal, into the mountains of Vandrew and Safer they searched for their own kind.

After the Shettee captives escaped, the Hutas swore to annihilate the Shettee race. Legions of Huta warriors were sent out into the kingdoms to hunt the escapees. The Hutas killed anyone they thought might have helped the Shettees. The Huta race had long thought of itself as the only pure race. They were driven by hatred and madness to eradicate other worlds that they judged were less worthy to survive. The Hutas' views of superiority and merciless cruelty made them a hated race among all the kingdoms; they had no allies in the Continent of Opots.

As the revenge driven Hutas hunted the Shettees; they rode through the other kingdoms without regard of boundaries. The Hutas burned villages and slaughtered hundreds of innocent people; all this they did in the names of hatred and fear.

Rumors spread through the kingdoms that when Xepoltr fell to the Hutas the Shettee women and children were hidden in the monastery at Avaide in the Kingdom of Norkv. This monastery was considered holy ground by all peoples. It was said that The Great Ruler Himself blessed this site. The monastery at Avaide was considered a sanctuary for all who needed help; regardless of race or standing. In all its centuries of existence no army or hoard of invaders had ever dared to desecrate this holy place. The Hutas now rode to Avaide.

Born of Nitreo descendants, Bastra, captain of the second platoon, third division of the Huta Army, was heir to the Caretes fortune. It was tradition for the men of his family to serve in the King's army. Bastra's father had fought in the Great War of the Andeas and made the rank of general. Bastra's brother was already a major, although he was only thirty two years old. Bastra was the only man in his family not to win a great battle.

Bastra was frustrated because he was determined to be promoted to the rank of general, but in order to be promoted he needed an exceptional victory to win the favor of the King. Bastra planned his career carefully, only to find himself stationed at a remote outpost in the kingdom. Bastra had little contact with people of influence out there. And he had to compete for promotion against sixteen other captains at that outpost alone.

Bastra's brother had only been in the army for ten years before he was promoted to a major. Bastra was going on his thirteenth year in military service and felt that he was a much better soldier than his brother. Bastra's desire to surpass his brother's achievements was even stronger than his desire to be promoted.

Bastra was confident that if he was responsible for the deaths of the last of the Shettee children he would be promoted and finally receive the recognition he so desperately craved. He was determined to promote his reputation at all costs; even if it meant killing the priests at Avaide or anyone else who stood in his way.

When Bastra and his troops reached the monastery they found no Shettees and only a handful of priests. Bastra was filled with rage; he could see his promotion slipping away. Bastra ordered his men to torture the priests. After long agonizing hours of torture the priests would not give any information about the Shettee refugees. Bastra ordered the execution of the priests and the destruction of the monastery.

With his dying breath, one of the priests cursed Bastra; a threat Bastra should have taken very seriously. Word of the destruction of the monastery spread quickly through every kingdom, making the Hutas the most despised and hated tribe in all of Opots. For hundreds of years believers from every kingdom would make great pilgrimages to that holy site. They believed the monastery pleased The Great Ruler and all pilgrims would be blessed and healed. Many were the stories of physical and spiritual restoration of visitors to that hallowed place.

Bastra finally received the recognition he so craved. Because of his actions he became one of the most hated men in all of Opots; he was cast out of every village and city. The weight of the Huta Army could not suppress the rage of all peoples towards him.

Some months later, the body of Bastra was found lying on a desolate roadside, surrounded by the paw prints of a great lion. It was said that the lion never tore the flesh of Bastra but Bastra's face was contorted into a mask of such horror, it is believed that he died of fright.

When King Roch, the feared dictator of the Kingdom of Stordt and the leader of the soldiers of Taperia, heard about the destruction of the monastery at Avaide, he was elated. Long had there been stories of great treasures hidden within the monastery, offerings of gold and jewels given to The Great Ruler.

Roch would never have dared to take on the wrath of the entire world by attacking that monastery; he felt fortunate that the Hutas had done that for him. Within hours of hearing the news, Roch sent Archetenus and a company of warriors to find Bastra and his men. Roch wanted any treasures the Hutas may have taken. Roch, himself led the troops that rode south to Avaide.

Tristt the Horrible led the platoon of Shettee warriors that Neputa dispatched to search the northern regions. Weeks they searched in the snow covered Safer Mountain Range. The bitter icy winds tore at their flesh.

Human-like in appearance, they walked upright with powerful bodies. Shettees were faster and stronger than most men, which enhanced the stories that they were descendants of lions. Both men and women wore their hair long and flowing, which gave them the appearance of a lion's mane. But as strong and fierce as this tribe was, the hearts of these warriors were broken because of the uncertainly about the plights of their families.

Tristt mourned the loss of his wife and children. Long had he yearned to see Samara's beautiful face and to hear the gleeful laughter of his three children. Reuniting with them was the hope that kept Tristt alive during the torturous months he was a captive of the Hutas.

Although, Tristt lost his right forearm as punishment for not submitting to his Huta captors, he was still a mighty warrior. Shorter in statue than most, Tristt had incredible strength, far beyond his size. A courageous leader, Tristt was the most decorated of Neputa's colonels.

Samara was the love of Tristt's life. A beautiful female, half his age, Samara brought Tristt utter delight. Cere, their daughter was a mirror image of her mother. Their sons Tabith and Korth favored their father in appearance and in strength. Eighteen months Tristt had been a captive of the Hutas. If his family was alive would he recognize his children? What would his sons be like?

The Kingdom of Stordt lay to the south of the Kingdom of Wetpr. Situated in the center of the continent; it was the second largest kingdom in the Continent of Opots. The capital city of Stordt was Taperia also home to King Roch. Roch's vast army was both feared and hated throughout Opots. Roch lived to conquer and to plunder other lands. He enslaved the peoples of the kingdoms he conquered and ruled through fear and intimidation.

Archetenus was a captain in the Taperian Army. His life had been devoted to the service of his kingdom since Archetenus was taken from his home at the age of six. The Taperian Army routinely took the first born son of each household and raised them to be soldiers. The army was the only life any of these boys would ever know. Archetenus grew to be a favorite among the Royal Family because of his fierce fighting skills in the Gefrey Games. These games were contests of sport, where men and beasts would fight to the death for the amusement of the crowds.

The Royal Family of Taperia would oversee the games and have the final decision as to the life or death of the fighters. Archetenus fought for the victory and the showmanship. He loved to entertain the crowds with feats of strength and savagery. Archetenus was a delight to Queen Vitomas, who asked her husband to promote him to captain of the northern legions of the Taperian Army.

Once promoted to captain, Archetenus ceased fighting in the Gefrey Games. The new position required all of his time and attention. Making the rank of captain at the age of twenty-six was quite a feat. But Archetenus' prestige also made him many enemies among the older army officers. There were few positions for advancement and the officers greedily strategized for each of them. King Roch valued unscrupulous men and encouraged jealousies and resentment between his top officers. Roch demanded complete loyalty of his men; yet Roch truly enjoyed watching his officers compete for his attention and favor.

Archetenus' promotion to captain took many by surprise. Some of the officers felt he had cheated them by taking that position. Although Roch admired many of Archetenus' qualities Roch was jealous of Archetenus' attraction to Queen Vitomas. Roch promoted Archetenus to please Vitomas, all the while knowing that same promotion would be Archetenus' doom.

Eighteen long months of captivity and Tristt still relived that battle; the sounds, the smells, the defeat at the hands of the Hutas. Never did Tristt believe the Shettees would lose that war. Still the anger swelled within him. The anger and the fear; what if the only survivors of their race, were the handful of warriors enslaved by the Hutas; a thought Trist could not bear.

The Hutas had attacked Vamur, the capital city of Xepoltr just before dawn. Under the cloak of darkness the Hutas surrounded the city and killed the sentries. With an army as vast as the horizon, the Hutas launched attack after attack for eleven days and nights.

Neputa ordered six of his bravest warriors to take the women and children out of Vamur which was the last stronghold of the Shettees. The warriors were ordered to take the women and children to Avaide, a holy place in the Kingdom of Norkv. Norkv lay north of Xepoltr and extended to the foot of the Safer Mountain Range.

Thousands of Huta arrows rained upon the Shettee warriors. The heads of the arrows were poisoned with the venom of the atha serpent; a poison that caused an agonizing death.

Vamur was in flames, black smoke filling the air, blinding and choking the warriors. The pounding of the Huta drums shook the earth. Blood ran through the streets as water, during the spring rains. Neputa sounded the Horn of Xepoltr, a signal for his army to fall back, but the sounds of war were deafening and many did not hear the mournful blast. Hutas overran the city and by dawn of the twelfth day the Shettees were defeated.

Archetenus and his men were at the garrison in Taperia when King Roch told him about the massacre at the monastery at Avaide.

"Take fifty of your best men and stop Bastra before they cross through the Gate of Isula," King Roch ordered. "I want you to take every treasure they have stolen from that monastery. Long have I dreamed of raiding that place and I will not let those barbarians deny me of my rightful inheritance."

"Yes My Lord, but they already have several days start on us and we have such a distance to cover, I fear they may reach the Gate well in advance of us," said Archetenus.

"Are you disobeying my orders?" snapped Roch.

"Never My Lord but I know you are a wise general and would never send your troops on a wild chase."

"Bastra and his men are still tracking the Shettee slaves which will deter them from returning to Marba; no matter how laden they are with treasures. I fear that you and your men will have to travel day and night to catch them," said Roch sarcastically.

"Yes My Lord, we will leave at once," replied Archetenus. He bowed before his King and turned to leave the war room.

As Archetenus was walking towards the door, he heard the King yell, "Archetenus do not fail me. If you do not acquire the treasure do not return to Taperia."

Archetenus turned and looked Roch in the eye, a cold stare. "Have I ever failed you My Lord?"

Roch approached Archetenus, both men staring at each other; their eyes betraying the hatred they felt for the other. "Do not let this be the first time; that treasure is mine. My wife cannot help your career anymore," sneered Roch. "You are dismissed."

Archetenus turned and walked out of the war room, he could barely consume his rage. Roch knew Bastra had over two hundred warriors with him; he was sending Archetenus and his men to their death. There were hundreds of miles of treacherous territory between Taperia and the Gate of Isula; it would be a difficult journey through the mountains. Archetenus knew he had to get his men through the Pass of Duvuk before the early snows or they would never get across the Safer Mountain Range.

Archetenus picked fifty of his best soldiers; they traveled light and rode hard for days. They traveled through the Kingdoms of Stordt and Puntd with little rest. As Archetenus and his men entered the northwestern section of the Kingdom of Ganz they stopped at the Village of Danji for fresh horses and supplies. Danji was thirty miles north of the foot of the Safer Mountain Range.

When they rode into Danji, Archetenus and his soldiers saw that many of the homes and stores had been burned; the buildings were in various degrees of destruction. Few people were on the streets. Archetenus saw a boy about thirteen leaning against the side of a building and called to the boy, who approached Archetenus and his men fearfully.

"What happened here?" asked Archetenus.

"The Hutas My Lord, they came in the night; demons they are," cried the boy. "They burned much of the village looking for Shettees. We have never seen any Shettees in our village My Lord but they would not believe us."

"How long ago did this happen?" asked Archetenus.

"Five days, My Lord."

"How many were there?"

"I'm not sure My Lord; they came in the night but there seemed like hundreds."

"Do you know which direction they headed?" asked Archetenus.

"South My Lord," replied the boy.

"My men need food and fresh horses; can you tell me where we can take rest?"

"My Lord, the Hutas stole or killed most of what we had but there is water in the well and you are welcome to take rest here."

Archetenus had his men search the village for any sign of the Hutas. Once Archetenus was satisfied that they had not ridden into an ambush; he told his men to fill their water bags. Several of the terrified villagers gave bread, wine, fruit and cheese to Archetenus and his men.

"We will not take rest in this village tonight, I feel as if we are being watched," Archetenus said to Hermanas, his second in command.

"My Lord there is a small hill overlooking this village to the west; we can make camp there. I agree something is not right here," said Hermanas.

"There are few villagers yet there are no bodies or new graves. They must be in hiding or are they concealing Huta soldiers from us?" Archetenus asked Hermanas quietly.

Hermanas ordered the soldiers to mount their horses and to be alert for Hutas. The men rode out of the village silently without seeing anything out of the ordinary. Archetenus was in the lead. The sun was lowering, casting shadows among the trees and boulders. Suddenly Archetenus saw a movement out of the corner of his left eye. Turning his head, Archetenus saw the grisly remains of the villagers of Danji.

Archetenus stopped his horse and raised his right fist as a signal for his men to come to a halt. To their left was a grove of huge old oak trees. Dozens of bodies were hung from the branches of the trees. Archetenus and Hermanas rode towards the bodies.

"These bodies have been here for days," said Archetenus. "I wonder why the villagers haven't cut them down and buried them."

"Fear," replied Hermanas. "Look at them, they didn't have a chance. They are just famers and peasants, not a soldier among them."

Tristt lay awake. His platoon had taken shelter under the lower outcroppings of the Cliffs of Borck. The wind was howling and driving the icy rain against the side of the boulder wall. Tristt listened to the sounds of the rain beating against the rocks and the fire crackling at their campsite. He was awakened by a dream that haunted him. Tristt had this same dream many times since beginning this journey northward. And never once did Tristt understand its meaning.

In Tristt's dream, huge crystal pillars reached from the heavens to the world below, shining with a radiant white light. The light had the warmth of the sun and a joyous quality. Samara was preparing a meal, in the glow of these crystals. He could hear the squealing of his children as they played. Tristt found that he was comforted by this sight.

But the dream was always interrupted by the appearance of a man. He was human-like in appearance but much taller than other humans Tristt had seen. The man appeared to be made out of crystal and the same warm glow emitted from him as from the crystal pillars. The sudden appearance of the crystal man always ended the dream, as if he was trying to prevent Tristt from seeing anything more.

Tristt felt a sense of hatred whenever the crystal man would appear in his dreams. He felt that the crystal man was trying to keep him from his family. "This icy rain will make it hard to climb tomorrow," Tristt thought. He had already lost two warriors from falls since they entered the high regions of the mountains. They were high in the peaks of the Safer Mountain Range, heading towards the Ice Caves of Mordv.

The Ice Caves were the last trek in Tristts' journey into the northern regions. He hoped the Rualas would be able to help them find the rest of their kind.

Tristt's platoon grew weary with despair for they had not seen any sign of their kinsmen since they regained their freedom. When Tristt's platoon first set out they went to Avaide, the holy place in the Kingdom of Norkv. For, Neputa told them the women and children had been taken there.

When Tristt and his men arrived at Avaide, they found nothing but burned ruins. An elderly priest remembered when the Shettees took refuge in their monastery. Although his memory was fading from age, he recounted many details. He told of a group of Shettee women and children brought to the monastery by six Shettee warriors. The priests gave them shelter for almost eighteen months, until they received word that Huta warriors were riding to the monastery to kill them.

While some of the priests diverted the attention of the Huta warriors, other priests led the Shettee refugees away from the monastery through underground tunnels. The tunnels led to the foot of the Safer Mountain Range. When the Huta warriors realized they had been tricked they killed the priests and burned the monastery.

The only priests who survived the massacre were the ones who had led the Shettee refugees through the tunnels, to safety. This priest said their tribal leaders did not plan to rebuild the monastery, because they wanted the ruins to be a reminder of what happens when hatred is unleashed and unfettered.

The Priest said that he and five other priests had led the refugees through the six tunnels to the northern border of the Kingdom of Norkv. The priests gave the refugees as much food and water as they could carry. The Shettee warriors guided the group towards the Pass of Duvuk, which led north through the Safer Mountain Range.

One of the Taperian scouts had tracked Bastra and his army along the Wall of Dorath within miles of the northern most point of the Kingdom of Xepoltr; then the trail suddenly stopped.

"They must have gone through the Gate of Isula and crossed into the Kingdom of Marba," Archetenus said to his men.

Archetenus commanded his men to split up as they searched for the Gate of Isula. He ordered Hermanas to take half of the soldiers and to retrace their steps by proceeding north along the wall in the Kingdom of Norkv. Archetenus would lead the others southward through the Kingdom of Xepoltr, towards the Highland Pass.

The sun had risen, warming the air and fanning away the fog. Gold and pink rays of light shown upon the grotesque scene before the soldiers, adding a supernatural aspect to the images of death.

The first group to find any sign of Bastra and his men or the Gate of Isula was to sound the Horn of Ire as the signal. The groups separated; each riding towards their destinies, each riding to Motfer, the land of the dead.

Archetenus drove his men southward until the noon sun was high in the sky. He ordered them to camp in the shade of a huge boulder. They would continue their journey in the cool of the evening. Archetenus dispatched a scout to ride ahead and to locate the Highland Pass. This was the only passage through the Rosu Mountains. This would be the last order Archetenus would ever give this soldier. The scout rode southward towards the passage.

Archetenus stood watch over the River Kya. He couldn't shake the growing feeling of uneasiness that was consuming him. Never had he felt such a way before, not even in the Gefrey Games when he had to fight a giant Tervator. Over fourteen feet tall, that creature dwarfed him in both size and strength. But Archetenus had the advantage in speed and skill. The fight was short and bloody and ended with Archetenus cutting off the creature's head and presenting it to King Roch.

The King was very pleased but it was the look on the Queen's face that Archetenus would always remember. Queen Vitomas had tears running down her cheeks and a look of genuine fear on her face. Archetenus remembered gazing into her beautiful green eyes and feeling as if he just conquered the world.

Archetenus thought of Vitomas often, she was always in his dreams. He started watching her after the first time he laid eyes on her at the Gefrey Games.

Archetenus still remembered what Vitomas wore that first day, a shawl which covered her hair and her body. The shawl was the color of a robin's egg and laid beautifully over her purple dress. From that day, Archetenus became obsessed with Vitomas. He followed Vitomas when she went riding and watched her when she was in the castle gardens. Sometimes Archetenus would watch Vitomas and Roch through their bedroom window.

Raised as a boy in Roch's army; Archetenus grew into a powerful warrior. He carried out the orders of the King without question, no matter how sadistic they were. But after the first time Archetenus saw Vitomas, he realized his love for her. Soon hatred for Roch filled Archetenus' being. Archetenus would plan ways in which he could kill Roch and take Vitomas for himself.

Many times during this journey, Archetenus wondered why King Roch had sent him on this long and seemingly suicidal mission. The King was not an ignorant man; perhaps he suspected Archetenus' adoration for the Queen. But at the same time, Archetenus had known the King his entire life and knew that if Roch perceived him as an enemy that Roch would want the pleasure of killing Archetenus himself.

The Safer Mountain Range was a dangerous realm not only because of the natural hardships but Trist had heard that these mountains were thought to be the home of the Rualas, a tribe of notorious fame. The Rualas lived in the Ice Caves of Mordv and were believed to possess supernatural powers. They were an ancient race, rumored to have been bred of men and eagles.

Rualas appeared to be human, but for the giant wings that protruded from their backs. They were considerably taller than most people in the world below and they were a race of exceptional beauty. Stories told of humans who had been placed in states of awe by the pure beauty of a Ruala warrior. In this tribe both the men and the women were now trained as warriors.

Legend tells of a time when the Rualas lived in peace with all other kingdoms in the world below. They were a tribe of hunters and farmers, ill prepared for the vicious acts of genocide committed against them by the xenophobic Hutas. The Sanuri of Tabrul, a powerful healer and benevolent being took pity on the tribe of the Rualas.

The Sanuri felt the Rualas had suffered greatly at the hands of the Hutas and he feared the Hutas' cruelty and hatred would not stop until they had exterminated the Ruala race. The Sanuri brought the survivors of the persecutions to the Ice Caves of Mordv, in the Safer Mountain Range. These caves ran throughout the entire mountain range and possessed a beauty not known to the world below. Many of the caves were large enough to hold entire cities.

The caves got their names from the giant crystals that grew inside. These crystals that were formed from the frozen ash of Mount Petrov grew from the floors of the caverns and extended to the tops of the mountains. The crystals not only provided light and warmth to the caves but they were filled with healing, spiritual life force; a blessing from The Great Ruler Himself.

Tristt and his platoon were almost drowned by flood waters in the Pass of Duvuk. The spring thaws caused severe flooding every year. He had directed his soldiers to climb above the flood waters and head upwards towards the highest of the Cliffs of Borck. The cliffs offered shelter for his cold and weary troops. The higher they climbed, the colder the wind blew.

Tristt and his men found shelter in the cliffs just as the icy rain started to fall again. The rain was freezing onto the rocky surfaces, encasing them under a layer of ice. Fortunately the Shettees were able to gather some dry wood and dried plants; that had been sheltered from the rain. Tristt and his men knew a night without a fire would be deadly to them all.

Sheltered from the wind and rain, the Shettees built their fire and ate what remained of their matu potage and opatu bread. These food staples of this tribe, had solely sustained this platoon for several weeks. But now the rations were declining and Tristt was worried. In this cold and barren northern region, the Shettees had little success finding fresh meat. Few plants or berries survived in the higher places of the mountains. Tristt knew they had to find food soon.

Archetenus and his men reached the southernmost point of the Wall of Dorath, where it butted up against the Rosu Mountain Range. They had not seen any sign of Bastra and his men, nor had they found the Gate of Isula to give them entry into the Kingdom of Marba. Archetenus' men were exhausted and needed rest.

Camp was made in the shelter of huge trees that lined the River Kya. It had been five days since Archetenus' troops split up. Archetenus had not heard Hermanas sound the Horn of Ire. If Hermanas and his men were still alive they had not found the Hutas they pursued or the Gate of Isula.

As his men took rest, Archetenus was troubled, thinking about this new land they had entered. He was not a fearful man but a prevailing sense of evil filled this place. Archetenus knew he was not the only one who felt it, for his men seemed just as unsettled as he was. Archetenus could not understand why they had not encountered any Hutas or any living creatures of any kind since they found the Wall of Dorath. "It is as if death permeates this place," thought Archetenus because they had not heard the sounds of birds or even insects for many days.

The trail of Bastra's men had been easy to follow for the trained Taperian scouts; until they reached the middle of the Wall of Dorath. "It's as if Bastra's army simply disappeared," thought Archetenus. "What evil is hiding these Hutas?"

King Roch's words rang in Archetenus' mind, "If you do not find the treasure do not return to Taperia." Archetenus thought of his men, many of them had families in the Kingdom of Stordt. As much as he hated King Roch, Archetenus did not want to be cast out of his homeland. He and his men would turn around tomorrow and head north to search the wall again.

Archetenus watched his men as they ate the last of their dried meat. Tomorrow he would also have to send warriors on a hunt. They had not seen any signs of animals for days and they were unable to catch fish in the river. Archetenus' men kept saying the wall was cursed with black magics. Archetenus did not believe in magic but he could see that his men were becoming weakened by hunger and exhaustion.

Later that night as Archetenus tried to sleep, the memories of his mother crying as the soldiers took him away, filled Archetenus' mind. His mother had run after them screaming until she fell down onto the road. Archetenus never had a chance to say goodbye to his father, who was cutting wood when the soldiers came.

Archetenus remembered having a toy wagon his father had made for him. Many years after Archetenus had grown into a young man he was allowed to return home to the City of Nora to visit his family. But Archetenus found his home burned to the ground without any sign of his parents. Archetenus could not find one person in the city who remembered his family or him.

Demons of the wind inhabited the mountains. They were said to be even more fierce and ruthless than the mountain demons. Tristt worried that the women and children could not have survived among so much evil. He did not voice his concerns to the troops but he knew it weighted heavily on their minds also.

The cold wind roared through the cliffs like a hungry lion on the hunt. The harsh conditions of the northern region would have made survival difficult for the refugees, especially the small children. Tristt's thoughts wandered to his own children; how he longed to see their faces again. Suddenly a deafening roar was heard from above the cliffs. A sound louder than anything Tristt had ever heard before. The entire platoon was on their feet ready to fight the unseen intruder.

The ground shook ferociously and rocks started falling down the mountainside. Darkness cloaked the Shettees, preventing them from seeing their foe. The sound of boulders crashing into boulders horrified the troops. They were torn between leaving their shelter in the cliffs and taking a chance of becoming trapped. Just as Tristt was about to command his troops to leave the cavern, the stone ceiling overhead collapsed on them. Tons of rocks buried the Shettee warriors.

Archetenus and his troops were traveling northward. Before they left camp, Archetenus had sent a hunting party of three soldiers westward in search of fresh meat. The hunters had orders to rejoin the group by night fall.

Archetenus thought he and his men must have missed some sign of the Gate of Isula when they traveled southward. As they retraced their steps northward, Archetenus had several soldiers walk next to the wall, even though this meant walking over remnants of bodies. He ordered his men to inspect the wall closely for any disguised portion of the gate. The troops talked among themselves of a great magic that hid the gate from them. Normally Archetenus would ridicule talk of magic; but in this time and in this place he wondered if such a thing could exist.

Queen Vitomas was over twenty years younger than King Roch and of exceptional beauty. She had long reddish blonde curly hair which flowed down her back; Vitomas often braided strands of pearls into her hair. Her slender build, green eyes and dimples brought her much attention. As she grew Vitomas realized that it was probably her physical beauty that had allowed her to live; as so many of Roch's other women were not as fortunate.

When Vitomas was but nine; Roch and his men ravaged her Village of Tadon, burning the monastery and murdering the priests before the eyes of the horrified villagers. Roch grabbed Vitomas from the arms of her terrified mother and took Vitomas for his wife. Three golden coins he threw at her mother's feet. Three golden coins is what he paid for the child.

King Roch inherited the throne of Taperia when he was just sixteen years old. He murdered his parents for the power of being king. A strong willed boy, he grew into an iron willed dictator of his people. Roch killed all who stood in the way of what he wanted.

But Roch's reign of terror was tempered as he grew to love Vitomas. She worked very hard to keep him happy, knowing the cruelty of his rage. As Vitomas grew into a young woman, Roch had gardens built at the castle for her pleasure. Roch loved to display his beautiful wife and gave to her the finest clothes and jewels. But as with everything in Roch's life; this generosity was more of a show of his power and wealth than of his feelings for his Queen. Vitomas cared little for the extravagant gifts; she would have eagerly traded all the riches for a life free of terror and pain.

By no means was Vitomas the only woman in Roch's life. Routinely he would have his men bring him girls and young women from the villages and cities. Their screams of terror and pain would fill the castle as Roch and sometimes his men tortured and raped them.

Shortly after Roch brought Vitomas to the castle; he abducted another little girl. Annabelle was the child of the former servants to Roch's parents. Annabelle was a beautiful girl, with long dark curly hair and large brown eyes; she was the same age as Vitomas.

Annabelle was to be a companion and servant to Vitomas but the two terrified little girls grew to be as close as sisters. Vitomas would often hide Annabelle when Roch was drunk so she would not become another of his victims. Annabelle would care for Vitomas and treat the many wounds inflicted upon her by Roch. These two little girls helped each other survive the horrors of their lives.

For the first years of her life Vitomas was never allowed to leave the castle. As she grew Roch would allow her to ride on the castle grounds and to take small shopping trips into the City of Taperia and the neighboring Village of Cana. Twice Vitomas had tried to escape from Roch. Both times his men caught her and she was punished severely. Roch took great pride in knowing what his victims feared most.

Vitomas was not allowed to speak to men other than the servants and the guards. The only events that Roch would take Vitomas to were the Gefrey Games which were violent battles between men and sometimes monsters. At these events Vitomas would sit at the right hand of Roch in the royal seats in the stadium.

Vitomas loved to watch the people and to feel the excitement but abhorred the violence. Many times she would close her eyes and pretend to watch the games. Roch wanted Vitomas at his side and she would do anything to please him, so Vitomas never told Roch how much the games disturbed and disgusted her.

At the age of fourteen Vitomas witnessed Roch's men beating a man and dragging him to the dungeons under the castle. The man's clothes were mere rags and he was crying and pleading for his life.

Vitomas' heart was touched by this man; she called to the soldiers to stop. Although the soldiers heard her calling, they would not look at her, nor did they stop. They dragged the man until she could no longer see or hear them.

Vitomas was sobbing when she found Roch in his war room, she told him of what she had seen and questioned him about the man. Roch was not happy that she had seen this peasant arrested by his soldiers and he did not want her questioning his authority. Finally to stop Vitomas from crying, Roch told her he would have the peasant freed. Vitomas was overjoyed and threw her arms around Roch's neck, kissing him with gratitude.

The next morning Vitomas heard that the peasant had been freed and that his family had been given money to buy food. Word spread among the people that Queen Vitomas had saved the peasant from certain death; soon she was considered the patron of the people of Taperia.

Over the next couple of years, Queen Vitomas would try to use her influence to help the peoples of Taperia and Cana. Annabelle and other servants warned her about the danger in helping the peasants. But Vitomas had so long ago lost all hope for herself; that these sporadic acts of helping others brought her a sense of value.

It was late into the night and the hunters had not returned. Archetenus and his men were hungry and tired. He doubled the guard around the camp. They would all be glad to return home after this mission. The morning light did not bring any sign of the hunters. The troops were rationing their food. They proceeded northward.

Three torturous days they traveled northward in the scorching sun. The decomposing body parts displayed on the wall and near it filled their nostrils and sickened their stomachs. The hunters still had not rejoined their group, neither had the scout that Archetenus sent out days earlier. The night of the third day was approaching. Archetenus was about to tell his men to set up camp, when one of the warriors yelled with horror. As Archetenus looked at the wall he realized the heads that were impaled on the spikes where those of Hermanas and his men.

Chapter II
The Children of Xepoltr

After many days and nights of travelling in the long tunnels that extended northward from the monastery at Avaide the Shettee refugees came out at the foot of the Safer Mountain Range. Fresh air and the warmth of the sun on their faces was a short lived luxury. Six Shettee warriors had to protect and relocate one hundred and twenty-two women and one hundred and forty-six children. The remnants of a once powerful kingdom. The enormity of their task weighted upon these warriors.

Before them loomed the Safer Mountain Range, a dangerous and difficult journey. They could not turn back because the Huta warriors were behind them. If they traveled east they would be in the Kingdom of Marba, which would mean certain death, as it was the homeland of the Hutas. To the west lay the Waste Lands of Manod. It was rumored, that no one ever returned from the Waste Lands. They had little choice but to move northward.

The six Shettee warriors were fearful; not for themselves but for the children, how would the children survive the arduous journey. The warriors talked in low whispers, concealing their conversations from the women and children. None of the warriors had ever been this far into the northern region. They had no maps or information about what lay ahead. The warriors had heard stories about demons that lived in the mountains and killed all who entered their lands.

Night was falling on the refugee camp. Children were crying while their mothers prepared the food. Long accustomed to the hardships of the land, these weary mothers cared for their children with love and patience. Thankful to be alive and to have their children with them, the women gladly performed their tasks. Scared of what the future might hold, the refugees cherished the peace of the evening. The warmth of the fires gave a sense of wellbeing to the group.

The Shettee warriors did not share in this false sense of security. They were planning the journey through the mountains and judging the strength of the group.

Though the concerns of the warriors were focused on what lay on the other side of the mountains, their talk centered on the journey itself. Realistically the warriors knew they could be planning a death march for perhaps the last of their kind.

Many of the children would have to be carried. The women were already carrying the food and water. The Shettee warriors had to scout the trail and fight any attackers so they could not be burdened with carrying the supplies. The Huta warriors were searching for them, so time could not be wasted. Night would soon be upon this band of refugees and they would have to extinguish the fires before the flames illuminated the darkness.

Archetenus and his men stared in horror at the sight of the mutilated bodies of their comrades displayed on the Wall of Dorath. Archetenus ordered three of his scouts to search for any sign of a trail of the attackers. He ordered a detail of men to bury the remains of Hernamas and his men; the rest of the army was to stand guard. The men worked quickly as they all wanted to leave the god forsaken place.

Paulas, the sergeant in charge of the detail that was burying the bodies, pulled Archetenus aside from the rest of the troops. Paulas reported that although the bodies of Hernamas and his troops were all accounted for, each body was missing the right forearm which bore a tattoo of the crest of the Royal Family of Taperia under the leather bracer.

"What do you make of such deviltry?" asked Paulas.

"This is a cursed place," replied Archetenus. "There is some evil here which stalks us. Prepare the men to move. I do not want to spend the night in such an open area." As Paulas and Archetenus were talking the scouts returned, "My Captain, we looked to the north, the west and the south and there is no sign of man or beast," replied one of the soldiers.

"How can this be?" asked Paulas.

"It is as if a demon attacked from the sky," said the second soldier.

"Or escaped through the Gate of Isula," said Archetenus. "Paulas it must be near; have your men carefully search this area, perhaps the gate is actually a tunnel."

Born into a wealthy family, Raul never experienced many of the hardships and sorrows of life. He was the only son born to Sudfad, King of Wetpr; the largest and wealthiest kingdom in the Continent of Opots. Raul was well educated; being taught by the best scholars in his kingdom. He was also a mighty warrior and a general in his father's army.

But Raul had a wild and adventurous side. After years of reading about other cultures and peoples Raul desired to travel to other lands. On his eighteenth birthday Raul left his kingdom to explore the continent. Against his father's wishes, Raul traveled alone.

Never being pretentious, Raul enjoyed being treated as an ordinary man and not as royalty. He dressed modestly and never told anyone his true identity as he traveled through the kingdoms. Raul knew the time would come when he would have to assume the responsibilities of being a king but before that time came he wanted to explore the world. Raul desired his freedom and adventure above anything else. He wanted to see the world as a free man; not as the heir to a throne.

The thick night air was heavy with moisture. Ground fog was billowing over the refugees as they lay sleeping. A lone Shettee warrior stood watch. Although exhaustion overtook most of the group of refugees, signs of restlessness were visible among the troubled protectors. Every two hours they changed the guard of the group.

Patrolling the perimeter of the refugee camp, Thedes a fierce and powerful Shettee warrior knelt down to examine some strange footprints in the soft ground. He heard the sound of wings flapping in the night air. Thedes' thoughts went to stories he had heard about the Rualas. The Rualas were thought to be a race of men with the wings of eagles.

But Thedes had never known anyone who had actually seen a Ruala, so he did not give much credence to the stories. Thedes was starting to stand up when suddenly the sound of roaring wind engulfed his being, as he heard the sound of hundreds of giant wings beating against the night air.

Before Thedes could move he was encircled by two giant wings and a hand was placed over his mouth. Thedes heard a soothing female voice whisper into his ear. The voice told him not to be afraid, that the Sanuri of Tabrul had sent them to help his kind. The woman continued speaking, never raising her voice above a whisper. She said the Sanuri had been watching the destruction of the Shettee race with great sadness in his heart and he had taken pity upon them.

"The Huta warriors have killed the priests of Avaide, only those who helped you escape survived the massacre," said the woman. "They are riding towards your camp now and will be here before morning light. The Hutas have sworn to destroy your entire race," she continued. "The Sanuri sent us to take you to safety."

The woman asked Thedes not to try to escape and removed her hand from his mouth simultaneously opening her wings to free him. Thedes stood up and turned to face his captor. To his utter amazement he saw the most beautiful human woman he had ever seen. She had long flowing, curly blonde hair that shined in the moonlight. She wore a dress of white with a belt made of spun gold and golden sandals. Behind each arm a huge white wing protruded from her body. Each wing was about eight feet long with tips of gold. An intoxicating smell engulfed her as if she herself was a flower.

Thedes was speechless for a moment, when he did speak all he could ask was "Why?" The female laughed and asked "What do you mean?"

Thedes asked "Why would the Sanuri send you to help us?"

"The Sanuri of Tabrul loves all creatures. He took pity on my race and saved us from destruction. He will save your race also, if you let him. We must hurry the Hutas are close at hand. Will you let us help you?"

"Follow me," Thedes said. "We must wake the others." He turned and walked towards the group of sleeping refugees.

35

Thedes woke the other Shettee warriors; who were amazed to see this beautiful winged woman with him.

Before Thedes could say anything, the woman spoke "I am Ibula of the tribe of the Rualas. Many of my tribe were sent here by the Sanuri of Tabrul to help you escape from the Hutas."

"The Hutas butchered the priests of Avaide and will be in your camp in less than two hours. We must move quickly."

Potomas spoke first "How do you plan to help us?"

"We are over three hundred strong and will fly you to our home. We live in the Ice Caves of Mordv," replied Ibula. "You will be safe there."

"Where is your army?" asked Thedes.

"Surrounding your camp," said Ibula and with a wave of her hand hundreds of Ruala warriors stepped closer to the camp; the moonlight glistening off their white wings and illuminating their bodies.

The Ruala army consisted of both men and women. All of whom, were dressed in white clothing with golden belts and golden sandals. Each had a sword sheathed to their side and a bow and quiver of arrows on their back. The sight of the Ruala army brought both a sense of relief and fear to the Shettee warriors. According to Ibula, each Ruala soldier planned to carry a Shettee in their arms as they flew to the Ice Caves. "The children, yes," exclaimed Potomas, "But how can you carry each of us?"

"My people are very strong," explained Ibula, "Do not fear my friend; we will get everyone out of here."

The Shettee warriors woke all of the women and children and explained that the Rualas were going to fly them to safety. The entire camp was evacuated in less than two hours. The Shettee warriors were the last to leave the campsite. As they were ascending into the night, sounds of horse hoofs could be heard in the distance.

After leaving his father's home, Raul decided to start his journey by riding southward. His people knew little of the lands that lay beyond their kingdom. Raul decided to explore the unknown and document what he saw so he could bring the wonders back to his people.

Raul was considered an exceptionally handsome man in his kingdom. Tall and muscular, his young body was filled with vitality and strength. His long dark hair hung to his shoulders. His hair was black as a crow, thick and straight. His eyes were an aqua blue. His skin was bronzed by the sun.

Many nobles wanted Raul to marry their daughters and many daughters wanted his attention. But Raul's heart had not been taken and he promised himself he would not marry for money or for land. Southward Raul rode towards adventure, never expecting how drastically his life would change.

The cool night air took Thedes' breath away as he flew to the Ice Caves. It was an exhilarating feeling to fly through the air but Thedes also felt fear, although he would not admit it. Ibula carried him with apparent ease, even though she was considerably smaller in statue than he was. Thedes was thankful for the arrival of the Rualas but he was worried that they were taking them to a refuge with no escape. Thedes had never heard of the Sanuri of Tabrul and questioned why this man would help his people.

The peaks of the mountains were becoming visible in the light of the sunrise. The sight of three hundred Ruala warriors in the sky looked like swarms of great birds. Thedes had never seen such a sight nor would he ever forget this moment. He estimated they were several hundred feet in the air. The rising sun warmed them with its rays.

"We will be at the Ice Caves soon," said Ibula. "The Sanuri of Tabrul hid the entrance to the caves to all but the Rualas and those with blessed sight. The Hutas will not find you there."

"How will we enter?"

"The Sanuri will assist you."

Archetenus watched as his men searched the area near the great wall. They held torches to illuminate the wall as they were moving piles of decomposing bodies to search the ground and the base of the wall. The men searched for hours without success.

Archetenus ordered his weary troops to mount their horses. "We will find no rest in this cursed place tonight," said Archetenus as he led his men northward. They traveled for several hours before Archetenus told his men to take rest. As Archetenus sat near the camp fire he thought about King Roch; never had Archetenus failed him before.

Archetenus knew the King's wrath would be terrifying; perhaps even cost him his life. It was not death that Archetenus feared, it was losing Vitomas.

Archetenus' heart knew Vitomas must feel love for him although the two of them had never been alone to talk about their feelings. "Perhaps I should leave the army," thought Archetenus. "I could take Vitomas far away and we could make a new life." Archetenus had gathered great wealth as a captain for Taperia; he could give her a good life, although not to the style she was accustomed to with King Roch.

Archetenus had doubled the guard around their camp, as weary as his men were; their sleep was restless and disturbed. That night Archetenus had a dream that would change his life. There was a woman in his dream but she did not look like a human woman, perhaps she was a spirit or an Angel. She warned him to leave this place and not to return to the Kingdom of Stordt. The woman said that King Roch had sent him on this mission to be killed, and if he returned, Roch would find another way to kill him.

The woman told Archetenus he had many choices in his life and to make them with care, as each would take him down a very different path. She told him he teetered on the brink of a great abyss and that if he went into the abyss his soul would be damned for eternity.

In the dream Archetenus kept asking the woman to explain what she was saying. She called him closer to the abyss, when he looked into the great darkness Archetenus felt as if he was burning alive. Archetenus heard terrified screaming. He didn't know if it came from the abyss or his own voice; as Archetenus awoke he realized it came from his men.

The sun had risen when the Ruala army reached the Ice Caves. Thedes watched with wonder as the Rualas appeared to fly into the side of a mountain and disappear. There were no openings to be seen to the outside world. Thedes clung to Ibula as she flew towards the mountain wall, which they passed through with ease.

"That was amazing," said a stunned Thedes.

"My people have been very blessed by The Great Ruler; our enemies cannot enter the caves," said Ibula. "We have a sanctuary as long as we choose to live here."

Unlike their names suggested, the Ice Caves were warm and comfortable. They were filled with lush forests and beautiful vegetation. There were waterfalls and pools. Fresh water from the caves flowed to Lake Manrt in the world below. Animals, birds, fish and insects of many species dwelled in these caves.

Huge crystal pillars originated in the bowels of the Ice Caves and protruded upwards, through the tops of the stone ceilings. They extended their forms to the heavens. Each pillar measured about thirty-five feet in diameter at the base and got bigger as it extended upwards. Some pillars measured as much as fifty feet in diameter at their top. Thousands of pillars were located throughout the Ice Caves, each radiating healing light and warmth.

There were over one hundred caves all connected by a series of tunnels in the Safer Mountain Range. The caves varied greatly in size. Legends say the tunnels were made by the ancient Prostra Tribe. The history of this tribe was recorded on the walls of the Ice Caves with pictures and symbols.

After the Great Separation, the Prostras fled to the mountains. They were a fearful people who chose to isolate themselves from other tribes but they grew increasingly paranoid as a result of their isolation.

After centuries of inbreeding and seclusion, the Prostras did what no invading tribe could do; they destroyed themselves. The paintings on the walls of the caves showed the Prostras killing their own families and neighbors as they fought over food and possessions. It was greed and jealousy that killed the race off; for the Ice Caves provided enough food to sustain them for centuries.

The cave paintings showed Prostras whose madness drove them to butcher and to hurl their young off the mountain tops. Their race vanished hundreds of years before the Rualas inhabited the Ice Caves.

Archetenus tried to jump up but something knocked him back down onto his back. He suddenly felt a crushing pressure on his chest; that took his breath away. As Archetenus gasped for air, he could hear the sounds of battle all around him but he could not see. Archetenus' sight was blocked by whatever was pinning him to the ground. Suddenly the monster shifted its weight and Archetenus could breathe again. Now to his horror Archetenus realized a large talon was holding him to the ground.

Archetenus freed his right arm and was frantically clawing at the ground trying to find his sword. The creature started to bellow and Archetenus could feel the vibrations through his body. Suddenly the great beast lowered its head and Archetenus found himself staring into the eyes of pure evil. The creature resembled a giant red serpent but it had enormous wings and talons like an eagle.

Struggle as he might, Archetenus could barely move under the weight of the creature's huge foot. As the beast was lowering its head towards him; Archetenus pulled a dagger out of his belt with his left hand and stabbed the creature repeatedly in the back of the leg that held him down. The creature screamed in pain and lifted its leg, allowing Archetenus to roll from under the creature's weight. Archetenus normally slept with his sword lying next to him; as he rolled twice to the left Archetenus grabbed his sword and stood up. He now faced the beast that had held him captive.

As the creature lunged at Archetenus, he stabbed it in the chest with his sword. Archetenus withdrew his sword and quickly moved to the right. Archetenus did a forward roll which brought him near the tip of one of the creature's wing that was resting on the ground. Archetenus brought the blade of the sword down in a slicing motion; with all his weight behind the swing Archetenus was able to cut off the end of the creature's wing. The beast screamed from pain and rage and lashed at Archetenus; attempting to bite him.

Archetenus had developed great skill and speed in the Gefrey Games; this was not the first monster he had fought. The creature lunged at Archetenus again and again and each time Archetenus was able to escape its huge teeth. Archetenus stabbed the creature several more times. The ground beneath them was slippery from the creature's blood. The creature lunged forward. Archetenus rolled underneath the creature then jumped up and lodged his sword into the creature's throat.

Archetenus jumped clear of the creature as it started to collapse, his sword remaining in its throat. The monster fell to the ground but it was still alive. Seeing no other weapons in sight, Archetenus ran up to the beast and grabbed his sword from its throat. Archetenus ran to the head of the creature and with all his strength he thrust the sword through one of the creature's eyes and into its brain.

Archetenus pulled his sword out of the creature and backed away from it. He was trying to catch his breath and to survey the scene before him. In the morning light Archetenus saw bodies littering the ground; bodies of his soldiers as well as several of the creatures. Archetenus ran towards his men.

Archetenus gathered all the surviving soldiers from battle. There was not a man among them, including Archetenus who did not have injuries. Archetenus was sure some of his ribs were broken and he had puncture wounds in his side from the claws of the creature. The exhausted men bandaged each other as they could. Archetenus and two of his soldiers walked through the battlefield again, they counted four dead creatures. All the creatures were similar in appearance.

"What are they?" asked Travor, a soldier seasoned in the art of battle.

"I don't know, I have never seen such monsters as these," replied Archetenus. "But I fear there is more evil here than these beasts."

"What do you mean, My Captain?" Travor asked.

"Look at them," said Archetenus as he pointed to one of the creatures. "They certainly could have killed Hermanas and his men but they could not have cut off their heads and impaled them on that wall. More devils walk this land than these monsters," Archetenus said and turned and looked at the wounded men in camp, "How many of us are left?" he asked.

"There are seventeen including us but Zorda and Compro will never make the journey home," replied Travor.

"There is not enough strength among us all to bury the dead," said Archetenus.

"We will leave them?" Travor asked with surprise.

"Yes, and we must find a safe place for our men to rest and to get some nourishment," said Archetenus. "The Village of Ort is a three day ride, we will head there and may the gods be with us."

The first night in the Ice Caves, the Rualas held a great feast for the Shettees in the Hall of Light. Food and drink of great varieties were served. The Shettee women marveled over these new foods and fed them to their children. The Shettee warriors, seated at the long tables listened to the music and speeches with suspicion. Ibula turned to Thedes, who was seated at her right. "What troubles your heart my friend?" she asked.

Thedes stared at Ibula for several moments. He was searching her face for any sign of the danger he and the other Shettee warriors anticipated. Finally Thedes replied, "I still do not understand why your people helped us and what you hope to gain by this gesture."

The warmth of Ibula's voice was a counterbalance to Thedes' cold demeanor. "I told you the Sanuri sent us; how else would we have known of your plight and where to find you?"

Thedes' eyes grew wide as he listened to her words. He had been so concerned that his people would be at the mercy of the Rualas that he did not question how the Rualas found them and knew of their situation.

"Your problem Thedes is that you see enemies everywhere; you cannot recognize a friend in front of you," Ibula scolded.

"Perhaps you are right," Thedes said. "But my people have been all but destroyed. We no longer have a home; and these children you see running in this room are the last our race. My men and I will protect them with our lives."

"I would expect nothing less," said Ibula. "But, do you not understand that the Sanuri told us to bring you here, so your people would be safe. You have a home now, if you choose to stay here. There is more than enough room in the caves for both of our peoples."

"Centuries ago our race was also on the verge of annihilation, by the same enemy that is destroying your people," continued Ibula. "Our homes were destroyed, and our lands taken, we were not trained as warriors then. Our numbers were few when The Great Ruler sent the Sanuri to our aid. He stopped the Hutas' attack and brought us to these caves. Here we were healed, here we are protected."

"I do not know of your Great Ruler or the Sanuri. For what purpose did they help you and what do they expect from us in return for their help?" Thedes asked suspiciously.

Ibula smiled and touched Thedes hand, "You have much to learn. The Great Ruler created this world and we are all His children, He cares for us. He does not expect anything in return for saving your people. And the Sanuri; he is a man but not like other men. You will have to meet him to understand what I am trying to tell you."

"Is The Great Ruler your god?" asked Thedes.

"Yes."

"And the Sanuri is a god also?"

"No, I told you he is a man," said Ibula.

"I still do not understand what makes him different?"

"Some of my people think the Sanuri is from an ancient race of people who were closer to The Great Ruler. He is very old yet you would not know it to see him. He is a great warrior; he is like a father to us. He can talk with animals, I have seen this myself. The Sanuri travels always, going where he is needed."

"He sees and knows things that other men do not; some say The Great Ruler Himself speaks to the Sanuri."

"Does he practice magic?"

"No, I don't think it is magic but he can do great things," said Ibula. "He stopped the Hutas from attacking us, he scared them away."

Thedes looked at Ibula with doubt in his eyes and asked, "How did one man scare Huta warriors?"

"We were few and with many wounded. We used to live in the Kingdom of Norkv. We were farmers and no match for trained soldiers. The Hutas burned our villages and farms and were killing us all, even the children."

"In our attempts to flee the Hutas we entered the Waste Lands of Manod. There was no water or trees to provide shade. We were seeking refuge in the Hills of Thermant, when our camp was surrounded by Hutas. We cried out to The Great Ruler to save us and He must have heard our pleas. Suddenly a fierce storm was upon us."

"The sky became black and there was great lightening and wind. Because of the darkness we were able to leave our campsite and hide in a cavern," Ibula continued. "One of the children screamed and pointed at a man who simply appeared in the middle of the cavern. He was a tall man in a light blue robe, with a dark beard. His voice was very calming as he told us not to be afraid, that he had been sent to help us. Then he walked out of the cavern."

"You were there?"

"No, this was long before I was born but this is our history; all of our children are taught about this," said Ibula.

44

"The Sanuri was gone for several hours; he returned to the cavern just as the storm ended. He told us the Huta army was gone and it was safe for us to leave the cavern. Of course, none of my people had ever met him before and were afraid to move. The Sanuri told us that The Great Ruler had taken pity on us and had prepared a new home for our people in the Ice Caves of Mordv."

"Many protested the journey because we were all so weak and there were many wounded. The Sanuri smiled and said 'he knew.' A great sleep fell upon us. When we awoke, we were in the Ice Caves and many of our wounded were already healing. Since that day, the Sanuri visits us frequently and teaches us of The Great Ruler. He came to us last night and sent us to help you."

Chapter III
The Sanuri of Tabrul

The Sanuri of Tabrul looked before him at the ruins of the monastery at Avaide and fell to his knees in despair. Never had he seen such desecration of a holy place. The ruins were still smoldering and the stench of burnt flesh was overpowering. The cobblestone pavement that surrounded the once beautiful buildings was covered with blood and bodies of priests.

Thousands of years had passed since the Great Separation from Divinity; which changed this world of Light to darkness. When the peoples chose to separate from The Great Ruler their worlds changed forever. They no longer honored The Great Ruler and did not want to follow His ways. The peoples divided into tribes of like beings, the tribes scattered throughout the world establishing kingdoms. Their fears and hatred consumed them.

The people built walls and developed different languages as they sought to separate from each other as they had separated from The Great Ruler. Allowed to create life, they valued only the lives of their own tribesmen. The people murdered and slaughtered all who were not of their kind; for power and for gain.

Legend tells of a time before remembrance when all manner of peoples lived together in peace. They recognized the holiness in all of The Great Ruler's creations. They listened to His Voice and followed His Teachings. Into this realm was born the idea of Xelope, the oneness of Spirit with all that lives. All that is living is from one source; all that is living is of equal value in the eyes of The Great Ruler.

When The Great Ruler saw what was befalling His children He wept. For those who had once lived together in peace were now separating and isolating themselves. The acts of isolation only fueled the flames of fear and mistrust between the beings. Their eyes became blind with hatred and conspiracy overtook their souls. Their descent into hell was already in motion; the nightmares had already begun.

Holy teachings said that The Great Ruler bestowed upon each kingdom special gifts that would bless and enrich each kind.

While some of these gifts were similar, no two kingdoms received exactly the same ones. To each kingdom The Great Ruler gave six Holy Scrolls written in the language of that kind. Each scroll was over six feet long and when unrolled. Every scroll was protected by a golden tube that was embedded with precious jewels. The designs of the jewels formed a holy code which was unique to the destiny of that kingdom.

Each scroll contained holy doctrine which explained the special gifts and powers bestowed on that kingdom as well as the teachings of The Great Ruler. The Great Ruler made an additional scroll. This scroll was made of spun gold and placed inside a tube that was made of rubies. It was said this scroll contained the gift of immortality for anyone who owned it; the power of this scroll was inconceivable to the beings of this world.

The Great Ruler called before Him the wisest and holiest beings from each kingdom. To each He gave the six scrolls for their kind. Each of these beings swore an oath to protect the scrolls and to honor the gifts they were given. Each being was given the responsibility of teaching the doctrines to their kingdoms and thus passing the teaching on to future generations.

The kingdoms scattered across the world. Their origins were soon forgotten as they grew and prospered. The kingdoms developed in different ways and at different rates. Many of them fell away from the holy teachings and sought to destroy the other kingdoms. Wars and chaos ensued.

Many beings questioned whether The Holy Scrolls ever existed. Some sought them as a means to connect with The Great Ruler, while others sought them as a means to obtain power and wealth. The legends of The Holy Scrolls never died. And the mystery of The Ruby Scroll ignited hunger and desire in the darkest of souls.

As a young priest, the Sanuri had studied at this very monastery which now lay in ruins before him. At an early age the Sanuri made a covenant with The Great Ruler. The Sanuri asked The Great Ruler to use him as His emissary in this world. With his promise to The Great Ruler, the life of the Sanuri changed forever. He was blessed with special gifts to aid him in his work. And his name was changed to Sanuri which means wise teacher in the old language.

The Sanuri lived many life times and yet now he saw a darkness in creation that made him weep. "Will they ever learn?" the Sanuri thought as he looked upon the remains of the monastery.

The Sanuri directed the team of horses that pulled his boca into the center of the ruins. He stopped before a building he recognized as the prayer directory. The Sanuri lowered himself from the boca and stood in the holy place remembering his last visit. The tears flowed down the Sanuri's cheeks, soaking the front of this tunic.

The Sanuri searched the ruins for any sign of life but as he expected, he found none. The pain of this sight weighed upon the Sanuri and made him feel exhausted. The bodies of his friends were everywhere and the Hutas had shown no mercy in their depravation. The Sanuri sought a place to take comfort and to grieve. Spying a large oak tree a couple of feet away, he walked towards it.

Just as the Sanuri was about to sit down, he saw a piece of white cloth on a branch of a bush. He picked it up and realized it came from a priest's frock. The Sanuri started searching the bushes and found another swatch of cloth a few feet away; this swatch had fresh blood on it. Pushing through the undergrowth, the Sanuri saw drops of blood on the ground. Soon he found more blood; the Sanuri could feel his heart racing as he followed the gruesome trail.

Vitomas secretly helped the people of Taperia behind her husband's back. Through her servants, Vitomas was able to give food and money to the poor. On more than one occasion Vitomas intervened in proceedings of law, preventing peasants from losing their homes or their lives but doing so brought great risk to her.

Annabelle was allowed more freedoms than Vitomas and often visited her parents in the Village of Cana. Annabelle's parents were students of The Holy Scrolls and would teach her of the writings when she was at home. Annabelle in turn shared the teachings with Vitomas; who would meet in secret with Annabelle to study the scriptures and to learn the words of The Great Ruler.

King Roch would never allow the words of The Great Ruler to be taught in his kingdom, especially to his Queen. Roch had destroyed all the holy buildings and schools in the Kingdom of Stordt. He outlawed education and all manner of religious practices. Roch wanted complete control over the minds and bodies of his subjects. As time went on, Roch started to think of himself as a god. Roch ordered his subjects to worship only him; his desire for power was insatiable.

After Roch murdered his parents and became King, the holy men of Stordt hid the sacred scrolls that had been given to that kingdom for they feared that Roch would misuse the power the scrolls contained. Although Roch was unaware of their actions he had the holy men butchered and their bodies displayed outside of the gates entering the City of Taperia.

The blood trail led the Sanuri past the monastery buildings and into a forest behind the Great Library. This was an old forest with a thick canopy which allowed little light to filter in. As the Sanuri searched the floor of the forest for blood, he heard moaning. The Sanuri stood very still trying to locate the sound as it was faint. He turned to his right and walked several hundred feet before he got a glimpse of a bare foot protruding from a thicket of berry bushes. When the Sanuri separated the bushes he found two bodies covered with blood.

The Sanuri quickly pulled the bodies out of the thicket and turned them onto their backs. They were both breathing, although the priest was having great difficulty. The Sanuri called to The Great Ruler to save this priest and this boy; he then leaned forward and breathed life force into their beings. With this act the blood stopped flowing from their wounds, the priest started breathing without difficulty and they both regained consciousness.

"My dear friend, The Great Ruler be praised," exclaimed Padre Bartholomew as he grasped the Sanuri's arm with both of his hands and tried to sit up.

"Lie still for a while and tell me what happened," said the Sanuri.

"The Hutas are the spawn of the devil himself they did this; they killed everyone," the old priest started to weep at his own words. "One night, about a year and a half ago, six Shettee warriors and hundreds of Shettee women, children and babies came to us for protection. They said the Hutas had captured their kingdom and King Neputa sent them to us. They were terrified and alone in the world, of course we took them in," said Padre Bartholomew.

"The children in particular brought us such joy and there was so much life at the monastery with them here. The warriors said that Neputa would send his men to the monastery if any of them survived the attack. After eighteen months the Shettees were losing hope of reuniting with the rest of their tribe. We told them they were welcome to make a permanent home here with us."

"Praises be to The Great Ruler," continued Padre Bartholomew, "For sending Petra to save us." As the priest said this he turned to look at the now conscious boy lying next to him. Petra sat up and stared at the Sanuri. "Petra, I want you to meet an old and dear friend of mine, a true holy man he is, we call him the Sanuri," said Padre Bartholomew. "Now Petra tell him about the Hutas."

Petra started to cry as he spoke, "I am from the Village of Ort. Yesterday a man came to our village to warn us that Shettee prisoners had escaped from the death camps of the Hutas and now the Hutas were attacking every village trying to find them. My entire village had heard stories for months that the priests were caring for Shettee refugees so I took one of my father's horses and rode here as fast as I could to warn them."

"This boy is a hero," said Padre Bartholomew. "Because of Petra we were able to get the Shettees away from the monastery before the Hutas came. We prayed to The Great Ruler to save them."

"The Great Ruler heard your prayers," said the Sanuri. "He sent the Rualas to carry the Shettees to safety."

"Oh thank goodness," Padre Bartholomew said with relief then his tone filled with sadness. "Six priests led the Shettees through the six tunnels under the monastery, if they are still alive they will be returning to this horror," the priest said sadly.

"I hid in the forest when the Hutas came," Petra was shaking and crying as he talked. "They took all of the priests and tortured them." Petra vomited as he relived the images. After a few moments Petra continued, "None of the priests told the Hutas about the Shettees, so they killed them, they killed them all." Petra wept.

Padre Bartholomew put his arm around Petra to console him. "Petra pulled me to safety before the Hutas could kill me. I don't understand how he was able to do such a thing because he is so small and well, as you can see I am not. It was a miracle."

"The Hutas are demons," cried Petra "They were smiling and laughing as they hurt the priests. Padre Bartholomew was lying near some bushes so I pulled him away while they were killing the others," Petra said with his head buried in his hands.

"Have you found any other survivors?" asked Padre Bartholomew as he hugged Petra.

"No, but I was still searching the grounds when I saw your blood trail," said the Sanuri. "Come my friends let me get you to my boca." The Sanuri lifted Padre Bartholomew to his feet. The Sanuri and Petra both helped the priest walk to the boca.

"Petra let me see your arm," the Sanuri said as he looked at a long gash on Petra's left forearm.

"How did you make the bleeding stop?" Petra asked in amazement.

"Petra tell the Sanuri what happened."

"I was trying to help Padre Bartholomew through the woods and a Huta came after us. He was really big and mean looking and we couldn't run fast enough to get away from him."

"The boy saved my life," said Padre Bartholomew. "He stood before me, unarmed, and faced the warrior. The warrior cut Petra with his knife then the earth shook with the roar of a lion. It sounded as if the lion was upon us. The Huta ran away and left us to die."

"Did you see this lion?" asked the Sanuri.

"No," said Petra. "As soon as the warrior left, me and Padre Bartholomew ran and hid in those bushes."

"My friends, I do not think you were alone in this fight," said the Sanuri. Then he helped Padre Bartholomew and Petra into his boca. The Sanuri dressed their wounds and gave them food and water. "Padre Bartholomew, we will need to get The Holy Scrolls and the other precious writings out of the monastery to protect them. After you finish eating do you feel up to such a task while I finish searching for survivors?"

"Regardless of how I feel it is a task that must be done."

"I'll help him," Petra said as he set down his bowl.

The Sanuri resumed his search of the monastery grounds. While he was walking back to the boca the Sanuri suddenly had a vision. He saw King Roch and his men at the monastery; they were searching through the buildings, stealing all they could carry. The Sanuri was not sure how close Roch and his men were so he ran to the boca calling for Petra and Padre Bartholomew. "Roch and his men are coming, quickly we must go. Padre Bartholomew did you find the scrolls?"

"Yes, they are in the back of the boca."

"I'll have to mark the tunnels so the returning priests know they might still be in danger. Finish your packing and hide in the back of the boca." The Sanuri quickly drew three X's with a line under them at the entrance of each tunnel; this was a code for danger. He hurried back to the boca. "Are you in there?"

"Yes," replied Padre Bartholomew. "We're all set."

The Sanuri walked quickly to the front of the boca; before he climbed into the seat he looked to the north and saw a great cloud of dust on the horizon.

Chapter IV
Journeys into Darkness

When Roch and his men arrived at the monastery, smoldering ashes and buzzards were the first things they saw. Remnants of bodies lay in the main court yard where they had been executed. The monastery itself was enormous as was the library. Many smaller buildings used for lodging, storage and animals were spread over the vast landscape. Roch turned to Jonas, his captain and second in command of the troops on this mission. "Go into Avaide and bring back as many peasants as you can find to dig through this rubble," ordered Roch.

"Are they to be paid, My Lord?" asked Jonas.

Roch laughed. "The question to ask is, are they to live? They have no choice in the matter and have them bring tools. They will do the digging for us," said Roch.

Jonas took half the soldiers and rode for Avaide, a small city that lay three miles south of the monastery. Roch ordered those who remained with him to start searching for anything that looked of value. Roch and six of his men entered the main body of the monastery. The structure of the building was sound, although most of the furniture and statues were damaged. Drapes had been torn from the walls and papers and books were scattered everywhere.

"The Hutas must have been searching for treasure," Roch commented.

"My Lord, perhaps the villagers are responsible," responded one of the soldiers.

"Nonsense," said Roch. "This monastery is considered holy to most of the kingdoms; the villagers would never do this."

Jonas and his men returned after a little more than an hour; they forced several dozen men and boys with wagons and tools to ride with them. The villagers were horrified at the sight of the dead priests.

"Should we bury the priests first?" asked one of the villagers.

"No, King Roch wants you to search for treasures first," replied Jonas. "Besides these priests have been dead for a while. If you were so concerned about burying them, why haven't you already done so?"

The men worked through the day searching the remains of the monastery for items of value. Jonas ordered both the villagers and the soldiers to put the items they found into piles in the courtyard.

After searching the monastery room by room Roch and his men were leaving when he spied part of a box hidden under a pile of drapery. Roch pushed aside the drapes exposing a box made of forged metal and wood. The box was about one foot by one foot and made of modest design. The box was secured by a padlock. Roch called to one of his men to bring an ax and to break the lock. Once the lock was broken, Roch ordered the soldier to leave.

Roch opened the box with eager anticipation, which was not in vain. The box contained large rubies, diamonds and sapphires. The gems appeared flawless. As Roch searched through the gems he found numerous gold nuggets. At the very bottom of the box lay a beautiful dagger, its handle was made of gold and encrusted with rubies.

Roch picked up the dagger to look at the symbols on it. The dagger reminded Roch of one he had once owned. The scene of his father lying in a pool of blood with the dagger protruding from his back now filled Roch's mind. This memory brought Roch both pain and pleasure. Roch could not keep that first dagger; he looked upon this dagger as a gift of fate. In the very bottom of the box was an old piece of tattered goatskin which was hidden by the dagger.

Roch picked up the piece of goatskin very carefully; he knew it had to be of great value if it was hidden under these treasures. Roch unfolded the goatskin and saw a very detailed map had been drawn on it. The map contained writing in a language Roch was not familiar with; but he did recognize many of the symbols drawn on the map. Thinking the map would lead him to even greater treasures; Roch folded the map and put it into a satin trimmed folder that he carried in his breast pocket.

With an army so close behind them the Sanuri traveled in the woods instead of the main road. Padre Bartholomew was sleeping in the back of the boca. Petra had climbed into the front seat next to the Sanuri.

"Where are we going?" asked Petra.

"I thought I would take you home," said the Sanuri.

"What about the Padre, where will he go?"

"Would your family take him in until his wounds heal?"

"Yes of course, but..."

"But what Petra?"

"Our house is small and well, it's not very fancy for a priest."

"Does your family love The Great Ruler?"

"Oh yes," said Petra.

"Then it is the perfect place for a priest."

Soon Petra was lulled to sleep by the moving of the boca. Petra leaned against the Sanuri who put his arm around the boy and smiled. "Sleep my brave little friend you have a long journey ahead of you," the Sanuri thought.

The Sanuri traveled in the concealment of the forest all day, although the travelling was much slower. As dusk was approaching he stopped the boca in a small clearing. Petra jumped down from the boca and started to gather wood. Soon they had a warm fire and a meal of beans, biscuits and dried meat. Petra was telling the Sanuri about his village when the Sanuri suddenly reached over and put his hand against Petra's mouth as a signal to stop talking.

Petra and Padre Bartholomew sat motionless; neither of them hearing anything but the normal sounds of the night. The Sanuri quickly stood up and walked to the front of the boca. He grabbed a long wooden staff from behind the front seat and brought it over to the campfire. The Sanuri stood still looking into the darkness; without turning he said, "Both of you need to go into the back of the boca now, we are not alone this evening."

Raul had been traveling for over two years, exploring other cultures and lands. He thrived on the adventure, always looking forward to what the next day might bring. But the same things that brought Raul such great pleasure also filled him with overwhelming guilt. Raul was heir to the throne of the Kingdom of Wetpr. His father was getting older and Raul knew soon he would have to return home and assume his responsibilities.

Raul loved his homeland but his heart yearned for another life. One in which he could be free to make choices for himself without having to be responsible for the lives of hundreds of thousands of other people. Instead of being grateful for the power and fame of his position in life; Raul sometimes felt a prisoner to his fate.

Raul's mother, Queen Renya, wrote to him often; keeping Raul informed on all the business and gossip at home. Renya warned Raul that the Hutas were attacking and destroying villages in many kingdoms. The Hutas had always been a hated and feared race but the destruction of the monastery at Avaide brought them new notoriety. The terror that the Hutas created in the hearts of many people was now turning to a defiance because of the brutal murders of the priests. Victims were now turning into enemies of the Hutas and the enemies were uniting.

Raul's mother was a loving woman and understanding of his heart's desires; although Renya reminded Raul in every letter that he could not change his destiny and that his kingdom needed him. Raul's father, King Sudfad was a loved and respected ruler as well as being a mighty warrior. But Raul's absence brought Sudfad such pain that it affected his life and his health. With every letter he received, Raul knew he would have to return home soon.

Lost and hungry, Raul decided to make camp near a grove of pine trees. The last few nights Raul had seen the tracks of a great lion that appeared to circle his camp. But to Raul's surprise the lion did not attack him or his horse. Raul gathered arm loads of wood hoping a big fire would keep the cat away one more night.

After Raul set up camp, he prepared to study his most prized possessions; six Holy Scrolls created by The Great Ruler. Raul came upon these scrolls in a cavern in the Kingdom of Puntd, shortly after he first started his journey. The scrolls were hidden in a basket made of reed and wood and buried behind a large wall of rock. Raul found them when he went into the cavern for shelter from a storm. The rock wall had collapsed exposing the basket.

All six scrolls were individually wrapped and lying side by side. The jeweled tube encasing each scroll was wrapped in a sheet of linen with a leather cord securing each end. On each end of the leather cords were fastened silver nuggets. A braided strand of pure gold was tied around the middle of each scroll on the outside of the linen.

The fire warmed Raul as he read the scrolls. The flames created illusions and shadows in the darkness of the night. Raul loved the crackling sound of burning wood. As Raul read, his studies were interrupted by thoughts of home and his parents. Raul had always been close to his parents, especially his father. Raul knew that he had angered his father and hoped to soon reconcile with him upon his return home.

There were moments when Raul regretted this journey, the loneliness and hunger were daunting at times. But Raul had seen things of such great wonder and had met such memorable people that the hardships were dwarfed in comparison. Raul learned that reading about people from other kingdoms was very different from walking with those people and sharing their lives.

Raul hoped that he would return home a better king for his experiences. Raul was starting to dose off when his horse suddenly started to snort and whiney. The horse was trying to pull away from the stake it was tied to. Before Raul could get to his horse he was struck from behind.

Roch and his men left the monastery at Avaide laden with great treasures. They had taken two wagons from the villagers to fill with their plunder. Roch now carried the jewel encrusted dagger in his belt. He found himself constantly touching his breast pocket as if to reassure himself that the map was still there. When they made camp, Roch sat away from his men so he could study the map.

Grudgingly, Roch began to realize he would need someone to translate the ancient text on the map. This would not be an easy task for him since Roch had all the holy men and all of the men of learning in his kingdom murdered years before. Roch had few friends among the royal families of other kingdoms but now he realized he would have to go beyond his borders to seek the help he needed. Roch was a man who always took what he wanted; politics was a game he didn't play yet it was a game that he would need to learn.

Petra and Padre Bartholomew crouched in the back of the boca. They could not see the campsite because of the wooden sides of the carriage. Petra found the silence stressful and after a few minutes he attempted to move to the rear door of the boca. As he was starting to move, Padre Bartholomew grabbed his right arm and held if firmly. Petra kneeled back down on the floor of the boca. Moments that seemed like hours passed before they heard the Sanuri's voice.

"You can come out now; our visitors are gone."

Petra jumped out of the back of the boca then turned to help Padre Bartholomew climb out. "What was it, what did you see?" asked Petra excitedly.

"All I saw were foot prints and honestly I do not know what made them," said the Sanuri.

"Do you think they were Hutas?" asked Padre Bartholomew.

"They certainly were not human," replied the Sanuri.

"Wolves or coyotes, you think?" asked Petra.

They all returned to the campfire where the Sanuri carefully added another small log to the fire. He was quiet for a few moments as if all his attention was devoted to the fire. "I do not want to scare you but I have never seen prints like those before. I will show them to you in the morning. Whatever the creatures are; they walk on two legs. The prints are shaped similar to a bear's but much, much larger and they have very long claws. This ground is moist, the prints sunk into the soil. Whatever the creatures are they are large and heavy."

"How many were out there?" asked Padre Bartholomew.

"From what I could see, I think three. It looked like they were watching us," replied the Sanuri.

"Why wouldn't the horses make any noise if the creatures were that close?" asked Petra.

"Why did they leave?" asked Padre Bartholomew.

"I am thinking about all those things," said the Sanuri. "And I do not have the answers yet. But you two need to get some sleep. I will stand watch."

"Sanuri I still don't understand; how did you know the creatures were out there?" asked Petra

"Yes, I wondered that too. I did not hear or see anything," added Padre Bartholomew.

"I could feel their presence."

Petra stared at the Sanuri with confusion and said, "I don't understand."

"And you won't tonight," the Sanuri said. "Now get some sleep."

King Roch did not take the time to inspect all the treasures they had stolen while they were at the monastery. But he did find a beautiful ruby and gold necklace that he put into his breast pocket; it would be a gift for Vitomas.

Roch demanded that Vitomas dress in a manner that befitted her standing because he felt that her appearance was a reflection of his own power and wealth. Many considered Vitomas to be the most beautiful woman in the kingdom; a sentiment shared by Roch and the reason she was still alive.

Unlike his predecessors, Roch was interested solely in personnel gain and power. Roch despised the weak and felt no sense of responsibility for those he ruled. Roch treated his army much better than the peasants. Not only did the soldiers earn a good wage and have lodging provided for them but they also shared in the spoils of conquest. Roch allowed his men to take whatever he himself did not want from the taxes of the villages and cities. Roch's men plundered the tribes they defeated. Many of the soldiers had become very wealthy from this way of life.

As hated as Roch was by his people, they feared him even more. All of his subjects knew that if Roch's men arrested someone, that person would never be seen again. Roch liked to make public examples of people who questioned his will. He would order public beheadings or hangings in the villages and cities and the bodies would be displayed as a means of intimidation. Roch's brutal tactics were effective as few of his subjects rebelled against his iron rule.

After a few hours, Petra climbed out of the boca and joined the Sanuri at the campfire. "I can't sleep," Petra said with a yawn as he sat down next to the Sanuri.

"Did you try?" the Sanuri asked. Petra gave the Sanuri a mischievous grin but did not answer. "We should reach your village by tomorrow evening. I will leave the Padre with your family but you must not let anyone know he is staying with you. The Hutas are still searching for the Shettees and if they find out the priest is staying with you they will kill all of you," warned the Sanuri.

"I know my parents will want to protect Padre Bartholomew but do you think we will be safe?"

"I think you were meant to save him. I think you will be safe. You just have to be careful," replied the Sanuri.

"I am starving, it will be dawn in an hour. What do you say about an early breakfast?" The Sanuri went to the back of the boca and grabbed coffee, beans, ham, bread and potatoes. "Why don't you wake the Padre," the Sanuri suggested as he started to prepare their morning meal.

Petra stood at the back of the boca and called Padre Bartholomew's name several times. The priest did not answer so Petra climbed inside of the boca and shook him; still the priest did not respond. "Sanuri," screamed Petra, "Something is wrong." The Sanuri ran to the back of the boca and climbed in. "He's cold, he's really cold," Petra cried.

"Petra get my staff, it's near the front of the boca." Petra was gone but moments, before he returned with the long staff. "Now point that staff in here towards the Padre. And I need you to hold very still."

Petra grasped the staff with both hands and tilted it towards the Sanuri and Padre Bartholomew. Within seconds the end of the staff started to glow, providing light inside of the boca. "Whoa," uttered Petra in amazement. The Sanuri examined Padre Bartholomew. The old man was breathing but his breaths were shallow and he was unconscious. The Sanuri opened up the priest's robe and stared at the bandages that covered a knife wound in Padre Bartholomew's chest.

"What is that?" gasped Petra as they watched something moving underneath the bandages. The Sanuri quickly cut the front of the bandages which wrapped around the priest's torso. When the Sanuri pulled the bandages back he heard a hiss. "Oh!" screamed Petra with disgust. "What are those things?"

The Sanuri did not answer Petra's question. "I should have suspected this," the Sanuri said to himself as he positioned his two large hands three inches above the priest's chest. The Sanuri closed his eyes and within moments his hands started to glow. The glow started as a soft white light that grew with intensity.

As the light became brighter the leech-like creatures on Padre Bartholomew's chest hissed more fiercely then they started to growl and to jump at the Sanuri's hands.

Petra watched in silent horror as dozens of the slimy creatures started crawling out of Padre Bartholomew's wound. The Sanuri remained motionless with his eyes closed as more and more of the creatures covered Padre Bartholomew's body. The light produced by the Sanuri's hands kept getting brighter until the inside of the boca was as light as day. Suddenly Petra realized that the creatures seemed to be coming out of the wound so they could attack the light.

As the small army of demonic creatures crawled out of Padre Bartholomew's wound they advanced on the Sanuri, who remained motionless. Soon the creatures started to attach themselves to the Sanuri. Little Petra watched the scene in horror; he was too afraid to speak. Within minutes the Sanuri's body was indistinguishable as he was covered with the creatures that were quickly growing in size. When the last of the slimy creatures moved from Padre Bartholomew's body to that of the Sanuri, the Sanuri quickly jumped out of the boca and stood a few feet away.

The Sanuri's entire body now, started to glow; a brilliant and intense light. The creatures that covered his body burst into ashes, one by one, from the intensity of the holy light. When the last creature had been destroyed the Sanuri ran to Petra and grabbed his bandaged arm.

"Petra, those creatures were born because of a poison that was on the knives of the Hutas," the Sanuri said as he ripped the bandages off the boy's arm. Petra screamed when he saw the head of a leech-like creature protrude from the wound on his arm. Petra fainted from fright as the Sanuri removed the hellish beasts from his arm as he had done with Padre Bartholomew. The Sanuri laid Petra in the back of the boca and cleansed and rebadged the wounds of both of his patients. Then the Sanuri packed up the campsite and hitched the team of horses to the boca.

As the Sanuri was climbing into the front seat of the boca, he stopped and looked around the campsite as he was feeling the eyes of unseen intruders. The Sanuri was not a man of fear but he was very curious about the strange footprints he had seen the night before.

Although he wanted to walk deeper into the forest and try to find the spies, the Sanuri knew he had to get the boy and the priest to safety. Within minutes they were on the road heading to the Village of Ort.

Every morning Vitomas would go riding on her stallion which she named Raven. This horse was the one and only gift that Roch had ever given her that she loved. When she was riding Raven, Vitomas felt free and happy. Her morning rides were an escape from the nightmare of her life. Vitomas was not allowed to leave the castle properties but fortunately for her the properties were vast.

Every morning when she mounted Raven, Vitomas desperately thought about escape but within moments this fleeting dream was crushed by the memories of how Roch punished her the two times she tried to run away from him.

After eight years of being a victim of Roch's depraved madness and his rage; Vitomas felt like a shadow of a person. Sometimes she didn't care what he did to her anymore. But Vitomas did care about what Roch did to Annabelle and to others. Roch was cunning; he knew that Vitomas cared more about others than she cared about herself and he used that against her. The great relief she had from her life with Roch; was that he would often leave for long periods of time in his quests for treasures. Greed was Roch's life's motivation.

On this morning Vitomas was feeling particularly free. Roch had not yet returned from his trip to the monastery at Avaide so she decided to explore some different areas of the royal properties. Vitomas had been riding for about two hours, enjoying the feeling of the wind blowing against her cheeks and the warmth of the morning sun when she realized there was a flock of vultures circling in the sky ahead of her. Vitomas squeezed her legs against Raven, commanding him to move faster; they headed towards the vultures.

Almost fifteen minutes later Vitomas rode up to the remnants of a camp site. She could see that someone had built a fire and surrounded it with small rocks. But now the logs and rocks were scattered around the ground as were cooking utensils.

Vitomas dismounted to get a better look at the many foot prints in the dirt; most of them belonged to men but there were also prints of a great lion. Vitomas saw blood on the ground and on some of the logs. The vultures were still circling overhead. Vitomas' heart started to race as she found a trail of blood on the ground. She followed the trail to a small ravine which was thick with vegetation.

Vitomas would not have found Raul's body had he not moaned. Frantically Vitomas tore through the bushes and weeds until she found him, lying face down in the dirt and covered with blood. Vitomas fell to her knees and turned Raul onto his back. He was a large man and not easy to move. Raul had many injuries and as swollen as his left leg was, Vitomas was sure it was broken.

"Can you hear me?" Vitomas asked as she gently touched Raul's cheek. Raul moaned again but did not open his eyes. Tears were running down Vitomas' cheeks as she tried to wake Raul. "How am I going to get him onto my horse?" she thought. "If you can hear me, I'm going to get my horse, I will be right back," Vitomas said.

Vitomas ran out of the ravine and back to the campsite where she had left Raven. "Help me, please help me," she prayed as she ran. Vitomas returned to Raul minutes later. She took water from her canteen and patted Raul's face. Then she shook his shoulder "Please wake up," Vitomas said and started to cry harder when she suddenly felt his hand grasp hers. "Are you awake?" she whispered.

Raul's face was bruised and swollen. When he opened his eyes he could barely focus his sight to see Vitomas. "You're badly hurt and I think your leg is broken," she said. "But I can't lift you to get you on my horse; do you think you can help me?" Raul nodded groggily and tried to sit up but winced in pain.

"Let me help you," Vitomas said as she put her arm around Raul's shoulders and helped him to a sitting position. She held her canteen to his lips so he could drink. Vitomas took off the scarf that she had holding back her long hair and poured water on one corner of it so she could wash the blood out of Raul's eyes. "Are you dizzy?"

"It's getting better," he said through swollen lips.

"I think your left leg is broken; my horse will kneel down. If I help you do you think you can get on him?"

Raul nodded, "Have him kneel on my right side."

With Vitomas' help and a great deal of pain, Raul managed to get on top of Raven. Vitomas had Raven stand and just as she was about to mount him she saw a large pouch that was lying on the ground; Vitomas put it into her saddlebag and mounted the horse behind Raul. Raul was in and out of consciousness as they rode to Roch's castle; at times Vitomas had great difficulty keeping him on the horse.

When they reached the castle, Vitomas did something she had never done before; she screamed orders at the soldiers to help her.

"Annabelle help me; the soldiers are getting the physician," Vitomas cried as she started to remove Raul's blood soaked clothing. Raul was unconscious.

"His wounds are still bleeding," Annabelle said as the two women lifted Raul to a sitting position and removed his shirt. "He has wounds on his back also."

Annabelle was the same age as Vitomas, another captive of Roch's; she had been taken at the age of nine to be a companion and servant to Vitomas. Annabelle was the only child of Alexander and Laurel, who had been the personal attendants to Roch's parents.

Alexander and Laurel had also taken care of Roch when he was young and in an uncharacteristic act of mercy he allowed them to leave the castle unharmed and return to their home in the small Village of Cana; after Roch murdered his parents.

Annabelle was born to the couple long after they had left the castle. Like Vitomas, Annabelle was a girl of exceptional beauty with large brown eyes and long curly black hair.

"Roch is not going to be happy about this," Annabelle warned as the two women were removing Raul's trousers.

"I couldn't leave him to die; he was on the castle properties. I suspect some of the soldiers beat him," Vitomas said with disgust.

"All the more reason," Annabelle scolded. "Vitomas you know he will punish you." Vitomas did not say anything. "But I do think it was smart of you to put him in the eastern wing," Annabelle said. "You have him as far away from Roch's chambers as you can." Annabelle stopped speaking as the Court Physician was led into the bedroom by a Taperian soldier.

Zorda died the next afternoon. Archetenus had his body concealed in a small cave that was near the path they were traveling; as he did not think the wounded remnants of his army had the strength to bury their dead. Archetenus' men needed food, water and medical attention. As they traveled towards the Village of Ort they saw the treachery of the Hutas, who often liked to display their dead.

Archetenus and his men stopped at the first farmhouse they encountered that was not completely burned to the ground. As the Taperian soldiers had seen earlier; the family that had lived in this house was now dead and their body parts were hanging from the trees that surrounded the small house.

Archetenus shook his head with disgust as his men searched the buildings of the farm for Hutas. "Check the well," Archetenus ordered. It was known that Hutas would throw bodies down wells to poison the waters. Archetenus walked into the remains of the blood soaked house where he found food and wine in the kitchen. He walked into the sleeping area and found a sheet that appeared to be unsullied, which he took to tear into bandages for his men.

Archetenus stood in the doorway of the farmhouse and said loudly, "We will take rest here." His men entered the house and devoured what food and drink they could find. These gifts from the dead helped to sustain them one more day.

Late that afternoon Raul opened his swollen eyes and looked around him. He had difficulty focusing his sight at first, as he was staring at the furniture in the bedroom and trying to remember how he had gotten there. Vitomas was sitting in a chair sewing when she heard him move. She flew to Raul's side and replaced the cool cloth on his forehead. Raul tried to speak but had difficulty because his mouth was so dry. Vitomas poured water from a pitcher into a glass that was on the table next to Raul's bed. She helped him raise his head and held the glass for him to drink.

"Thank you," Raul said in a whisper as Vitomas lowered his head back to the pillow. He stared at her, "I thought you were a dream."

"Do you remember what happened to you?" Vitomas asked as she stroked his dark hair.

Raul was quiet for a few moments as he tried to unlock the memories of his attack. "No, where am I?"

Vitomas did not want to tell Raul that he was in the castle of King Roch for fear it would upset him. "You are safe, that's all that matters now," she said soothingly. "I'll take care of you." Raul reached over and took Vitomas' hand into his then immediately fell asleep. Vitomas sat at Raul's side, holding his hand and wondering who this handsome young man was.

"Roch hasn't been gone two weeks and his queen brings home a stray," Cerephus bellowed. Cerephus was the general who Roch left in charge of the kingdom in his absence. A vile and merciless man, Cerephus followed Roch's orders without question.

"The man is almost dead," Crispus said. "He cannot be of much trouble."

"Crispus your job is to watch the Queen, make sure her attention to this man goes no farther than being a nursemaid."

"Yes, My Lord."

When Archetenus saw the ruins of Ort, he lost hope. The village had been destroyed by fire. There was no sign of life. His men had not eaten for two days, they drank the last of their water a day earlier and they all were suffering from exhaustion and their wounds.

"Have the Hutas destroyed the whole damn world," Archetenus spat as he sat on his horse and surveyed the desolate street before them. There was no sign of movement other than a windmill screeching in the wind.

Archetenus and his men started to ride down the main road going through Ort. Archetenus was in the lead and they were all on alert for signs of trouble. Suddenly Archetenus heard a thud behind him and turned to see the soldier directly to his rear, fall from his horse with an arrow in his throat.

Archetenus yelled to his men to take cover. His horse lunged into the air as his eyes searched the ruins for the attackers. Archetenus rode into the remains of a large barn; three of the original walls were still standing. He dismounted at the rear of the barn and crouched behind a stone wall, looking for any sign of movement.

Archetenus could see some of his men across the street slowly searching through the ruins of buildings. The village was quiet, too quiet thought Archetenus. He was about to move forward to the burned out shell of the next building when Archetenus thought he heard a sound inside of the barn. Even with the fourth wall of the barn partially collapsed, the interior was very dark.

Archetenus stared into the darkness. He slowly walked back into the barn with his right hand on the hilt of his sword. Archetenus strained to accustom his eyes to the darkness. He did not want the bright sunlight in the doorway to silhouette his body, so Archetenus quickly jumped behind a pile of rubble that leaned against the eastern wall.

After a few moments Archetenus moved around the edges of the barn. He did not see any sign of movement. He started to walk towards the rear door of the barn when he heard a hissing sound. Archetenus stopped and looked at the floor expecting to see a snake.

As he looked down Archetenus felt a searing pain to the back of his head, he fell forward. The last thing Archetenus remembered was suddenly feeling nauseous.

Hours later Archetenus regained consciousness. He felt cold; his hands were wet and sticky. Archetenus tried to open his eyes but all he could see was darkness. He tried to push himself up with his forearms but he collapsed into a pool of his own blood.

Chapter V
A Family of Kings

Raul had regained consciousness on and off during the next two days. But his periods of clarity were brief. Either Vitomas or Annabelle was at his side always. They feared that Roch's men would harm Raul if they left him alone. The morning of the third day, Vitomas stepped out of Raul's room to get some clean towels and to fill his water pitcher.

"Well, if it isn't my angel," Raul said with a smile as Vitomas entered his room. She was so startled by his voice that she spilled some of the water on the floor and almost dropped the linens. They both laughed. Vitomas set the items she was carrying on the table next to Raul's bed and stared at him in amazement. "You look as if you have seen a ghost," Raul said.

"I think I have. For the last few days you haven't been conscious for more than a few moments and now you are sitting up and talking to me, I can't believe my eyes." Then as an afterthought Vitomas remembered the water she had spilled on the carpet. She grabbed a towel and quickly cleaned up the mess as Raul watched her. When Vitomas turned around and saw how intently Raul was staring at her she blushed. "Are you hungry?" Vitomas asked.

"I'm starving," Raul said with a big smile. Vitomas smiled and turned, walking towards the door. "Wait," Raul called. Vitomas turned around and looked at him. She felt very excited but she did not understand why. "What is your name?"

"Vitomas," she answered and walked out the door.

Roch had forced his men to push their horses to their limits as they rode to Avaide. But there was no urgency to return to Taperia and the wagons of treasures that they now pulled; slowed them down considerably. Roch led his men when they were riding but when they would stop for a rest, he would wander off by himself so he could study his precious map. Roch would carefully fold and unfold the tattered goatskin as if he was afraid it would shatter. Roch was mesmerized by this map and found himself stopping the movement of his troops more often so he could study his new found treasure.

"Well, it's about time you two woke up," the Sanuri said as he was preparing breakfast. "You've been sleeping for two days."

"Two days!" gasped Padre Bartholomew as he and Petra walked over to the camp fire.

"We had monsters in us," Petra said and looked like he was going to cry.

"Petra, both of you will be alright now," the Sanuri said in a calming voice.

"What are you both talking about?" asked Padre Bartholomew as he poured himself a cup of coffee.

"You wouldn't wake and when I examined you I found hundreds of Jacars in your wound."

"They looked like giant leeches," Petra said with disgust. "I had them too!"

"I don't understand," Padre Bartholomew said. "What are Jacars?"

"Hutas often dip their weapons in different types of poisons to intensify the torture of their victims. When they stabbed both of you they must have dipped their knives in a poison made from the Jacept plant. It causes those creatures to grow in the victim's body and like leeches they drain the body of blood," the Sanuri explained.

"But that makes no sense, how is that even possible?" Padre Bartholomew asked.

"It's possible if the poison is made by a dark lord."

Vitomas returned to Raul's room carrying an enormous tray of food. She cleared the table next to his bed and set the tray on the table.

"There's enough food there for several people," Raul said with a laugh that hurt his mouth.

"Well, you said you were starving and besides I didn't ask you what you like to eat. Now which plate do you want first?"

"The pancakes and some coffee, please."

"Do you want me to cut them for you?"

Raul laughed. "No, my leg is broken not my arms." Vitomas turned red. "I didn't mean to embarrass you, I was just joking. Please sit down and eat with me." Vitomas sat on the edge of the bed and laughed as she watched Raul hungrily devour the plate of pancakes. Then Vitomas handed him another plate that contained a small steak and fried potatoes.

"What is your name," Vitomas asked as she refilled his cup of coffee.

"Raul, I am the son of Sudfad, King of Wetpr."

"What are you doing here?" Vitomas gasped in horror.

Raul stopped eating when he saw the look on her face, "Well, I guess I don't know where 'here' is."

"This is the castle of King Roch. I found you on his property. We should not tell anyone who you are. How did you get here?"

Raul now understood the seriousness of his situation. King Roch was Raul's uncle. Raul's father, Sudfad, was Roch's older brother and heir to the throne of Stordt. Roch was a mere child when he started to torture and kill animals. It wasn't long before Roch started attacking the staff of the castle but his real hatred was always directed towards Sudfad. Their parents King Jaretta and Queen Lillian feared for Sudfad's life, as he too was but a small boy and unable to defend himself from his brother's sadistic viciousness.

To protect Sudfad, his parents sent him to the Kingdom of Wetpr to live with Jaretta's brother Alexandras and his wife Sumona, the King and Queen of Wetpr. Alexandras and Sumona never had children and fell in love with Sudfad instantly. They adopted him as their son and raised him.

Roch and Sudfad reigned over the two largest kingdoms in the Continent of Opots. Yet these men were extreme opposites of each other in every respect, except for two similarities. They were both fierce warriors and brilliant military leaders. The two brothers had never reconciled after Roch murdered their parents.

"I have been traveling among the kingdoms," Raul said. "Trying to learn of the world before I am to become king. I didn't realize I was on Roch's land."

"It was probably his men who beat you," Vitomas said. "I am amazed they didn't kill you." Vitomas was quiet for a few moments as she was trying to think of a plan. She leaned closer to Raul and whispered, "There is only one person here who you can trust and that is Annabelle, she has been helping me take care of you. Trust no one else with your secret. I will find a way to get you out of here."

"Who are you?" Raul asked.

"I told you my name," Vitomas said evasively. "Now you must eat to regain your strength. King Roch left two weeks ago to go to the monastery at Avaide. General Cerephus is in charge in Roch's absence."

"Why would Roch go to a monastery?"

"You have not heard?" Vitomas asked sadly. "The Hutas heard that the priests were giving shelter to Shettee refugees; the women and the children. When the Hutas couldn't find any Shettees at the monastery they murdered the priests and destroyed the monastery."

"That is awful but I still don't understand why Roch would go there."

"To steal the riches that had been given to The Great Ruler."

"You're looking exhausted," Vitomas said as she gently touched Raul's face. "We've been talking for hours; I should let you get your rest."

As Vitomas started to stand, Raul grasped her hand and said, "No, please don't go, stay a little longer." Vitomas smiled shyly as her body was surging with excitement. Never before had she felt this way around a man.

"How old are you?" Raul asked as Vitomas resumed her seat next to him.

"I just turned seventeen."

"Seventeen why you're just a girl," Raul joked.

"And how old would you be My Lord," she replied in a teasing manner.

"Twenty."

"I see," Vitomas said. "Well you certainly look good for your age."

Raul stared boldly into her eyes, "So you like how I look?" he asked with a grin. Vitomas' eyes grew wide as she stared at him with utter embarrassment. Raul was squeezing her hand and Vitomas looked at him unable to speak. "Are you being silent because you are trying to be polite and not hurt my feelings?"

"No," Vitomas said in a whisper. "I," Vitomas was so embarrassed she was starting to stammer. "I think you are very handsome."

Raul continued to stare intently at Vitomas, who was visibly uncomfortable. "Good, because I think you are the most beautiful woman I have ever laid eyes upon. And you seem to be just as sweet on the inside."

Vitomas was filled with emotions; never had she been so attracted to anyone. Raul took her breath away as she looked at his muscular, shirtless chest and his handsome features. But it was his aqua eyes that made her feel like she was melting before him. Vitomas knew she could never care for this man for Roch would certainly kill him; and that thought broke her heart.

"Vitomas are you afraid of me?" Raul asked as her silence was confusing to him. Raul could tell by the way Vitomas looked at him that she was attracted to him; yet he could see fear in her eyes also.

"No," Vitomas said and looked like she was going to cry. "I should go now."

"Why? What is wrong?"

"You wouldn't understand."

Raul was still holding her hand and now he kissed it softly. Tears started to run down Vitomas' cheeks. She wanted so badly to kiss Raul. "I have to go," Vitomas said and ran out of the room.

Raul couldn't sleep; he knew he should be concerned about his situation but it was Vitomas he could not stop thinking about. He was captivated by her. "She's the most charming person I have ever talked to," Raul thought as he remembered how Vitomas' face lit up when she laughed. Suddenly the door to his room opened.

"You look disappointed," Annabelle said with a laugh. She put the pile of linens that she was carrying on a table then returned to the door and looked both ways in the hallway before she closed it.

"I'm sorry," Raul said as Annabelle moved the tray of breakfast dishes from the table next to his bed and replaced it with the stack of linens she had been carrying.

"I'm Annabelle," she said with a grin. "I'm your other nurse." Annabelle sat down on the side of the bed and leaned close to Raul. "Vitomas told me about you; we will get you out of here."

"What did she say?"

Annabelle had a mischievous glint in her eyes as she said with a grin, "That you are a handsome and charming prince. Of course I think you will be more handsome when those black eyes go down."

Raul laughed, he liked her sassy nature. Annabelle turned to the stack of linens that she had put on the table. She lifted a folded sheet off the top of the pile and handed it to Raul.

"A gift for our prince." Raul unfolded the sheet and found two daggers in their sheaths and a map. As he unfolded the map, Annabelle pointed features out. "This is where you are, in the eastern wing. The doors that we have put an 'x' by are doors that lead outside. This is the front of the castle, you don't ever want to sneak out there because directly across from the front doors is Roch's war room. He is usually in there when he is home. Roch's chambers are here in the western wing. There is a stable here. And these two big 'X's' are the gates to the wall.

"Where do you and Vitomas stay?" Raul asked seriously.

Annabelle stared at him and grinned, "You are going to be trouble. Here," she said as she pointed to a room in the west wing.

"You both stay in the same chambers?"

"Yes. But I have more gifts." Annabelle reached back to the stack of linens. "Whoever beat you stole all of your things. We cleaned your clothes. There is a pouch of gold coins in the front pocket of your pants." Annabelle handed Raul his pants which were folded. Raul pulled a heavy leather pouch out of the pocket of his pants.

"How did you get this?"

"Don't ask," Annabelle said as she handed Raul his cleaned shirt and socks. "Your boots, belt and a pouch that Vitomas found are in that cupboard," Annabelle said and nodded towards a cupboard on the other side of the room.

"Annabelle would you get that pouch for me?"

"This is heavy," Annabelle commented as she retrieved the pouch. "Vitomas said you were lying on it."

Raul sighed with relief when he found the six Holy Scrolls in the pouch. He handed the large leather bag back to Annabelle and she returned it to the cupboard.

Annabelle returned to the bed and once again sat close to Raul; she leaned towards him and whispered. "We are being watched here always. Trust no one and be very careful."

"Annabelle, you and Vitomas need to be careful helping me," Raul paused for a second. "Did Vitomas tell you why she is so upset with me?"

"Raul, we are all in great danger here; she is trying to protect you."

"I don't understand." Raul said. When Annabelle didn't respond he continued. "Why do you stay here, in this place?"

Annabelle stared at Raul incredulously. "Do you not understand where you are? We are prisoners here. We cannot leave."

"Have you ever tried to?"

Annabelle was quiet, then she looked down at the floor, "I have never been that brave but Vitomas has and when they caught her the punishment was," Annabelle looked back at Raul. "It was too horrible to talk about. You have to understand; when Roch administers punishment he will hurt or kill all that you care about first, then hurt you. He is a very cruel man."

"And what will he do to the two of you for helping me?"

"And what will he do to you if we don't?" Annabelle said as she started to examine Raul's bandages. "I want to tell you something," Annabelle wanted to change the subject. "My parents used to care for your father when he was small. They were the personal attendants of King Jaretta and Queen Lillian."

"What are their names?"

"Alexander and Laurel."

"I have heard my father speak of them."

"Really?" Annabelle said with surprise. "After you are gone I will have to tell them. It will please them greatly."

"Do they live in Taperia?"

"No, in the Village of Cana, it's not far from here."

Annabelle was wearing a pink dress with a blue shawl tied around her waist. "What is this?" Raul asked as he saw something that looked like rope fall under her shawl.

Annabelle started laughing, "I forgot to give that to you." She stood and took the shawl off which exposed a great deal of rope, wound around her tiny waist. "You know we don't know if you can use these things we are just bringing them to you in case you want them." Annabelle said as she removed the rope from her waist and wound it tightly. "This should be strong enough to hold your weight. You are on the second floor of the castle; hopefully this is long enough to allow you to escape if you need to."

Raul laughed, "You girls think of everything."

"Trust me; we have spent a lot of time thinking about how to escape from here."

The Sanuri, Padre Bartholomew and Petra had been travelling since the first light of dawn; now they were about to enter the Village of Ort. Because the Sanuri traveled through the woods, they did not enter Ort from the main road but instead from the western side of the village. The Village of Ort was surrounded by farms. Petra cried out when he saw the first farmhouse that had been burned to the ground.

"No, no they didn't," cried Petra.

Petra was sitting in the front seat of the boca between the Sanuri, who was driving the team of horses and Padre Bartholomew. Padre Bartholomew put his hand up to Petra's mouth and said, "My son, you must be quiet, we do not know what we are riding into."

The Sanuri spoke to the horses in a language that neither Petra nor Padre Bartholomew recognized. The horses suddenly became very quiet. As the three entered the village, they could see that most of the buildings had been burned but were in varying stages of ruin. Some of the buildings were a mere remembrance while others were still standing.

The Sanuri stopped the team of horses when they reached the west side of what had been the main road in the village.

Tears were running down Petra's face but the boy did not make a sound. As they looked at the remnants of the village they all were keenly aware of the silence. A few doors squeaked as they were moved by the wind gusts but there were no other sounds coming from the village, not even a bird's song.

"I do not like this; it is too quiet," said Padre Bartholomew.

"Petra is there a designated place the villagers would go to in times of trouble?" asked the Sanuri.

"The monastery but that no longer exists," said Petra through his tears.

"No, is there some place closer? Would they hide in the forest?" asked the Sanuri.

"Perhaps they are dead," said Padre Bartholomew.

"Where are the bodies?" asked the Sanuri. "This village looks as if it were deserted."

"Sanuri, the Forest Yar is very old and many of my people believe it is haunted," said Petra. "I have hunted in there, but many of the villagers would never consider entering those woods."

"Even if their lives depended on it?" asked the Sanuri.

"I don't know," replied Petra softly.

"Petra we will find your parents," said the Sanuri as he dismounted from the boca. "But we must search these buildings; both of you stay with me." The Sanuri walked into the middle of the roadway and was studying prints in the dirt.

"There were many horses here recently. We need to be on the lookout for Hutas," the Sanuri warned.

Together the Sanuri, Padre Bartholomew and Petra searched building after building. They found Huta arrows impaled in many walls. In some areas they saw blood stains but they did not find any of the villagers. As they were walking out of the building that housed the school, Petra said, "Even the animals are gone. It is as if everything vanished."

79

The Sanuri, Padre Bartholomew and Petra shared a sense of uneasiness. Their eyes searched the landscape for any sign of life as they walked down the road. As the three entered the remains of an old barn, they heard moaning. The Sanuri pushed Petra behind some rubble and motioned to Padre Bartholomew to hide. The Sanuri slowly walked forward in the darkness, clutching his staff in his hand.

Vitomas returned to Raul's room with a tray of food for his midday meal. She thought Raul was sleeping as she tidied his room and adjusted the drapes. Suddenly Vitomas looked towards the bed and saw Raul sitting up and smiling at her.

"Did you get any sleep at all?"

"A little but it was difficult because all I could do was think about you. I believe you are stealing my heart, My Lady."

"My Prince are you always so bold with women?" Vitomas asked as she was trying to sound more confident than she was.

"Actually no but then I rarely find myself in a situation like I am now," Raul said. "Vitomas please come and sit near me so we can talk." Vitomas hesitated then slowly walked across the room and sat down on the edge of the bed. Raul took both of her hands in his. "Vitomas you act like you are scared of me and that makes me feel awful. I am sorry for whatever I did that upset you so badly. That was never my intention."

"You have done nothing wrong and you certainly do not scare me," Vitomas replied but she would not meet his gaze.

"Then why won't you look at me?"

"Raul, you don't understand how it is here."

"I understand that you and Annabelle are both prisoners here and that your charity to me is putting both of you in a great deal of danger. I understand that my heart jumps in my chest every time you walk into this room and I can't stop thinking about you. I understand that both you and Annabelle are the two most beautiful and charming girls that I have ever met and how such beauty of spirit can survive here is beyond my comprehension."

Tears started to well in Vitomas' eyes as Raul spoke. She wanted so desperately to tell Raul the truth but she was afraid that he would hate her if she confessed that she was Roch's queen. "Vitomas I know you don't know me but know this, that I will never lie to you," as Raul spoke he put his hands on both of Vitomas' shoulders and stared into her eyes. "If you and I were back home I would ask to court you. But we both realize we do not have the luxury of a normal life right now. We are going to have to make decisions quickly based on our instincts."

"Raul I really don't know what you are talking about," Vitomas said as she stared back at him.

"We have only known each other for a couple of days," Raul said seriously. "But already I know I want you in my life. I want you and Annabelle to come home with me. I am a good man and neither of you have any reason to fear me. I will take care of you both."

"I cannot leave you two behind, not only because of my feelings for you but also my fears of what Roch will do to you for helping me. I don't expect you to have feelings for me so quickly; in fact I realize I must sound rather insane to you. When we get to Wetpr perhaps you will allow me to court you and we can establish a relationship like people would under normal conditions."

Vitomas stared at Raul with tears running down her cheeks. She moved closer to him and put her hand on his cheek. "Raul, I don't think you are insane," Vitomas said with a laugh. "For my heart has been saying the same words that you are speaking to me now."

"I cannot understand how I can care so deeply for someone who I have known for such a short period of time. I know you are a good man, I would trust you with my life. But my dear there are many things that you do not realize here. You are in such great danger that it frightens me always. We must get you out of here before Roch returns. I have been trying to figure out a plan."

Raul pulled Vitomas closer to him as he interrupted her, "We will work on a plan together. Vitomas all I can think about is how much I want to kiss you." As he said these words, Raul put his arms around Vitomas and kissed her passionately on the lips. Vitomas pulled her head back and stared into Raul's eyes, then at his lips as her passion and loneliness overcame her fears.

81

Vitomas put her arms around Raul's neck and kissed him with a passion she did not know dwelt within her. Within moments the two young lovers were losing themselves to their emotions. The world no longer existed with its danger and its fears. All they could feel was the love that was consuming them both.

Suddenly the bedroom door flew open. "Cerephus is coming," Annabelle said frantically as she ran into the room.

Padre Bartholomew hid behind a stack of bales of hay, which gave off a pungent smoky odor. He stood motionless listening to a soft moaning in the darkness of the barn. The Sanuri had motioned to him that he would search the barn and that Padre Bartholomew should stay hidden. There was no sound of movement in the barn. Moments passed and Padre Bartholomew wondered if something had happened to the Sanuri or Petra; just as Padre Bartholomew was about to leave his hiding place to look for his friends he heard a voice in the darkness.

"It is safe to come out but we have a young man here who is quite injured," said the Sanuri. "Padre, Petra help me move him out into the light."

"He is so wet," said Petra. "Is that from his blood?"

"I believe so but I won't really know until I can get a good look at his injuries," replied the Sanuri.

The Sanuri lifted the shoulders of the injured man while Padre Bartholomew and Petra each lifted a leg. They carried the man into the street, where they had entered the barn. They lowered the injured man onto the ground and the Sanuri immediately started to check him for wounds.

"Petra run to the boca and get my medicine bag. It is a brown leather bag behind the front seat," ordered the Sanuri.

"He wears the insignia of the soldiers of Taperia," remarked Padre Bartholomew.

"I know, he is a long way from home," said the Sanuri.

Petra returned with the medical bag and a bowl of water. "You are a smart lad," said the Sanuri "Place the bowl by his head."

The Sanuri took a cloth out of the medical bag, wet it in the bowl of water and started washing blood off the face and neck of the soldier.

"See those brass pins?" the Sanuri was pointing to pins of a crossed battleaxe and arrow on either side of the soldier's tunic. "He is a captain in the Taperian Army. I am wondering where his men are," said the Sanuri with concern.

"Should Petra and I continue searching the village?" asked Padre Bartholomew.

"No it is too dangerous for you," the Sanuri said to Padre Bartholomew, then he turned to Petra and asked. "Petra do you think you can drive the boca here?"

"I can drive it," replied Padre Bartholomew with a smile "I'm not in that bad of shape."

"Good, bring the boca here and clear a space in the back for our guest," said the Sanuri. "I feel we are too in the open here; although no one has tried to harm us yet."

"I feel like we are being watched," said Petra uneasily. The Sanuri finished dressing the soldier's wounds and they moved him into the boca. "What do you think happened to him?" asked Petra.

"He looks like he has seen battle in the last few days because he has several wounds which are healing. But someone hit him many times in the back of the head when he was in the barn; he has lost a great deal of blood," said the Sanuri.

"Do you think it was Hutas?" asked Petra.

"No, the Hutas would have killed him and taken his armor," replied the Sanuri.

As the Sanuri climbed into the front seat of the boca he asked, "Petra where is your home?"

Cerephus burst through the bedroom door, his massive body filling the frame of the doorway.

"Cerephus, I'm so glad you are here, can you help us get him into a sitting position so he can eat. He is so big for Annabelle and me to move alone," Vitomas said. Cerephus looked around the room and did not see anything that seemed unusual for the situation.

"Please Cerephus will you help us? The poor man needs to eat," Annabelle asked.

Cerephus grunted and walked to the side of the bed where Vitomas was standing. He grabbed Raul under the arms and roughly pulled him up to a sitting position. Raul moaned in pain. Cerephus grunted again and started to leave the room.

"Cerephus can we get you if we need help again?" Annabelle asked.

"No," he said gruffly. "Get one of the men."

Annabelle waited a few moments then walked to the door, which Cerephus had left open. She looked both ways down the hallway then closed the door. "That man is very dangerous," Vitomas warned. "Did he hurt you?"

"A little, it's nothing," said Raul as he was still wincing with pain.

Annabelle sat on the bed opposite of Vitomas. Annabelle had a huge smile on her face; first she looked at Vitomas, then at Raul, then back at Vitomas. "You two were kissing, when I walked in," Annabelle said mischievously. Vitomas blushed and smiled and Raul laughed. "You two fools if you're going to kiss lock the door, anyone could walk in here," Annabelle said in a scolding manner then started to laugh. "So?" Annabelle asked and stared at Vitomas.

"So? What?" Vitomas asked.

"So how was it?" Annabelle asked and giggled.

"Annabelle," Vitomas said with embarrassment. "I can't believe you said that."

"It was great," Raul said sincerely. He took Vitomas' hand in his left hand and Annabelle's in his right.

"I am really afraid you girls are going to be punished for helping me. Annabelle, before you came in, I asked Vitomas if the two of you would come to Wetpr with me."

"Really," Annabelle said as her eyes grew wide with excitement. Then her entire demeanor changed. "If I go, Roch will kill my parents. Take Vitomas and never come back here."

"If I go, he will kill Annabelle," Vitomas said. "I won't leave without her. And Raul we have to have a good plan because if they catch us..." she didn't finish her sentence.

"Do you have family here?" Raul asked Vitomas. She shook her head from side to side to indicate no.

Vitomas and Annabelle sat with Raul as he ate lunch. He asked them many questions about the castle, the area and Annabelle's parents

"Outside of Cana there is a hunting cabin that no one ever uses; it is on the Lake of the Pors," Annabelle said. "I think we could hide Raul there, if we can get him out of the castle. I'll draw a map."

"We have to leave, if we spend too much time in here they will get suspicious," Vitomas said. Raul pulled her to him and the two stared at each other for a moment before they kissed.

"Come back," Raul whispered.

Vitomas smiled and the two women grabbed his dishes and walked out of the room. Raul felt as if he was floating on a cloud.

Petra was overwhelmed with emotions, as much as he wanted to see his family he was afraid of what they would find. "Keep going through the village on this road, we are only a half mile down the road," Petra said with a quivering voice. The Sanuri put his arm around Petra. Padre Bartholomew rode in the back of the boca with the wounded soldier.

They did not see any sign of life as they passed the last few burned buildings in the village. "I too felt like something was watching us," the Sanuri said to Petra.

"If it was the Hutas they would have attacked us and if it was the villagers they would have come out of hiding, seeing you."

"Do you think it was Taperian soldiers?" asked Petra.

"No, they would never have let us take their captain away."

"It is there," cried Petra. He stood up in the boca and pointed at a smoldering farmhouse on the right side of the road. Petra started to jump out of the boca but the Sanuri held onto his left arm until the team of horses had stopped. The Sanuri stopped the boca in front of the house and Petra jumped down and ran towards it screaming for his parents.

The Sanuri stayed seated in the boca as he surveyed the area; looking for any signs of danger. When he felt satisfied that they were alone, the Sanuri climbed down from the boca and entered the house. Padre Bartholomew had already followed Petra inside and the Sanuri could hear the priest trying to console the crying boy.

The roof of the small farmhouse was completely destroyed by fire but only one wall of the structure was burned. Much of the furniture inside of the house was toppled over but there were no signs of blood or arrows. The farmhouse was empty.

"They left everything, my mother's jewelry and the family Bible are still here; my parents would never leave these things behind. Perhaps they will return soon," Petra said hopefully as the tears ran down his face.

"Does your family have animals?" asked the Sanuri.

"Yes, we have chickens, pigs, sheep, horses and a few cows why?" asked Petra.

"There are no animals here," said the Sanuri.

"Why would they leave these things and take the animals?" asked Petra.

"Son, your parents may have been taken," said Padre Bartholomew softly. Petra threw his arms around the Priest's waist and cried. Padre Bartholomew put his arms around Petra and looked at the Sanuri sadly.

86

"I am going outside to search the barn and to look for tracks," said the Sanuri.

The Sanuri stood on the front porch of the farm house, his staff in hand. He gazed uneasily over the immediate landscape. "Something is wrong here," he thought to himself. "It is as if all life has left this place." The Sanuri did not hear any birds singing in the meadow; there were no insects buzzing and the air felt unnaturally heavy.

The ground was hard and dry, leaving no evidence of footprints. When the Sanuri entered the barn, he saw tools thrown around the floor. A milking stool was lying on the floor shattered into pieces; the Sanuri saw marks on the wall above the broken stool. "Someone must have thrown this with great force," he thought. The Sanuri walked through the barn and opened a door at the rear of the building. Approximately ten yards in front of him, the Sanuri saw the remains of a human body lying on the hard ground.

Although Vitomas had to share Roch's bed when he demanded, she had her own chambers in the west wing of the castle. Vitomas and Annabelle had shared these chambers since they were nine years old. These two young women had spent their lives trying to protect each other in the castle of a madman. After Vitomas and Annabelle left Raul's room they returned to their chambers.

Vitomas and Annabelle trusted no one in the castle, least of all the cook, Sophie. Sophie prided herself on knowing everything that was going on in the castle as well as in Taperia. She was a source of information for Roch, which he valued. As was their routine, Vitomas and Annabelle searched their rooms for unwanted visitors; then met in the center of the inner room in the chambers and talked in whispers.

Vitomas and Annabelle discussed various ways they could get Raul out of the castle and what they would need to get him out of the kingdom. Both of them were avoiding talking about his offer to take them to Wetpr because it was too painful for them. Raul offered them freedom from Roch, the one thing they desired most, yet if they took him up on his offer; most assuredly innocent people would die.

87

"Annabelle you told me once that your parents were in the castle the night that Roch killed his parents, did they ever tell you about that night?" Vitomas asked.

"Yes and it was awful."

"Do you remember what they said?"

"Vitomas are you sure you really want to hear this story?"

"Yes."

"My parents said that Roch was never a normal child, he was cruel and violent even as a very young boy. They said everyone suspected there was something terribly wrong with Roch, including his parents."

"What did they think was wrong?"

"My mother said that as soon as Roch could walk he was killing animals and stabbing people with knives and scissors. What child acts like that? Mother said that everyone in the castle believed that Roch was possessed by a demon. But no one could figure out how that could happen because his parents were such wonderful people and his brother Sudfad was a normal child. You already know that King Jaretta and Queen Lillian sent Sudfad to Wetpr because Roch kept trying to kill him. Sudfad was nine when they sent him away which means that Roch was only six."

Annabelle continued, "Father said that Roch would get into horrible arguments with his father and that he threatened to kill his father and take the throne many times. And this is when Roch was still a boy, can you believe that?"

"Roch was sixteen when he murdered the King and Queen; my parents say they will never forget that night. One of the soldiers yelled that there was a fire in the King's library. Father was among the people who ran to the library. Father said when they got there the drapes were burning and they found King Jaretta's body on the floor of the library. He had been stabbed in the back many times and a dagger was still in his back."

"The guards recognized the dagger because it had been a gift from King Jaretta to Roch; the handle was gold and encrusted with rubies. Many of the servants and guards heard Roch and his father arguing in the library shortly before the fire was discovered," said Annabelle.

"Mother told me that when she saw the King's body she was filled with fear for Queen Lillian and searched the castle for her," continued Annabelle. "My mother found the Queen's body in her bed chamber. The Queen had been beaten so badly that her face was not recognizable and she had been stabbed in the heart several times."

"That night, after the Queen's body was found, the guards split into groups to search the castle and grounds for Roch. My father joined six of the guards in the search. He said when they reached the back garden they found another group of the King's guards standing near the pool watching Roch. My father pushed through the group expecting to find Roch dead; instead he found something that horrified his soul."

"Father said that he saw Roch sitting near the pool, screaming at his own reflection in the water. Roch was crying and telling his reflection he should not have murdered his parents. Roch yelled at the reflection threatening to kill it. Then Roch lowered his head and started to laugh; a low, chilling laugh. My father said he felt as if he was in the presence of the devil himself."

"Father said that suddenly Roch turned and looked at the men standing behind him then he jumped up from the pool and started yelling commands to the guards. The guards stood in place staring at Roch as he approached them screaming and pounding his blood soaked chest. Roch was commanding the guards to bow before him as he was now King."

Chapter VI
Monsters

In each kingdom live the ruthless and savage Rogetts, tribes of nomads who roam the earth taking whatever they need to exist. Once humans, these creatures were so fearful of the worlds above ground that they chose to make their homes in the bowels of the world. After centuries of living in utter darkness and isolation they lost their humanity. Their bodies adapted to their environments and became smaller and better equipped to travel through tunnels and caves. Rogetts now stand four feet tall. Their skulls became smaller and elongated. Their nails and teeth are long and prominent; giving them a rat-like appearance.

Each and every Rogett carries the Mark of Satan on their chest, a seal of their covenant with the demons. This is a mark of red, shaped like a snake poised to strike. The eyes of the snake are brilliant green with red pupils. The snake's tongue is forked and bright yellow.

These creatures of darkness are cannibals; they will eat their own kind when other meat is unavailable. The sweet flesh of humans is a delicacy for them and highly desired. Rogetts are despised in all of the kingdoms for there are no warriors among them. Instead of fighting face to face and man to man as a warrior, they attack in packs and usually prey on the weak and the defenseless. And even under these circumstances they often hide their faces behind masks of death. Their actions betray the fear that still permeates their souls.

Although Rogetts prefer to live in caves and tunnels they have been known to take over entire mining sites, trapping and eating the miners underground.

The Sanuri turned the body over to expose its face which was partially eaten away. As the Sanuri was examining the corpse, Petra and Padre Bartholomew ran up beside him.

"Petra do not worry it is a Huta warrior and not your father," said the Sanuri.

Petra was both relieved and horrified as he was staring at the corpse. "What killed him?" Petra asked.

"I think it was a large animal, look at these claw marks," saying this, the Sanuri turned the body onto its stomach exposing the shredded back of the warrior.

"The Great Ruler be with us," said Padre Bartholomew. "What manner of creature could do that?"

"The ground is too hard for me to see any foot prints," said the Sanuri as he stared at the body.

"What are you thinking?" asked Padre Bartholomew.

"I was thinking about those strange creatures that were watching us the other night and wondering if they could have done this," said the Sanuri.

"My parents," said Petra anxiously. "We have to find my parents."

"Not tonight my young friend," said the Sanuri as he put his hand on the boy's shoulder. "It will be dark soon; we will spend the night in your home and start our search in the morning." The Sanuri turned to Padre Bartholomew. "You and Petra should gather a great deal of wood for the fire tonight; the fire may have been what kept those creatures out of our camp. The sun will be going down soon so you will have to hurry," continued the Sanuri. "I will check on our patient."

"What about the body? Shouldn't we bury it?" asked Padre Bartholomew.

"That too can wait until the morning," replied the Sanuri as he turned and started walking towards the boca.

"I have known the Sanuri for many years and there is something he is not telling us," said Padre Bartholomew.

"I am scared Padre," said Petra.

"My son, we couldn't be in better hands," replied Padre Bartholomew. "Now we need to gather wood."

"My father has a wood pile on the other side of the house," said Petra and the two walked towards the remains of Petra's home.

The Sanuri was sitting near the wounded soldier in the back of the boca, praying to The Great Ruler to heal the young man. The soldier was still unconscious. As he prayed, the Sanuri suddenly knew this soldier had a significant role to play in the journey ahead and much of his role would be shrouded in darkness.

"Petra, Padre can you help me move this man?" the Sanuri yelled from the boca. The three of them carried the soldier from the boca into Petra's house. "Put him near the fire," said the Sanuri. They lowered the soldier onto the floor in front of the hearth.

"My parents left a lot of food in the house," said Petra as he returned to the kitchen area. "I'll fix supper."

"Do you know how to cook?" the Sanuri asked.

"I used to help my mother a lot."

"I'll help him," Padre Bartholomew said.

"Padre, my parents keep the wine and a lot of food in the cellar, if you want to get something." After Padre Bartholomew descended into the cellar, Petra looked at the Sanuri. "I hope my parents are hiding in the forest."

"I do too Petra, but what are they hiding from?"

As Padre Bartholomew, Petra and the Sanuri finished their meal the soldier started moaning loudly, then suddenly sat up. When the soldier saw them sitting at the table he grabbed for his sword, which the Sanuri had removed from the soldier's belt.

"We are friends," the Sanuri said soothingly "You have nothing to fear with us; do you think you can eat?"

The soldier looked at them, an old man, a Priest and a boy and relaxed his body. "I don't know but I am very thirsty," said the soldier as he tried to stand up. The soldier grabbed his head in pain as Petra and the Sanuri each grabbed one of the soldier's arms to help him walk to the table. Once the soldier was seated in a chair, the color quickly drained from his face.

"Do you feel like you are going to pass out?" asked the Sanuri.

"I am just very dizzy," replied the soldier. "I have not had anything to eat or drink in several days."

"You lost a lot of blood," Padre Bartholomew commented.

The soldier suddenly looked at them, his head clearing. "Where are my men?"

"We found you unconscious in a burned barn in Ort; we searched the village and found no others," said the Sanuri.

"Where am I now?"

"This is Petra's home," said the Sanuri pointing to the boy. "We are trying to find his family; the entire village has disappeared. Do you know what happened here?"

"No, when my men and I rode into the village it was destroyed," said the soldier. "As soon as we entered the village one of my men was shot with an arrow. We searched the village looking for the attackers; the last thing I remember is entering a barn."

"I seem to have forgotten my manners," said the Sanuri. "Petra please fix our guest a plate." The Sanuri turned back to the soldier. "I am the Sanuri of Tabrul, this is Padre Bartholomew and that young man is Petra, what is your name?"

"Archetenus."

"I see you are a captain in the Taperian army," said Padre Bartholomew.

Archetenus looked at Padre Bartholomew then at the Sanuri before answering, "Yes."

"You are a long way from home," said the Sanuri as he filled his pipe.

Petra put a plate of food in front of Archetenus and a cup of wine, "Thank you," said Archetenus as he ravenously devoured the food.

"King Roch sent me with a small detail of men to hunt for the Hutas who attacked the monastery at Avaide," Archetenus said between mouthfuls of food.

93

"That was very noble of him," said the Sanuri suspiciously.

"Padre Bartholomew was almost killed at the monastery," said Petra.

Padre Bartholomew reached over and patted Petra's head, "Yes this brave young man saved me."

"Why did King Roch send you after those Hutas; to avenge the deaths of the priests?" asked the Sanuri.

Archetenus drank his cup of wine in one gulp, he reached across the table and grabbed the bottle, as he was filling his cup he said, "King Roch wanted the treasure that the Hutas had taken from the monastery."

"To return them to the holy place?" asked Padre Bartholomew innocently.

"You must know nothing of the King," Archetenus said with a sneer. "He has long coveted the treasures belonging to that monastery but he would not attack a place considered holy by the entire world. No, he feels like those treasures are his property and he wants them returned."

"Why would he think they are his property?" Padre Bartholomew asked. "Those things were given to The Great Ruler."

"Roch thinks everything is his property. Could I have some more food?" Archetenus held out his plate to Petra, who refilled it.

"Roch looted the monastery after the Hutas left," said the Sanuri.

"How do you know?" asked Petra.

"Roch and his men were approaching the monastery as we were leaving," said the Sanuri. "So were you successful on your mission?"

Archetenus laughed, "Do I look like I was successful? We lost the trail to the Hutas at the Wall of Dorath. That is the place of demons. We were attacked by winged monsters and there were others which we did not see."

"Monsters?" Petra asked fearfully.

"I split my men into two groups to look for the trail of the Hutas," said Archetenus as he continued to eat. "We couldn't find the trail or the Gate of Isula. That place is cursed. We saw no living creatures of any kind; there were no fish in the river or birds in the air and there was a quietness that felt like we were in another world." As Archetenus spoke, the Sanuri thought about his similar observations outside of Petra's house.

"My men were starving," Archetenus continued. "I sent hunters out but they never returned. After several days we found the remains of the other group; their heads were displayed on the Wall of Dorath and their forearms were missing. The winged monsters would not have been able to impale the heads on the wall as they were. We were returning to Taperia when we came to Ort looking for food and water."

"I don't understand why the forearms of your men were taken," Padre Bartholomew said.

"Neither do I," said Archetenus as he grabbed some more bread. "But it was the right forearms that were cut off and all the Taperian soldiers have a tattoo of the crest of the Royal Family of Stordt on their right forearms, under their bracers."

"That must be of significance but how I do not know," said Padre Bartholomew.

"You must have lost a great deal of men. Were they all killed by the monsters?" the Sanuri asked.

"I only had fifty to start with."

"Why did Roch send so few of you after the Hutas?" asked the Sanuri.

Archetenus did not answer the question but said, "It is true, from following their trail; we were greatly outnumbered."

"I find that curious," said the Sanuri. "It appears he did not give you enough men to perform the mission he sent you on. I believe Roch to be a madman but he is also known for his military astuteness."

Archetenus and the Sanuri stared at each other for a moment. "I too, found it curious that the King would send us on an ill-fated mission," said Archetenus.

"What will happen if you return to Taperia without the treasure?" asked the Sanuri.

"King Roch will have me killed."

"Then why go back?" asked Petra.

Archetenus hesitated for a moment, "There is something in Taperia which I need to get."

Padre Bartholomew noticed the tension between Archetenus and the Sanuri and wanted to change the subject. "We were being watched by some strange creatures a few nights ago and we think they may have killed the Huta warrior lying near the barn."

"What sort of creatures?" asked Archetenus, glad to change the subject.

"The Sanuri sensed we were being watched and he found three sets of foot prints in the mud," said Petra. "They were similar to a bear's print but twice the size of the Sanuri's foot with long claws."

"And you all saw these?" asked Archetenus. "Anything else?"

"The Sanuri saw them," Petra said. "Padre Bartholomew and I got attacked by monsters too, so we couldn't see the prints."

"What?" asked Archetenus.

"Both Padre Bartholomew and Petra have knife wounds from the Hutas; who must have dipped their knives in a poison made from the Jacept plant. Because Jacar started to grow in their wounds and spread in Petra's and Padre Bartholomew's bodies eating their blood," the Sanuri explained.

96

"I have heard of the Jacar but no one ever survives their attack. Is this some kind of magic?" Archetenus asked.

"The beasts were a result of magic the healing was the result of The Great Ruler," the Sanuri said.

Archetenus stared at the Sanuri in disbelief, after a few moments Archetenus said, "Tell me more about the creatures that were watching you."

"They walked on two legs as a man," replied the Sanuri.

"Why do you think they killed the Huta?" asked Archetenus.

"He has claw marks on his body larger than any bear could make," said Padre Bartholomew.

"And part of him was eaten," said Petra.

"What do you make of this?" the Sanuri asked Archetenus.

"I don't know. The beasts that attacked us had wings and were the Mark of Satan."

"What do you mean?" asked Padre Bartholomew.

"They looked like giant red serpents with wings, their eyes were green. They killed many of my men."

"I have never heard of such beings," said Padre Bartholomew with astonishment.

The Sanuri took another puff from his pipe, "I have and Archetenus is right they are beasts of Satan. They are called the Talmuth and are servants to the unholy. They would not have attacked you and your men unless they were directed to by a very powerful being."

"Who could summon such creatures?" asked Archetenus.

"A powerful sorcerer or demon," replied the Sanuri. "Do you know why someone would have sent them against you?"

"The Wall of Dorath is an evil place. Have you ever seen it?" asked Archetenus. The Sanuri nodded his head in affirmation.

"There are heads of hundreds of beings impaled on the top of the wall, as far as you can see. The bodies are piled at the base of the wall. There is no sign of life in that place and there is a feeling of evil that chills your soul. Perhaps we disturbed the evil there," continued Archetenus.

"As far as I am concerned that wall is a symbol of the evil of mankind but I have been there many times and not encountered those creatures," said the Sanuri.

"Archetenus and his men were following the Hutas, could the Hutas have called those creatures forth?" asked Padre Bartholomew.

"The Hutas are butchers but I have not heard of them having someone powerful enough in their tribe to summon the Talmuth," said the Sanuri. "Archetenus it is well known that King Roch has many enemies but he also has great power and wealth is it possible that he had the Talmuth summoned?"

They all looked at Archetenus as the color drained from his face. "You asked me before why I had so few men," Archetenus said as he looked at the Sanuri. "I did wonder if King Roch sent us on a suicide mission."

"Why would he do such a thing to his own men?" asked Petra.

Archetenus hesitated "I used to compete in the Gefrey Games and gained the favor of Queen Vitomas; she urged the King to promote me."

"Is there more?" asked the Sanuri.

"Why do you ask?" asked Archetenus angrily.

"Because it could be important," replied the Sanuri.

Archetenus looked down and responded, "I am in love with Queen Vitomas."

"Does she feel the same about you?" asked the Sanuri.

Archetenus looked the Sanuri in the eyes confrontationally, "We have never spoken but I believe in her heart she does; why?"

"If Roch sent you on a death mission because of his hatred and jealousy he will not stop until you are dead; he will have you hunted down," said the Sanuri. "He killed his own parents; there is nothing he would not do."

"Archetenus you cannot go back to Taperia," said Petra.

The Sanuri looked at Archetenus intently, "You my son have many choices before you; consider your actions, for every choice will take you on a different path."

Archetenus looked at the Sanuri suspiciously as he uttered the same words as the woman in his dream. "I have heard those words before," Archetenus said in a low voice. "The night we were attacked by the flying monsters I had a dream. In that dream a woman said those same words to me."

The Sanuri smiled. "The Great Ruler has sent you two messengers with the same message, you should take heed."

No one spoke; they all sat in silence for a few moments before Petra asked. "What about my parents?"

"We will look for them tomorrow," replied the Sanuri.

"But what if we don't find them?" cried Petra.

"Now don't think like that," said Padre Bartholomew as he put his arm around Petra's shoulders.

"You may stay with us as long as you like," the Sanuri said to Archetenus.

"Thank you but I need to find my men."

"Perhaps we could look for them and Petra's parents together as it seems the entire village disappeared," suggested Padre Bartholomew.

"Let us see what tomorrow brings," said the Sanuri. "We should get some rest now."

"Sanuri you and Petra stood watch last night, I will take watch tonight," said Padre Bartholomew.

"I will take the second watch," said Archetenus.

"You are in no shape," said the Sanuri to Archetenus. "Padre wake me and I will take the second watch."

Padre Bartholomew threw another log onto the fire and pulled his blanket tighter around his shoulders, the chill of the night air made him shiver. His eyes felt heavy from weariness as he stared out the window into the darkness of the night. A few moments passed and Padre Bartholomew realized he must have dozed off in his chair near the window.

The priest stood up and walked around the house looking out the other windows; peering into the darkness. "It is difficult to know if shadows are real or an illusion of the mind," thought Padre Bartholomew as he walked around his sleeping friends. After several minutes he returned to his chair, unaware of the eyes that were watching him.

Vitomas had great difficulty sleeping because she could not stop thinking about Raul. She was overwhelmed with emotions. Vitomas finally met a man who she could care for, a man who she truly was attracted to and now he was immersed in the nightmare of her life. Vitomas wanted so badly to escape with Raul but the consequences of her previous attempts to escape were burned into her soul. Could she put so many others at risk for her own happiness?

Vitomas got up before sunrise and put on her favorite skirt and blouse. Vitomas realized she was humming as she was dressing; this was something she had not done for a very long while. Vitomas grabbed a stack of linens and walked down the hallway and into Roch's chambers.

Vitomas checked to make sure she was alone, then she entered the bedroom and put her hand inside of the fireplace. She pulled down on a hidden lever which opened the door to the secret room behind that wall. This was one of the rooms where Roch hid his treasures. Quickly Vitomas filled two leather pouches with gold coins. Then she left the room and returned to her chambers.

"You're up early," Annabelle said as she was getting dressed. Without saying a word, Vitomas pulled Annabelle into the middle of the inner room of the chambers and showed her the two bags of gold coins.

"If any of us are to escape we will need money," Vitomas whispered. "Annabelle can you slip out today to look at that cabin you were talking about?"

"Of course."

"Raul will need food and blankets, will you start putting items in there?" As Vitomas said this she gave Annabelle a handful of gold coins.

"Vitomas this is a lot of money,"

"What you don't spend, give to your parents. But you know people will get suspicious if you spend it all at once."

"I know. I will leave after sunrise," Annabelle said as she helped Vitomas move the large carpet in the center of the room. Under the carpet, the women had made a hiding place in the floor boards, where they now put the pouches of gold.

"I made two maps showing the location of the cabin," Annabelle said, "One is for you and the other for Raul."

Vitomas walked through the long cold hallways of the castle without seeing any guards. When she opened the door to Raul's room, he appeared to be sleeping. She quietly closed the door behind her and walked over to the fireplace. The fire was dying. Vitomas took blocks of wood from a nearby basket and added them to the fire; when the blaze was roaring she turned around and saw that Raul was sitting up in bed watching her and smiling. "You are certainly here early My Lady."

"I didn't want you to get cold," Vitomas said flirtatiously.

"Why don't you lock the door and come here."

Vitomas opened the door and looked in the deserted hallway before she closed and locked it. Then she turned to Raul. Her heart was pounding wildly as she walked up to him but Vitomas said nothing.

Vitomas had barely sat on the side of the bed, when Raul grabbed her with both of his massive arms and kissed her. He pulled her closer to him as their passions took control. Vitomas had never experienced such feelings before and surrendered to them.

Vitomas completely lost herself in his embrace; neither time nor the world existed anymore, it was only her and Raul. He pulled her on top of him. Both of them were sweating as they caressed each other's bodies. Suddenly Raul stopped kissing Vitomas. They both stared at each other trying to catch their breath. "We need a break before this goes any farther," Raul said and kissed Vitomas on the forehead. "I couldn't stop thinking about you all night."

"I know, I thought about you all night as well," Vitomas said with a mixture of love and sadness. "I have something for you." She reached into the pocket of her purple skirt and took out the map that Annabelle had drawn. "This is a map to the cabin that Annabelle was telling us about. I have one also. This morning I gave Annabelle some money to start buying provisions to put in that cabin."

Raul had never asked Vitomas what her position was at the castle but from watching her work and the knowledge that she was a prisoner of the King's; he thought she was a servant. Now Raul's demeanor changed and he looked very seriously at her. "Vitomas where did you get the money from?"

"Don't ask."

"But I am asking; don't tell me you stole it from Roch?"

A guilty look overtook Vitomas' face. "He will never miss it, he has great treasures here."

"Honey, please don't do things that are going to put you in harm's way. I am already so fearful of what he might do to you and Annabelle."

Vitomas' heart melted as she listened to this young man, who she barely knew. Other than Annabelle, no one had ever worried or even cared about her before. Suddenly tears started to roll down Vitomas' cheeks.

Raul thought he was responsible for her tears and felt badly. "I am sorry to make you cry but I mean it; you have to be careful."

"It's not that you scolded me."

"Then why are you crying?"

"Because I'm not used to anyone caring about what happens to me."

Raul stared at Vitomas in disbelief and for just a moment he began to understand how hopeless she felt. Raul put his arms around Vitomas and hugged her tightly.

The two young lovers cuddled, giggled and kissed for another hour. "I should get your breakfast before Sophie tries to bring it to you," Vitomas explained. "She is Roch's biggest spy and I have been trying to keep her away from you."

Vitomas stood up; Raul watched her as she straightened her clothing and pulled back her long, flowing hair. "You have the most beautiful hair," Raul said admiringly. "Come back here." Vitomas sat down on the bed again. "I'm afraid I'm going to mess your hair again," Raul said as he started to kiss Vitomas' neck.

Vitomas giggled and melted under his touch. "I just don't want to let go of you," Raul said and kissed Vitomas on the lips. Then he pulled back and looked into her eyes. "Vitomas, you say you won't leave without Annabelle and she can't leave because of her parents. Do you think they would come with us?"

"Laurel and Alexander, well, I don't know."

"Are they happy living here?"

"No one is happy living in Stordt except for the monsters. I just mean I have never heard them talk about leaving."

"Talk to them, please. Find out if they will leave with us," Raul said earnestly. Vitomas looked at him without saying a word. "Vitomas I know you have not committed to leaving with me. But I will not leave you behind. I am falling in love with you; you have to come home with me." Vitomas did not speak but stood up and walked out of the room.

Vitomas had barely left Raul's room before she returned again, carrying a large tray of food. "It's a good thing I left when I did," Vitomas said as she placed the tray on the table next to Raul's bed. "I met Sophie in the hallway, she was coming here with your breakfast."

"Is that so bad?"

"Raul, that woman prides herself on knowing everyone's business and telling it to Roch. And it is truly remarkable the things she knows."

"What do you mean?" Raul asked as he was filling his cup with coffee.

"Why that woman only leaves the castle one day a week to go shopping and she can tell you everything that is going on not only in Stordt but every other kingdom. It's as if she has spies herself. If she even suspects who you are, they will kill you."

"Perhaps Sophie isn't who she pretends to be?"

"What do you mean?" Vitomas asked as she sat next to Raul on the bed.

"Well, Roch does have a lot of enemies, perhaps she is a spy,"

"She is a fat, old woman," Vitomas said incredously.

"And all the more unsuspecting," Raul said teasingly.

As Raul ate, Vitomas was straightening his beding and tidying up the room. "I'm going to change your bandages after you finish eating," she said. "Would you like a bath?" Vitomas turned and looked at Raul because he did not answer her question. He was staring at her intently and grinning.Vitomas blushed and became flustered, "I gave you a bath before," she said as if defending her question.

"And I wish I would have been awake for that," Raul said suggestively.

Vitomas was becoming more embarrased by the moment and Raul was enjoying it. "Annabelle gave you a bath too."

"So you have both seen me naked?"

"Oh just, just never mind," Vitomas said and walked over to the windows to open the drapes.

"No, you asked me," Raul said with a laugh. "And yes, I want a bath and make sure you lock the door."

"Where is the body of the Huta?" asked Archetenus the next morning.

"It's behind the barn," said Padre Bartholomew. "I will show you; we have to bury that poor soul today."

"Breakfast will be ready soon," yelled Petra from the kitchen area.

"We won't be gone long," said Padre Bartholomew as he and Archetenus walked into the early morning light.

"Sanuri I have been thinking; there might be a place my parents would go if they were in danger," said Petra. "It is not far from..." Petra did not have a chance to finish his sentence before they heard Padre Bartholomew yelling. Both the Sanuri and Petra ran out of the house and towards the sound of Padre Bartholomew's frantic voice.

Padre Bartholomew was running back to the house when he met the Sanuri and Petra. "Sanuri the body is gone," said Padre Bartholomew as he tried to catch his breath.

"What do you mean?" asked the Sanuri. "Where is Archetenus?"

"He is trying to find a trail of whoever took the body, there are no foot prints," huffed Padre Bartholomew. "Come now."

The Sanuri, Petra and Padre Bartholomew ran to the area where they had last seen the body. Archetenus walked towards them, coming from the edge of the woods. "There are no foot prints or drag marks anywhere and the earth does not look like it has been swept," said Archetenus.

"This ground is so hard and dry it is impossible to see anything," said Padre Bartholomew.

"If other Hutas took the body they most certainly would have killed us," said Archetenus.

The Sanuri was looking up at the sky as Archetenus spoke. "Have any of you noticed how still it has been here?" asked the Sanuri. "Not a bird or insect to be heard since we have been here and the air seems so thick. Archetenus you spoke of something similar near the Wall of Dorath." All three men and Petra now looked around in silence.

"You are right Sanuri, we have seen no signs of life since we came here," Padre Bartholomew said in wonderment. "And last night I never heard so much as a night bird."

"At the wall there was almost a green haze to the air and a sense of evil that unsettled us all. Every man among us remarked about it."

"I don't think it was Hutas who stole the body," the Sanuri said as he looked towards the forest.

"Do you think it was those creatures who watched us?" asked Padre Bartholomew.

"I don't know," said the Sanuri as he turned towards Archetenus. "Archetenus search around the house for any sign of our intruders; Padre take Petra and check both the inside and outside of the boca and horses."

"What are you going to do?" asked Archetenus.

"I am going to have a little talk with nature," said the Sanuri with a smile. As the Sanuri was walking towards the woods he yelled, "Petra stay with the Padre no matter what happens."

Archetenus looked at Padre Bartholomew and Petra with surprise. "What does he mean he is going to talk with nature?" scoffed Archetenus.

"Do you know who he is?" asked Padre Bartholomew.

"Only the name he gave me," replied Archetenus with a dubious look.

"The Sanuri is a holy man sent here by The Great Ruler," said Padre Bartholomew. "He possesses gifts that normal men do not have."

"He is hundreds of years old," added Petra enthusiastically.

"I find all that difficult to believe," said Archetenus as he looked at Petra. "And he sure doesn't seem very holy to me."

Padre Bartholomew smiled, "Have you ever met anyone who was holy before?"

"You and other priests."

"Oh no my son, we are nothing in comparison," said Padre Bartholomew. "You feel uncomfortable around him because he can see into your heart. The Sanuri can see many things; you should talk with him." Archetenus did not answer but turned and walked towards the house.

"Raul I can't believe we did that," Vitomas said as she got out of his bed and started to dress.

"Are you sorry we made love?" Raul asked as if he expected her to break his heart.

Vitomas quickly sat down on the bed and put the palm of her hand on his cheek, "No, my darling, it's just, it's just that it is so dangerous here. We will both be killed if we are caught."

"Then we will have to be careful not to get caught," Raul said and kissed Vitomas on the lips.

"Raul I need to get dressed and leave this room for a while or Cerephus will get suspicious."

"If you must leave me, go to Annabelle's parents and speak with them. And can you find me a sword?"

"Yes, do you want anything else?"

"Some paper and pen and a crutch."

"There's paper and pen in this desk," Vitomas said as she brought the items to Raul. "I will return with the rest." Then she looked at him seriously, "Raul I know you are a warrior but you are in no shape to fight or even to ride; we will have to get you to that cabin until you are better."

"Well, this is what I am thinking," Raul said as he pulled her back down on the bed and spoke in a whisper. "What if Annabelle's parents drove a boca across the border, while we hid in the back?"

"They are poor and do not own a boca," Vitomas said more to herself. "But I will give them the money to buy what we need. Oh, but we will need papers or the border guards will not let us cross."

"What kind of papers?"

"Everyone must have written permission from the King to leave this kingdom; you see we are all prisoners here."

Raul heard someone at the door and quickly hid his paper and pen under the covers. Expecting to see Vitomas, he was quite disappointed to see an older woman enter his room, carrying a tray of food. Besides the fact that Vitomas had warned Raul about Sophie there was something about this woman that made the hair on the back of Raul's neck stand up. Her eyes were black and intense as she stared at Raul.

"The Queen is not back from her errands, so I brought you a snack."

"The Queen?"

"You mean she didn't tell you?" Raul could tell that Sophie was deliberately searching for his reactions so he did not know if he could believe what she was saying.

"Which one is the Queen?"

Sophie laughed as she put his tray on the table next to his bed. "I forgot that Annabelle is taking care of you too. You are a lucky man to have the Queen of Stordt as your personal nurse."

Raul suddenly felt a great pain in his chest, as if his heart was breaking but he did not want Sophie to realize his feelings. "And who are you My Lady?" he asked politely.

"Sophie, I am the King's cook," she said with pride.

Raul smiled, trying desperately to hide his pain. "And a wonderful cook you are. The only person I know who could cook like you was my mother."

Sophie blushed and seemed quite flattered by Raul's comments. Sophie sat down on the side of the bed next to Raul, staring into his eyes boldly but to Raul's surprise Sophie's words sounded sincere. "You seem like a nice young man so I am going to give you some advice. I am sure the Queen did not tell you who she was because she didn't want to scare you. King Roch's jealousy knows no bounds. He barely let's her speak to other men, when he learns that she has been spending time with a handsome young man you will regret that she saved you."

"But neither woman has done anything wrong."

"It doesn't matter. Tell me, do you have family I can contact to come and get you?"

"No, Vitomas asked me the same thing," Raul said trying to protect Vitomas. "My parents are dead and I have been traveling around getting small jobs."

"Young man you have to leave this castle and soon. Is there no one I can contact?"

"Perhaps if I had some crutches I could walk."

"And where will you go?"

"Taperia. What little money I had was stolen, so I would need to get work."

"Eat your lunch," Sophie said as she stood up. "I will get you some crutches."

109

"Sophie I thank you but why would you help me?"

"Because we all suffer when the King is angry."

The Sanuri returned more than two hours later. When he entered the house Padre Bartholomew, Petra and Archetenus were all sitting at the table. "How was nature?" asked Archetenus sarcastically.

The Sanuri smiled, "I have something to show all of you. Petra we will need some lanterns do you have any?"

"In the cellar," Petra said as he got up from the table.

"We did not see any signs of the intruders near the house or boca," said Padre Bartholomew.

Petra returned with four lanterns, he lit them and handed them to each man. "I will not need one," said the Sanuri. "Come, follow me."

The four walked deep into the woods behind Petra's house. They were not speaking but listening for any sounds. Finally Petra whispered, "Sanuri it is too quiet here."

"I agree," said the Sanuri as he walked in front of the group.

"What do you make of this?" asked Padre Bartholomew

No one answered his question. The group walked almost another mile before they came to a mountain. The side of the mountain facing them appeared as a huge stone wall instead of the normal terrain of a mountain. It was smooth and vine covered and gave an appearance of suddenly jutting out of the earth; it seemed most unnatural with the rest of the surroundings.

The Sanuri walked forward running his hand along an area of the wall. "Here," he said as he moved a mass of thick vines exposing an opening into the mountain. Archetenus entered first, followed by Padre Bartholomew, Petra and the Sanuri. "Look at the drawings on the walls," said the Sanuri.

Archetenus turned to look at the Sanuri and was amazed to see the end of the Sanuri's staff glowing brightly in the dark. "Look here," said the Sanuri pointing to a drawing high on one of the walls. "I believe these are the creatures that were watching us a few nights ago."

"Look there are many pictures of these creatures," said Petra.

"Yes, their history is written on these walls," said the Sanuri. "These creatures are called Centras. They are ancient beings that once roamed freely in the world. But men hunted them for sport and captured them until their species became almost extinct. They are gentle, intelligent creatures that now shun the world of men."

"So they live in caves now?" asked Petra.

"Yes and high in the mountains," answered the Sanuri.

"They are huge and walk on two legs," said Padre Bartholomew as he studied the wall paintings. "They certainly could have made the foot prints you saw."

"Do you think they had anything to do with my parents disappearing or that dead Huta warrior?" asked Petra.

"I don't know but something is terribly wrong here," said the Sanuri.

"I want to know who made these paintings," said Archetenus.

"The Centras did, they are documenting their history," said the Sanuri.

"You mean they are smart enough to do this?" Archetenus asked with amazement as he looked at the thousands of paintings on the walls of the cave.

"Yes," said the Sanuri. "There are tribes of men who are not as intelligent as these beings, yet they were hunted for sport."

"Why?" asked Petra.

"The species of man does not appreciate the gifts of The Great Ruler; they do not coexist with nature," said the Sanuri. "There are many men who mock The Great Ruler and live to destroy all that is good; like the King who you serve," the Sanuri said as he looked at Archetenus.

"I am not King Roch," Archetenus said angrily.

"That is true," said the Sanuri. "But some say a man can be measured by the demons he serves."

Chapter VII
The Face of Death

Two hours later Vitomas and Annabelle came into Raul's room; both women were smiling and seemed excited. They both stopped abruptly when they saw the look on Raul's face.

"What is wrong?" asked Vitomas.

"I don't know, perhaps you should tell me My Queen," Raul growled through clenched teeth.

Vitomas started to cry, "Who told you?"

"Sophie, and that is all you can say is 'who told me'. You let me fall in love with you and you couldn't even tell me you were married." Raul's face was red with anger.

"I should go," Annabelle said.

"No," Raul yelled. "You are part of this too."

"Raul please keep your voice down, or the soldiers will come in here," Vitomas said as she sat on the bed near him. "You have every right to be angry with me but not Annabelle, I begged her not to tell you." Annabelle walked to the door to listen for the soldiers. Raul was seething and just kept staring at Vitomas, who couldn't stop crying.

"Roch stole me from my parents when I was a small child and as young as I was he took me for his wife. I am not with him because I want to be. I despise the man, he is a monster."

"Is this the truth?" Raul asked sternly.

Before Vitomas could answer Annabelle walked up to the bed with her hands on her hips and said angrily, "Raul, I told her you would be angry and you have every right to be. But you have no idea of what Roch has done to Vitomas or the beatings she has taken to protect the rest of us. Her life is a nightmare; he hurts her all the time. Yes, she should have told you but she was afraid; so don't you judge my friend."

Raul looked at Vitomas. "Why didn't you tell me?" he asked in almost a whisper.

"Because I was afraid you would hate me," Vitomas said between sobs.

Raul grabbed Vitomas and pulled her to him, hugging her tightly. "You too," he said to Annabelle as he held out his right arm. Raul hugged both of the women for a couple of minutes. "Vitomas do you have feelings for me?"

"How can you even ask?" Vitomas asked as she looked into his eyes, through her tears.

"Because you have not told me and you are another man's wife."

"She loves you," said Annabelle with a grin. "She's just been too afraid to tell you that too."

Raul enjoyed Annabelle's personality and smiled at her words. "But I need to hear it from Vitomas."

"I do love you Raul but I fear that our feelings for each other will result in your death." Raul kissed Vitomas on the lips then turned to Annabelle. "Are you spoken for?"

Annabelle was shocked by his question. "Raul I like you a lot but I don't love you."

Raul laughed loudly. "I have an adopted brother named Simon, who is just going to adore you."

"Does he look like you?" Annabelle teased.

"He and I are built alike but he has blonde hair and blue eyes. He's my closest friend as well as being my adopted brother." Annabelle gave Raul an approving smile and a wink.

"So what are you saying?" Vitomas asked.

"I want you to come back to Wetpr with me and be my wife."

Archetenus was filled with rage; he took a step towards the Sanuri and both men stared into each other's eyes. The silence was broken by Padre Bartholomew. "No good will come of us fighting among ourselves; we have bigger problems to solve."

114

"Sanuri, Padre, look at this," said Petra who had wandered deeper into the cave. "This creature is holding a box in many of these pictures; now look over here, it looks like a Huta warrior is riding away with the same box."

"There is a scorpion with a sword next to the warrior," said Archetenus. "That is the symbol of the Huta army."

"What does this mean?" asked Padre Bartholomew as he studied the wall paintings.

"That is The Box of Itifer," said the Sanuri. "It is a powerful gift that The Great Ruler gave to this world. But as with many of his gifts, when men discovered they could misuse and distort the power they sought if for their personal agendas. Since the Centras have always been faithful and pure of heart, The Great Ruler gave it to their tribe to protect until a time when mankind was ready for such a miracle."

"Does this mean that the Hutas now have this gift?" Padre Bartholomew asked with horror. "I have heard stories that they worship demons and from what I have seen I believe this is the truth. We cannot let them desecrate a holy gift."

"The Hutas have always been a hate driven race which is how they were easily influenced by powerful demons. As a race they have sold their souls to darkness which is why we are now seeing so many changes in them," the Sanuri explained.

"What do you mean?" Archetenus asked.

"The Hutas have always been the scourge of this continent with their hatred and intolerance. But there was a time when they thought for themselves as other men. But since they have sold their souls to the demons they have no will of their own. Their King in a mere puppet whose reign is soon to end. The Huta generals no longer command the warriors. They are commanded by dark lords and demons and this makes them more dangerous than ever."

Vitomas could not believe Raul's words. She stared at him with her lower lip quivering, unable to speak. Annabelle too, stared at Raul but she was the first to break the silence. "I can't believe this," Annabelle said excitedly and kissed Raul on the cheek.

Then Annabelle ran around to the other side of the bed and kissed Vitomas on the cheek. "I'm so very excited," Annabelle said as she ran to the door to make sure no one would walk in on them.

"Well, are you excited?" Raul asked Vitomas.

"I cannot believe my ears, please say it again."

Raul's face lit up with a smile, "I want you to be my wife." Vitomas started crying harder as she put her arms around Raul and whispered into his ear, "I want you to be my husband."

"So are these creatures, the Centras, killing the Hutas to get their box back?" asked Archetenus.

"I do not know," said the Sanuri. "But that might explain why they have not bothered us."

"But what about my parents?" asked Petra with fear in his eyes. "I don't see any paintings on the wall that look like these creatures attacked our village."

"Archetenus is it customary for the Hutas to leave their dead behind?" asked the Sanuri.

"They usually will not bury the bodies but they will strip them of valuables."

"Let us leave this cave," said Padre Bartholomew. "I do not like it here."

They continued their conversation as they walked out of the cave and back into the forest. "Did any of you notice valuables on the body of that Huta warrior?" asked the Sanuri.

"I didn't see any," said Padre Bartholomew. "But there was so much blood perhaps I missed something."

"I did not see any valuables either," said the Sanuri. "So from what Archetenus said, it probably was not Hutas who took the body."

"If that Huta warrior would have been the one who stole The Box of Itifer wouldn't there have been a painting on the wall that the box was returned?" asked Padre Bartholomew.

"Yes, and a painting that showed great celebration," replied the Sanuri.

"We have not seen any signs of bodies, neither my men nor the villagers; if these creatures have them, well, what would they do with them?" asked Archetenus.

"The Centras have never been a violent species but with their spiritual connection gone I don't know what they might do," said the Sanuri.

Archetenus was walking in the lead; he suddenly stopped and held up his hand for the others to stop also. The group was silent, all eyes searching the woods for any sound or sign of movement. Then they heard it.

The beating of the drums.

"You two can kiss later," Annabelle teased. "Raul we have much to tell you. We talked to my parents today and we went to the cabin I told you about. The cabin is still deserted and my parents will help you." As Annabelle talked her voice was filling with excitement.

"My parents loved your father and his parents. They were thrilled when we told them about you but then almost immediately they were worried for you. They want to meet you but it is not safe for them to come to the castle so we have to find a way to get you to the cabin tomorrow. When we described you to them they said you must look like your father."

"Yes, I am a mirror image of my father," Raul said with a proud smile.

"Will Roch recognize you?" Vitomas asked as she tried to stop crying.

"He hasn't seen father since they were small boys, I don't know how he could."

Vitomas was wiping the tears from her face, when she suddenly jumped up and ran over to a chair. She had dropped her shawl on the chair when she entered the room. Now Vitomas walked up to Raul and showed him a sheathed sword that was wrapped in her shawl.

Raul pulled the sword from its sheath and examined the blade and the balance. "This is a beautiful weapon, where did you get it?" Neither girl said anything, they both smiled at him.

"You didn't steal it from Roch did you?"

"It belonged to your grandfather; Alexander had it hidden all of these years," Vitomas said with a huge smile.

"My parents have some other things that belonged to your grandparents. They didn't steal them, they have been hiding them from Roch; hoping someday they could get them to your father."

"This sword will go to my father when we get home," Raul said and was surprised how emotional he felt holding something that belonged to a grandfather he never knew.

"Vitomas gave my parents money to buy a boca and some horses and provisions for the journey as well as provisions for the cabin. I already took some baskets of food and blankets to the cabin; we have to figure out how to get you out of here now."

"Raul what did Sophie say to you besides to tell you I was Roch's wife?" Vitomas asked.

"I didn't know if I should believe her because it was obvious she was looking for reactions from me. I don't believe I gave her what she wanted. But once I started to compliment her cooking she seemed, I don't know, like she was telling the truth after that. She told me it was not safe for me here because Roch was such a jealous person."

"I told her that neither of you had done anything that should anger him but she said just because you were around me was enough. She asked if I had some family who could get me out of here and offered to contact them for me. I figured this was a trick so I told her my family was dead."

"Sophie told me again that I needed to leave. I said that I could if I had some crutches. She said she would get me some."

There was a knock on the door and both Vitomas and Annabelle jumped. Vitomas walked over to the door and opened it. To her surprise Sophie walked into the room carrying two crutches. "I don't know if you two girls are just stupid or if you are up to something but you know there will be hell to pay for all of us if you don't get him out of here. Cerephus expects Roch back any time now. You need to hurry."

"Sophie, do you think the guards will stop us?" Annabelle asked.

"They don't want him here either. Believe me no one wants to tell Roch you spent the entire time with a handsome young man, even if he is injured."

"Sophie would you come here?" Raul asked.

Sophie walked up to the side of Raul's bed. "Please sit down," Raul said. When Sophie did, Raul leaned over and kissed her on the cheek. "Thank you Sophie." The old woman blushed and became so flustered she didn't say anything but stood up and walked out of the room. Both Vitomas and Annabelle stared at Raul in amazement. "She's nicer to me than she is to you two," Raul said jokingly. "Hand me my clothes."

Raul was getting dressed when they suddenly heard Sophie's voice in the hallway. "My Lord you must be hungry wouldn't you like something to eat?" Sophie said loudly. Annabelle grabbed the sword and threw it under the bed just as Roch burst through the door.

A low thundering boom echoed through the forest, then silence then another and another. Petra grabbed Padre Bartholomew's sleeve. "What is that?" asked Petra fearfully.

"I don't know but I fear whatever it is will be upon us soon," said the Sanuri. "Quickly, everyone back to the house."

The group was silent as they moved through the woods; listening for sounds of attack. Archetenus pulled his sword from its sheath. Petra was about to ask a question, when the Sanuri motioned for him not to speak. The sounds of drums could still be heard in the distance when they arrived at Petra's house. Archetenus searched the inside of the house as the others watched for attackers, through the windows.

"Would the Hutas beat drums?" asked Padre Bartholomew.

"I think every tribe beats drums but Hutas usually don't let you know they are coming," Archetenus said.

"What about those creatures?" asked Petra.

"I have never heard of them using drums and I did not see any drums in their paintings," said the Sanuri. "Petra have you ever heard of villagers or farmers in the area beating drums?"

"No, but my parents told me about a tribe of people who live deep within the Forest Yar. They are supposed to be very friendly and they trade wares with the villagers of Ort; that is where I wanted to look for my parents."

"I know the village you speak of Petra but it is almost to Lake Manrt, that is a great distance," said the Sanuri. Petra's eyes started to fill with tears.

"Don't worry, we will find your parents my son," said Padre Bartholomew.

"I have not seen any movement," said the Sanuri. "I am going to check on the boca and the horses." The Sanuri left through the back door.

A few moments later the Sanuri opened the back door. "Archetenus you need to come here." Archetenus, Petra and Padre Bartholomew all followed the Sanuri. "We have had company," said the Sanuri as he led them to a fenced area behind the house. "Is that your horse?" There were two horses tied to the fence both had saddles that displayed the colors of the Taperian Army.

The Sanuri was in the lead and walked between the two horses. He turned to Archetenus and pointed to one of the saddlebags on the horse. On the flap of the saddlebag was painted a red serpent with green eyes. "I think someone is telling you that you have been cursed," said the Sanuri.

Archetenus looked at the Sanuri, "These are not my saddlebags," said Archetenus as he untied the strap and reached inside the bag.

"Wait," yelled the Sanuri. But it was too late; Archetenus quickly pulled his hand out of the saddlebag and it was covered with blood. "Are you hurt?" asked the Sanuri.

Archetenus looked at his right hand, "It is not my blood."

"Step back," said the Sanuri as he took the pair of saddlebags off from the horse. He walked a few yards away from the horses and held the bags upside down, so that the contents would fall out.

"Great Ruler save us," cried Padre Bartholomew. "Petra do not look."

Roch entered the room like a raging bull. Cerephus, Sophie and two soldiers stood behind him in the hallway. "What the hell is going on here Vitomas?" Roch was screaming but as he entered the room he stopped dead in his tracts and stared at Raul, who was dressed, standing with his crutches and staring confidently at Roch. Even with Raul's black eyes, cuts and bruises, Roch could see his brother in the young man. Their audience stared at both of them in wonder of what was happening.

"Are you Sudfad's boy?" Roch growled.

"Yes and I can see my father's resemblance in your face," Raul replied. Cerephus and Sophie looked at each other with wide eyes at the revelation.

"Why are you here and what happened to you?"

"I have been traveling in all of the kingdoms. The last thing I remembered was sitting at my campfire then I woke up here."

"Your father did not send you?"

"No, why would he? You beheaded the last messenger he sent to you."

"Yes I suppose he wouldn't take a chance of me doing that to his only son. Were you traveling alone?"

"Would I look like this if I had help?"

Suddenly Roch laughed, which amazed everyone in the room. "You may look like your father but you sound like me." Then Roch turned to Vitomas. "Tell me what happened," he growled. This was the first time that Raul looked away from Roch. Raul now saw the looks of terror on the faces of Vitomas, Annabelle and even Sophie.

"My Lord, I was on a morning ride when I saw vultures circling overhead and went to investigate. I found a campsite that was torn up, there were prints of men and the prints of a lion and blood. I heard moaning and found this man."

"A lion?" Raul asked.

"Yes," Vitomas said fearfully.

"Where did you find him?" Roch demanded.

"Near the river, close to those caves."

"How did you get him on your horse?" Roch asked suspiciously.

"I poured water from my canteen on his face and he came to a little. I had Raven kneel next to him and I told him to climb on Raven's back. Which he did but then he was unconscious again and it was very difficult keeping him on Raven."

"Why didn't you just leave him?"

"My Lord, I am sorry this displeases you and you have every right to be angry with me but you know me; I could not leave an animal to die, much less a man."

Roch finally believed Vitomas' word and the anger seemed to drain from him. Then he turned to Annabelle. "What is your role in this?" he asked gruffly.

Before Annabelle could speak Vitomas walked closer to Roch, standing between him and Annabelle. "You can see for yourself that your nephew is as big as you are. He has wounds everywhere and a broken leg; I could not move him and bandage him by myself. Remember that time you came home almost dead, I couldn't take care of your wounds without one of the soldiers helping me. She did nothing wrong. And besides as you can see he is dressed and on the crutches we just brought him. He was preparing to leave and resume his journey."

Raul wanted to fight with Roch but he knew his actions could cause Vitomas and Annabelle to suffer.

"You can't ride like that," Roch said to Raul.

"My horse was stolen, I was going to walk to Taperia."

"So you wouldn't feel my wrath?" Roch asked contemptuously.

Roch's words angered Raul but he tried not to show it. With the use of his crutches Raul walked up to Roch and gently pushed Vitomas out of his way. The two men stood but inches apart and glared at each other. "No," Raul said calmly. "I was going to leave so you wouldn't punish anyone for helping me."

Roch grinned. "Your father never had the balls to stand up to me like that," Roch said still trying to goad Raul. "Truly you should be my son not his." Raul just kept staring at Roch. "It is getting dark soon you can't walk on crutches in the dark. You can stay until you are better but my wife will no longer be your nurse." Roch grabbed Vitomas by the arm and dragged her out of the room, Vitomas looked at Raul and shook her head from side to side, trying to tell him not to do anything.

Cerephus and the soldiers walked away with Roch, Sophie remained in the doorway and Annabelle stood motionless in the bedroom.

"Sophie, I am sorry I lied to you," Raul said. "I did not know this was Roch's castle until you told me and I was afraid I would endanger you if I told you who I was."

Sophie looked at Raul and smiled. "I understand. I will bring your dinner later," she said and walked away.

Annabelle closed the door and stood with her back to it staring at Raul. "No one has ever challenged Roch like that and you can't even fight. I couldn't believe my eyes," she said in awe. Then Annabelle asked "Why did you say that to Sophie?"

"Because I would rather have her as an ally then an enemy."

"I will admit she does seem to like you and she doesn't like anyone." Annabelle could see that Raul was still angry. "Raul sit down, there are some things I should explain to you. But you might not like to hear them."

"Do you know him?" the Sanuri asked Archetenus as they looked at the decapitated head lying at their feet.

"His name is Travor, he was one of my men," said Archetenus sadly. "The last time I saw him was in the Village of Ort."

"What?" cried Petra.

"Padre would you please take Petra into the house?" asked the Sanuri.

As soon as Petra and Padre Bartholomew were gone Archetenus screamed, "Would someone kill my men as a curse to me?"

"What was this man doing the last time you saw him?" asked the Sanuri.

"All my men split up and we were searching the buildings in Ort."

"Archetenus whatever is after you is watching all of us; I need you to be honest with me. Do you know of anyone who might be after you because this is not the work of the Hutas?"

"When I was promoted to captain, there were jealousies among many of the other soldiers but this is not how a warrior fights," said Archetenus with frustration.

"The question is would any of those men employ the assistance of a witch? Think back to the battles you have fought; the villages your men commandeered for King Roch."

Archetenus was silent for a few moments, the furrows in his forehead deepening with his frustration. The Sanuri studied Archetenus' face waiting for an answer.

"I cannot think of anyone other than Roch. He would not want Queen Vitomas or the men who are loyal to me, to know of his involvement in my death," said Archetenus angrily. Then he quickly stepped towards the Sanuri and glared into his eyes. "You are supposed to be a holy man with special powers, why don't you tell me who is behind this," Archetenus demanded confrontationally.

Vitomas did not struggle as Roch dragged her down the hallway and stairs, he stopped in front of his war room. "Go to my chambers and wait for me," Roch ordered. "I think you need to be reminded whose wife you are."

Vitomas looked Roch in the eyes. "I never forgot My Lord," Vitomas said and started to walk towards the west wing.

"Wait," Roch said. "I have been traveling a great deal, make sure there is whiskey and wine in my chambers and wear something nice."

"Yes, My Lord."

Sophie now joined Roch and Cerephus in front of the war room. "My Lord I have fixed your favorite, leg of lamb and potato pie would you like me to serve you in the war room?"

"Sophie I know that you won't lie to me, were they telling me the truth?"

"To the best that I know everything they told you was the truth My Lord. That boy was unconscious for days, when I brought him some food today I told him where he was because he didn't know. Ask Cerephus, he checked on them, in fact he had to help those girls sit that boy up so he could eat."

Roch looked at Cerephus who replied, "Everything that Sophie says is true My Lord. I did not think she should bring that boy here but she is still your queen. I did not stop her but I did watch her. If I would have seen anything inappropriate I would have killed him myself."

125

"My Lord you know how Vitomas is, that girl cries when she sees a dead bird," Sophie said in an uncharacteristic act to defend Vitomas.

"I see," Roch said as his suspicions were put to rest. "Sophie, Cerephus and I will eat dinner in the war room."

"Are you really going to let that boy stay here?" Cerephus asked as he shut the door to the war room."

"Actually I kind of like him," Roch said as he filled two glasses with whiskey. "He reminds me of me. But that doesn't mean I won't kill him. Cerephus this could be a gift; I have Sudfad's only son prisoner in my castle. I will have to think about this."

"So we should stop him if he tries to leave?"

"Yes, I wonder what my dear brother will give up to save his son."

The Sanuri smiled, "I believe you don't know who is behind this butchery but you have aligned yourself with evil."

"Do you mean King Roch?" asked Archetenus. "His men took me as a small boy, I did not have a choice in that matter."

"Archetenus you are no longer that boy and you have made many choices in your life; a man is only a slave to destiny if he allows himself to be."

"I had to stay or they would have killed me."

"You do not strike me as a man who fears death."

The two men stood silent for minutes, Archetenus thinking about the Sanuri's words. "I am sorry I brought this curse upon you and your friends; I will take leave of you," said Archetenus.

"My son, stay with us, it is no accident we are all together at this time; The Great Ruler has a reason for everything," said the Sanuri with sincerity.

"Then what would be the reason for this?" demanded Archetenus.

"I do not yet know. But have faith, it will be revealed."

"Do you hear that?" asked Archetenus as he visually searched the landscape for signs of intruders.

"The drums have stopped," said the Sanuri anxiously. "Quickly into the house." As the two men entered the house the Sanuri yelled, "Petra, Padre get near the windows."

"What is happening?" asked Petra.

"The drums have stopped beating which means whoever was beating them may be ready to attack," said Archetenus as he pushed the table against the back door.

"Help me," yelled Padre Bartholomew as he was trying to push a heavy wooden cupboard against the front door. Both Archetenus and the Sanuri helped him with the cupboard.

"I don't suppose you have any magical weapons on you," said Archetenus sarcastically.

The Sanuri laughed, "Always my son."

"Archetenus we have the bows and arrows from the boca," said Petra as he ran to the kitchen to gather the quivers and bows.

"Well, that is something," said Archetenus. "Petra get that fire going we may need it."

"Padre do you know how to use a bow?" asked the Sanuri.

"I should say so; I will have you know I used to provide all the meat for my family before I entered the monastery," replied Padre Bartholomew with pride. "You will be surprised to know this old priest is also well versed with the staff."

"Good to hear," said Archetenus smiling.

"Petra do we have enough water in here to last for a day?" asked the Sanuri.

"I brought in three buckets and we have plenty of food. Sanuri, there is a tunnel in the cellar that goes to the barn," Petra said.

The three men all looked at each other and then at Petra. "Show me," said Archetenus. Petra and Archetenus climbed down the ladder into the cellar.

"What do you think is out there?" asked Padre Bartholomew.

"I really have no idea," said the Sanuri as he was walking from window to window.

"Petra is a fine boy," said Padre Bartholomew. "Sanuri, if something happens to me will you help him find his parents?"

Before the Sanuri could answer, Archetenus and Petra climbed out of the cellar. "The door in the barn is well hidden, no one will find it unless they know what they are looking for," said Archetenus. "The barn is close to the forest, I think we should leave this place once darkness falls."

"Something has been watching us and we have yet to get a glimpse of it; I think we cannot wait until nightfall," said the Sanuri as he looked at Archetenus.

The Sanuri motioned for Petra to come to him. "Petra," the Sanuri said as he put his hand on the boy's shoulder. The Sanuri knelt down so he could look Petra in the eyes. "We will find your parents but right now we are all in grave danger. Gather your belongings and the keepsakes you would have and put them into the boca; do you understand that we have to leave here now?" Petra threw his arms around the Sanuri's neck and hugged him, then ran to the sleeping room.

"I will pack the food," said Padre Bartholomew.

"Can you hitch up the horses without making any sound?" Archetenus asked Padre Bartholomew.

"I will hitch the horses to the boca," said the Sanuri.

"Well, I think you might want to hurry; there is a lot of smoke coming from behind that hill," said Archetenus as he pointed out a side window.

Petra ran from the sleeping room with two satchels. The Sanuri grabbed the satchels, "Petra I will take these to the boca; you help the Padre."

Within minutes the group was leaving the barn, the Sanuri driving the boca with Petra in the front seat and Padre Bartholomew watching through the rear curtains. Archetenus was riding his horse and pulling the second horse. They escaped into the forest without seeing any intruders. Deeper and deeper they rode into the darkness of the old forest; the forest sounds silencing as if the creatures sensed danger.

Archetenus motioned to the Sanuri that he was going ahead of the boca to check the area. He returned about thirty minutes later. "Luck must be with us," said Archetenus. "There is a cave up ahead, big enough to hold the boca and the horses; follow me."

Inside the cave, Petra and Padre Bartholomew were feeding the horses and preparing dinner. Archetenus motioned for the Sanuri to follow him outside. "When I was looking for a place to make camp I saw a hill. I crawled to the top of the hill so as not to be seen. I could see quite a distance and all I saw was thick smoke coming from the direction of Ort. I did not want the boy to see it," said Archetenus.

"Are they burning the forest?"

"I do not think so but I believe Petra's home was attacked."

"Did you see or hear anything else?"

"No. You go in; I am going to gather more brush to cover the cave's entrance."

Annabelle and Raul had just sat down on his bed when she quickly jumped back up, "I almost forgot," Annabelle said as she walked to the other side of the bed and picked up a covered basket which she now set on the bed near Raul.

"My father sent you this," Annabelle said as she pulled a bottle of fine whiskey out of the basket. "Do you want me to pour some for you?"

"Yes, please." Raul was listening to Annabelle but thinking about Vitomas. "Join me."

"I've never tasted whiskey," Annabelle said and poured just a few drops into a glass for herself. "Raul I know you are worried about Vitomas, but let her handle him. If Roch even suspects the two of you have feelings for each other he will torture and kill both of you. And honestly, when the two of you are in the same room, it is obvious that you care about each other. You will have to be careful."

"What do you mean, let her handle him?"

"Roch took Vitomas when she was nine years old and treated her terribly. There were nights that I thought she would die at his hands." Annabelle got tears in her eyes as she talked. "He brought me here to be her companion but he never treated me as badly as he treated her; mostly because Vitomas would hide me when he was drunk or angry. Many times I would hear her screaming terribly. When it got quiet I would sneak out and look for her. I would find her naked and bleeding, one time he threw her outside like that." Raul stared in horror as Annabelle talked.

"As long as I have been here, Roch will have his men bring women and children here, and sometimes other men. He rapes and tortures them in front of his men because he likes an audience. Sometimes when he is done he lets his men have them. Roch often makes all of us watch what he does. In a way I guess you could say that Vitomas and I were lucky because he never killed us; he usually killed the others." Raul took Annabelle's hand and held it.

"Four or five years ago, Roch suddenly changed, we don't know why. I mean he still does all of those awful things but it was like he fell in love with Vitomas. He started to treat her better and to do things to make her happy. He likes to hear her laugh. He had more gardens built around the castle and he gave her Raven. But even though he seems to love her he still beats her; it's hard to understand."

Annabelle continued, "Now Raul I don't know if you can truly understand what I am going to tell you. When Roch has his fits of temper he hurts not one or two people but many. Vitomas can keep him calm. She hates him but she tries to keep him happy just to protect everyone else. She has saved people's lives. The peasants say she is their patron saint."

"Don't mistake her kind heart for affection towards Roch. One of the reasons she didn't tell you she was Roch's queen is that she is very ashamed that she is forced to sleep with a man she hates. Vitomas didn't want you to think badly of her."

Later that night, Padre Bartholomew, Petra and Archetenus slept in the cave as the Sanuri took the watch. The Sanuri was standing near the opening of the cave, peering through the brush they had put up as concealment; when his head was flooded with visions. The visions were coming so fast that he couldn't understand what he was seeing. Suddenly the visions slowed down and the Sanuri realized he was watching beings crawling around in the darkness, many, many beings.

The Sanuri strained his mind's eye to see what these beings were; finally they came into focus and he could see the geometrically cut tuffs of hair protruding from the heads of the invaders. Their faces were eaten away by the cancers of their souls leaving gaping holes that distinguished the Zendoti from other demons. Their hands were nothing more than three long fingers but it was what the Sanuri saw them holding that interested him. Many of these hell beasts were holding the forearms of slain Taperian soldiers, the bracers had been removed exposing the crest of the Royal Family of Stordt.

Raul got little sleep that night, so much was going through his head. All he could think about was how terrified Vitomas looked when Roch found them and the stories that Annabelle told him. Raul had heard many things about Roch, his cruelty, his insanity, his violence towards his people but until tonight Raul never really understood.

Raul wanted to run to Roch's chambers and kill him and take Vitomas. But Raul knew Annabelle was right when she told him that impulsive actions on his part could put many people in danger.

Raul sat up and grasped the hilt of his grandfather's sword; that Annabelle had hidden under his blankets before she left. Raul was sleeping with his trousers on, his boots and crutches were next to the bed and the daggers that the women gave him were under his pillows. Raul knew he had to be prepared for anything.

The Sanuri quickly walked out of the cave into the darkness of the night.

"I see you got my message," a voice said.

The Sanuri turned and smiled when he saw his old friend. The Lion, as old as time itself was an emissary of The Great Ruler. A warrior Angel who took the form of a great lion when he walked in these dark worlds. The Lion had been a teacher, a guide and a protector to the Sanuri for hundreds of years. The Sanuri had never seen The Lion's true form but the Sanuri understood that he was unworthy to gaze upon such holiness.

"Have you figured out who the boy is yet?" The Lion asked.

"No."

"He is one of The Seven Sons of the prophesy. You must protect him at all costs. If you do not find his family you will know where to take him."

"Are those beasts after Petra?"

"They are after all of you."

"Why do they carry the forearms of Taperian soldiers?"

"Roch's darkness knows no limits. As if his army of mercenaries is not enough for him; he has employed a witch of great power to help him. He wants Archetenus dead. But the witch in her ignorance thought she could control the demons she unleashed. They will be stopped tonight. But know there are more monsters here than these Zendoti. Go back to your friends and keep them inside of the cave."

Padre Bartholomew, Archetenus and Petra all jumped up; startled from their slumber as the Sanuri entered the cave.

"By the saints what is that sound?" asked Padre Bartholomew.

"Lions," replied the Sanuri calmly.

"Lions," repeated Petra fearfully. Archetenus grabbed his sword.

"There is no need for that," said the Sanuri as he touched Archetenus' forearm. "They are not our enemies."

The four stood in silence listening to the earth shaking roars outside of the cave.

The next morning Roch got out of bed first, he walked around the bed and opened the drapes; the first rays of the rising sun were barely visible. Vitomas stood up as she was putting on her robe, Roch put his left arm around her thin waist and grabbed her throat tightly with his right hand. "I don't want you to go near my nephew again; do you understand?" Vitomas nodded because she was unable to speak.

"That's my girl," Roch said and kissed Vitomas on the forehead. I have gifts for you. Roch walked over to his saddlebags that were setting on one of the chairs. He pulled out two pouches, Roch set one on the table and opened the second. Roch held up the gold and ruby necklace he had stolen from the monastery.

"It's beautiful."

"Turn around and hold up your hair," Roch said as he fastened the necklace on her. It was a large and heavy necklace; that Vitomas would never have worn if she had a choice. "Turn around. It's beautiful on you," Roch said admiringly. "I want you to wear that today."

"Yes My Lord, thank you."

"Oh I have more, these I found on the way back to Taperia. Roch held up two large sapphire earrings that were surrounded with diamonds and rubies.

"I love these," Vitomas said. Roch handed her the matching necklace, brooch and ring. "Thank you but why so much?"

"Because you're my favorite girl." Roch kissed Vitomas on the cheek and walked out of the room.

When Vitomas was sure that Roch had gone down to his war room she ran to her chambers, hoping Annabelle was still in the room.

"Are you alright?' Annabelle asked as Vitomas entered the room.

"No, but he didn't really hurt me too much, apparently Sophie and Cerephus told him that we were telling the truth."

"Sophie has never defended us before," Annabelle said. "I think she likes Raul. After you left they talked and she really was nice to him."

Annabelle was still in bed and Vitomas sat on the bed beside her, "Did you see the way that Raul stood up to Roch?" Vitomas asked. "I was so afraid that Roch would kill him but I couldn't believe my eyes."

"I know, I told him the same thing last night." Annabelle said. "He was so worried about you. I told him, well, basically about our life here and that you can keep Roch somewhat sane so he shouldn't do anything rash."

"That was probably good," Vitomas said. "But we have to get Raul out of here; you know how fast Roch can change. He has forbidden me to go near Raul. So I need you to give him a message for me, then go to Cana and help your parents prepare for the trip. I'm going to try to figure out how we can get the paperwork for the border guards."

Raul jumped when Annabelle entered his room with his breakfast tray. "Have you seen Vitomas? Is she alright?"

"Yes she's fine but he has forbidden her to come near you. She told me to tell you that she loves you and to be ever watchful because Roch is so tretcherous. She wants me to go to Cana and help my parents prepare for the trip."

"Vitomas is going to work on the paperwork we will need to get across the border. Raul you have to be patient but we have to get you out of here."

"Can't I just walk out the door?"

134

"I don't know. I wouldn't trust anything Roch says."

"Well, I guess there is only one way to find out," Raul said and started to get out of bed.

"What are you going to do?"

"See if the guards stop me."

Annabelle stood between Raul and his crutches. "Will you sit down, honestly Raul you aren't King here, just sit down." Raul reluctantly sat down as Annabelle continued, "So what, you are going to start a fight with the guards and lose because you are so injured and because of your actions, Vitomas and I will be beaten and locked away for a couple of days."

"Now please tell me how that helps anything?" Raul angrily stared at Annabelle. "So what was your plan Raul, to walkout in the dark and make your way to the cabin or were you thinking of trying to find Vitomas?" Annabelle now softened her voice. "Raul you know I am right. Put your energies to use by helping us plan the escape."

Chapter VIII
Holy Men

"My Lord, Jonas and others did not return with you, were they killed?" Cerephus asked as they ate breakfast in the war room.

"No, we didn't lose any men," Roch replied as he gulped down a cup of coffee. "I sent them on an errand."

"What sort of errand?"

"Why?"

"Well they are still under my commnand I should know where my men are."

"You all are under my command and I sent them out to find holy men."

"All the holy men in this kingdom are dead, you mean you sent a handful of men to raid other kingdoms?" Cerephus was becoming angry at the absurdity of the idea.

"Settledown, stealing a holy man shouldn't be that hard."

Cerephus stared at Roch for a few moments waiting for him to say more before he asked, "Why do you want a holy man?"

Roch smiled, knowing he was really irritating Cerephus. "Because I found some ancient text at the monastery that I want translated."

Cerephus knew that Roch was not a religious man so the text must have something to do with treasure. "You do know that not every holy man will be able to translate that text, especially if it is very old."

"Well then, I will just work my way through them until I find one who can help me," Roch said smiling as he sliced a piece of ham on his plate.

That morning Raul and Annabelle drew maps of the surrounding areas as well as the routes they should take to Wetpr.

"Yes, yes I will check on her but Raul you should know that once Roch goes to his war room he either spends his time in there or on the road. She will be fine the rest of the day."

"Please just go check on her," Raul begged.

Annabelle stared at Raul for a moment, as if she was trying to read his thoughts, "You really love her don't you?"

"Yes, I do," Raul said softly.

"Roch is nice to her sometimes but I have never seen him look at Vitomas like you do. He thinks of her as his property; your eyes are filled with love when you talk about her. Raul I hope so much that we can all escape from here and have real lives." Annabelle kissed Raul on the cheek.

"Have you figured out what you are going to do about the boy?" Cerephus asked referring to Raul.

Roch smiled and leaned back in his chair, "I am really savoring this moment; do I want to kill him now and send his head back to his father or do I want to make Sudfad work to get him back and then kill him."

Cerephus was silent for a moment, "My Lord, need I remind you that your brother commands an army much greater than ours and he is known throughout the continent for his strong abilites as a military leader. I know you hate him but he isn't that same little boy anymore."

Roch stared at Cerephus angrily. "I am well aware of these things."

"My Lord going to war against your brother's army would deplete your treasures; I am just looking out for your interests," Cerephus said.

Cerephus knew exactly how to get Roch's attention, nothing mattered more to Roch than his treasures. "I know you are Cerephus, you above all have always watched out for my interests."

"My Lord, might I speak freely?"

"Go ahead Cerephus."

"Well, most of my contact with the boy was well, when he was unconscious. I know how badly injured he is and I saw how he challenged you last night. As he heals I suspect he will be trouble."

To Cerephus' surprise, Roch laughed, "I suspect so too. Cerephus when he challenged me I felt exhilerated; it has been a long time since I have had a worthy opponent. And as I stared at him, it was like looking in a mirror. My nephew is the man I would have liked my son to be. For just a moment I actually felt proud of him."

"Sanuri, Sanuri," yelled Petra as he shook the Sanuri's shoulder. "He's gone Sanuri, wake up."

"Who is gone?" asked the Sanuri as he sat up.

"Archetenus, he took his horses and some food," said Petra.

"When did he leave?" asked Padre Bartholomew who was also awakened by Petra's voice.

"He was gone when I got up," replied Petra. "Should we look for him?"

"No, let him go," said the Sanuri. "Archetenus believes the creatures that have been following us are after him, he left to protect us."

"Why are they after him?" asked Petra.

"He says he does not know."

"Do you know where he is going?" asked Padre Bartholomew.

"I suspect he is returning to Taperia, he said he had to get something there," said the Sanuri. "He is a grown man and able to make his own choices. Do not worry about him. But, there is something I need to tell you. Petra, your house was attacked after we left, Archetenus saw the smoke. It is not safe for you here. I am going to take the both of you to the monastery in Malga in the Kingdom of Puntd; you will be safe there."

"But what about my parents?"

"I promised you I would look for them and I will but you and the Padre do not need to be travelling always, as I do."

"I know some of the priests at Malga, we will be treated well," said Padre Bartholomew trying to reassure Petra.

Petra was quiet through breakfast. When they were ready to leave the cave, Petra rode in the back of the boca while Padre Bartholomew rode in the front with the Sanuri.

"I think the boy is very upset but you are making the right decision," said Padre Bartholomew.

"He is afraid he will never see his parents again."

"Now that we are alone, tell me about the lions last night."

"The Great Ruler works in mysterious ways. I believe he cleared our path for us."

Raul was anxiously pacing in his room on his crutches; which caused him great annoyance. He was trying desperately to keep himself from doing something that would only end up putting Vitomas and Annabelle in danger. Raul had never been the kind of man to sit back and let others do his fighting for him. And now he felt so helpless; he couldn't even protect the woman he loved. Vitomas filled Raul's thoughts always; he felt as if his heart was melting every time he saw her. Raul thought about the previous night and how brave she had been to stand up to Roch and protect Annabelle.

"You're going to exhaust yourself."

Raul had been so absorbed in his thoughts that he did not hear Sophie enter the room. She put his lunch tray on the table next to his bed.

"Thank you Sophie; that smells really good."

"Are you trying to figure out what you are going to do?"

Raul now stared at Sophie; there was something about the tone of her voice that peaked his interest. "Yes, you are very astute. Sophie how long have you worked here?"

"Since Roch was a boy."

"So you know this castle well?"

"Like the back of my hand," Sophie said with a smile as she straightened Raul's bedding. "Yes, these old drafty castles are a lot of work to keep clean, what with all the back staircases and hidden areas."

"Sophie you have been very kind to me and I don't want to get you into trouble."

"You know I cannot tell you how to escape; so choose your questions carefully."

"I never seem to see any guards in this hallway, am I missing something?"

"No, your observations are correct." Sophie was straightening the drapes as they spoke. "Yes, you could walk freely up here if you were to choose to do so."

"I am sure Roch wants me watched, so if there are not guards up here they must be at the bottom of the staircase."

"You are an intelligent young man but I am assuming you are referring to the main stair case. You know I started my employment here after your father was gone but the staff would tell me stories of the two young princes playing. Apparently they liked to hide in the closets where the staff keep the cleaning supplies and linens. One time Roch locked his brother in one of the back stairways that led to such a closet. Little Sudfad was sitting in that dark stairway for two days before his parents found him."

"And if he would have walked to the bottom of the stairs what would he have found?"

"The butler's pantry near the main kitchen. There is almost always someone in the kitchen, if only little Sudfad would have realized that."

140

"And I assume there is a door from the kitchen that leads outside for deliveries."

"Of course it is a large kitchen."

"Sophie I know you are loyal to your King; why are you helping me?"

Sophie now walked up to Raul and stared into his eyes. "You remind me of someone I used to know; learn from an old woman. We all have choices to make in this world, choose wisely because the fates rarely give you a second chance."

"You were in love with this man Sophie?"

Sophie did not answer the question. "If you feel the need to clean your room, the supplies are in a closet five doors down to your left." Sophie started to turn towards the door, then turned back to Raul. "Last night I saw the look on your face when Roch was dragging Vitomas from this room. You are most fortunate that he did not see it."

"What do you mean you cannot find any holy men?" screamed Roch. He grabbed his goblet of wine and threw it at Jonas' head. Jonas quickly moved to the right and the goblet smashed into the wall. Red wine spilled onto a pile of maps that were stacked on top of a leather topped table.

"It has been days," screamed Roch, "And you still have not found anyone." Roch pushed over a chair that stood between him and Jonas. As Roch quickly moved towards Jonas he grabbed the ruby handled dagger out of his belt. Roch held the point of the dagger to Jonas' throat. "Perhaps I should find another for this task," Roch screamed into Jonas' face.

"My Lord, you killed all of the holy men in the kingdom. I have had soldiers travelling to the surrounding kingdoms but their holy men hide in fear," said Jonas as he looked Roch in the eyes with an unwavering stare. "I have heard stories that there is a great holy man living in Calix in the Kingdom of Puntd but he is protected by the King." Jonas continued. "It is said this holy man is an advisor to King Tobias; I dare not capture him for fear of starting a war."

Roch lowered the dagger from Jonas' face and walked across the room to the window. Roch stood for minutes looking through the window into the royal courtyard; the redness fading from his face as he calmed down. "Jonas, gather one hundred good men we will pay King Tobias a visit."

"Are we going to war with only one hundred men?"

"No," laughed Roch. "I will be bearing gifts; perhaps King Tobias will allow his holy man to do me a small favor." Roch turned and faced Jonas, "Have the men ready to leave in two hours."

"Yes My Lord," said Jonas and he exited the war room.

Roch walked up the stairs of the west wing. He wanted to see if Vitomas was following his orders. When he found Vitomas she was soaking in a hot bath in her chambers. The vision of her, stirred the passions within him.

"My Lord is something wrong?" Vitomas asked as she was surprised by his visit.

Roch walked across the room and sat on the edge of the tub. He caressed Vitomas' cheek with his right hand which was cloaked in a thick leather glove with spikes of metal on the knuckles. "I will be leaving this afternoon for Calix; I should be back after a few days. Why don't you get out of the tub?"

Vitomas stood up and covered herself with a towel. "You just got home, why are you leaving so soon again?"

"I want to see if King Tobias will loan me some of his holy men," Roch said with a laugh. Roch watched as Vitomas dried herself and took the ribbon out of her hair that had secured it to her head. Her golden locks fell around her shoulders. Roch loved Vitomas' hair.

"Why?" Vitomas asked in amazement at his statement.

"Nothing to worry yourself about," Roch said as he pulled her close to him. "I just need something translated. But we have some time before I go, I don't want you to forget who your husband is while I am gone."

142

After Sophie left his room, Raul walked up and down the hallway looking into rooms. He did not trust Sophie but in this case she appeared to be telling him the truth. Every door he entered opened into a bedroom chambers. While richly decorated, these rooms looked as if they had been closed up for years. White dust covered everything and showed every print, Raul was very careful not to touch anything in these rooms.

When Raul felt satisfied that soldiers were not lying in wait for him he found the closet that contained shelves of linens, and some cleaning supplies. Raul examined the walls and found a small knob in the back of the closet. He had to push hard against the wooden door which had warped over time.

Raul was pushing so hard that when the door finally flew open, he lost his balance and almost fell down the dark stairway; causing great pain in his broken leg. Raul shut the door that opened into the hallway and slowly made his way down the dark staircase. The wooden steps were narrow which made balancing on his crutches difficult.

Raul counted the steps, seventeen in all. He came to a stop at another closed wooden door. Quietly Raul turned the knob. This door was easier to open. Raul pushed the door open just enough for him to look out. Sophie had told him the truth; Raul was in a pantry that was lined with cupboards filled with dishes and silver.

The young prince held his breath as he listened for even the faintest sound. Finally Raul opened the door and walked through the pantry. The pantry had two doors, one opened into the formal dining room, which Raul found dark and empty and the other opened into the kitchen. There were two huge hearths with blazing fires in the kitchen. The room was large and filled with tables and cupboards. Baskets and pots hung from the walls.

Raul peered out of one of the windows in the kitchen and saw soldiers patrolling the area. Raul noted that he would have to cover a great distance before he could get to the wall that surrounded the castle but there were many large bushes and trees that he could use for concealment.

Raul tried to time how often the soldiers walked past that area but then he heard voices from inside the house and quickly made his way back to the staircase.

Roch was often gone from the castle, sometimes for months at a time. General Cerephus was always put in charge of Roch's properties and interests when the King was away.

"Cerephus I want you to double the guard watching the Queen while I am gone," said Roch.

"Of course My Lord, no harm will come to her."

"I am more concerned with her activities Cerephus; I expect a full report when I return."

"Yes My Lord," replied Cerephus warily.

"And Cerephus, our guest has over stayed his welcome but do not let the Queen know I was involved."

"I understand My Lord. He will not be here when you return."

"What do you mean that Sophie told you about a hidden staircase?" Annabelle asked.

"She told me the truth although I am not sure what her motivation is." Raul said as he peaked into the hallway from his bedroom. "I searched all of the rooms on this floor to make sure there weren't any soldiers spying on me. Then I found the closet and made it down to the kitchen. Come I'll show you."

Annabelle followed Raul down the hallway and into the closet. He shut the door to the hallway behind them which left them in the dark. "There is a door straight ahead of you, it opens immediately to a narrow staircase. There are seventeen steps before you come to the door of the pantry.

"You stay here and let me try," Annabelle said.

"Are you alright," Raul called after he heard Annabelle trip.

"Yes, I don't know how you made it down these steps on those crutches."

Annabelle would normally be free to walk in the castle so her presence in the kitchen would not cause suspicion. Annabelle looked in cupboard drawers until she found some candles. She grabbed a handful, then walked over to one of the kitchen hearths and lit one candle in the flames. Annabelle walked back into the stairway and closed the door behind her.

"Just as I thought, there are holders on the walls," Annabelle said as she quickly inserted unlit candles into the holders. When she ran out of candles Annabelle put the candle that was lighted in a metal holder and returned to the pantry. This time she grabbed a small plate in addition to more candles. As Annabelle walked back up the stairs towards Raul, she filled all of the candle holders. "This one we can keep in your room to use to light the others."

"I saw soldiers patrolling but I think I can work my way to the wall by hiding behind bushes."

"Raul, you are on crutches, we have to think of something else."

Later that night, Vitomas sat in her room trying to figure out what clothing she could take with her on their journey to Wetpr. Vitomas was trying to keep busy as she waited for Annabelle to return with a message from Raul. Vitomas sent Annabelle to tell him that Roch had left and would be gone for several days and perhaps this was the break they needed.

"Vitomas, Vitomas," Annabelle screamed as she ran into their chambers. "Come quickly something is wrong with Raul."

"What do you mean?" Vitomas asked as fear seized her heart.

"Raul is really bad, like he was when you first found him. I think the Court Physician gave him something because there is a medicine bottle on the table next to his bed." Vitomas grabbed her head as she tried to think.

"Annabelle do you know any healers in Cana, someone we can trust?"

"Yes, Gala is a great healer, should I get her?"

"Yes, but you will have to sneak her into the castle and here," Vitomas pulled a small pouch of gold coins out of a drawer and gave it to Annabelle. Tell her I will pay her much more when she gets here."

"Should I tell her why we need her?"

"I believe you will have to."

Annabelle, tried to calm herself as she grabbed her cloak and shopping basket. She still had to get past the guards and out of the castle walls. Annabelle took a deep breath and walked out of the chambers, her heart was pounding so loudly it seemed deafening.

Vitomas ran out of her chambers and to the eastern wing. No one stopped Vitomas as she entered Raul's bedroom. He was lying in bed, unconscious. Raul was fully dressed and his clothing was soaked with sweat. His lips had a strange purple color to them. Vitomas looked up and saw the bottle of medicine on the table. "Hurry Annabelle," she whispered to herself.

Vitomas grabbed a towel and soaked it in cold water, as she was placing it on Raul's forehead one of the soldiers entered the room. Crispus was supposed to watch Vitomas always. Crispus thought he was doing a good job; he did not realize that both Vitomas and Annabelle knew he spied on them.

"My Lady, the King said you are not to be with this man," Crispus said as he stood in the doorway of the bedroom.

"Crispus, my patient is dying, now you can either run your sword through me now or just report to the King like you always do; because I am going to take care of him. In fact I could use some help. Crispus will you come here and help me pull him to the center of the bed?" Crispus did not move. "Crispus please help me."

Crispus helped Vitomas move Raul in the bed. "What do you think is wrong with him?" Crispus asked as he stared at Raul.

"I don't know but he is burning up with fever," Vitomas said as she took Raul's boots off from his feet.

146

"Do you think it's ketchy, My Lady?"

"Crispus I really don't know what is wrong with him. Now you better go and tell Cerephus I am in here before you get into trouble."

"Yes, My Lady."

Vitomas opened Raul's shirt and was pressing the cold wet towel against his chest, desperately trying to cool his body.

"My Lady, you know what the King said," Cerephus said as he entered the room.

"Yes Cerephus and I expect that he will punish me severely when he returns but this man is dying and I am going to take care of him," Vitomas said as she started to cry. "Please Cerephus, have you no mercy?" Cerephus grunted and turned and walked back down the hallway.

Annabelle hitched a single horse to a small boca and drove across the court yard. Her heart was racing as she neared the gate. Annabelle was not afraid for herself but she was afraid that if the soldiers stopped her she would be delayed getting Gala. Annabelle had become very close to Raul in this short period of time; she was filled with fear that he would die.

Annabelle waved and smiled flirtatiously as the soldiers opened the gate for her. Annabelle waited until she was out of sight of the tower guards before she made the horse run.

Archetenus stayed off the main roads as he traveled back to Taperia. The Sanuri had told them all about the demons that were coming for them in the cave. Archetenus didn't believe the Sanuri's story but after the lion's stopped roaring and the sun started to show its face to the world, Archetenus left the cave and found the ground littered with the bodies of the demons.

Archetenus did not like or understand the Sanuri but he did not want to bring his curse upon the Sanuri, the priest and the boy. Archetenus started his journey to Taperia before sunrise. While he was riding, Archetenus thought about what he would do next.

Vitomas cried and prayed as she tried to cool down, Raul's burning body. He was thrashing around the bed and mumbling incoherently. When she ran out of water, Vitomas ran down to the kitchen to refill the pitcher. Sophie was alone in the kitchen when Vitomas entered.

"How is our patient?"

"Don't you know?" Vitomas said accusingly, in a tone she never used with Sophie.

Sophie's demeanor changed, "No, what are you talking about?"

"He's dying and I am sure you know nothing about it."

Sophie stared at Vitomas, "How?"

"If I had to guess I would say he had been poisoned." Vitomas filled the pitcher and started to leave the room.

"Vitomas, I had nothing to do with it. I showed him a hidden staircase, I hoped he would escape. But I don't think he was ready to leave you behind."

Vitomas did not say any more to Sophie, she just turned and walked out of the kitchen. Vitomas was crying so hard she could hardly see as she walked down the long hallway to Raul's room. Just as Vitomas got to the door, she heard a sound inside of the room. Fear seized her as she thought the soldiers were with Raul. Vitomas flew through the door, startling both Annabelle who was holding Raul's head up and Gala, the healer, who was pouring a bottle of liquid down his throat. Vitomas quickly shut and locked the bedroom door.

"Gala figured out what the poison was from me describing Raul's symptoms. She just gave him an antidote," Annabelle said happily.

"What!" Vitomas gasped. "You mean he will live?"

"Yes My Lady but it appears this bottle is filled with more of the poison. The one dose will not kill him just make him horribly sick but if he was given more from that bottle he would surely have died," said Gala.

"What is the poison?" Vitomas asked.

"The physician ground the root of the asp tree, which is very poisonous and mixed it with this medicine. You can tell because of how purple the Prince's mouth is," Gala explained.

"Gala did Annabelle tell you who Raul is?"

"Yes My Lady and you more than anyone else knows that he will die if he stays here."

"Gala I can't thank you enough for helping us. I will pay you greatly but we may need more of your services," Vitomas said. "How soon can he be moved?"

"Tobias certainly we can come to some kind of compromise," said Roch as he raised his goblet of wine to his lips.

"Roch every kingdom knows you murdered the holy men in your kingdom to quash all religions. Now you come to my kingdom and ask me to present you with holy men. Would you murder them also?" asked King Tobias, his voice rising with anger.

"Tobias I do not mean any harm to your people, I simply have an ancient text I need translated," said Roch calmly. "You are correct I forbid all religious activity in my kingdom," Roch continued "But I have no intention of pushing my beliefs on you or your people."

"Then I do not understand why you come to my home with an army and demand to see my holy men," said Tobias as he held out his goblet for the servant girl to fill.

"I want to speak with a holy man for a purely personal reason. As I said earlier I have come into the possession of a very old manuscript in one of my conquests. I believe it to be written in the language of the ancients and I have not found anyone who can translate it for me," said Roch as he took a bite of chicken.

149

Tobias sat quietly eating his dinner, he did not respond to Roch's statement. "All the continent knows how you value education, I am sure you have someone who can translate this manuscript for me," continued Roch.

"Have you asked your brother, it is said he has the finest universities in all the continent," replied Tobias without looking up from his plate of chicken.

Roch was filled with rage at Tobias's comment but he was too close to finding a translation of his beloved map to alienate Tobias now. Roch sat quietly for several minutes calming himself before he spoke again.

"Roch while I respect you for your abilities as a commander and a soldier I do not trust you in this matter; I will not hand over any of my people for you to slaughter," said Tobias as he stared into Roch's eyes.

"How can I persuade you to believe me?"

"Send all your men home except six," said Tobias, "You will stay as a guest in my home and my holy men will attempt to translate your manuscript here in the castle with both of us present."

Roch stared at Tobias for a few moments then responded, "I am sure you have many obligations and do not need to waste your time in this venture."

"Roch, those are my terms besides I am becoming curious as to what you think this manuscript says."

Roch gritted his teeth then managed to smile as he motioned for Jonas to come over to him. Jonas had been standing along the wall in the great dining hall. Jonas stood at attention next to Roch at the dining table.

"Jonas pick five men to stay with us and send the others back to Taperia."

"Yes My Lord," said Jonas. He took one step backwards, then turned to his left and marched through the Great Hall.

"Jonas, one of my men will go with you and show you and your men to your quarters," said Tobias before Jonas exited the room. Tobias motioned for one of his guards to go with Jonas and the two men left the room.

"Roch, I know you are not happy with my terms but I am still unclear as to why you chose to come to my kingdom on this quest."

"This manuscript is very important to me and honestly you are the first King I have come to with this request."

Tobias motioned for the servant to pour more wine into Roch's goblet. "If this manuscript is truly written in the language of the ancients my people may not be able to translate it; you need to understand that," said Tobias. "Very few men have that knowledge, it has unfortunately been lost in our history." Tobias handed Roch a pouch of tobacco.

"Perhaps your holy men will know of someone with this knowledge," said Roch as he filled his pipe.

"I know of someone who would have such knowledge."

Roch quickly looked up from his pipe, "Who do you speak of?"

"Surely you must have heard of the Sanuri of Tabrul?"

"I thought he was a legend."

"By no means, I have met him myself. Some say he has walked this world for hundreds of years, working for The Great Ruler Himself," Tobias continued. "It has even been said that the Sanuri is the messenger who gave The Holy Scrolls to each kingdom; if this is true he would be able to read the language of the ancients."

"Tobias are you telling me this story so I leave your kingdom?" asked Roch with a laugh.

"No, this is why your actions confuse me. I would have thought you would have sent for the Sanuri first," stated Tobias as he continued to try and light his pipe.

"In what kingdom does he live?"

"He lives everywhere and nowhere. He has no permanent home but travels the continent doing the will of The Great Ruler; I have heard he spends much time in the Ice Caves of Mordv."

"With the Rualas?" asked Roch with astonishment.

"Why do you act so surprised Roch, the Sanuri saved the Rualas and relocated them to the Ice Caves."

"I had heard that story but I did not believe it."

Tobias leaned forward as if he was afraid someone would hear what he was to say to Roch. "Roch you are a fierce warrior but the Sanuri is a very powerful being, perhaps the most powerful being you will ever meet; he cannot be intimidated."

"Why do you call him a being and not a man?" asked Roch. Then he added with a sneer, "I have beaten many powerful men."

King Tobias leaned back into his chair and looked at Roch for a moment before answering. "What man do you know who has lived more than five hundred years, my friend?"

"And you believe that Tobias?"

"Roch I have been in his presence. He may look like an ancient holy man but The Great Ruler has bestowed upon him gifts that normal men do not possess; just be careful."

"If he possess such great powers, perhaps I should have him in my court," replied Roch with a laugh.

"Roch I am serious."

"Tobias you must know I don't believe the legends about The Great Ruler. I think fearful people cling to such stories because they are weak and looking for someone to save them."

"Then I must be a fearful person," said Tobias as he stared boldly into Roch's eyes.

"I do not want to start a conflict with you; how would I find this Sanuri?"

"You will have to send messengers out to the kingdoms as I said he is always travelling. I will have a servant show you to your room, I will call my holy men to appear at the castle first thing in the morning."

"Cerephus he is dead; surely you will allow me to give him a proper burial," Vitomas said as she sat across from Cerephus in the war room. Vitomas was sobbing, which seemed to make Cerephus very uncomfortable. "Cerephus if you don't believe me, look at his body, you can send men to the gravesite with us," Vitomas offered, then she paused for a moment. "I am prepared to pay you."

"What?" Cerephus uttered in surprise.

"Roch gives me money but I never go any place to spend it except to the market once in a while, here see," Vitomas said as she handed Cerephus a small pouch of gold coins.

"I don't think the King would approve," Cerephus sputtered.

"Does he have to know?" Vitomas knew that like Roch, Cerephus was obsessed with riches. That was one reason the two men understood each other so well. If her tears didn't work to soften Cerephus' heart, Vitomas knew the gold coins would entice his greed.

"I am sorry you did not find the information you seek," said King Tobias as he walked Roch out of his castle the next morning. Jonas and the other five soldiers were mounted on their horses and waiting for King Roch to join them. Roch was visibly angry as he walked towards his horse. Just as Roch and his men were starting to ride, King Tobias called out to Roch. Roch turned back to the castle and rode up to Tobias.

"Roch, perhaps your trip was not in vain after all," said Tobias as he handed Roch a piece of dried leather. "While you were speaking with my holy men, I asked my soldiers to locate the Sanuri for you. They did not find him but they did hear of an ancient monastery located in Rubar in the Kingdom of Ryed, here is the map."

Roch took the map. "If I find the information I seek, I will be in your debt."

King Tobias and several of his ranking soldiers watched Roch and his men ride away from the castle. Tobias turned to his Captain. "Double the sentries on the walls tonight, I do not trust Roch."

"I will prepare the men at once My Lord," replied the Captain.

"Also, have your men gather all the holy men in the kingdom and bring them to the castle. Tell them they will be staying here for their own protection," said Tobias.

"For how long?" asked the Captain. "You know they will ask."

"I don't know yet."

"They will not like that. You know they are preparing for the holy quest My Lord."

"Tell them it is by order of the King," said Tobias. "Besides, they may be more willing to come than you think; many of them saw the rage in Roch's eyes when they could not give him the information he wanted. Roch is a madman, never trust him," said Tobias as he turned and entered the castle.

Jonas rode to Roch's right. "My Lord you seem angry," said Jonas.

"Tobias is a pompous fool!" exclaimed Roch. "I should kill him, perhaps I will one day."

Jonas was silent as Roch ranted loudly. "Tobias and his soldiers sat between me and each of his holy men; I could not get them to tell me anything I wanted," Roch said his voice rising with anger. "I know they were keeping things from me. If we were in my kingdom they would have been in the dungeons. And one morning, he gives me one morning to question all of his holy men; you know there were more that he did not bring to me." Roch was spitting as he yelled, he was so angry.

They rode in silence for several minutes before Roch spoke again, "Jonas there was one man who told me an interesting story," said Roch. "Have you ever heard about the legend of The Ruby Scroll?"

Jonas was startled by the question because Roch did not make normal conversation with his subordinates, at least not without an ulterior motive. Jonas hesitated, knowing a wrong answer could have dangerous consequences with Roch. "Yes My Lord, it is a legend as old as the beginning of time."

"Tell it to me."

"It is said that at the beginning of all things that men lived together as one. When people started to separate into different kingdoms The Great Ruler gave gifts of great power and wisdom to each kingdom. These gifts are called Holy Scrolls and six were given to each kingdom. Legend says The Great Ruler gave the scrolls to the holiest men of each kingdom to keep safe and to teach the people of The Great Ruler. It is said that these scrolls hold great power but The Great Ruler also made another scroll that was encrusted with rubies and which holds the power of immortality."

"Do you believe this nonsense?"

"My Lord, I have seen The Holy Scrolls in the Kingdom of Ganz; in the Monastery at Leven."

"When was this?"

"My parents took me on a pilgrimage when I was twelve," replied Jonas.

"So you believe each kingdom was given these scrolls?"

"All I know is that I have heard about them since I was very young and I saw the scrolls in Ganz."

"If these legends are true then what became of the scrolls given to Stordt?"

"I am sure your father would have been aware of them My Lord, perhaps he left some documents behind."

Roch rode in silence for several minutes. "Jonas do you know if Annabelle's parents are still alive?"

"No My Lord, I do not know."

"They served my parents for many years; I no longer needed their services after my parents died in the fire; so they left the castle. Later I had them bring Annabelle to the castle as a companion for Vitomas; that was the last time I saw them."

"Would you like me to find them My Lord?"

"Yes and find out if there is anyone else still living that closely served my parents. Jonas you have done well, I am pleased."

"Thank you My Lord."

"Don't try to sit up," Gala said softly.

Raul tried to focus his eyes. The image of a middle aged woman with long dark hair was becoming clearer to him. "Who are you? And where am I? And where is Vitomas?" suddenly there was panic in Raul's voice.

Gala was sitting in a chair near the bed that Raul was in. "My name is Gala. I am a healer in Cana. Annabelle and Vitomas brought me to the castle after Roch's physician poisoned you. You are a very lucky young man that they got me when they did."

"Are they alright?"

"Yes, but I have much to tell you. Do you want something to eat first?"

"No, please just tell me."

"I am supposed to tell you that you are in the cabin that Annabelle told you about. I have been staying with you and so has Annabelle. But Cerephus doubled the guard on Vitomas so she cannot come as often but she has been here several times in the last few days."

"Few days! How long have I been out?"

"You were poisoned five days ago. We knew Roch's men would keep trying to kill you so Vitomas came up with an extraordinary plan. You will be so proud of her. She had me make a potion of the Ycan plant. It is a sleeping potion but if given in large enough quantities it makes a person appear dead. Vitomas and Annabelle told the guards you had died and had several of them look at you. Then she paid that corrupt general to let her give you a proper burial."

Gala continued, "There is a grave in the cemetery in Cana with your name on it. You are to stay here until they can get you out of the kingdom. Roch left the same day that you were poisoned but Vitomas does not know when he will return. Sometimes he is gone for months at a time. We couldn't move you to Wetpr because you were just too sick."

Raul tried to sit up and fell back down on the bed clutching his head. "Everything is spinning and I have such a headache."

"That is because of the poison, I will give you something for the pain but you must also try to eat and you must drink lots of water to help flush that poison out of you."

Gala walked over to a table that was in the middle of the one room cabin. The table had many small bottles setting on it. Gala poured some of the contents of two bottles into a cup of water and brought it over for Raul to drink. Gala had to help Raul sit up and he was afraid to drink for a few moments because he felt sick. "Do know that getting some food and water in you will make you feel better," Gala said softly.

Raul started to feel better shortly after he drank the medicine. "Gala how did you stop the poison?"

"I made an antidote."

"How did you know what to make?"

"Annabelle described your symptoms to me and when she told me your mouth turned purple I knew it was the poison of the asp tree."

"Thank you but you must know it is dangerous to help me."

"I know."

"I will pay you well."

"Raul I do not want your money. Vitomas has already paid me more than enough. I come from a long line of healers. And the healers in my family have been friends with the Sanuri for generations. Why, I have heard so many stories about you and Simon; that I feel like I know you. And from what I have heard, your father is the greatest King in all of Opots, how could I let his son die."

Chapter IX
Surrounded

At noon Roch and his men took shelter from the searing sun, under a grove of oak trees. Roch sat apart from his men so he could study the ancient map that was becoming his obsession. He now wondered if the treasure he sought was The Ruby Scroll. "Immortality, I really would be a god," Roch thought to himself and smiled. Roch now studied even the smallest detail on the map for a symbol of a scroll. "If such a scroll exists it is possible," Roch thought as he looked at the many religious symbols on the map.

"My Lord I do not mean to disturb you but..." said Jonas.

Roch quickly folded the map and put it into the pouch, "You are disturbing me Jonas!" Roch barked.

"I am sorry My Lord but I sent a scout out this morning because I heard about Huta war parties in the area; he just returned."

"Yes," replied Roch impatiently.

"Not five miles up the road, he saw a group of Hutas, fifty maybe more riding in this direction."

"Mount up," yelled Roch as he ran to his horse. "Quickly the Hutas are upon us."

"My Lord, they ride from the north," yelled Jonas

"They ride from my kingdom?" yelled Roch with disgust.

Roch's men quickly gathered their belongings and mounted their horses. "Jonas we will ride east towards the River Oja; we can conceal ourselves in the cliffs," said Roch. Roch and his small band of men rode as fast as their horses could carry them. They rode through fields, hard and dry from the torturous summer sun. Dust clouds rose from their passage which were easily seen from a distance.

Roch looked over his shoulder and saw giant dust clouds in the distance. He knew this meant the Hutas were following them. Roch had no choice but to lead his men to the River Oja for there was no place for them to hide and they were considerably outnumbered. The horses ran as if they sensed the death that followed them.

"Ahead My Lord," yelled Jonas as he pointed to the tree line of woods that lay just west of the River Oja.

Roch again looked over his shoulder; the Hutas were still in pursuit but had not closed up the distance between the two groups of riders. This gave Roch relief; he knew his men's horses were exhausted which meant the horses of the Hutas would be also, forcing them to slow their pace or kill their horses. Roch knew that the more distance they had from the Hutas the better their chances of escape. "Jonas into the trees," yelled Roch.

Roch and his men rode into an old forest. The tall tree tops blocked the sun so that only filtered rays of light shown through the trees. "Perfect," thought Roch. "This forest will hide us."

The seven soldiers from Taperia rode in silence but listened intently to the sounds of the forest. The sounds the forest creatures make when they have intruders. Trees long fallen, lay in decay on the forest floor forcing the soldiers to ride around them.

"My Lord this forest is now quiet, I don't like it," said Jonas. Roch looked at Jonas and nodded in agreement for he too thought the silence unusual. The forest slowed their movement but within an hour they saw the rocky cliffs that bordered the River Oja. Soon they were riding single file up a rocky embankment. Emerging from the forest their eyes were strained by the harsh sunlight reflecting off the rocky surfaces.

A rattlesnake lunged at one of the horses causing it to rear up on its hind legs throwing the rider. The soldier fell over the side of a cliff, his body bouncing off boulders as it descended. Roch yelled, "Grab his horse, we may need it." The six soldiers continued on.

"Your friend is awake," Gala said with a smile when Annabelle entered the cabin.

"You look pretty good for a dead man," Annabelle said and ran to Raul and hugged him tightly. Then she turned to Gala, "I can stay with him for a couple of hours if you need to go home."

"I do need to get a few things," Gala said as she grabbed her shawl.

"I brought two baskets of food and here," Annabelle handed Gala a small pouch of gold coins.

"The Queen has paid me more than enough already."

"Take it, we know you can use it Gala."

"I brought you a surprise," Annabelle said as she went to one of the baskets she had carried in and took out an apple pie. "I stopped at the market first." Annabelle cut a large slice and brought it to Raul, who devoured it quickly. Annabelle laughed. "I will get you some more. How do you feel?" Annabelle asked as she sat in the chair next to his bed.

"Horrible but Gala said that I will feel better as I get food and water in my body."

"She is a great healer, she saved your life."

"How is Vitomas?"

"Gee, I've been here for five minutes and you are just asking now," Annabelle joked.

"Actually Gala was telling me just before you came."

"They believed that you died but there are more guards watching her than before. She has to work really hard to get here. Last time she went into Cana and changed her clothes and horse at Gala's before she came here. She misses you and is so worried about you. She will be happy when I tell her you are awake. Raul you look like you're getting sick, do you want to lie back down?"

"No, I will be alright in a few minutes."

"Did Gala tell you that since your body is trying to heal from all of your injuries and the poison that you are going to be really weak and sick for a while?"

"Yes," Raul replied with frustration.

"Raul every time I come I bring weapons, I have your grandfather's sword and the daggers you had in your room at the castle."

Raul suddenly looked in a panic, "Annabelle did you get my pouch from the room?" Annabelle opened a cupboard door and brought the pouch to Raul, who immediately opened it and checked the contents. "Annabelle I need you to make me a promise."

"Of course, anything?"

"Have you ever heard of The Great Ruler?"

"Yes, my parents taught me about him."

"Look in the pouch."

Annabelle was speechless as she pulled out one of the bejeweled tubes that held an ancient Holy Scroll.

"I found those hidden in a cave. Gala said she is friends with the Sanuri. If anything happens to me you have to get those scrolls to him or to my father, will you do that for me?"

"Of course, I promise," Annabelle said. "Raul can we show these to my parents? Oh, they really want to visit you; would that be alright?"

"Yes to both. I would like to meet your parents besides we need to work out the plans of our trip." Raul paused and Annabelle could clearly see that the color was draining from his face. "Annabelle I think I need to sleep"

Raul was asleep within moments. Annabelle returned the pouch to the cupboard, emptied the baskets that she had brought and put the food away. She took Raul's two daggers and placed them under his pillow like he did at the castle. Annabelle took his grandfather's sword which was in a sheath and hid it under Raul's blankets. Then Annabelle pulled a chair up to the window and watched for intruders in the shadows of dusk.

"Jonas there is a cave just over this ridge, we will take refuge there," yelled Roch.

The entrance to the cave was partially blocked by a fallen boulder concealing it from the ridge. Jonas ordered one of the men to go into the cave. The man emerged within minutes. "From what I can see there is plenty of room for the horses," yelled the soldier. Jonas motioned for the men to enter the cave; they each dismounted and led their horses into the darkness.

"My Lord how did you know about this cave?"

"Years ago a group of bandits stole a shipment of my gold. We found them hiding in this cave," said Roch with an evil grin that lit up his face. "We threw them off the cliffs; no one steals from me!"

Once inside the cave the soldiers automatically assumed duties, one tending to the horses, one gathering wood, another preparing food and a fourth standing guard.

"What do you make of these?" said one of the men as he held a torch up to one of the cave walls.

"My Lord all the walls are covered with them," said a second soldier as he illuminated the paintings with his torch.

Roch and Jonas stood before one of the walls. "Give me that," growled Roch as he grabbed a torch from one of the men.

"I have never seen anything like these," exclaimed Jonas as he looked at the elaborate paintings.

"I don't recognize most of these creatures," said Roch. Roch continued to study the wall paintings long after the others lost interest. While some of the paintings were vibrant with color others were being lost to age. Roch was turning from the last wall to take food when he saw a shape in the corner of his eye that took his breath away.

There in a shadow was a painting of a scroll in a red container. Roch frantically searched the walls again for any other paintings of scrolls without success. Roch's frustration turned into anger because he could not understand the meanings of the paintings. Roch decided to step outside of the cave to get some air.

The sun was falling, lighting the western sky with rays of red and gold. A cool breeze blew against Roch's face; a welcomed relief from the heat of the day. Roch walked about one hundred yards from the cave's entrance. He stood quietly looking for any sign of movement. "It is too quiet," he thought. The hair on the back of Roch's neck started to raise, he knew he was being watched. His eyes searched the landscape, still no sign of movement. Roch quickly returned to the cave.

"Jonas there is no sign of the guard," Roch said as he entered the cave. "And I felt something watching me."

"The Hutas?" Jonas asked as he and the other men quickly stood up.

"I think the Hutas would have attacked me," said Roch as he was looking out the cave entrance.

"Then we are not alone; do we take our chances here or try to get down the cliffs in the daylight that is left?" asked Jonas.

The decision was made for them when a Huta spear landed in the ground in front of the cave's entrance. Roch motioned for the others to be still as he leaned back into the shadows, pulling his sword from its scabbard.

A lone Huta warrior appeared about twenty yards from the cave. A huge man with both his breast plate and his shield bearing the distinctive emblem of the Huta military, the scorpion with a sword. His helmet was leather and fit over the top portion of his face like a hideous mask. The helmet as well as his arm braces were decorated with bones; trophies from those he had killed in battle.

Roch and his men remained quiet as the Huta warrior slowly approached the entrance to the cave. Roch was wondering why the warrior had not alerted the other Hutas. Roch turned towards Jonas and motioned for him to hand over his battle axe. Roch put his sword back into its sheath and grasped the leather handle of the axe. From his hiding spot Roch could see the immediate area around the front of the cave; he did not see any other Hutas or any sign of movement.

The Huta warrior was almost to the cave's entrance when Roch threw the axe; impaling the Huta in the forehead. The warrior made a slight moan as his life force left him and he fell onto his back. Roch and Jonas each grabbed one of the warrior's feet and pulled him into the cave. Jonas striped the Huta of his weapons as Roch pulled at the axe trying to dislodge it from the skull.

After several attempts, Roch put his left foot on the Hutas head and pulled the axe handle with both arms, successfully removing it. He handed the bloody axe to Jonas; "Have the men saddle up; I don't want to be trapped here. And Jonas saddle my horse while I keep watch," Roch ordered.

Roch knew it would be dangerous for them to ride down the rocky embankment once the sun set. Leaving now they would not reach the bottom before the darkness settled. Subconsciously Roch grabbed his pocket containing the map; feeling the map's pouch gave him a sense of security. "It is still there," Roch thought. "My destiny." Roch knew the area well and led his men down the steep and rocky slope towards the River Oja. They rode single file, no one spoke. The only sound was that of the horse's hoofs hitting the rocks.

Darkness was starting to fall, the setting sun making a brilliant display in the western sky. They only had about a quarter of a mile to travel before reaching the bottom of the embankment. Suddenly Roch heard the sound of a thud behind him, as the body of one of the Taperian soldiers hit the ground.

"Ride!" yelled Jonas.

The Taperian soldiers rode as fast as they could down the steep embankment as arrows landed around them. Roch felt a stabbing burning sensation as an arrow lodged itself in the back of his right shoulder. Roch's horse stumbled but caught itself without falling. There were no sounds to be heard other than the horses and the barrage of Huta arrows hissing through the air. Seconds seemed like hours as the soldiers made their escape. The thick darkness of the night sky wrapping itself around the soldiers; withholding any light to guide them down the rocky slope.

Roch was still in the lead when his horse fell, causing both horse and rider to roll to the bottom of the embankment. Roch lay on the ground temporarily stunned from the fall; he could hear horses running past him.

Roch jumped up only to fall back to the ground as an arrow lodged itself in the back of his left leg, just above the knee. The pain in Roch's leg was searing; he reached behind him and broke the shaft of the arrow off leaving the head of the arrow in his leg.

Roch tried to push himself up but his right arm was numb from the arrow lodged in his shoulder. Pushing himself up with his left arm and right leg Roch was able to stand. He looked around him and could not see his men or any Huta warriors. Roch could hear the moving water from the River Oja to his left; he turned and started to run towards the river.

Roch fell twice the second time he was not able to stand again so he crawled; pulling his bloody body over the rocky ground. The sound of water was getting closer. Roch reached out and immersed his left hand in the cold river water. The sound of the water drowned the steps of the Huta warrior.

Cold water splashed against Roch's face, waking him. As his consciousness started to return; pain seared through his body; awake, he was suddenly awake. Roch tried to jump up but was restrained by the back of his belt which was caught on a large tree branch which was hanging over the river. Roch's feet and his legs had been submerged in the cold water of the River Oja all night and most of this day. Roch tried to move his legs but could not feel them.

Starting to panic, Roch looked around for something to grasp onto. The hot afternoon sun was beating down on him. The branch he was caught on hung over the water for ten feet from the shore line. Roch reached for his sword but the sheath was empty. He reached into his belt for his dagger and that too was gone. "The map," Roch thought as he grabbed the inside of his shirt pocket. A sense of relief filled him as he felt the pouch that contained his precious map.

Roch could barely move his right arm but he managed to unfasten his belt. As he slid out of the belt he grasped it with his right hand and held onto the tree branch with his left arm. Roch put his leather belt over the tree branch and held onto it with both hands as a way to keep himself afloat in the water as he slowly worked his way towards shore.

Roch's head was pounding as he tried to stay focused on his task. He was very weak and fighting the small current of the river was difficult. Finally Roch reached the rocky shore line. He pulled himself out of the water and managed to crawl about one hundred feet before he lost consciousness.

The small Village of Cana was built two miles south of the City of Taperia and lay between that great city and the Lake of the Pors. Legend said this lake was haunted with the spirits of two young lovers who were separated by an evil king but united in death.

"Vitomas are you sure you were not followed?" asked Annabelle who had arrived at the cabin earlier in the morning.

"I was very careful," replied Vitomas as she removed her black cloak and placed it over a chair in the cabin. "How is he?" asked Vitomas as she moved towards the bed.

"He is doing much better. Gala has been taking good care of him."

Annabelle and Vitomas each sat on opposite sides of the bed that Raul was lying on. Vitomas placed her hand on Raul's forehead to check for a fever. To her surprise Raul reached up and grasped her hand. Holding onto her hand, Raul slowly opened his eyes. He looked at Vitomas then turned and looked at Annabelle. Raul reached out his right hand and grabbed Annabelle's hand.

"Am I dead?" Raul joked. "Because it looks like I am surrounded by Angels."

Both of the women laughed. "You are not dead," said Vitomas, her heart filled with joy. "Raul I am so sorry I can't be here more but the guards are watching me always."

"I understand," Raul said as he sat up in bed with the help of both Vitomas and Annabelle.

"How are you feeling?" Vitomas asked as she brushed back a strand of his black hair.

"Vitomas is that a bruise on your cheek?"

167

"It's nothing, it's almost gone," Vitomas said softly as she gazed into his eyes. "Your black eyes are almost completely healed."

"I'll leave you two alone," Annabelle said as she walked over to one of the windows to watch for soldiers.

Raul gently kissed Vitomas on the lips then he moved her long hair and started to kiss her neck, "Vitomas!" She looked at him guiltily as she realized he saw the remnants of the bruises around her neck. The blouse that Vitomas was wearing was light green with a collar that stood up and a small 'V' neck opening before reaching a row of buttons. "Honey unbutton your blouse."

"Raul."

"Please."

Vitomas unbuttoned her blouse and pulled it open. Raul started to shake with rage when he saw the bruises on her light skin. "Are there more?" he asked through clenched teeth.

"Yes but Raul don't worry about them. You need to concentrate on getting better."

"Did he beat you because you helped me?"

"He said he wanted me to remember who my husband was while he was gone."

"I will kill that monster!" Raul spat then he grabbed Vitomas and hugged her tightly. "I am so sorry that he hurt you. It is killing me that I can't protect you."

"Vitomas started to cry as she caressed Raul's hair."

"Lay down with me," Raul said as he tried to slide over to make room for her.

"Raul, I don't know."

"Honey, I just want to hold you for a while."

Vitomas took her shoes off and got under the covers next to Raul. The young lovers held each other and cried.

The sun burned into Roch's back through his clothing, adding to the pain of his body. He dragged himself further up the shoreline so he could take shelter under some trees. The shaft of the arrow in Roch's shoulder had broken off leaving the arrow head still lodged in him. He tried several times to pull the arrow head out of his shoulder but he could not reach it. Roch checked himself for other wounds. He found a great deal of dried blood in his hair. Under the blood he felt a deep gash to the back of his head, which had stopped bleeding.

Roch felt weak and exhausted. He was afraid he was going to lose consciousness again and moved himself under some bushes so he would not be easily seen. Roch positioned himself so he could see the river and the shoreline; then he reached down and pulled a dagger out of a sheath in his right boot. "They didn't find this one," he thought. Roch fell asleep clutching the hilt of his dagger.

Hours later Roch suddenly jumped, awaking from a dream. The same dream he had so many times before. "The Lion, always The Lion," thought Roch. "What does it mean?" Then he saw them in the moonlight; Huta warriors near the shoreline. He counted six. The rocks he dragged himself over would not leave much of a trail unless he left blood behind. Roch knew that in the moonlight a good tracker would find the blood.

Roch lay in the bushes watching the Hutas. They were filling their canteens and letting their horses drink. Roch wondered where the rest of the Hutas were. The Hutas did not linger; when the horses had drank their fill, they mounted and rode south towards Malga. Roch remained in the bushes all night, afraid to fall asleep; clutching his dagger.

"Annabelle you're here so early," Gala said as Annabelle arrived at the cabin just after sunrise.

"Oh Gala whatever you are making sure smells good," Annabelle said cheerfully as she crossed the small room. "And how's my favorite patient?" Annabelle asked and kissed Raul on the cheek.

"You seem so happy this morning," Raul said with a grin. "Are you up to something?"

"Yes, my parents should be arriving here any minute to meet you and I am so excited and so are they, Raul."

"Well, it's a good thing I made a morning cake," Gala said as she put more eggs and ham on Raul's plate.

"Good, I am looking forward to meeting them too," Raul said. "Did you warn them about how I look?"

Annabelle's demeanor became serious, "I told them everything that has been going on and that is one of the reasons they want to see you. They are worried about you."

"They're here," Gala said as she looked out the window. "Did you tell them to put the horses in back?"

"Yes," Annabelle said as she walked to the backdoor of the cabin. Annabelle stood in the open doorway waiting for her parents.

Raul guessed that Annabelle's father was in his sixties. Her father was a tall man who looked to have great strength even at his age. He had gray hair and steel gray eyes. His skin was darkened from the sun. Annabelle's mother was short and petite like Annabelle, with the same big brown eyes and dark curly hair.

"Raul this is my father Alexander and my mother Laurel."

"Alexander he is the image of Sudfad," Laurel said in awe and sat on the bed next to Raul. "Excuse me for staring but I loved your father so. All these years Alexander and I have thought about him and wondered what kind of man he grew into. And now I look at you," she said sentimentally.

"Father looks much better than I do right now," Raul said and laughed.

"Oh you are a beautiful boy even with all of those bruises," Laurel said. "Tell me how do you feel?"

"Like I fought a whole army and lost but I am doing better every day. I have great nurses," Raul said with a warm smile.

Alexander sat in one of the chairs next to Raul's bed. "Laurel and I were talking and we certainly can come out here and help too, especially if Gala needs to do other things."

"If Raul doesn't mind that would help us," Annabelle said.

"Mind; I love the company but I have to warn you I'm not always the best company to be with."

"He means because he needs to sleep a lot not because he is of ill temperament," Gala said as she handed Laurel and Alexander cups of coffee.

"You do realize it is dangerous to be found with me?" Raul asked seriously.

"My dear, we were in that castle until Roch murdered his parents and we were there that night. Believe me we understand," Laurel said. "Raul when you feel up to it we want to hear all about your father. We have some gifts for him. Things of his parents that we didn't want Roch to destroy."

"Thank you for the sword. I will give it to Father when we get home. It is a wonderful remembrance."

"Your grandfather was a man to be proud of and your grandmother was a wonderful woman," Alexander said. "They were loved by everyone in Stordt except their own son. When he murdered them, I, well, I don't know how to explain it, it's like the heart of this kingdom died."

"We have something for you; whether you want to keep it or give it to Sudfad is up to you," Laurel said. "Alexander tell him."

"Raul, first I want you to understand that Laurel and I worked for your grandparents from the time we were young, that's how we met. We respected and loved them as family. It broke our hearts when they sent Sudfad away but we certainly understood. It was Roch that should have been sent away. So I want you to understand why we took some of their possessions."

"Father I think you should tell Raul about that night and he will really understand," Annabelle said.

"I would like to hear everything about the time you were there," Raul said.

Laurel and Alexander looked at each other and smiled, "We are happy to hear that. A man should know his history and Sudfad was so young when he was sent away, I don't know what he remembers," Alexander said as he reached inside his shirt pocket. Alexander pulled out a small silk cloth that was wrapped around an object and handed it to Raul.

"That ring was handed down in your family for generations; it was always given to the first born son," Alexander said then his voice hardened. "And a son does not butcher his mother and father. I was not going to let Roch take that from Sudfad too."

Raul listened to the passion and intensity of Alexander's voice before he unwrapped this precious gift. The golden band of the ring was intricately detailed. Both sides of the ring had elaborate designs of vines, hearts and swords. The center of the ring was an extremely large and flawless emerald surrounded by six descending rows of small diamonds. In the center of the emerald was a golden crown with a diamond at its peak.

After three days Roch regained consciousness. The wound in his leg was infected and he was delirious with fever. Weak and disoriented Roch did not recognize his surrounds. He dragged himself out of the bushes and to the river's edge; this effort stole all of his energy. Roch lost consciousness before he could swallow any of the cold river water.

Raul improved slowly over the next few days. Alexander and Laurel came to the cabin every day to visit and to help; allowing Gala to spend less time at the cabin. Raul enjoyed their company and would tell them stories about his parents and their life in Wetpr. In turn, Alexander and Laurel would tell Raul about the history of his family. It was mid-morning. Laurel was making stew and biscuits, while Alexander cut wood for the hearth.

"Raul if you feel up to it, I think we should try to get you out of bed and into a chair," Laurel said. "I'm concerned about your leg mending properly."

"I would like that. I have to admit it angers me how weak my body is. I usually heal faster than this."

"It's the poison dear, you should just be thankful you are alive."

Raul and Laurel heard voices outside. Raul grabbed the hilt of his sword, which was under his blankets. Within moments, Alexander and Annabelle entered the cabin. Annabelle first kissed Laurel on the cheek then she kissed Raul's cheek as Alexander filled the wood box.

"Alexander we should get Raul out of bed today," Laurel said.

"First I have much to tell you," Annabelle said. She had brought two baskets into the cabin and put them on the floor; now she took one over to Raul and set it on the bed. "Last night Roch's horse returned to the castle; the saddle was covered with dried blood. Cerephus has taken over one hundred soldiers and they are searching for Roch. The bad part of this is Cerephus has greatly increased the guards around Vitomas and has now forbidden her from going on her morning rides."

"Is he afraid that she will escape?" Laurel asked.

"Roch has many enemies," Raul said. "I would guess he is afraid she might be in danger."

"In danger?" Annabelle asked.

"Yes, there could be a couple of reasons," Raul explained. "If someone killed Roch because they were planning to conquer this kingdom, Vitomas would be in danger. Or if someone is trying to destroy Roch they might think that killing his queen would weaken him. Although we know Roch doesn't care about her. Actually that was a smart move on Cerephus' part."

"Except it is almost impossible for her to come here now," Annabelle said. "Vitomas said she just feels like there are always eyes upon her. But with Cerephus gone she was able to sneak into Roch's war room and go through his things." As Annabelle spoke she reached into the basket and pulled out six small scrolls and handed one to Raul and the rest to her parents. "These are the papers we need to get past the border guards. They all say the same thing and have Roch's signature."

Annabelle reached into the basket again. "Here are some blank sheets of paper that have Roch's Royal Seal and his signature. Vitomas thought if we got into trouble that perhaps we could find a use for them. And here are two more pouches of gold coins; she wants to make sure we have enough money in case we need to bribe the guards. She thinks we should plan to leave soon, while Roch is away."

"We have been buying things slowly as not to draw suspicion," Alexander said. "But later today I will start getting things prepared."

Roch woke up shivering from the cold rain that was pelting his body. As he shook his head he suddenly remembered where he was. He instantly grabbed for his shirt pocket to make sure the map was still there. Reassured the map was secure; Roch crawled closer to the river and drank of the cold water. Roch was hungry and in pain but he knew he could not find food until the sun came up. He turned to look behind him but the darkness of the night camouflaged the bushes he had previously taken shelter in.

Roch knew he could not stay near the river's edge for he would easily become prey to the creatures who hunted at night. Roch felt around the ground, looking for a fallen tree branch that he could use to support himself for walking. Thunder was rolling in from the east. Bolts of lightning lit up the sky.

In a moment of light Roch saw there were no branches for him to use as a crutch. He lay still, trying to get his sense of direction. Soon a second lightning flash revealed the bushes he had been hiding in. Roch dragged himself over the rocky ground and once again crawled into his hiding place. Although the bushes concealed his presence they did not afford him shelter from the rain.

Chapter X
The Monastery at Malga

The monastery referred to as the monastery at Malga is located three miles north of the small Village of Malga. While the monastery lies within the Kingdom of Puntd the village sits on the border of Puntd and the Kingdom of Ganz. Peace exists between these two great kingdoms now but that has not always been the case. The Village of Malga has changed ownership many times over the generations; currently King Tobias of the Kingdom of Puntd is the ruler.

The monastery at Malga is one of the oldest and most revered monasteries in the Continent of Opots. While the monastery at Avaide was considered a blessed and holy site; where peoples from all the kingdoms would do pilgrimages and claim to be blessed with miracles; the monastery at Malga became the location for the head of the church.

This monastery located in such a remote section of the continent contained rooms upon rooms of religious art, treasures and religious and historical relics. Like many men who claim to be religious leaders, the high priests who were in charge of the monastery at Malga acquired great wealth and power. And like many men who claim to be religious leaders, their power and decisions were unquestioned.

Senior High Priest Dominic Petlov had overseen the monastery at Malga for one hundred and eighty one years. The Great Ruler often blessed people of great holiness and purpose with unnaturally long lives. But in direct contrast people who sold their souls to demons too were granted long lives and the appearance of not aging. High Priest Petlov was a holy and devout man. He and his cabinet which was comprised of High Priest Vincent, High Priest Samuel and High Priest Timothy all died in the same two week period of time by most unusual circumstances.

After Petlov's death, High Priest Marcus Meekos assumed the position of Senior High Priest of the monastery at Malga, a position he has held for almost three hundred years. His senior cabinet includes only High Priest Tenebrae and High Priest Pravis.

One of the first laws that Meekos declared was that all of the holy teachings of The Great Ruler would be locked away from both the priests and the peoples. Meekos deemed that he would read these manuscripts and tell the world what they said. This law enabled Meekos to maintain unquestioned power as neither the priests nor the people understood which laws and covenants were created by The Great Ruler or which were merely a ruse of man.

Ultimately both the priests and the people of Opots were afraid to question anything that Meekos said for fear their questions would be an offense to The Great Ruler. If the devout and faithful would have questioned Meekos' words and actions they would have discovered the demons which hid behind the sacred doors of that monastery. But since this type of behavior by religious leaders was common among numerous religions of the World of Nunc; the peoples of Opots whispered among themselves and lived in great fear but did nothing to stop the horror that soon touched them all.

Like most monasteries of that age, the monastery at Malga had a large stone wall surrounding the grounds. Unlike many monasteries it did not have a ditch or moat surrounding the outer wall for increased protection. Until the Hutas destroyed the monastery at Avaide and butchered the priests there, the holy men at Malga never thought they would need protection.

"In all my years I have never seen the gate to this monastery locked," the Sanuri told Padre Bartholomew and Petra as he dismounted from the boca. The Sanuri pulled on a long rope that was hanging to the left of the massive wooden gate. The rope was attached to three large metal bells, the ringing of the bells resounded through the entire monastery.

After a few minutes a priest opened the gate for the Sanuri's boca to enter. The priest was an older man with a thin frame, red hair with streaks of gray and round spectacles. A grand smile filled his face when he saw the Sanuri, who stopped the boca just inside of the monastery walls.

"My old friend it is so good to see you after all these months," the priest said as he clasped the Sanuri's hands.

"Padre Bartholomew and Petra I want you to meet an old and very dear friend of mine, Padre Thomas." Both Petra and Padre Bartholomew had climbed down from the boca and now walked up to Padre Thomas and shook hands with him.

"Padre Bartholomew is one of the few survivors of Avaide, thanks to our young friend Petra here. Both are wounded and need rest," the Sanuri explained. "Padre Thomas can they stay here for a few days while I search for Petra's family who have gone missing?"

"Of course, and I hope you plan on staying a little while yourself," Padre Thomas said with a gentle smile. "Come let's take care of your horses then I will take you to the Great Hall to eat and after that I will get you some rooms."

During their meal Padre Bartholomew and Petra told Padre Thomas and others who joined their table, about the attack at Avaide. The priests sat in stunned silence as they listened to the horrors that were beyond their comprehension.

"The Hutas were not alone in their loathsome behavior," explained the Sanuri. "We left just before King Roch of Stordt and his men looted the monastery."

"King Roch, why he was here just days ago," Padre Thomas said.

"Here at this monastery?" the Sanuri asked with concern.

"No, he met with King Tobias. Roch wanted a priest who could translate an ancient text for him. King Tobias called us to the castle so Roch could ask us questions. But King Tobias and some of his soldiers sat in between us and Roch, which made Roch quite angry. After Roch left the castle King Tobias had the soldiers bring us all to the castle for protection for several days," said Padre Dibon, one of the priests who had joined the group.

"Did any of you see this text that Roch wanted translated?" the Sanuri asked.

"No," replied Padre Thomas. "Roch asked us questions about our abilities to translate ancient languages; he didn't show us anything."

177

"The fact that he did this so soon after looting the monastery at Avaide makes me believe he has something from that monastery," the Sanuri said.

"Not The Holy Scrolls!" Padre Dibon gasped.

"No, we saved those and many other things," Padre Bartholomew said assuredly. "I wonder what Roch could have gotten his hands on."

As the Sanuri, Padre Bartholomew and Petra sat in the Great Hall eating and talking with other priests Padre Thomas said. "Sanuri there is something that we must tell you. Padre Philip is not in this room now but he told us that when he was being questioned by Roch that King Tobias suggested that you would know how to translate the text. We were all horrified that our King would betray you in such a manner."

The Sanuri smiled, "Tobias did not betray me. I have known him for a very long time. Did you know that his brother-in-law is King Sudfad of Wetpr? Tobias said that to save all of you. He knows that Roch has no power over me."

"What do you mean?" Petra asked.

"King Roch will stop at nothing to get what he wants. Tobias knows that. So if Roch wants one of the priests from this monastery he will find a way to get him. But if he comes after me, well, that is a story for another time," the Sanuri said then he looked at the priests sitting around the table. "You are fortunate to have a King who is trying to protect you but still be cautious."

"As you can see, we now lock the gate and we patrol the towers on the wall," said Padre Simpson.

After they finished their meal, Padre Thomas took Padre Bartholomew, Petra and the Sanuri to small rooms on the second floor of the monastery. Petra decided he did not want to stay by himself so they moved a small bed into Padre Bartholomew's room for Petra.

"Padre Thomas would you allow me into the Hall of Antiquities so I can do some research?" the Sanuri asked after he had been shown his room.

"What is the Hall of Antiquities?" asked Petra.

"It is a section of the monastery that houses holy treasures and ancient texts," said Padre Thomas.

"And King Roch does not know about it?" asked Petra.

"No and he never will," replied the Sanuri. "We have come across some interesting things in our journey and I need to do some research."

"By all means; you always have permission to enter the hall my friend," said Padre Thomas. "Would you like me to take you there now?"

"Yes if you do not mind."

"After I return I will give the two of you a tour of the monastery," Padre Thomas said to Petra and Padre Bartholomew.

Padre Thomas led the Sanuri into the northern most wing of the Building of Song, in the monastery complex. Torches lit the dark stone passageways. "From the size of these spider webs I assume this area in not well traveled," said the Sanuri with a laugh.

"One does need a valid reason to enter the Hall of Antiquities. All new priests need the authorization of a high priest to enter," said Padre Thomas.

"Why?"

"Having access to this hall is a great privilege as it contains irreplaceable holy objects."

"But it also contains the Word of The Great Ruler, which should be shared and taught," said the Sanuri.

"A priest here must earn the right to learn the teachings of The Great Ruler."

"And who deems that priest worthy of learning the Word?" asked the Sanuri with disdain.

"High Priest Meekos; you do not agree with our procedures?"

179

"I believe The Great Ruler gave us His written words so they could be shared and taught to His children, and is this monastery not filled with His teachers?" asked the Sanuri. "This is a matter I should like to bring up with Meekos is he here?"

"I don't believe so. He travels a lot."

"He has never been here during one of my visits. I find it curious that he travels so much. Where does he go?"

"Surely you don't think that the Senior High Priest confides such information with us?"

"I don't see why he wouldn't tell any of you where he is going. Don't you consider that strange?"

"We are used to it. But I do believe he tells High Priest Pravis and High Priest Tenebrae where he goes."

"But don't they travel with him? I mean they too are always gone when I am here."

"You are right; they do travel with him a lot."

The hallway they were walking in ended at two huge wooden doors. Although the doors stood side by side they each had seven locks. Padre Thomas pulled a large metal ring filled with keys, from inside his robe. Each lock required a separate key to open it. When all the locks were unlocked it took the strength of both men to push the two doors open. "These doors have not been opened in a while," the Sanuri said.

"Wait here while I light the candles," Padre Thomas said. Padre Thomas slowly moved through the darkness and lit candelabra after candelabra as the majesty of this great hall unfolded before them. There were beautiful murals painted on the walls and ceilings of this enormous room. Heavy wooden shelves lined all the walls and were organized into seven rows down the center of the room. There were heavy wooden tables piled with books, scrolls and other objects.

The floors were covered with thick brightly colored rugs. There were great varieties of chairs, benches and chests in the room. The room was large enough to have two huge hearths, although neither was lit. All the windows were covered with thick purple drapery with golden trim. The candelabras on the tables and hanging from the walls and ceiling were made of gold.

"Do you have any information at all about the text that King Roch wanted translated?" asked the Sanuri.

"Yes but I did not want to speak about it in front of the others," said Padre Thomas. "King Roch showed each of the high priests an ancient map which contained many unusual symbols."

"Do they know where the map came from?"

"No, no one said. High Priest Zophar and I have been friends for many years; he confided this information to me."

"When I heard about the massacre I went to Avaide as quickly as I could," explained the Sanuri. "I will tell you my heart broke when I saw what had been done there. The buildings were still smoldering. Bodies of my friends lay everywhere; Padre Bartholomew and Petra were the only two who I found alive. We saved The Holy Scrolls. Padre Bartholomew and Petra saved as many manuscripts and items as they could while I searched among the dead. Suddenly I had a vision of Roch and his men and within minutes I saw the dust from their horses as they rode towards the monastery."

"You think the map was from the monastery?"

"Perhaps; where would he obtain a map that he needs a holy man to translate?"

"Do you have any idea what this map leads to?"

"No but if it is written in the ancient text of The Great Ruler, Roch has no idea of the journey he is about to take," replied the Sanuri.

"What do you mean?"

"Roch is a demon who wears the face of a man; darkness does not hunt down and capture holiness," said the Sanuri. "This map could be his undoing."

The Sanuri had spent the entire day and long into the night studying in the Hall of Antiquities. For centuries this hall had become the final resting place for unimaginable numbers of religious texts and items, not only from the Kingdom of Puntd but from all of Opots itself. The inventory was so vast that the priests had long ago forgotten what secrets lay within the walls.

The Sanuri was always annoyed at the overall disorganization of the hall. Things were shoved into boxes and piled indiscriminately on top of other items. The shelves and tables were covered with thick layers of dust and there were spider webs everywhere.

Towards midnight, the Sanuri was searching in the western back corner of the huge room. He walked from behind some huge bookcases and found a table that had been pushed up against the wall. The table had but one chair pulled up to it. The table was clean, free of dust and had a single candle setting on it. "Well, someone comes here to study," the Sanuri thought then resumed his search among the shelves.

"Sanuri where have you been?" Petra asked as the Sanuri joined Padre Thomas, Padre Bartholomew and Petra in the Great Hall for breakfast the next morning.

"I was studying all night. Did I miss anything of interest?"

"I took them on a tour of the monastery," Padre Thomas said. "But Petra can't seem to think of anything but his family. Sanuri is there anything I can do to help you find them?"

"If you could just keep him safe until I return, I would be in your debt."

"But Sanuri I want to go with you," Petra pleaded.

"Petra you know of the dangers we have already encountered. Your parents will be very cross with me if they think I put you in danger. Please stay here and watch after Padre Bartholomew until I return."

Petra looked down at his food without speaking. Padre Bartholomew was sitting next to Petra and put his arm around the boy. "Petra you know the Sanuri speaks the truth. Besides he can travel faster if he doesn't have to take care of us." Petra still did not speak.

"Did you find what you were looking for?" Padre Thomas asked the Sanuri.

"It is difficult to find anything in there. When was the last time the Hall of Antiquities was cleaned and organized?"

Padre Thomas smiled and said "I thought of that when I took you in there yesterday. Perhaps that is a project that Petra and Padre Bartholomew would like to help me with. It will make the time go by faster."

"I fear you will need more help than that," the Sanuri said as he refilled his cup with coffee.

"Perhaps we could help you look," Padre Bartholomew offered.

"I would welcome the help. I was trying to find information about The Box of Itifer as well as information about the Talmuth and those strange footprints I saw."

"What about those demons that came after us, what did you call them again?" asked Padre Bartholomew.

"The Zendoti," replied the Sanuri. "Perhaps you could help with research while I search for Petra's parents."

"We would be happy too," Padre Bartholomew said as he looked at Padre Thomas who nodded in agreement.

"Oh by the way, Padre Thomas someone has been in there studying besides me because I found a table in back that was cleaned off with a chair pulled up to it and a candle for light," the Sanuri said. "I hope that fellow had better luck finding what he was looking for than I did."

Padre Thomas stared at the Sanuri, "That can't be."

"What do you mean?" asked the Sanuri.

"Because I am the keeper of the keys and I have not let anyone into the Hall of Antiquities for a very, very long time," replied Padre Thomas with a puzzled look on his face.

"Are there other sets of keys?" Padre Bartholomew asked. "Or another entrance?"

"There are fourteen locks on the two front doors of the Hall, I have no knowledge of another entrance," Padre Thomas said.

"Then there must be more keys," the Sanuri said. Then as an afterthought he added. "Although it did seem like those front doors had not been opened in a while."

"The high priests all have keys but I have rarely seen them in there," Padre Thomas said.

As the men talked, Petra remained silent; staring at his plate of food. "Petra, I am leaving after breakfast," the Sanuri said. "I will do my very best to find your parents and when I do, I will bring them here." Petra still did not say anything. "Petra I know you are angry with me but it just is not safe for you to accompany me."

Padre Stephens quickly walked up to the table and whispered into Padre Thomas' ear. Padre Thomas left the table and followed Padre Stephens out of the Great Hall. Padre Thomas returned minutes later and looked visibly upset.

"What has happened?" asked Padre Bartholomew.

"Petra they found the villagers of Ort," said Padre Thomas softly.

"My parents are they all right?"

"Petra, I am so sorry but they are all dead," said Padre Thomas with tears in his eyes.

"No!" screamed Petra and ran through the Great Hall and out into the courtyard.

Padre Thomas looked at the Sanuri and Padre Bartholomew, "Their bodies were mutilated and hung in trees outside of the village."

"I am going to find the boy," said Padre Bartholomew and left the Great Hall.

"There is more," said Padre Thomas. "Dozens of dead Huta warriors were found outside of Ort, their bodies were torn apart."

"Were there footprints?" asked the Sanuri.

"We did not receive any information about prints," replied Padre Thomas.

Padre Thomas and the Sanuri walked through the Great Hall in silence. When they reached the courtyard they saw Petra crying in Padre Bartholomew's arms. The Sanuri remembered the words of The Lion, if Petra's parents were gone, the Sanuri would know where to take the boy. The Lion said that the boy was one of The Seven Sons of the great prophesy. That meant that the Sanuri would have to protect Petra until he grew into a man and fulfilled his destiny.

This prophesy was as old as time itself and because of that; it was known not only to the holy men of all the lands but also to the demons and the dark lords, who had spent centuries murdering those suspected of being one of the holy sons.

Padre Bartholomew, Padre Thomas and the Sanuri took Petra to the room that he shared with Padre Bartholomew. They sat with the boy trying to console him until Petra ultimately cried himself to sleep. The Sanuri left the room and returned to the Hall of Antiquities.

The Sanuri walked into the Great Hall and joined Padre Bartholomew, Padre Thomas and Petra as they ate their breakfast the following morning. "Did you get any sleep last night Petra?" the Sanuri asked as he looked at Petra's red and swollen face.

Petra did not answer. "He got some sleep but he kept waking up and crying," Padre Bartholomew said as he reached over and patted Petra's hand.

"Petra, we will stay here at the monastery for a while, then I am going to take you on a journey," the Sanuri said. "Padre Bartholomew you are welcome to join us or I can take you any place you would like to go."

"I asked Padre Bartholomew to stay with us here," said Padre Thomas. "I also asked Petra if he wanted to stay here and study to become a priest." Petra looked at the Sanuri and shook his head from side to side, indicating he did not want to stay at the monastery.

"Sanuri I am an old man and my body has not yet mended," Padre Bartholomew said. "I believe I will stay here."

"Where are we going?" Petra asked.

"I am going to take you to Wetpr to visit my dear friends King Sudfad and Queen Renya. You will like them very much."

"Do they have any kids to play with?"

"Their sons are grown men but both the King and Queen love children."

Chapter XI
Eyes in the Darkness

Roch suddenly awoke, thinking he had heard movement. He grasped his dagger and peered through the bushes. Roch realized he was shivering even though the heat of the morning was upon him. He waited in the bushes for several minutes, just as he began to think it was a dream; he heard something move in the brush. Roch lay perfectly still.

Another couple of minutes passed before Roch heard something again but this time it sounded like a human voice moaning. Roch did not move as he searched the landscape with his eyes, looking for an ambush. The sound of the voice moaning continued and when Roch felt it was safe for him to move; he started to crawl towards the sound.

Roch deliberately crawled slowly, so his movements would not alert anyone or anything that might be in the area. The sound was getting louder. The undergrowth of the forest was thick in areas that were exposed to more sunlight. Roch must have crawled for twenty minutes before he located the area where the sound was coming from. The sound appeared to be coming from a small thicket where several trees had fallen, allowing sunlight to reach the ground and nourish the plant life.

Roch clenched the dagger in his teeth as he inched forward, parting the vines and grasses when he saw a bloody hand. Roch stopped and listened then moved closer to the body. As soon as Roch saw the arm brace he realized the man was one of his soldiers. Roch now moved quickly and grabbed the man's shoulders to turn him onto his back. Although the man's face was covered in dry blood, Roch recognized Jonas.

There was a large gash on the right side of Jonas' head and his right ear had been cut off for a Huta trophy. Roch searched the man for signs of other injuries and for weapons; he found neither. Roch knew they were exposed to anyone on horseback. He was too injured to drag Jonas to his hideout in the brush. Roch looked around and saw some large leaves from the ginga plant. He crawled over to the leaves and saw they still held water from the heavy rain. Roch broke a leaf off from the plant and carefully returned to Jonas, trying not to spill any water.

Roch poured the rainwater onto Jonas' face. Jonas jumped up and grabbed Roch by the throat. Roch grabbed Jonas' wrist, "Jonas, its Roch," said Roch sternly. Jonas released his hold on Roch's throat. "My Lord, I thought I was dead," Jonas said in a dazed manner.

The two battle weary soldiers dragged themselves to the seclusion of Roch's hideout. Exhausted and injured they never realized how many pair of eyes were watching them.

"I have never seen anything like this," Gala said as she was fixing Raul his lunch. "There are soldiers everywhere searching for the King. I am so very frightened that they will come here. Raul I was thinking; everyone knows that I am a healer. If the soldiers come here, I am going to tell them that you have a great fever and that I have you here so you cannot give it to others."

"Gala I will never forget how you have put yourself in such danger to help me," Raul said seriously. "You should come to Wetpr with us. I will worry about you if we leave you behind."

"Raul, I thank you but my home is here as are my patients."

"Well, you will always have a home at my father's castle. If you change your mind and can make it to Wetpr, tell the guards that you are a friend of mine and that I have asked for an audience. They will let you in without delay."

Roch and Jonas were barely able to make it to Roch's hide-out. Both men were weak and exhausted from their wounds, hunger and dehydration. They slept during the heat of the afternoon. In the evening they both crawled to the river to drink. Although the two were unlikely friends they both took comfort with each other's company. Neither man wanted to die alone.

Shrouded in the darkness of the night Archetenus leaned against the stone wall surrounding the garden courtyard outside of Vitomas' chambers. He longed to gaze upon her beautiful face and lovely body.

Archetenus dwelled on the same thoughts that filled his mind always; that Vitomas was his sole purpose for surviving the Gefrey Games each month. As she watched him fight her eyes were filled with both admiration and fear. Although Vitomas had never expressed her feelings for him; Archetenus knew she must care for him, why else would there be fear in her eyes when he fought.

As Archetenus watched the balcony to Vitomas' chambers he saw light through the windows. He watched as Vitomas lit the candles in her rooms. She was wearing a light blue dress with her long hair flowing. Archetenus could feel his heart pounding in his chest as he watched Vitomas.

So many nights Archetenus had stood in this exact same spot and watched his Queen. Archetenus had always known that if he was caught watching Vitomas that he would be put to death. But what started out for him as simple attraction turned into an obsession that he lost control of. In Archetenus' mind this beautiful young girl, yearned for him as strongly as he wanted her. Archetenus was convinced that if he could take Vitomas away from King Roch; they would live happy lives together. Lost in his thoughts, Archetenus did not hear the footsteps behind him.

"Who goes there," yelled a castle guard as he pointed his sword at Archetenus' back. Archetenus had not thought of what he would do if he encountered other Taperian soldiers; after all he was still in the service of the King. But would the King kill Archetenus if he knew of his return? As these thoughts filled Archetenus' head he swiftly turned to the right and stepped towards the guard.

Archetenus hit the forearm of the guard with his right forearm, causing the guard to drop his sword. In a fluid movement Archetenus was behind the guard; locking the guard's neck with his forearms. Archetenus kept putting pressure on the guard's neck until his body became limp and motionless. Archetenus lowered the guard's body to the ground and ran from the royal gardens.

Annabelle and Vitomas were both wakened by loud knocking at the front door of the chambers. The sun was not yet up. There was a second knock and both women got out of their beds and walked into the sitting room of the chambers; both of them fearful that the soldiers had found Raul.

"My Lady it is Crispus, I need to see if you are alright."

Vitomas opened the door as she was tying her robe. Crispus and six other soldiers burst into her chambers and immediately searched it.

"Crispus what is the meaning of this?" Vitomas asked.

Crispus was the first to reenter the sitting room. "I apologize My Lady but one of our men was murdered last night and his body was found outside of your chambers," replied Crispus. "My Lady did you see anyone in the garden last night or hear anything unusual?"

"Outside of my window!" Vitomas gasped. "Where? Show me."

"My Lady it is still dark but my men are out there with torches so perhaps you will be able to see. Crispus led Vitomas and Annabelle to the balcony. "Behind that large oak tree, the one to the right," Crispus pointed the tree out as he spoke.

"How was he killed?" Annabelle asked.

"There were signs of a fight."

"So there was more than one person outside of my balcony?"

"Yes My Lady, but whoever it was swept the ground so we could not find any tracks." Vitomas and Annabelle looked at each other fearfully but neither spoke. "My Lady," Crispus continued. "I believe there was an intruder outside of your window and the guard found him. They fought and the guard was killed. You never answered me; did you see or hear anything unusual?"

"Crispus I did not. I mean I felt like I was being watched but I just thought that was you and the other soldiers."

"Crispus, you and the other men are watching the Queen so closely she feels as if she cannot breathe so tell me how could an intruder get this close to her?" Annabelle asked accusingly.

"I don't know that is what I am trying to find out."

Archetenus walked through the southern gate of the castle grounds and entered his cabin. The soldiers had to live in barracks but each of the officers had a small cabin on the castle grounds. Archetenus was both surprised and relieved that nothing looked out of place in his quarters. He searched the three rooms of his sparse cabin. Just as he was entering the kitchen the front door opened. Archetenus pulled his sword with his right hand while grabbing the person entering through the door with his left hand.

"Oh My Lord!" exclaimed the woman with fright.

"Tega I am sorry," said Archetenus as he put his sword back into its sheath. Tega was one of the servants who cared for the quarters of all the captains. Tega quickly knelt down to pick up the armful of clean towels she dropped when Archetenus grabbed her.

Tega was a stout woman in her forties. Her straight hair was pulled into tight braids that wrapped around her head. "My Lord you look awful," said Tega. "Do you need the Court Physician?"

"No, a hot meal and a bath will do," said Archetenus with a smile.

"Yes My Lord," said Tega as she quickly placed the towels in a cupboard and turned towards the door.

"Tega."

"Yes My Lord."

"Do not tell anyone I am here."

Tega looked confused and slowly said, "Yes My Lord."

"I am so exhausted I just want to rest and eat before I speak with anyone."

Tega smiled, satisfied with that explanation and left the cabin. Archetenus watched Tega walk out and wondered why he did not see any soldiers in the area. When she was out of sight Archetenus walked into the sleeping room and pulled up the rug. Under the rug were two loosened wooden boards. Archetenus moved one of the boards and pulled out a large leather pouch. He opened the pouch to make sure no one had robbed him, in his absence.

The pouch was filled with gold coins. Archetenus reached back into the hole under the floorboards and pulled out another large leather pouch, this one contained jewels of all manner; with the exception of the small wooden toy wagon that lay on top of the jewels.

Archetenus' father had made him that wagon. Archetenus could still remember that day. He was a small boy, sitting in the yard just outside of the kitchen door of his home. He was playing with that toy wagon when a group of Taperian soldiers rode up to the house. One of the men grabbed Archetenus and the men turned and rode away. Archetenus was trying to get out of the grasp of the soldier as his mother ran out of the house screaming and crying. Archetenus remembered seeing his mother fall in the road; that was the last time he ever saw her.

"Tega thank you this is the best meal I have had in a long time," Archetenus said as Tega was filling the bathtub for him in the next room.

"I got it from the main kitchen. There is certainly more food if you want some, what with all the soldiers gone."

"I wondered why it seemed so quiet around here. Where are the soldiers?"

"Oh My Lord did not you hear what has been going on?"

"No, Tega please come in here and talk to me."

"Almost two weeks ago the King took a small army and traveled to the Kingdom of Puntd; it is said he wanted to speak with any holy men King Tobias had," said Tega.

Archetenus interrupted Tega, "Holy men? Why in the world would King Roch want to speak with holy men?"

"I really don't know My Lord, I am just telling you what I was told."

"I'm sorry Tega, please continue."

"Well, the troops returned three days later except for King Roch and six men; they said King Tobias did not trust King Roch and made him send the soldiers back."

"I am surprised Roch would do such a thing," said Archetenus. "He must have really wanted something from Tobias to let him dictate conditions."

"No one had heard from Roch," continued Tega, "Then a couple of days ago his horse returns to the castle and there is blood on the saddle. General Cerephus is leading men to the Kingdom of Puntd to search for the King."

"Did he take all of the soldiers with him?"

"No, he sent four other search parties out looking for the King also. And there is more My Lord this morning the guards found a dead guard in the garden underneath Queen Vitomas' window."

"Do they know how he died?"

"I overheard some guards say his neck was broken and there were signs of a fight; whoever killed him is gone."

"Do the guards have any idea who killed him?"

"No," said Tega. "My Lord I am glad you are back, I feel safer now." Tega smiled and returned to filling the bath tub. When the tub was filled with hot water, she walked back into the kitchen.

"My Lord would you like me to clean your armor?"

"Yes Tega, thank you and remember tell no one I am here yet. Archetenus paused, "Tega, before you go, is the Queen alright?"

"Yes My Lord, Cerephus doubled the guards around her before he left," said Tega. "That poor thing first her friend dies and now her husband is missing."

193

"What friend?"

"My Lady was riding one day and found a poor soul left to die along the road; you know what a big heart she has, she brought the man home and cared for him," said Tega. Then in a whisper she added, "Some say the King was furious but did not kill the man because he was the son of his brother, King Sudfad of Wetpr."

"The Prince of Wetpr, what would he be doing here?"

"I really don't know My Lord but Sophie told me that Annabelle and the Queen were caring for him day and night while King Roch was gone because he was so badly injured. Sophie said it was her that told the man he was in Roch's castle, she said he had no idea where he was."

"What happened to him?"

"I do not really know. I heard he suddenly died and the Queen had him buried near Cana."

"I'll bet Roch had something to do with his death."

"That is what many people think. Some have wondered if we will go to war with Wetpr when King Sudfad finds out."

"Is there anything else Tega?"

"No My Lord."

"Then I will take my bath now, thank you."

Archetenus watched Tega through the window as she walked away from his quarters. Tega did not act like she thought anything was suspicious with Archetenus. "This should be easier than I thought," Archetenus said to himself as a big smile crept over his face. He walked into the next room and prepared to take a bath.

Every day Alexander would help Raul out of bed. The young prince would sit up a little longer each day as his strength slowly returned. Raul was becoming anxious and impatient. He expected himself to heal faster than he was.

Raul also worried greatly about Vitomas, Annabelle and the others who were risking their lives to help him. Raul was a large and powerful man, a great warrior and a fierce fighter. Although Raul had been wounded many times he had never been incapacitated like this before and he did not like feeling weak and helpless. As the days wore on his temperament was becoming strained, although he worked hard not to let the others notice. And every day an overwhelming feeling of apprehension was growing within him. Raul wanted to leave Stordt soon.

Chapter XII
Miranda

The next three days were a struggle of survival for Roch and Jonas; rarely were they both conscious at the same time. Roch cleaned and bandaged Jonas' head wound using his inner shirt, which was the cleanest piece of cloth he could find. Jonas removed the two festering arrowheads from Roch's shoulder and leg. He cleaned the wounds and treated them with a paste made from herbs he found near the river.

Jonas used Roch's dagger to carve some small pieces of wood into containers to hold water. Neither man had eaten anything besides berries and leaves for days. But the morning of the fourth day brought great hope.

Roch awoke to the smell of wood burning. He opened his eyes and peered through the bushes to see Jonas cooking fish over a fire. Roch crawled out of the bushes and suddenly realized the pain in his wounds was considerably diminished.

"Good you are awake," said Jonas. "I thought the smell of food would wake you."

"How did you catch these?" asked Roch as he looked at the fish cooking over the flames.

"With my hands, I felt like a bear wading into the cold water and diving for fish," said Jonas with a laugh.

The two men devoured the fish in silence; both intent on eating. After they ate they both sat back, looked at each other and started to laugh; the laughter of men who have narrowly defeated death.

"This is the first day I can think clearly, that Huta almost took my brain out," said Jonas. "Before I caught the fish I checked the area. I did not see any sign of Hutas but I saw a great deal of strange footprints."

"What sort of prints?"

"They almost looked like a bear's prints but were three times the size, whatever the animal is it walks on two feet like a man and My Lord the prints surround our camp."

"What!"

"Whatever those creatures are, they did not want us. Which is lucky for us because neither of us are in any shape to fight."

"I can't believe we didn't hear them; especially if they are as big as you say."

"Look at the prints yourself. I don't know what to make of them," Jonas said as he stared at the river. "My Lord do you think you are strong enough to help build a raft? We could take the river north to the Lake of the Pors and to Cana."

"What are we going to use to connect the logs?"

"There are lots of old vines on those trees," said Jonas as he pointed to the forest.

"And the logs?" Roch asked as he tried to envision the project when they only had one dagger as a tool.

"We'll have to drag logs out of the forest. What I wouldn't give for an axe right now."

Vitomas stood on her balcony overlooking the royal gardens; lost in her thoughts. Going days without seeing Raul was breaking her heart but she realized how dangerous it was now, more than ever. The guards were watching her so closely. Crispus didn't want Vitomas to leave the castle after they found the body of the guard outside of her window.

A tremendous feeling of uneasiness overtook Vitomas, she again felt as if she was being watched. She looked down at the garden. Suddenly Vitomas caught her breathe, was she imagining things? For a moment she thought there was a movement by the large oak tree where the guard's body was found.

Vitomas turned when she heard the door to her chambers open. Annabelle walked into the chambers and out onto the balcony.

"How is he?" Vitomas asked. "I miss him so much."

"He is still very weak but he wants to leave soon," Annabelle said. "We have to find a way to trick the guards so you can get away."

"Do your parents have everything ready?" Vitomas asked as she nervously looked behind her at the garden.

"What is the matter?"

"The hair on my neck is raising. I just feel like I am being watched by more than just the soldiers."

"I don't see anyone," Annabelle said as she looked down at the garden. "My parents have almost everything ready, they are just waiting for word on when we should leave. Vitomas I think we should leave soon also. Raul wants me to return with an answer."

"Tell him tomorrow morning. I will find a way to get there."

As Archetenus watched Vitomas and Annabelle on the balcony he wondered what they were talking about because they both had such serious looks on their faces. Archetenus almost let Vitomas see him but then he thought better of it, in case there were guards in her chambers. Archetenus was monitoring the men who were guarding Vitomas, as he waited for his chance to get close to her.

In their weakened states, Roch and Jonas found dragging small logs and large branches from the forest exhausting. They had to take breaks often as they spent days working on their raft. Roch made some snares that provided meat to their diet of fish. Finally on the morning of the ninth day they were ready to sail the raft. The sun glistened on the water as they made their way up the river. The sounds of birds and the splashing of fish gave them both a sense of peace.

"Jonas when we get to the Lake of the Pors, there is a small fishing cabin on the shore that we can take shelter in," Roch said. "We can get some horses in Cana."

"Where is she?" asked Raul as the fear welled within him.

"I don't know," said Annabelle. "She said she would meet us here."

"Everything is packed," said Alexander as he entered the cabin through the back door.

"Someone is coming," said Laurel who was standing near a front window.

Vitomas ran inside of the cabin. When Raul looked at her he thought she had never looked more beautiful; then he realized she had been crying. Vitomas hugged Laurel and Alexander then she walked over to Annabelle and kissed her on the forehead. Annabelle started to cry.

"Vitomas what has happened?" Raul asked. "Something is wrong."

Vitomas ran to Raul, threw her arms around his neck and started to cry. He held her tightly thinking he never wanted to let her go. "Talk to me," implored Raul. It took Vitomas several moments to compose herself. "I am being watched closely, if I leave with you now they will discover I am gone and catch us." Vitomas started to cry again, then stopped herself but she could barely speak. "A boca cannot outrun their horses; I will tell the guards that Annabelle left to care for a sick aunt and hopefully they will not find out she is gone for several days."

Annabelle ran to Vitomas crying, "I will not leave you behind."

Vitomas hugged Annabelle and stroked her hair, "You have to go now you know that."

"We can get away," Raul said anxiously.

Vitomas turned back towards Raul and put both of her hands gently on his face, "My love you are a general in the military you know we cannot escape the soldiers in a boca. If I go with you it will be a death sentence for us all. You are a wise man but your emotions are blinding you. You know I speak the truth."

"You cannot stay here," Raul said with anger and fear rising in his voice.

"My love, I want to go with you so badly but everyone I care about is in this cabin and I will not risk your lives."

Raul pulled Vitomas tightly against him. "Then I will stay with you."

"It is just a matter of time before the soldiers find you and you are in no condition to fight," cried Vitomas as she looked into his eyes. "If they kill you I have no reason to live Raul," Vitomas sobbed. "I was dead and you gave me life again, I cannot lose you."

Raul leaned down and kissed Vitomas on the lips, a long passionate kiss. "I love you," he whispered. "And I will come back for you."

"I love you also," said Vitomas and kissed Raul. "I will be waiting for you but please take Annabelle and her family to safety."

"I think we should leave them alone," said Alexander as he ushered Annabelle and Laurel out the back door of the cabin.

"I do not want to leave you," said Raul with tears in his eyes.

"If you do not go we will both be killed, you know that," said Vitomas as tears ran down her cheeks. Vitomas fought to compose herself. "Roch has not returned from Calix, I do not know if he is alive. If he is dead I will send a messenger to your father's castle," said Vitomas. "If Roch returns, he often leaves me for months at a time; perhaps I can send you a message through Gala."

"No matter what happens do not lose hope; I will return for you," said Raul as he hugged Vitomas tightly.

Vitomas pulled out of Raul's grasp and took off one of her earrings, a gift from Roch. It was a large sapphire earring surrounded by small diamonds and rubies. She put the earring into Raul's hand, "This is a symbol that I pledge my heart to you forever."

"I have nothing to give you my dear," said Raul with his voice shaking.

"You have already given me your heart, I do not need more," said Vitomas as the tears streamed down her face.

Raul grasped Vitomas and pulled her against him again, "I don't want to let you go."

"I know," sobbed Vitomas with her head buried in his chest.

Alexander opened the back door of the cabin, "Gala was just here and said there are soldiers in Cana we need to go."

Vitomas pushed Raul away from her, "Go quickly."

Raul did not move so Alexander grabbed his arm and walked Raul to the door. Vitomas watched as Alexander helped Raul into the back of the covered boca; her heart sinking in her chest. She watched the boca until it was out of sight; then Vitomas collapsed on the bed crying. Vitomas heard a noise at the front door of the cabin; without thinking she jumped off the bed and quickly opened the door.

"Hello My Lady," said Archetenus with a grin.

"My Lord look," said Jonas as he pointed to the western bank.

"Pull the raft in," said Roch.

The two men steered the raft to the western bank of the River Oja. Jonas got off the raft first and tied it to a small tree. Roch and Jonas looked for any sign of movement before they searched the bodies that littered the ground. Five Huta warriors and one Taperian warrior lay dead. The Taperian warrior had three arrows in his body. The Huta warriors were disemboweled. Jonas and Roch went from body to body taking weapons and anything of value.

"What happened here?" asked Jonas more to himself than to Roch.

"Jonas are these the same tracks that surrounded our camp?" Jonas walked to where Roch was standing. The ground near one of the Huta warriors had been softened by the man's blood, and preserved several large footprints.

"Yes My Lord, and these bodies have not been dead more than two days," Jonas said as he looked around the area for signs of the creatures. "My Lord I feel like we are being watched."

"I know Jonas I was thinking the same thing. We need to return to the raft."

The two men hurried to the raft and maneuvered it to the middle of the river. "Why do you think the Hutas would remain in this area?" asked Roch. "I have not heard of any Shettees or treasure here."

"I don't know My Lord. I am more disturbed as to why the Hutas were torn apart and not our soldier and why the creatures did not attack us."

"I would like to know what those creatures are; never in my days have I seen prints like those."

"At least I feel better with some weapons," said Jonas with a laugh.

"I would feel better with some food and wine," replied Roch and they both laughed.

The two men paddled in silence; they were moving against the current which was getting stronger as they headed north. Roch's shoulder and arm were still weak from his wound and he was becoming fatigued. "Jonas we may have to go to shore, I am having difficulty holding the paddle," Roch said after several hours.

"I was about to say the same thing; look at those storm clouds," said Jonas as he pointed to the eastern sky which was black. The storm was moving quickly and causing waves to rise and fall. The two men paddled the raft to the western shore and tied it to two trees on the bank. They scarcely got off the raft before torrential rain fell and blinded them. Roch and Jonas had difficulty standing against the wind as they ran for cover into the forest. No sooner had they entered the forest when a tree to their right was struck by lightning.

The tree tops acted as a canopy and sheltered Roch and Jonas from some of the force of the storm. They ran deeper into the forest; the thunder of trees falling violently shook the ground as they ran. Roch grabbed Jonas' left arm and pointed at a cabin that was made visible by a lightning bolt. Both men ran towards the structure. Roch fell and Jonas helped him to a standing position. The two men burst through the front door of the cabin.

"I knew you were coming," said the old woman seated at the hearth. Slowly she turned and looked at the men. She was about four and a half feet tall with raven black hair that she wore in one long braid down her back. Her piercing eyes were steel gray. The wrinkles that were deeply embedded in her leathery skin made her look older than her years.

"My Lady we are sorry for barging into your house, we are merely seeking shelter from the storm," said Jonas.

"By all means my sons; come closer to the fire and warm yourselves," said the woman kindly. "Are you hungry?"

"Yes My Lady," replied Jonas as he walked towards the fire. Jonas realized that Roch was not with him and looked over his shoulder. Roch remained standing at the door staring at the woman as if he had seen a ghost. "My Lord," said Jonas.

"Yes, I will be right there," answered Roch but he continued to stand in the doorway. "Have we met before?" asked Roch of the woman who smiled but did not answer. Roch continued to hesitate.

"Come in or stay out in the storm but shut the door," the woman said to Roch as she walked over to a chest and took out two blankets. Roch entered the house and took a seat near the fire with Jonas. The woman gave them each a blanket. She then set the long wooden table with three plates. "As soon as you warm up come to the table," said the woman as she put a pitcher of wine and three goblets on the table.

Roch and Jonas moved from the warmth of the fire to the wooden benches on either side of the table. The woman ladled hot stew onto their plates from a boiling black pot hanging over the fire. She took two large loaves of bread from a rack near the fire and handed one to each of the men. The woman joined them at the table without speaking.

"Thank you for your kindness," said Jonas as he broke off a large piece of bread.

The wind howled through the cracks in the walls, causing the flames in the hearth to dance. Roch and Jonas looked around the one room cabin. The cabin was clean and orderly; there were bunches of dried herbs and flowers hanging from various areas of the ceiling.

"This stew is wonderful," said Jonas. The woman still did not look up from her plate of stew. "My name is Jonas and..."

"I know who you are," interrupted the woman.

Roch and Jonas looked at each other quizzically. "How do you know who we are?" asked Roch.

"I told you I saw you coming," replied the woman without looking at them.

"I do not understand," said Jonas.

"I am a seer," replied the woman. "My name is Miranda."

The three ate in silence for a few minutes then Miranda stood up from the table and walked to the hearth. Without turning towards them she said, "You may stay here tonight but be gone in the morning."

"Is that any way to speak to a king?" asked Roch arrogantly.

Miranda spun around so quickly that it took both men by surprise. She stared at Roch until the hair on the back of his neck rose. "You may be a king but you bring darkness wherever you go; there is death all around you."

Miranda walked towards Roch with defiance. "You want to ask me about that map in your pocket. Be very careful my king you have many choices to make and many you will regret through eternity." There was such power and authority in Miranda's voice when she spoke that both men remained silent. Miranda turned and stared at Jonas, a penetrating cold stare. "I did not recognize you at first. I do not fear you; you have no power here."

"You need not fear me, My Lady," replied Jonas with a sly smile.

"Roch you are so arrogant you do not even know the company you keep," said Miranda as she turned back to the fire.

"I do not know what you are talking about woman," Roch replied angrily.

"Of course you don't," Miranda said with disdain. "Those who created you are preventing you from seeing many things. You are surrounded with spies; you should trust no one."

The small cabin shook as a tree fell nearby. Neither Roch nor Jonas wanted to stay in Miranda's cabin but to go out into the storm was suicide. The men finished their meal in an uneasy silence. Jonas stood up and walked over to Miranda. "Thank you," said Jonas as he handed her two gold coins. Miranda did not take the money but stared at Jonas for a few moments then a smile came across her face.

"What is it?" asked Jonas with puzzlement.

"I just saw your future," Miranda said with a power that unnerved Jonas. He backed away from the woman, not wanting to ask what she saw.

Miranda slept in the only bed in the cabin. Both Roch and Jonas slept on the wooden floor near the hearth. Roch's sleep was often disturbed by nightmares; this night was no different. As Roch tossed and turned he kept seeing the face of a lion in his dreams; this night The Lion kept asking him 'Why?'

Miranda was awake and cooking breakfast long before the sun rose in the sky. She had to walk around Jonas and Roch but neither man woke until they smelled the coffee and the meat frying in a pan of grease. Miranda set the table and served the men their breakfast in silence. Miranda's presence gave both Jonas and Roch an unusual feeling of uneasiness that neither man was accustomed to.

The storm had subsided so Roch and Jonas decided to leave as soon as they finished eating. Both men had an overwhelming need to flee Miranda's cabin. They thanked Miranda for her generosity; Jonas walked outside first. As Roch was walking through the doorway Miranda said, "That is the emissary of The Great Ruler that you see in your dreams do not take that lightly." Roch stopped dead in his tracts but said nothing. "That Lion that you see is a most powerful Angel you would do well to listen to what he says."

"It is merely a dream of a lion," Roch scoffed but his voice was barely audible.

Miranda turned and stared into Roch's eyes, "Are you so blinded by darkness that you do not realize that things are often not what they appear and people are not who they claim to be?"

"What are you talking about?" Roch demanded although his voice was surprisingly weak in her presence.

"Ask your travelling partner," Miranda said and turned away from him.

Roch stood in the doorway of the cabin a few more moments. He did not respond to Miranda's statement, but the cold chill of fear filled his being.

Chapter XIII
Going Home

Vitomas awoke to the sound of a crackling fire. When she first opened her eyes Vitomas did not know why she was lying on the ground or why her head hurt. Her vision was blurred at first; Vitomas tried to sit up but the pain in her head caused her to feel nauseous and she quickly fell back to a prone position.

Vitomas tried to put her hand to her aching head; then fear seized her as she realized her hands were tied together in front of her. Vitomas opened her eyes and fearfully looked before her. She was lying on a blanket in front of a large fire. Vitomas could smell meat frying and coffee brewing but she saw no one. Vitomas tried to sit up again but slowly this time so that she would not get sick.

"I was wondering when you would wake," said a male voice.

Vitomas swung her head around which caused her blinding pain; she fought against shutting her eyes. With her vision still blurry, Vitomas stared into the darkness and saw a large man walking towards the fire with an armful of wood. "Who are you?" she demanded.

"Do you not remember?" the man asked with a laugh as he walked closer to the fire.

"I can barely see; what did you do to me?"

"I am sorry about that," the man said as he came closer to Vitomas. "You fell and hit your head on the bed post in the cabin."

"Bedpost," Vitomas repeated as images flooded her memory. "Archetenus."

"See you didn't forget me," Archetenus said as he put the armful of wood near the fire. Archetenus walked up to Vitomas and squatted down so he could look into her face.

"Archetenus what is the meaning of this?"

"You mean you don't know?" Archetenus asked as he untied Vitomas' hands.

207

"Archetenus I don't understand what you are saying and I don't know why I am here."

"Here drink this," said Archetenus as he handed Vitomas a cup of coffee. "The food will be cooked soon, of course it is not what you are used to at the castle." Vitomas put the cup of coffee on the ground and shifted her sitting position, when she did this she winced in pain. "Are you alright?"

"My head really hurts."

"You took a bad fall; you have been out for hours."

"Archetenus where are we and why are we here?"

"You do not know?"

"You keep saying that, Archetenus I really don't understand any of this."

Archetenus handed Vitomas a plate of food, "Here we can talk over dinner." As they ate Archetenus told Vitomas about the mission Roch had sent him on; he told her about his men dying and the monsters. Archetenus told Vitomas about the Village of Ort and the Sanuri. He finished the story by telling her that Roch sent him on that mission to be killed.

"Archetenus I am sorry you had to endure such hardship and horror but why would Roch send you on a mission to be killed?"

Archetenus sat in silence for a moment looking into her green eyes, "Because of you My Lady." A shocked look came across Vitomas' face that surprised Archetenus.

"Archetenus what are you talking about?"

"Vitomas the only thing that kept me alive on that mission was the thought of you." Vitomas' eyes grew wide but she remained silent. "Vitomas I love you and I have been in love with you since I first set eyes upon you at the Gefrey Games." Tears started to well in Vitomas' eyes but she did not speak. "See there, you would cry when I was in danger at the games; that is when I knew you loved me too."

Vitomas put both of her hands to her face and looked at Archetenus, tears running down her cheeks. "I don't know what to say, you are a brave and honorable warrior and I did not want to see you hurt," whispered Vitomas. "But I do not love you Archetenus." Vitomas became frightened as she could see the fury creeping into Archetenus' face.

"Well then, you will learn to," Archetenus growled.

The next morning after breakfast the Sanuri and Petra rode out of the gate of the monastery at Malga, heading towards the Kingdom of Wetpr. "I am going to miss Padre Bartholomew," said Petra as he sat next to the Sanuri in the front seat of the boca.

"I will too, we can certainly visit him any time you want," replied the Sanuri. "Petra, I was thinking that I could pick up where your mother left off with your education while we travel." Petra started to cry and the Sanuri put his arm around the boy's shoulders. Petra leaned against the Sanuri and the two rode in silence for a while; soon Petra was sleeping peacefully.

As the Sanuri drove the boca his mind was filled with thoughts of all that the priests had told him at Malga. While the Sanuri believed what the priests said about their recent encounter with King Roch; he also heard many inconsistencies. As the Sanuri was pondering on what Roch was involved in he saw men riding towards them.

"Petra wake up," whispered the Sanuri. "Do not say anything."

Petra quickly opened his eyes. The Sanuri had stopped the boca which was now surrounded with soldiers on horseback.

"What are Taperian soldiers doing this far south in the Kingdom of Puntd?" asked the Sanuri.

"We are looking for some of our men who may be hurt," replied Cerephus. "Have you seen any Taperian soldiers?"

"We found Archetenus injured in Ort; we cared for him and he left us about a week ago," said the Sanuri. "He is the only Taperian we have seen but we have seen signs of Hutas."

"Archetenus lives?" replied Cerephus. "Where was he headed?"

"I thought he said he was returning to Taperia," said the Sanuri. "You seem surprised."

Cerephus ignored the Sanuri's comment. "Where are you two headed?" asked Cerephus.

"Calix," replied the Sanuri.

"Be careful, we found the remains of a Huta war party east of Calix," said Cerephus. "They looked like they had been torn apart by animals."

"What kind of animals?" asked the Sanuri.

"I don't know but we found thirty Huta bodies; I cannot imagine how many animals there had to be to kill them," said Cerephus then he turned and led his men south towards Malga.

"There is more to that search party than that General said. Taperians do not normally search for their wounded soldiers," the Sanuri said to Petra.

"Who do you think they are looking for?"

"The priests said King Roch was in Calix a few weeks ago, I wonder if he did not return to Stordt."

"How long will it take us to get to Calix?" asked Petra.

"We aren't going to Calix," replied the Sanuri.

"I am sorry I just cannot stop crying," whispered Annabelle as she and Raul rode in the back of the boca.

"You love her very much," replied Raul sadly.

"So do you," said Annabelle wiping tears from her cheeks. "It has been two days and I am still crying," she added with frustration.

"Quiet! There are soldiers ahead," Alexander yelled to Annabelle and Raul in the back of the boca.

Alexander pulled the team of horses to a stop as six Taperian soldiers blocked their passage on the road. Laurel sat quietly next to Alexander in the front seat of the boca.

"Why are you leaving Stordt?" demanded one of the soldiers.

"My wife's sister is dying and we are travelling to be with her in the last hours," said Alexander. Laurel started sobbing as Alexander was speaking.

"It is against the law to leave this kingdom without permission of King Roch," stated the same soldier.

"But we have permission, I will show you," said Alexander as he reached into his vest pocket and grabbed one of the small scrolls Vitomas had stolen for them. Alexander handed the scroll to the soldier, who appeared to read it. After a few moments the soldier handed the scroll back to Alexander.

"You are free to go," said the soldier. Then as an afterthought the soldier asked, "Where are you traveling to?"

"Salar," replied Alexander.

"Very well," said the soldier as he and his men turned and headed west along the border.

"Thank The Great Ruler that Vitomas got us that scroll," said Alexander with a sigh of relief. He turned to Laurel and said, "That sobbing almost sounded real." Both Annabelle and Raul laughed. Raul moved to the front of the boca so he could speak with Alexander.

"We will be across the border soon then I should ride in the front," said Raul.

"Very well," said Laurel. Then with a loud laugh she added, "But you will have to practice your sobbing." They all laughed again and Raul returned to Annabelle in the rear of the boca.

"I love your parents and my father will be so glad to meet them," said Raul. Annabelle smiled. "He will be glad to meet you also," said Raul trying to reassure her.

"No it is not that, I am so thankful that we are leaving Stordt; it is just that I am so afraid for Vitomas."

"I am also," said Raul in a whisper. "But I will return soon to get her, in the meantime I need you to draw me another map of the castle, mine must have been left behind in that bedroom."

"It is up just a little bit further," said Roch.

"I will be so glad to get on dry land and stay there," said Jonas. Both men were exhausted and badly burned from the sun. "There, by that tree hanging in the water," said Roch, pointing as he spoke. They pulled the raft up to some stone steps and tied it to a tree. "The cabin is just on the other side of those trees," explained Roch.

The two men grabbed their weapons from the raft and walked a few hundred feet into the forest. In the fading light of the evening they could see the outline of a cabin. They entered the cabin through the back door.

"Is there anyone here?" yelled Roch. There was no response. "I will light the hearth," said Roch. "If I remember there were candles on a table." Roch felt along the wall until he found the hearth. He put his hands out, "We are in luck, there is wood in the hearth," said Roch with a laugh.

"If we are really lucky perhaps there is some food in here too," added Jonas as he felt his way around the dark cabin until he bumped into a table. He felt two plates with candles on them. Grabbing the candles Jonas walked over to the hearth where Roch had just ignited the wood. Jonas handed the candles to Roch who lit them and returned them to Jonas. "What happened in here?" asked Jonas as he turned around and saw the disarray of the cabin.

Roch turned and saw the furniture thrown around the room. "Either a fight or an animal got in here."

"Either way I hope they left some food," said Jonas as he started to pick up some of the furniture. "Well, we are in luck; here is a basket with apples, wine and honey," said Jonas as he put the basket on the table.

Roch turned from the fire and picked the mattress up from the floor and put it back on the bed. He saw a small reflection in the corner of his eye. Roch bent down and picked up a sapphire earring which was surrounded by diamonds and rubies.

Petra put another log on the campfire and watched ashes swirl around in the night air. "You have been quiet for a long time my young friend," said the Sanuri.

"I am just thinking."

"Know that you can talk to me about anything," said the Sanuri. "I will always be here for you." Petra continued to poke at the fire and cry softly. The Sanuri watched him for a few moments then returned to reading one of The Holy Scrolls. Suddenly they heard the sound of something large moving loudly through the forest.

The Sanuri jumped up and handed Petra the scroll and told him to go into the boca. The Sanuri stepped to the front of the boca and grabbed his staff. The sound of movement stopped; then the Sanuri heard a voice cry for help. The voice seemed to come from the darkness just past the circle of light which radiated from the campfire.

The Sanuri walked into the darkness listening intently. He heard the muffled voice again, just a few feet to his right. The Sanuri carried the wounded man into camp and laid him down next to the campfire.

"Petra bring me my medicine bag and some water and cloths," the Sanuri called.

The Huta warrior was covered in blood. He had deep claw marks and bites covering much of his body. Some of his hair looked like it had been pulled out at the scalp. The warrior went in and out of consciousness as the Sanuri cleaned and bound his wounds.

"What happened to you?" asked the Sanuri.

"We were attacked by demons," whispered the warrior. "Demons they were everywhere."

"Those creatures are not demons and they are attacking you because your soldiers stole the most sacred possession of their tribe, The Box of Itifer," said the Sanuri. "The box must be returned or blood will not stop flowing." The warrior had a look of recognition in his eyes as the Sanuri spoke. "Do you know where the box is?" asked the Sanuri. The warrior started to speak then lost consciousness.

"What language are you speaking?" Petra asked the Sanuri.

"The tongue of the Hutas," replied the Sanuri as he washed blood from the warriors face.

"How do you know that language?"

"I can speak every language," said the Sanuri. "It is a gift from The Great Ruler." The Sanuri paused as if listening to a voice that Petra could not hear. "Petra go to bed, I will stay with this man," said the Sanuri as he was sensing the presence of other beings in the darkness.

"Vitomas, I am going to teach you how to cook," Archetenus said. "I haven't decided yet if we will have servants."

After Archetenus' initial outburst of anger, he had been very nice and accommodating to Vitomas although he kept talking about their life together. "Archetenus it has been a couple of days and you still haven't told me where we are going. I know we are traveling west now."

"We are going to Port Friada; I've heard it is a good place to start over. Come here and I will show you how to make biscuits."

Vitomas knelt next to Archetenus, near the fire. She was trying not to anger him because the rage she saw in his eyes that first night reminded her of Roch. Archetenus always tied her hands and led her horse when they were traveling. But this night he untied her as soon as they stopped to make camp.

Vitomas had never been out of the Kingdom of Stordt and had no idea where they were or where Port Friada was located. All she could think about was how difficult it would be for Raul to find her now. "Where is Port Friada, I have never heard of it."

"You've never heard of Port Friada?" Archetenus asked with amazement.

"Archetenus you know Roch barely let me out of the castle."

Archetenus stared at her for a moment, as he was beginning to realize the extent of her imprisonment. "It is the largest port city in all of Opots. It's in the Kingdom of Ganz on the Inlet of the Sea of Grevtd."

"Why do you want to go there?"

"It's a large and busy city. With all kinds of people who come from all over the world to trade their wares."

"Have you been there before?"

"No, but I have heard much about it."

They were kneeling side by side near the fire as they prepared food together. Archetenus became quiet and Vitomas turned and looked at him. Archetenus was staring at Vitomas and as soon as she looked up at him he put both of his arms around her and pulled her close to him. Archetenus was a huge man, much larger than Roch. Vitomas tried to struggle as he kissed her on the lips but she could barely move. Vitomas did not return his kiss and after a few moments Archetenus stopped kissing Vitomas and stared at her. She could see the anger in his eyes.

"You cannot tell me that you love Roch," Archetenus said with disgust.

"I hate Roch; he is worse than a demon."

"Then why won't you kiss me?"

"Because I have given my heart to another."

Archetenus was not expecting that answer from Vitomas. He now let go of her and stared at her angrily. "Who would you love instead of me?"

Vitomas took a deep breath and looked into his eyes. "Archetenus I love Prince Raul from Wetpr. I am pledged to be his wife."

"I heard he died in the castle."

"Roch's men beat him then they poisoned him, he did almost die." Vitomas explained. "Gala the healer from Cana gave him a potion that made him appear dead. Annabelle and I got him out of the castle and Annabelle and her parents are taking him back to Wetpr."

Archetenus sat back and stared at Vitomas as she spoke. "I actually believe your story. What condition was he when he left?"

"Not good, there was no way he could have fought Roch's men."

"So you really don't know if he will live."

Vitomas' eyes grew wide; she had never thought that Raul might later die of his injuries. "He will live," she said with conviction.

"Vitomas tell me; did he say he would come back for you?"

"Yes."

"And you believed him?"

"Yes and don't say it like that. Raul is a brave and honorable man. As injured as he was he stood up to Roch with defiance."

"Then he sounds like a man I would like," Archetenus said. "But I am not willing to give him my woman."

"What happened to the Huta?" asked Petra after he climbed out of the boca early the next morning.

"He died during the night; I just finished burying him," replied the Sanuri.

"You look really tired, I can drive the boca while you sleep," said Petra as he started preparing breakfast.

"Actually we have a change of plans my young friend," said the Sanuri as he took a seat near the fire. "I need to do some research so we will stay here for the day."

"What are you researching?"

216

"That warrior told me who has The Box of Itifer before he died; I need to determine what direction we will take."

"Can I help?"

"You can watch," said the Sanuri. "This will be the beginning of your lessons."

After they finished breakfast the Sanuri grabbed his staff, "Come Petra lesson number one."

"Where are we going?"

"I will know when we get there," replied the Sanuri. The two started walking to the east. "The Great Ruler created all life, every flower, every animal, every person he created," said the Sanuri. "So we should respect what he created."

"Even the Hutas?"

"Petra The Great Ruler does not create bad people they become bad by the choices they make in this life. Today I am going to show you a gift I was given by The Great Ruler," said the Sanuri as he pointed to a small hill. "We are going to the top of that hill, when we get there I want you to stay about one hundred feet behind me and do not speak, just watch."

Petra did as he was instructed. The Sanuri stood in a clearing at the top of the hill. He placed his staff on the ground next to him and raised both his arms towards the sky. Petra could not hear if the Sanuri was speaking. Soon the sky around the Sanuri was filling with flocks of different kinds of birds. The various flocks started to circle around in the air, around and around they flew, then they started to land.

Most of the birds landed on the ground but many landed on the Sanuri. When the birds landed, Petra could hear the Sanuri's voice but could not make out what he was saying. The flocks of birds left, each flying in a different direction. The Sanuri turned and walked towards Petra.

"Were you talking to the birds?" asked Petra his eyes wide with amazement.

The Sanuri laughed loudly, "Yes I was, I asked them to look for the Huta warriors who have The Box of Itifer."

"How did you do that?"

"Actually it is easier than you would think," replied the Sanuri. "Would you like to learn how to speak with creatures?"

"Oh yes, yes I would," said Petra beaming with excitement.

"When you love and respect the creatures and remove the fears that put boundaries on us all; you will be able to speak with them," said the Sanuri with pleasure in his heart. "I will teach you."

Raul awoke to the smell of coffee brewing and bacon and eggs frying. He opened his eyes and saw Laurel, Annabelle and Alexander working around the campfire. "You should have woken me," Raul said as he sat up and grabbed his crutches. Alexander quickly walked over to Raul and helped him stand up.

"Raul, I don't know if I can explain how we feel," Laurel said, her voice almost singing. "This is the first morning of our lives that we have awakened as free people. It is like we are in a different world."

Raul smiled at their happiness. "Laurel, Wetpr is a very different world than Stordt. You can do as you please and you won't have to live in fear any longer. I want you all to stay at my father's castle until you decide where you want to live."

"Raul that is so very generous of you," Laurel said but don't you think you should ask your father first?"

"He will be so grateful that you helped me that he will extend the invitation himself, just wait and see. Now he may not be so happy with me."

"What do you mean?" asked Annabelle as she handed a plate of food to Raul.

"I will be the next King of Wetpr and have many responsibilities. My father was not happy at my decision to travel the kingdoms."

Alexander walked up to Raul and put his hand on Raul's shoulder. "Raul as a father I will tell you that Sudfad will be so proud of the man you are."

"There are riders," Laurel announced. From Raul's position behind the boca, he could not see them. "They look like soldiers," Laurel added as the men came closer.

Raul heard the horses stop, then he heard a voice that was very dear to him say, "Good morning."

"Simon," Raul called out and started to walk towards the front of the boca.

A handsome young officer quickly rode around the boca, his mouth dropping open when he saw his Raul. "What happened to you?" asked Simon as he jumped off his horse and ran up to his brother. Raul and Simon hugged and laughed. "Do Father and Mother know you are coming home?"

"No, it's a long story," Raul said. "Simon I want to introduce you to these people who saved my life. This is Laurel and Alexander, they were the personal attendants of King Jaretta and Queen Lillian, our grandparents and they took care of Father when he was young."

"We have heard a great deal about you," Alexander said as he shook hands with Simon.

"Where is Annabelle?" Raul asked.

"She went down to the river to get some water," Laurel said.

"Annabelle is their very beautiful daughter," Raul said with a grin. "And almost the sister of the woman I want to marry."

"What!" Simon said with a laugh. "You come home looking like you have been in a war and now you tell me you want to get married. You have some explaining to do."

Annabelle now appeared from behind the boca carrying a wooden bucket of water. Simon saw her first and quickly went up to Annabelle and took the bucket from her hand. Simon and Annabelle stared at each other admiringly, neither of them speaking.

"Simon this is Annabelle and Annabelle this is my brother Simon; who I told you about," Raul said with a grin.

"So he told you about me?" Simon said with a flirtatious smile. Annabelle just kept staring at Simon and nodded, she did not speak. Simon held out his arm for Annabelle to take and he escorted her back to the campfire.

"Thank you," Annabelle said in almost a whisper.

Simon put the bucket of water on the ground and walked over to his men. "You may not recognize him but your future King finally came home; come over and greet him," Simon joked. The six men who were riding with Simon all dismounted and walked around the boca and greeted Raul. Alexander, Laurel and Annabelle all stared in amazement at the affection and respect Raul's men showed him.

"Lt. Markus will you take the troops back to the castle and tell the King and Queen, Raul is coming home and that we will be having guests?"

"Yes, My Lord. Your mother will want to know what time."

"Tell her noon," Simon said. "That should give her enough time to organize something."

Raul was laughing at Simon's comments. When Simon returned to the fire he said with a grin, "You know Mother would kill me if I didn't give her advance notice." Simon sat down on one of the stools that had been placed around the fire.

"Would you like some breakfast?" Laurel asked.

"Yes I would," Simon said. "It smells great."

As they all ate breakfast, Raul was telling Simon about his attack and Vitomas and Annabelle helping him. When Simon interrupted.

"I don't understand why you left her behind; you said you asked her to marry you." Simon noticed how everyone in the group became quiet after his comment.

Annabelle looked at Raul and saw how emotional he suddenly became. "Vitomas stayed behind to save us all," Annabelle said as she started to cry. "She knew that if she came with us, the soldiers would find us and kill us."

Simon looked at everyone's faces. "I am sorry but I don't understand how her staying behind saved you."

"Vitomas is Roch's Queen," Raul said.

"What!" Simon said loudly. "Raul do you know what you are doing?"

Annabelle now walked up to Simon with her hands on her hips and anger in her voice. "Don't you ever say a bad thing about Vitomas. Roch stole her when she was a child. She hates him as we all do, she does not want to be his queen. He beats her and tortures her, yet she is the kindest person you will ever meet. She saved me from being raped several times and she saved Raul, and Roch punished her for it. We would all be dead if it wasn't for her."

"Did something happen that you have been in such an ill temperament?" asked Jonas as he and Roch walked towards Cana the next morning.

"No, we need to get some horses," Roch growled.

The two men continued to walk in silence. Just as they entered the Village of Cana, a young man rode past them on a horse. Roch yelled for the man to stop. The man stopped immediately and before he could say a word, Roch pulled the man off his horse and threw him to the ground.

"I am King Roch and I need your horse," yelled Roch at the man. Roch mounted and turned to Jonas. "Get a horse or walk, but I need to get to the castle." Roch headed for Taperia at a full run.

"Annabelle I certainly did not mean to offend you," Simon said.

"Annabelle, that was very disrespectful," Alexander scolded.

"I'm sorry I yelled at you," Annabelle said softy and turned around, walking back to her seat near the fire.

"We all love Vitomas and none of us wanted to leave her behind," Laurel explained. Then she looked at Raul. "It broke Raul's heart and Annabelle can't stop crying."

"Roch stole Annabelle also," Raul said to Simon. "Somehow those two little girls kept each other alive in that nightmare. Simon you would not believe what it is like there. I have never been to such an evil place before. As soon as I can walk I am going back for her."

"You mean we are going back for her," Simon said with a smile.

"I'm coming with you," Annabelle said.

"I don't think that is a good idea," Raul said as Simon stared at Annabelle with surprise at her statement.

"Raul, I know the castle and the people. You will need me and you know it."

"What is going on here?" screamed Roch as he burst through the front doors of the castle. "Where are the guards?"

"My Lord you are alive," gasped Sophie as she ran to Roch. Sophie started to curtsy but Roch grabbed her arm. "Tell me woman what is going on, where are the guards, where is my wife?"

"My Lord, Cerephus took many men and they have been searching for you?" cried Sophie in pain.

"Did they all leave?" yelled Roch angrily.

Sophie looked at the floor and tears came to her eyes, Roch let go of her arm and asked, "Sophie what happened to the Queen?"

"She is gone My Lord and so is Annabelle; the guards have been looking for them for a week."

"What of the man that was injured?"

"He died shortly after you left My Lord, I saw the body myself."

Roch ran up the stairs to Vitomas' chambers with Sophie behind him. Sophie followed Roch into Vitomas' bedroom. "My Lord there is something you have to know." Roch turned and looked at her, his eyes were filled with rage. "Before the Queen went missing a dead guard was found underneath this window," said Sophie as she walked towards the balcony. "The guards said there were signs of a fight near the body."

Roch screamed with rage. He picked up a vase of flowers and smashed it against the wall. Then he kicked a chair and started to tear the quilts off Vitomas' bed, throwing them around the room.

"My Lord, none of her belongings are missing, it is as if she and Annabelle just disappeared," said Sophie.

"So are you saying someone took them?" Roch asked without looking at Sophie.

"That is what many think, My Lord."

"And who would dare to steal my wife," Roch screamed with rage.

"My Lord, no one knows."

Just before noon, Alexander was driving the boca towards Salar. Raul sat in the front of the boca next to Alexander and Simon rode his horse on the passenger side of the boca so he could talk to Raul. Laurel and Annabelle were in the back of the boca changing into their finest dresses.

Alexander pulled the horses to a stop as a group of soldiers approached the boca. The soldiers came to a stop and only Markus rode forward to the passenger side of the boca. "My Lord the King has sent us to escort you to the castle."

Simon looked at Raul with a grin, "Told you he would be glad to see you."

"Thank you Markus," said Raul. The soldiers turned and led the way to Salar.

"It's a shame they didn't bring you any clean clothes to wear," Simon kidded and all three men laughed.

"Are you two about ready?" Alexander yelled into the back of the boca.

"Father it is very hard to get dressed when the boca is moving," Annabelle called out. "Listen, Mother listen."

The sound of trumpets could be heard as they got closer to Salar. The soldiers had been riding in three vertical lines in front of the boca, upon Markus' orders they now rode single file in front of the boca. Cheers could be heard before Raul and Alexander could see the people lined up on either side of the road. Women and children were throwing flowers into the air. Raul smiled and waved to the people of Salar.

The cheering crowds started about a quarter mile outside of the city gates and continued to the gates of the castle. Only the soldiers and the boca entered the castle yard. Simon dismounted so he could help Raul down from the boca then Simon walked to the rear of the boca and lifted Laurel down to the ground.

A few moments later Annabelle peeked her head out of the back of the boca. Simon felt his heart race when he saw her. He boldly stared at her which made Annabelle blush and look away. After a moment, Simon said, "Annabelle come closer and I will help you down." Annabelle leaned down and put her hands on Simon's shoulders and he grabbed her small waist and lifted her out of the boca.

Annabelle was wearing a blue silk dress, the color of dark sapphire. Her long curly hair flowed freely except for two jeweled hair clips in front. "You look like a princess," Simon said with an admiring look in his eyes. Once Simon set Annabelle's feet on the ground he did not let go of her waist and the two stood looking at each other and smiling; until they heard a trumpet sound. "The King," said Simon as he took Annabelle's hand and they both hurried to the castle steps.

Two huge wooden doors opened and the King and Queen of Wetpr walked out to a platform at the top of the steps. Soldiers lined each side of the stairway.

224

Queen Renya displayed a beauty and elegance that time could not alter. She wore an emerald green dress with golden trim. Her earrings and necklace were made of emeralds and gold. Her black hair showed strands of gray and was pulled back and up into an elegant hair style. King Sudfad held her left hand as they walked through the doorway.

King Sudfad wore the dress uniform of the military. The scarlet sash accented his graying hair and mustache. A handsome and powerful man, he was showing the signs that only age can bring.

Raul stood at the bottom step, while Simon directed Alexander, Laurel and Annabelle to stand behind Raul. Simon stood next to Annabelle. King Sudfad and Queen Renya gracefully walked down the steps hand in hand as they had done for countless ceremonies. But the formality of the ceremony ended when they reached the bottom step and Raul grabbed and hugged them both. Queen Renya was crying tears of joy. The sight of Raul brought a light back to King Sudfad's face which had been long missing.

"My son what has happened to you," asked Queen Renya as she brushed some of Raul's hair out of his face.

"Mother and Father I have so very much to tell you but first I want you to meet the people who saved my life." Raul turned around and motioned for the others to step forward. "Father you already know them," said Raul with a warm smile. "This is Alexander and his wife Laurel they were the personal servants to your parents and to you as a small child."

Alexander bowed and Laurel curtsied before the royal couple. King Sudfad walked up to Alexander and looked into his eyes. "By The Great Ruler I never thought I would see you again," said Sudfad as he grabbed Alexander and hugged him tightly. Raul motioned for Annabelle to come closer and waited to speak until Sudfad had finished hugging Laurel.

"This is their daughter Annabelle." Annabelle curtsied. "Father these people risked their lives to help me, I asked them to stay with us until they can get settled," said Raul.

"By all means," said King Sudfad. "Come let us all go inside."

"My Lord before we go inside, Laurel and I have brought you something," said Alexander. "Simon will you help me get it from the boca?" Alexander and Simon carried a golden chest that was three feet long and two feet wide. The chest had the word Lillian artfully painted on it. The two men held the chest as Alexander presented it to King Sudfad.

"This chest contains possessions of your parents that we hid from King Roch," Alexander said proudly. King Sudfad did not speak. Raul thought it was the first time he would see his father cry. Queen Renya stepped closer to King Sudfad, who reached out and touched his mother's name that was painted on the chest and his hand started to shake.

"We saved these for you, hoping our paths would cross again one day," said Laurel as tears ran down her cheeks. Laurel looked at Queen Renya, "I put some of the King's baby clothes in there also." With this statement the entire group broke into laughter.

"Father they gave me this but I believe it should be on your hand," Raul said and handed King Sudfad the family ring.

"That ring has been handed down to the first born son of your family for generations. After Roch murdered your parents I took it off from your father's hand. I did not want Roch to take everything from you," Alexander said.

Now Sudfad got tears in his eyes as he looked at the beautiful keepsake in his hand. "I don't know what to say," he whispered.

Renya could see how overwhelmed Sudfad was for he never understood why his parents had abandoned him as a young child. The most powerful King in Opots now stood speechless. "Come we have much to celebrate," Renya said enthusiastically. "Simon have the soldiers put that chest in your father's study and help your brother up all of these stairs." King Sudfad and Queen Renya turned around and ascended the long staircase with Alexander and Laurel walking behind them. Annabelle got on Raul's left side and Simon on his right, as the two helped Raul walk up the stone staircase.

"Raul you look exactly like your father," Annabelle said. "When my parents said you looked like him I never thought they meant you were identical." Raul and Simon both laughed.

"I need to go to my chambers and change," Raul said more to himself.

"Raul you have been up more than you are used to," Annabelle said. "I should probably change your bandages first then I can help you get dressed. But you should probably rest a little."

Raul looked at Simon and winked. "I have had the two most beautiful nurses in all of Opots taking care of me. Actually Annabelle, I was thinking that Simon should give you a tour of the castle and grounds since I can't."

"Simon, this is the first day that Raul has been out of bed for more than a couple of hours. He is not as strong as he would like you to think. He needs help getting dressed."

"I just let her think that," Raul said with a grin; but both Simon and Annabelle could see the color draining from Raul's face.

"Fortunately his bedroom is close by," Simon said as they were walking through the front doors of the castle. Simon and Annabelle took Raul straight to his bed and helped him lay down. Annabelle unbuttoned Raul's shirt and examined his bandages, while Simon took Raul's boots off from his feet.

"Raul, do you want to get a little rest before I change your bandages," Annabelle asked as she felt his forehead.

"I think that would be best. But I would like some water."

"Simon will you show me where I can get a pitcher of water?" Annabelle asked.

"Oh and Annabelle will you go back to the boca and get grandfather's sword and my pouch and give them to Father?" Raul asked.

"Of course, now you lie down and I will be right back," Annabelle said as she covered Raul with blankets and kissed him on the forehead.

"You and Raul seem very close," Simon said as he and Annabelle walked to the kitchen.

"We have been through a lot together. I kind of feel like he is my brother; I suppose that sounds silly to you," Annabelle said and smiled shyly at Simon.

"Not at all," Simon said as he took her hand in his own; a move that both surprised and pleased Annabelle. The two walked down the hallway holding hands and neither of them speaking for a few moments. Then Simon said. "Annabelle I hope you aren't going to start thinking of me as your brother." Annabelle stopped walking and turned and looked at Simon; her face was red and Annabelle was so flustered she didn't know what to say. Simon laughed loudly and said, "Well, I guess I got my answer."

Petra and the Sanuri had returned to the boca to wait for the birds to return with the information that the Sanuri had asked for. The Sanuri started to read a scroll but soon both he and Petra fell asleep in seats they had placed outside of the boca. The sound of rushing wings woke them; when Petra opened his eyes he saw that dozens of huge black birds had landed in their camp. The birds were about two feet tall with purple tail feathers and blue bills. One of the birds was talking with the Sanuri and Petra could understand what the bird was saying. Petra stood up slowly because he did not want to startle the birds.

"Thank you my old friend," said the Sanuri to one of the birds.

"You are most welcome and please return the box to the Centras, much of nature is out of balance when demons take what is holy," said the bird. As soon as the bird had finished speaking the entire flock flew away.

"What kind of birds were they and why could I understand what it was saying?" Petra was so excited he was almost yelling.

The Sanuri laughed loudly, "They are Enrops, they have been here since the beginning of time and they are so intelligent that they can speak in many human tongues."

"Really," said Petra his eyes wide with amazement.

"Most humans greatly underestimate the intelligence of creatures," said the Sanuri. "Someday they will learn."

Chapter XIV
Unseen Enemies

Roch left Vitomas' chambers and continued his destructive rant throughout the castle. Sophie followed behind him picking things up. Roch marched into his war room and slammed the door behind him. Not far from the door was a large table, surrounded by wooden chairs. Roch kicked one of the chairs with such force that the wood splintered. He, then poured himself a glass of whiskey, took one gulp of the liquid and smashed the glass against the wall. Roch paced back and forth for several minutes before he opened the door and yelled to one of the guards, "Bring me Jonas!"

Jonas was a captain in the Taperian military. A man of that rank did not socialize with the King. Jonas had been in the King's service for many years and he knew how unpredictable and violent Roch was. Jonas was not sure what to expect as he entered the war room.

"Jonas come in and have a seat," Raul said with anger in his voice. "Have you heard the news?"

"No My Lord I just arrived at the castle."

"Vitomas and Annabelle have disappeared into thin air. There are search parties looking for them as well as for you and me which is why there are so few soldiers guarding my castle."

"My Lord what do you mean they just disappeared?"

"That is what I am being told, all of their things are still in their rooms; they just vanished."

Sophie entered the war room with a large tray of food. As she set the food on the table she stopped and stared at Jonas.

"Sophie, what is the matter you look as if you have seen a ghost?" Roch asked.

"Nothing, it's nothing My Lord."

"Well, then bring another plate of food for Jonas."

"Yes My Lord," Sophie said as she started to walk out of the war room.

"Sophie wait," Roch called. "Tell Jonas what you told me about, you know about the dead guard."

Sophie returned to the table. "The morning before Vitomas and Annabelle disappeared, some of the soldiers found a dead soldier on the ground under the Queen's window. They said the soldiers' neck had been broken and there were signs of a fight."

"Apparently I have unseen enemies," Roch said angrily with his voice raising. "No one steals from me, who would have the guts to come to my castle and steal my Queen?"

"Where is Raul?" Renya asked when Simon and Annabelle entered the parlor.

"He had to lie down," Annabelle explained. "He is excited to be home but he hasn't been out of bed for more than a couple of hours at a time. He is weaker than he lets on."

"Is he alright?" Renya asked.

"Oh yes, he just needs some sleep. I will change his bandages when he wakes," Annabelle said.

"I've already sent for the Court Physician," Sudfad said then he saw the look on Annabelle's face. "Why child what is the matter?"

"I am sorry, I, well, I've been taking care of Raul since Vitomas found him. I guess I just thought I would take care of him here too," Annabelle said with disappointment in her voice.

"She's very good with him," Simon said. Then he added sarcastically, "He actually does what she tells him."

"Annabelle you certainly can continue being his nurse if you like but don't think you have to," Sudfad said.

"No, I want to take care of him, thank you."

"Annabelle is too small to hold Raul up when he gets weak like he just did," Simon said. "I'll stay with him too." Sudfad looked at the young couple, who were holding hands and smiled. "Raul asked us to bring you some things from the boca," Simon continued. "This is your father's sword. Alexander gave it to Raul for protection."

Sudfad took the sword and carefully examined the sheath and the sword itself. "This is a fine sword," he said. "My parents never told me why they sent me away and they never gave me anything to remember them by. Alexander and Laurel I thank you so very much for saving these things for me and my family," Sudfad said genuinely.

"Annabelle has something for you too," Simon said.

Annabelle let go of Simon's hand and walked closer to the King. "Raul found these in his travels. When Vitomas found him, he was almost dead but he was still protecting this pouch. When he was so sick from the poison he made me promise to get these to you or to the Sanuri," Annabelle said as she handed the pouch to Sudfad. Laurel and Alexander smiled as the King took the contents out of the leather bag.

"There are six Holy Scrolls here," Sudfad said with amazement.

"My Lord, this morning, well, it was almost like you knew something had happened here," Jonas said as he poured coffee into his cup. "How could you have known?"

Roch took the earring out of his pocket and showed it to Jonas. "I found this on the floor of the cabin we stayed in. I gave Vitomas these earrings, they were her favorites," said Roch angrily.

"My Lord do you have any idea who would have taken her?"

"I have many enemies," said Roch irately. "At first I thought my nephew talked her into leaving but I am assured that he is dead."

"My Lord, you saw that cabin, the Queen did not go willingly," said Jonas. "But why Annabelle?"

"They are like sisters and very protective of each other, that is why I trust Annabelle as her maid," said Roch. "Annabelle would die before she would allow someone to capture Vitomas." Roch paused then said in a low growl. "Jonas find me the men who were charged with protecting my wife."

"Yes My Lord," Jonas did not finish his meal, but stood up and left the war room.

After Roch finished eating he returned to Vitomas' chambers. Now that he had calmed down, Roch looked around the chambers for clues as to what may have happened to her. Just as Sophie had said it appeared that all of Vitomas' belongings were in their places. "She could not have been taken from these rooms," thought Roch. As he was walking towards his war room he thought, "Her horse," and left for the stables.

Jonas returned to the war room an hour later. "Well, what did you find out?" Roch demanded.

"Before Cerephus left to search for you he put Crispus in charge of watching Vitomas."

"And where is he?" asked Roch as he filled two glasses with whiskey and both men sat down at the table in the war room.

"Crispus organized the other soldiers into six search parties and they are looking for the Queen."

"Well he did something right but he should not have left the castle unprotected," growled Roch.

"My Lord I spoke with the members of your house staff and they all said the Queen was scared and feeling like she was being watched."

"So whoever took her may have been waiting for the perfect opportunity," said Roch. "Her horse is missing from the stable."

"If she was taken while on a ride, what happened to Annabelle?" asked Jonas thoughtfully.

"I do not know but I mean to get to the bottom of this, if I have to kill every one of the castle guards to do it."

Jonas looked across the table at Roch and could see the rage in his eyes. "My Lord if you kill them all there will be no one to search for her," Jonas said trying to soften Roch's temperament.

Roch smiled, "You are right my friend." Roch gulped down his drink and refilled his glass. Jonas was vividly aware that Roch had never called him 'his friend' before.

"My Lord let me go into Taperia and talk to the people; if there were strange soldiers here someone would have seen them."

"That is a good idea," said Roch as he glanced at the sapphire earring lying on his desk.

"Jonas do you think any of my staff or soldiers are behind this treachery?"

"No My Lord, your staff and your men are very loyal to you."

"But everyone has a price," snapped Roch.

The Sanuri and Petra started travelling shortly after the Enrops left their camp. "Where are we going?" asked Petra.

"We are heading west to Bastar. The Enrop said there is a small band of Hutas camped on the River Cenja who were seen with The Box of Itifer."

"Why didn't they go back to Marba?"

"This is how they live; they attack and steal from others," replied the Sanuri. "And perhaps they are still searching for Shettee survivors."

"I hope the Hutas don't find them."

"They will not," said the Sanuri. They traveled for a short distance in silence.

"Sanuri how old are you?"

"Why do you ask?"

"Padre Bartholomew said you were hundreds of years old but your hair isn't even all gray."

The Sanuri laughed loudly, "I am five hundred and thirty three years old."

"Really!"

After a few minutes the Sanuri realized that Petra was staring at him. "What is the matter?" asked the Sanuri with a grin.

"I have never seen a five hundred year old person alive before. I want to see if you look different."

"Have you ever seen a five hundred year old person dead?" asked the Sanuri as he laughed.

"Well no," replied Petra thoughtfully. "How come you're so old?"

"I guess The Great Ruler still has work for me to do here," said the Sanuri still laughing.

"How do you know if The Great Ruler has work for you?"

"How did you know you should go to the monastery at Avaide and try to save the Shettees and the priests?"

Petra thought for a couple of minutes before answering, "I don't know, something inside of me just knew I had to warn them."

"The Great Ruler talks to everyone, some people do not listen and some do not want to hear. But very often The Great Ruler talks to you through a small voice in your heart."

"So you think The Great Ruler told me to go to Avaide?"

"I know he did," replied the Sanuri. Petra thought about the Sanuri's words for several minutes before he spoke again.

"How does The Great Ruler speak to you?"

"Sometimes he speaks to me like he did to you but most of the time he sends me images in visions or in dreams."

"Can't he talk to you in a voice?"

"Do you want to hear his voice?"

"I sure do. Actually I would like to talk to him"

"About what?"

"Oh, all kinds of things but most important I would like to know if my parents are with him and how they are." The Sanuri put his arm around Petra's shoulders and they rode in silence.

Later that afternoon, Raul returned to bed after sharing a late lunch with his family. During the meal he held everyone captive with his stories of his travels. Although he talked about Vitomas, even telling his parents that he wanted to marry her; Raul did not tell them that Vitomas was Roch's Queen. Raul wanted to explain Vitomas' relationship with Roch when he and his parents were alone.

Annabelle and Simon helped Raul return to bed then they went in search of some large overstuffed chairs to put into Raul's bedroom. Annabelle was laughing as she opened the door to Raul's chambers so Simon could carry a chair in. They immediately saw Renya sitting on the bed next to Raul holding his hand.

Simon set the chair next to Raul's bed. "He didn't wake up," Renya said as she wiped tears from her eyes. Simon put his hand on his mother's shoulder.

"I'm sorry," Renya said as she was trying to stop crying. "It's just difficult to see your child like this."

"You would be proud of him My Lady," Annabelle said. "Even as injured as Raul was, he walked up to Roch and challenged him. They stood inches apart staring at each other. Never have I seen such a thing. Vitomas and I were so scared for Raul because we know how violent Roch is."

"What did Roch do?" Simon asked

"Well, that is what was so peculiar. I think Roch was shocked that someone actually stood up to him. He didn't do anything he just stared at Raul then he laughed and said that Raul should have been his son; then he left the room. But later he had the physician poison Raul."

"The physician!" Renya gasped. "Why I have never heard of such a thing."

"That's why Vitomas and I stayed with him always; we couldn't trust anyone. We sneaked Gala into the castle once but she and my parents couldn't help with Raul until we got him out of the castle."

Renya took Annabelle's hand, "I believe my son is very fortunate to have such a good friend. And Annabelle my name is Renya, call me Renya."

Vitomas always rode behind Archetenus because he led her horse. Archetenus bound her wrists together every morning before they started to ride. Vitomas tried to keep Archetenus talking as they rode so he would not get suspicious that she had been dropping small pieces of her skirt along the trail. Vitomas was wearing a skirt that was the color of a robin's egg; a color that was not commonly worn by peasants and farm women. She hoped that Raul would remember what she was wearing the last time they saw each other.

"Archetenus, I am surprised that we travel at such a leisurely pace; aren't you afraid that Roch's men will follow us?"

Archetenus laughed, "Vitomas are you saying you are eager to start a new life with me?"

"You know what I am saying."

"Let them come."

"You seem awfully confident," Vitomas said. "I know you are a powerful warrior but you cannot take on an army."

"As long as I worked for Roch, he never sent his men this far east. And I doubt that he will now." Vitomas did not say anything, she was curious as to why Archetenus seemed so confident. "We will marry when we reach Port Friada," Archetenus said with a voice of authority.

"I'm not going to marry you Archetenus. I am going to marry Prince Raul."

Archetenus quickly dismounted and walked up to Vitomas' horse. He reached up and pulled her off the horse so that Vitomas was standing but he held her arms tightly. "I have not touched you or hurt you because I want you to love me. But my patience will not last forever and it would benefit you to realize you will never see your prince again."

Late that night, Simon entered Raul's chambers. Raul was sleeping soundly in his bed and Annabelle was curled up in a large chair, sleeping. Simon picked up one of the folded blankets that was placed at the foot of Raul's bed. Simon knelt down by Annabelle and started to cover her with the blanket when Annabelle suddenly jumped up, swinging her right arm towards him; Annabelle held a dagger in her right hand. Simon grabbed her right wrist tightly.

"Annabelle its Simon," he said. Simon knew she was not awake and had reacted instinctively.

"Simon, oh I am so sorry," Annabelle cried as her consciousness returned.

"Give me the dagger," Simon said as he took the weapon out of Annabelle's hand. "Now give me the sheath."

Annabelle reached to her left side and grabbed the sheath and handed it to him. "Simon did I hurt you?"

"No," Simon said as he put the dagger into the sheath and but the sheath inside his belt.

"I'm sorry," Annabelle repeated. "Simon are you mad at me?"

"No Honey I am not mad at you," Simon said as he took hold of both of Annabelle's hands. "Is this what you have been doing? Sleeping near my brother so you can protect him from attack?"

"We both have, Vitomas and me."

Simon spoke softly, "Annabelle, Raul would not be alive if you and Vitomas had not taken such good care of him and protected him so. But he is home now and he is safe and so are you. Annabelle you don't have to be afraid anymore."

"I think I will stop being afraid when we find Vitomas."

Simon looked at Annabelle for a moment then he stood up, pulling her to a standing position. "Here we go," Simon said as he draped the blanket over Annabelle's shoulders. "There is a bed in the other room, get some sleep. I will watch over him."

Annabelle didn't move. "Simon I really want to stay here."

"Well then, we will watch him together," Simon said and sat down in the chair that Annabelle had been in. "There's room, sit with me," Simon said as he moved to make room for her.

Annabelle took the blanket off from her shoulders and squeezed into the chair next to Simon. She covered them both with the blanket.

"Would you think it bold if I put my arm around you?" Simon asked with a grin.

Annabelle giggled, "I thought you were bold when you held my hand. Tell me Simon do you always hold hands with a girl when you first meet her?"

Simon laughed, "Not usually." Annabelle kept looking at Simon as if waiting for him to say more. "You want me to tell you why I have been holding your hand don't you?" Now Annabelle blushed and looked away from Simon with embarrassment.

"Simon don't make fun of me," she said meekly.

"Oh Honey I didn't mean to embarrass you and I wasn't making fun of you," Simon said sincerely. "I just wasn't prepared to answer your question." Simon gently lifted Annabelle's chin so she was now looking at him. "Annabelle I think you are very sweet and also incredibly beautiful and I love how you have looked after my brother. He is very dear to me."

Annabelle's eyes grew wide. "You think I'm beautiful?" she asked incredulously.

"Why do you say that with such surprise?" Simon asked.

Annabelle blushed again and looked away as she spoke, "I don't know I guess no one has ever told me that before."

238

Simon watched Annabelle for a few moments before he spoke again, "Annabelle has anyone ever held hands with you before?"

"Not a man," she said shyly.

Simon now chose his words carefully as he did not yet understand the life Annabelle had at Roch's castle. "Annabelle have you ever had a suitor?"

"Why no Simon," gasped Annabelle. "I was a prisoner; I was not allowed such things. And besides the men at the castle were horrible and frightening; I tried to stay away from them."

"Annabelle I don't want to frighten you so I need you to tell me if I am being too bold with you. Do you want me to hold her hand?"

"Yes," Annabelle said as her eyes smiled. "I like holding your hand. You know Raul talks about you all of the time and he told me that he thought you and I would like each other. For my part, he is right."

"Good," Simon said with a large smile. "Because I am very attracted to you." Simon and Annabelle stared into each other's eyes for a few moments before Simon leaned down and softly kissed Annabelle on the lips. Annabelle put her arms around Simon's neck and gently kissed him. The gentleness of their kisses slowly transformed as they allowed their passions to take over.

After Simon and Annabelle had been kissing for several minutes, Simon stopped. "This position is too awkward, why don't you set on my lap or we could lie down on the other bed." When Simon saw the look of shock on Annabelle's face he said, "Oh no, Annabelle I meant we would just kiss, nothing more, I promise."

"It is hurting my back sitting in this chair like this," Annabelle said shyly. "What do you want to do?"

"I think we would be more comfortable lying down," Simon said then he reached to his belt and pulled out Annabelle's dagger which was in the sheath and handed it to her. "Here, if we do more than kiss you can use this on me."

239

Annabelle laughed loudly then stood up. "Do you think we will be able to hear Raul if he needs us?" she asked as they walked into the next bedroom hand in hand.

"I'm sure we will," Simon said. "I'm a light sleeper."

Simon and Annabelle kissed and laughed and held each other for some time before Annabelle eventually fell asleep in Simon's arm. He lay next to Annabelle watching her sleep and feeling like he wanted to protect her from all that was evil in the world.

Jonas had sent men out to find Crispus, who was leading one of the search parties that was looking for Vitomas and Annabelle. Crispus reported to Roch's war room early the next morning.

"My Lord after we found the body of the guard we searched the castle and the grounds and found nothing unusual," said Crispus as he stood before Roch. Jonas was the only other person in the war room and he stood at the door to prevent others from entering.

"You were put in charge of her," yelled Roch.

"I am sorry My Lord, she just disappeared," said Crispus. With the back of his right hand Roch slapped Crispus across the face almost knocking him to the ground. Crispus regained his balance and wiped the blood from his mouth.

"The servants said she was afraid and felt like she was being watched," Roch growled.

"Neither the Queen nor the servants told me that but My Lord we had guards outside of her window and in the castle."

"Then how do you explain her disappearance Crispus?"

"I cannot My Lord; I have six details of men looking for her. I am only here because I heard you had returned."

"You are here because I had Jonas summon you," screamed Roch. Roch was pacing around the room and waving his arms, he was getting more and more agitated by the answers Crispus was giving him. "What happened to my nephew?"

"The physician's poison worked; he died a few days after you left."

"And you saw the body?" growled Roch.

"Yes My Lord and so did the physician, the man was dead."
This appeared to be the only answer that did not anger Roch.

"How does the Queen think he died?"

"The physician told everyone that your nephew died of infections in his wounds."

Roch walked to the window, turning his back on both Crispus and Jonas. Jonas was relieved to see Roch's body becoming less tense and agitated. No one spoke for several minutes. Roch turned towards Crispus and in a calm and deliberate voice said, "Crispus you failed me."

"I am sorry My..."

Roch grabbed a dagger from his belt and lunged at Crispus driving the blade deep into the soldier's chest. Roch pulled the dagger out and stabbed Crispus over and over again until the floor and desk were covered in blood and pieces of flesh. Blood splattered onto the walls, the ceiling and the furniture. Jonas stood at the door watching the savage attack. Blood splatter was dripping down onto Roch from the ceiling but he did not notice as his frenzy escalated.

Roch finally stopped stabbing Crispus when he was too exhausted to stand. Roch stood upright over the remains of the body then fell a couple of steps backwards against his desk. Roch was soaked with sweat and the blood of Crispus.

"Jonas get someone in here to clean up this mess."

Raul was getting out of bed when he saw Simon and Annabelle walk out of the second bedroom in his chambers. A large grin took over Raul's face as he watched them walking towards him. Simon had his arm around Annabelle's shoulders and they were both smiling.

"Is there anything that you should be confessing to me?" Raul teased.

Annabelle blushed as she walked up to Raul to help him out of bed. "We did nothing wrong Raul," Annabelle said. "We just slept and kissed."

"Actually we kissed a lot," Simon said with a grin and kissed Annabelle on the top of her head.

"Annabelle you aren't leading my brother astray are you?" Raul asked with a laugh as he knew he was embarrassing her. Annabelle blushed a darker shade of red and laughed but did not answer.

"Simon, Annabelle is never lost for words, I don't know what you did but I like it."

"Raul you just wait," Annabelle warned and punched him on the arm. The three were still laughing when they entered the dining room to have their breakfast with the family.

"What's so funny?" Sudfad asked. "We could hear you laughing down the hallway."

"Raul is just teasing Annabelle," Simon said as he pulled Annabelle's chair out for her. After Annabelle sat down, Simon helped Raul take a seat at the table.

"We have wonderful news," Renya said excitedly. "Laurel and Alexander are going to live here at the castle with us. Sudfad and I are so pleased."

"Good," said Raul with a big smile.

"I'm happy about it," Simon said as he looked at Annabelle, who was sitting next to him.

"Annabelle what do you think?" Renya asked. "Do you want to live here?"

"Oh yes," Annabelle stammered. "It's just, well, all of this is like a dream. First to be free from Roch and then to meet all of you."

Annabelle squeezed Simon's hand as she spoke. "And now to live in such a wonderful place; why I could never have imagined all of this. I just wish Vitomas was here to share it with us."

Vitomas had said few words to Archetenus after he pulled her off from her horse the afternoon before. They had eaten dinner in silence. He let her sleep undisturbed. Now that she was preparing breakfast, Vitomas was looking for more ways to leave a trail for Raul besides dropping pieces of cloth. Archetenus had momentarily left the campsite and Vitomas was looking at her surroundings trying desperately to think of some way to leave a message for Raul.

"So are you ever going to speak to me again?" Archetenus asked as he put a pile of wood near the fire.

"You act like this is all a game," Vitomas said without looking at him.

Archetenus squatted down by the fire and poured himself a cup of coffee. "You know you never did tell me why you were at that cabin. I saw a boca drive away. Was that Annabelle's parents?"

"Yes," Vitomas said in a horse whisper as she handed him a plate of food. Vitomas still did not look at Archetenus' face."

"Were Annabelle and your prince in the back of that boca?" Vitomas sighed and nodded her head. The memory made her want to cry. "Why didn't you leave with them?"

"Because I love them all and didn't want to put them in more danger. You know the guards would have caught us if I left too."

"I killed the soldiers who were following you," Archetenus said. "You might have been able to get away with it, at least with them; I mean. I would have followed you."

"You killed your own men?" Vitomas gasped in disbelief. "How could you do such a thing?"

"I wasn't going to let anything stand in the way of what I wanted."

243

Vitomas now stared into Archetenus' eyes with horror as she realized how much he sounded like Roch.

"Is someone calling us?" Raul asked as he and Simon studied maps in Simon's chambers. Simon walked over to the door and opened it. He heard Annabelle's voice and walked out into the hallway. "Annabelle we're in here," Simon called and waited in the hallway until she came up to him.

"I've been looking for you two," Annabelle said with a flirtatious smile. "I have something for Raul and I have a question for you. Whose chambers are these?" Annabelle asked as she entered the parlor where Raul was sitting at a large table that was covered with maps.

"Simon's," Raul answered as he looked up at her.

"Here, I finished the map of the castle," Annabelle said as she handed a large piece of folded paper to Raul. "I had Mother and Father look at it in case they could remember something I had forgotten?"

"Good idea," Raul said as he unfolded the map and spread it on the table. "You are very good at drawing, Annabelle."

Annabelle did not answer because she was looking at the maps that Raul and Simon had been studying. "You're already planning your trip to get her. Raul I am going with you."

"No you aren't," Raul said. "It's too dangerous."

Annabelle was visibly angry. Her voice was rising as she spoke. "Raul I know the castle, the guards and the people in Cana and some in Taperia. You need me to get back into that castle and you know it, so don't you tell me I'm not going!" Simon started to grin as he listened to Annabelle yelling at Raul. "Simon don't you dare laugh at me, I am serious."

"I'm not laughing at you Annabelle; I'm just enjoying you scolding my brother. But Raul is right, it is too dangerous."

"Listen to the two of you. I have been living in that horror since I was nine years old; don't you think I know how dangerous it is."

"I don't want to be caught by Roch's men but I want to find my friend more than anything else. You are both strangers in that area. Do you really think you will be able to talk the people into giving you information or helping you?"

Neither Raul nor Simon said anything as Annabelle spoke; they both realized she was right. "I thought you might say, 'no'; so I am just going to tell you that if you don't take me I will just follow you. And that brings me to the other reason I came here. Simon will you teach me how to fight with a sword before we leave?"

"No Annabelle," Simon said seriously.

"Then I am going to ask one of the soldiers," Annabelle turned and quickly walked out of the room.

Simon stood dumbfounded as he watched Annabelle leave his chambers. "You better go get her," Raul said with a grin. "Because she means what she says."

Simon walked quickly to the door and looked down the hallway; Annabelle was running down the hall. Simon called to her twice but Annabelle did not stop or act like she heard him. Simon ran after Annabelle and quickly caught up to her. Simon grabbed her arm. "Annabelle just stop." Annabelle stopped moving but she stood with her back to him. "Will you turn around and look at me?" When Annabelle faced Simon, he could see that she was crying.

"I know you are worried about Vitomas, we will find her." Annabelle glared at Simon without speaking. The tears were running down her cheeks.

"Will you please stop crying," Simon said as he tried to pull Annabelle close to him but she resisted. Simon and Annabelle both stood in silence looking at each other for a few moments. "Ok, I will give you some lessons but that doesn't mean you are coming with us," Simon said which made Annabelle smile. "When do you want to practice?"

"Can we start now?" Annabelle asked enthusiastically.

"Alright, I'll wait while you change."

Annabelle was confused by Simon's statement. "Why should I change?"

"Well, do you have some other shoes to wear?" Simon asked as he looked at the flimsy slippers she was wearing.

Annabelle looked embarrassed, "No these are my only shoes."

"Annabelle do you have any boots or riding clothes?"

"No," she said shyly.

Simon took Annabelle's hand and said, "Come on." They returned to his chambers. "We're going to Salar," Simon said to Raul as he grabbed a pouch of gold coins out of a cupboard.

"Why are we going to Salar, Simon?" Annabelle asked as they were walking down the hallway.

"So I can buy you some things."

"Simon I can't let you buy me clothes."

Simon stopped walking and turned to Annabelle. "Annabelle if you are serious that you want to learn how to fight and you want to come with Raul and me; you have to have some different clothing and some boots. And there is no reason you can't let me buy you something. I have plenty of money and think of it as a gift for saving my brother." They walked down to the first floor and entered the main parlor in the castle. Sudfad, Renya, Laurel and Alexander were sitting in the parlor talking. They all smiled when they saw Simon and Annabelle walk into the room holding hands.

"Mother where is that store that you like to buy clothes?"

"What kind of clothes do you want to buy?"

"Annabelle wants me to teach her how to fight with a sword; I need to get her some boots and riding clothes."

Before Renya could say anything, Sudfad said, "Simon I am sure she needs a lot more than that. Buy her a wardrobe and make sure she gets some gowns, it's the least we can do. Let me get some money for you."

"No Father I will pay for it," Simon said.

"Simon you cannot buy me these things," Annabelle said uncomfortably.

Simon turned and looked down at her. "Annabelle will you just let me take care of you?" Simon said with a hint of frustration in his voice. Annabelle was so surprised at his statement that she did not say anything else. Simon turned back to Sudfad and asked, "Do you need me to pick anything up while we're in Salar?"

"I hope you plan on taking a boca," Sudfad said.

"Yes."

"Then stop at the armorer's and check on my order."

Renya was smiling as she said, "There are several wonderful stores on the main street in Salar. But the one you should go to first is on the left side of the street and has a large sign that extends from the building. The sign is in the shape of a hat with a feather in it." As soon as Simon and Annabelle left the room, Renya turned to Sudfad and said proudly, "Dear, I believe our son is falling in love."

"Wake up sleepy head, it is time for our midday meal," said the Sanuri as he steered the boca underneath some trees.

"How long did I sleep?" asked Petra as he rubbed his face.

"All morning," replied the Sanuri with a laugh. The Sanuri cared for the horses as Petra started the meal.

"Sanuri, what is so important about The Box of Itifer?"

"Petra most people can never know the power of that box so if I tell you, you can tell no one," the Sanuri said very seriously.

Petra was not used to the Sanuri speaking in that tone of voice; so he was deep in thought for a few moments before answering. "Sanuri I will keep the secret, I promise."

"At the beginning of time all of The Great Ruler's children and creatures lived together peacefully but as darkness crept into their souls His children sought to separate from Him and His rules. In His wisdom The Great Ruler sent gifts to this world to help keep creation connected to Him, like The Holy Scrolls."

"Is The Box of Itifer a gift from The Great Ruler?" asked Petra with excitement.

"Yes and he gave it to the creatures we call the Centras to protect because not only are they extraordinarily intelligent but their hearts are not lured by the darkness that controls men." The Sanuri continued. "The Box of Itifer possess many powers, it restores balance in creation as men are always distorting the balance but to do this it has a powerful connection to the hearts and minds of creation."

"I don't understand what you mean."

"Since The Box of Itifer has been stolen it appears that there has been a great change in the nature of the Centras. They have always been peaceful, non-aggressive creatures. But I now suspect that they have been killing Huta warriors while they are searching for the box. That would be a change in the balance of nature."

"But there is more Petra. The Great Ruler understands how men are driven to obtain power. Every gift that He has given to His children with love can be distorted in evil hands. So for many of His gifts He made a second gift or key that is needed to access the true powers of the original gift. In the case of The Box of Itifer; The Great Ruler created a small scroll called The Scroll of Imari. This scroll contains the secrets to unleash all of the powers of the box."

"Do you know what this scroll says?"

"I don't know all of what is written in the scroll but I do know that if someone is in possession of both The Scroll of Imari and The Box of Itifer they can actually dictate the behavior of much of creation; and that is why we are going after the box."

"Do you think the Hutas know how powerful it is?"

"The Hutas worship demons and all forms of darkness; a powerful demon named Sporos may have sent the Hutas after the box and the scroll," said the Sanuri with sadness in his voice.

"Why do you look so sad?"

"Because Sporos and I were boyhood friends and as we grew we both pledged ourselves to The Great Ruler and became priests."

Petra interrupted the Sanuri, "Sporos is a priest?" Petra asked in disbelief.

"He was a priest a very long time ago but he changed and he gave himself to darkness and that makes me sad."

"Why would he do such a thing?" gasped Petra.

"When a person is seeking a spiritual path as Sporos and I were, The Great Ruler tests you and the tests are difficult; my old friend could not resist the temptations of the demons."

"Sanuri we cannot allow Sporos to get the box and the scroll," said Petra with a commanding voice.

The Sanuri looked at the boy with adoration, "Petra we will not allow him to get those items but you understand it may be a long hard journey for us; do you think you are prepared?"

"Is this going to be like a spiritual test?"

"It might be."

"Yes Sanuri just tell me what I need to do."

"Vitomas, you haven't said a word for hours," Archetenus said as the two were riding westward.

"I don't know what to say to you."

"I will treat you much better than Roch did."

"Archetenus you already have, although he stole me too."

"I am not Roch!" Archetenus yelled angrily.

"I didn't say you were. Archetenus can I ask you a question without you getting angry?"

Vitomas' question made Archetenus angry, "Go ahead."

"I know that first night you told me some things but my head hurt so badly I don't remember everything you said. Did you think I was in love with you and that is why you stole me?"

Archetenus was silent for a moment before he answered, "Yes."

"Then the real reason you're so angry with me is because I hurt you; because I am not in love with you." Archetenus did not speak. "I'm sorry that I hurt you," Vitomas said sincerely.

Chapter XV
Confessions

"Simon I have never been in such a store," Annabelle said with amazement as they entered the luxurious building.

"How did you get your clothing?"

"Mother would make my clothes and Vitomas would give me her things but we had to be careful that Roch didn't find out."

"My Lord this is a surprise," said a well-dressed woman of middle age. "Your mother shops here often."

"I know," said Simon with smile. "What is your name?"

"Eloise, I own the store."

"Eloise, this is Annabelle; she and her parents are close friends of our family. When they were traveling here there was an accident and many of their things were destroyed. Father told me to get a complete new wardrobe for Annabelle and I would not be surprised if Mother doesn't bring Annabelle's mother in soon."

Annabelle pulled Simon away from Eloise. "Simon I don't feel right letting you buy me these things and they all look so expensive."

"You would defy the orders of the King?" Simon asked with a smirk.

"Simon, I've never been shopping for clothes before, I'm embarrassed."

"Do you want me to help you?"

"Would you?"

Simon turned to Eloise, "Eloise I am sure you are much better at sizes than I am. Will you start picking out clothing while Annabelle tries on some boots and shoes?"

"Of course My Lord," Eloise said with a large smile.

"She needs some riding clothes and some gowns also."

Shortly after Simon and Annabelle left for Salar, Raul walked into the main parlor of the castle where Renya, Sudfad, Laurel and Alexander were still sitting. Raul looked at Laurel and Alexander then at his parents. "Father, Mother there is something that I have to tell you; I have just been waiting for the right time."

Alexander stood up and said, "Laurel and I should go."

"Alexander do you and Laurel know what Raul wants to tell us?" Sudfad asked suspiciously.

"Yes we do," Alexander replied.

"Well then, you might as well stay," Sudfad said.

Alexander helped Raul sit down since he was still on crutches, then Alexander sat next to Laurel on one of the sofas.

Raul told his parents every detail that he could remember about his condition when Vitomas found him and how she took care of him and protected him. Raul told them of how Roch stole Vitomas when she was a child and of her life with him. At this point in Raul's story Alexander added a great deal of information about Vitomas; how she had helped others and protected Annabelle. Neither Sudfad nor Renya spoke as they listened to Raul and Alexander.

When Alexander had finished, Sudfad looked at them both. "From what you have said she sounds like a wonderful woman who is in an awful situation. But what are you not telling us?"

"Father she is Roch's Queen and we love each other. I asked her to marry me."

Renya gasped but said nothing. "Son, I am old but not stupid I expected something like that after you told us how she stayed behind so you could escape," Sudfad said.

"Are they married?" Renya asked.

"I would greatly doubt it," Alexander said. "Roch has no respect for such things."

"I am going back to get her as soon as I can walk," Raul said with passion.

"And who are you taking with you?" Sudfad asked.

"Simon; and Annabelle is demanding to come along."

"You are not taking that poor girl back there," Renya said.

"I don't want to but Annabelle has a good argument; she knows the people, the guards and the castle."

Sudfad was quiet for a moment then said, "Son do you understand the delicacy of this situation? I do not want you to start a war between our kingdoms."

"But Father..."

Sudfad held up his hand for Raul to stop talking. "You will be King someday and you have to think about the welfare of your people. I have never seen you act like this before and I believe you truly love this woman. So if you plan on saving her you must think with your head Raul not with your heart. You, Simon and Annabelle cannot rescue Vitomas by yourselves. If Roch knows that Annabelle, Laurel and Alexander are missing, he will have his suspicions and will be waiting for you. You are an excellent general now look at this mission as you would any other in the military. Now tell me again how you would plan to rescue her."

Raul smiled because he understood that his father had just given him permission to use the military. "I would probably ask for volunteers for a personal mission," Raul explained. "I would have the men dress in civilian clothing and cross into Stordt in small groups as not to draw attention. I would determine a place that we could meet up, probably outside of Cana. The healer there, Gala, saved my life. Vitomas said I could get a message to her through Gala. If Vitomas is still allowed to take morning rides that would be the best time to get her."

"And if Vitomas is not permitted to ride anymore?" Sudfad asked.

"Annabelle has drawn a map of the castle and grounds. I will have to see what the situation is before I can make other plans."

253

"Every Tuesday there is a huge market in Cana," Laurel said. "That is the only day that Sophie, Roch's cook leaves the castle. That woman talks to everyone and knows all of the gossip of the kingdom. Gala knows Sophie, perhaps Gala could find out some information."

"I approve of your plans," Sudfad said.

"Raul, I almost lost you once. And now you and your brother are planning what sounds like a suicide mission and my heart wants to scream out, 'No you can't go.' Then I listen to Annabelle, Laurel and Alexander and hear how these wonderful people risked everything to save you, a total stranger to them. And the stories you tell about Vitomas make me want to weep. When you go after that girl, you plan well and you take enough men to ensure that you will all come home," Renya said.

"Son, did Simon tell you about last night?" Sudfad asked.

"No, what happened last night," Raul asked with surprise.

"Annabelle had asked that she could continue to be your nurse. She has been sleeping in a chair near your bed."

"Yes, I know Father, every night it was her or Vitomas."

"Last night Simon walked into your room to tell Annabelle she should go to bed and he would watch over you. When he saw her sleeping in the chair he started to cover her with a blanket. She attacked him with a dagger."

"Annabelle!" Raul said in utter disbelief.

"She was not awake and reacted instinctively. Simon took the dagger from Annabelle and she told him that she and Vitomas slept near you to protect you from being attacked," Sudfad said.

"Father those girls couldn't stop the guards, they probably would have been hurt or killed."

"They knew that," Laurel said.

Later that day, Simon and Annabelle walked into the family dining room of the castle holding hands and laughing.

254

"We just finished eating," Renya said. "I'll have Marie bring you some plates."

"No, we ate in Salar," Simon said.

"Mother, Renya I want you to come and see all of the beautiful things Simon picked out for me."

"Simon picked out your clothes?" Raul asked with a grin.

"She was too shy," Simon said.

"He is being kind," Annabelle said. "I have never been shopping for clothes before and I felt embarrassed in such a fancy store."

"You did just fine," Simon said.

"Laurel I don't believe my son has ever bought women's clothes before, perhaps we should see what they got," Renya said with a smile as she stood up.

"I'm coming along too," Raul said.

Annabelle's chambers were in the same hallway as the family dining room, so they did not have far to walk. "Simon," Laurel gasped. "I don't believe this." Boxes were stacked on the bed, all of the tables and chairs and on the floor.

"I kept telling him not to spend so much money," Annabelle said. "If he really liked something he would buy it in every color."

"Simon this is beautiful," said Renya as she held up a gown. "I am sorry but I am surprised."

"Mother what did you expect?" Simon teased and laughed.

"He bought me a lot of gowns. I don't know what I am going to do with all of these beautiful dresses."

Simon looked at Annabelle and smiled, "I have to attend a lot of functions and I would like you to accompany me."

"Really?" Annabelle asked; her eyes wide with excitement.

"Would you go with me?"

"Oh yes Simon," Annabelle said excitedly, then she paused. "I have never been to a function and I don't know how to dance."

"Well My Lady, I can certainly teach you how to dance and when my brother is off his crutches he can teach you too," Simon winked at Annabelle and continued. "Raul does believe he is a better dancer than me."

Renya grabbed Laurel's hand and squeezed it as they listened to the young couple talk. Raul was grinning. "Annabelle since you have become a little sister to me; I want you to understand. When Simon says that he wants you to attend functions with him, he is saying that he wants to court you."

Annabelle's eyes grew wide and she blushed. "I guess I didn't realize that, I've never had anyone want to court me before."

"Actually I will bet there were men who wanted to court you in Stordt but Roch probably had them killed," Raul said sarcastically. Raul walked over to Annabelle and kissed her on the cheek. "Annabelle I don't think you realize what a beautiful woman you are." Annabelle turned dark red with embarrassment.

"Well?" Simon asked as he walked up to Annabelle.

"I don't understand," Annabelle said in a shy whisper.

"Do you want to be my girl?"

Annabelle started to cry and nodded her head.

"Petra stay in the boca and do not come out for any reason," said the Sanuri sternly.

"But I want to help."

"You will be the most help if you stay here. Do not leave the boca no matter what you see or hear," said the Sanuri as he quickly vanished into the night.

Petra climbed into the back of the boca and grabbed a sword. He sat in silence listening to the sounds of the night. After an hour, Petra's eyes were getting heavy and he was having great difficulty staying awake; when he heard a sound that chilled his being. Petra sat very still and listened as lions roared in the distance.

"Please Great Ruler protect the Sanuri," prayed Petra. As his curiosity overcame his fears, Petra crawled to the front of the boca and peered through the curtains. To the west Petra saw a light as bright as day. The light grew brighter and bigger all the while the lions were roaring. Petra was captivated, he could not look away. Suddenly the light was gone and the forest was silent.

That night Archetenus and Vitomas sat quietly near the campfire. As usual they prepared the meal together since Archetenus was teaching Vitomas how to cook. They had not spoken since they finished eating their meal more than half an hour earlier.

Vitomas was trying to be strong but she was feeling the weight of her fears and anxieties. What Vitomas feared most was never seeing Raul again and that brought her great sadness.

"I have been thinking about what you said before," said Archetenus softly. "That I was angry at you because you do not love me. I believe you are right."

Vitomas turned and looked at him with surprise. "Archetenus you seem like a good man and you certainly are a brave warrior. I would never want to hurt you. But I am not going to lie to you. Please tell me why you believed I was in love with you?"

Now it was Archetenus who was surprised at her question. "Because I saw the way you would watch me at the Gefrey Games; you would shed tears for me. And you persuaded Roch to promote me to captain."

They were sitting side by side and now Vitomas moved so she was facing him. "Archetenus I hated the Gefrey Games, the violence sickened me. Roch demanded that I go with him and honestly it was nice to get out of my prison, which is what that castle was."

"I did cry for you but I also cried for others because I didn't want to see anyone killed before my eyes. And you always seemed to fight the most dangerous creatures. Archetenus did you never wonder why you were always chosen to fight the worse monsters?"

Archetenus stared at Vitomas suspiciously. "I thought it was because I am an excellent fighter but are you going to tell me something else?"

"Archetenus, I don't need to tell you that you are a very handsome man and that you became the most popular fighter in the games. The people of Taperia and Cana love you and the games draw people from many other places. Roch, Cerephus and some of the other commanders thought the crowds at the Gefrey Games were becoming larger every week. Your popularity among the people was a threat to them and from comments that I overheard, many were jealous of you."

"They were talking about ways that they could have you killed at the games. Archetenus I do admire your courage and skill as a warrior and I did not want to see an innocent man murdered. I talked to Roch and suggested that it would be easier to promote you and move you, than to murder you and have an uprising of not only the people of the kingdom but the other soldiers. I asked him to promote you to save your life not because I love you."

Simon and Annabelle helped Raul to bed and sat in his room as Raul told them of his conversation with his parents about Vitomas.

"When are we leaving?" Annabelle asked.

"The physician told me it would be another two weeks before I can walk again and that I need to slowly practice putting weight on my leg. He said I will be fine but that I need to eat and get a lot of sleep to regain my strength."

"That will give us time to prepare," Simon said. "Tomorrow I will ask for volunteers."

"Annabelle I don't think you need to sleep in here anymore. Sleep in your own room where you will be more comfortable," Raul said.

"You told him," Annabelle said accusingly to Simon.

"No, I told Father," Simon said. "And Raul is right. He is doing much better and you don't need to protect him here."

"But what if he needs something during the night? He does sometimes, you know. I don't think I can hear him in my room."

"She is probably right," Simon said. "Why doesn't she stay in the other bedroom in here for at least a couple of nights until you are better?" Then Simon winked at Annabelle. "Perhaps I should stay here also in case Annabelle needs some help."

Raul laughed loudly, "Be my guests."

Simon continued, "Besides Mother said she was going to move Annabelle to one of the larger chambers upstairs."

"Why?" Annabelle asked.

"It might have something to do with the fact that you and Simon are courting now," Raul said with a laugh. "Or that you need bigger chambers because of all the clothes he bought you."

"So Roch and others have been conspiring against me before this last mission I was sent on?" Archetenus asked angrily.

"Yes and you know what kind of men they are."

"I know because I am one of them," Archetenus said. "I have been a loyal soldier to King Roch my entire life. It greatly angers me that they plot against me behind my back."

"Archetenus they would have killed you sooner or later. I am glad for you that you did not return to your position."

"Well it seems that I owe you my life My Lady," Archetenus said. "But that does not change my feelings for you."

"Archetenus perhaps if I had never met Raul I would be happy that you stole me from Roch. But I miss Raul so, my heart is breaking."

"And you don't think you could ever feel that way about me?"

Vitomas looked at Archetenus with tears in her eyes, "I don't know, my heart is filled with love for Raul."

Petra awoke to the smell of coffee brewing and wood burning. He climbed out of the boca and saw the Sanuri cooking breakfast over the open fire. "Did you get the box?" asked Petra.

"No they did not have it," replied the Sanuri without looking up from the frying pan of eggs and ham.

"Was the Enrop wrong?"

"No Petra," replied the Sanuri sadly. "Sporos already has it."

"What!" yelled Petra. "Are we going after it?"

The Sanuri laughed loudly as he put the food onto plates and said, "You are such a joy." The Sanuri stood up and handed a plate of food to Petra. "Yes we are going after it my young friend." Petra stared at the Sanuri for several minutes without speaking. "What is on your mind?" asked the Sanuri.

"Last night I prayed to The Great Ruler to help you because I heard lions roaring and I saw a great light in the direction of the river; what happened out there?"

"Well, I guess The Great Ruler answered your prayer," said the Sanuri smiling. "I had help getting the attention of the Hutas." The Sanuri sat down to eat his breakfast and to read The Holy Scrolls.

"Are you going to tell me more?"

"Nope," responded the Sanuri. Petra's patience was not lasting as he watched the Sanuri studying the holy text.

"So are the lions your friends?"

"All creation is our friend," said the Sanuri without looking up from his text.

"That is the third time that I remember the lions helping us."

"And what did you learn?"

"What do you mean, what did I learn?" The Sanuri did not answer Petra's question. Petra sat in silence for a few moments thinking about what the Sanuri had asked.

"Is the lesson that they helped us when we needed help?"

The Sanuri smiled and put down the scrolls. "Petra think of all the times you or someone you know needed help and suddenly a person or animal or act of nature provided that help. The lesson I want you to learn here is that people pray to The Great Ruler and think that He does not answer their prayers because they do not recognize how He answered them."

"So the lions were an answer to my prayer?"

"Yes and an answer to mine also. They did not hurt the Hutas but they surrounded the camp, protecting me and scaring the Hutas into telling me about the box."

"And that great white light?"

"You have had enough lessons for today," said the Sanuri as he picked up the scrolls.

"Does Sporos have The Scroll of Imari too?"

"I do not believe so; I think a great darkness would fall upon this world if he was in possession of both of those holy items."

The next morning Archetenus watched Vitomas as she was preparing their breakfast. "I know I can't make you love me Vitomas and I don't want you to hate me either."

Vitomas looked at him sadly. Archetenus continued, "So this is what I am proposing. You come with me to Port Friada and stay with me and if you do not learn to love me, I will return you to the Prince of Wetpr myself."

"Why would you do this?" asked Vitomas softly.

"Because I have been seeing myself in your eyes and you look at me as if I were Roch."

Vitomas was both happy and suspicious of his proposal. "So if I agree to this, what is it that you want from me?"

"I want you to give us a chance. I want you to kiss me back when I kiss you. I want you to act as if you were mine."

Vitomas' heart sank with his words.

After breakfast Raul and Simon met in Raul's chambers to work on their plans to rescue Vitomas. "This morning at inspection I told the troops a little about our mission and I asked for volunteers. I told them that you would pay them double what their normal pay would be. And they would get a bonus if the mission was successful."

"A bonus?" Raul repeated.

"Yes, that is from Father," Simon said. "The Lieutenants are collecting the names of any volunteers. I would not be surprised if we did not have a lot more volunteers than we need. Besides the money, some of our men are looking forward to some action."

"You know I am really glad about you and Annabelle. I thought the two of you would fall in love," Raul said sincerely.

"That's what she said."

"But I am a little surprised at how fast things are going."

Simon looked at his brother and laughed, "Raul tell me how long it took for you to realize that Vitomas was the one?"

Raul laughed, "I think after that first morning that I talked with her. But I also think the danger of our situation made things move faster. Wait until you meet Vitomas. In some ways she and Annabelle are very much alike and in others they are the complete opposite. I think Vitomas is the most beautiful woman I have ever met, both physically and her nature. It truly amazes me that either of those girls could survive the horrors of their time as Roch's captives and turn out to be so caring and wonderful. Has Annabelle told you about her life there?"

"Very little but the night that Annabelle almost stabbed me made me realize how terrified she must have been always. She was not at all awake, so her fears to protect you are ingrained. Annabelle is so beautiful and petite and yet she would fight to the death for you brother."

"That night we talked and held each other. I love her spunk and honestly she makes my blood boil. But after Annabelle fell asleep I found myself just holding her and watching her sleep. I don't know how to explain it but I just wanted to protect her from everything. It was then that I realized I wanted to take care of her forever."

"Do you love her?" Raul asked.

"Yes but I haven't told her and I don't know if she loves me."

"From all of the time that I have spent with Annabelle, I would say that she loves you." Raul's comment made Simon smile.

"I am taking her on a picnic later today. I think the two of us need to get away from the castle for a little while. I plan to tell her how I feel then."

"Simon, I lived in their world even though it was just briefly. They grew up trying to survive and to keep each other alive because that is all either of them had. They aren't like the other girls we have dated. They have been prisoners, I think you realized that yesterday when you took Annabelle shopping."

"It was fun taking her shopping. She was so full of wonder it was like I saw everything new again through her eyes. But what are you really trying to say to me?"

"Annabelle is very smart but she has been so sheltered; so don't assume that she always understands your meaning. You may have to explain some things to her."

Chapter XVI
Terror in the Night

"My Lord I came as soon as I got word," Cerephus said as he walked into Roch's war room. "What happened?" Cerephus was surprised to see Jonas sitting at the table.

"Jonas pour Cerephus a glass of whiskey, I am sure he is dry from riding. I will take some more also."

Jonas handed Cerephus a glass of whiskey. "Cerephus have a seat, we have much to discuss but first tell me if you encountered anything unusual while you were searching for me," said Roch.

"My Lord in the weeks we were gone we encountered groups of Huta warriors many times. I only lost twenty men in all our battles."

Jonas interrupted Cerephus, "We too were attacked by Hutas, are they still searching for Shettees?"

"That is something I was about to tell you, we captured two Huta warriors and tortured them to find out if they had seen you," said Cerephus. "These warriors said they had not, so I wanted to know why they had crossed over our borders." As Cerephus talked he pulled a folded piece of leather from his shirt pocket and handed it to Roch. "These men said that they were sent to search for two things of great religious value The Box of Itifer and The Scroll of Imari."

"What would Hutas want with religious relics, they worship demons," asked Roch.

"That is what is interesting; they said Sporos sent them on the quest and that he gave them maps," Cerephus pointed to the piece of leather that he had handed Roch.

"I have heard stories about Sporos but I did not think he really existed," said Roch as he unfolded the map.

"I haven't heard of him," said Jonas deceitfully.

"Some call him a demon others say he is a powerful and evil sorcerer; he was once a priest," said Cerephus.

264

Roch sat in silence for a few moments trying to contain his excitement as he realized the map in his hand was identical to his prized map that he kept in his shirt pocket; the one he had stolen from the monastery in Avaide. Roch folded both maps and put them into his shirt pocket. "Why is Sporos after these items?"

"The Hutas said Sporos needed the scroll to open the powers of The Box of Itifer and whoever was in control of the box could control much of creation," Cerephus said smugly.

"Do you think such a thing exists?" asked Jonas.

"Sporos and the Hutas believe it does," answered Roch. "Did the Hutas say if they found either of these objects?"

"No, they were still searching," replied Cerephus.

"You got a lot of information from those Hutas," Jonas said with a grin.

"I am good at what I do," said Cerephus and all three men broke into laughter.

Jonas filled their glasses with whiskey again as Roch told Cerephus that Queen Vitomas was missing and that Crispus was dead. Cerephus was about to drink from his glass as he listened to Roch talking about the body that was found under Vitomas' window before her abduction. Cerephus instantly stopped his arm in motion and held the glass near his mouth.

"What is it?" asked Roch suspiciously. "You look like you just saw a ghost."

"A few weeks back we stopped an old man and a boy near Malga; they said they had found Archetenus injured in Ort and took care of him until he could ride again," said Cerephus.

Roch leaned towards Cerephus. "Archetenus is alive!" Roch yelled.

"My Lord the old man said that Archetenus was returning to Taperia."

Jonas kicked the door open to Archetenus' chambers. He entered the cabin followed by three soldiers who searched the rooms.

"What are you doing?" screamed Tega as she was being dragged to the doorway by two soldiers.

"Let her go!" ordered Jonas.

"Thank you My Lord. What on earth is going on?" asked Tega with disdain.

"Have you seen Captain Archetenus?"

"Yes My Lord; he returned to the castle a few weeks back. He looked awful and said he wanted to rest before he spoke to anyone."

"How long did he stay here?"

"Just a few days My Lord."

"When did he leave?"

"I am not really sure. I came in one morning with his breakfast and he was gone."

"How long ago was that?"

"I think two to three weeks ago."

"Was he here when the soldier was killed outside of the Queen's chambers?"

"Why, yes he was My Lord; that was the first morning I saw him and I told him about the attack as he ate breakfast." Tega saw the look on Jonas' face. "Oh you do not think Captain Archetenus had anything to do with that do you?" Jonas did not respond. "He seemed shocked when I told him about it," said Tega.

"Where is he now?" asked Jonas.

"When we talked he made it sound like he was home for good. I was surprised that he left again."

266

"Thank you Tega; if you see him again come and tell me," said Jonas as the men left the cabin. Jonas ordered the soldiers back to their posts and returned to the castle to talk to Roch.

"Well, if Archetenus took Vitomas that would explain how he could move around the castle without anyone noticing," said Roch angrily as he paced back and forth in the war room.

"Where is his home?" asked Jonas.

"He has no home anymore," replied Roch. "But where would he take her?"

"I certainly hope he is lucky enough to avoid all the bands of Hutas."

Roch looked at Jonas with shock as this was the first time he realized the Hutas too could be a threat to Vitomas. "Jonas have we heard any word from the search parties?"

"No but he will know we are tracking him and cover his trail."

"But he has two women with him and they must have supplies," stated Roch. Then Roch walked over to the corner table that held the containers of wine and whiskey. He poured two large glasses of whiskey and handed one to Jonas. "Jonas I have another assignment for you. Go to Cana and bring Annabelle's parents to me."

"Padre Thomas, Padre Thomas," yelled Padre Bartholomew as he tried to catch up with the priest in the main garden of the monastery at Malga. Padre Thomas was in deep contemplation and did not hear Padre Bartholomew calling him. Padre Bartholomew was out of breath when he caught up with Padre Thomas.

"My friend what is the matter?" asked Padre Thomas with concern when he saw the look on Padre Bartholomew's face.

"Look," said Padre Bartholomew as he unfolded a leather map. "King Tobias sent soldiers here to give this to us; they said they took it off a dead Huta."

"I can't understand all of the words because it is a very old language but this is a symbol of a scroll and that word 'Sanctus' means sacred or holy and that word over there 'Ostendo' means to reveal. Why would Hutas have something like this?"

"Padre Bartholomew, I am wondering if this is the same map that Roch has. We should show this to High Priest Zophar because he saw Roch's map. Then I think we should go to the Hall of Antiquities and look for information about these other symbols."

"We should contact the Sanuri," Padre Bartholomew said. "But I am not really sure how."

"I would prefer to try and gather as much information as we can before we send any messages to the Sanuri."

"This is so much fun," Annabelle said as she and Simon spread a tablecloth on the ground near a small pond. "I can't believe how beautiful it is here."

"Since we have the picnic baskets, I thought we should take a boca but next time we will ride horses so I can take you to more places," Simon said as he took two large baskets of food out of the back of the boca. "I can't believe how much food Marie packed," he said with a laugh. Simon set the two baskets on the ground near Annabelle and turned back towards the boca.

"There is more?" Annabelle asked in amazement.

"Oh yes, besides food, she packed water, wine and blankets. We have enough here to last a couple of days."

"I like Marie, she is really funny," Annabelle said as she started to put food and dishes on the tablecloth.

"She helped raise me and Raul," Simon said with a laugh. "We would make her so mad, she always called us hellions." Simon opened a bottle of wine and filled two glasses.

"I really don't drink very much," Annabelle said as she took a glass and sipped the wine. "This is really good," she said in amazement.

"If you're not used to drinking, drink slowly."

Annabelle fixed Simon a plate and handed it to him. "I can't even imagine you and Raul as kids. I bet Marie was right, you were hellions."

"Sure she was right," Simon said. "We used to get into so much trouble that our parents sent us out to work so that we would learn to be responsible."

"What do you mean they sent you out to work?"

"Well, if someone in Salar needed help, like a widow, we would have to go and do chores at their home. They were always sending us to the orphanage to work. It was good experience but we still got into trouble even working on those jobs."

"I have never heard of such a thing, sending princes out to work. Your father is very different from his brother."

"Speaking of Roch, I know you and Vitomas had horrible lives. Annabelle I want you to know you can always talk to me about what happened there."

Annabelle didn't say anything for a few moments. "Simon it's not that I am hiding anything from you; it's that talking about that is difficult and right now I am enjoying everything so much. I have never been this happy or felt this free. I would like to forget that other world."

"But I can't stop thinking about Vitomas, you cannot even imagine what Roch will do to her if he finds out she helped us escape. When Vitomas was little she tried to escape twice and both times Roch's men found her. The things he did to her as punishment, terrified me so that I never tried to escape."

"I am very much hoping to meet Roch when we go for Vitomas. You know he tried to kill my father when he was a boy, he tried to kill my brother and he murdered my grandparents. And he hurt the women that Raul and I love. He does not deserve to live," Simon said passionately.

"Simon did you just say that you loved me?" Annabelle asked shyly.

269

"Yes, does that surprise you?"

"I love you too Simon," Annabelle said without hesitation and moved the two plates that were setting between them. Annabelle leaned close to Simon and kissed him on the lips. It was a shy kiss at first but within seconds the passion of the two young lovers overwhelmed them. After several minutes, Simon moved more dishes so they could lie down. Time was lost to them as they embraced. When both of them were sweating and breathless; Simon stopped kissing Annabelle and pulled away from her.

"Annabelle we need to stop now before this goes any farther."

"Simon I have never felt like this before. I feel like I am going to explode."

"So do I," he said with a smile.

"Simon do we have to stop?"

Simon looked at Annabelle for a moment then he walked over to the boca and grabbed the blankets that Marie had sent along. Simon spread the blankets on the ground then took Annabelle's hand. "Let's move over here," he said.

"I think this is the best we can do in this storm," Archetenus said as he led the horses under a large rock outcropping on the side of a hill. He dismounted and helped Vitomas off from her horse and untied her hands. They were both completely soaked by the cold pouring rain.

Archetenus cared for the horses then turned to Vitomas who was huddled against the rock wall shivering. Archetenus sat down close to Vitomas. "Lean against me, I will warm you up," he said as he put his arm around her. Vitomas did not move so Archetenus pulled her tightly against him.

"We won't be able to make a fire here and the blankets are wet; so I am afraid we are in for a cold night," said Archetenus. As reluctant as Vitomas was to touch Archetenus she found herself huddling against him to get warm. Vitomas fell asleep with Archetenus' arms tightly around her.

"Vitomas," Archetenus whispered into her ear. She groggily looked up at him. "I can't sleep in this position all night; I need to stretch out."

"Alright," said Vitomas sleepily and moved away from him.

Archetenus lay down on the ground. "Come here," he said and pulled Vitomas down next to him. Archetenus could feel her resistance. "It is the only way you are going to stay warm," he said. They were both lying on their sides, Vitomas had her back to Archetenus and he held her tightly against him.

Vitomas suddenly awoke; her heart racing. She lay perfectly still listening for sounds. When Vitomas first opened her eyes she did not know where she was because of the darkness of the rock enclosure. Vitomas heard the rain falling and started to remember; then as she realized what woke her; fear seized her heart.

Vitomas could feel Archetenus' hands gently moving over her entire body and he was kissing the back of her neck. Vitomas could feel her breathing quicken as she tried not to cry out; she pretended to still be sleeping. Thoughts were racing through Vitomas' head as she was trying to figure out what to do. She had no weapons and Archetenus was such a large man she knew she could not fight him and win.

Archetenus pulled the bottom of Vitomas' blouse out of the waistband of her skirt. He put his hand under her blouse and felt both of her breasts, tenderly at first and then much harder. "I know you're awake," he whispered into her ear. Vitomas could feel his hot breath on her neck.

The tears were running down Vitomas' cheeks as Archetenus rolled her over onto her back. "Archetenus please don't do this," Vitomas whispered but her fear made it difficult for her to speak.

Archetenus moved his weight on top of Vitomas and kissed her passionately on the lips. She did not respond. "Kiss me back," he whispered.

"No, please don't do this Archetenus, please." He kissed her on the lips again and Vitomas could feel that Archetenus was unbuttoning her blouse. Again Vitomas did not respond to his kiss. Archetenus started kissing her neck and her breasts.

271

Vitomas gathered all the strength she could and yelled angrily, "You do not want me to look upon you as Roch and yet you would be him." Archetenus stopped moving. Vitomas could feel his entire body stiffen as he was consumed with anger. Archetenus raised his right arm and Vitomas closed her eyes thinking he was going to strike her; then she felt his large hand tightly grasp her throat. Vitomas lay perfectly still with the tears flowing down her cheeks. In that moment the irony of the situation struck her; it would not be Roch who killed her.

Neither of them spoke. Archetenus did not choke Vitomas nor did he drop his tight hold on her throat as he was trying to contain his rage. After what seemed like an eternity to Vitomas, Archetenus said angrily, "Your problem is that you do not realize you love me."

Vitomas was trying to think of something to say, she did not want to die this night. "Then give me time to realize it," she whispered. Archetenus did not speak or move for several moments. Eventually he let go of Vitomas' throat.

"If you want me to stop now then I want something from you," Archetenus said, his voice so filled with anger it was as if he was spitting out the words.

"What?" whispered Vitomas as she was terrified to hear the answer.

"I want you to kiss me and I mean really kiss me like you love me." Archetenus leaned down and kissed Vitomas on the lips. After a moment he said angrily, "Vitomas that was not a kiss."

"I am sorry," Vitomas cried. "I am just so frightened."

Archetenus kissed her on the lips again and she kissed him back, her lips trembling. After a few moments he said sarcastically, "I will bet that is not how you kiss your prince." Vitomas could hear the anger rising in Archetenus' voice and could feel his body tensing more and more. "You have one more chance," he growled.

"Alright, I am sorry," said Vitomas. "I will do better, please let me sit up."

Archetenus moved off from Vitomas. The two sat looking at each other for a moment. All Vitomas could think about was staying alive until Raul found her. Vitomas raised her arms and put them around Archetenus' thick neck and his long wet hair. Then she leaned upwards and kissed him on the lips. As Vitomas kissed Archetenus she tried to imagine that he was Raul and as she put more passion into her kiss he responded aggressively.

Archetenus kissed her so roughly that it hurt Vitomas and she was having difficulty breathing. Archetenus held Vitomas tightly with his left arm; while he felt her body under her skirt with his right hand. Vitomas tried to push herself away from Archetenus but she could not move. The tears flowed down her face. After what seemed like a very long time to Vitomas; Archetenus ended his assault on her. "That is how I want you to kiss me from now on; do you understand?" he asked sternly. Vitomas did not answer but nodded her head.

"And from now on you will sleep at my side," Archetenus growled, then he lay back down on his side and pulled Vitomas tightly against him. He enveloped her with his massive arms and crossed one of his legs over hers so she could not move. Vitomas laid like that the rest of the night, too afraid to move; the tears running down her face. Vitomas was overwhelmed with despair and hopelessness.

"How cruel this world is," Vitomas thought. "I finally find love and it is taken from me so quickly. Am I doomed to live among these monsters?" Vitomas tried to think about Raul so she would be less afraid but this night it was not working.

When Archetenus awoke he released the holds he had on Vitomas with his arms and leg. He rolled her onto her back and stared at her. Vitomas could see the anger in his face.

"For so long I dreamt about making love to you and in my dreams you wanted me too," Archetenus said angrily. "Vitomas you have ruined everything." He got up and started to saddle the horses. "We might as well move until we can find some dry firewood," Archetenus growled.

"My Lord did you work through the night?" asked Sophie as she placed a tray containing Roch's breakfast on a table in the war room.

"Yes, thank you Sophie." Roch folded the two identical maps and returned them to his shirt pocket. He had just sat down to his breakfast when Jonas entered the war room.

"I am sorry to interrupt your breakfast My Lord but I think you will want to hear this," said Jonas.

"Sophie bring another breakfast," Roch said.

"I went to Cana and Annabelle's parents are gone," said Jonas.

"What do you mean gone?" yelled Roch.

"Most of their belongings were gone from the house; some neighbors said they left weeks ago in a boca."

"What of Annabelle?"

"The neighbors said they just saw her parents in the boca."

"A few weeks ago around the same time my wife and Annabelle went missing; this is most odd," said Roch suspiciously. "Did they tell the neighbors where they were going?"

"No they did not."

"Sophie!" yelled Roch.

"Yes My Lord," said Sophie as she ran into the war room.

"Did Annabelle tell you that her parents were planning a trip?" asked Roch.

"Not that I remember My Lord but Annabelle did mention she had an aunt who was gravely sick."

"Did she say where her aunt lived?"

"No My Lord and I did not ask."

"Thank you Sophie that will be all."

"Do you think it is a coincidence?" Jonas asked.

"Honestly I don't know what to think," said Roch sincerely. It was the very first time Jonas had ever heard Roch speak in that manner.

"Also My Lord, the last of the search parties returned this morning. Many were wounded from a battle with a party of Hutas; but they found no sign of the Queen."

Roch threw his coffee cup against the wall with rage, "Jonas it is as if she just disappeared, how can this be?" Jonas did not respond. Roch got up from the table and stood before the window behind his desk. He turned back to Jonas after he had regained his composure.

"Jonas send men out to villages, monasteries I do not care but have them find the location of Sporos," said Roch. "I do not want them to contact Sporos I just want them to find his location."

"Of course My Lord but we might have more success by taking more Huta prisoners."

"Very well Jonas, whatever you think will be more successful; just get me that information. Also Jonas I will be leaving in two days for Tadon, I will be taking fifty men with me. I want you to have information about Sporos when I return."

"Are you looking for the Queen My Lord?"

"No I am going to the old monastery to find help translating that Huta map."

"But all the priests are dead."

"I know," said Roch with a smile. "But I did not have all the manuscripts destroyed."

This morning Annabelle got out of bed quietly and walked into Raul's sleeping quarters and sat next to his bed. She had once again slept in the second bedroom in Raul's chambers.

"I'm awake," Raul said. "You don't have to be so quiet."

"How do you feel?" Annabelle asked as she examined his bandages. "Sit up and let me look. I think you are healed enough to remove this bandage. Annabelle was silent as she removed a large bandage that was wrapped around Raul's shoulder and upper arm. "You are healing quickly Raul. This is good. I am taking the last of your bandages off."

Raul stared at Annabelle for a few moments without speaking. She looked at him and blushed. "Why are you smiling like that Annabelle?" Raul asked kiddingly.

"No reason."

"You must have come back from your picnic very late because I didn't see you before I went to bed."

"We did come back late," Annabelle said with a happy smile.

"Annabelle did you and my brother make love?" Raul asked with a grin.

"Yes," Annabelle said with a sigh. "Raul it was the most wonderful thing. I just feel; I don't know how to explain it. I feel like I am floating."

"Annabelle I am really happy for you and Simon but I wouldn't tell our parents."

"Of course not Raul, I'm not stupid. Raul you are standing so well," Annabelle said happily as she watched him get out of bed and balance on both legs without the use of his crutches.

"I am going to try walking with only one crutch today."

Simon entered Raul's room, walking briskly with a huge smile on his face. "Did Annabelle tell you?" Simon asked as he put his arm around her shoulders.

"You mean that you made love? Yes."

"No, that we are getting married."

"Did you ask Father?" Annabelle asked as she looked up into Simon's face.

"Yes, he gave us his blessing. All of our parents know and Mother and Laurel are going to start planning the wedding. I said we will be married after we come back with Vitomas."

"I am really happy about this," Raul said with a large smile. "Did you tell Mother to plan a double wedding?"

"No, I think that you should tell her but I know she has already been thinking about ideas. You know how Mother loves to plan celebrations." Simon turned to Annabelle. "We are moving into one of the biggest chambers today."

"What do you mean?" Annabelle asked. "Do you mean we are going to share chambers?"

"Yes, we'll be married soon; why not?"

"And our parents approve of this?"

"They didn't say 'no'. I think they are all so happy we're getting married, nothing else matters."

"Besides they probably know that Simon would be sneaking into your chambers all the time anyways," Raul said and winked.

Vitomas did not speak; she could see how angry Archetenus was and she did not want to provoke him further. The morning was gray and cold but the rain had stopped. Vitomas was shivering as the two rode in silence. About midmorning the sun started to show its face in the sky. Vitomas felt grateful for the warmth. Slowly the sun started to dry out her clothing and hair.

Close to midday Archetenus stopped the horses. He helped Vitomas down from her horse and untied her hands. "Gather wood for the fire and do not try to run away; I am not feeling very merciful today," he barked at her. Archetenus unsaddled the horses as Vitomas found wood. He started a fire. "Make coffee and put the blankets out to dry," Archetenus ordered. "I am going to find food."

As soon as Archetenus walked into the forest with his bow and arrows; Vitomas started to cry loudly. She did as he ordered. As Vitomas was hanging the blankets on tree limps she was trying to calm herself. "He is not as bad as Roch," thought Vitomas.

"I can do this until Raul finds me." Then a thought filled her with terror and grief, "What if Raul never finds me?"

"I am taking you back to Malga to stay with Padre Bartholomew for a while," the Sanuri said.

"But why?" cried Petra. "I want to go with you."

"I have some business that is too dangerous for you to be with me."

"What business?" asked Petra angrily.

"I am going to pay Sporos a visit."

Petra grew quiet. "Why?" he asked.

"Last night I had a vision, I saw what could happen if Sporos obtains The Box of Itifer and The Scroll of Imari."

"What could happen?"

"Hell my young friend, hell unleashed on this world," replied the Sanuri solemnly.

"Do you know where to find him?"

"In the vision I was told he is near Casmer in the Kingdom of Marba."

"But that is the kingdom of the Hutas; you will be killed," whispered Petra.

Archetenus returned to the campsite carrying three dead rabbits. He walked past Vitomas but he did not speak or look at her. Vitomas watched him as he skinned the animals and saw how tense and angry he was. "I am going to get more wood," Vitomas said. Archetenus did not acknowledge that he heard her.

As Vitomas was picking up small branches from the floor of the forest she stopped and looked around at her surroundings. Vitomas thought about escaping but she had no idea where she was.

Vitomas had never been out of the Kingdom of Stordt or even seen a map of the continent. Vitomas cried softly as she filled her arms with wood. When Vitomas brought the wood to the campsite Archetenus still did not look at her. Vitomas returned to the forest three more times for wood for their fire.

"That's enough wood," Archetenus growled as he was placing the rabbits on a long stick to cook over the fire.

Vitomas nervously sat down on the ground. "Is there anything you want me to do?" she asked.

"Just stay away from me."

"What?" Vitomas asked because she wasn't sure she heard him correctly.

Now Archetenus looked at her, his eyes ablaze with anger. "Vitomas I don't want to hurt you but I am so damn mad that you need to just stay away from me."

Chapter XVII
Passages

"Padre Thomas we have company," Padre Bartholomew announced happily as he escorted the Sanuri and Petra to one of the gardens surrounding the monastery.

"Your flowers are beautiful," the Sanuri commented as he looked at the lush and colorful garden before him.

"Every morning he is out here by sunrise working in the gardens," Padre Bartholomew said proudly of his friend. "I have tried to help but I am afraid I kill and break more plants than I cultivate."

"Don't let him fool you as to his talents," Padre Thomas said as he brushed the dirt off from his robe and walked towards their guests. "Did you know what a talented artist he is? Padre Bartholomew has painted some extraordinary pictures of the gardens and he is putting his talent to use restoring some of our oldest documents." As soon as Padre Thomas was close to the Sanuri he whispered, "It is a miracle you came because we have something for you. Let's go to my room."

Padre Thomas' room was small and frugal. His room contained the bare necessities, a small bed, a dresser, a small writing desk, several chairs and two small tables. The only items of color in his room were four unframed, stretched canvases that were hung on the wall. Each canvas contained a brightly colored painting of a garden.

"Did you paint those?" Petra asked of Padre Bartholomew.

"Yes, what do you think?"

"I like them; they look just like Padre Thomas' gardens.

While Petra and Padre Bartholomew were talking, Padre Thomas took a folded piece of leather from a compartment in his writing desk and handed it to the Sanuri. "King Tobias sent this to us it was taken off a Huta warrior."

The Sanuri looked at the map carefully. "Do you know what this is?"

"We have our suspicions but first I must tell you that High Priest Zophar said this map is identical to the map that Roch wanted translated," said Padre Thomas.

"Padre Thomas and I went to the Hall of Antiquities and tried to translate the words and symbols on that map," Padre Bartholomew explained. "See that symbol of the scroll near those caves. I believe two of those words written above it mean 'holy' and 'to reveal'. And look at those drawings of creatures and the word 'monstrum', does that mean monster?"

"This is a map to The Scroll of Imari," the Sanuri said. "The scroll is hidden in the Caves of Muldun, in the Kingdom of Stordt. You are right, that word does mean monsters and it is talking about the Giant Gants that dwell in those caves and the nearby forests. The Gants protect The Scroll of Imari like the Centras protect The Box of Itifer. But the creatures could not be more different. The Gants are giant savage beasts."

Roch and his small army entered the tiny Village of Tadon just before dawn. They had traveled through the night and were eager to reach their destination. Roch dismounted in front of an ancient monastery in the center of the village. He ordered two men to accompany him and the rest to remain mounted. The iron gate to the wall surrounding the monastery was rusted shut and one of the soldiers had to kick it repeatedly before it would open.

One of the two huge wooden doors to the monastery was destroyed allowing access to the building. Roch stopped and looked at the remains of the door remembering when his men broke it down and dragged the priests out so many years before.

The rooms inside the monastery were dark. One of the soldiers found some candles which they used for light as they searched the rooms. "How can this be?" yelled Roch angrily. "A monastery without scrolls or books."

"My Lord most of the furniture is gone also; perhaps the villagers took these things," said one of the soldiers.

Roch exited the monastery and told his men to take rest in this place. He walked to the gate of the monastery and sat in the shade of a huge tree. Roch took one of the maps from his shirt pocket as was his daily ritual. He caressed the map as if it were the face of a loved one. Roch often dreamed of this map as it was always in his thoughts. Roch placed the map on his lap and leaned back against the trunk of the tree; his eyes were heavy from exhaustion. As Roch's eyes were closing he spied something that jolted him to a standing position.

The iron archway over the monastery gate contained a series of symbols that matched symbols on the map. Roch held the map up and saw the same series of symbols: a five pointed star, a quarter moon followed by a six pointed star. Roch walked up to the gate and compared the map to the surrounding scenery.

To Roch's right he saw a hill which was pictured on the map; to his left Roch saw a small ridge which was also depicted on the map. Left of the ridge a forest was drawn on the map which was consistent with the location of the Rodite Forest which connected with the Forest of Bach. West of the forests the map had a symbol of a scroll drawn amidst a series of caves.

Roch's heart was beating and his hands started to shake. "Finally I have found my fortune," Roch said out loud then he quickly turned to see if any of the soldiers had heard him.

"The Saints be with us!" gasped Padre Bartholomew. "How would a Huta have such a map?"

"Sporos," the Sanuri said. "A few nights ago I encountered a group of Hutas who told me that Sporos has The Box of Itifer and has sent the Hutas in search of The Scroll of Imari also."

"Wait, you encountered a group of Hutas and you got them to talk to you," said Padre Bartholomew in amazement.

The Sanuri smiled, "Yes, they were actually quite willing to give me information. Petra can fill you in on the details. I would like to leave him here with you for a little while."

"Of course," replied Padre Thomas. "Are you going after the scroll?"

"No, I believe the Gants will protect it from both the Hutas and Roch," the Sanuri answered. "I am going after Sporos."

"Do you have any idea where he might be?" asked Padre Bartholomew.

"I had a vision of him in a castle near Casmer in the Kingdom of Marba."

"Come with me," Padre Thomas said to the Sanuri. "I have something that will be quite useful for you."

"I will take Petra to the stables to see our new colt," said Padre Bartholomew as he ushered Petra into the hallway.

Before Petra walked through the doorway he turned around and said, "Sanuri you will come back for me, won't you?"

"Yes Petra, I promise I will come back and get you."

"That boy is very attached to you," said Padre Thomas.

"And I to him," replied the Sanuri sincerely.

"I believe I know of the castle that Sporos lives in, it was once left to the church to be used as a monastery," said Padre Thomas as the two men were walking to the library. "Of course that was long before the Hutas conquered the Kingdom of Marba. As you know that kingdom was a battleground for many decades and that castle was fortified for war."

The two men entered the library. The Sanuri started to light the candles as Padre Thomas searched for materials on the shelves; it took Padre Thomas almost a half hour to find what he was looking for. "Here is a map of both the exterior and interior of that castle," said Padre Thomas as he unrolled the map on top of an oak table. "Of course Sporos may have made some changes and as you can see these drawings are very old and fading. But hopefully they will be of some use to you."

"There are two sets of exterior walls," said the Sanuri as he studied the map. "But the guard towers are only on the most exterior walls."

"Yes, but you still have the moat to contend with and who knows what manner of creatures he has living in that moat."

As the Sanuri studied the map Padre Thomas dropped a heavy metal ring of keys on the table. "I do not know if he changed the locks but it is worth a try. It is terrifying to think of two such forces of evil vying for the same holy objects. Perhaps they will destroy each other," Padre Thomas said wistfully.

"Perhaps," said the Sanuri as he was concentrating on the drawings. The Sanuri stood up quickly. "Padre Thomas I thank you for these things, they will greatly aid me. I have a friend who is an Enrop his name is Nica and he is the leader of his flock; use him to send me messages."

"But how do I contact him?"

"Fly the purple flags, he will get word that you need to speak with him."

"And if it is dark or an emergency, will the flags do?"

"Then pray and The Great Ruler will send him."

"I will be praying for you my friend," said Padre Thomas as the Sanuri left the monastery.

Gathering his men, Roch headed towards the Caves of Muldun. They headed northwest into the land of the Gants, a tribe of giant creatures which resembled apes. The males of this species could weigh as much as seven hundred pounds and averaged about ten feet in height. These creatures lived mainly in the Forest of Bach although some small tribes traveled throughout the Rodite Forest also. An ancient species these creatures were intelligent and aggressive hunters who lived in family units that were led by the oldest and strongest male.

Ancient civilizations named the Gants the Watchers of the Caves because the Caves of Muldun were the sacred burial place for this species. Gants routinely slept during the day and fed at night. They hunted in packs and were capable of killing entire herds of animals in one hunt.

Roch planned to travel at night and to sleep during the day to stay ahead of the Gants. Traveling just a few miles, Roch ordered his men to make camp.

"What is this place?" asked Vitomas as she tried to break the silence. For two days they had barely spoken and Archetenus still seemed angry.

"It was called Norta, it was a mining town; the diamond mines are just north of here," said Archetenus with a sweep of his hand.

"Where is everyone?" asked Vitomas as she felt relief that Archetenus did not sound angry anymore.

"A dozen years ago Rogetts attacked the mines and killed or captured all of the inhabitants. No one will work those mines for fear the Rogetts will return."

"It is sad to see something like this," said Vitomas as they rode on the outskirts of the abandoned town.

A once prosperous and highly populated area, Norta was reduced to a shamble of old buildings in various states of disrepair. A sign that was once grand and welcomed people to the town was hanging from a single hinge on a pole and banging in the wind.

"This place scares me," whispered Vitomas.

"Perhaps it is not your fear you feel. The people who lived here died awful deaths at the hands of the Rogetts."

"Let us put this place behind us quickly."

Archetenus and Vitomas rode for several more hours before making camp on the western shore of the River Toba.

Queen Renya wept bitterly as Raul, Simon, Annabelle and the soldiers prepared to leave. "I feel like I am losing all my children," she cried. Raul stopped his packing and put his arms around his mother. "When we return you will be adopting another daughter," Raul said as he hugged Renya. "You will love Vitomas." Raul kissed his mother on the forehead.

285

"Laurel already thinks of Vitomas as a second daughter," Renya said trying to force a smile.

"Mother I am truly sorry I did not ask you or Father if Annabelle and her parents could stay with us before they were on the doorsteps."

"Nonsense having them here is like having your grandparents; they are such a joy. And now they will be family. Raul your father and I know you are a young man who must experience life but after you left it was as if your father's life source left with you. I beg of you find Vitomas and return to us quickly." This comment broke Raul's heart for he loved both of his parents dearly.

"Mother I know you are already planning Simon and Annabelle's wedding. Would it be too much of a burden to plan my wedding also?"

"Burden, how could you even ask such a thing? I am thrilled that both of my sons are getting married," Renya winked at Raul. "Actually I started planning your wedding right after you told us that you asked Vitomas to marry you. You know Raul I love that little Annabelle. She is so shy and sweet but I think she can keep Simon on his toes," said Renya and they both laughed loudly. "And I am sure that I will love Vitomas just as much."

Vitomas sat by the fire lost in her thoughts of Raul. She missed him dearly and believed Raul when he told her he would come back for her but now Vitomas' fears were overtaking her. "How will he ever find me?" Vitomas thought with despair. Vitomas looked across the fire at Archetenus as he slept. He filled her so with fright at times. But Archetenus' anger had so consumed him that for the last few days and nights he wanted nothing to do with her.

In her rejection of him, Vitomas had shattered Archetenus' fantasy. Archetenus had planned so much of his life around his unrealistic dream that he now felt lost. Archetenus had imagined a world where he would be Vitomas' hero, saving her from Roch. It had never entered Archetenus' mind that Vitomas would not want him.

Archetenus desired Vitomas greatly and fought his own desires to take her by force; he had certainly done that before with other women. But it was his own image that Archetenus saw in Vitomas' eyes that stopped him because Vitomas looked at Archetenus as if he was a monster.

As Vitomas sat by the fire, overwhelmed with her sadness she heard Archetenus moaning. He was tossing around the ground as if he was having a nightmare. The thought struck Vitomas ironically, "Do the monsters that create nightmares, have nightmares of their own?" Archetenus now settled back into his slumber.

Archetenus could not wake himself from his dreams this night. The woman appeared again, the one who had warned him about his choices. Her piercing eyes filled Archetenus with guilt. Although her appearance looked considerably different Archetenus recognized her. In his dream she came to him as an old, haggard woman but now she was incredibly beautiful with a light that seemed to glow from inside of her.

"Archetenus you did not heed my words," Miranda said accusingly. "Your own darkness will be your downfall. This woman belongs to another; her destiny is not entwined with yours. You can yet save yourself but your path becomes darker every day." Now it was as if Miranda was showing him images. Archetenus saw himself on top of Vitomas' dead body, his hands still around her warm neck. In the vision, Archetenus sat back and was filled with regret for what he had done.

As Archetenus watched his own image he was flooded with sadness. Then Archetenus realized he was watching his face changing. In the vision, Archetenus' body remained the same, but his face changed to that of Roch's, then back to Archetenus then to another face. This was the face that he saw in the eyes of Vitomas. His face repeatedly changed between the three countenances.

Archetenus called out to the woman in his vision, "I am not Roch but who is the other? That face fills me with fear."

"You do not recognize it?" Miranda asked sarcastically.

"Tell me woman, who is it that you show me?"

"It is the demon within you and you should fear him Archetenus because you are quickly losing yourself to him." Then Miranda's face was gone.

Archetenus sat up so quickly that he scared Vitomas and she jumped. Archetenus looked around the campsite, his eyes wide with fear.

"I think you were having a dream or a nightmare," Vitomas said softly.

"A nightmare yes, but I do not think it a dream."

Then both Vitomas and Archetenus jumped as they heard a lion roar.

Two hundred strong, the army from Wetpr rode in disguise. Raul had been overwhelmed when he learned that most of the two hundred thousand troops that were stationed at Fort Salar had volunteered to help rescue Vitomas. The group originally left Wetpr divided into three groups; Raul, Simon and Annabelle remained together with a detail of men.

Lieutenant Klass led the second detail while Lieutenant Markus led the third. Each detail broke into smaller groups that crossed the border into Stordt virtually unchallenged. The groups crossed the border at different locations as not to raise the suspicions of the border guards.

"The more that we look like bandits, the easier it is to get across the border," Lieutenant Klass said with a laugh to the sergeant who rode to his right.

The plan was for the troops to regroup in the Mangee Forest which was north of Cana and east of Taperia on the third night, after they crossed the border.

"Great Ruler give me speed," prayed the Sanuri as he rode south from Malga. The vision the Sanuri had, still disturbed him considerably. In the vision The Lion was in Sporos castle and it was as if the Sanuri could see through The Lion's eyes. The Lion had shown the Sanuri how dark Sporos' heart had become and what great pleasure Sporos now achieved from horror.

It was as if Sporos' being grew and fed on the fear of others. The Lion showed the Sanuri the future and what would happen if Sporos obtained both The Box of Itifer and The Scroll of Imari. This vision made the Sanuri weep; not only for the cruelty that was inflicted upon the innocent but also for the loss of someone he once called his friend.

Both the Sanuri and Sporos had been taken to the monastery at Avaide as children. They grew into men at that monastery, learning the Word of The Great Ruler as well as receiving the best educations that could be taught. The Sanuri thought about the many fighting matches the two had with their staffs and swords. They would spend long hours together talking of philosophy and the stars. It was as if the Sanuri could still hear his old friend laugh. He always thought that Sporos had a hardy contagious laugh. "What happened to you?" thought the Sanuri sadly as he drove the boca towards the Safer Mountain Range.

Riding at night, Roch and his men traveled by way of an old dried river bed that skirted the Rodite Forest and would lead them to the Forest of Bach. A full moon illuminated the landscape allowing the soldiers to see their surroundings. This was the second night they heard bloodcurdling screams coming from the forest. The men were on edge and the horses were restless.

"It is as if this place is cursed," said Sampson as he rode next to Roch.

"They are merely animals," said Roch, although he too felt the presence of death among them. "We should be alright as long as we stay out of the forest." Roch touched his shirt pocket, a move that had become a comforting habit.

Suddenly a horse squealed at the rear of the formation. Roch ordered, "Weapons drawn!" As all the men turned and looked towards the rear of the formation. Only Roch and Sampson broke formation and rode to the rear. As a horse struggled to get back on its feet they heard the terrifying screams of a man.

In the few moments it took Roch to reach the rear of the formation one of his soldiers was being dragged into the forest by a giant shadow. "Stay put!" yelled Roch to his men who would follow their friend to their deaths. "We stay out of the forest." Sampson quickly dismounted and checked the horse.

"Does the horse need to be put down?" snapped Roch.

"No My Lord, it is merely frightened," responded Sampson, who tied the reigns of the horse to his saddle.

Roch's small army continued its march towards the Caves of Muldun; fear filled the hearts of the men as they rode in the moonlight. The screams of the Gants pierced the air throughout the night. Roch rode in silence fantasizing about the power that would be his once he had The Scroll of Imari.

"What do you mean she is gone?" asked Annabelle in a horrified and loud whisper. Raul and Simon were both standing at different windows in Gala's house watching for Taperian soldiers. When Raul heard Annabelle's words he ran to Gala.

"What did you say?" demanded Raul with fear in his voice.

"Shortly after you left, groups of soldiers were searching for the Queen."

"Are you sure Roch did not do something to her?" asked Raul.

"The King did not return for almost two weeks after she went missing," said Gala tearfully. "It is said that he killed the guard who was responsible for watching her."

Annabelle put her hand on Raul's arm. "I did not want you to worry any more than you already were," said Annabelle with tears in her eyes.

Raul interrupted her, "Annabelle what happened? What have you not told me?"

"Shortly before we left one of the castle guards was found dead underneath her window. The guards that found him said there were signs of a fight. They think the guard found someone watching Vitomas." Annabelle watched as Raul's face turned white. "I am sorry there is more," cried Annabelle. "Vitomas said she felt like she was being watched but she never saw anyone watching her; she thought she was being foolish."

Raul turned and walked to the window trying to regain his composure. "Did the soldiers find anything?" Raul asked without turning around.

"King Roch and Jonas traveled up the River Oja to return home. They arrived at night and stayed in the same cabin you were in Raul. According to Sophie, when they entered the cabin the furniture was thrown around as if there had been a fight," Gala explained. "When they were picking up the furniture Roch found one of Vitomas' earrings on the floor, so he knew something had happened to her before he reached the castle."

"Did anyone say what the earring looked like?" asked Raul softly.

"Sophie said it was the Queen's favorite earrings, sapphires surrounded by diamonds and rubies," Gala said.

Raul pulled Vitomas' earring out of his shirt pocket and showed it to everyone. "She gave this to me as a promise of her love; she was wearing the other one when I left the cabin." Raul's voice was barely audible when he finished speaking.

"I speak with Sophie every market day and she said Archetenus had returned and was staying at his cabin on the castle grounds for a few days; and now he is gone too," said Gala. "Sophie said the King thinks Archetenus took Queen Vitomas."

"Who is Archetenus?" asked Raul.

Gala poured coffee for everyone as Annabelle walked closer to Raul. "Archetenus is a captain in the Taperian Army. Roch sent him on a mission a few months ago and no one expected Archetenus to live through it," said Annabelle. "The reason Roch sent Archetenus on a mission of death is because of his jealousy. Archetenus always looked at Vitomas with love in his eyes and everyone including Roch saw this."

"How did Vitomas feel about him?" Raul whispered.

"She only saw Archetenus when he fought in the Gefrey Games. Vitomas admired his courage but she was not in love with him," said Annabelle. "Raul, Vitomas loves you and you alone. In fact Vitomas has never even spoken to Archetenus."

Simon saw the looks of despair on the faces of both Raul and Annabelle and it broke his heart. "Gala am I to understand that no one had any idea where Archetenus would have taken her?"

"That is what Sophie said," replied Gala.

"Who is this Sophie?" Simon asked.

"She is the King's cook, she spies for him and knows everyone's business," Annabelle said with disgust.

"So we need to find out where the soldiers are looking," said Simon.

"All the search parties returned to the castle last week," Gala said.

"Did Roch stop looking for Vitomas?" Raul asked incredulously.

"I think so; I heard he left for Tadon a few days ago and it appears that the soldiers have stopped searching," replied Gala.

"Is he looking for Vitomas in Tadon?" Raul asked.

"No, Sophie overheard him talking about following a map that was taken from a Huta."

"Tadon is where Vitomas used to live; that's where he stole her from," Annabelle said. "Roch is always looking for treasure. Vitomas said Roch had become so obsessed with one of his maps that he would get up in the middle of the night to study it."

"You mean he is searching for treasure instead of his wife?" Raul asked angrily.

"I like this man more and more," said Simon sarcastically. "Gala can you speak with this Sophie and find out if she knows where the soldiers have already searched?" asked Simon. "Our other choice is to talk to one of the Taperian soldiers."

"Let me talk with Sophie first. Tomorrow is market day in Cana and I always see her there. I will try to get better information for you," Gala said. "You are welcome to stay the night here or you could stay in that cabin by the lake."

"We have more men in the area," Raul said more to himself than to Gala.

"I don't want to get Gala in trouble; we should stay at the cabin," Annabelle said looking at Simon.

"Annabelle you cannot show your face here, the soldiers will take you to the castle; they already know your parents are gone," Gala said.

"How do they know about my parents?"

"The King sent soldiers to their house."

Simon motioned to Raul that the two of them should go into the adjoining room. As soon as they were alone Raul looked at Simon with tears in his eyes. "I should have forced her to come with us; if Archetenus hurts her I will never forgive myself," Raul choked out. Simon put his hand on Raul's shoulder, "We will find her my brother. Now you and Annabelle stay here until I return," said Simon. "I will go to the men and tell them we will be spending the night here. We should not stay with Gala but she has to be able to contact us. Do you think we can stay in that cabin without detection?"

"Yes, I stayed there for some time." Raul was flooded with emotions and Simon could see that in Raul's eyes.

"Raul, everything will be all right. I will return soon."

Cheers rang throughout the Ice Caves as the Rualas realized the presence of the Sanuri. Throngs of Rualas ran to greet him and to introduce their Shettee neighbors to him.

"This is the Sanuri who saved your race from extinction," said Ibula with pride to her new husband Thedes.

The Sanuri was overwhelmed at the loving response he received and he was pleased to see how well the Rualas and Shettees had learned to live together. The crowd grew so large around the Sanuri that he could no longer walk through the caves. "My children, although my visit is long overdue, it is with remorse that I say I have come here to speak with your Grand Council; for this time it is your help that I need."

The crowd parted to allow the Sanuri to walk to the Hall of Light, the meeting place of the Grand Council. The members of the council, which now was comprised of both Rualas and Shettees quickly gathered and took their assigned seats at the large U shaped table. Trays of refreshments were brought into the chambers before the meeting was to begin. The Sanuri stood in the center of the U table and addressed the council. He told them of Sporos, The Box of Itifer and The Scroll of Imari and of his plans.

"Of course we will help you in whatever way we can," said Manu the Chief of the Grand Council and the King of the Rualas.

"It will be a dangerous mission, I would prefer you ask for volunteers," said the Sanuri.

"I would be very surprised if every Ruala and Shettee warrior did not volunteer," replied Manu. "I will have you taken to your quarters while we get the volunteers, then we will meet back here in two hours. And my dear friend you look exhausted you should try and get some rest."

As Manu predicted he summoned the Sanuri two hours later. The Hall of Light was filled with warriors and the Grand Council was sitting at the table. Manu smiled as the Sanuri entered the room. "It is as I told you, these are only the volunteers that can fit into the hall," Manu said with a wave of his hand. The Sanuri told the warriors the same information he had shared with the Grand Council. "If anyone would like to change their mind about this mission you may do so without disgrace," said the Sanuri. No one left the room.

As soon as the meeting was finished two legions of Ruala warriors were dispatched to flight. The first group headed northwest to the Caves of Muldun; their orders were to prevent Roch from obtaining The Scroll of Imari if the Gants failed to stop him.

The second legion flew south to the Kingdom of Marba with orders to obtain information about Sporos' castle; this group was instructed not to do battle with Sporos unless they were attacked. After the two legions left the Ice Caves the Sanuri reviewed the maps of Sporos' castle with the leaders of both the Rualas and the Shettees.

Chapter XVIII
The Caves of Muldun

Simon left Gala's house and proceeded to the Mangee forest to speak with the troops. Gala put a platter of biscuits on the table along with some honey and butter. The women were talking about Archetenus but stopped when Raul entered the room.

"Simon left to speak with the men, he will return shortly," Raul said as he took a seat at the table.

"Will he be alright?" asked Annabelle.

"Yes," said Raul. "Our men will remain in the forest tonight and we will stay at the cabin."

"Good," said Gala. "Sophie will get suspicious if I talk to her other than our usual meetings at the market."

"What were you saying about Archetenus?" Raul asked.

"Roch maintains the strength of his army by stealing sons from their families and forcing them to be soldiers; Archetenus was one of those boys," said Gala.

"After years of being in the military Archetenus was allowed to go to his home to see his family and found they had all died and the house had been burned to the ground," said Annabelle. "We were trying to remember if we had ever heard of him having more family."

"Roch is a barbarian," stated Raul with disgust.

"Yes he is," said Gala. "But Archetenus is different. He is more like a hero to the people here."

"What do you mean," Raul asked as he poured honey on his biscuits.

"He fought in the Gefrey Games every week," Annabelle explained. "He would fight horrible beasts and he always won. The crowds loved him. In fact people started to come from all over just to see Archetenus fight. He is a brave warrior."

"He also loved the attention of the crowds," Gala said. "He liked to perform."

"Vitomas overheard Roch and some of his men plotting to kill Archetenus because they were threatened by the following he had. So Vitomas suggested to Roch that it might be wiser if he promoted Archetenus and gave him a new assignment. Which is what Roch did," Annabelle continued. "People soon forgot about Archetenus but Roch still hated him."

"Tell him the rest," Gala said.

"Roch always made Vitomas attend the Gefrey Games and sit at his side. She hated the games but it was one of the few times he allowed her out of the castle. Archetenus saw her there and well, everyone could tell that he was attracted to her."

"Why did she save him from being murdered?"

"Raul, Vitomas was always helping others," Annabelle said. "She once told me that she could not free herself but she could use her position to help others. You know how her heart is."

"I need to understand this," Raul said. "Before Simon left, you said that Roch had sent Archetenus on a suicide mission because he was jealous. So do you think that Archetenus took Vitomas because he is in love with her or because this is a way to get back at Roch? Because if he took her for retribution, Archetenus will probably kill her."

The Sanuri stopped his boca at the Wall of Dorath and looked at the impaled heads that were displayed to instill fear in all. He had a ways to go before he would reach the Gate of Isula; the Sanuri wondered if he would come upon the same evils that had plagued Archetenus and his men. The Sanuri had traveled along this wall many times and every time he thought that the wall epitomized the fear in all mankind.

As the Sanuri traveled south along the wall, he thought about the stories Archetenus had told. Now that the Sanuri knew that Sporos dwelled on the other side of the Wall of Dorath he knew who sent the Talmuth against the Taperian soldiers.

Only a demon or dark lord of great power could summon the Talmuth. But why would Sporos go to that trouble to call forth such ancient beings when he could have destroyed Archetenus and his men in other ways?

And why were the forearms cut off from the Taperian soldiers; the forearms that carried the brand of the Royal Family of Taperia? The same forearms that were carried by the Zendoti when they tried to attack the cave that Archetenus, Petra, Padre Bartholomew and the Sanuri were hiding in.

As the Sanuri thought about these questions he remembered the words of The Lion. The Lion had explained that Roch had employed a powerful witch to help him kill Archetenus but she was not powerful enough to control the demons that she called forth. At the time the Sanuri thought the Zendoti were the demons the witch had called forth but now he wondered if that was accurate. Why would Roch kill his own men and have the demons carry their forearms with the brand that showed their allegiance to him.

The Sanuri pondered many questions as he drove his team of six white horses southward, parallel to the wall. But every time the Sanuri came up with an answer it raised several more questions. Then the Sanuri remembered the decapitated head that had been put into Archetenus' saddlebag, and the sign of a curse. These two things seemed more like the work of a witch but again why not just kill Archetenus? The one thing that was becoming clear to the Sanuri was that something considered Archetenus a threat; perhaps something more powerful than King Roch.

Simon returned to Gala's house. "Annabelle where is your parent's house?" Simon asked as soon as he entered the kitchen.

"In the northern section of Cana, why?"

"I was thinking that perhaps some of our men should stay there, they would be closer and perhaps they would hear something. I sent some of them into Taperia and others into Cana to see if they can find out any information," Simon said.

"Won't they be recognized?" Gala asked.

"None of them are in uniform," Raul replied. "I assume you told them to stand around in the taverns and on the streets?"

"Yes, they are travelling in groups so it should be safer for them," said Simon.

"I can take you to my parent's house," Annabelle offered.

"Remember you can't be seen here," Simon said. "Just draw a map." As Annabelle was drawing the map, Raul told Simon what the women had said about Archetenus.

"I don't think Archetenus would hurt Vitomas," Annabelle said.

"Honey, you said that Archetenus had been in Roch's command since he was a small boy and he had worked his way up to captain," Simon said. "Even if Archetenus had help with the last promotion, I would assume that he was very loyal to Roch to be promoted at all. That tells you a lot about the man."

"I don't understand," Annabelle said.

"If Archetenus is working for Roch and being promoted by Roch, then he is doing all of the things that Roch wants done; and probably doing them well. And what does Roch have his men do? From what you all have been saying they murder, rape and terrorize their people," Simon continued.

Annabelle and Gala looked at each other with concern. "I guess I hadn't thought of it like that," Annabelle said.

"Annabelle do you think you would be able to draw a picture of Archetenus so we know what he looks like?" Raul asked.

"I'll find some more paper," Gala said and started to stand up.

Simon took the map from Annabelle and was about to walk through the door when he turned to Gala, "When you talk to Sophie tomorrow try to find out where the troops have already searched for Vitomas, that will help us narrow down our search areas."

Annabelle described Archetenus as she drew a picture of him. "Archetenus is a mountain of a man, tall and very muscular. He is taller than you and Simon. He has long curly brown hair that hangs past his shoulders. He has many scars from battle wounds," Annabelle continued. "Including a long scar on his right cheek. But even with all of these scars he is very handsome." Gala was standing over Annabelle's shoulder watching her draw.

Annabelle looked up from her drawing, "Raul this man has fought savage creatures and always won. He has been in love with Vitomas for a very long time and may not give her up easily. Please be careful." After a few minutes, Annabelle held the drawing up for Gala to see, "What do you think?"

"That's him," Gala said. "I didn't realize you were such a talented artist."

Annabelle handed the drawing to Raul who stared at the likeness of the man he was to kill. Raul studied the picture like he would a map. Raul wanted Archetenus' face permanently stamped in his mind; for he would hunt Archetenus down if it took the rest of his life.

"This is where the girls hid me for weeks," Raul said to Simon as the three of them entered the cabin. Annabelle immediately started to straighten things up since there were still signs of the struggle between Vitomas and Archetenus.

Simon saw the look on his brother's face as Raul watched Annabelle clean up the signs of the crime. "I'll get some wood, why don't you open that bottle of wine. I am sure we all could use a glass," Simon said.

"I'm glad that Gala gave us some clean bedding," Annabelle said as she changed the sheets and blankets on the bed. "I wouldn't want to sleep on any sheets that Roch might have slept on." Annabelle quickly turned and looked at Raul, "Perhaps I shouldn't have said that."

"It's alright Annabelle," Raul said as he sat down in a chair, suddenly feeling the weight of his despair. "You and Simon take the bed tonight; I will sleep by the fire."

"There are no fresh prints around the cabin," Simon commented when he walked in with an armload of wood. Simon started a fire as Annabelle prepared the food that Gala had sent with them. Raul drank his glass of wine and stared into the flames, wondering where Vitomas was and what nightmare she might be living through.

Once again Archetenus had not heeded the words of Miranda. A third night she came to him and this time her eyes were ablaze. "You fool of a man," Miranda screamed in his dream. "Do you not realize that I am sent here to warn you and who do you think sends me? I am a messenger for the greatest being of all, as is that lion you heard last night. Why do you not heed my words?" As Miranda yelled her hair as well as her eyes burst into flames. Archetenus was sweating as he tossed and turned on the ground trying to wake from his dream.

Suddenly Miranda became calm and in his dream she walked through a sort of doorway but it was unlike anything that Archetenus had seen before. It was as if Miranda walked between worlds. Now Archetenus could see Miranda's entire body instead of just her head. Her long black hair was flowing and somehow blowing back.

Miranda wore a light blue gown that also appeared to be blowing back in a breeze, although Archetenus did not feel a wind. Miranda was so beautiful that for an instant she took Archetenus' breath away; then Miranda held her hand out to him and Archetenus froze with fear.

"The man who fears no one, fears me?" Miranda asked in a sarcastic tone. "I am going to give you a rare gift this night Archetenus. Do not doubt that what I am about to show you is the truth. Take my hand." Archetenus fearfully took the Angel's hand and they instantly were transported to what appeared to be a giant maze.

"What is this place?" Archetenus asked fearfully.

"Each and every person makes choices in this life and every choice leads down a different road. This Archetenus is a map of your life." Miranda pointed to a dot that was close to their feet. "This is where you started, follow the paths and see the choices you have made that may determine where you will end up. Every man controls his destiny by the choices that he makes. If I were you I would study this map carefully."

The map appeared to stretch out for miles before them. "You can walk upon it," Miranda said. The map reminded Archetenus of branches of a tree with all of the different limbs. Suddenly dots of lights appeared on the map.

"The lights have different colors what do they mean?"

"Before I tell you, I want you to notice how the lights affect the directions of the paths in your life," Miranda said. Suddenly a cold wind blew across them causing Archetenus to shiver and Miranda's voice became as icy as the wind. "These lights represent every choice that you make in your life that so affects others that they create their own energy."

"Behold Archetenus the soul of every man, woman and child that you have murdered." Dozens of dark blue lights grew with intensity across the map. "Each person that you killed, had a purpose, had a destiny that you altered. And by altering their destinies you have altered the tapestry of The Great Ruler.

Archetenus started to shake as Miranda continued, "The Great Ruler put those beings here; you not only killed them but their future generations of offspring."

"What are the red lights?" Archetenus asked, wanting desperately to change the subject.

"They are the men, women and children that you have raped to prove your domination over all."

Suddenly Archetenus was terrified and he spun around and faced Miranda. "Who are you and who sees all that I have done?"

Miranda smiled, "You have said that you do not believe in The Great Ruler so you will not believe in me."

"That did not answer my question," Archetenus demanded.

"Do not demand of me; I am not of your world you have no power over me," Miranda said sternly. "In your world I am called many things, an Angel, a messenger, a guide. And to answer your second question, heaven sees all. There is no place that you can hide from The Great Ruler; He sees your actions, He knows your thoughts and He knows the voices that you listen to. And it is not His voice that you have been heeding."

Archetenus suddenly felt as if he was naked; to think that everything he was, had been exposed to heaven.

"The yellow lights are those poor souls who you injured and maimed but did not kill. The violet lights are every time you stole from others. The orange lights symbolize your deceptions." As Miranda spoke the map became a collage of bright lights.

"Have I done nothing good in this life?"

"The aqua lights, but you can hardly see them because of the others."

Archetenus walked slowly along the map of his life. "Are these choices I have made or choices I will make?"

"These are the paths of the choices you have made. I want you to walk to the end of this map," Miranda said.

Archetenus noticed that although there was a great deal of empty space at the end of the map all of his paths were pointing to the same dot. A dot that had a color he had never seen. "What is that dot? I have never seen that color before."

"You helped create that color," Miranda said. "It is the color of horror, the color of pain, the color of treachery. It is the color of hell."

Suddenly Archetenus' fear turned to rage. "If I am such a beast and you are an Angel why are you showing me these things?"

Miranda was instantly next to Archetenus, staring into his eyes as if she could read his soul. "Because you Archetenus are such a beast that you will do more harm to this world dead than alive. I am showing this to you to give you a chance to alter your course."

"And if I do not?" Archetenus asked defiantly.

"You will be dead by morning and you will know of hell more than that ghoulish light."

"So the Angel will kill me?" Archetenus asked challengingly.

"No the Angels have been protecting you. The Lion that you hear roaring every night is keeping the demons that hunt you away from your camp."

Now his eyes grew wide "Why?" asked Archetenus in amazement. Miranda did not answer him but stared into his soul.

"Vitomas? Is it because Vitomas is with me?"

"I told you that your destinies were not entwined. She is a light that we will not let you put out."

"What would you have me do?"

"Turn around, ride back that way you came." As soon as Miranda had uttered these words she was gone and Archetenus was awake and back at his campsite, although he found himself farther away from the fire and on the opposite side of the fire than his bedroll. Archetenus walked closer to the fire and stood over Vitomas, who was sleeping soundly. As he looked upon her, the beast in Archetenus arose. He knelt down near Vitomas but stopped when he heard Miranda's voice, as if she was whispering into his ear. "Thirteen levels, thirteen doors."

Archetenus quickly stood up and walked away from Vitomas. "Thirteen levels, thirteen doors, what does that mean?" Archetenus thought as he sat on his blanket. "What does any of this mean?"

"We have lost three men and two horses and not killed a single Gant," Sampson reported to Roch.

"Sergeant we will have our chance to battle with the Gants; we are close to the caves now," replied Roch as he led his men on another night march. Every night had been the same since they left Tadon, the screams, screams of hell coming from the forest as they kept riding westward. The only thing that differentiated the nights was whether Roch and his men suffered casualties.

They had been riding for about four hours when one of the soldiers yelled a warning. In an instant they were surrounded by Gants. These dark figures loomed as high as buildings. The Gants ran to the soldiers, grabbing them off their horses, and devouring the men. Roch yelled for his soldiers to run to the caves that were only a few hundred yards away.

Roch could hear his men screaming in agony as he rode towards the caves; he did not look back or consider helping them. After he entered the first cave; Roch looked behind him and realized that only a handful of his men had made it to safety. Roch ordered his men to dismount and to take battle positions. The soldiers dismounted and readied their bows. The cave was dark except for a few rays of starlight coming in through the entrance. Roch and his men were tense with anticipation but the fight did not come.

Sun light started to seep into the cave, allowing the soldiers to see their refuge for the first time. The cave was small with three passageways leading to different directions within the earth. There were piles of bones littered throughout the cave. One of Roch's men tripped over a huge skull and fell into a pile of bones causing a loud noise. Before the soldier could get up, movement was heard outside of the cave entrance.

Roch ordered his men to be quiet and to stand fast as the sound of heavy creatures walking, intensified. So focused were they on the sounds outside of the entrance that they did not hear death walking behind them. Suddenly a loud cracking sound came from their rear; turning Roch saw the shadow of a Gant against the wall of the passageway on the right. As the creature roared, Roch's men turned to do battle.

The giant creature entered the cave and grabbed the nearest soldier. To everyone's horror the Gant raised the soldier up to its mouth with ease and bit off the soldier's head. The Gant threw the lifeless body on the ground and moved towards the others.

Roch yelled at his men to shoot their arrows at the Gant's neck and heart. As the arrows pierced its throat and heart, the creature fell onto its knees clutching its throat; then it fell forward. Dead, the creature no longer posed a threat, so Roch yelled at his men to turn and to shoot their arrows at the Gant entering through the front entrance to the cave.

Their arrows pierced the second Gant in the heart. This creature too, fell dead. Roch and his men stood fast, prepared for another attack, but after twenty minutes Roch told his men to relax. They stripped jeweled belts off of the dead Gants. The soldiers pried the jewels out of the belts and put them into pouches and the pockets of their shirts. Roch then ordered them to search the passageways in teams of two.

Gala entered the front door of the cabin at midday. "I was careful that I was not being followed," she said as she took a seat at the table. Both Raul and Simon had drawn their swords when they heard Gala approaching the cabin, they now returned their swords to their sheaths and joined the women at the table.

"Sophie was particularly talkative this morning; I am sorry I am late," apologized Gala. "She took great pride in the fact that she was eavesdropping on conversations between Roch and Jonas, one of his men." As Gala spoke, Simon unfolded a large map and spread it out on top of the table.

"Sophie said the guards started looking for Vitomas the first evening she did not return to the castle; at that time they did not know that she had been in this cabin and thought she may have been hurt on one of her rides," Gala continued. "They first searched the castle grounds then expanded the search to the surrounding areas; which sounds true because they did not show up in Cana for three days after you left."

Annabelle filled everyone's coffee cups as Gala continued to talk. "Sophie said the soldiers searched the Kingdom of Stordt as far as the Tange Mines to the west and from the castle to the eastern boundaries of the kingdom. They rode south as far as Malga in the Kingdom of Puntd and north across the border into the Kingdom of Wetpr."

"They could not have come too far north because we did not hear about it," Simon remarked.

"Gala is there anything else you can think of?" Raul asked. "Any little detail might be important."

"Only that Sophie said the soldiers kept talking about the fact there were no signs or trails; they kept saying it was as if she vanished into the air. Sophie said that Roch even said Vitomas had just vanished."

"So did you find out for certain if Roch is looking for Vitomas?" Raul asked.

"He is not. According to Sophie he took fifty soldiers and headed west. She overheard Roch say he was going to get some manuscripts from that old monastery at Tadon."

Simon was studying the map while Gala was talking. "Raul if you wanted to leave this place without a trail what would you do?" asked Simon with a smile. Raul looked at the map for a moment then he smiled also.

"What are you two smiling at?" Annabelle asked anxiously.

"If Archetenus is as great a warrior as you say, he knows how to conceal a trail," replied Simon.

Raul pointed to the Lake of the Pors on the map. "He would want to leave this kingdom as soon as he could; Archetenus walked the horses in the water of the lake then south in the River Oja."

"Why not north along the river?" asked Gala.

"Because he would come too close to Roch's castle," Raul replied.

"Now to figure out where he would leave the river," Simon said as he studied the map.

"If Archetenus really cares about Vitomas as you say," Raul said as he looked at Annabelle. "He would not take her south of the Safer Mountains into the lands overrun by Hutas. If I were Archetenus I would stay on the river until I could cross over into the Kingdom of Ganz; I have traveled that way and there are few people until you reach Port Friada," said Raul.

"You do not think he would go north into the Kingdom of Zorta?" asked Annabelle as she studied the map.

"That is a possibility," said Simon. "But in that area where the three kingdoms meet there are bands of Rogetts."

"Would Archetenus know that?" asked Annabelle.

"From how the two of you describe Archetenus he is a smart and experienced warrior; he would know these things," replied Raul.

"Annabelle said Archetenus has been in love with Vitomas for a very long time. I am willing to bet he has a well thought out plan and was just waiting for the right opportunity," said Simon.

"Which he got if he followed her to this cabin, she was alone and off from the castle grounds," said Raul. "I wonder where he was hiding and how many times he may have followed her here."

"Raul, you could not have prevented this," Annabelle said. Raul looked at her but did not speak.

"Annabelle, we are going to be traveling in some pretty dangerous lands. Bands of Hutas and Rogetts travel in the lands east of the River Oja. You can't go any farther with us. I am going to send you back to Wetpr," Simon said.

"Simon, you can't, you promised," Annabelle said angrily. "You both promised I could help find her."

"That was when we thought she was in Roch's castle," Raul said. "Simon is right. You need to go home." Annabelle stared angrily at both Simon and Raul, tears started to well in her eyes.

"Honey it is just too dangerous, you have to go home," Simon said again.

Annabelle stood up and walked out of the cabin, slamming the door behind her.

Roch and Sampson walked into the passageway on the right, the one where the dead Gant had come from. They were about a quarter of a mile into the passageway when they heard screams coming from the other soldiers. Both men turned and ran back towards the center of the cave, moving as fast as they could. Before Roch and Sampson reached the cave the screams stopped.

Still in the passageway, they listened for any sound of movement. Soon they heard a crunching sound, someone or something was walking on the bones in the cave.

Rounding a corner, Roch peered into the cave. His eyes had long been accustomed to the darkness. Before him stood a giant Gant eating the remains of one of his soldiers. Roch backed up and leaned against the wall. "Our only hope is to get out of this cave," he thought.

Roch signaled to Sampson to go back down the passageway. They crept along the stone corridor trying not to make any noise. They did not know where the passageway led. The horses had run out of the cave while the soldiers were fighting with the Gants. Fear gripped Roch's heart, a feeling he was not accustomed to.

Roch and Sampson were silently moving through the passageway, which seemed to be going deeper underground as no light was entering through the rocks. The thick darkness slowed their process, preventing them from seeing where they were walking. As they inched their way along the cold stone they would hear the sounds of movement in the distance.

After what seemed like hours, Roch and Sampson saw a shaft of light coming from above. They hurried towards it and found a hole in the ceiling of the tunnel. They could see the doorway to their freedom but they could not reach it. They looked for something to stand on, when Sampson spied what looked like a wooden beam lying in the tunnel ahead.

Sampson could not drag the beam by himself so Roch attempted to help him but the size and weight of the beam was too much for them to budge. They decided to try to climb up the side of the tunnel walls but the walls were too steep and Roch and Sampson kept falling; which was creating noise.

Desperate, Roch decided to send a signal through the hole in the ceiling of the passageway. Roch hoped that some of his men were still alive and would see it. Roch and Sampson gathered rocks from the floor of the tunnel and threw them through the hole. After several minutes of throwing rocks, they heard a loud bellowing sound coming from outside of the hole. Suddenly the light was blocked by a huge ape-like head.

309

The passageway became dark as night with the Gant's head blocking out the sun light. Roch and Sampson backed up and ran from the escape hole. They ran down the passageway, in the opposite direction of the cave. Running as hard as they could in the darkness they tripped time and again over rocks and bones on the ground.

Finally collapsing from exhaustion on the floor of the tunnel, Roch and Sampson laid there for several minutes gasping for breath. Suddenly they felt the ground vibrate from the footsteps of the giant Gants. Both men jumped to their feet and continued down the passageway, not knowing what they would find at the end.

As they ran through the darkness, Roch and Sampson heard screaming coming from all around them. Running for their lives, they saw a ray of light in the tunnel ahead. Quickening their steps, they reached the end of the tunnel to find an opening large enough for them to crawl through.

Roch crawled through the hole first and turned to help Sampson. Roch grabbed Sampson's right hand and pulled him almost completely out of the hole when Sampson screamed and kept screaming as a Gant was pulling him back into the tunnel. Roch saw the look of terror in Sampson's eyes before he turned and ran from the caves.

Roch ran for his life, jumping boulders and fallen trees finally he came to the edge of a cliff that was overlooking the River Cheban. Turning Roch saw three Gants quickly approaching him. With no choice left, Roch jumped off the cliff and fell fifty feet to the water below.

Roch lost consciousness when he hit the water. He went under the water then popped back to the surface. The cold water revived him and he started to swim to the eastern shore; which was the same side of the river as the caves. Roch kept watching the shoreline for signs of movement. Suddenly he realized there were two Gants on the shoreline watching him; they seemed reluctant to enter the water. Roch turned and swam towards the western bank.

Swimming as hard as he could, Roch was trying to put distance between himself and the eastern shore. He was getting tired; the western shore was a distance away and the water was cold. Roch had always been a strong swimmer but he was getting weak and his muscles were starting to cramp.

Roch was feeling himself slipping under the water when he spied a sand bar about twenty yards to his right. Gathering the last of his strength Roch swam to the sand bar. Pulling himself onto the sand, Roch collapsed. He lay on the warm sand for some time; the heat of the sun warming his body and drying his clothes. As Roch was feeling his strength return, his thoughts went not to the men he had just lost or even to his own peril but to the treasure he did not find.

Angrily Roch sat up and watched the eastern shore. He had not seen any movement or Gants for several hours. Roch knew that Gants usually slept during the heat of the day. He needed to get back on the eastern shore to find his horse and any of his men who may have survived the attack. Around midday Roch saw a large tree limb floating down stream. He swam to the limb and climbed on top of it.

The river current was moving quickly because of the power of the Terga Falls, which was further up the river. Roch estimated it took him close to two hours to get to Zurlag; a village known for fishing and trading. This village sat on the shore of the Cheban River; once Roch swam to shore he was already in a busy section of the village.

Roch walked to a nearby stable, announced he was the King and demanded one of the man's horses. For just a fleeting moment Roch thought about returning to the caves to look for survivors but instead he rode east towards Taperia. Roch's mood fluctuated between anger at not getting his treasure and relief that once again he had cheated death.

Chapter XIX
Battles

"Gala we will be leaving soon," said Raul. "And I want to thank you for everything you have done for us. I fear for your safety here and want you to know you are welcome to return to Wetpr with Annabelle."

"Thank you Raul but my home is here. But I do appreciate your concern."

"The invitation is always open, our castle is in Salar," Raul said sincerely as he handed Gala a map showing the location of both the city and the castle. "I can never repay you for all that you have done."

"What is this?" Gala asked as she realized there was a second piece of paper with the map.

"It is a letter from me stating you are friends of the Royal Family of Wetpr. If you can cross the border show that to any of our soldiers and they will make sure you get to us." Raul reached into his pants pocket and pulled out a small pouch of gold coins, handing it to Gala.

"Find Vitomas and give her a good life; that will be payment enough," Gala said and did not take the pouch. Raul set the pouch on the table for her. Gala nodded towards the door. "Will they be alright?" she asked because they could hear Annabelle and Simon arguing outside.

"Annabelle will you listen to me?" Simon asked loudly. "The chances are great that we will run into Rogetts or Hutas, I cannot focus on battle if I am worrying about you; I love you too much."

"And I love you, I just cannot stand by and let something happen to you."

"And you want to come along to protect me?" Simon asked with a big smile.

Annabelle put her arms around Simon's neck and searched his eyes. "Please come back to me," she said and kissed him passionately on the lips. They kissed as if they would never see each other again. "You have my heart, my husband," Annabelle whispered.

"And you have mine," Simon said and kissed Annabelle again. "When you get home, tell Father and Mother everything that we have learned. Tell them we will head east towards Port Friada. And keep yourself busy working on our wedding so we can be married as soon as I come home. And don't be afraid to tell Mother what you want, it is our wedding."

"But Simon I don't know what I want, I never thought about such things. What do you want?"

"I just want to marry you," Simon said with a grin and kissed Annabelle again. "Perhaps we should just let Mother plan everything."

"I want to say goodbye to Raul and Gala before I leave," Annabelle said and they walked back inside the cabin.

Clouds of noxious gases rose from the defiled ground around Sporos' castle. The ground blackened with a tar only recognized in hell. Devoid of any life forms, the castle grounds announced the terror that awaited inside. The blackened stone walls stood ominously against the night sky.

The light of the moon allowed the Ruala warriors to see the open windows in the towers of the castle. The first Ruala who flew into the castle was carrying the Sanuri of Tabrul. He was followed by hundreds of Ruala warriors; some of whom carried their Shettee brothers.

The warriors had their orders; no one was to interfere with the Sanuri when he confronted Sporos and they were to search for The Box of Itifer. The Sanuri could feel the presence of evil in the castle. He walked down the old stone steps from the castle tower. There were no torches attached to the walls, so the Sanuri used the light emitted from the end of his staff to lead the Ruala and Shettee warriors into the bowels of the castle.

The stone stairway was old and narrow forcing the warriors to walk single file. Suddenly the Sanuri stopped and instantly the light of his staff was extinguished. Ahead of them, the reflection of torches danced on the stone walls. "Sanuri, let us in front," Thedes whispered into the Sanuri's ear. "You have to find Sporos."

The Sanuri moved to the side and the giant Shettee warrior leaped down to the landing below. Welding his sword in one hand and a battle axe in the other, Thedes landed directly in front of two Huta warriors. Revenge was his; Thedes fought with a fire that he had never felt before. He was killing the monsters that had destroyed his people.

There were few Huta warriors in the tower; for they never thought that anyone would dare attack them. The invaders quickly made their way to the fourth floor of the castle; this was the floor at the base of the tower steps. The Rualas and Shettees had the advantage of surprise and quickly overpowered the Hutas guarding this floor. But the sounds of battle soon alerted the Hutas on the floor below. The sound of a Huta horn rang out, a call to arms; and Huta forces swarmed the invading army.

The Hutas were a violent race of warriors. They butchered their own people if they were not strong enough. The Hutas did not tolerate infirmities or differences of any kind; not among their own tribe or others. Their hatred of all things burned within them; motivating the Hutas into an unstoppable force. But this night the remnants of civilizations that had been persecuted, imprisoned and murdered rose up against their oppressors with a passion that the Hutas could not overcome.

The Sanuri found Sporos on the first floor of the castle, sitting behind a desk in his war room. Sporos looked so very different from his youth. A tall and skinny man, he was now bald except for one long pony tail of dark hair which hung all the way down his back. He had a thin mustache and wore two golden earrings in each ear. Sporos was sitting calmly staring at the doorway as the Sanuri entered the room. "My old friend I wondered when you would visit me," Sporos said mockingly.

"Is there any of my old friend left inside of you?" asked the Sanuri. "Or did you sell everything to the demons?" The Sanuri walked up to Sporos' desk.

314

Sporos laughed, "Perhaps you are right there is none of your friend left."

With a note of sadness in his voice the Sanuri asked, "Why?"

Laughing Sporos replied, "Because the benefits are better on this side."

"It looks to me like you live the life of a recluse in a crumbling castle that is surrounded by the stench of hell," replied the Sanuri with disgust. "You used to enjoy life and people and now do you hide from them?"

"I despise them," snapped Sporos angrily. "Their weaknesses and their whining; always crying and complaining because someone isn't taking care of them or protecting them. This world is meant to be grabbed by the balls and that is what I have done. What I don't understand is how you have been able to put up with them all these years."

"They are the children of The Great Ruler and I help take care of them and protect them. And I do it out of love. You used to have a great deal of love in your heart Sporos, what happened to it?"

"You say you protect the children, well, I got sick of wiping their noses and Sanuri you will too. Join me; we could rule this world together."

"This world is not ours to rule Sporos. All those many years that we were friends, I never saw it in you. I don't know how I missed it."

"Missed what? What are you talking about?"

"Fear. Ultimately it is fears that make men call out to darkness. I never saw your fears. Perhaps if I had I could have helped you."

"Enough!" yelled Sporos as he pounded his fist on the desk.

"I did not see any mirrors as I walked through your castle; are you afraid to see the monster you have become?" asked the Sanuri as he walked closer to Sporos. "You know it is never too late, you can come back."

"And the great Sanuri is going to save me," replied Sporos mockingly as he stood up from behind his desk. "I do not think so."

"That is your choice," said the Sanuri and with these words the room filled with a blinding white light. The holiness of the light burned the skin of the demon. Sporos could not see the Sanuri but he could hear the Sanuri's commanding voice. "You have learned nothing you fool; the darkness of hell shall never conquer the Light of The Great Ruler." As Sporos strained his eyes to see his adversary through the intensity of the light; Sporos was suddenly thrown on the floor with such power that his breath was knocked out of him.

"Do you hide from me?" Sporos screamed in a sarcastic tone.

"I hide from no one, you have been long blinded by your hatred and greed. I am still standing before you."

Sporos tried to jump to his feet but an unseen force was weighing down on him, preventing him from moving. "Magic tricks my old friend," laughed Sporos. "I would have thought them beneath you." The Sanuri did not respond. "What, are you afraid to fight with me?" mocked Sporos. "Are you afraid to find out just how powerless you really are? The Great Ruler will not protect you. All these years you have served a master who does not care about you."

"And a demon is going to teach me about The Great Ruler? I cannot believe you can even utter his name. Tell me old friend, what master do you serve?"

"I serve no one," yelled Sporos as he tried to stand up a second time.

"You fell to darkness because you could not pass the holy tests. You could not rise above the demons. You could not conquer your fears," said the Sanuri. "You are here now because you failed at everything you spent your life training for. And what has it gotten you?" The Sanuri's voice was getting louder as he spoke. "I look around me and I do not see riches, or a splendid castle. I see no loved ones, or even signs of power. I see a frightened, broken man who turned to darkness to feel empowered."

316

Sporos screamed with rage. His screams surpassed the war room and filled the castle. His screams transcended the castle walls and echoed off the surrounding hills. His were the screams of the hell beasts that bellowed from below. His were the screams of the dark lords as they were being exposed. His were the screams from the hell dimensions as they withered before the holy light.

"Are those screams of defeat or are you summoning your army to save you?" asked the Sanuri sarcastically.

"You think you are so superior," said Sporos with a chuckle. "Your power is nothing compared to that of the dark world. You have been so brainwashed that you can't see what is before your eyes. There is a world here for the taking. And we have the power to take it."

"It is not my power that I put my faith in. Sporos I once loved you as a brother and a friend. I know that means nothing to you but I am curious when did you sell your soul and who was the demon that conquered you?"

Sporos smiled, "I will tell you only because I know it will bring you great pain. Remember all those hundreds of years ago when we were studying to become priests? And you and I decided we wanted more, we wanted to test ourselves as the ancients did; to see if we could stand against the darkness and to conquer it." The Sanuri did not respond.

"You and I studied the ancient rites of purity and ascension. We studied the quests of manhood and the initiation rites to becoming a warrior. And after all that studying we decided to go to the desert," Sporos said. "We fasted and we prayed. We saw illusions and had dreams and nightmares of all sorts. And the demons came to us; they attacked us, they challenged us and they seduced us."

"They seduced you Sporos," said the Sanuri sadly. "And the dreams only become nightmares when you let your fears take control."

"I watched you fight those thirteen demons and that looked like a nightmare to me," Sporos said mockingly. You fought them day and night. They pierced you and tore you to shreds, yet I will admit I admired you when I saw one of the demons try to flee the battle and you pulled him back into the fight. Twenty one days you fought with those demons, a fight you could only do alone. I saw you bloodied and outnumbered. And while you fought for your soul, you know what I did?" Sporos asked with a salacious grin. The Sanuri did not respond. "I danced my brother, I danced with those demons."

The Sanuri's heart was heavy as he listened to Sporos speak. "I fought for more than my soul," replied the Sanuri. "The quest was to expand the boundaries of my existence. I fought to save the souls of others; I fought to be more than my birthright. And tell me Sporos do you remember how that battle ended or were you too busy dancing?"

Sporos did not respond immediately. "You grew stronger and the demons grew weaker. You beat them all and when the battle was over both of your legs had been broken. I saw you try to walk and I called out that your body was broken and you answered, 'darkness cannot break me'. And slowly and with great pain you put one foot in front of the other and started to walk; and as you walked your body was healed."

"And you learned nothing from that?" asked the Sanuri. Sporos did not answer. "When we were in the desert did you resist the demons at all?"

"I saw your struggle and thought it was easier just to give in," replied Sporos with a moment of sincerity.

"So you are telling me that you had sold your soul before you even became a priest?" asked the Sanuri in horror.

"Yes," laughed Sporos.

"Then why become a priest?"

"Are you really asking me that?" Sporos asked mockingly. "Think of the advantages I had in obtaining everything I was asked to. Besides the demons think it a major blow in the battle to recruit the holy."

"And my pious friend, I hope you are not so naïve as to think I am the only one who was recruited. In fact I did some recruiting of my own," Sporos said then started to laugh hysterically.

"Sporos, you know it is never too late, you can come back to the light."

"My old friend, I have made my choices and I rather like the side I am on," replied Sporos. "So are we going to talk about old times all night or are we going to fight?" Sporos challenged.

Suddenly Sporos could feel himself floating through the air. "What are you doing?" growled the demon. "We are going to have a battle of old," replied the Sanuri as he dragged the demon through time and space. "In The Abyss."

Sporos cursed and growled and tried to free himself from the Sanuri's grasp as they traveled to The Abyss. "You do not think you can defeat me alone," screamed Sporos with rage.

"I am never alone; that was the point of the quest in the desert," replied the Sanuri. "But I guess you were too busy dancing to have understood that."

The Sanuri and Sporos wrestled for seven days and seven nights in the vast emptiness of The Abyss. Without weapons these two powerful beings tore at each other with all their strength. The Abyss was an ancient battle ground between the forces of good and evil, where the winner alone could escape the eternal darkness. No being except The Great Ruler Himself could help the combatants once they entered this arena. The darkness lit up with the energies that were emitted from the powerful blows of these two beings. They fought as men, they fought as immortals and the worlds shook from their fury.

Raul led his men southward along the River Oja then turned east at a point that would lead them into the Kingdom of Ganz. They traveled just south of Norta and the abandoned diamond mines. Raul sent two soldiers ahead to look for signs of a trail. Three hours later the soldiers met up with Raul and his troops.

"My Lord we found a trail heading east. There are two riders; it looks like one is leading the other. The rider in front is, considerably heavier than the rider following on the second horse. The trail looks old but we also found these," said the soldier as he handed Raul small pieces of robin egg blue material. "There were lots of them all along the trail."

Raul clutched the material in his hand and his face lit up in a broad smile. "That's my girl," he said out loud. Raul turned and proudly showed Simon the pieces of material, "That is the color of the skirt she was wearing at the cabin; she is leaving us a trail."

"So she must be smart and beautiful," said Simon as he smiled at his brother's happiness.

"Simon at least I know she is alive and we are on the right trail," said Raul in disbelief. "You know as well as I; the chances of us finding her in this wilderness if Archetenus really wanted to hide her."

The scouts guided the men eastward to the trail they had found. When Raul saw all of the tiny pieces of blue material dropped on the ground and bushes his heart began to race. He ordered his men to quicken their pace. Although they covered a great deal of territory, Raul was reluctant to stop and make camp.

"Raul, it is too dark to see the trail anymore and the men and horses need rest," Simon said. "We need to make camp now. Don't worry we will find her."

"I know, you are right," Raul said with a sigh. "I am just letting my emotions get the better of me. I just feel like we are so close now." They continued to travel a little farther until they found an area they felt they could defend if attacked.

"I doubled the guards," said Raul as he joined Simon at a camp fire. "I don't want any Hutas surprising us."

"Actually I am surprised we haven't seen any signs of Hutas or Rogetts, since they both travel this area," said Simon as he handed Raul a plate of food. Raul saw the look on Simon's face.

"Just go ahead and say it, we are both thinking it," Raul said with disgust.

"I know Archetenus doesn't want Roch to find him," said Simon angrily. "But what is he thinking not only traveling alone in this area but bringing a woman with him? Both the Rogetts and Hutas travel in packs; he isn't going to be able to defend her if they get attacked."

Annabelle entered the front door of the castle, as she walked across the foyer she heard Renya calling her name. Annabelle entered the dining room and saw her parents eating with Sudfad and Renya.

"My child please come in and join us," said Renya. Annabelle kissed her mother on the cheek and took a seat at the table.

"So tell us where are the others?" Sudfad asked.

"When we got to Cana we found out that Vitomas was missing. Everyone thinks that Archetenus stole her from the cabin after we left. Simon and Raul think they know which path Archetenus took so they are going after them and they made me come back."

"Wait Annabelle," Sudfad said as he interrupted her story. "Who is Archetenus and why do people believe Vitomas was stolen from the cabin?"

As they ate; Annabelle told them every detail of the events that had occurred on her journey to Cana. Sudfad, Renya, Laurel and Alexander listened intently to the bizarre story.

"That poor girl," Laurel said. "First Roch and now Archetenus, I hope the boys find her soon."

"Archetenus is a monster," Alexander said. "Vitomas is in great danger with him."

"I can't get past the part where Roch went treasure hunting instead of looking for his queen," Renya said.

"He doesn't care about her," Annabelle said. "He thought of Vitomas as a beautiful trophy that he owned."

As they finished their meal Sudfad asked Annabelle, "Did the boys ever tell you how Simon came to live with us?"

"No," replied Annabelle shyly.

"When they were about nine years old they used to meet at the river every morning and fight," said Sudfad.

"Why did they fight?" asked Annabelle.

Both Sudfad and Renya started to laugh, "Those two boys lived to fight, it was a sport to them," Sudfad said.

"It wasn't like they hated each other," Renya said. "They were friends."

"They were the same size with similar abilities and they just loved to challenge each other," Sudfad said. "Then one morning Simon didn't come to the river. So Raul walked several miles to Simon's home, which was in the countryside. When Raul got there he found the remnants of the house smoldering and Simon in the yard crying over his dead parents."

"Hutas?" Annabelle asked.

"No," Sudfad explained. "There had been an awful storm the night before and their house was struck by lightning. Simon was sleeping on the porch and able to escape. He ran back into the burning house and got his parents out but they did not survive."

"Simon got burned badly when he ran back into the house," Renya said as tear came to her eyes. "It still upsets me so."

"Even though Raul was just a boy he carried Simon home; all those miles," Sudfad said with obvious pride. "Simon required a great deal of medical treatment and was bound to bed for several weeks. Raul never left his side. The boys had been friends before this happened but they became so close afterwards. And of course we fell in love with Simon and adopted him immediately."

"Annabelle have you noticed how much alike they are?" Renya asked.

"I saw that more when we traveled," Annabelle replied. "But I have never seen two men care about each other so. When Gala told us that Vitomas was gone, Raul took it badly. Simon was so worried about him; I guess I'm not explaining it well. I could just see in their eyes how much they love each other."

The next two days Raul, Simon and their men traveled hard through the eastern tip of the Kingdom of Stordt and into the Kingdom of Ganz. Heavy rains had washed away some of the trail they were following but they continued to find the tiny strips of material from Vitomas' skirt to guide them on.

"We have traveled for three days and not seen another soul," Simon said. "That really does surprise me because I expected to run into Hutas by now."

"I know and believe me I am grateful," Raul said. "But something does not seem right about this. We haven't even seen any other tracks besides Archetenus and Vitomas."

"Why does that seem peculiar to you?"

"I have traveled this way before, it is isolated but there are usually signs of more life. I wonder if something is scaring things away."

"You mean like the Rogetts?"

"Yes and if they are in the area; we have to get to Vitomas first."

The second night after Roch escaped from the Gants he was lying next to a fire, thinking about what he would do differently when he returned to the caves for the scroll. Slowly he drifted off to sleep only to walk in the world of nightmares. Roch kept seeing the face of the Seer Miranda; she was scolding him for abandoning his men to the Gants. The face of this woman terrified Roch.

Roch suddenly sat up, awake and sweating. "I knew I had seen her before," Roch said out loud. "I have seen her in my dreams." Roch shook his head back and forth several times as if he could shake himself free of the images in his mind.

"But how could this be?" thought Roch as he pondered upon meeting a woman who had haunted him in his dreams for years. Afraid to return to sleep, Roch pulled his beloved map out of his pocket and studied it. "What if this scroll was The Ruby Scroll," thought Roch as the excitement surged through his body.

Roch started to fantasize about what he would do if he became immortal. "The first thing I will do is attack Wetpr and kill Sudfad," Roch said out loud. Hearing is own words, made the idea even more exciting to him. Roch continued to imagine the various ways he could kill his brother. Then the most satisfying thought consumed him. "I have heard his queen is of rare beauty; I will take her as my wife before his eyes, then I will kill him."

Several hours passed before exhaustion overtook Roch's fears and he fell asleep. Again Miranda came to him in his dreams but this time she did not speak. Roch kept seeing images of Miranda's face with those piercing eyes that saw through him and chilled his being.

Then suddenly her face was replaced with the image of The Lion. "Stop your quest for the scroll," said The Lion with a voice of authority. "Your destiny is not yet sealed, you can change it." Roch tossed and turned and called out in his sleep as these illusions haunted him.

The third morning of their journey since they were travelling southeast towards Port Friada, Raul and his men were riding across a large open area. They had been watching two people on horseback riding towards them. As the riders got closer Raul's heart leaped with excitement. "I think that is Vitomas," he said to Simon. Suddenly they heard a woman's voice cry out "Raul."

Raul stopped his men; turning to Simon he said, "This is my fight." Raul untied his shield from his saddle and rode forward until he was about ten feet from Archetenus. The two men stared at each other with hatred in their eyes. Raul looked at Vitomas then dismounted and pulled his sword out of the sheath.

Simon ordered the soldiers to stay back but he rode closer to the impending battle.

Archetenus dropped the reigns to Vitomas' horse and grabbed his shield. He too dismounted and pulled his sword from its sheath. The two men circled each other slowly, prepared to strike.

Vitomas jumped from her horse screaming, "Archetenus this is not what you promised." Vitomas ran towards the two warriors but Simon dismounted and grabbed Vitomas by the waist pulling her towards him.

Vitomas struggled to free herself of Simon's grasp until he whispered into her ear, "If you love him do not distract him." Vitomas stopped struggling and turned and looked up into Simon's face; that was when he realized how truly beautiful she was.

Archetenus looked at Vitomas and thrust his sword into the ground. "I did not come here to fight," he said angrily. "Although my heart wants to kill you." Raul did not respond and he did not lower his sword. Archetenus looked again at Vitomas and stepped towards Raul, "This woman loves you and if you hurt her I will come back and kill you."

Before Raul could respond a loud war cry pierced the air, looking to the south they saw a Huta war party coming at them at great speed. Simon yelled, "Hutas" and the soldiers charged the advancing Hutas which were quickly upon Archetenus and Raul.

As Raul used his shield to block a blow from a battle axe wielded by a Huta on horseback, he yelled, "Simon." Simon responded, "I have her." Simon quickly pushed Vitomas behind him and pulled his sword.

Several Huta warriors were riding towards Archetenus and Raul simultaneously. Archetenus grabbed a warrior off his horse and threw him to the ground; then he thrust his sword into the man's chest. He pulled the sword out of the Huta and with a continuous motion swung it high and to his left slicing another Huta across the stomach.

At the same time Raul was fighting with two Hutas on the ground. One Huta was in front of Raul and the other at his back. Raul swung his sword and disarmed the Huta in front of him then quickly grabbed that Huta and used him as a shield. Raul turned to face the Huta behind him just as that man thrust his sword into the human shield. Before the second Huta could withdraw his sword Raul ran his sword through the man's throat.

Raul heard Simon yelling his name; when Raul looked up he saw Simon on the ground fighting with a Huta and two other Hutas running towards Vitomas. "Archetenus!" yelled Raul. "Vitomas."

Archetenus looked up as he was breaking the neck of a Huta warrior and saw Raul running towards the two Hutas who were within feet of Vitomas. Raul tackled the Huta closest to her and thrust a dagger into the man's back. Archetenus swung his sword and hit the second Huta in the small of the back, causing him to drop to his knees. Archetenus took a second swing and cut the man's head off.

Simon was back on his feet and the three men made a triangular formation around Vitomas as it was apparent that many of the Hutas had centered their attention on her. Simon blocked a spear with a shield he took off a dead Huta, pulling the spear out of the shield he threw it and killed a Huta riding towards him. The bloody and vicious battle ended as quickly as it started. Raul's men outnumbered the Hutas and killed them all.

Raul yelled for several of the men to check the bodies of their attackers to ensure they were dead. He ordered the others to tend to each other's wounds and to report back to him. Raul turned and looked at Vitomas who was looking at him and crying. Vitomas flew into Raul's arms and kissed him.

"I knew you would come for me," she whispered into his ear.

"Did he hurt you?"

"No."

Raul then turned to Archetenus as he did not trust him. Archetenus was standing but a few feet away watching them. "I told her if she could not find it in her heart to love me I would bring her to you; I have my answer," said Archetenus with his heart sinking.

Raul walked towards Archetenus and said, "Thank you."

"Where will you go now Archetenus?" Vitomas asked.

He smiled and said "I have heard that Port Friada is a good place to start over." All of the men were covered in the blood of combat; as Archetenus spoke Vitomas realized he was bleeding from wounds to his chest.

"You are injured," said Vitomas.

"It is nothing," replied Archetenus as he walked towards his horse.

"There may be more Hutas in the area you are welcome to ride with us," Raul said. Archetenus did not respond. "Archetenus, Roch knows you took her but he has stopped searching." Archetenus turned and looked at Raul and nodded to him before mounting his horse and riding towards Port Friada.

Raul turned to Simon, "Vitomas this is my brother Simon and soon to be Annabelle's husband."

Vitomas squealed with delight and reached up and gave Simon a hug. As she pressed her body against Simon's, Vitomas felt something warm and sticky. She looked down at her blouse and saw that it was drenched in blood. Vitomas quickly looked at Simon's shirt; and saw that the entire right side of his shirt under his arm was wet with blood and the blood was spreading to the front of the shirt. "Raul," screamed Vitomas. "He is hurt." Vitomas grabbed Simon, "Simon sit down and open your shirt," Vitomas said as she helped lower him to the ground.

"Raul I need some water and do you have a physician's bag?" yelled Vitomas as she started tearing strips of material off from her underskirts.

Exhausted and bloodied the Sanuri left Sporos to endure eternity in The Abyss. A pang of sorrow surged through the Sanuri's heart as he thought of the man Sporos could have been. "To lose a friend to such darkness," thought the Sanuri. "Is a horror I hope to never again experience."

When the Sanuri returned to Sporos' castle he found that the Rualas and Shettees had defeated the army of Hutas that protected the demon Sporos.

Many of the warriors were wounded and the most seriously injured had already been flown back to the Ice Caves; as the remaining warriors waited for the Sanuri's return.

"I am sorry I was gone so long," the Sanuri said wearily as a large group of warriors gathered in the huge front entrance of the castle. "How many warriors did you lose?"

"The Great Ruler was with us," said Prince Hadar, one of Ibula's older brothers. "We lost two, but many are wounded."

Thedes stepped forward to the Sanuri, "This battle was an honor for our people; the Shettee sword is always at your command." The Sanuri smiled and bowed to Thedes. When the Sanuri bowed Ibula saw the blood on this robe and ran to him, "You are hurt, we need to get you back to the caves."

"First, did you find The Box of Itifer?" asked the Sanuri weakly.

A Ruala warrior stepped forward; he was holding a small gilded chest which he handed to the Sanuri. The Sanuri did not take the chest from the warrior but merely opened it and saw The Box of Itifer undamaged. The Sanuri smiled then he looked at the faces of the Ruala and Shettee warriors who surrounded him. All of them had sustained some types of wounds and they were weary from battle.

"I don't know if you fully understand the significance of your deeds. You few, stood before the entire world and protected them from horrors you cannot even imagine. Be proud, you walked where others would not go. You my brave warriors and honored friends, you sent the demons back to hell."

"Raul he is losing a lot of blood," cried Vitomas as she was pressing material from her underskirts against the gushing gash on Simon's side. Raul handed Simon a bottle of whiskey and said, "You know what I have to do, drink this to kill the pain."

Simon grabbed the whiskey and took a long drink. "Annabelle is going to be so mad at me," Simon said with a grin as he watched Vitomas try to stop his bleeding. Raul had a couple of his men quickly build a fire.

"Raul, cut more off my underskirt," said Vitomas frantically.

Raul looked at both of Vitomas' hands that were pressing against Simon's wound. Raul could see the blood oozing through the material and through Vitomas' fingers and running down her hands. Raul pulled up the side of Vitomas' tattered blue skirt and cut some large pieces of material with his dagger. He folded the material into large squares and handed them to her.

Vitomas replaced the cloths and said anxiously, "Everything I am wearing is so dirty, we should have clean cloths."

Raul did not respond to her comment but spoke to Simon. "Simon keep drinking, I am heating the sword now."

"Raul perhaps Simon should lay down, he is getting awfully pale," Vitomas said.

Raul quickly grabbed a blanket that was tied to his saddle and unrolled it on the ground near Simon. "I am alright," said Simon as he tried to stand but suddenly Simon's legs started to collapse and both Raul and Vitomas caught him and lowered Simon onto the blanket. Vitomas tore off more of her underskirt and pressed it tightly against Simon's wound. Simon looked at the fear on Vitomas' face and said, "You know Annabelle never stops talking of you." Simon tried to force a smile.

Vitomas looked into Simons' eyes and started to cry. "Simon I am so sorry that you got hurt protecting me." Then she leaned over Simon and kissed him on the forehead.

"Raul your girl just kissed me," Simon called out, jokingly. Raul stood up from the fire and walked towards Simon with the heated sword. Vitomas moved to Simons' other side and grasped both of his hands.

"Simon I will not leave you," Vitomas whispered as she tried to stare into Simon's eyes and not watch Raul as he put the searing sword against Simon's skin.

Simon screamed in pain as Raul cauterized the wound, then Simon lost consciousness. The smell of burnt flesh pierced their noses. Vitomas was stroking Simon's hair and crying. Raul stood up and walked around Simon to Vitomas. Raul took her hand and pulled Vitomas up to a standing position then pulled her against him and hugged Vitomas tightly. "It is not your fault," Raul whispered and kissed her hair.

329

As Vitomas was putting her arms around Raul's neck she saw blood running down his right arm. Vitomas quickly pulled away from Raul, "You are bleeding also," Vitomas said as she tore his sleeve; exposing the large gash on his bicep.

"Raul, I don't think I can burn you," Vitomas said between tears. She tore more material from her underskirts and pressed it against Raul's wound. Raul called to one of the soldiers and handed him the sword. As the sword was being reheated, Vitomas said, "Raul no one has ever protected me before, ever; and now you and Simon are both hurt." Vitomas was crying as she held the cloth against Raul's arm. "I am so sorry to bring this upon you."

Raul took one of Vitomas' hands off from his wound and kissed the back of it, then turned her hand over and kissed her palm. "My love, we are all alive and going home." Vitomas moved to Raul's other side as the soldier walked over with the heated sword; her heart cried as the metal of the sword was put to Raul's flesh.

A second soldier approached as Raul's arm was being cauterized. "My Lord, Tegman and Jess are both dead, seventeen others have wounds of varying sorts."

Sadness gripped Raul as he stood up and walked towards the soldier. "Take their personal items that I may return them to their families; and bury them." Raul turned around and saw Vitomas sitting next to Simon, holding his hand.

"Do you think he will be alright?" Vitomas asked as Raul knelt down next to her.

"He is a strong man with much to live for," said Raul in a hoarse whisper. "I certainly hope so." Raul stared at Simon for several moments then turned and looked at Vitomas, "We cannot stay here tonight; this place is too open and hard to defend."

"But what about Simon, he should not be moved," Vitomas replied fearfully.

"Do you think you can hold him on a horse if I lead it?"

"Yes, but we must ride Raven, he will not let one of your soldiers ride him and he is strong enough to carry us both. I know because I carried you on him," Vitomas said with a slight smile.

After the dead were buried and the wounded cared for; Raul helped Vitomas mount her horse. Three soldiers put Simon, who was still unconscious, on Raven in a sitting position in front of Vitomas. She put her arms around Simon's waist and held on to him tightly.

The journey home began.

Chapter XX
Hauntings

Archetenus only rode west for a short time before he stopped to tend to his wound. Archetenus made a fire and heated one of his daggers. He pulled a bottle of whiskey out of one of his saddle bags and took off his leather vest and his shirt. A Huta spear had sliced his left shoulder. Archetenus built the fire near a large boulder; he now sat down, leaning his back against the boulder.

Archetenus took the dagger from the fire and pressed it firmly against his wound. Archetenus yelled out, the pain was excruciating but he managed to continue to press the hot blade against his wound until the bleeding stopped. After Archetenus was sure that he had cauterized his wound he dropped the dagger on the ground and leaned his head back against the boulder. Sweat poured down Archetenus' face. The trees around him started to spin, then everything went dark.

Raul and his men moved slowly that morning because of the injured soldiers. Raul rode on Vitomas' left side and Lieutenant Marcus rode closely on her right. Raul and Marcus stayed close to Vitomas in case she had difficulty keeping Simon on the horse. Simon was still unconscious and heavy for Vitomas to hold.

But Vitomas did not complain; she was so grateful to have been rescued and reunited with Raul that she could not hold back the tears. But Vitomas' tears were a mixture of happiness and sadness because of the injuries that Simon and some of the other men had received in their battle with the Hutas.

Raul and Vitomas kept looking at each other and smiling but they spoke little. They had so very much to talk about but this was not the time, not in front of the soldiers and not with Simon in such a precarious condition.

The morning sun woke Roch. He sat up feeling as exhausted as he did when he went to sleep; Roch started to search through the pouches of food he had stolen from some peasants. As Roch started to tear apart a loaf of bread he was filled with terror. In the morning light Roch could see the prints of a great lion that had walked around his campsite.

It was The Lion in his dreams that terrified Roch, not the normal cats that prowled the night. Convinced that the paw prints were connected to his nightmares; Roch quickly saddled his horse and headed towards Taperia at a full run.

Renya and Laurel kept Annabelle busy with errands partially to keep her from worrying about Simon. Renya called the best dress makers in the city to the castle as well as carpenters, painters and a long list of others. Since they did not know when Simon, Raul and Vitomas would return to the castle; Renya and Laurel worked late into every night with preparations for the weddings and for the new homes for the couples.

"Sudfad and I decided to give the eastern wing of the castle to Annabelle and Simon and the western wing to Raul and Vitomas, there is plenty of room for grandbabies," said Renya as she and Laurel worked on Annabelle's veil.

"That is so gracious of you."

Renya laughed, "Oh Laurel you know what we are doing; Sudfad will give them land also but wouldn't you rather have them living in the castle with us?" Both the women laughed.

"Renya I will tell you I could not be happier that Annabelle fell in love with Simon. Do not tell anyone what I am about to tell you," continued Laurel in hushed voice. "But as much as I love Vitomas; when I first met Raul I thought he would make a wonderful husband for Annabelle but that idea ended soon after I saw the two of them together," said Laurel and laughed. "Raul and Annabelle act like they have been brother and sister all their lives."

"I did notice that right away. It is as if The Great Ruler brought us all together as a family; and I will tell you that is an answer to my prayers."

"What do you mean?"

"When the boys were young they were so wild and mischievous that the castle was always filled with laughter and people; but they have grown into young men. We understood that Raul had to find his own way in this world but when he left it was like a death had occurred."

"Raul told us he feared he hurt you and Sudfad greatly."

"Simon is so thoughtful and he tried to do extra things with us; but he too was affected," said Renya reflectively, then she started to laugh. "When Raul and Simon are together they bring out the craziness in each other and I am afraid that Annabelle and Vitomas will have their hands full."

Roch stopped at a farm house in the middle of the afternoon. A young woman walked out of the door and onto the porch. "Do you need help?" the woman asked as she was shielding the bright sun from her eyes.

"I need a fresh horse and some food and water," Roch said as he dismounted.

"You are certainly welcome to food and water but I am afraid my husband has our only horse and he is in Zurlag."

"So you are alone here?" Roch asked as he entered the small farmhouse. Roch saw that there was a baby in a cradle that was setting in the kitchen. The house was small but clean and organized. There were several water pitchers in the kitchen that contained large bouquets of flowers.

"Please have a seat," said the woman as she pulled a chair out from the kitchen table. "I will get you some food."

"What is your name?" Roch asked as the woman put a platter with roasted chicken and a bowl of hard boiled eggs on the table.

"My name is Noreen," she said then set a loaf of bread and a plate and eating utensils in front of Roch.

Noreen was a beautiful young woman with long auburn hair and large hazel eyes. Roch watched Noreen as she moved around the kitchen. He guessed her age at perhaps eighteen.

"When do you expect your husband back?" Roch asked as he hungrily devoured the food in front of him.

"Not for another two days," Noreen replied as she filled Roch's cup with coffee.

"Is there anyone else here?" Roch asked as he continued to stare at Noreen.

"No just me and baby Jacob," Noreen said and nodded towards the infant in the cradle. Noreen turned and walked over to the hearth, where she was cooking a kettle of stew.

Roch wiped the grease from his mouth on the dirty sleeve of his shirt. He had not had a woman in several weeks and this opportunity was too great for him to resist.

Roch got up from his chair and walked up behind Noreen. Roch grabbed Noreen by her shoulders and quickly spun her around so that she was facing him. Roch grabbed the back of Noreen's head with his left hand and put his right arm around her waist. He held Noreen tightly as she tried to struggle.

Roch looked at her face for a moment and smiled. Seeing the fear in the eyes of his victims always excited Roch. He bent down to kiss Noreen on the lips then suddenly screamed and let go of her. Roch took three steps backward staring at Noreen as if he had seen a ghost. But it was not a ghost that was staring at Roch; it was the face of Miranda with those piercing steel gray eyes.

"Roch leave this place at once," Miranda said in a powerful voice.

Roch fell backwards into the table, then tripped over the chair that he had been sitting on. Roch ran out of the house and jumped on his horse, quickly riding away from the farm house.

After Roch left, Noreen ran to the front door and bolted it, then she did the same to the back door. Noreen closed all of the shutters on the windows and bolted them. Then she picked up baby Jacob and sat down on the floor and cried. As Noreen rocked back and forth and sobbed, she saw something out of the corner of her eye. There on the floor next to the chair that Roch had tripped over was a ring. Noreen reached over and picked the ring up. It had a silver band with a large ruby stone. The silver band was wide and decorated with unusual markings.

After Vitomas helped to clean and bandage the wounds of several of the soldiers she returned to the campsite that Raul had set up for them. Raul and his men made several campsites, each in an area that afforded them some sort of protection from attack. Raul made his camp for just Simon, Vitomas and himself.

"The sun is starting to set, I am glad you returned before it got dark," Raul said. Simon was still unconscious and Raul had not left his side.

"The men that I helped with, all had minor wounds, none as serious as Simon's," Vitomas said as she reached over and put the palm of her hand on Simon's forehead. Raul kept putting wood on the fire to keep Simon warm from the evening's chill. Raul picked up a blanket and put it around his shoulders and arms. He enveloped Vitomas with his arms and the blanket as she now sat between his legs, leaning tightly against him. They sat in silence for several moments; each watching Simon sleep.

"Don't ever let go of me again," Vitomas whispered.

Raul kissed the top of her head, "I promise I never will." They sat long into the night watching over Simon and taking comfort in each other's presence.

That night Roch huddled over his fire trying to stay warm. A fierce wind was blowing up a storm. Roch felt fortunate that he had found a cave for shelter. The cave was just large enough for Roch and his horse. Roch pulled the map out of his shirt pocket and studied it as was his ritual. He was studying the symbols to determine a more direct route to his treasure.

As Roch held the map he noticed that his ring was gone. "What the hell!" he exclaimed loudly and stood up. Roch searched the small cave, then he searched his saddle, blanket and bags. But he did not find it. Roch had worn that ring since he was a boy. Sophie said she found it when she was cleaning his father's room. Once Roch put the ring on he never took it off. He sat down again by the fire and tried to remember the last time that he saw the ring. He decided that he had either lost the ring at the Caves of Muldun or at the farm house and either way he was never going back for it.

Roch returned his attention to his beloved map. As he looked at the map the symbols started to move and to dance on the piece of old leather. Roch rubbed his eyes several times but the symbols still moved. "I must be too tired," thought Roch and started to fold the map. Suddenly he jumped into the air, dropping the map near the fire.

"Who is there?" yelled Roch as he drew his sword. He saw no movement. "Show yourself," he ordered, still no movement. Roch started to return his sword to its sheath when he heard his name called again. Roch crouched down and stared into the darkness outside of the cave. "Show yourself," he yelled again. Roch walked out of the cave into the storm and searched the immediate area. He returned to the cave soaked from the rain.

"It must be the wind that I am hearing," thought Roch as he sat down by the fire. Roch put the map back into the silk pouch that he kept it in. He removed his wet clothes and laid them by the fire to dry. Then he lay down to sleep.

Sleep came quickly to Roch but once again he tossed and turned all night, at times yelling into the darkness of the cave. Roch yelled so loudly that he woke himself up. Shaking and sweating Roch sat up and put more wood on the fire. "What was I dreaming?" Roch asked out loud when he suddenly jumped back from the fire.

"There it is, that is the face in my dream," yelled Roch out loud. But the face did not disappear. Roch did not know if he was dreaming or awake as he looked into the fire and saw an image of a man, a tall thin man, bald except for a dark ponytail down his back. The man had a thin mustache and was wearing two golden ring earrings in each ear.

When Archetenus awoke it was nightfall. His fire was all but out and his left shoulder caused him considerable pain. Anticipating that he would pass out after cauterizing his wound, Archetenus had stacked some wood near the fire. He now grabbed a branch and stirred the ashes causing a few flames to rise up. Then Archetenus placed more dry wood on the fire and some dry plants he had found; soon the fire was blazing again. Archetenus grabbed the bottle of whiskey that was next to him and took a long drink.

Archetenus had previously unsaddled his horse and now he reached for his saddlebags which he had placed close to the boulder. Archetenus reached into one of the bags and pulled out three biscuits that Vitomas had made that morning. As soon as Archetenus took a bite from the first biscuit he thought about her.

Archetenus became filled with both anger and sadness when he remembered the way Vitomas looked at Raul. That was how Archetenus wanted her to look at him. Archetenus took another long drink from his whiskey bottle. He missed her company; it seemed so quiet.

Archetenus finished eating the biscuits and drank more from his bottle of whiskey. Then he thought about Miranda and the dreams he had. Archetenus remembered Miranda saying that the Angels were protecting him because he had Vitomas with him. Archetenus was becoming drunk and he was already light headed because of his wound. "What was it she said they were protecting me from?" Archetenus was trying to remember her words. After several moments the answer came to him; Miranda said the Angels were protecting him from the demons that hunted him.

"Angel," Archetenus called out. "I want to talk with you." Archetenus looked around the campsite but saw nothing out of the ordinary. "Hell you haunt my dreams when I don't want to talk to you. Why can't you come when I do?" he yelled into the darkness. Archetenus took another drink from his bottle. "Hell she probably wasn't real anyways," he said out loud and laid his head back against the boulder.

"Archetenus you sound like you're disappointed you haven't seen me," Miranda said sarcastically.

Archetenus' head shot up and he smiled, a drunken smile, when he saw Miranda standing on the other side of the campfire. Miranda looked as she had the night she showed him the map. Her long dark hair blowing in the night breeze and wearing a blue dress.

"I can't remember what you told me your name is," Archetenus said.

"I didn't tell you my real name I told you to call me Miranda."

"Miranda did I get an aqua light today?"

Miranda smiled, "Yes, but you still must change the path you are on."

"Miranda are you real or am I crazy?" Archetenus was slurring his words.

"You are crazy and I am real," she said still smiling.

"Miranda did you see them, Vitomas and her prince?" Miranda did not answer. "They looked so in love, that is what I wanted," Archetenus said as he started to swing his head back and forth.

"Archetenus if you want to be loved you have to learn to love others."

"I loved her," he growled.

"No, you were obsessed with a fantasy, an illusion. You made up a world in your mind and expected her to know what role you wanted her to play. Then you became enraged when she did not understand. That is very different from loving someone."

"Miranda do you hate me?" Archetenus was so drunk now he could barely form his words.

"I do not hate you Archetenus."

"Good." He said and laid his head back against the boulder for a moment. "You said you were protecting me from the demons that hunted me. What demons and why are they hunting me?"

"You saw some of the demons at that cave when you were with the Sanuri. Roch paid a witch to curse you. But the witch was not powerful enough to control the demons she brought out of hell, now they walk in this world."

"Did that witch call forth the demons at the Wall of Dorath?"

"No, a power much greater than you will ever realize called forth those demons."

"Why? They killed my men."

"Archetenus you are a threat to Roch and there are those who would protect him."

"The other soldiers?"

"No, Roch is not in this world as other men, those who created him have a purpose for him."

"Those who created him? I don't understand."

"I have told you enough this night."

"Miranda don't go. Will you stay with me?" Archetenus said then his head fell back onto the boulder as he lost consciousness."

When Vitomas awoke she was wrapped in a blanket and lying on the ground. As soon as she opened her eyes she heard Raul's and Simon's voices. Her heart leaped, knowing Simon was still alive. Raul was helping Simon to a sitting position, Vitomas went to them. The first thing she did was to check Simon's wound. "Thank The Great Ruler it's not bleeding," Vitomas said as she knelt next to Simon and felt his forehead and cheeks. "You don't seem to have a fever, which is good." Then Vitomas softly took Simon's head in both of her hands and kissed him on the forehead.

"I'll say you are the prettiest nurse we have ever had in the field," Simon said as he weakly squeezed Vitomas' hand. "You are much prettier than Raul." Simon tried to laugh but instead winced in pain.

"I wish we had something to give you for your pain," Vitomas said sympathetically. "In Cana there is a wonderful healer, I wish we could take you to her."

"Are you talking about Gala?" Simon asked.

"Yes," Vitomas said with surprise. "Did Raul tell you of her?"

"Yes but she also helped us as we searched for you."

"Oh Simon, I fear she is in great danger for her kindness."

"Raul asked her to come to Wetpr but she wanted to remain in Cana."

Raul was stoking the fire. Vitomas took the blanket that she and Raul had shared and gently put it around Simon's shoulders to protect him from the damp morning air. "Raul he is very weak, he will need something to lean against if he remains sitting." Vitomas held on to Simon as Raul put a saddle behind Simon for support.

"Raul do you want me to help with the food?" Vitomas asked as she worried about Simon's condition.

"No, you just stay with Simon, I will get it."

"He is actually a very good cook," Simon said trying to smile.

"Simon you are shivering; would it hurt you if I lean against you to keep you warm?" Vitomas asked.

"I don't know, will my brother think I am trying to steal his girl?" Simon said in a louder voice for Raul to hear.

Raul laughed. "Vitomas make sure you hold on to him from his good side; I will have some coffee for him soon."

"I know Honey," Vitomas replied to Raul, as she snuggled against Simon on his uninjured side. "Simon tell me if I hurt you," Vitomas said as she was adjusting the blankets around him. Suddenly Vitomas felt Simon go limp in her arms. "Raul he is unconscious," Vitomas said anxiously as she checked his breathing and his wound again.

Simon regained consciousness on and off during both that day and night. Vitomas and Raul made Simon drink water and eat, when he was awake. Between them they had only three blankets. Two blankets they put over Simon, while Raul and Vitomas huddled together under one. Raul held Vitomas as she slept in his arms. The relief that he felt to have found her alive was sullied by his concern for Simon.

A cold wind started to stir the flames of the fire. Raul got up and put more logs on the fire, then he walked over and checked on Simon.

As Raul knelt over his brother the hair on the back of his neck started to rise. Something was not right. Raul grabbed Simon's sword which was lying next to him and stood up. Raul knew they were all exposed by the light of the campfire.

"Raul," Vitomas said groggily as she started to sit up. Raul quickly went to her side and put his fingers against her lips.

"I think we are being watched," he whispered. Before Raul and Vitomas fell asleep, Raul took off his weapons and placed them next to their blanket. Now Raul grabbed one of the daggers and slipped it into his belt, then he handed a second dagger to Vitomas. "Go near Simon, I am going to look around."

Raul slipped into the darkness of the night. Vitomas put the blanket over her shoulders and grabbed Raul's sword that he left on the ground. Vitomas walked over to Simon and sat down next to him, placing the sword on the ground in between them. Trying not to be seen, Vitomas took both the sword and the dagger out of their sheaths.

As Vitomas watched over Simon, she strained to hear the sounds of the night. It was then that Vitomas realized how incredibly quiet it was. She did not hear the normal birds of the night or even insects. It was as if the world was dead. The only sounds that Vitomas could hear was Simon's breathing and the beating of her own heart.

Raul crept through the dark forest. He was aware that whoever had been watching them, saw him leave the ring of light made by the campfire and was probably looking for him. Like Vitomas, Raul noticed how quiet the forest had become. He stopped now and listened; being a highly skilled warrior, Raul's senses were keen and alert.

There was a strangeness to the night air, almost like it was thickening. And there was something else about the heavy air which made the hair stand up on the back of Raul's neck. He stood motionless for several moments then he moved to the left to alter his course.

Raul walked an entire circle around their campsite without finding anyone. At times he would peek through the trees to make sure Vitomas and Simon were safe.

Just as Raul was about to return to their camp, he sensed a presence ahead of him. Stealthily Raul crept forward, prepared for attack. Suddenly he was overwhelmed with an intense putrid smell that made his eyes water. Raul was careful where he placed his steps but as he lowered his left foot to the ground it was immersed in a sticky, tar-like substance.

Raul quickly pulled his leg back, causing him to lose his balance. Raul started to fall to his right; as he reached out to balance himself he grasped something that felt like an arm. Raul jumped back but nothing came at him. In the darkness of the forest it appeared that there were dark forms lying on the ground; but he heard no signs of life.

Raul quickly returned to the campsite and grabbed the Horn of Cass, which Wetprian troops used to communicate. He blew three short breaths into the horn; within moments dozens of soldiers were running into his campsite.

"Markus, double the guards I believe we have intruders," Raul ordered. "Six of you stay with Vitomas and Simon and the rest come with me." Raul picked up a log from the fire to use as a torch and led the men into the forest.

"What on earth are they?" one of the soldiers asked as he covered his nose and mouth to keep from breathing in the putrid air.

"I think they're demons," another soldier said, who was kneeling down next to one of the dead Zendoti. "Look at their faces, they're eaten away."

"I stepped in something sticky, I wonder if that was their blood," Raul said as he illuminated the ground with his torch. "What I am really wondering is what killed them."

"Well, they haven't been dead long," said the soldier who was kneeling down. "Their bodies aren't cold."

"I felt something watching us and entered the forest," Raul explained. "I didn't hear anything and I mean anything; it was like all of the forest sounds had stopped. There were no sounds of fighting."

Raul and his men returned to their campsites, no one slept that night except for the wounded soldiers. As soon as the sun started to rise, soldiers went into the forest and found more dead Zendoti, dozens of them.

"My Lord, our campsites were surrounded with those creatures," Markus reported to Raul. "But there are no signs of a struggle. I don't know who killed those beasts but I would sure like to thank them."

"There's no logical cause for their deaths," Raul said. "I'm beginning to think we have guardian Angels."

The Sanuri stayed at the Ice Caves for several days as he healed from the wounds he received in his battle with the demon Sporos. The Sanuri was pleased and impressed at how the Shettees and Rualas had blended two such different cultures. Both tribes seemed intrigued with learning the ways of the other. And both races seemed stronger as a result of their coexistence. Now that the two races were starting to intermarry, the Sanuri was looking forward to see what this new species would be like.

The third day that the Sanuri was at the Ice Caves, the Ruala warriors returned from the Caves of Muldun and told the Sanuri all that had happened to Roch and his men. "He will be the death of so many more if he stays on the path he is on," said the Sanuri about Roch.

"Can you not stop him?" asked one of the Rualas.

"Roch still has choices he must make," replied the Sanuri without further explanation.

"But he is such an evil man," said another Ruala warrior. "I don't understand why you can't destroy him or imprison him in The Great Abyss."

"I am just an emissary of The Great Ruler, I get information as He chooses to share it with me," said the Sanuri. "I cannot explain the purpose Roch has here but I do know that he is connected to a great evil. And that he has a role here that is yet to be played out."

When the Sanuri had healed, the Rualas and Shettees asked him to stay on with them. The Sanuri loved them as his children and a part of him wanted to stay at the Ice Caves but his work was calling to him. The night before the Sanuri left, the Rualas and Shettees held a feast for him in the Hall of Light. There was music and dancing and delicacies served by both cultures.

Many of the Shettees had questions of him about The Great Ruler as they had not heard of him before coming to the Ice Caves. The entire hall grew quiet as the Sanuri answered their questions and shared the teachings of The Great Ruler. At the end of the feast the Sanuri spoke to Manu, the Chief of the Grand Council and the King of the Ruala people.

The Sanuri now stood up from his place at the front table and walked in front of the large crowd. Then he turned and faced the leaders of the tribes who were sitting at the long front table. "It is the order of The Great Ruler that the gifts I am to present to you be given to the wisest and holiest beings of each kingdom," said the Sanuri in a voice the reverberated in the huge building.

"The Great Ruler is pleased with the choices you have made and the paths you have taken. The Rualas have been faithful children for a long time and now they are teaching the holy ways to the Shettees. So Manu I bestow upon you and all your peoples gathered here, the set of Holy Scrolls that had long been protected at the monastery at Avaide."

Everyone at the front table stood up as the Sanuri walked up to Manu and handed him a small chest made of gold and encrusted with precious jewels. Manu's hands were shaking as he accepted the gift. He carefully placed the chest on the table and lifted the lid. Manu saw six golden, jewel encrusted tubes that each contained one of The Holy Scrolls.

"These are the scrolls that were originally given to the holy men of Norkv at a time when the Kingdoms of Norkv and Xepoltr were one," the Sanuri explained. "At that time the kingdom was called Samona. The peoples of Samona were the ancestors of your tribes." As the Sanuri said these words, there was loud whispering throughout the hall as none of the beings were aware of their history.

The Sanuri continued, "The information and blessings contained in these scrolls are as timeless as The Great Ruler Himself. Manu please pick up the scrolls and show them to the others. You will see that the golden tube containing each scroll is embedded with jewels. The designs made by the jewels form a holy code, which is unique to the destiny of that kingdom."

The Sanuri now turned around and faced the crowd. "Your tribes were saved from annihilation and brought to the Ice Caves to start new lives. And you have done well. But your former kingdoms, the lands below, are overrun with Hutas. Whether you realize it or not you are forming a new kingdom here in the Ice Caves. Hundreds of years ago your tribes peacefully coexisted in the Kingdom of Samona. So I think it only fitting that you honor your heritage and your ancestors and name this new kingdom New Samona."

Loud applause rang from the group. The Sanuri turned back to Manu and the others at the front table. "Now that you are leaders of the Kingdom of New Samona, you will be wise to study the designs on the tubes and to translate the codes. I cannot help you with this work but I trust The Great Ruler will give you guidance if you but ask," the Sanuri said.

Every being in the Hall of Light was allowed to examine the golden containers of the scrolls but Manu would not allow anyone to take a scroll out of its container; as he wanted to hold special ceremonies for the reading of each scroll.

Many of the Rualas and Shettees talked long into the night trying to determine what type of structure they should build to house such holy gifts. The Sanuri left the Hall of Light in the early hours of the morning and started to pack his boca. By the time he finished packing a large crowd of Shettees and Rualas had formed to see him off.

The Sanuri spoke to the crowd, "Thank you again my friends. It is not often one can say they helped to change the world but you can boast such a claim; you should be proud. Use the power of The Holy Scrolls wisely and never forget there are others who covet such treasures."

The Sanuri was about to step up into the front seat of the boca when he changed his mind and turned back to the crowd. "There is a darkness that is coming upon us, such that I have never seen before; men are calling to it and the darkness is answering," said the Sanuri sadly. "You will remain safe in the Ice Caves but the world below is changing and it makes my heart weep."

Chapter XXI
Shelter

After discovering the bodies of the Zendoti demons surrounding their camp, Raul pushed his men hard. They rode eastward in the Kingdom of Ganz towards the western tip of the Kingdom of Stordt. Raul planned to enter Stordt and travel north along the River Oja into Wetpr. This route was considerably shorter than his other options and he would be able to avoid areas known to be inhabited with Rogetts.

Midmorning of the third day after they found Vitomas, they came to the border of the Kingdoms of Stordt and Ganz, where the River Oja divided the two kingdoms. Raul decided to make camp on the bank of the River Oja for a few days so the wounded soldiers could rest. They made camp on top of a small hill that overlooked the river. The area between the top of the hill and the riverbank was a thick forest.

"Raul I am so glad we will be stopping for several days, Simon and some of the others need to rest," Vitomas said. "I am very concerned about him."

"I know but we had to move until we found a site with water, that we could defend," Raul said as they were setting up their camp. Raul finished building a fire and turned to Vitomas, "Honey, I know you and I haven't had a chance to really talk yet; you do understand why?"

Vitomas walked over to Raul and kissed him on the cheek. "Of course I understand; we will have plenty of time to talk later," she said. "Raul, when we have the camp set up I would really like to clean up in the river. I have not had a bath in weeks, would you tell the men to stay away for a few minutes?"

Raul looked at Vitomas' as if seeing her with new eyes; both her blouse and skirt were ragged and torn and covered with dried blood and dirt. The blouse that had once been white was now a worn grayish color. Vitomas' underskirts were exposed by the tears in both her blouse and skirt and they too were in tatters. And her long beautiful hair was matted in spots.

"I was so thankful to find you I didn't really pay attention to the condition of your clothes; I wish now I would have thought to bring you something to wear," Raul said as he walked over to his saddlebags

"I would give anything for some clean clothing now; I know I am a sight," Vitomas said apologetically.

"I have an extra shirt in my pack which you can wear while you wash your clothes in the river. Raul said as he pulled a rolled red shirt out of one of his saddlebags. Raul unrolled the shirt as he walked towards Vitomas. "Of course this will look like a dress on you," he said with a grin. "But know you look beautiful no matter what you wear." Raul leaned down and kissed Vitomas on the lips.

"Oh thank you so much, I cannot tell you how dirty I feel; I was afraid to bathe when Archetenus had me."

Raul stared warily at Vitomas. "I thought you said he treated you honorably." Vitomas looked at the ground and did not speak. "Vitomas tell me what happened," demanded Raul.

"He never hit me and we did not have sex but there were times when he frightened me greatly," Vitomas said in almost a whisper.

"I want you to tell me what happened, everything," Raul said softly.

"Raul I will tell you everything I promise but it is a long story; can I tell you tonight after we have settled in?"

Raul searched Vitomas' eyes for a few moments then he grasped her hand and kissed it. "I will tell the men to leave the river as soon as they are done watering the horses," Raul said and walked away. Vitomas went to Simon because he was moaning; she looked at his bandages then sat next to him holding his hand. Raul returned to the campsite about fifteen minutes later with Lieutenant Markus.

"You two go take a bath, I'll watch over Simon," Markus said as he sat down next to his friend.

"The coffee should be ready soon," said Vitomas as she picked up a blanket and the red shirt.

"I have soap," Raul said with a smile, as he took a large bar out of his saddle bag. "I have a comb and brush too. I am sorry Vitomas I have been so worried about you and Simon that I didn't think to offer you these things before."

Vitomas smiled and took his hand. The two walked down the hill to the water's edge. Raul found a spot that he felt was the most secluded and spread the blankets out. They both took off their clothes, dropping them on the shore and ran into the water. Vitomas squealed because the water was cold. Raul and Vitomas swam, played and kissed. Their laughter resounded through the trees.

Vitomas put her arms around Raul's neck, "I have never laughed like this with anyone before." The sadness of her statement pulled at Raul's heart. He picked Vitomas up and kissed her passionately. After a few moments he said, "Let me help you wash your hair and then we should go back to shore." They both laughed and giggled as Raul tried to help Vitomas wash her long tresses. But Raul's attention was soon diverted as he started to kiss the back of Vitomas' neck and down her spine. Vitomas moaned and leaned back into Raul.

Roch had stayed awake all night and now tried to sleep in the heat of the morning sun. The Lion and the face of Miranda had long plagued his dreams but the addition of Sporos' face drove Roch into madness. Roch had slept little for several nights. He did not recognize Sporos nor could Roch understand what Sporos was trying to say.

The Lion and Miranda spoke to Roch with voices of authority; he could clearly understand their words although they created fear within him. But the face of Sporos was filled with rage and pain and his voice muffled. Roch did not want Sporos haunting him yet at the same time not being able to understand what Sporos was saying was unnerving for Roch.

Shortly after Sporos was imprisoned in The Abyss, he started appearing to Roch. Sporos was one of Roch's creators, a secret which Roch would never learn.

For centuries Sporos and others had worked on a mission to create a human of such diabolical proportions that the human form could house the essence of a powerful demon. An ancient demon, one of the Old Ones who came to this world at the beginning of time. The Old Ones were the true demons, the most powerful of their kind. Their power was so great that the sheer energy of one could not be contained in a normal human body. So members of the Recupero Sect of the secret society of the Insidiae worked to create the perfect human vessel to hold the essence of their master Omnibus.

Roch had no idea of his destiny nor did he realize that members of the Recupero were spying on him as well as demons from other worlds. There were spies in his own castle that sometimes guided his actions without Roch being aware of it. The time was fast approaching for Roch to fulfill his destiny. The timing had to be perfect, for the demon Omnibus was imprisoned in The Great Abyss and no demon had ever escaped from that vast nothingness.

Sporos and other members of the Recupero Sect had to make sure that Roch lived to fulfill his destiny; which was not always an easy feat. Roch was impulsive, explosive and violent; characteristics that usually led to a short life span. Sporos had been watching Roch from his eye into the world of men. But now the great demon was trying to communicate with Roch but The Great Ruler muffled Sporos' voice to the world.

Archetenus knew he had to move from his campsite. He had not had the strength to ride since he was injured by the Huta spear. Archetenus knew there were more Hutas in the area and it was just a matter of time before they found him. This morning he found the strength to saddle his horse and resume his journey to Port Friada.

Archetenus traveled directly east instead of southeast because it was a more direct route to the shores of the River Toba. Archetenus needed water, he needed food and he needed shelter. Archetenus did not try to cover his tracts for he was more concerned with staying on his horse. Dehydration and the fever Archetenus was developing from the infection in his wound clouded his thoughts.

Archetenus could not stop thinking about Vitomas; he was still obsessed with her. It both angered him and hurt him every time he thought about the way she looked at Raul. That look of undying love was the way Vitomas always looked at Archetenus in his fantasies.

"And Miranda," Archetenus suddenly said out loud. "I still don't know if she is real." Miranda made Archetenus enraged at times. Like most humans Archetenus did not like having a mirror held before him; a mirror revealing his true image. Yet, there were times when Archetenus took great comfort in Miranda's presence. In a way she was like his enemy and his only friend, a thought that made Archetenus laugh out loud.

The heat of the afternoon woke Roch; he sat up with sweat pouring profusely from his body. Agitated to be awakened, Roch started to throw his few meager belongings around his campsite. "I finally get some damn sleep and the heat wakes me!" he yelled out loud in disbelief. Roch stood up, grabbed the blanket he was lying on and walked over to a large tree. He spread the blanket on the ground and sat down.

Roch took his beloved map from his pocket and studied it. After almost twenty minutes Roch looked up from the map and glanced at his campsite. There on the ground where he had been sleeping; Roch saw something that appeared to be moving. He walked over to that area to get a better look.

It appeared to be a talisman made from sticks and feathers; it was crude in design except for the enormous ruby stone in the center. Roch greedily grabbed the talisman and was about to tear the ruby from the piece when the stone became hot to his touch; so hot that he dropped it on the ground.

Roch swore and reached to pick the talisman up again when he saw the face of Sporos appear in the gem. Only now the face was not screaming but seemed to be staring at him, intently staring at him. Roch moved to the right and Sporos eyes appeared to follow Roch's movements. Roch then moved to the left and watched as Sporos' eyes followed him again. "What sort of magic is this?" Roch thought to himself as he reached for the ruby stone. The heat emitted from the stone was now searing and burned Roch's hand before he touched the ruby.

Enraged Roch stomped on the ruby stone with the heel of his boot; he was immediately thrown back as if there had been an explosion. Roch landed hard on the ground about ten feet from the talisman and to his amazement the talisman and the stone were both intact. Roch jumped to his feet and charged at the talisman only to be thrown to the ground again.

Rage now blinded Roch as he stood up and again charged his invisible adversary. This time Roch was thrown into the tree he had been sitting under. Roch's head hit the tree with such force that it momentarily dazed him. Roch sat on the ground, shaking his head, trying to clear his thoughts when he heard a voice that was so diabolical it sent shivers of fear through him. The voice was not speaking but laughing.

Archetenus made camp in the shade of a grove of trees. The heat of the sun scorch his skin. His thirst was overwhelming but Archetenus had run out of water the day before. The combination of dehydration and heat was causing Archetenus to feel dizzy and light headed. As he lay on the ground Archetenus was trying to focus his thoughts on anything besides the throbbing pain in his wound.

Archetenus knew he needed to get to the River Toba or he would die. He lay on the ground drifting in and out of consciousness when he heard a slight movement in the brush. Archetenus grabbed his sword and tried to stand but fell back to the ground.

"Miranda, Miranda help me," Archetenus whispered as his eyesight was becoming cloudy. "I want to die as a warrior, not like this."

The voice continued laughing and laughing which further enraged Roch. "I demand to know who you are," Roch screamed as he stood up.

The voice stopped laughing and was silent for a moment before it spoke. "I am known by many names in your world as you too are known by many names," the voice said sarcastically.

"I am King Roch," Roch screamed arrogantly.

"Well, I'm not going to call you King Roch, let's see what oh what should I call you? I have it; I will call you My Little Tyrant," the voice said and laughed again.

"I am not yours and you will not speak to me like that."

"Oh, but there you are wrong; you were created for one purpose and one purpose alone. And those who created you, well, let's say they work for me."

Roch remembered Miranda's words when she spoke of 'those who had created him.' And now fear was overtaking Roch's anger. "You speak in riddles."

"That's all you have to say?"

"You still haven't told me who you are."

"I know; you will find out soon enough."

"What does that mean?" The voice laughed but did not answer Roch's question.

"Are you the face I saw in the ruby?"

"No, he was one of those who worked for me. You do not recognize him?"

"No, I don't know who the hell he is."

"Hell such an interesting word, don't you think?"

"You are just playing games. Tell me what you came here for," Roch demanded.

"I really don't like the way you talk to me; you should cower before me," the voice said tauntingly.

"I cower before no one and besides I don't know who the hell you are."

Roch suddenly felt as if there were hands around his neck choking him. He couldn't talk, he couldn't breathe. Roch was lifted off the ground, the unseen hands lifted him higher and higher then they let go of him. Roch fell to the ground and screamed in pain as he broke his right ankle. The voice laughed, then it was gone.

"You two certainly look happy," Simon said as he and Lieutenant Markus watched Raul and Vitomas walking into the camp hand in hand. "From the way you are blushing Vitomas, should we assume there was more than bathing going on?" Simon asked with a grin.

Vitomas turned bright red but did not say anything. Raul smiled and kissed her on top of her head. "Honey you are as red as that shirt now," Raul said. "You are going to have to learn to give it right back to Simon." Then Raul turned to Simon and said, "Yes we had a very enjoyable bath. How are you feeling? You're certainly looking better."

"He woke up right after you left and has been talking my ear off," Markus said as he stood up. "I'll be going now."

"You can stay for lunch," Raul offered as he was cutting some potatoes. "Vitomas found some herbs and onions; she has a good eye for plants."

Vitomas finished hanging her wet clothes on some tree limbs and turned to Raul. "If we have a container, I'll go back and pick those raspberries we saw." Raul handed Vitomas a small dish, "Don't be gone long," Raul said. "Lunch will be ready soon." Vitomas kissed Raul on the cheek and walked back towards the river.

"Markus, I have never seen my brother in love before," Simon said with a grin. "Is he actually humming while he is cooking?"

Markus laughed and poured more coffee into his cup. "When did you have time to go fishing?" Markus asked as he watched Raul prepare lunch.

"I didn't, Thompson gave them to us," Raul replied. "He brought them earlier this morning." Then Raul's voice became more serious. He looked up from his cooking to see if Vitomas was near, when Raul was sure that she could not hear him, he turned to Simon and Markus. "Vitomas and I need to have a talk tonight. I believe that Archetenus was a lot less honorable than she originally made him to be. She told me she hadn't taken a bath since he took her because she was too afraid of him. I knew I should have killed him," Raul said through clenched teeth. "I don't know why she didn't say anything."

"I think you were a little busy fighting Hutas," Simon said sarcastically. "Raul you know why she didn't say anything. You are doing well but you are no way near your normal strength. You've been limping and winching in pain ever since you fought the Hutas. Archetenus looked like a small mountain with legs. Vitomas didn't want anything else to happen to you. You would have to be blind not to see how much she loves you. In fact I'm surprised that Roch couldn't tell the two of you are in love."

"That's what Annabelle and Sophie said too," Raul was putting fried fish on plates. "Markus would you check on Vitomas, lunch is almost ready."

"I'm right here," Vitomas said as she walked carefully into camp, so as not to spill her heaping bowl of berries. "There are so many more berries down there I will get more for us. And I found a cave but I didn't go inside because I didn't have a torch."

"We can look at it after lunch," Raul said as he handed her a plate.

Vitomas sat down near Simon, so she could cut his food. Simon grinned as he watched her. "I walk into camp and all of you are acting like I just caught you at something and now no one is talking," Vitomas said without looking up from Simon's plate. "What is going on?"

"I was telling them that you and I are going to have a talk about Archetenus later tonight."

"Well, if it is bothering you that much, we can talk now," Vitomas said as she handed Simon his plate.

"I'll leave," Markus said as he shoveled his food into his mouth.

"You really don't have to," Vitomas said.

Markus looked at Raul. "You can stay," Raul said.

"That day that you left," Vitomas explained. "I stood in the window of the cabin and watched all of you drive away. My heart was breaking. I felt so alone. When you were out of sight I laid on the bed and cried. I heard something at the front door, I don't know why but I thought it was you, so I ran over to the door and opened it. Archetenus was in the doorway. He grabbed me and tried to kiss me. I pushed him away and we fought. The next thing I remember is waking later that night. I was tied up and laying in front of a campfire and my head was so painful."

"Did he hit you?" Raul yelled.

"Archetenus said I fell and hit my head on the bed post. I believed him because he kept apologizing. You have to know that I had never even spoken to Archetenus before he stole me, but in his mind he was convinced that I was in love with him. Archetenus thought I would be happy to see him and that I would want to run away with him."

"The first couple of days he didn't believe me when I told him I didn't love him. But as he began to realize I was telling the truth he became angrier and angrier. One night I thought he was going to rape me, I yelled at him that he was just like Roch and he stopped. But I could see how enraged I had made him. Archetenus put his hands around my throat and Raul all I could think of was that I was never going to see you again."

"Honey why don't you sit over here," Raul said. Vitomas stood up and walked over to Raul and sat down. She paused for several moments, "What I am to tell you next will probably make you very angry." Vitomas said as she looked into Raul's eyes. "He told me that if I wanted him to stop trying to force me to have sex that I had to give him something." Vitomas stopped talking and looked down at the ground.

"What did he want?" Raul asked angrily.

"He wanted me to kiss him like I loved him. Raul I didn't want to kiss him but I didn't want him to rape me either. I tried but I couldn't do it and he got so angry, I, well, I didn't know if I was going to live through that night." Raul reached over and held Vitomas' hand. "I kissed him but I thought about kissing you, it was the only way I could do it."

"Did he hurt you?" Raul asked.

"Not very much but he really scared me. The rest of the trip he would be really angry with me then he would want me to kiss him and a couple of times, I thought, well, there were times I thought he would finally rape or kill me. But then he started to act so strangely. I believe he is crazy. Twice when Archetenus was hurting me he suddenly stopped and started yelling, like he was arguing with another person in camp. Then I would hear him at night talking to someone but there was no one there."

"Was he talking to himself?" Simon asked.

"No because he kept calling the imaginary person Miranda. He was arguing with her and would get really mad at her. I pretended like I was sleeping because he scared me."

"Was he drinking whiskey?" Markus asked.

"No, I mean I am sure he does drink but he didn't drink whiskey when he was with me."

"I don't understand why he brought you back?" Raul asked.

"I was getting more and more depressed. I was crying all of the time and talking about you. Near the beginning he told me that he really wanted me to love him and if I stayed with him a while and things didn't work out that he would bring me to you. But that was in the beginning before he became so angry and crazy. At the end, he told me he had to bring me back because Miranda told him to."

"Miranda you look so bright," Archetenus said as he tried to focus on the Angel standing before him. "Am I dead?"

"No, Archetenus you are not dead."

"I will be soon, I have no water and my wound is infected. I always thought I would die in battle, not like this," Archetenus said sadly.

"Archetenus pick up your water bag and drink. It is setting near your right hand." To his amazement a full water bag was lying next to him. As Archetenus drank, Miranda talked to him.

"Your horse has been given water also. I find it curious that a man who has spent his entire life calling to demons is now calling to an Angel. When most people call to Angels they ask for things, what is it you would ask for Archetenus?" Miranda's voice sounded challenging.

Archetenus continued to drink as he thought about her question. He slowly put down the water bag and wiped his mouth. "Thank you for the water. Before when I was riding," suddenly Archetenus chuckled. "You can probably read my thoughts so I don't know why I am saying this. But before, I was thinking about you. I think about you a lot Miranda. It's like you are my enemy and my only friend at the same time. No one has ever talked to me the way you do. And although you make me angry at times, I take a strange comfort in your presence. Now I have a question for you."

"Ask your question."

"Actually I have two questions," Archetenus said as he tried to sit up. "Why do you come to me now that I released Vitomas, why do you bother?"

"Before I answer that question ask me the second one."

"You told me I would be more dangerous dead than alive, what did you mean?" Miranda was quiet. "Oh, you are trying to change me so I don't become whatever it is I am becoming," Archetenus said as the thought just entered his mind.

"Although your questions sound simple the answers are not. Remember that map I showed you?"

"Yes."

Suddenly Archetenus jumped because Miranda was now sitting next to him and staring into his eyes. He had never been this close to her before. "Archetenus I want you to stop for a moment and think about this, do you really want answers to those questions. Because you may not like what I am about to tell you and it may change your life for either the good or the bad."

Archetenus sat up straighter; he reached out and gently touched Miranda's hand. "You feel real," he said. Now Archetenus stared into her gray eyes. "Miranda if you indeed are real; there must be a very important reason that an Angel would come to me. I have never known anyone who said they met an Angel before."

"Actually a lot of people encounter Angels, it's just that they don't realize it because the Angels look different than the people expect. It is the same with demons; people don't always realize they are walking among demons either. And you Archetenus have walked among real demons."

Archetenus shook his head from side to side. "I feel as if my head is clearing, maybe it was the water." Then he stared at Miranda again and asked seriously, "Miranda what would you have me do?"

"Take my hand."

When Vitomas finished telling her story about Archetenus, Raul hugged her tightly. "Vitomas I think what you did was very smart," Simon said. "You may not have wanted to kiss him but you had to survive until we found you. From the way you describe his behavior I am surprised he didn't hurt you more than he did."

"So was I. Sometimes it was like something was stopping him."

"Who do you think Miranda was?" Markus asked.

"I don't know," Vitomas whispered.

"Markus, after lunch would you stay with Simon while Vitomas and I look at that cave?" Raul asked. "The wind is changing; we might need a shelter for the night."

Roch screamed with rage after the voice left him. Roch picked up anything that was near him and threw it as his tantrum escalated. Roch's ankle was swelling up quickly and was already purple. "What the hell is going on here," he screamed over and over. Roch hobbled over to his saddlebags and pulled out a bottle of whiskey. He had been commandeering food and drink from people during his journey. The last person he stole from did not have any food but had four bottles of whiskey which Roch took.

Roch sat back down under the shade tree. He propped his broken ankle up on his saddle bag and uncorked the bottle of whiskey. Roch leaned back against the tree and drank several large gulps; the whiskey burned his throat all the way down. The throbbing pain in his ankle made Roch angrier. Roch took several more gulps of whiskey as he tried to figure out what had just happened to him.

The extreme heat of the day intensified the effects of the whiskey. As Roch was starting to fall asleep he suddenly remembered the words of the Seer Miranda, when she told him that he was so arrogant he did not even know the company he kept. For the first time, Roch thought about her words. "Jonas, I must talk to Jonas," Roch said as he passed out.

"Where are we?" Archetenus asked as he and Miranda were walking down a dirt road.

"You do not recognize this?"

"Wait, this can't be. Miranda am I alive?"

"Yes."

"Then how can we be here, this is my house from when I was a child; it was destroyed a long time ago."

Miranda did not answer as the two walked to the rear of the house. "My parents," Archetenus yelled. The excitement Archetenus had at seeing them soon drained from him as he watched the scenario in front of them. Both of his parents were young and they were crying as his father lowered a small casket into the ground.

361

"Can they not see us?"

"No."

"Miranda who is in the casket, is that me?"

"No, Archetenus. You thought you were an only child but you had an older brother who died when he was six of a fever. You were the second son born into your family. Your father was a second son as was his father and his father before him."

"Why are you telling me this?"

"Because it is significant in understanding who you are now."

"My mother was so beautiful," Archetenus said as he gazed lovingly at the image of his parents. "She was a good woman."

"And your father was a good man. Archetenus tell me what would they think of you now?" Archetenus quickly swung around and glared at Miranda with rage in his eyes. "It was a simple question Archetenus; call back your demons," Miranda scolded.

Raul held a torch in his right hand and Vitomas' hand in his left as they walked through the cave. "Luckily this is big enough for us and the horses if a storm comes up," Raul said as they walked around the cavern. "There's only the one way in," Raul commented.

"Looks like someone else has stayed here," Vitomas said as she looked at the remnants of an old campfire in the middle of the cave.

"I'm taking you back by Simon, then I am going to put wood in here in case we need to use it," Raul said as they walked out of the cave and into the afternoon light.

"You know I can walk back to Simon by myself."

Raul turned and looked at Vitomas and then he brushed a strand of her hair from her eyes. "When Gala told us that you were missing, well, I have never felt fear like that before."

"I just don't want to take a chance of something else happening to you. We are so close to the border of Stordt and anyone could recognize you."

Vitomas squeezed Raul's hand then kissed it. "I love you," she said softly.

As soon as Roch fell asleep he was plagued by dreams. Roch kept seeing the number thirteen in different forms such as thirteen lit candles and another time thirteen large red snakes moving towards him. Again he saw the face of the bald man with the dark pony tail; but in his dream the man was chanting in a language Roch did not understand.

Then Roch saw men wearing little but hoods over their heads dancing around a huge fire. The man with the ponytail was there standing before what looked like an altar made of bones with bowls of blood and snakes everywhere. Roch broke into a sweat as the man with the ponytail raised one of the bowls before the altar and then drank of it. The man handed the bowl to the dancers; each drank from the bowl of blood.

In his dream Roch was in the same cavern as these men, watching the ceremony. The bowl was passed to him. Roch drank of the bowl as had the others. Suddenly Roch sat up, his eyes wide with fear; sweat pouring down his body. "I must die," Roch said out loud.

In an instant Miranda and Archetenus were transported to a different location. "This I have seen in my dreams or I should say nightmares," Archetenus said as they looked at a large dark cavern. In the middle of the cavern was a huge fire pit and a group of naked men were dancing on the very edge of the ring of light. The men wore hoods over their faces and carried a variety of items such as spears and bones decorated with feathers.

"Do you know what that is?" Miranda asked as she pointed to an altar in the far corner of the cavern. The altar was crudely made. It was decorated with bones of humans and bowls of human blood. There was a circle around the altar made up of bones and bowls of blood and live snakes slithered over it all.

"No but I have seen that too in my nightmares."

"Archetenus you are an astute and observant man. Do you notice anything unusual in this scene?"

"I think it is all unusual," he said sarcastically. "The hoods, I don't trust anyone one who has to hide their faces, a real man does not hide behind a hood," Archetenus said with disgust.

"Keep looking."

Suddenly Archetenus' eyes grew wide, "The shadows aren't dancing but the men are." Archetenus quickly looked around the cavern. "Miranda what is making those giant shadows?"

"Those shadows are waiting for men like you to die, Archetenus. That is your fate if you keep on the path you are on."

"I don't understand; why are they waiting and what are they?"

"They are demons but not all of them are from the world that you know. They are waiting to enter this realm but for some the transition will not be easy and they will need, shall we say a vessel to pour their essence into in order to maintain a form in this world."

"What do you mean; a vessel?"

"Your body is a vessel that contains your essence, Archetenus."

"They want my body?" he gasped loudly. "But why mine?"

"People can willingly give their bodies over to demons and many do. But the demons, whose shadows you see on this wall are not like other demons. They are called the Old Ones. They are the original demons; they are much stronger and considerably more evil than the demons that walk with men."

"For the Old Ones to take over a human body the human must die and in that instant when the soul is between worlds the demon takes over. But these demons are so powerful and so evil that an ordinary human body cannot contain them; they need the body of a human who has virtually lost his humanity to the darkness. A human who is close to becoming a demon of this world."

Roch was filled with terror; a part of him didn't understand why he was so scared. As soon as Roch awoke he saddled his horse; the entire time Roch was swearing because of the throbbing pain in his broken ankle. As Roch grabbed everything from his campsite he saw the talisman lying on the ground; Roch made no effort to pick it up. This would be the first time that Roch would leave a treasure behind. Roch painfully mounted his horse and rode towards Taperia and into an impending storm.

"Are you telling me one of those demons is waiting for me to die so he can take over my body?" Archetenus asked incredulously.

"Yes, and if you allow this to happen you will be opening a door between worlds and bringing a monster of great proportions into this world. Archetenus the choice is yours."

"What do you mean the choice is mine?"

"You still have time to change your course; that is why I come to you."

"And if I can't?"

"You mean if you won't," Miranda said coldly. "Your body will remain in this world but it will be inhabited by a beast. You will not be the same man you are today. The real you, Archetenus will be a prisoner of one of these powerful demons, a fate you should wish on no man."

Archetenus was quiet for a while as he stared at the scene of the men dancing before the shadows of the demons. Archetenus was trying to process all that Miranda had told him. After a few moments he asked, "Miranda I don't understand how the two scenes that you have showed me are related."

"These men who you see dancing and others like them belong to a secret society called the Insidiae. The name is of the old language and means conspirators. They conspire against The Great Ruler and mankind itself. They are the first humans to call the Old Ones into this world, and the world has never been the same."

365

"After murdering hundreds of innocent people the members of the Insidiae realized, centuries ago, that the Old Ones would need special humans to inhabit."

"So the Insidiae master-minded an insidious plan. For centuries they have coerced certain individuals to sell their souls to demons in order to start a strain of humans that would make perfect vessels for the demons. This strain is handed down from the second son to the second son to the second son. Archetenus you were chosen by the demons to be a vessel; but as every human you have free will, or at least you will until the demons completely own you. You are at a crossroads the decision is still yours to make."

"I'm glad you found this cave," Simon said as they heard a tree crash to the ground. "This storm came upon us so quickly."

"I'm just glad the men found other caves also," Raul said. "This hill is riddled with them and they are all the same, fairly small with one entrance."

"I think it is unnatural that there are so many similar caves in one hill, they must have been dug out by men," Markus said as he peered out of the entrance to the cave. "It's black as night out there."

"Well, I think it is cozy," Vitomas said with a smile as she looked at the seven men and their horses that were crowded inside the cavern.

"Did you see these?" Tyson asked as he held a torch up to one of the walls of the cave. "There's drawings all over these walls."

Simon remained seated as the others grabbed torches and examined the walls. "Raul tell me what you see," Simon said.

"They look like very old paintings. I think it's the history of a tribe," Raul said as he was scrutinizing the paintings.

"I'll bet every one of the caves has drawings," Markus said as he was studying them.

"Maybe each cave housed a family and those paintings are the history of each family," Simon suggested.

"Whoever these people were I think they sacrificed humans," Tyson said. "Look at these drawings."

"I wonder what happened to these people," Raul said. "Has anyone seen drawings that look like the last ones painted?"

"I found a painting you all should see," Simon said and pointed to the ceiling above the fire pit.

"Oh my god!" Vitomas gasped as she looked at a huge painting of a horrid face. The creature had horns and a long tongue that protruded from its mouth. "What is that?"

"It's some sort of demon," Raul said. "If these people sacrificed other humans I'll bet they worshipped demons."

"Now I don't want to sleep in here," Vitomas said as she held Raul's hand.

"Don't think there is much of a choice," Simon said. "You can't go out in that." Simon was referring to the storm with its strong wind gusts and lightning strikes.

"Look at this," Markus said loudly. "I think I know what happened to these people. It looks like some of their demons got them."

Everyone except for Simon crowded around two pictures in the very back of the cave. "What do you think those things are?" Vitomas asked.

"I have no idea," Raul replied as he stared at the primitive drawings. "Whatever they were they came into the caves and dragged the people out."

The next three days and nights Noreen lived in fear that Roch would return. She was afraid to go outside or even to unlock the doors and shutters. Her husband Henry should have returned home the day before, now Noreen was becoming fearful that something had happened to him. She tried to keep herself busy with chores and taking care of little Jacob, but fear was now consuming her.

Noreen kept thinking that Roch would return for his ring; after all it looked like a great treasure. There was something very strange about that ring. After Noreen found it she set it on top of the kitchen table; twice, out of the corner of her eye, she thought she saw movement in the stone. Fearing she was driving herself crazy, Noreen put the ring in a wooden cupboard and shut the door.

Chapter XXII
Astras

In the old language the word Centras referred to the center; thus The Great Ruler named this tribe of special beings since they dwelled between the darkness of mankind and the light of the heavens. The tribe of Centras has inhabited the world since its creation. A nonhuman race, the Centras' advancements both spiritually and intellectually so surpassed their human counterparts that they changed the course of their own destiny.

The Centras had always been a peaceful and nonviolent race but their lack of aggression soon made them ideal prey for mankind. The Centras were hunted for sport and captured for slaves and entertainment until their species were nearly annihilated.

As a means of preservation, the Centras left the world of man and made their homes in caves, either underground or in mountain peaks. Over the centuries the Centras thrived in their new environments and their population grew and became strong again. They created great cities that rivaled those above ground.

Although a persecuted race, the hearts of the Centras were so pure that they held no malice for their persecutors. The Centras simply sought to remove themselves from the world of man. After the Great Separation as men called to darkness, the Centras surrendered to the light of the heavens; a choice that greatly advanced their species.

Because they were not tempted by the darkness that dwells within the hearts of men, The Great Ruler bestowed upon them a precious honor. The tribe of the Centras would be the Keepers of one of the most powerful and extraordinary gifts that The Great Ruler had given His children. The Centras were the Keepers of The Box of Itifer.

The Box of Itifer, as all the gifts from The Great Ruler contained great powers on its own but when used in conjunction with The Scroll of Imari these two gifts could affect the nature of all mankind. When The Great Ruler created the worlds He created all life forms with a symmetry; a balance that would allow them to live in harmony with all.

But of all His creations, man alone deliberately chose to destroy this balance without realizing the dire consequences. The Great Ruler could see that man was destroying all that sustained their world, so He sent to them The Box of Itifer to help restore the balance of creation. Through the centuries the Centras had protected this great gift; it took a demon with the knowledge of a priest to put into motion plans of such diabolical proportions that The Box of Itifer was stolen from the Centras.

The Centras as a race towered over humans. The average height for a male Centra was nine to ten feet, while the female Centras averaged seven to eight feet in height. Their weights ran from five hundred pounds to seven hundred pounds, most of which was muscle. These creatures walked on two legs and also like humans, the Centras had hands.

Their bodies were covered with a beautiful long silvery brown fur, which was one reason they were hunted by men. Their faces were beautiful; all Centras had large brown eyes and high foreheads. They had noses and lips like humans and high cheekbones. These creatures truly were a race that balanced between humans and animals.

On this day the Sanuri drove to the underground City of Astras, the capital city of the Centras which was located in the Kingdom of Norkv, northeast of the Village of Ort, near the River Kya. The Sanuri drove through the Village of Ort with sadness in his heart. No one had returned to the village after the Huta massacre. No one had buried the bodies, remnants of which still hung from those grisly trees. The ghosts of the murdered victims cried out to the Sanuri. "Great Ruler give peace to their souls," he prayed. "For there is nothing else I can do for them."

The Sanuri stopped the boca several hundred yards from the cave where he had seen the paintings of the Huta warrior with The Box of Itifer. Slowly he walked towards the cave holding the small chest that contained the holy gift. The Sanuri could feel the eyes of many upon him.

When he reached the entrance of the cave, the Sanuri turned and said in a loud voice, "I am the Sanuri of Tabrul and I beseech an audience with the leaders of the Centras." He turned and entered the cave.

The Sanuri stood in the center of the dark cave with his eyes closed and chanted; soon the light from his presence spread and grew filling the entire cave. When the Sanuri opened his eyes he saw hundreds of Centras filling the cave and all of the passageways.

The Sanuri held out the precious chest with both of his hands. "What was once given to you by The Great Ruler has been returned." With these words all of the Centras bowed down except for one who walked up to the Sanuri to receive the chest.

"How is it that you can speak our language?" asked the Centra.

"I can speak with all creatures; I am an emissary of The Great Ruler."

"I am Atomos I am an elder and Keeper of the Box of Itifer," replied the Centra. "I have heard about you Sanuri, it is an honor to meet you."

Without speaking the Sanuri opened the lid of the chest, exposing The Box of Itifer. "The Great Ruler has answered our prayers," said Atomos gratefully.

"The demon that is responsible for stealing this has been banished to The Abyss; but take heed there are others who would have it and The Scroll of Imari also," warned the Sanuri.

"We understand and this will never leave our possession again," said Atomos as he stared deeply into the Sanuri's eyes. "You desperately want to ask me something, I can see it in your eyes. Please, we owe you everything we have no secrets; ask your questions."

"During my travels I have seen footprints that could have been made by your kind, footprints outside of my campsite and near bodies of Huta warriors. Something has been hunting Hutas and tearing them to shreds. Has the hearts of the Centras been touched by such darkness because the box was stolen?"

"Sanuri our hearts were broken and our spirits crushed when this most holy gift was stolen from us. Yes we searched for The Box of Itifer but we too came upon the bodies and saw the footprints that you speak of."

"So it was not your tribe that killed them?"

"Sanuri you in particular should know things are often not what they seem; there are many monsters that walk this world on two legs."

"I found a Huta warrior who was dying and said he had been attacked by demons. I found his statements strange since the Hutas worship demons. Do you have any idea what has been killing the Hutas?"

"Sanuri as you know, our tribe has been in this world since the beginning of time. And we document our history in both paintings and oral history. Follow me, there are things you must see and hear."

Atomos and the Sanuri walked through the maze of underground tunnels which separated the world above ground from the spectacular city below. "Sanuri we will have a great celebration tonight because this gift has been returned, please honor us with your presence."

The Sanuri smiled, "I would be honored Atomos. As we walk I am trying to remember the last time I paid a visit to Astras, it has been far too long."

As Atomos and the Sanuri walked through the tunnels; Centras bowed before the presence of The Box of Itifer. Atomos stopped before a giant door made of wood and bronze. The door was covered with ornate carvings. Without saying a word, the door suddenly opened before them and Atomos and the Sanuri entered a room of spectacular beauty.

A thick red carpeting covered the floor. The walls and ceilings were adorned with incredibly vibrant paintings. Red curtains hung from some of the walls. Giant golden candelabras hung from the ceilings, while smaller versions were attached to the walls.

Pillars of marble formed a pathway from the entrance of the room to the altar where The Box of Itifer was usually displayed. The Sanuri watched as Atomos placed the box on top of the altar, which was made of marble and gold.

"How did the Hutas get The Box of Itifer, there are no signs of battle here?" asked the Sanuri.

"The box was taken out of this room so it could be seen in the procession for the Celebration of Days; when we give thanks to The Great Ruler for the gifts and blessings He has bestowed upon us. Somehow the Hutas were aware of our customs and they attacked our tribesmen who were taking the box to the celebration.

Atomos led the Sanuri out of the room that contained the altar. Now after the huge wooden and bronze door closed behind them; the Sanuri heard a loud noise. Both Atomos and the Sanuri stood still and watched as a portion of stone wall slid in front of the wooden door, concealing its presence. "That is very clever," said the Sanuri approvingly. Atomos led the Sanuri down another long dark tunnel that ended at a huge wall of stone.

"Sanuri these doors open by thought; but only the thoughts of one blessed by The Great Ruler," Atomos explained. "If you need entrance simply imagine, the walls of stone moving and you will gain entrance." Within moments the stone wall before them split in half and each side receded exposing the entrance to the ancient City of Astras. The city of splendor before them stood in direct contrast to the cold, dark tunnels they had been walking in.

Like the Ice Caves of Mordv, these caves had giant crystal towers that grew from the floors of the caves through the ceilings. Also like the Ice Caves, these crystal towers filled the caves with light and healing energy allowing forests and gardens to flourish below the surface of the world. The caves and tunnels that the Centras had dug out to build their homes were filled with gold and that gold could be seen everywhere within the city. Atomos and the Sanuri walked down a stone roadway which was lined with beautiful buildings and rich gardens.

"The cave drawings that we have above ground, while accurate are more of a ruse, so people do not suspect there is this world below them," Atomos explained. "I am taking you first to the Hall of Understanding so that you may read our history yourself. There are some pictures there that I want you to see before I take you for an audience with our elders."

"Is Romos still among you?"

"Yes, he is an elder and my great uncle."

"I wondered at the similarity of your names. I knew him as a boy. As I said I have not visited your city in many years."

After the Sanuri and Atomos walked the equivalency of two city blocks they came to one of the largest buildings in Astras. They walked up a long flight of stairs and entered the building by one of the three sets of double doors. This building was ornately decorated with marble floors and gold everywhere. The building was divided into sections and each section held the drawings of a particular period of time in the history of the Centras.

"Sanuri as you can see, you could spend months in here looking at the drawings and know that you are always welcome to come here and study the history that we present. But I am first taking you to the drawings of the creatures that killed the Hutas." As Atomos talked he opened two ornately carved doors and they entered a room that matched the design of the building but this was the first room they were in that had the historical pictures displayed on the walls.

"Sanuri we will start here," said Atomos as he was pointing out particular drawings. "These drawings here tell of our lives before the Great Separation, when all manner of beings lived as one. Then we move over here. This is when mankind started to separate from The Great Ruler, notice the darkness and chaos that is depicted. This series of pictures to your left show the world as humans started calling to the demons and the arrival of the Old Ones into this world. That is the first time my race encountered these creatures," Atomos said as he pointed to a series of drawings in the middle of the wall.

On the wall before them were drawings of hideous beings that were tall and thin with an almost transparent appearance. These creatures had large feet and hands that had long claws and long protruding fangs. Their eyes were dark and hollow yet they were filled with an evil of great intensity. These creatures were the same ghoulish color of hell but there was something about their countenances that emitted an evil far greater than that of normal demons.

"Atomos you will have to forgive me for jumping to conclusions," the Sanuri said as he looked at the drawings. "It was not until I saw you that I remembered that your race had hands similar to a human's unlike the clawed hands we see before us. Do you know what these creatures are called?"

"They are the Teragon, the demons who stalk and kill other demons, although we do not know why."

"I have read about them in ancient texts. They are also called the Death Terror. They are created as a consequence when evil begets evil of incredible proportions. So the Teragon were first seen when the Old Ones came to this world?" asked the Sanuri as he studied the paintings. "It looks as if these beasts killed the humans who called to the Old Ones but I don't see any pictures of them killing the demons themselves."

"Sanuri, remember these are the drawings of things my race has seen, our ancestors witnessed them murdering humans in this world. We do not know what happened in the hell dimensions. And we do not know if the Teragon have been among us more than the two times we have experienced them," Atomos said. "After the Great Separation and now. Sanuri my question to you is what is happening now that is so evil that these creatures have returned to our world?"

The Sanuri spent the next seven days in Astras meeting with the elders and studying their historical drawings. The first night, the Sanuri attended a lavish celebration that was held for the return of the precious Box of Itifer, a celebration that lasted throughout the entire night. After the first night, the Sanuri stayed in the home of Romos as an honored guest. During this week the Sanuri only returned to the surface of the world once and that was to retrieve his boca and horses, which he brought down to Astras.

Now as the Sanuri drove his boca toward the monastery at Malga he reflected on the many things he had learned from the Centras. The Sanuri enjoyed his time among these unique beings and had promised them he would visit regularly. But the Sanuri was haunted by the words of Atomos, 'What was happening now that was so evil that the Teragon had returned to this world?'

Chapter XXIII
Crossroads

Raul allowed his wounded soldiers to rest for two days then they resumed their journey home. Vitomas was extremely worried about Simon; he was conscious for longer periods of time but Simon was not getting his strength back. Vitomas feared Simon might be developing an infection in his wound or worse perhaps there was more damage than they had initially realized. Vitomas urged Raul to hasten home so they could get Simon to a physician.

Raul led his men north along the River Oja. They had been traveling in the Kingdom of Stordt for two days without seeing any Taperian soldiers. Raul did not know how long their luck would hold out. He did not fear a battle for he had many well trained soldiers with him but Raul feared a delay in getting the wounded home.

Simon was still riding on Vitomas' horse with her holding him. Raul too, worried about Simon's condition but he didn't want to push his wounded men too hard. They would be in Cana the following day; Raul hoped that Gala could help his men.

After five days of traveling Roch crossed the River Nebu and took lodging in the Village of Jarta. He paid for a room that was on the second floor of a tavern. Roch put his belongings in the room then walked down the stairs into the tavern. Roch searched the faces of every man and woman he saw; then decided on a table where he could sit with his back against the wall and watch the front door.

Roch could not rid himself of the overwhelming feeling that he was being watched; a feeling that had plagued Roch since his escape from the Caves of Muldun. He ordered several plates of food and a large container of wine. He stared at the other patrons with suspicion. Roch overheard three men at another table talking about several Huta raids then he heard one of the men say Taperia.

"What did you say about Taperia?" Roch asked loudly. The men turned and looked at him but did not answer. "I am King Roch and I demand to know what you were saying."

The men were surprised to hear Roch's words since he looked so dirty and disheveled. "Last week a large war party of Hutas attacked Taperia, My Lord," said one of the men. Now it was Roch who looked surprised; never had the Hutas dared come that far north into his kingdom before.

"Do you know what happened?" asked Roch.

"We have not been there but some travelers said the city was taken by surprise and many were killed," replied a second man at the table.

"My Lord, we were told the Hutas attacked your castle," said a third man.

"Outrageous, how could they?" yelled Roch as he got up from the table. Roch's broken ankle was painful and very swollen. Roch limped up the stairs as fast as he could manage and got his belongings from his room. After retrieving his horse from the stable, Roch rode towards Taperia.

Archetenus had not spoken with Miranda since she showed him the scene in the cave. After that night, the infection in his wound seemed to heal. Miranda provided Archetenus with food and water; items that simply appeared in his camp. Archetenus stayed at his camp for two more days then headed southeast towards Port Friada.

Archetenus believed that Miranda was keeping him alive until he could make a choice. He did not want the destiny that Miranda had shown him, yet at the same time Archetenus did not believe that change would come easily for him. The more that Archetenus thought about the things that Miranda told him the more he wondered how he could change or if he really wanted to.

Archetenus had been trained to be a killer since the age of five, when Roch's men kidnapped him. Archetenus knew no other life. In the Gefrey Games Archetenus had fought monsters and won because sometimes he was more of a monster than the creatures. Archetenus could not really imagine living another type of life. Then he remembered the shadows on the walls of the cave.

Raul and Markus rode into Cana alone after leaving their men and Vitomas in the dense forest that was north of Cana and east of Taperia. Their men were making camp on the northwestern shore of the Lake of the Pors. Gala was behind the house feeding chickens when she heard horses approaching. Gala walked to the front of the house and was pleasantly surprised to see Raul.

"Gala, we found Vitomas but Simon and some of my other men are wounded from a battle with Hutas, will you help us?" Raul asked as he dismounted.

"Of course, just let me get my things," Gala said as she turned and ran into the house.

Markus stood watch outside as Raul followed Gala inside. "Do you need help?" Raul asked as he saw Gala filling two baskets with bottles, herbs and bandages.

"You could saddle my horse," Gala said. "I have only one, the gray mare, she is grazing in back. The saddle is in the barn." Within minutes the three were heading towards the forest.

"You said your men were wounded battling Hutas," Gala said. "Just days ago Hutas attacked Taperia and King Roch's castle."

"What? How bad was it?" Raul asked.

"Those devils killed many in Taperia and burned a great deal of the city before the soldiers got there. I was told the soldiers were busy fighting with the Hutas at the castle so they were delayed going to Taperia. Sophie said that the Hutas entered the castle grounds through some secret tunnels that none of Roch's men knew about."

"Was Roch there?" Raul asked.

"No he hasn't returned from his trip to Tadon," Gala said. "Which is strange because Tadon is a tiny village, Roch must have gone somewhere else."

"Did the Hutas attack Cana?" Markus asked. "Because we didn't see any signs of damage."

"No, that is what is so strange," Gala said. "No one in or near Cana has seen any Hutas, it's like they disappeared after they attacked Taperia."

"Gala now I am even more worried about you staying here than I was before," Raul said. "I wish you would come home with us."

"Raul I told you this is my home. Four generations of healers have lived in my house, I cannot leave it. But I do appreciate your concern," Gala said then after a pause asked, "So Raul, tell me how you found Vitomas."

By the time Raul finished telling Gala about Vitomas' experience with Archetenus, how they reunited and the battle with the Hutas; they had arrived in the camp. Vitomas ran up to Gala and hugged her tightly.

"I am so glad to see that you are alive and well," Gala said. "I was so worried about you."

Vitomas pulled Gala aside and spoke to her in a whisper so that Simon would not hear, "Gala all the wounded seem to be healing except for Simon. He was stabbed in the side with a Huta spear and Raul burned the wound but I know something is not right. I don't know if he is getting an infection or if there is more damage inside of him. Please help him."

"Take me to him," Gala said to Vitomas. Then Gala called over her shoulder, "Raul will you bring my baskets?"

Simon was sleeping and did not wake as Gala cut off his bandages. She examined his wound, then the rest of his body. "Vitomas in my saddlebags are clean blankets and towels please bring them to me." Gala reached inside of one of her baskets and brought out a rolled towel which contained surgical instruments. "Raul please cleanse these instruments in the fire; I am going to have to open his wound."

"Is there something I can do?" Markus asked.

"It is unnatural that Simon is sleeping this deeply. It concerns me. Markus I will need you to hold him on his side for me. You should probably get two more men to help."

"I'll hold him," Raul said without turning from the fire.

Markus left and returned in a few moments with Tyson and Denks, who rolled Simon onto his left side so Gala and Vitomas could put clean blankets and towels under him. Gala washed Simon's wound then took one of the sterilized knives from Raul. Vitomas could no longer watch and turned away.

Roch was screaming with rage as he rode home. No one had dared to attack his castle since he had become king. "I will kill them, I will kill them all," Roch kept repeating over and over. So consumed was Roch with anger that he paid little attention to the road he was on.

Roch was travelling north along the River Nebu which flowed past his castle. Both Roch's castle and Taperia lay to the east of this river. On the western bank of the River Nebu, just five miles south of Roch's castle were a series of caves. Roch cared little about these caves since they contained nothing of wealth. The Insidiae cared a great deal about the caves.

For generations the Recupero Sect of the Insidiae had been taking prisoners from the villages and forcing them to work in these caves. It was not for precious metals or stones that the prisoners dug; but it was to create a series of underground chambers. These chambers would someday house the masterminds of one of the most insidious plots against mankind.

Vitomas cried as she listened to Simon's screams of pain. Four men tried to hold Simon still as Gala performed surgery on him.

"It is as I thought," Gala said as she was looking inside of Simon's wound. "The Hutas are known for putting poisons and other substances on the tips of their weapons to increase the pain and agony of their victims."

"Has he been poisoned?" Raul gasped.

"No but something just as bad." Gala reached into Simon's wound and pulled out a worm-like creature that was two inches long. The spear must have been dipped in a tincture made from the redeti plant. The tincture contains tiny insects that lay eggs in the wound. When the eggs hatch you have these creatures that eat the organs of the victim."

"Oh my god!" Vitomas cried.

Gala reached into one of her baskets and brought out a small bowl, which she filled with four different liquids and some dried herbs. "Fortunately only a few of the eggs have started to hatch. I can kill these creatures but it will be painful for Simon, so please hold him tight." Simon screamed in pain as Gala flushed out his wound several times. When Gala was convinced that she had destroyed all of the larva and worms, she treated his wound with herbs that would help him heal, then sewed his wound closed.

Raul stayed with Simon while Gala and Vitomas tended to the other wounded soldiers. The sun was starting to set when Vitomas and Gala returned to Simon. "Raul if you would have waited another two days I would not have been able to help Simon," Gala said. "I will sit up with him tonight."

"I think we all will," Vitomas said. Raul was sitting next to Simon. Vitomas put her arms around Raul and kissed him on the head.

"Dinner is ready," Markus said as he started to fill plates.

Roch rode late into the night. Continual nights of sleep deprivation were causing Roch to see shadows where there were none. Several times Roch stopped his horse and drew his sword but the wind turned out to be the only spirit of the night that was haunting him. Twice Roch caught himself as he started to fall from his horse when his eyes closed.

Finally Roch made camp; he started a fire but was too exhausted to cook; so he pulled a bottle of whiskey from one of his saddlebags. Roch drank half of the bottle down hoping it would deaden the pain in his ankle. As exhausted as Roch was, he found himself afraid to go to sleep. At night Roch was plagued by visions and nightmares. Roch did not really understand who all the images were that he kept seeing or what they wanted with him. Roch just knew that they created fear within him and that only added to his rage.

"Sanuri!" yelled Petra as he ran down the pathway to meet his friend. The Sanuri knelt down and gave Petra a big hug. "Do not leave me again," scolded Petra.

"Petra you will have to understand sometimes I must go places where you cannot follow; at least not until you are older," the Sanuri said. Then he laughed as Petra grabbed his hand and pulled the him towards the monastery.

"Padre Bartholomew, Padre Thomas he's back, he's back," yelled Petra excitedly.

The two priests came out into the courtyard to welcome the Sanuri. "You look well, I am so relieved," said Padre Bartholomew.

"I take it all went as planned?" Padre Thomas asked.

"Yes, I will fill you in on the details later," said the Sanuri as he glanced down at Petra.

"Petra why don't you get your staff and show the Sanuri what you have learned," suggested Padre Bartholomew. Petra ran to his room.

"I will tell you more when Petra has gone to sleep but know that Sporos is in The Great Abyss and the Gants prevented Roch from finding The Scroll of Imari," the Sanuri said.

"And The Box of Itifer?" asked Padre Thomas.

"I returned it to the Centras; in fact I stayed with them for a week," the Sanuri explained. "They told me it was not their tribe that was killing the Hutas but a type of demon called the Teragon. They showed me ancient pictures of these demons in their cave drawings and the elders of the Centras told me what they could remember. The Centras said they were searching for The Box of Itifer and some of them saw Teragon stalking and killing Huta warriors."

"They said the last time anyone from their tribe had seen one of those demons was after the Great Separation when men were calling the Old Ones into this world. They showed me the pictures of Teragon killing the men who called to the Old Ones."

"I remember reading about the Teragon in some ancient texts but that was so long ago I don't remember all that was said. If it is alright with you I would like to stay here for a few days to rest and to study," the Sanuri said.

"You are always welcomed here," Padre Thomas said. "And we are more than willing to help you."

"Watching Petra is of tremendous help to me," replied the Sanuri. "Because I really need some time to do research. The Teragon concern me greatly. If I remember correctly they are created only as a consequence when evil beings create some sort of evil of incredible proportions. I understand why the Teragon came here when the Old Ones where invited into this world. Why they are here now should be of great concern to all of us."

Raul and Vitomas huddled together under a single blanket as they sat next to Simon, watching him sleep. Gala too was not sleeping this night; she was keeping busy tending to all of the wounded soldiers. The guards around the camp changed every couple of hours so there was activity even as the majority of men slept.

"The coffee should be ready now," Vitomas said. "Do you want some?"

"Yes but I can get it," Raul said.

"No, you stay here," Vitomas said and walked over to the fire and poured two cups of coffee. As she stood up from the fire Vitomas could hear coyotes howling in the distance. The night birds were screeching and a light wind was blowing.

"The evening is beautiful," Vitomas said as she slid under the blanket next to Raul. "When you told me the stories of your adventures I admired you so and I wished that I was with you. But now that I have been living off the land for weeks, I will be so glad to get to Wetpr, to sleep in a bed and to be warm and dry. I don't know how you endured such hardships for such a long time."

Raul smiled. "It was lonely and difficult at times but the adventures, the things that I saw and the people I met were worth it. I never would have met you if I had not ventured on that journey. But don't worry; I will be staying home with you now." Raul leaned over and kissed Vitomas on the lips.

"Are you sure that is what you want?"

"More than anything; and I want a family, a very large family," he said with a grin. "Vitomas what is the matter, did I say something to upset you? Don't you want a family?"

"I do want a family but all the years I was with Roch I never gave him a child."

Raul looked deep into Vitomas' eyes, "You said that Roch had many women, did he ever get any of them pregnant?"

Vitomas was quiet for a few moments as she thought about the answer to Raul's question. "No, he didn't and Roch wanted children so I believe I would have heard if he got a woman pregnant."

"He is probably too evil to create life," Raul spat.

Archetenus was surprised that he had not seen any more Hutas as he journeyed towards Port Friada. He wondered if Miranda was protecting him from being killed. Archetenus had not seen Miranda for several nights but he had not called to her either. Tomorrow he would be in Port Friada. Archetenus sat before his camp fire thinking about what he was going to do once he arrived in the city.

Archetenus had planned everything around building a life with Vitomas, now he wasn't sure what he wanted. He had enough money to purchase land or a house or a business. As Archetenus pondered the possibilities of his future he felt lonely, he wanted to be around people again, to have someone to talk to.

"Miranda," Archetenus yelled into the darkness of the night. He called her name three more times but Miranda did not appear. "I don't want anything from you, I just want to talk." Archetenus was surprised that he felt disappointment that she had not come, and this thought made him laugh.

Suddenly the hair on the back of his neck rose. Archetenus knew he was being watched. Archetenus took a dagger out of his belt with his left hand and grasped the hilt of his sword with his right. Archetenus listened intently to the sounds of the night. There he heard it, movement behind him. Archetenus jumped to his feet and quickly turned around with weapons drawn. No attack came. "Who goes there?" Archetenus yelled. "Come out and fight like a man." Nothing.

Archetenus left the ring of light that was made by his fire and disappeared into the darkness of the night. He searched the area around this campsite and found nothing. Archetenus returned to his fire and found Miranda sitting near it.

"It was you," Archetenus said with a laugh.

"It was not my presence you felt," Miranda said seriously. "You should check your blanket before you lie down."

Archetenus walked over to his blanket that was spread out on the ground. Using his sword Archetenus moved the blanket back. "What the hell; is that what was watching me?"

"Do you know what that is?" Miranda asked.

Archetenus stared at the huge red snake that was lying under his blanket. The snake was dead but was still in a position coiled to strike. The snake had green eyes and a bright yellow tongue. "That is the Mark of Satan, I have seen that before."

"Tell me."

"I have seen that tattooed on Rogetts. But also the monsters that attacked us at the Wall of Dorath looked like this but were larger and with wings. And when I was with the Sanuri there was a smaller snake like this on my saddlebag; that contained the severed head of one of my men. The Sanuri said that I had been cursed."

385

"And you saw them the other night in the vision I showed you of the cave, they were crawling on the unholy altar."

"Miranda you haven't told me everything have you?"

"There is much that I have not told you Archetenus; if you have questions of me, ask."

"The Sanuri said I had a curse placed upon me; was he talking about the witch that Roch hired to send demons after me?"

"Yes."

"Have I escaped from those demons?"

"You are safe from them now."

"Is this snake related to that witch?"

"No, and that witch is dead. She was killed by the demons she called out of hell."

"You told me before that something more powerful than the witch sent the monsters against us at the Wall of Dorath because I was a threat to Roch, is that correct?" Archetenus asked as he sat down by the fire, near Miranda.

"Archetenus the reason I make you ask questions is because it is your choice what information you want to know. To tell you the answer to that question will put you in great danger, are you sure you want to know this information?"

"I believe I am already in great danger," Archetenus replied with a grin. "But most of the time I know who my enemies are, this time I am not sure."

"Before I answer your question I should explain some things to you. People talk about hell but few understand that there are many different hell dimensions. And demons are very much like humans, they fight and kill for power and greed. There is not one devil as many believe but many devils and like humans they compete for riches, territory and to feed their egos. They have their individual goals and agendas," Miranda said.

Before she could continue Archetenus asked, "Miranda are there other human worlds also?"

"That is an answer I will not give you now. I told you about a secret group called the Insidiae; they have been selling out their world of humans for centuries. And they have many diabolical plans in progress. To cultivate men of great evil so their bodies can be sold as vessels to demons is but one conspiracy they are developing. That is the conspiracy you have been chosen for."

"There are others and King Roch is an integral piece of a demonic puzzle that could destroy this world as you know it. There are eyes from many worlds watching Roch. The mutual hatred that you and Roch share with each other would be no concern for the demons if you were a normal human but you are not. You are one of the Second Sons you have the capacity to hurt or kill Roch and this would ruin plans that have been in the works for centuries. A demon named Sporos set the monsters upon you at the Wall of Dorath. But he is no longer a threat."

"What do you mean he is no longer a threat?"

"The Sanuri of Tabrul fought with him in a battle of old. Sporos is now imprisoned in The Great Abyss."

"The Sanuri; that old man fought with a demon and won?" Archetenus asked in amazement.

"You really have no idea who the Sanuri is and yet you spent several days with him," Miranda said. "Archetenus you put your faith in the powers of your body, a body that can be weakened and die. The Sanuri puts his faith in The Great Ruler; His powers are beyond your imagination. His appearance is humble; do not take him lightly."

"So some of the Insidiae want to sell me to be a slave of a demon and others want to make sure I don't ruin their plans for Roch. So the Insidiae are my enemies."

"It's not that simple, as I told you the demons have their own plans and agendas, perhaps not every demon wants the Insidiae's plans for Roch to succeed. Think of your world as a large game board, the demons are the players and the humans are the pawns. You Archetenus have been used as a pawn and you did not realize it."

387

"Miranda are you using me as a pawn?"

Miranda stared into Archetenus' eyes with such power that he felt as if he was a small boy before her. "I am trying to save you and to save others from you. I have not deceived you or seduced you. I tell you the truth whether you like to hear it or not."

Archetenus did not comment on her statement but changed the subject. "Does Roch know about the Insidiae and what they have planned for him?"

"No. The Great Ruler has sent him many messengers but Roch ignores them."

"Perhaps The Great Ruler should send you to him."

"He has."

Roch's sleep was plagued with nightmares as usual but this night he kept hearing the laughing of the demon that broke his ankle. Tonight Roch did not see The Lion or Miranda in his dreams. He saw Sporos, he saw red snakes and unholy altars and he saw himself dead and through all the visions Roch heard the diabolical laughter of one of the most powerful demons in all of the hell worlds.

Roch woke up in a cold sweat. He saddled his horse and started for his castle long before the sun rose in the sky. Roch the man who always boasted that he feared nothing, was afraid to sleep. From Jarta Roch followed the River Nebu north which would take him to the western gate of his castle. As Roch was riding near a section of the river that was riddled with caves; he suddenly decided to veer east and to ride through the City of Taperia first. Roch never heard the drums beating in the caves as the men danced before the altar made of bones.

The Sanuri suddenly awoke; he had fallen asleep at a large wooden table in the Hall of Antiquities. Before he fell asleep the Sanuri had been praying to The Great Ruler to give him a sign of the evil that was to come so that the Sanuri could stop it. Now as the Sanuri walked around the great room lighting candles he tried to remember all the details of his dream.

In his dream the Sanuri kept seeing the same images over and over. These images repeated for what seemed like hours to the Sanuri. He saw eyes peering out from the darkness watching all creation. The eyes were everywhere and in the few instances when the Sanuri was shown a partial face it was covered with cloth.

The Sanuri also saw a man on horseback who was standing on a hill watching a village burn below, the man was handsome with dark curly hair and muscular and the man embodied pure evil. But what disturbed the Sanuri the most were the images he saw of Sporos.

Two different images kept playing out before him. In the first image the Sanuri saw Sporos lost in the darkness of The Abyss, screaming with rage. In the second image the Sanuri saw Roch sitting before a campfire looking at the exact same image of Sporos that the Sanuri had been shown.

"What can this mean?" the Sanuri cried out to The Great Ruler. "Is Sporos calling to Roch from The Abyss?" As the Sanuri studied the ancient texts he prayed to The Great Ruler over and over, "Please give me clear sight that I might understand the meaning of these images."

Chapter XXIV
Reunions

"My Lord, My Lady," screamed Marie as she ran into the family dining room.

"What is it Marie?" asked King Sudfad as he jumped up from the breakfast table.

"One of the soldiers just said the boys have returned and many of the men are badly wounded. I told the soldier to fetch the physician."

"Oh my god!" gasped Renya as everyone at the table now jumped up and ran to the front door of the castle.

"Simon, Simon," screamed Annabelle hysterically as she ran down the long flight of steps in the front of the castle and towards Vitomas' horse. Simon was unconscious and seated in front of Vitomas; who held Simon from the back while Markus rode close on Vitomas' right side and Raul on her left. Six other soldiers rode with them; the rest of the troops had already taken the wounded soldiers back to the military physicians at the garrison.

"Annabelle he is not as bad as he appears," Vitomas yelled to her friend. "Gala gave Simon some medicine to make him sleep."

Annabelle could not get near Simon because of the way the soldiers were riding around Vitomas' horse so Annabelle ran back to the castle steps. The soldiers dismounted and took Simon off from Raven. "Put him in his old bedroom it is closer," Renya said as she ran ahead of the men to show them the way. Raul helped Vitomas off of her horse and they ran into the castle, as did Markus.

"What is wrong with him?" cried Annabelle who was sitting on the bed next to Simon and stroking his hair.

"We battled with Hutas," Raul explained. "Simon was cut with a Huta spear that had a potion on it that caused worms to hatch inside of him. If Gala would not have killed them, the worms would have eaten Simon's organs. Mother are you alright?" Raul asked as he noticed Renya suddenly became very pale. Sudfad grabbed Renya and helped her to a chair in the bedroom.

"Gala killed the parasites and packed his wound with healing herbs," Raul continued. "Gala said the process was very painful for Simon so she gave him pain medicine that makes him sleep. He has his color back and looks much better than he did before we found Gala."

"So he is going to be alright?" Annabelle asked as tears streamed down her face.

"Yes," Vitomas said as she put her arm around Annabelle and kissed Annabelle on top of her head. "Annabelle he was hurt protecting me from the Hutas, I am so sorry." The two women hugged each other and cried.

"Raul the Court Physician is here, tell him what you just told us," Sudfad said as he left Renya and walked closer to his son's bed.

"Annabelle, Simon's clothes are filthy and we should give him a hot bath," Vitomas said. "I am concerned about the dirt near his wound."

"As well you should be," said Philip the Court Physician gruffly as he walked up to Simon's bed. Philip had been the physician to the Royal Family for many years. His unfriendly nature was overlooked because of his extraordinary medical skills. Philip liked to brag about his education and medical proficiencies and he resented anyone touching his patients.

"Who is this healer?" Philip demanded as he removed Simon's bandages.

Annabelle was extremely upset because of Simon's condition and now defended her friend with great emotion, "Gala is the healer who saved Raul after he had been poisoned. And the same healer who made the potion so Raul would appear dead, so we could sneak him out of Stordt. She is a great healer and if she says Simon will be alright, he will be!"

"Please excuse our daughter for the way she spoke to you," Laurel said. "She is very upset."

"And I agree with Annabelle," Raul said. "I have repeatedly asked Gala to come to Wetpr Father. Not only because of her skill as a healer but she has put herself at great risk multiple times to help our family. We owe her greatly."

Philip gave Raul a disapproving look, then stood up as he had been examining Simon. "Well, Simon has no signs of infection and his wound does seem to be healing nicely. I will leave some pain medicine."

"We still have medicine from Gala," Vitomas said as she frowned at Philip.

"Very well," Philip barked. "My work is done here."

"Perhaps you could go to the garrison and help those physicians with the wounded," Raul suggested.

Philip was more than insulted by Raul's suggestion because Philip considered providing medical care to anyone other than the Royal Family beneath him and a waste of his talents. Philip picked up his medical bag and put his hat on his head, then he slowly turned towards Raul. "I do wonder why a woman who has no ties to you would put herself at such great risk, did you pay her well?"

Annabelle's face turned dark red and she started to walk towards Philip but Vitomas held her back. Annabelle was starting to speak when Raul interrupted her.

"I asked Gala the same question. Besides being a friend to our wives and to Annabelle's family, Gala comes from a long line of healers who have all been friends with the Sanuri. Gala said the Sanuri talks about our family so much that she felt like she knew us. Gala also said that Father was the greatest king in all of Opots and she would not let his children die."

"I don't like him," Annabelle said after Philip left the room.

"That is obvious," Sudfad said with a broad grin. "Raul are you planning at all on introducing us?"

Raul took Vitomas by the hand and they walked up to both of his parents. Renya stood up from the chair. "Mother and Father this is Vitomas, Vitomas my parents King Sudfad and Queen Renya."

"I am sorry I am such a sight," Vitomas apologized shyly as she was painfully aware that not only was she meeting Raul's family but the King and Queen in her dirty and tattered clothes.

"Nonsense child," said Renya and grabbed Vitomas and hugged her tightly. "We have been looking forward to meeting you."

After Renya and Vitomas finished hugging, Vitomas looked shyly at Sudfad who boldly stared into her eyes as if trying to read her thoughts. "We have heard a great deal about you Vitomas, not only did you save my son's life but you devised a brilliant plan so he could escape from Roch. And you stole his heart in the process. This room is filled with your friends who talk constantly about your kindness and your courage. We welcome you to the family." Vitomas started to cry as Sudfad spoke; he grabbed Vitomas and hugged her tightly. "Thank you," Sudfad said.

Roch rode into Taperia and what he saw angered him. All about Roch were signs of the attack. Burned buildings, broken windows and dried blood. There were many arrows still lodged in walls and barrels along the walkways. No one spoke to Roch as he rode through the streets; the citizens were so blinded by their despair they did not recognize their King.

Roch rode through Taperia without speaking to anyone; he was consumed with rage as he rode towards his castle. As Roch got closer to the castle he could see a thick column of black smoke rising in the air. Roch quickened the pace of his horse and soon the smell of burning flesh pierced his nostrils. In front of the castle gates Roch saw a huge pile of bodies being burned.

"The King has returned," called out one of the guards in the towers, and the gates to the outer wall of the castle were opened to allow Roch's entrance.

"What happened here?" demanded Roch as he dismounted.

Cerephus walked up to Roch and started to explain, "Four nights ago a large party of Hutas stormed the castle in the middle of the night. As we were doing battle, we saw the flames and smoke coming from Taperia."

"So they attacked the castle and Taperia simultaneously?" asked Roch angrily. "That is unheard of; they are such barbarians they are not known for planned attacks like this."

"My Lord there is more, perhaps you should speak with Jonas in your war room."

When Roch and Cerephus entered the war room they saw Jonas sitting at the table looking at drawings. Jonas' left arm was in a blood stained sling.

"My Lord, you have returned," said Jonas as he stood up to greet Roch.

"You are injured," commented Roch.

"A Huta spear; but we have much to discuss," said Jonas gravely.

As Jonas and Roch sat down at the table, Cerephus handed each man a glass of whiskey, "You are going to need this," said Cerephus as he looked at Roch.

"There are many disturbing things here My Lord, the Hutas not only carried out two well-planned attacks but they entered the castle grounds by hidden tunnels," explained Jonas.

"What!" screamed Roch.

"Neither Jonas or I knew about the tunnels and could not find how the Hutas were gaining entrance," said Cerephus.

"I found these old maps of the castle My Lord and they do not show the tunnels," said Jonas.

Roch grabbed the plans of the castle and studied them for a few moments, "Show me these tunnels you speak of."

Cerephus and Jonas took Roch through both of the tunnels; Roch was bewildered. "How could the Hutas know about these tunnels when I did not and I have lived here all my life?" Roch asked in amazement. "Are there others?"

"Not that we have found yet," replied Cerephus.

"The hinges on these doors are ancient and appear to have had little use," said Jonas as he was inspecting one of the doors to a tunnel.

"How many men did we lose?" Roch asked as they walked through one of the tunnels.

"Almost two hundred," replied Cerephus.

"Two hundred!" yelled Roch. "How big was that war party?"

"Hundreds My Lord," replied Jonas.

"What did they take?" asked Roch.

"Nothing that we know of," replied Cerephus, "But there is another problem."

"We killed all of the Hutas that came through the tunnels but some of the others got away," said Jonas. "So there are others out there that know about the tunnels."

"This does not make any sense," said Roch. "A huge war party of Hutas with secret knowledge of this castle travel this far north, attack and take nothing. Honestly I do not understand the meaning of any of this."

"Perhaps they did not take anything because we did not give them a chance; the men fought valiantly," said Jonas.

"Cerephus get explosives and destroy these tunnels," ordered Roch.

"What happened to the men who were with you?" asked Jonas.

"Gants," replied Roch without further explanation.

"Father we lost two soldiers, I am going to speak with their families now," said Raul sadly. "And I am giving additional bonuses to the men who helped me rescue Vitomas."

"That is the responsible thing to do my son," said Sudfad. "Although it is no consolation for their grief; tell the families they will never want, we will take care of them."

Raul walked up to Vitomas as she talked with Laurel and Alexander. "I have to go but I am sure Laurel can show you to a room and find you something clean to wear," Raul said then kissed Vitomas on the forehead.

"Where are you going?" asked Vitomas.

"To see the families of the men who died," Raul said gravely.

Vitomas smiled warmly, "Would you like me to come with you?" Raul took her hand and the two walked out of the castle with the King and Queen watching proudly. "Honey, what will those poor people think, the way we look?" asked Vitomas.

"They will think we are honoring their families by coming straight from the battlefield," said Raul as he kissed the back of Vitomas' hand.

"I need to be alone," yelled Roch to Jonas and Cerephus. Both men left the war room and closed the door. Roch picked up a glass from the table and threw it against the wall; again and again Roch picked up items and smashed them against the wall until his anger had lessened.

"Who would know of those ancient tunnels?" Roch yelled as he tried to pace back and forth but the pain of his ankle was too great. Roch sat down on one of the chairs surrounding the table in his war room. He pulled another chair towards him and propped his right leg on it. Roch tried to think of the names of people who would have been at the castle when his parents were alive. But he had to dismiss every name he could think of as he remembered the person was dead.

"Sophie!" screamed Roch.

Sophie could hear the King screaming through the closed doors. She ran to the war room and entered.

"Yes My Lord," said Sophie fearfully.

"Sophie clean up this damn mess," yelled Roch angrily as he pointed to the pile of things he had thrown against the wall.

"Yes My Lord," replied Sophie as she started to pick up books from the floor.

"On second thought bring me something to eat first, a steak would be good," snarled Roch.

"Yes My Lord," said Sophie as she backed out of the room.

"And Sophie send word for Jonas to join me."

"Yes My Lord."

Raul and Vitomas were exhausted when they returned to the castle after visiting the families of the slain soldiers. Hand in hand they walked down the hallway and into Simon's bedroom. Simon was sleeping and Annabelle was sitting in a chair at his bedside. Annabelle jumped out of the chair and ran to Vitomas, both women hugged again and cried.

"I am so glad you both are safe," said Annabelle as she let go of Vitomas and gave Raul a hug.

"Has he awakened?" asked Vitomas.

"No."

Vitomas stroked Annabelle's hair, "You know what he said after he was injured?" Vitomas continued with a gentle smile. "Simon said Annabelle is going to be so mad at me." But instead of seeing the humor in the statement Annabelle started to cry again.

"I was so angry at Simon because he would not let me go with them," Annabelle said and wiped the tears from her eyes.

"Annabelle you should not have been there it was horrible," said Vitomas.

"I wanted to help," cried Annabelle.

"Do you know what Simon said to me; he said if I loved Raul not to distract him when he was fighting," Vitomas started to cry as she continued. "I think Simon was hurt because he was trying to watch over me as he was fighting and I am so sorry."

Raul put his arms around both women and hugged them. "Annabelle would you take Vitomas to the room next to yours and could you find her something clean to wear; I would like to sit with Simon for a while," said Raul wearily.

"Of course," said Annabelle as she took Vitomas by the hand and led her from the room.

Vitomas fell asleep on Annabelle's bed as they were looking at clothes. Annabelle returned to Simon's room and saw Raul sleeping in the chair next to Simon's bed; Simon was also sleeping. As much as Annabelle wanted to be near Simon, she decided to leave the two brothers alone. Annabelle was quietly closing the door when Renya walked up and peeked into Simons' room. Annabelle and Renya looked at each other, then back again at Simon and Raul and smiled.

Renya put her arm around Annabelle's shoulders and said, "My child you need to eat, come I will walk you to the kitchen." As the two women were walking through the castle, Renya said, "Do you remember us telling you about Simon getting burned in the fire that killed his parents?"

"Yes," replied Annabelle.

"He suffered some horrible burns on his legs and back and had to stay in bed for weeks; Raul never left his side all those days," said Renya with a tear in her eye. "Those boys are so close."

Annabelle touched Renya's hand softly and asked, "How are you doing?" The Queen started to sob.

Sophie served platters of steaks and potatoes to Roch and Jonas in the war room. Always fearful of Roch's wrath she served the food quickly bringing large pots of coffee and loaves of bread.

"My Lord would you prefer I finish cleaning after your lunch?"

"Yes Sophie, that will be all," growled Roch.

"Thank you Sophie," said Jonas smiling. Sophie turned to smile at Jonas and stopped abruptly. Sophie took a step closer to Jonas and stared into his eyes."

"Sophie what is it?" growled Roch. "You look as if you have seen a ghost."

"Nothing My Lord, I am sorry, enjoy your meal," said Sophie as she hurried from the room.

"She is acting peculiar today," commented Roch.

"She was worried about you and of course all the staff were frightened by the Huta attack," said Jonas as he piled food onto his plate.

"Jonas have someone talk to the older staff and people in the city; find out if anyone can remember hearing about the tunnels or men working on the tunnels."

"Yes My Lord. And if I might say you may want to reconsider destroying those tunnels."

"Why?" asked Roch without looking up from his food.

"Whoever had them dug obviously thought of them as escape routes. They may benefit us someday. We could simply put guards at the doors."

"Your suggestion is not without merit, let me think about it. Tell Cerephus not to destroy the tunnels until I tell him."

"Also My Lord, you said Gants killed the men," said Jonas as he took a drink of his coffee. "So I take it you went to the Caves of Muldun?"

"Yes, what of it?"

"To go to such a place you must have been looking for something of great importance."

Roch stared at Jonas. "Perhaps I was."

"Did you find what you were looking for?"

"No," growled Roch. "Those damn Gants stopped us."

"Do you plan to return to those caves?"

"You certainly are asking a lot of questions Jonas. What is it your business anyways?"

"Do you remember years ago when the Rogetts were attacking the western villages?" asked Jonas but before Roch could respond Jonas continued speaking. "We chased a large group of Rogetts into those caves; we did not enter, we just listened to the screams as the Gants and Rogetts battled."

"The Gants must have won because I didn't see any Rogetts in the caves."

"You know you are going to have to distract the attention of the Gants to give you time to search for whatever it is that you seek.

"An interesting idea Jonas, I really do like how you think," said Roch smiling. "So what are you thinking of as a diversion for the Gants?"

"You are going to have to make the Hutas pay for attacking your castle, perhaps you could drive a band of Hutas into the caves as we did the Rogetts; or force Huta prisoners into the caves," said Jonas as he sipped his coffee. "Actually," he added. "You could force any group of people into the caves."

"There would have to be a great number to distract the Gants for any length of time; they killed all my men very quickly," said Roch as he thought about Jonas' idea.

"Do you know where in the caves you need to go?"

"No, I am still having difficulty translating the map," replied Roch with frustration.

"I may have heard of someone who can help you."

"A holy man who can read the ancient language?" asked Roch with keen interest.

"Yes but I am still trying to find him."

"Is it the Sanuri that Tobias spoke of?"

"No but I heard that the Sanuri is an old friend of the one I am looking for," said Jonas with a sly smile. "They studied as young priests together, then went their separate ways."

Vitomas woke up from her nap. Annabelle was no longer in the room so Vitomas walked through the door that separated the two adjoining sets of chambers. Vitomas looked around at the beautiful room that was now hers and tears started to run down her cheeks. She was free, finally free. "Roch will never hurt me again," Vitomas thought. "It doesn't seem real yet, maybe I am just dreaming." Vitomas opened the double glass doors to the balcony and looked down at one of the castle gardens. Then she went into the bathing room and prepared a hot bath.

Vitomas had not taken a hot bath in weeks. She thought she would never take the experience for granted again. Vitomas lay in the bathtub with her eyes closed. Vitomas was almost asleep when she thought she heard a knock at her door. Vitomas listened but heard nothing so she closed her eyes again. Then Vitomas heard Raul's voice although she could not understand what he was saying.

"Wait, wait," Vitomas yelled as she got out of the tub. The towel she had was too small and she had no robes. "Do not come in," Vitomas yelled as she ran to the bed and grabbed a blanket and wrapped it around her. Water was dripping from Vitomas as she opened the door.

Raul stared at Vitomas' bare shoulders and arms and smiled. "You could have dried off," He said as he walked into her room.

"I couldn't hear who was at the door and I don't have a robe," said Vitomas as she closed the door behind him.

"So you would come to the door like this for anyone?" Raul asked with a smile as he put his arms around her waist.

"I did recognize your voice, I just couldn't hear what you were saying, so I didn't know if you were alone," Vitomas said as she leaned up and kissed him on the lips.

"Borrow something from Annabelle and I will take you shopping later this afternoon," Raul said as he kissed her neck. Then Raul cradled Vitomas' face in both of his hands and stared at her for a moment before he kissed her forehead, the tip of her nose and then her lips. Vitomas moaned and leaned into him as they kissed. Suddenly Raul stopped. "We can't do this now, I have to meet with Father in a few minutes but I must speak with you first," Raul said seriously.

"What is the matter?"

"Why don't you sit down," Raul said and nodded towards the bed as there were no chairs in the room. Vitomas sat down on the edge of the bed and watched Raul pace back and forth for a few moments before he spoke. "After Roch stole you, did you ever have a wedding ceremony of any kind?"

"No," said Vitomas softly as she shook her head from side to side.

"Then you were just living with him?"

"Raul this is embarrassing," Vitomas said blushing.

"Vitomas this is important," said Raul seriously. "If you are officially married to him then we cannot marry as long as he is alive. And although I very much want to kill him my father is concerned about starting a war between the two kingdoms."

"We never married; Roch took me as his woman and called me his queen."

Raul sat down on the bed next to Vitomas and smiled with a look of relief, "Good, this has been weighing on my mind because I want us to marry as soon as possible."

Vitomas looked at him and started to laugh, "Raul you have not asked me yet."

Raul started laughing, "Well, this is a good start, isn't it?" He moved off from the bed and got down on one knee before her. Raul took both of Vitomas' hands in his and said, "Vitomas I fell in love with you the first day that I saw you come into my room. Before that day was over I knew I wanted you as my wife. I promise I will protect you and care for you for the rest of your life and I will always love you. Will you marry me?"

Vitomas was crying and could scarcely say "Yes." Vitomas put her arms around Raul's neck and they kissed. "I am sorry I cannot stop crying," Vitomas said with a joyful laugh. "My Love, I knew you were the one that first day also. I never knew love until I met you and I want to be with you always. I promise to be a good wife and to give you many children and I love you so much I don't know if even death could end it." They kissed for several minutes, then Raul stood up.

"I have to meet with Father; get dressed and I will come back in an hour," said Raul. "Annabelle is still in Simon's room downstairs. Did you know you can enter her chambers from yours?"

"Yes," said Vitomas as she stood up.

"Simon has bought her a lot of clothes, you two look about the same size; I am sure she won't mind if you borrow something for the day."

"Annabelle told me that she and Simon share those chambers. Does he have two bedrooms?"

"The room Simon is in now was his until he asked Annabelle to marry him. Simon told her parents and ours that they wanted to stay together. Our parents are allowing it since they are to be married soon," Raul said then he looked at Vitomas and smiled. "I will start moving my things in here tonight."

"Good, I want to be with you, but..." Vitomas hesitated for a moment. "But also, I only feel truly safe when I am with you Raul."

"Raul close the door," said Sudfad as he handed his son a small glass of whiskey. Raul entered his father's study and sat down.

"I know why you called me in here," Raul said.

"Then you know we must talk," said Sudfad solemnly. "Vitomas is a lovely girl and I can understand why you fell in love with her but I need to know if you have brought my brother's wife under this roof and what will Roch do to gain her back."

"Father that question has been weighing on me also but I did not bring his wife here, I brought his prisoner here; they were never married."

"And you are sure of this?"

"Yes."

Sudfad sat in a chair across from Raul and studied his son's face. "Then if that is the case, you have my blessing to marry the girl. But because Roch did not marry her does not mean he will not start a war to get her back."

"We were told that Roch stopped searching for Vitomas several weeks before Simon and I reached Taperia."

"I find that curious, don't you?"

"I find that outrageous. If someone kidnapped your wife would you go hunting for treasure?" asked Raul with disgust.

"What type of treasure?"

"We were told he was going west towards Tadon, following a map that was taken from a Huta."

"Roch always was obsessed with riches," Sudfad said, then paused for several moments before speaking again. "Son there are a couple more things I wanted to speak with you about," Sudfad continued. "Your mother and I have been talking and while Vitomas seems like a very strong person she has experienced some horrible things; you would be wise to remember that."

"I know that Father," said Raul with a look of confusion.

"I mean you will have to be understanding of her."

"Father I am not sure I understand what you are trying to say."

"I guess I am trying to say that perhaps your mother should be having this conversation with you," said Sudfad smiling.

"I love Vitomas I will not hurt her."

"I know son but sometimes it takes more than love to build a marriage. Your mother and I had some difficult times at the beginning."

"I would never believe that," said Raul with surprise.

"I will have to say this to Simon also, but both of you boys are strong willed and adventuresome; your lives are about to change drastically, especially once you start having children."

"I think we understand that Father."

Sudfad smiled warmly, "I hope you do my son."

"Father I believe I do know what you are trying to say to me," Raul said softly. "I had heard stories about Roch but to be in his castle and to see the fear in the eyes of all who were around him was disgusting. If you knew what he did to Vitomas and Annabelle it is truly hard to believe they could both be such loving and wonderful girls. Neither of them really show their scars but Vitomas has horrible nightmares. She won't tell me about what she dreams but Vitomas says she only feels safe when she is me. Father I plan to move my things into her chambers tonight."

"I understand. Perhaps you could let both of the girls know that they can always talk to me or Renya about anything."

"Are you ready?" asked Raul as he walked into Vitomas' chambers.

Vitomas walked into the room smiling but before she could answer Raul put his hands around Vitomas' waist and pulled her tightly against him. "My father has given us his blessing to marry; I am very pleased," he said and kissed Vitomas.

Vitomas put her arms around Raul and hugged him tightly. "Was there a chance he would not?"

"Yes, if you were still his brother's wife. You understand that don't you?"

"He would not have sent me back would he?" Vitomas asked fearfully.

"No, I would never let him do that," whispered Raul. Vitomas grew quiet. "Come," said Raul happily. "We have a lot of things to buy you."

"Why are you so quiet?" asked Raul as they walked through the castle.

"I guess I never considered how your father would look at things."

"Vitomas he is a good man but he is also a king and he has to watch out for the interests of the kingdom."

Vitomas looked at Raul, "Your father must be a very different sort of king than his brother; Roch never thinks about his people."

"My father is the exact opposite of Roch. He is a great man who is admired by his people because he is such a wise ruler. His people do not cower in fear before him. In fact, he and Mother have grand celebrations and open up the castle to the people who come from all over the kingdom to bring them gifts and to pay their respects."

"Annabelle told me that your parents have been wonderful to her and Laurel and Alexander," Vitomas said. "She said your parents have treated them like family since the moment they arrived at the castle."

"My parents already think of all of you as family. In fact Mother was telling me that she and Father are so excited to have two daughters now. They always wanted a big family and regretted not having one."

Chapter XXV
Disguises

Sophie waited for Jonas to walk out of Roch's war room, where he had been all evening drinking whiskey with the King.

"Jonas may I speak with you in the kitchen?" Sophie asked coldly as she led the way to the kitchen. Jonas walked behind her smiling. The kitchen was large with two small pantries attached to it. Sophie looked through every room to make sure they were alone before she spoke to Jonas. "I did not realize who you were at first. How long have you taken over Jonas' body?"

"Why Sophie you're talking crazy," Jonas said with a laugh.

"Don't give me that crap Demetries. Do you forget who I am?" Sophie asked with an air of authority. "Did my brother send you here?"

Demetries laughed, "You got me Sophie, I knew I couldn't get anything past you. Yes Meekos sent me and I took over Jonas' body when he died in the forest after they were attacked by Hutas."

"And I assume you orchestrated that attack so you could get close to Roch," Sophie said suspiciously. "You do know that Jonas and Roch were never close; some of the others are getting suspicious."

"By others I assume you are talking about that windbag Cerephus."

Sophie did not respond to Demetries comment. "What I want to know is why Meekos sent you here without telling me. Has something happened to Meekos or the plans?" Sophie asked.

"Sophie you know that Meekos isn't going to confide in me. He is paying me to make sure Roch stays alive until the chosen time. He knows you are doing a good job but you are tied to the castle; where I have the freedom to ride with Roch."

"Did you orchestrate the attack on the castle and Taperia too?"

"Yes, got his attention wouldn't you say," Demetries said with a gloating smile.

407

"You killed a lot of innocent people to get his attention."

"And when did the witch become so compassionate? If your plans work out, all these people will die anyways. You are just mad because I am stepping in your territory."

"No Demetries, I have never trusted you. And I have worked too hard on this to have an arrogant, self-serving demon come in here and mess things up."

Renya opened the door to Simon's room, and saw him sleeping peacefully. Tears filled her eyes as she thought how easily she could have lost her beloved son. Renya was the daughter of a king and knew well the responsibilities of their positions; yet every time her husband and sons rode to battle her life stopped until they returned.

Renya walked into Simon's room and smiled as she saw Annabelle curled into a ball sleeping in a chair next to Simon's bed. "That girl has not left his side," thought Renya. "She will make him a fine wife." Renya took a blanket from a large chest at the foot of the bed and covered Annabelle and kissed her on the forehead.

Then walking to Simon's bed, Renya looked at the bandages on his right side to make sure there was no fresh blood. Renya pulled the blankets up to Simon's shoulders as the night's air was cooling. She kissed Simon on the forehead and stood at his bedside looking at him. "Such a big and strong man he has become," Renya thought. "Yet I always see Simon as that little boy who Raul carried home." Tears were running down her cheeks as Renya left Simon's room and closed the door behind her.

The Sanuri relentlessly read through shelves of manuscripts in the Hall of Antiquities trying to find references to the Teragon. He remembered reading of them once, a vague passage in a manuscript but that was so many hundreds of years earlier that the Sanuri barely remembered the words.

Late into the night the Sanuri grabbed an old and dusty scroll from the back of a shelf. The Sanuri became fearful that he would damage the ancient text since the goatskin was frail and cracking. He was surprised that the text was written in Amark the ancient language of The Great Ruler. A language the world had long forgotten.

The Sanuri found that he was having difficulty translating some of the words since it had been centuries since he read that language. *The creation of evil,* translated the Sanuri, *begets an evil unto itself of such great proportions that the demons feed upon their own.*

The Sanuri pondered on these words. "Does that mean the Hutas somehow created the demons that are killing them?" he thought. "What evil could they be creating that is that powerful?" As the Sanuri read further he discovered another passage; the words were worn but he translated them as *True evil knows no boundaries, not even of its own kind.*

The Sanuri looked through the shelves for texts that identified demons. He found a book that contained images of monsters of various kinds. The images were drawings that had been handed down through the centuries; some of them were copies of cave paintings. As the Sanuri looked through the book he questioned the accuracy of the images as he had always found that fear distorted the perceptions of man.

Towards the middle of the book The Sanuri saw a drawing of a creature that looked similar to the drawings he had seen in Astras. "This one walks on two legs and would be about the size and weight to make the footprints I have seen," thought the Sanuri as he moved the book closer to a candle so he could read the caption under the drawing. "*A Teragon,* I found it," thought the Sanuri. "I have the picture and these vague phrases; there must be more information about these beasts."

Cerephus sat in his small cabin on the castle grounds, writing a letter and drinking a large glass of whiskey.

Erebus old friend, some things appear to be disrupting my plans. I may need your services sooner than I had anticipated. Start to prepare yourself for the journey.

Can you travel by carriage or do you want me to send men with a boca to carry the things you will need? I will make arrangements for quarters for you until I can bring you into the castle. Cerephus

The Sanuri jumped up from the table where he had been sleeping in the Hall of Antiquities. He was awakened by Padre Thomas calling his name.

"There you are, we have been looking all over for you," said Padre Thomas as he sat at the table next to the Sanuri.

"Excuse me I must have fallen asleep," said the Sanuri with a yawn.

"Come down for breakfast and afterwards Padre Bartholomew and I will help you search for the answers you seek."

"Actually I must show you and Padre Bartholomew what I have found," said the Sanuri as he picked up the book containing images of demons and walked to the dining hall with Padre Thomas.

"Where is Petra?" asked the Sanuri as he sat next to Padre Bartholomew.

"He already ate and is outside."

The Sanuri motioned for the two priests to lean closer to him as he spoke. "Last night I found an ancient manuscript written in Amark; it said *The creation of evil begets an evil unto itself of such great proportions that the demons feed upon their own.* This phrase was similar to what I remember reading before. Then I found a second passage, *True evil knows no boundaries, not even of its own kind.* I was having such difficulty finding information on the Teragon that I decided to take a different approach and I found this book of pictures."

The Sanuri placed the opened book in front of the priests. "This creature is the Teragon and there is a remarkable similarity between this picture and the drawings I saw in Astras. I truly believe that the Centras have seen the Teragon. The passages I just told you are not the same ones I remembered reading years ago. There must be more information about these demons."

"Sanuri I still don't truly understand how these demons came to be. Are you saying the Hutas were creating some kind of great evil and as a mistake created the Teragon too?" asked Padre Bartholomew.

"Well, from what I have been reading it was not that the Hutas made a mistake but this is the consequences of their actions," said the Sanuri. "You might say a byproduct of their actions."

Padre Bartholomew was quiet for a few moments as he contemplated the Sanuri's words. "I hear what you say but I find the entire concept very confusing," Padre Bartholomew admitted.

"If there is a picture and references to these demons someone besides the Centras have seen them," said Padre Thomas. "Padre Bartholomew and I will take turns taking care of Petra and helping you do research. We must find out what horrors the Hutas have created that have brought the Teragon back to this world."

High Priest Meekos sat at his breakfast table with High Priest Pravis and High Priest Tenebrae in the Great Hall of the monastery at Malga. The three watched intently as the Sanuri was talking to Padre Thomas and Padre Bartholomew.

"I wonder what he is up to now," Pravis said. "We should just kick him out of here."

"Are you crazy Pravis?" Tenebrae asked. "To kick the emissary for The Great Ruler out of the monastery would not only expose us but call the wrath of The Great Ruler upon us."

"The Great Ruler hasn't punished us yet and we have done a lot worse than kicking the Sanuri out," Pravis responded sarcastically.

"Will you two shut up? You sound like a couple of children," Meekos snapped. "And watch what you say in front of the others. For now we will just watch them until my men arrive and can take over."

That night Roch tossed and turned in his bed as nightmare after nightmare plagued his sleep. Sweat poured out of him as images of his precious map were intertwined with images of Vitomas, the Gants devouring his men and that face in the fire, that haunting, terrifying face. Roch sat up in bed soaking wet. Then after a few minutes he got out of bed and walked down the stairs to his war room for a glass of whiskey; a nightly behavior that was becoming routine.

Sitting at his desk and studying his map; it wasn't until Roch poured his second glass of whiskey that he realized Jonas was standing in the hallway outside of the open door of the war room. "It is the middle of the night is something wrong?" Roch asked.

"I couldn't sleep so I decided to take a walk, it looks like I am not the only one," said Jonas as he entered the war room and boldly poured himself a glass of whiskey. "You look awful," Jonas said as he sat in one of the chairs facing Roch.

"I feel awful, I can't remember the last time I got a good night's sleep," said Roch as he drank the entire glass of whiskey in one gulp.

"So what keeps you up at night?" asked Jonas nonchalantly.

Roch stared angrily at Jonas as he again filled his glass with whiskey. "Nightmares."

"You have nightmares," replied Jonas in disbelief. "I didn't think you were afraid of anything."

"I'm not," growled Roch. "Besides these are not those kind of nightmares."

"I cannot imagine what would keep a man like you up at night."

Roch leaned back in his chair and stared at Jonas. "If I tell you, you will think I am crazy. But I fear someone has put a curse upon me. It's not just in my nightmares that I see the faces but when I am awake I see them in my campfire and I have heard them calling my name. That is how I broke my ankle, it was daylight and a voice came out of nowhere and started talking to me then it was like an invisible hand started to throw me around. And as if that wasn't bad enough the voice never stopped laughing."

412

"You said the voice was laughing?" Jonas asked as he started to suspect who Roch's attacker was. "Did you find out who it was?"

"No, he wouldn't tell me but I am sure it was a demon because he was talking about hell. But he did tell me that one of the faces I have been seeing used to work for him; although he wouldn't tell me why I was seeing that face or who it was I was seeing."

Roch definitely had Jonas' interest. "If you don't mind my asking what do these faces look like?"

"Well, one of them is that seer we met, Miranda. But most of the time it is either the face of a huge lion that talks to me or the face of a man. The demon said it is the man that worked for him."

"You are saying the demon said the man used to work for him, so he no longer does?"

"I am just telling you what the demon said," Roch growled. "He certainly wasn't answering any of my questions. Every time I asked him something he answered in riddles."

By this time, Jonas was convinced that Roch had an encounter with Ahriman; the most powerful Old One in this world. But Jonas had no idea why Ahriman would reveal himself to Roch. The Old Ones rarely revealed themselves to humans; they sent underlings for such tasks. "And what did this man look like?" Jonas asked, trying to sound like he was just making conversation.

"He is bald except for a long thin ponytail down the middle of his head. He has a thin mustache and two gold earrings in each ear."

"And does this man speak to you also?" Jonas asked as he realized Roch had described Sporos.

"No he is surrounded by darkness and looks like he is screaming with rage."

Jonas held his glass up to his mouth, yet he did not drink. Jonas did not move, nor did he speak; he just stared at Roch. For now Jonas realized why he had not been able to contact his friend and benefactor Sporos.

413

Jonas knew that Sporos must be a prisoner in The Great Abyss, where their lord Omnibus was also imprisoned. This knowledge filled Jonas with both fear and anger. Yet Roch's words confused Jonas, for it was not Ahriman that Sporos worked for but Ahriman's old rival Omnibus and to Jonas' knowledge Ahriman had taken no part in the plans to help Omnibus escape his eternal prison. Jonas wondered what treachery Ahriman was planning.

Noreen jumped out of bed and grabbed a knife that she had placed on the small table next to her bed. She ran to her infant son Jacob, who was sleeping in a cradle in her room. Then Noreen hid behind the bedroom door as she listened to something pushing on the front door of their home.

"Noreen Honey, it's me, Henry," a voice called out. "Unlock the door."

With great relief Noreen ran into the kitchen and opened the door. She jumped into her young husband's arms and hugged him tightly. "Where have you been?" Noreen cried. "I thought you were dead, you should have been home two weeks ago."

Henry was barely eighteen years old, although a man physically he was not prepared for the responsibilities of a wife and child. Henry hugged Noreen and walked into the kitchen without speaking.

"Henry what is wrong? Did something happen to you?" Noreen asked as she stared at him. There were no candles lit but the flames from the hearth provided enough light for her to see the look of guilt on her husband's face.

"Noreen you are going to be so mad at me."

"Henry what did you do?" Henry did not answer so Noreen repeated the question in a louder voice, "Henry what did you do?"

"I lost our horse in a card game; I had to walk home," Henry said with shame.

"Henry how could you, we have nothing as it is and now you lost the horse!" Noreen quickly sat down on one of the chairs that surrounded the kitchen table. "And I suppose you didn't find work either."

"No," Henry replied in a hoarse whisper.

Noreen covered her face with both of her hands and cried. Henry was afraid to comfort his wife. After a few moments she looked at him. "You have not asked about your son or me. I will have you know that while you were gone, playing cards, a crazy man came here and attacked me. That is why everything is locked up; I have been afraid he will return."

"Honey are you alright?" Henry asked as he walked closer to Noreen.

"I have been terrified but otherwise alright, if you care at all. The man was going to rape me; he had a hold of me but suddenly stopped and ran out of the house so fast that he tripped over the furniture. He was a big man too, I could not fight him off."

Henry stared at Noreen, he believed her yet the story was so strange. "Why did he run off?"

"I don't know, I told you he was acting crazy." Henry did not say anything. "You don't believe me do you? I can't believe this, I could have been raped and killed and you don't even believe me. I will show you," Noreen said as she got up from the chair and ran to the kitchen cupboard. "I found this on the floor after he left." Noreen said defiantly as she took Roch's ring from the cupboard and threw it at Henry.

Henry was shocked as he picked up the ring and examined it. Then his countenance began to change, "Noreen this ring must be worth a fortune," Henry said with a devious smile.

"Have you two been up all night?" Sophie asked as she walked into the war room before sunrise.

"Yes," Roch growled and I am starving.

"My Lord I will be right back with your breakfast. Will Jonas be eating also?"

"Yes," Roch replied with annoyance. His continual lack of sleep was making his temperament worse.

Within minutes Sophie carried the first of three large trays of food into the war room. She set platters of eggs, pork chops, potatoes and biscuits on the table. Sophie returned again and again to the war room with coffee and morning cakes. Sophie was filling Roch's cup with coffee when she gasped in horror, "My Lord your ring!"

"Yes, I lost it someplace," Roch growled.

Both Sophie and Jonas understood the significance of the blood ring, although Roch did not. "Perhaps I could help you look for it," Jonas offered.

"No, I realized it was missing when I was returning from the Caves of Muldun. I could have lost it any number of places. I was swimming for my life, trying to escape the Gants, I stopped at several farm houses to get food; there are so many places I could have lost it." Roch was looking down as his plate as he spoke; now he looked up at both Sophie and Jonas. "Sophie you look so upset, it was a beautiful ring but it was just a piece of jewelry."

Chapter XXVI
Husbands

Simon healed quickly over the next week. He was still weak and in pain but Simon was now able to walk without assistance and he moved back into his chambers with Annabelle.

"Where are you two going?" asked Marie as she saw Simon and Raul walking out the front door of the castle.

"We were going to visit the wounded troops, why?" asked Raul.

"Because your father just sent me to get you two. He and your mother are waiting for you in the study."

"Do you know why?" asked Simon.

"No, they just told me to get you now," said Marie as she turned down the hallway.

"For some reason this is reminding me of when we were kids and they would send Marie for us," Raul said with a laugh. "We always knew we were in trouble then."

"I heard you," Marie said laughing. "And it reminded me of that too."

When Raul and Simon entered the study, Sudfad was sitting behind his large wooden desk and Renya was sitting next to him. "Please be seated boys," said Sudfad. They sat in the two chairs that had been placed directly in front of the desk.

"You both know that we love you and are very proud of you," Sudfad said. "You have devoted your entire lives to becoming great leaders and fierce warriors but now you must learn to become good husbands." Simon smiled and was about to say something when Sudfad held up his hand and said, "I am still talking." Sudfad continued. "Your mother and I are aware of our responsibilities to the kingdom and we are very pleased with your choices for wives; not only are they lovely girls but either of them will make a fine queen some day."

"You both proposed to those girls but did either of you think of giving them a ring?" asked Renya. Simon and Raul both looked at each other then at their parents sheepishly.

"That is what we thought," said Renya. King Sudfad opened a desk drawer and took out two small boxes, handing one to each son. "Your father and I had these made and fortunately Laurel knew the favorite stones of each girl," said Renya. Raul and Simon opened the boxes and stared at the beautiful rings before them.

"For Annabelle the dark sapphire with diamonds and for Vitomas the ruby with diamonds," said Sudfad, then with a laugh he added, "And trust me sons it is things like this you will want to remember."

Both Raul and Simon got out of their seats and leaned forward to hug their mother when Queen Renya said, "You two sit right back down your father needs to talk to you." Both sons quickly took their seats feeling much like they were kids again.

"Where do you plan to live after you are married?" Sudfad asked.

Raul and Simon looked at each other with embarrassment. "You are right Father, we have been so happy just being with the girls that we haven't taken the time to think anything out," said Simon.

"That is what we thought," said Renya. "And that would be fine but both of you have said you want to have the weddings as soon as possible and if that is truly the case you need to make some plans. You cannot live with them in your little bedrooms forever," Renya added with a warm smile.

Sudfad handed each son a small scroll. "These are deeds to fine pieces of land that are more than suitable for family homes," said Sudfad then he reached over and took Renya's hand and continued speaking. "But we had hoped you would consider staying in the castle; your mother has had workmen here day and night for weeks," said Sudfad smiling. "Raul we are giving you and Vitomas the west wing of the castle and Simon, you and Annabelle the east wing."

"The wings have been redesigned for families and now have private entrances," said Renya. "And they have nurseries; sons your father and I want lots of grandchildren."

"Of course the choice is yours, talk to the girls and look at the wings; and if you decide to live here I am sure you can persuade your mother to help the girls decorate your new homes," Sudfad said and laughed.

Both Raul and Simon sat speechless for a moment. "We are stunned by your generosity, "said Raul.

"Thank you," said Simon sincerely.

"So when are you getting married?" Renya asked. Neither Raul nor Simon answered for a moment. "We haven't really talked about it," Raul said with embarrassment.

"I have started some preparations but you both know that as princes and heirs to the throne these weddings have to be spectacular. Both those girls are so sweet and so happy just to be here I will bet neither of them will bring the subject up first. Talk to them, then come back and tell Sudfad and me what your decisions are."

"I felt like I was ten years old and getting a scolding again," said Simon as he and Raul left their parents in the study.

"I did too," said Raul with embarrassment. "But they are right. As detailed as we are with everything else I cannot believe neither of us thought of these things. Did Annabelle say anything to you?"

"Are you kidding, she is so humble and grateful for everything; I can't even get her to tell me when she needs things. How about Vitomas?"

"She's so happy to be here with me and to be safe; she has not asked me for anything," said Raul as they walked towards the center wing. "The other day when I took her shopping she was so happy she just kept crying."

"You know both of the girls have probably been thinking about these things," said Simon. "Do you want to talk to them together; maybe we won't look like such asses that way."

"Oh, we will look like asses."

Raul and Simon found Vitomas and Annabelle sitting in one of the castle gardens. "I thought you were leaving," Annabelle said as she jumped up and kissed Simon.

"What is the matter, you have such peculiar looks?" asked Vitomas.

"We need to talk with both of you," said Raul seriously. Both Vitomas and Annabelle became worried.

"Annabelle why don't you sit down," suggested Simon. Annabelle returned to the bench she had been sitting on.

"Our parents just had a talk with us," Raul said.

Smiling, Simon said, "The good news is they love the two of you."

"And the bad news?" asked Vitomas with concern.

Raul and Simon looked at each other sheepishly. "They think we need lessons in being good husbands," said Raul. "And after talking with them we agree. Simon and I have just been so happy being with the two of you that we had not considered any of the responsibilities connected with getting married. And we are truly sorry for that."

"Neither Raul or I have ever considered marrying anyone before, which is not an excuse," said Simon. "But we need you two to help us out. Tell us what you want and do not assume we know anything about weddings."

Before either of the women could speak Simon said, "We are sorry we did not think to give you rings." Simon and Raul handed each woman a small box. Annabelle squealed with delight when she saw her ring and threw her arms around Simon's neck.

Vitomas started to cry as she put her ring on her hand. She put her arms around Raul's neck and asked, "How did you know?"

"I didn't know and that was the point of the talk," said Raul with embarrassment.

"Our parents had these rings made for you," admitted Simon shyly. "You will want to thank them too."

"Do not be so hard on yourselves, things have been so crazy," said Vitomas.

"That is not an excuse, there are other things we didn't think of also," said Simon sincerely. Simon and Raul handed Annabelle and Vitomas the small scrolls. "These are deeds to land our parents gave to us to build homes on but they would prefer we live in the castle."

"They have redesigned two wings of the castle and given them to us; Vitomas you and I have the west wing and they have the east wing," said Raul as he nodded towards Simon and Annabelle.

"They said the choice was ours to decide where we wanted to live," Simon added.

"Your parents are so generous," Annabelle said with amazement.

Simon laughed loudly, "Oh there is a catch we have all been ordered to give them lots of grandchildren."

They all laughed except Vitomas. "Are you alright Honey?" said Raul putting his arm around her.

"I am just so overwhelmed I don't even know what to say," said Vitomas with tears in her eyes.

"Do you want to look at the wings?" asked Raul. "Simon and I have not seen them either. And girls we need you to be honest with us as to where you want to live." The two couples walked inside the castle.

"We are closer to the east wing," said Simon. "As he led the small group in that direction. They were all taken by surprise when they entered the living quarters. "It never looked anything like this before," said Simon as they walked through a beautiful parlor, dining room and kitchen.

"I have a study," Simon called out with a grin.

"Look at all of these bedrooms," said Annabelle in awe.

"I told you they wanted lots of grandbabies," said Simon with a laugh.

"Look at this," said Vitomas as she and Raul stood in the master bedroom, which included a fireplace, a seating area, an attached nursery and a garden entrance.

"This is so beautiful," said Annabelle. "I think I am going to cry."

Simon put his arm around Annabelle and asked, "What do you think?"

"I think your parents have put so much work into this home that we should live here," replied Annabelle happily.

Simon kissed Annabelle on the forehead and said, "I do too."

When the two couples reached the west wing they saw that it was the same design but with different furniture and decorations. Raul and Vitomas walked through the home hand in hand; finally he turned to her and asked, "What do you want to do?"

"Raul for the first time in my life I have a family, I want to live here with them," said Vitomas with tears in her eyes. Raul kissed her on the lips and said, "I agree." He kissed Vitomas again and said, "We should tell our parents."

The group was standing in the master bedroom. Simon sat down on the bed. "We can't talk to them until we set dates for the weddings," Simon said with a grin. The others sat down on the bed with Simon.

"Actually Annabelle and I have been talking about that," said Vitomas.

"What would you think about a double wedding?" asked Annabelle.

Raul and Simon both looked at each other and smiled. "That sounds fine to me," said Raul.

"Of course we will have to ask your parents, there might be some royal protocol about weddings," Vitomas said.

"Did you pick a date?" asked Simon, relieved that Annabelle and Vitomas had already discussed these things.

"The physician said it will be at least two more weeks before you are healed," said Annabelle to Simon "We shouldn't have anything before you are ready."

"Your parents and Annabelle's parents are working on all of the preparations," Vitomas said. "We need to ask them when everything will be completed."

Raul looked at the others, "I think we should hold the ceremonies as soon as all of the preparations are completed and as quickly as mother had these wings redesigned I suspect the wedding preparations are moving quickly also. Who is in agreement?" Vitomas hugged Raul and happily said, "I agree dear."

"I agree too," said Annabelle excitedly.

Simon got off from the bed and took Annabelle's hand, "I think we are ready to see the King and Queen."

Raul, Vitomas, Simon and Annabelle found Renya and Sudfad sitting in their parlor. Both Vitomas and Annabelle ran to Renya and hugged her then to Sudfad and hugged him. They were talking and laughing at the same time; thanking the King and Queen and telling them how much they loved the homes and the rings.

Sudfad and Renya were filled with joy when Raul said, "We are all staying here."

"Let me see your hands," said Renya and the two women showed off their rings.

"Marie," called Sudfad. When Marie appeared at the door he said. "Marie would you please ask Alexander and Laurel to join us and then bring us a couple of bottles of our finest wine."

"Yes My Lord," said Marie as she was preparing to leave.

"And Marie, bring a glass for yourself we are celebrating," said Sudfad happily.

"Marie the children are staying here," exclaimed Renya with joy.

Marie looked at Raul and Simon with a broad smile on her face and said, "I am glad." Then turned and left the room.

"Did you decide on the dates for the weddings?" asked Sudfad.

"We were thinking about a double wedding if that would be alright," said Annabelle shyly.

Renya looked seriously at Vitomas and Annabelle and asked, "Was this your idea or the boys?"

"Ours," replied Vitomas. Simon and Raul glanced at each other when they heard the tone of their mother's voice."

"Well, then it sounds wonderful to me," said Renya.

"We would like to be married as soon as possible," said Simon, squeezing Annabelle's hand.

"The physician said it will be at least two weeks before Simon is healed," said Annabelle.

"Since you are putting all of the work into the weddings, we decided to be married as soon as the preparations are completed," said Raul.

"That is if it is alright with you," added Vitomas.

Sudfad and Renya looked at each other smiling. "We are both very pleased with all of your decisions," said Sudfad.

"Girls, tomorrow we will have the dressmakers come to the castle, once we find out how long it will take to make the dresses we can set a date," said Renya with tears in her eyes. "I think the boys told you that I always wanted daughters too, you are my daughters now." Both Vitomas and Annabelle hugged Renya tightly.

"The two of you," said Sudfad looking at Raul and Simon. "Will be married in your military formal uniforms; which neither of you have worn for a while. Tomorrow go to the tailor's and have new ones made." Both Raul and Simon were smiling as their father spoke.

"I know these are your weddings but as the Royal Family we have responsibilities to our subjects also, never forget that," Sudfad continued. "The wedding will be open to all. We will have a grand celebration and you will ride through the streets after the ceremony."

The two young couples were overwhelmed by the words that Sudfad was saying. When Renya saw the looks on their faces she said, "Your father is right, ceremonies like this help to unify the people and to uplift their spirits; it is the least we can do."

"Sanuri are you going to spend all of your time in the Hall of Antiquities?" Petra asked as they ate lunch.

"I am trying to get as much work done as I can because we will be leaving soon," the Sanuri replied and winked at both Padre Bartholomew and Padre Thomas.

"We will? Where are we going?" asked Petra with excitement.

"Petra you don't have to be so happy about leaving us," Padre Bartholomew joked.

"It's not that I want to leave you, I am just excited to go traveling."

"We need to be in Wetpr in a few weeks," the Sanuri said. "I told you before that we would travel there."

"Wetpr, I've never been to Wetpr before," said Petra as his eyes grew large with anticipation.

"What is in Wetpr?" asked Padre Bartholomew.

"It is the Time of Kings," replied the Sanuri.

"Truly the Time of Kings?" Padre Thomas asked.

"Yes, the Princes of Wetpr are both getting married on the same day and I have been asked to perform the ceremonies."

"You mean the Princes of Wetpr are the kings that the prophesy speaks of?" Padre Bartholomew asked.

"What are you talking about?" asked Petra.

"Can I tell him?" Padre Thomas asked.

The Sanuri looked at Petra and asked, "Petra can you keep a secret? This is the kind of secret that if you tell; people will get hurt."

"Then I won't tell anyone," Petra said with determination.

"There is an ancient prophesy called the Prophesy of The Seven Sons. The prophesy predicts that seven sons of goodness will lead armies and destroy the demons of the night. They will save the people of all the kingdoms from great horror. The prophesy says that The Time of Kings will usher in this era," explained Padre Thomas.

"Petra I told you about my friends the King and Queen of Wetpr, the princes that we are talking about are their two sons Raul and Simon. So you my young friend are going to experience your first royal wedding and all of the celebrations that will be planned. And you will experience everything first hand with the Royal Family," the Sanuri said with a smile.

"Whoa," said Petra as his eyes grew wide with anticipation.

"Henry I thought you said we were going to sell that ring," Noreen said. "There are so many things that we need."

"We will, I am just not ready to part with it yet," Henry said as he looked at Roch's ring which Henry was wearing on his right hand.

"I wish you would look at me like you do that ring," Noreen said without humor. "I'm beginning to think it is bewitched, it's almost like it has a hold over you."

"Shut up, just shut the hell up!" Screamed Henry as he jumped out of his chair and raised his hand to strike Noreen; something he had never done before.

Noreen stared at Henry with fear and concern; she no longer recognized the man she married.

Chapter XXVII
Gifts

"After breakfast I am going to need Vitomas and Annabelle to stay with me for a while," said Renya as the entire Royal Family sat around the huge dining table. "Girls the dressmakers will arrive around ten but before that you have to choose the invitations." Vitomas and Annabelle looked at each other with confusion.

"We have no one to invite to the weddings," Vitomas said shyly. "Except for Gala but it would be too dangerous for her to come here."

"Oh my dears, we will be inviting a lot of people. These are royal weddings; we will be inviting dignitaries from many kingdoms," said Renya gleefully. "And I have a large family."

"Mother, Father I just realized I never finished telling you about my travels," said Raul. "Forgive me; there is so much to tell you. Mother I stayed with your brother Mathas and his family for several weeks." Raul turned to Vitomas and said, "Mother's brother is king of the Kingdom of Lentz, his wife's name is Rosa and they have three children Matthew, Juleta and Margarit."

"Oh Raul, how could you have forgotten to tell me about that; I have not seen Mathas and his family for years," said Renya. "I want to hear every detail."

"Actually I decided to visit them at the beginning of my journey. Mother, Mathas and Rosa looked very much like they did the last time they came to visit. The years have been kind to them," said Raul. "Matthew is two years younger than Simon and me and I will tell you he could be our brother." Raul turned to his left and looked at Simon. "Simon, he is exactly like us, I told him he could come and stay with our family any time. Mother, Father I think you would really enjoy him."

"Is he the oldest?" asked Annabelle.

"No, Juleta is the oldest and just a horrible person."

"Raul, surely you are joking," Renya said with surprise.

"No, I am very serious," Raul said as he looked at his father. "The best way I can describe her is to say she is a female version of Roch."

"Raul!" exclaimed Sudfad.

"Father she is consumed with a desire for power and she will do anything to get it," continued Raul. "I actually warned Matthew to watch his back with her. Juleta is rude, demanding and speaks in a condescending manner to everyone including her parents. I hope she does not come to the wedding but if she does, I will guarantee Mother will be appalled and offended."

No one at the table spoke so Raul continued with his story. "Actually I probably exaggerated," Raul added. "I can't imagine Juleta could be as cruel as Roch. But wait until you meet her. Their third child is Margarit, who would be about ten now. She is a charming and sweet little girl. Matthew wanted to travel with me but Mathas would not allow him to miss his studies."

"Raul it's getting late; the girls and I have to be going but I know we all would very much like to hear about your travels," Renya said as she stood up from the table.

"If everyone is planning to be here for dinner tonight, perhaps Raul would continue," Sudfad offered. Renya took both Vitomas and Annabelle by the hand and ushered them out of the dining room.

"And you two should have fittings for your uniforms today," Sudfad reminded his sons.

Simon looked at Raul and said with a grin, "Well, that does sound better than picking out invitations."

Raul laughed and said, "Perhaps we should leave before Mother makes us get involved with the preparations."

Laurel joined Renya, Vitomas and Annabelle for the dress fittings. Both of the prospective brides were overwhelmed with all of the beautiful dresses they had to choose from.

"Now girls, if you don't like any of these we will get others," Renya said as she beamed with pride. Although Renya had known Annabelle and Vitomas for such a short period of time, the girls had stolen her heart. Renya already thought of them as her daughters and wanted to make their weddings wonderful for them.

"Renya the problem is that we love them all," Annabelle said. "You and mother are going to have to help us pick the right ones."

"I'm sorry," Laurel said as she was both crying and smiling. "You girls just look so beautiful. If I am crying this much now I don't know what I will be like at the wedding." Renya put her arm around Laurel and hugged her tightly.

"More dresses," Vitomas gasped as attendants were carrying armfuls and laying them on tables and over chairs. "Maybe we should have Raul and Simon help us choose."

"You will not," Renya said with a laugh. "You don't want them to see the dresses until you walk down the aisle and take their breath away."

The Royal Family of Wetpr sat around the dining room table for hours after they had finished their evening meal; drinking wine and listening as Raul told them of the adventures and hardships of his travels. Raul told them of his encounters with wild beasts and his narrow escape from a band of Hutas.

Raul described a tribe of people that he met in the Kingdom of Zorta, who so adorned their bodies with tattoos that they did not feel the need for clothing. Raul told them of a tribe of exceptionally tiny people who lived near the river Tpra in the Kingdom of Gandt. And he told them of a group of giants who dwelled in Port Friada.

"I wish I would have gone with you," Simon said wistfully.

"Well, I am glad you didn't," said Renya. "It was difficult enough to endure the absence of one son; I don't know what I would have done with both of you gone."

Raul got up from the table and walked over to his mother and hugged her tightly. "But Mother, if I would not have left we would not have Vitomas, Annabelle, Laurel and Alexander here." Renya patted Raul's hand, "Yes you are right my son but we still missed you greatly."

"So you said several times you awoke to find the prints of a huge lion in your camp and yet you and your horse were never attacked," said Sudfad. "I find that rather astonishing. The Great Ruler must have been watching out for you."

"I know," replied Raul. "Vitomas said that when she found me there were prints of a great lion in the dirt near me and I even found lion prints by the back door of the cabin I was hiding in near Cana, it is so odd. Father what do you make of this, is it possible that a single lion followed me during my travels? It is incredible to think I had that many encounters with different lions and never received so much as a scratch."

"Honestly son, I don't know what to make of it; I have never heard of such things."

"It just scares me to think of how many times you could have been injured or killed and we would never have known," Renya said fearfully.

"My dear he is home now," said Sudfad as he reached over and squeezed Renya's hand.

"Mother before I forget, I visited your sister Tasha and Tobias," Raul said. "I stayed with them and their family for almost a week."

"Raul, I just cannot believe it slipped your mind to tell me these things," Renya scolded.

Sudfad looked at Vitomas and Annabelle and explained, "Raul is talking about King Tobias and Queen Tasha of the Kingdom of Puntd."

"Renya are all your family kings and queens?" asked Annabelle.

"No, I have two sisters and one brother. My brother Mathas is King of Lentz, my sister Tasha is Queen of Puntd and my youngest sister Isabella married Josef, a captain in the Royal Lentz Army," replied Renya. "Raul the last I heard, Isabella and her family were still living in the castle with Mathas and Rosa is that true?"

"No, they have a castle on the southeast portion of the kingdom; they live on the shores of the Sea of Grevtd. Josef is stationed at Fort Castor. They have four small children, Geoff would be seven now, Tabitha is five, Ottillia is three and Jasper is probably a year and a half." Raul said with a partial laugh. "Isabella told me they could not stand to live under the same roof with Juleta."

"I am beginning to hope Juleta comes to the wedding just so I can meet her," Simon said sarcastically.

"I don't," said Annabelle. "She sounds horrible."

"Raul, tell us about Tobias, I really don't know him very well," Renya said.

"He seemed like a fair and honorable man. He takes care of his subjects and has a large army. But Father," Raul said as he looked at Sudfad. "His entire army is garrisoned at his castle so it takes them a long time to respond to situations in other areas of their kingdom. I told him that you established military posts throughout our kingdom for better protection of the people and he merely said he found the concept interesting."

"What kind of husband and father is he? And how many children do they have now?" asked Renya.

"Mother from what I saw he seemed like a good man, Tasha seems very happy. They have three children, Sasha is the oldest and should be about seventeen now. Nicolas is ten and Philp is seven."

Renya looked at Laurel and said. "My sister and Tobias had great difficulty conceiving. She had five miscarriages before their first child was born."

"Renya are you inviting all of your family to the wedding so we can meet them?" Vitomas asked.

"Oh, yes my dear."

"Renya has hired extra staff to prepare all of the rooms in the castle and the cottages for guests and to serve them during their stay," Sudfad said.

"This all sounds so wonderful yet I have to admit it is a bit overwhelming," said Annabelle. "I would be happy with a quiet little ceremony."

"Honestly Honey, we all would," said Simon as he put his arm around Annabelle. "But ceremonies like this are more for the people of the kingdom than for us."

"I don't know if I would go so far as to say they are more for our people than for you," said Sudfad. "But your mother and I feel a great responsibility to our people. We want them to feel like they are a part of our family."

Sudfad looked at Annabelle and Vitomas. "Girls wait until you see the excitement and happiness this event brings to people who are total strangers to you. We always open our ceremonies to the people and hundreds of thousands of them attend in some fashion."

"How can that many people attend?" asked Annabelle.

"The wedding will be held outside. And the royal grounds and the area around the castle will be filled with people. After the ceremony you will ride through the streets of Salar so the people who could not get close to the castle can see you and celebrate with you," said Sudfad.

Roch walked into Vitomas' chambers. Nothing had been touched since her disappearance. Sadness touched his heart as Roch looked at Vitomas' beautiful dresses and her hair brush still lying on a dressing table. Roch opened the drawers to Vitomas' dressers and writing tables looking for any clue of what had happened to her. All Roch found were the usual items that he would expect to find in a young woman's room.

Roch searched Vitomas' closet looking in boxes and pockets of clothing. Then he spied her saddlebags pushed in the back of the closet; finding this curious Roch opened the saddlebags and found them filled with clothing. He pulled the clothes out; there was nothing extraordinary in the bags, a couple of sets of clothing, a hair brush, soap and perfume. Roch sat down on the bed looking at these items wondering why Vitomas would pack them. "If she was not kidnapped and left him, then why did Vitomas leave the saddlebags behind?" he wondered.

Finally Roch just placed all the items on her bed. He walked over to Vitomas' dresser and took the box that still contained all of her jewels. Roch locked the box of jewels in the secret treasure room, behind the hearth in his bedroom and returned to the war room.

The Sanuri sat up in bed. "The eyes, the eyes of the terrorists what were they looking at?" thought the Sanuri as he sought to understand his dream. Then he saw the vision again; the two young princes of Wetpr were seated in a grand boca with their brides. They were being driven through the crowded streets of Salar, surrounded by thousands of cheering people. And in the crowds, on the streets and in the windows were the eyes of the terrorists watching the royal couples.

The Sanuri was suddenly filled with a sense of great danger. He jumped out of bed and quickly packed his belongings. The Sanuri ran to Petra's room and woke him. "Petra you must get up now, we have to leave for Wetpr."

"Now, I thought we weren't leaving for a couple of days," said Petra, who was not fully awake.

"The time is now, pack your things and meet me at the boca quickly."

The Sanuri knocked on Padre Bartholomew's door and told him they were leaving and he would explain on his next visit. The Sanuri hitched the team of horses to the boca and he and Petra sped off into the darkness of the night.

Annabelle jumped out of bed the next morning and ran to the window. The sun was just beginning to rise as she searched the landscape.

"Where are you going?" Simon called sleepily.

"Simon, Simon you have to get up now," said Annabelle excitedly as she quickly got dressed. "Simon, really get up."

"Yes Honey."

"Simon please get up now."

When Annabelle realized that Simon had pulled the covers over his head she ran to the bed and started to shake him. Simon started to laugh and pulled Annabelle down on top of him, kissing her neck. "Simon, we don't have time for this, you need to get up now."

There was a knock at the door that separated Vitomas' and Annabelle's chambers. "Are you two up?" called Vitomas through the closed door.

"Simon won't get out of bed," Annabelle called out with a giggle.

"Simon," Vitomas scolded. "If you don't get up right now I am coming in there and helping Annabelle get you up." Simon could hear Raul laughing on the other side of the door.

"Vitomas you are welcome to come in but I am afraid both of you girls will end up in bed with me," Simon said laughing. There was silence for a few moments then Simon heard Vitomas talking to Raul. "Raul will you get him up we have a surprise for you two?"

"Did you hear Brother?" Raul yelled through the closed door.

"Yes, I am getting up now."

As soon as Simon put his pants on Annabelle opened the door so Vitomas and Raul could enter her chambers. Vitomas walked up to Simon as he was buttoning his shirt and hit him on the chest. "What was that for?" Simon asked with a grin.

"It's for what you said," Vitomas replied as she turned and walked back towards Raul. Both men broke into laughter.

"Come on," pleaded Annabelle who was waiting in the hallway outside of her chambers.

"Annabelle here," said Vitomas as she handed Annabelle a long scarf.

"What is this for?" Annabelle asked.

"We are going to blindfold them."

"Well, this is certainly sounding like more and more fun," Raul joked.

After the two couples had descended the staircase that led from the front door of the castle to the front court yard; Vitomas asked Raul and Simon to bend down so that she and Annabelle could blindfold them. Once the women were certain the blindfolds were secure they led Simon and Raul through the gardens to the side of the castle where Sudfad and Renya were waiting. Both the King and Queen started laughing when they saw their sons blindfolded.

"Are Mother and Father here?" asked Simon when he heard the laughter.

"Yes," replied Annabelle. "They are a great part of this surprise."

Vitomas and Annabelle led Simon and Raul to one of the barns on the royal grounds. This particular barn had fenced corrals on each side of it. Vitomas led Raul to the corral on the right side of the barn. Sudfad was following them so Renya started to follow Simon and Annabelle to the corral on the left side of the barn but Sudfad touched Renya's arm and whispered into her ear, " Stay here; you are about to see something you won't believe."

Annabelle stopped Simon when he was just a few feet from the corral. "Ok Honey you can take your blindfold off now."

"Annabelle," gasped Simon softly as he walked towards the corral. A wild white stallion was racing around the corral looking for a way to escape the enclosure. The horse was large, muscular and unblemished.

"Do you like him?" asked Annabelle anxiously.

"Yes," said Simon as he lifted Annabelle off the ground and kissed her on the lips. "He is incredible, how did you get him?"

"Your mother asked Vitomas and me what we were getting you and Raul for wedding gifts and we were both embarrassed and told her we had no money."

"Oh Honey," Simon interrupted. "I am so sorry I never thought to give you some."

"Renya said that she and Sudfad would pay for whatever we wanted to get you. Vitomas and I agonized for days over the gifts since you and Raul have everything you could possibly want. Finally we decided to get both of you horses befitting kings. Sudfad took us shopping until Vitomas found the ones she wanted. You know I don't know very much about horses," Annabelle said apologetically. "But I do like this one for you, look at the way he carries himself, he acts as if he is a king."

Suddenly the horse started to kick the air with its back legs and to snort. The horse charged towards them but stopped several feet before it reached the front of the corral. "Oh my," said Annabelle fearfully. "Perhaps this wasn't the best horse to get you."

"Nonsense," said Simon as he put his arm around her waist. "He is just putting on a show; I like a horse with spirit. And he is the perfect gift," Simon said as he bent down and kissed Annabelle on the head.

"You can take the blindfold off now," said Vitomas.

Raul's breath left him for a moment when he saw the beautiful black stallion running around the corral. "He is majestic," uttered Raul as he stepped closer to the corral.

"Vitomas picked both of the horses out," said Sudfad. "She has a keen eye; you would do well to take her along when you buy stock."

"But how did you pay for him," asked Raul with astonishment.

"Your wonderful parents said they would pay for whatever we decided to give you for wedding gifts."

"I might say, you boys could give these girls some spending money," said Renya with a grin.

"I don't know why I just didn't think about that, I will start giving you money today," Raul said as he hugged Vitomas. "And Father I will pay you for the horse."

"Nonsense," said Sudfad, "But there is something I want you to see."

The four watched the horse as it aggressively charged at the fence that stood between it and freedom. "Simon, Annabelle could you come here a moment?" Sudfad called out.

"We wanted to get gifts worthy of kings," said Vitomas as she leaned upwards and kissed Raul on the cheek. "Do you like him?"

"You could not have gotten me a better gift."

"I could help you break him," Vitomas offered.

Raul looked down at his petite wife, "Honey look at that horse he could kill you. I appreciate the offer but it would be too dangerous."

Simon and Annabelle were walking towards Raul and the others with their arms around each other when Sudfad said, "Raul you might want to reconsider. Vitomas show him."

As Vitomas started to walk towards the horse, Raul reached out his hand to hold her back. "Let her be," said Sudfad with a smile. Vitomas walked up to the corral and stood on the bottom rail of the fence. She started speaking softly to the horse which was racing around the corral and kicking. The others could hear the sound of Vitomas' voice but they could not hear the words she was saying.

As Vitomas spoke the horse started to pay attention to her. His movements became less aggressive and he kept looking at Vitomas as he ran.

Suddenly the horse stopped in the middle of the corral and looked at Vitomas for a few minutes then he started to slowly walk towards her. The entire time Vitomas kept talking in a soft and soothing voice. Raul gasped when the horse walked up to Vitomas and leaned his head over the fence. Vitomas stroked its head and nose then kissed the horse. Vitomas appeared to lean forward and whisper into the horse's ear before she climbed down from the fence and turned back towards her family.

"Have you ever seen such a thing?" asked Sudfad proudly. "She did that with both of those horses."

"That was incredible," said Simon. "I would not have believed it had I not seen it with my own eyes."

"She has always been able to do that," Annabelle said with pride.

Vitomas smiled as she saw the look on Raul's face. Raul did not say a word as Vitomas walked towards him. When Vitomas was directly in front of Raul, he put his arms around her and said, "You never cease to amaze me, girl." Then Raul kissed Vitomas. "Seriously how did you do that?"

"I don't really know. When I lived at Roch's castle I always felt closer to the animals than the people, except for Annabelle of course. I thought the horses just responded to me because I was as much of a captive as they were."

"Vitomas it looked like you whispered something into that horse's ear," said Renya.

Vitomas blushed. "I asked him to take care of my husband."

"Padre Thomas and Padre Bartholomew, how good to see you," called out High Priest Meekos with a smile. "Would you care to join us for breakfast?" Both priests looked at each other then put their trays of food on the long table and sat down, joining Meekos and four other High Priests in the dining hall at the monastery at Malga.

"I am sorry if we seemed startled," said Padre Thomas. "It is not often we are extended such an honor as to dine with the High Priests."

"Well, it is our fault for not inviting you," said Meekos graciously. "So tell me is it true that the Sanuri left the monastery in the middle of the night because of some emergency?"

Padre Thomas looked at Meekos warily but before he could respond Padre Bartholomew spoke. "I don't know why he left so quickly, he said he would explain later but that he had to get to Wetpr as soon as possible."

"Wetpr, why would he need to get to Wetpr?" asked Meekos.

"All I know is the two young princes of Wetpr are getting married soon," said Padre Bartholomew without looking up from his plate of eggs.

"I am sure that will be a grand affair," Meekos said. "Do you know what days the weddings will occur?"

"Not the exact dates but the Sanuri made it sound as if the weddings would be held within the next few weeks," said Padre Bartholomew.

Meekos turned to the man seated at his right hand, "Pravis did you not say you would be in Wetpr in a few weeks for business?" Pravis gave Meekos a blank stare. "Perhaps you will be fortunate enough to partake in the wedding celebrations."

Pravis stared at Meekos as he spoke then replied, "Yes, yes you are right, it must have slipped my mind. But I doubt if I will receive an invitation."

"Nonsense you will not need an invitation," said Meekos. "It is well known that King Sudfad and Queen Renya share all of their grand celebrations with the peoples of their kingdom. The weddings will be open to the public. I would expect thousands of the King's loyal subjects to be filling the streets."

"Simon your horse is beautiful," remarked Renya. As the entire family walked around the barn to look at Simon's stallion.

"They are both excellent horses," said Sudfad. "You boys should be proud of your wives for coming up with such fine gifts."

"We are," said Simon as he squeezed Annabelle's hand.

"Simon what do you think; should we give the girls their wedding gifts now or wait until the wedding?"

Simon turned and looked at both Annabelle and Vitomas. "I think they deserve to get them now."

"Why don't all of you go into the main parlor and Simon and I will join you in a few minutes," Raul said with a wink.

By the time Renya, Sudfad, Annabelle and Vitomas reached the parlor, Alexander and Laurel were up and joined them.

"Wait until you see the stallions the girls bought for the boys," Sudfad said to Alexander and Laurel. "They are exceptional horses."

"Morning," Simon said as he and Raul entered the parlor. Simon walked up to Laurel and kissed her on the cheek. Then he walked up to Annabelle and handed her a gift. Vitomas was already opening the gift that Raul gave to her.

"Raul," gasped Vitomas as tears came to her eyes.

"They are for you to wear with your wedding dresses," Raul said. "Mother helped us pick them out."

"Simon I have never had such things before," gushed Annabelle as she too started to cry. "These are the most beautiful jewels I have ever seen."

"Can we put them on now?" asked Vitomas.

"Of course," said Raul as he picked up the diamond and ruby necklace out of one of the boxes and put it around Vitomas' neck. Simon helped Annabelle with her necklace which was made of diamonds and sapphires. After Vitomas and Annabelle put on the matching earrings and bracelets, Renya turned to her sons.

"Wasn't there more?" Renya asked.

441

Raul smiled and stepped into the hallway, when he reentered the parlor he handed one large box to Simon and the other to Vitomas. Both women were speechless as they took tiaras out of the boxes that matched the rest of their jewels. Vitomas hugged Raul as she cried.

"I don't even know what to say," said Annabelle before she hugged and kissed Simon.

Sudfad, Renya, Alexander and Laurel smiled lovingly as they watched the two young couples.

Padre Thomas and Padre Bartholomew met in the eastern garden of the monastery for their morning walk.

"Is something bothering you my friend?" asked Padre Bartholomew.

"This morning when High Priest Meekos invited us to join them for breakfast; did you think there was something odd about the whole thing?"

"I will admit it was highly unusual," replied Padre Bartholomew. "But I just thought Meekos was being generous."

Padre Thomas stopped walking and turned towards his friend. "May The Great Ruler forgive me for the words I am about to utter," he said. "I have known Meekos for many years and I have never seen him act in a generous manner, or even a kind manner for that fact. I have often wondered why such a man became a priest."

"What exactly are you saying?"

"Just watch him and you will see what I mean," Padre Thomas said. "And when Meekos asked us questions about the Sanuri the hair on the back of my neck stood on end. I believe he only asked us to join him to get information about the Sanuri but for what purpose I do not know."

"You should be careful what you say," scolded Padre Bartholomew. "Meekos is a High Priest of the fourth order, he could make a lot of trouble for you."

"It is not me that I am worried about."

Jonas entered the kitchen of the castle at Stordt and looked around the room to make sure that he and Sophie were alone before he spoke. "Have you heard from Meekos yet?"

"No," replied Sophie. "And that concerns me also; it has been days since I sent him the message about Roch's ring."

"Do you think he is having another made?"

"I don't see how he can. That ring was different from the other blood rings. Roch's ring actually had a drop of Omnibus' blood in the stone," explained Sophie. "It was my understanding that ring was one of a kind and now that the master is imprisoned we cannot get more of his blood."

"I have seen so many members of the Insidiae wearing similar rings; can't we just give one of them to Roch? Or does he have to have one with the master's blood?"

"I was told the blood in the ring would bind Roch with Omnibus at the time of the ascension. I am hoping that Meekos can explain this to us."

"Your brother is such a perfectionist I am sure he had a backup plan. I mean people lose jewelry all of the time. Meekos must have anticipated that this could happen."

"I hope you are right. And there is something else that concerns me. What if someone found that ring and is wearing it; would that person be bound to Omnibus?"

Chapter XXVIII
Matthew

The Sanuri walked to the back of the boca and checked on Petra, who was curled up in a quilt sleeping. The Sanuri returned to his seat near the fire and filled his pipe with tobacco. He blew smoke rings into the still warm air and watched them dance above the fire for several minutes. Then the Sanuri poured himself another cup of strong coffee and leaned forward staring into the fire.

Often The Great Ruler sent him information in dreams and visions. Sometimes the Sanuri clearly understood the messages and other times it was like constructing a puzzle. This night he was examining pieces to such a puzzle. Night after night the Sanuri had experienced similar dreams which he did not understand. The Sanuri felt that he was missing something that should be obvious to him; so he tried to remember every detail of the dreams.

In his mind the face of a young man kept appearing. "Why do I keep seeing Petra as a man?" thought the Sanuri. Suddenly the Sanuri's eyes widened with recognition. "None of this has made sense because I thought that was Petra, I was limiting myself." The Sanuri closed his eyes and said, "Great Ruler give me clear vision, help me to understand the messages you are sending to me." In an instant the Sanuri saw a single word that flashed before his minds' eye, 'Matthew'.

"My Lord, High Priest Pravis is here to see you."

"Thank you Angela, please show him in," said Meekos to his housekeeper. Pravis entered Meekos' study and waited to speak until Angela had shut the door behind her.

"I have gathered one hundred and fifty men," Pravis said. "We are prepared to leave in the morning."

"Good, remember to blend in with the crowds; we do not want to look conspicuous. I don't care about the brides, kill them if they get in the way," Meekos said. "It is the Princes we have to eliminate."

"Do you think there is any truth to that prophecy?"

Meekos seemed lost in thought for a moment, then he looked at Pravis, "You mean the one about The Seven Sons? I don't know what to believe but the Insidiae believes that entire family is a danger to our cause. And we have our orders. Kill the sons; kill the King and anyone else who gets in our way."

"But what about the Sanuri? It is said that he protects that family."

"And doesn't that make you question why? Why is that particular family so important to him? I know I have my suspicions."

"What if the Sanuri tries to stop us?"

"Some of the members of the Insidiae will be inside of the castle as guests while you and your men will be in the crowds. The Sanuri cannot watch all of you."

"But Meekos I have heard stories about the Sanuri's abilities."

"And that is what they are Pravis; stories, don't fill yourself with foolish fears. Just do your job."

Roch suddenly sat up in bed soaked with sweat. He walked down the stairs to his war room and poured a large glass of whiskey. "Am I going crazy?" He thought. "Or has a curse been placed upon me?" Roch sat at his desk as thoughts raced through his head, "Did that seer place a curse on me? I will have her killed," Roch said out loud.

Then he remembered the image of The Lion that had been haunting him for years. But the face in the fire, that damned face, it called to him every night. There was a familiarity about that face that Roch did not understand. And now Roch saw that face from the fire in his dreams and he would hear that laugh, that demonic laugh. That laugh is what filled Roch with terror and made him afraid to go to sleep.

As Roch sat at his desk trying to figure out what was happening to him a single thought filled his mind. Roch walked quickly to the door of the war room and opened it.

445

"Guard come here at once," demanded Roch.

"Yes My Lord," said one of the castle guards.

"Wake Jonas and tell him I want to see him now."

"Yes My Lord."

Roch returned to his desk and poured himself another glass of whiskey. He waited impatiently for Jonas to arrive. "What took you so long?" Roch growled when Jonas entered the room.

Jonas walked through the door yawning, "My Lord I came as soon as the guard woke me. Is something wrong?"

Roch handed Jonas a glass of whiskey. "Jonas I want you to take some men and leave tonight."

This statement sent a rush of adrenaline through Jonas which woke him completely. "My Lord, what is of such importance?"

"I want you to find him and bring him to me," said Roch angrily.

"Who My Lord?"

"The Sanuri of Tabrul."

All of Wetpr was filled with excited energy as the kingdom prepared for the royal weddings. Inn keepers and merchants were preparing for the numbers of people who would be descending on the city. The mayor of Salar was having all the streets cleaned and planned to have them decorated with flags and thousands of flowers. The wedding was to take place on the castle grounds as there were no buildings large enough to hold the expected crowds.

The King was having carpenters build hundreds of tables to hold food and drink for the spectators. Many musicians had been brought into the city for entertainment. All of the dressmakers and tailors were busy making clothes for the Royal Family, the Royal Army and many of the guests. Flowers and food delicacies of all types were arriving in Salar by bocas and by boats.

Many of the citizens of Salar knew Raul and Simon personally and had watched them grow into young men; so they felt a particular kinship to the royal couples. King Sudfad and Queen Renya were loved and adored by the people of Wetpr who felt honored to be included in the celebrations of the royal weddings.

The castle was complete chaos and the staff and workers were just as excited as the Royal Family. Vitomas and Annabelle worked hard alongside the staff not only to prepare the castle and the grounds for the celebration but also preparing their new homes. The young couples had decided not to move into the newly decorated wings until after the weddings.

Neither Vitomas nor Annabelle had ever run a household before and neither of them had much experience cooking. Marie, the longtime cook to Sudfad and Renya was flattered when the Princesses asked her to teach them how to cook and how to prepare their households.

Although Raul and Simon told their wives they would be more than happy to hire servants, Vitomas and Annabelle wanted to care for their homes and their husbands themselves. Vitomas and Annabelle adored Marie not only for her kindness and sense of humor; but Marie was always telling them stories about Raul and Simon when they were boys.

Renya's true talents as a manager were tested as she oversaw the remodeling of the wings of the castle as well as all the preparations for the wedding celebrations. Laurel never left Renya's side and the two women became as close as mother and daughter. Laurel was a talented seamstress and was kept busy making all manner of outfits and linens for the grand event. As busy as these two women were, they decided to make the veils for both of the young brides.

Although not a carpenter by trade, Alexander was quite the craftsman and worked diligently on all the various projects. The King's duties kept him busy as usual but Sudfad loved to sneak out of his office and work with Alexander. "Somehow this relaxes me," Sudfad would say every time he helped Alexander on a project. Sudfad promised Alexander that after the weddings, he would have a carpentry workshop built for Alexander on the castle grounds. This was the most precious gift that Sudfad could have given to his friend.

Padre Thomas was pulling weeds in one of the flower gardens behind the monastery at Malga while Padre Bartholomew sat under a shade tree, painting a picture. As Padre Thomas was pulling up handfuls of weeds from around the roots of flowering bushes he saw a dead raven that had been hidden by the weeds. Padre Thomas picked up the bird with his shovel and was going to remove it from the garden when he saw a piece of paper in the bird's beak. He pried the paper from the bird and unfolded it.

After reading the note, Padre Thomas looked around to see if anyone was watching them, then he put down his shovel and walked over to Padre Bartholomew. Padre Thomas knelt down and pretended he was looking at the painting.

"I am going to show you something," Padre Thomas said quietly to Padre Bartholomew. "In case we are being watched; just act nonchalant as you read the note."

"What are you talking about and why are you whispering?"

"I found a dead raven in the garden. The Sanuri once told me that dark lords use ravens as messengers. I found a note in the bird's mouth. You must read it, then you will understand."

Padre Bartholomew's eyes grew wide as he read Sophie's note. *My dearest Meekos, it is with great concern that I am sending you this note. This morning I saw that Roch was no longer wearing the blood ring that I gave him. He said he realized it was missing as he was returning from the Caves of Muldun. I know that ring held the blood of our master; can the ascension go forth without it? Can we get another? And should we be concerned if someone finds that ring and wears it. Please reply to me swiftly so I know what to do.*

With all my love

Sophie

"I think we need to get this to the Sanuri right away," Padre Bartholomew said as he stood up. "And your suspicions about High Priest Meekos were correct." Suddenly Padre Bartholomew stopped as the gravity of the note took hold. "Padre Thomas does this mean that Meekos is a dark lord?"

Renya, Laurel, Vitomas and Annabelle were walking through the front foyer towards the parlor. They had decided to take a small break from the activities. Marie approached them with a tray containing coffee, sweet rolls and a small glass of milk.

"Marie how did you know we were coming to the parlor?" asked Renya.

"I didn't My Lady; you have guests," replied Marie with a smile.

Sudfad, Alexander, Petra and the Sanuri were seated in the parlor when the women arrived. The Sanuri got out of his chair and walked over to Renya and kissed her on the cheek. "It is always a pleasure to see you Renya," he said. "Let me introduce you to my friend Petra." Petra stood up and bowed before the Queen.

"Your friend?" Renya asked quizzically but before she could say anything else Sudfad stood up and introduced the Sanuri to the rest of the women.

"Sanuri this is Laurel, Alexander's wife and the mother of one of our new daughters Annabelle. And this is Annabelle," Sudfad said.

"You look exactly like your mother," the Sanuri said. "And which of the boys are you marrying?"

"Simon," Annabelle said shyly.

"And this is our other daughter Vitomas," Sudfad said. "She saved Raul's life and devised a brilliant plan to get Raul out of Stordt and away from Roch." Sudfad turned to the women. "Alexander and I were just telling the Sanuri about how you all met."

The Sanuri looked deeply into Vitomas' eyes. "You and Annabelle will now have the families and homes that you have prayed for. It was no accident that you found Raul; you were all meant to be together." Tears came to Vitomas' eyes as she listened to the Sanuri speak but she remained silent.

"Vitomas isn't that who Archetenus talked about?" Petra asked. Suddenly all eyes were upon him.

"How do you know Archetenus?" Vitomas asked.

"We found him badly wounded in the Village of Ort. We cared for him until he was strong enough to leave us," replied the Sanuri as he studied the looks on everyone's faces. "When he left us he said he was returning to Taperia to get something."

"He came back and stole me," Vitomas said. "Raul and Simon searched for us and saved me."

Sudfad quickly changed the subject as he could see that Vitomas and Annabelle were getting upset. "The Sanuri came early because he has some business to attend to."

"Well, I couldn't be happier, Sanuri you know we love having you here. Tell us about your friend," said Renya as she watched Petra eating a sweet roll. "Is he travelling with you?"

"Yes, he is my new traveling companion," the Sanuri replied. "Petra is an orphan and we have become quite attached to each other."

"An orphan," Renya repeated.

"This brave young fellow rode to the monastery at Avaide and warned the priests that the Hutas were coming for the Shettee refugees. Because of his actions the Shettees escaped but the priests were not as fortunate," said the Sanuri as he looked over at Petra. "As the Hutas were murdering the priests, Petra pulled a dear friend of mine, Padre Bartholomew to safety. But while Petra was at Avaide saving lives, the Hutas murdered his parents and his entire village."

No one spoke for several moments before Renya asked Petra, "How old are you?"

"I am nine My Lady."

"Petra do you have any other family?"

"No My Lady," Petra's eyes started filling with tears.

"Oh my child, come here," said Renya as she stood up and took Petra's hand. "Let's go into the kitchen and see what wonderful delights Marie has made up." The Sanuri and Sudfad watched Renya and Petra as they walked out of the room and then the Sanuri looked at Sudfad and winked.

Sudfad turned to Annabelle and Vitomas, "The Sanuri is not only an old and dear friend of the family but he is..." Sudfad paused and looked at the Sanuri. "How exactly would I describe you?"

The Sanuri smiled, "I work on behalf of The Great Ruler."

"We asked him here to perform your wedding ceremony," Sudfad said as Raul and Simon entered the room.

"Oh we have heard of you," Annabelle said. "You are a most powerful holy man."

"Sanuri we met another one of your admirers," Raul said kiddingly. "A healer in Cana named Gala. She said you have been friends with generations of healers in her family."

"Ah Gala, a wonderful woman and a powerful healer. What she tells you is true," the Sanuri said. "Your father was just starting to tell me about your escape from Stordt and how you met your wives."

"Gala played a major role in all of that," Raul said. "We owe her our lives."

Renya and Petra returned to the parlor. Petra was carrying a plate containing a large piece of chocolate cake; he sat down next to Renya. "Raul why don't you tell Sanuri what happened," Sudfad said.

Pravis had his men enter Salar in small groups so as not to draw attention to them. They rented rooms in the various hotels and inns along the route that the royal couples would take after their weddings. Many of the citizens of Salar were renting out rooms in their homes as there was not enough lodging available for all the people arriving in the city.

Pravis and his men paid well to get lodging in homes that afforded them good views of the main streets as well as the designated route. Pravis had a small group of men camping outside of Salar. These men guarded the weapons until they could be smuggled into the city.

Every night Pravis planned to have some of his men sneak weapons into their rooms. Pravis knew that the Royal Family was beloved by the citizens of Wetpr and he fully expected these citizens to report any suspicious behavior to the army.

It was not difficult for Pravis and his men to get current information about the wedding and the Royal Family as the entire city was filled with excited anticipation. "Talk with people, they truly are our eyes and ears," Pravis told his men. Feeling confident that everything was falling into place; Pravis decided to send Meekos a message.

Pravis went into the courtyard of the home he was staying in. Standing in the garden, Pravis softly mumbled the words of the dark lords. He was beckoning the messengers of darkness. Soon the sky over the courtyard filled with ravens, casting shadows on the garden. One of the large birds landed on Pravis' arm. Pravis handed the bird a piece of paper which contained a single message; *All is in place.*

"My Lord, there is someone here to see you," said Marie as she entered the parlor.

"My goodness more company, how wonderful," said Renya.

"Marie did you get his name?" asked Sudfad.

"No My Lord, he told me to tell you he was Raul's little brother."

Upon hearing Marie's words Raul quickly left the parlor. "Matthew," Raul said loudly as he ran up to his cousin and gave him a hug. "I am so glad you could make it. I've been telling the family about you."

"I wouldn't miss your wedding for the world," Matthew said.

"Marie this is my cousin Matthew," Raul said with pride. "He will be staying with us, for a long time I hope."

Raul entered the parlor with Matthew. "We heard you," said Renya as she ran up to Matthew and hugged him then she stepped back. "Let me look at you. Matthew you were just a boy the last time I saw you. What a handsome man you have become." Matthew was a large man with the same muscular build as Raul and Simon, although he was slightly shorter than them. Matthew had short brown hair and brilliant blue eyes that danced against his tanned skin.

"Matthew this is my father," Raul said as they walked towards the King. The Sanuri stood up as Matthew was shaking Sudfad's hand. Both Matthew and the Sanuri stared at each other; the Sanuri walked towards Matthew smiling.

"Do you two know each other?" Raul asked as he saw the incredulous look on Matthew's face.

"I saw you in a dream," Matthew could barely utter the words.

"Yes you did," said the Sanuri smiling.

"What is going on here?" Sudfad asked.

"Sudfad, you will need to adopt Matthew as one of your own, I will explain later," said the Sanuri as he stood very close to Matthew and stared into his eyes. The Sanuri's face began to beam as he took a couple of steps back from Matthew. "Sudfad this son will lead The Great Ruler's children out of darkness."

Matthew looked at Raul, "I do not know who this man is but he is the reason I am here. He came to me in a dream and told me I had to come here immediately that I had an important role to play; I thought perhaps you were in trouble."

"You mean you didn't come because of the wedding invitation?" Raul asked.

"I was planning on coming for the wedding with the rest of the family until I had that dream," Matthew said. "It was so real I could not ignore it."

"Matthew I did come to you in that dream because your presence is needed here. I will be meeting with all the men of this family to discuss some matters, at that time I will explain your dream," the Sanuri said.

"Matthew this is the Sanuri of Tabrul, you may have heard of him," Sudfad said. "He is an emissary of The Great Ruler." Matthew continued to stare at the Sanuri with a mixture of amazement and disbelief.

"Excuse me My Lord but lunch is ready. Would you like me to serve it?" Marie asked as she entered the parlor.

"Yes, yes," said Sudfad as he walked over to Renya and took her hand. The King and Queen held hands as they walked to the dining room, an act that made Matthew smile. As Marie served lunch, Raul finished the introductions with Matthew.

"It figures that you two would marry the most beautiful girls in the continent," Matthew said as he flashed a smile at Vitomas and Annabelle. "Tell me do either of you have any sisters?" Both women blushed and giggled.

"I do believe our wives are taken with you," Simon said with a grin.

Then Matthew turned his attention back to the Sanuri. "I have heard of you but I will admit I thought the stories of the Sanuri of Tabrul were just that, stories."

"Well, depending on what you have heard, they very well could be," replied the Sanuri.

Then Matthew got a serious look upon his face. "What did you mean by those things you said? Why should Sudfad claim me as a son and what did you mean I would lead children out of darkness?"

"The first question I will answer later tonight, when I speak with Sudfad and his sons, which now includes you," the Sanuri said smiling. "The second question you will answer for yourself."

"And why did I see you in my dream?"

"I don't mean to be vague but as I said, that will be answered tonight also."

"What is this mysterious meeting we are having after dinner?" asked Simon.

"Sons, you might say it is a rite of passage," replied Sudfad "I guarantee it will be something you will never forget."

Padre Thomas and Padre Bartholomew waited until dusk to call Enrops to take the note they had found to the Sanuri. They were both fearful of being seen giving the Enrops messages, especially now that they suspected High Priest Meekos of being a dark lord. The note they had found with the dead raven disturbed both priests greatly; since neither of them could sleep they decided to go to the Hall of Antiquities to study.

After several hours Padre Bartholomew gasped and jumped up from his chair; startling Padre Thomas. "Oh no, look at this," said Padre Bartholomew as he showed a passage of an ancient text to Padre Thomas. "We must warn the Sanuri, he could be riding into a trap."

"Tear that page out, we must go to the courtyard," said Padre Thomas as he understood the seriousness of the situation. Both of the old priests ran out of the Hall of Antiquities and down the stone hallways of the great monastery.

The courtyard and gardens were almost as light as day because of the full moon which hung directly above the monastery. Both priests prayed to The Great Ruler to send an Enrop messenger. Their prayers were answered quickly. The priests were both relieved and pleased to see giant bird after giant bird landing in the courtyard.

"We have a very important message for the Sanuri of Tabrul, would you deliver it?" asked Padre Thomas who was never really sure if the Enrops understood what he said.

An Enrop stepped forward. Padre Bartholomew walked quickly up to the bird and held out the piece of ancient paper, which the Enrop grabbed with his beak. "The Sanuri was heading to the royal castle in the Kingdom of Wetpr, he should have reached his destination by now," said Padre Bartholomew.

"The Sanuri may be in grave danger and needs to see that message," said Padre Thomas.

Both priests stood and watched as the flock of Enrops took to the skies. "I think they understood everything we said," Padre Bartholomew said in disbelief. The priests said a quick prayer of thanks to The Great Ruler, also asking Him to protect the Sanuri.

"Let us return to the Hall of Antiquities there may be more we need to find," said Padre Thomas.

Chapter XXIX
The Keepers of the Scrolls

After dinner the Sanuri and Sudfad met in his study. "Sudfad you have not told them anything about their duties?" asked the Sanuri.

"No, I was going to wait until after the weddings; when all our lives settle down a little."

"It cannot wait any longer," said the Sanuri as he looked out of the window in Sudfad's study.

"I understand," said Sudfad as he turned to open the door.

"Sudfad before you call them," said the Sanuri as he turned around. "I wanted to tell you that you and Renya have done a fine job raising those boys, you should be very proud of them."

"I am," said Sudfad smiling.

"And before this is over you will be very proud of their wives also," said the Sanuri.

"They are but girls, will they have to be involved with this?"

"They are the wives that were sent to your sons and they too have their roles to play," replied the Sanuri. "And one more thing," added the Sanuri smiling. "The Great Ruler is very pleased that you and Renya have kept your word to Him and you are being blessed with many grandchildren."

Jonas led twenty Taperian soldiers to the City of Salar in the Kingdom of Wetpr. They did not dress in their Taperian uniforms, but they dressed to blend in with the thousands of travelers who were in the city.

Jonas ordered his men to break into groups of two and to go into taverns and restaurants and to engage people in conversation. He wanted information about the wedding, the Royal Family and the Sanuri. Jonas left the city and looked for a suitable site where his men could camp without being observed.

The Sanuri waited for Raul, Simon and Matthew to be seated before he spoke. Sudfad poured glasses of whiskey and handed them to each of the men.

"Your father was waiting until after the weddings to explain some of the responsibilities of this holy family but unfortunately there are forces at work that cause me to come to you sooner," said the Sanuri. "But before I start to explain these responsibilities Sudfad needs to adopt Matthew."

Sudfad stood up and handed Matthew a small scroll. Matthew unrolled the scroll and read it. Then he walked over to Sudfad's desk, took a pen and ink and signed the scroll. Matthew handed the scroll to Sudfad who looked it over and handed it to the Sanuri to read.

"Before we begin, I must tell you that what we are about to speak of will be repeated to no one. Raul and Simon after you are married there will be a time when we share this conversation with your wives."

"This is sounding very mysterious," Raul said with a grin.

"He is very serious my son," Sudfad said.

"Shortly before your father's marriage to Renya, I came to him as I come to you now and I asked for his promise to continue a covenant made between his forefathers and The Great Ruler. I will be asking the same question of you that I did of Sudfad but before you can give me an answer I have a great deal to tell you."

"Some of what I am going to say may be very difficult for you to believe and I understand that. First you must know that The Great Ruler has watched all of you closely during this life; to make sure you are capable of performing the tasks He will ask of you."

The Sanuri continued, "As you know The Great Ruler gave one set of Holy Scrolls to each of the original twelve kingdoms; what you may not know is that The Great Ruler has also bestowed other gifts upon His children."

"He gave these gifts with love and the understanding that His children would have to transcend the darkness of their nature to fully use these gifts for their intended purposes. But as you can imagine any gift from The Great Ruler possesses powers beyond the imaginations of many beings."

"Your family," said the Sanuri. "Entered into a covenant with The Great Ruler hundreds of years ago to protect these gifts until such time that the world of man is ready for them. Your father, as his adopted father before him and so on, has been the Keeper of the Scrolls for The Great Ruler."

Both Raul and Simon looked at their father with surprise. "We knew nothing of this," said Raul.

"You were not meant to know these things until the designated time, which is now my sons," replied the Sanuri. "As certainly as there is the Light of The Great Ruler there is darkness in these worlds and there are many emissaries of darkness seeking to obtain these gifts and to distort the powers they possess."

"Also there are those who suspect the holy responsibilities of your family and are a threat to you. In my five hundred years in this world I have worked with your forefathers on behalf of The Great Ruler. And until now, only the King and Queen of Wetpr have been the Keepers of the Scrolls."

"The Queen?" asked Simon. "You mean Mother has been doing this also?"

Before Sudfad could reply the Sanuri said, "Sons, you have no idea who your mother really is or what a remarkable person she is. During your lifetimes both your mother and father have risked their lives on multiple occasions to do the work of The Great Ruler."

"What!" exclaimed Raul.

Sudfad laughed, "Actually I feel a sense of relief that the boys now know; Renya and I have been leading secret lives for far too long."

"Before I go any farther on this subject I want to explain something," said the Sanuri. "I swore a covenant with The Great Ruler many lifetimes ago. He communicates with me in various ways, sometimes I clearly understand His messages and sometimes they are very confusing to me. Although I have given my life to work for The Great Ruler I am but a man, which means that much of the time The Great Ruler gives me only the information I need for a particular moment in time."

"And this leads me to speak about Matthew. As I said, until now only the King and Queen have been Keepers of the Scrolls. Raul and Simon since you were born you were meant to help your parents with this role; which would be the first time in history there were three kings protecting The Great Ruler's gifts."

"A couple of weeks ago I started having a series of dreams which I found quite confusing. In each dream Matthew's face appeared. When I finally rose above my ego and asked The Great Ruler to clarify the messages He was sending to me; I was told that Matthew also had been chosen to serve with the rest of you."

"Sanuri why does The Great Ruler need all of us now?" Sudfad asked.

"I do not have all of the answers to that question but I do know that there is darkness upon this world now that has not been seen since the ancient times. There are many who are calling to darkness and it is answering."

"Sanuri, I have several questions," said Simon. "First what are you referring to when you say darkness and second I was not born into this family. Are you saying my parents were killed so I could be a Keeper of the Scrolls?"

"First and this may be hard for you to believe, there are demons in your worlds. Various types of demons with different levels of power. The demons are not to be confused with the dark lords, which are men who serve the demons. Then there are men like Roch who are so evil, one would believe they are a demon but they are men; men with little humanity left in them. This is a very complicated subject which I will be glad to go into more detail about later."

"I am sorry but I do find this difficult to believe," said Raul.

"As I would expect a logical man to say," replied the Sanuri. "I have a great deal to tell you and I will answer your questions. Please bear with me as it may appear that I am changing subjects quickly but I am trying to paint a picture for you. Now I am going to try to explain something else which can be confusing; your lives."

"The Great Ruler gives us freedom of choice; that is how He created us. You must understand that He does not force us to say or to do anything. But He does call to us, each and every one. But only a few choose to answer His call. The Keepers of the Scrolls, for example have answered His calls. When I say you have been chosen for this task that is because of the choices you have made throughout your lives that have brought you to this place in this time."

"You are all men of great faith, courage and integrity and each of you in his own right has answered The Great Ruler's calls on many occasions whether you realized it or not. And each of you has earned your place to be called upon for such an important purpose. Now before I go farther I want to tell you that before this night is through, I will ask you if you will answer The Great Ruler's call to be Keepers of the Scrolls; the choice is yours."

"It is difficult for men to understand how The Great Ruler works and why things happen as they do. But I will try to show you how The Great Ruler has been watching over you and playing a part in your lives. Simon," continued the Sanuri. "The Great Ruler did not kill your parents but when you were lost and alone he led you to a loving family. I do not believe it was an accident that Raul found you that day. And look at the man you have become; I will tell you that The Great Ruler is as proud of you as are your parents."

"Simon and Raul, some people have said it is like you two are different sides of the same coin. You both have strong personalities, are leaders of men and great warriors. Usually men who share such equal characteristics compete with each other. But you have transcended such petty jealousies with a strong bond of love and respect. You may not realize how much both of you are like Sudfad."

"And Raul, there are so many things we have to talk about. Do you remember that night shortly after you started your travels when you prayed to The Great Ruler to guide your way?"

"Yes," replied Raul with a look of astonishment that the Sanuri would know about this.

"You really had no idea what you were asking. There is an emissary of The Great Ruler who often communicates with me and gives me help and guidance. He is not of this world and when he does appear in this world he often chooses to take the form of a lion," the Sanuri said. "All those mornings you woke up and saw lion prints around your camp, you never realized that was a message from The Great Ruler that He was watching over you."

"Vitomas said that when she found me there were lion prints around my body but the lion did not protect me from being attacked," Raul said.

"Oh my son," said the Sanuri. "This is exactly what I am talking about. Raul how many times did you get lost during your travels?"

Raul thought for a moment before answering, "Only the time I ended up near Roch's castle."

"Raul, you thought that Vitomas saved you but in reality you were sent there to save her and Annabelle and Laurel and Alexander. Under what other circumstances would you ever have been allowed inside of Roch's castle? Not only did you save those people but you and Simon found the loves of your lives, the wives that The Great Ruler intended for you."

"I will tell you what happened. Roch has been sending spies into your kingdom for years to watch your family and to determine the strength of your defenses. His men had been watching you and they attacked you. The Lion stopped them from killing you and sat next to you until Vitomas arrived. The Great Ruler did not have you injured but He used a bad situation for good. Also it was no accident that you found that set of Holy Scrolls in that cave in Puntd. The men who attacked you stole all you had, except for those scrolls."

Raul stared at the Sanuri as he remembered all of the dangerous situations that he had eluded during his travels and the many times he saw the prints of The Lion. "This is incredible," Raul said thoughtfully. Then he added, "I am beginning to see it, how it all unfolded."

"Raul you were horrified when you discovered that Archetenus had taken Vitomas. As Simon thought, Archetenus had been planning on kidnapping her for several years. But taking her at the time that he did actually saved Vitomas' life because Roch would have killed her for helping you escape. Archetenus is a vile and dangerous man, who has spent his life murdering and raping people. He scared Vitomas but he did not hurt her. Have you not wondered why?"

"Actually I have thought about that a great deal and so has Simon," Raul said.

"As The Lion watched over you, another messenger was watching over Vitomas and stopping Archetenus from hurting her."

"Miranda!" Simon gasped. "Vitomas told us that Archetenus kept talking to what seemed like an imaginary person. She said Archetenus would argue and yell at thin air; then he told her he was bringing her back to Raul because Miranda told him to."

The Sanuri smiled, "Yes, she is an emissary of The Great Ruler and has taken on the name of Miranda in this world. She is still with Archetenus and will prevent him from bothering your family again."

"When you say an emissary of The Great Ruler, do you mean she is an Angel?" asked Matthew.

"Yes," replied the Sanuri.

"Why would an Angel stay with a man like that?" Raul asked.

"To stop him from doing great harm to this world."

Sudfad got up and poured more whiskey into everyone's glasses. His sons sat in silence, overwhelmed by the words of the Sanuri.

"And Matthew, an impressionable young man who was at a crossroads in his life; when his cousin Raul came to visit him. You were so impressed with your cousin that you vowed to become like him. Matthew you needed Raul to visit you exactly when he did."

"What you did not know was that your evil sister had paid the dark lords to bring you to ruin; but your conviction and integrity were so strong that you rose above the challenges and adversities and became the man you wanted to be. It is the blood line of this family that is a credit to your forefathers."

"We have much more to discuss so I will be meeting with you several more times before the weddings. Understand your father is not giving up any of his responsibilities as Keeper of the Scrolls; you will be joining him because the need is great. And The Great Ruler needs men of your strength of character and abilities to perform these tasks," the Sanuri said.

"Now I will ask you the same question I have asked your forefathers for generations. In the presence of your father and The Great Ruler will you thrust down your swords and stand before the heavens? Will you answer The Great Ruler's call? You do not have to give me an answer tonight, if you would like to talk it over."

The three young men looked at each other without speaking a word. "We are ready to answer," said Raul.

"Simon what is your answer?" asked the Sanuri.

"I will."

"Raul what is your answer?"

"I will."

"Matthew what is your answer?"

"I will."

"Well, what did they say?" Renya asked as Sudfad entered their bedroom chambers later that evening. Renya was sitting up in bed reading.

Sudfad smiled and walked over to his wife and kissed her on the forehead. "They are our sons, what do you think they said?" Sudfad replied with a father's pride.

"And Matthew?"

"And Matthew is our son now also and he too will make us proud," Sudfad said as he was disrobing.

"The girls are having a little welcoming party for Matthew in Simon and Annabelle's chambers," Renya said smiling. "They invited us but I thought the children should all get to know each other without us spoiling their fun."

"So that was the message that Petra brought into the room for Simon," Sudfad said with a grin as he slid under the covers.

"Speaking of Petra," Renya said with a coy smile. "He really is a sweet child and living on the road with the Sanuri, well the boy should have a home and a family."

"And what are you really saying my dear?" Sudfad asked while he put his arm around Renya's shoulders. Sudfad already knew what his wife was about to ask. Renya turned so she was fully facing Sudfad. "What would you say about us adopting the boy? We have so much to offer and well, our sons are starting families of their own and don't need us like they used to."

Sudfad took Renya's hand into his own. "My dear I am going to let you in on a little secret. I do believe the Sanuri brought Petra here hoping that we would adopt him. I have not been able to spend as much time with the child as you have but I too have become fond of him in this short time. I agree, I think we should adopt him." Renya squealed with delight and threw her arms around Sudfad's neck and kissed him.

When Simon, Raul and Matthew entered Simon's chambers they found both Annabelle and Vitomas dressed in fancy dresses. The rooms were lit with dozens of candles. There was now a large table in the middle of the parlor which was filled with platters of food and bottles of whiskey and wine.

"What is this?" asked Simon with a grin.

"We thought we would have a little party for Matthew," Vitomas said as she walked up to Raul and kissed him.

"And Marie is teaching us how to cook, so we prepared all the food," Annabelle said with a proud smile.

"Oh, Matthew this may not be good," Simon said jokingly. "Our wives don't really know how to cook."

Annabelle softly punched Simon on the arm before she kissed him and they both laughed. "Well, everything looks wonderful to me," Matthew said with appreciation.

"Come sit at the table," Vitomas said as she led Raul by the hand. "So this secret meeting is it to teach you how to be good husbands?" Vitomas winked at the others as she spoke.

"What?" Matthew asked as he took a seat at the table.

When Simon finished laughing he said, "Matthew before we explain first you have to know that both Raul and I are known for the thought and detail we put into everything we do. Well, that is except for getting married. We asked the girls to marry us but forgot to give them rings and didn't make plans for the wedding or where we were going to live. So our parents gave us a good scolding."

"And we deserved it," Raul said. "But now I am going to confess to something." Raul reached over and held Vitomas' hand as he talked. "I forgot to ask Vitomas to marry me. I told her we would marry but I forgot to propose."

"What!" yelled Simon as he roared with laughter. "Now I don't feel like as much of an ass."

"Oh no Simon, you should still feel like an ass," Raul joked.

The next day as the Sanuri was walking down the hallway to Sudfad's study he heard Petra calling.

"Sanuri, Sanuri," yelled Petra as he ran down the hallway towards him.

"What is it Petra?"

"Sanuri, there are Enrops in front of the castle, and there are a lot of them. I think they are talking to one of the soldiers." The Sanuri walked quickly to the front of the castle with Petra running to keep up.

The Sanuri saw hundreds of Enrops in the front courtyard and a soldier was walking up the steps towards him. "My Lord I know this is hard to believe but one of those birds spoke and asked for you."

"Those birds do talk," said the Sanuri, although his response did not lessen the confusion of the soldier. "Thank you," said the Sanuri and started to descend the staircase. When he got to the bottom of the steps, four Enrops walked forward. Nica was in the lead, the three Enrops that followed him each had a piece of paper in their beaks.

"Nica it is always good to see you but why are there so many of you here?" asked the Sanuri.

"Sanuri it too is good to see you and my entire flock is here because we bring you many messages," Nica said. "First your friends, those two priests from Malga summoned us to give you a message." As Nica spoke one of the great birds stepped forward and the Sanuri took a piece of paper from its beak but did not read it.

"Only a few Enrops were delivering that message to you. The Lion told them to wait. Within hours those priests summoned us again with this second message." Again one of the Enrops walked forward and gave the Sanuri a piece of paper. "This time the priests said you might be in great danger and that we should deliver that message to you quickly.

"I was with this second group," Nica continued. "After we started our flight here, The Lion told my group to meet up with the first group of Enrops. By the time we found them the rest of our flock had joined us at The Lion's direction. He then told us to intercept a large flock of ravens that were carrying a message from a dark lord in Salar. And that message is the last one we are now handing over to you."

"Did The Lion tell you where the dark lord was sending the message to?" the Sanuri asked.

"Yes, the monastery at Malga," Nica replied. "Sanuri, The Lion also told us to stay close to you and the Royal Family, that is why he sent the entire flock."

King Sudfad had been standing next to the Sanuri listening to the conversation. "Forgive me but I am rather confused about what is going on here," Sudfad said.

"King Sudfad this in Nica, he is an old friend and a leader among his tribe," the Sanuri said. "And Nica this is King Sudfad of Wetpr." The Sanuri now turned and faced Sudfad. "For centuries The Great Ruler has used the tribes of Enrops as messengers. For their faithfulness he has blessed them with the ability to speak many, many languages."

"Just as The Great Ruler uses the Enrops, dark lords use ravens as their messengers. Nica and his flock have brought us two messages from my friends in Malga. The Lion diverted the Enrops and had them do battle with a flock of ravens who were transporting a message from a dark lord in Salar to the monastery in Malga. The Lion has also ordered them to stay with us for protection."

"For protection?" Sudfad repeated. "I don't understand."

"The Enrops are fierce fighters and they can be your eyes, in places you cannot go," the Sanuri continued. "Sudfad these birds have flown a great distance and have been in battle; they could use some food."

"Of course," Sudfad said to the Sanuri, then Sudfad turned to one of the soldiers and said, "These birds can talk, give them whatever they want. And they can have access to the gardens and orchards."

The Sanuri and Sudfad walked into the King's study and closed the door. They did not want to read the messages in public. The Sanuri read the messages in the order the Enrops had received them. First he read the message that Sophie had sent to Meekos.

"What is it?" Sudfad asked as he took the note from the Sanuri. "I have never seen that look on your face before."

"High Priest Meekos is in charge of the monastery at Malga. I know he has lived for hundreds of years. There are only two ways a being can have such a prolonged life, one is to surrender to The Great Ruler and the other is to sell your soul to demons. I have long had my suspicions about this man, now from this note I believe him to be a dark lord."

"No, that can't be," said Sudfad. "A senior high priest is a dark lord!"

"Sporos became a demon. If you would have known the man he was before he surrendered to darkness; you would know that anything is possible," the Sanuri said gravely. The Sanuri now read the ancient page of text that Padre Bartholomew and Padre Thomas sent to him. Neither of these priests took the time to annotate the passage of their concern but as the Sanuri read he found it in the middle of the page.

"This is the page of text that my friends gave to the Enrops with the warning that I might be walking into a trap." The Sanuri read the passage out loud to Sudfad; *"As they lay in waiting for the time to strike, the lords of darkness watched the kings of light."*

"What does it mean?" asked Sudfad.

The Sanuri was already reading the third note, the one taken from the ravens and did not immediately answer Sudfad's question. "It means we need to prepare for an attack," said the Sanuri as he handed Pravis' note to Sudfad. "This is the note that a dark lord was sending from Salar, *All is in place.*

For the second night, the men of the Royal Family of Wetpr met with the Sanuri in the King's study. Sudfad handed everyone a glass of whiskey as the Sanuri continued talking. "I feel you may be in danger on your wedding day although at this point I cannot fully explain it."

"What!" exclaimed Simon.

"I told you last night that The Great Ruler sends me information in various ways and sometimes I do not fully understand the messages at first. The reason I arrived here early was because of a dream I had about your wedding."

"In this dream I saw both of you with your brides riding in a grand boca through the streets of Salar. There were huge crowds in the streets, on the balconies and standing near windows of buildings. Then I saw the eyes of terrorists, many eyes, hidden in all of these crowds. At the same time I was overwhelmed with a sense of danger for all of you. The feeling was so prevalent that I instantly jumped out of my bed and came here."

Matthew started to speak but Sudfad interrupted him, "Son, let him finish there is more."

"This morning a huge flock of Enrops brought me three notes, two of them were sent from two friends who I trust implicitly who thought I might be walking into a trap and the other was intercepted from a flock of ravens."

"Sanuri you will have to explain the significance of the birds to them," said Sudfad.

"The Enrops are an ancient race of birds which are highly evolved creatures. They are faithful to The Great Ruler so He has blessed them with the gift of being able to speak many languages. The Great Ruler, as do I; often use them as messengers. Ravens are the messengers of the dark lords. Nica is the name of the leader of the flock of Enrops which is currently on the royal grounds."

"Nica said that as the Enrops were flying here to give me the messages from the priests at Malga, The Lion, who I told you about last night, told them to intercept a flock of ravens that were flying from Salar to Malga. The birds did battle and the Enrops brought me the message that a dark lord was sending from Salar."

The Sanuri first handed the ancient text to Simon, who was sitting the closest to him. Simon read it and passed it to Raul. "The note you are now reading is one of the messages my friends sent to me," explained the Sanuri. "Now this is the note that was taken from the ravens," the Sanuri said and handed this note to Simon.

"It certainly sounds like someone is planning to attack us," Simon growled.

Raul became visibly angry when he read the papers. "Simon and I do not fear battle but we will not put our wives in harm's way. We must call this off."

"I do not think that is wise," said the Sanuri. "The terrorists will only try again, at least now we know where they are. And my sons, this is a time when you must have faith. Remember The Great Ruler Himself is sending us this information. I say we prepare for the attack."

"I am sorry to interrupt but I really must tell you all some things," said Matthew earnestly. "The first thing I must tell you brings me great shame. I have witnessed with my own eyes, my sister Juleta using ravens as messengers. I will admit I thought it odd but I did not understand the significance."

"And the second thing, well, perhaps the Sanuri can explain. When I told you all that I had seen the Sanuri in a dream that was only partially true. I have seen him in a number of different dreams. I did not know who he was or if I just imagined him."

"In these dreams the Sanuri spoke directly to me at times but there were some dreams where I watched him. Last night as you spoke," Matthew looked directly at that Sanuri. "My heart was filled with fear for I have seen the tracks of a lion around my campsites many times also and I have seen a lion in my dreams."

Matthew turned and looked at Raul, "The Sanuri was right when he said I strongly bonded with you during your visit. To me you represented everything a true king and warrior should be. After you left the castle I would have dreams about you on your journey and always in the dreams there were eyes watching you from the darkness."

"And there is another dream which I have seen over and over since I met you. There is a great battlefield. On the eastern side of the field are legions upon legions of warriors. In front of the warriors is a line of ancient chariots. I have seen all of us in this room in those chariots but we are not alone as there are others who I do not recognize driving chariots also. We lead the warriors to the west. Then I see the other side of the battlefield that we are charging towards; it is filled with dark clouds and fire and monsters that surpass the imagination."

471

Everyone in the room stared at Matthew as he spoke, then as one they turned and looked at the Sanuri. "Matthew," said the Sanuri with a warm smile. "I believe The Great Ruler has given you a gift of prophesy. Do not take it lightly. Every time The Great Ruler sends you a vision, there is a reason."

"Also, I only sought to call to you in the dream that beckoned you here for the weddings. If you can remember the other dreams I would like to talk with you about them later. I know you are heir to the throne of Lentz but from what you have told me I believe your place is here as Sudfad's son, at least for now."

"Simon and I do not want the girls to know anything about the threats, they deserve to enjoy their wedding day," Raul said. "And I don't think you should tell Mother either." Raul said as he turned to his father.

"I think we all agree that the women should not know of any of this," Sudfad said.

"Renya is a very astute woman, do not be surprised if she doesn't realize something is going on," the Sanuri said.

"While I am on the subject of your wives there are a few things I should tell you. First you boys have to realize that Sudfad is as protective of his family as you are of yours. You will not be able to keep your responsibilities from your wives for long, nor should you. As I have told you, The Great Ruler sent you the wives you were meant to have. You will find they will be invaluable to you as Keepers of the Scrolls and one day I will come to your sons as I have you."

"We will have sons?" Simon asked.

"Do you want sons?" the Sanuri asked.

"Of course, both Raul and I want many children."

"And that you shall have," the Sanuri said. "You know that Renya and Sudfad always wanted a large family so The Great Ruler is answering their prayers through you, their children. Also Raul and Simon you both feel so protective of your wives because of the horror they have lived through. Not only have they fallen in love with you but with your family."

"Vitomas and Annabelle have never experience what most people would consider a normal life and they greatly desire that. Both girls long to have large families and I tell you this now because there will be times when you are concerned about how close the babies are coming; trust in The Great Ruler. But remember that just like your mother, the women of your family are very much more than mothers and wives."

"Sanuri do you know what our futures hold?" asked Matthew.

"Only small bits and pieces that The Great Ruler allows me to see."

"From what you have told us, it sounds as if Raul and Simon were led to their wives. Should I expect the same? Should I seek your guidance on the matter? Have I already met her?"

"Matthew I don't have the answers that you seek. But I do believe that since The Great Ruler appointed you as a Keeper of the Scrolls that He will lead you to the love of your life just as He did Raul and Simon. And do not be surprised if you meet her when you least expect to fall in love with someone."

"Now I want to change the subject for a moment and talk about Petra. Sudfad with Matthew you now have three sons, are you open to adopting Petra also?"

"Just last night Renya and I decided to adopt him. We wanted to speak with you before we said anything to Petra."

"Sudfad I am so glad to hear that. I will meet with you and Renya after this meeting. Sudfad you know Petra's story, your sons do not. While I tell them I want you to think if there are any similarities between Petra's story and that of your other sons."

The Sanuri continued. "That incredible young boy was a peasant who lived on a farm outside of Ort. When he heard that the Hutas were planning to attack the monastery at Avaide he rode there and warned the priests. Because of him, hundreds of Shettees, mostly women and children were able to escape a massacre. When the Hutas arrived at the monastery they tortured and murdered the priests; that boy pulled an injured priest to safety and saved his life also," said the Sanuri.

"But he is just a small boy," said Simon.

"He is the same age you were when you tried to pull your parents from that burning building," replied the Sanuri. "And the same age as Raul when he found you near death and carried you on his back all those many miles to the castle. While Petra was at Avaide, the Hutas murdered his parents and all the inhabitants of Ort."

"He is an orphan," said Sudfad.

"Simon would you take the time to get to know him; your stories are so similar I think it would help him to heal?" asked the Sanuri.

"Of course," replied Simon then he looked at Matthew and said, "Raul and I were both nine when the things he speaks of occurred." Simon turned back to the Sanuri. "Sanuri did you know that although Annabelle is a couple of months younger than Vitomas both the girls were taken as prisoners at the age of nine. Are we to believe that the fact that all of these major events happened when we were all the same age is a coincidence?"

"Sudfad your children are as brilliant as they are brave," the Sanuri said. Then looking at Matthew the Sanuri asked, "Matthew what happened in your life at that age?"

Matthew stared at the Sanuri for several moments without speaking. "I saved my sister Margarit from drowning. She was just a baby and had fallen into a pond."

"Who was watching Margarit when she fell into the water?"

"Juleta, wait, do you think Juleta deliberately tried to drown Margarit?"

"Yes, I know she tried to kill her because that was not the only attempt. Juleta is very jealous of both you and Margarit."

"Then I should warn Father, or bring Margarit here."

"She is safe, at least for now. The Great Ruler is watching over her. But I tell you this so you do not underestimate the darkness in Juleta."

"But I still do not understand the significance of the age of nine," said Simon.

"At this time I do not have that answer for you Simon but I will tell you that I learned long ago there are no coincidences with The Great Ruler."

The third night in a row, Raul, Simon, Matthew, Sudfad and the Sanuri met in the King's study. "I have been trying to keep these meetings short so as not to overwhelm you and also so you can spend time with your wives and wedding preparations," the Sanuri said.

"Actually we have been trying to get out of the wedding preparations," Simon said. "So this is fine with us."

"Last night I showed you two messages that I had received," explained the Sanuri. "There was a third also and this one I want to present to Raul first as he might be able to give us some insight into its significance." The Sanuri handed Raul the note that Sophie had sent to Meekos. Raul read it then handed the note to Matthew, who was sitting the closest to him.

"Who is Meekos?" Raul asked.

"He is the Senior High Priest of the monastery at Malga," the Sanuri responded. "And you should know this message was taken out of the beak of a dead raven."

"So Sophie is a dark lord?" Raul asked in amazement.

"What can you tell us about the woman?" the Sanuri asked.

"Well, she is Roch's cook. She is an older woman and heavy set but a fine cook. The girls said that Sophie was a notorious gossip and always knew what was going on not only in the castle but also in Cana and Taperia and she would report everything to Roch to gain his favor."

Raul paused for a second. "In fact Annabelle and I had a conversation as to how Sophie could know all of these things when she only left the castle on Tuesdays to go to the market in Cana. I jokingly said that perhaps Sophie was a spy or had her own spies."

"Has she been with Roch long?" the Sanuri asked.

"She arrived right after Roch murdered his parents," Raul answered. "But there is something else you should know. Both Vitomas and Annabelle tried their best to keep Sophie away from me, they said she was cruel and never liked anyone. But truth be told, she visited me on several occasions and appeared to have taken a liking to me. We had conversations and Sophie gave me information as to how I could escape the castle. Sophie also brought me crutches and kept warning me to leave before Roch returned."

"At first I thought it was some kind of trick but Sophie noticed how Vitomas and I looked at each other and she never told Roch. And well, from some of our conversations I started to suspect that I reminded Sophie of someone she once cared for but lost."

"You girls certainly don't have to help with this," said Marie as Vitomas and Annabelle helped her polish silver pieces that would be used the day of the weddings.

"Marie we are both so nervous we just want to keep busy," said Vitomas.

"And you certainly can use the help," added Annabelle as she looked at the long table of pieces still unpolished.

"Well, I will tell you, I started to believe that neither of those boys would ever settle down. I am so proud of them for waiting until they found the perfect wives. I have never seen them so happy and whether you realize it or not they have changed greatly."

"What do you mean Marie?" asked Annabelle.

"Just ask Queen Renya. We have never seen the boys home this much. They were always out with the troops. And well, it is hard to explain, it's like they grew up some. I teased Raul about having sons as wild as he and Simon were. And Raul said that they both wanted big families, well, you could have knocked me over with a feather."

"Why?" asked Vitomas.

Marie looked at Vitomas for a moment then said, "As I said they were pretty wild."

"Marie do you know why they are meeting with the Sanuri every night after dinner?" asked Annabelle.

"No, haven't they told you?"

"No and it has been almost a week now," replied Vitomas.

"Do you girls think something is wrong?"

"I don't know," Annabelle said. "Not all of the meetings are long but Simon always seems so serious afterwards. And I see him and Raul and Matthew talking a lot, like they don't want anyone else to hear."

"I agree, Raul has been acting like something is heavy on his mind," added Vitomas.

"Girls they are the princes of this kingdom; I think they will deal with many things they probably won't tell you about, I would not worry."

"Marie you are probably right," said Annabelle.

"So tell me what do you two think of Matthew?" Marie asked with a grin.

Annabelle and Vitomas both smiled. "He is very handsome and charming," Vitomas said.

"If I had not met Simon, I would be quite taken by him," Annabelle said with a sly smile.

"Marie, I have not seen Renya or Laurel all day, do you know where they are?" asked Vitomas.

A broad smile brightened Marie's face. "They took the boy Petra into Salar to buy him some clothes and things. You mark my words, Queen Renya will adopt that poor child; she has such a big heart. I will tell you I got a tear in my eye when she told me his story."

Pravis never learned that his message to Meekos had been intercepted. After a few days, Pravis was surprised that he had not received a response but it was merely a fleeting thought. Pravis himself watched Sudfad's castle.

One day he followed a large boca that held Queen Renya, an older woman and a young boy. There were two soldiers in the front of the boca, two on each side and two in the rear. Pravis wondered if the newlyweds would use the same type of formation of soldiers when they rode through the streets after the weddings.

Pravis did not wear the attire of a high priest so he could blend in with the crowds. He watched the Queen as she and the other woman were buying clothes and toys for the boy. Pravis noted that the soldiers always remained close to the Queen. He followed her boca back to the castle and hid as he watched the routines of the guards.

Vitomas lay on her side watching Raul sleep. She loved him so much that at times Vitomas felt like her heart would burst. A fear that always permeated her thoughts was that Roch would somehow pull Vitomas back into the hell her existence had been for so long. This fear filled Vitomas' being more and more as the day of their wedding grew closer. Raul seemed so worried as of late, that Vitomas feared Roch was somehow a threat.

Vitomas reached up and started to softly caress Raul's thick black hair. "He is such a handsome man," she thought. Vitomas wanted to kiss Raul but she was afraid of waking him. As Vitomas was lost in her thoughts she suddenly realized Raul was smiling.

"Did I wake you?" Vitomas asked apologetically.

Raul rolled onto his side so he was facing Vitomas and propped up his head with his hand. "Is everything alright Honey?"

"Yes, I was just admiring my handsome husband; that is all. I am sorry that I woke you." Raul started to play with strands of Vitomas' long hair. "Raul is everything alright? Both you and Simon have been acting like something is weighing on your minds."

"It is just business, nothing for you to worry about."

"It's not the wedding is it? I mean you haven't changed your mind have you?"

Raul moved closer to Vitomas and stared directly into her eyes. "I cannot believe you could even think such a thing. If I had my way we would already be married." He paused for a moment then said, "You know the Sanuri said that we were going to have lots of children. How do you feel about that?"

"I hope he is right," Vitomas said as she leaned forward and kissed Raul. "Have I told you today how much I love you?" Vitomas whispered into Raul's ear as he kissed the side of her neck. He gently lowered Vitomas onto her back and moved on top of her.

Chapter XXX
Something Borrowed

Raul and Simon wanted nothing to do with the wedding preparations. Although their responsibilities as military officers and princes of the largest kingdom in Opots kept them busy, they made time every day to spend with Matthew. The three young men bonded quickly because of their similar interests and similar personalities.

Sudfad looked across the dining room table at Matthew and smiled. "So Matthew how was your first day as a captain in the Wetpr Military?"

"I will admit I am glad to be doing something familiar; I never have been one for sitting around."

"Matthew has been training with us since he got here and he does know what he is doing." Raul said as he passed a large platter of ears of corn to Simon.

"He has been teaching us an ancient form of fighting, which we had never heard of," said Simon. "And it is effective Raul and I both have the bruises to prove it."

"None of you boys better have black eyes or injuries for the weddings," scolded Renya. Raul, Simon and Matthew all grinned when she said this.

"So tell me about this fighting technique," said Sudfad.

"It was developed by an ancient tribe called the Asherane. They inhabited the northern areas of our kingdom. In fact the Tombs of Mercha, which we visited Raul, are their burial grounds."

"Sanuri are you familiar with this tribe?" asked Sudfad.

"Yes, but by legend only; their kind was already extinct by the time I was born. They are said to have been fierce warriors, who lived only for the kill."

"What destroyed them?" asked Renya.

"I believe their own lifestyle," remarked the Sanuri.

"The form is called Tabutu and I have been studying it since a child," Matthew explained. "It utilizes the traditional punches and kicks but it also teaches you how to use an opponent's energy and force against them. For example if a warrior is coming at me, I can grab him and throw him to the ground using his own momentum. The idea of this type of training was so a single warrior could fight many combatants without draining his own energy as quickly."

"It sounds interesting," said Sudfad. "I would like to see a demonstration."

"Sudfad," said Renya in a scolding manner.

"Darling, the boys are all experienced fighters; I am sure they can give us a demonstration without seriously injuring each other."

Renya looked at Vitomas and Annabelle. "Just so you know, when the boys were growing up we rarely went a week without an injury of some kind. Why you would have thought we sent those boys off to war the way they looked."

"Who were you fighting?" asked Annabelle.

Both Raul and Simon got sheepish grins, "Mostly each other," Raul said.

Jonas and his men made a camp almost two miles from Salar, which they returned to every night. During the day Jonas would assign groups to watch different members of the Royal Family or to gather information in the city.

Although many of the men had noticed and even commented on how differently Jonas was acting, none of them discovered the truth. It was beyond the comprehension of these men to realize that the body of their captain was now controlled by an ancient and vicious demon.

High Priest Meekos as well as High Priest Pravis and High Priest Tenebrae had sold their souls to the demon Omnibus hundreds of years earlier. For this price they received prolonged life, power and riches.

As members of the Insidiae these High Priests kept their titles within the church; honored disguises that brought them power and respect. They pretended to work for The Great Ruler, while they denounced and sullied everything that was holy.

Meekos had hired the demon Demetries to spy on Roch and to make sure Roch did not get himself killed before his destiny could be fulfilled. But Demetries had his own agendas also. It was long rumored in the underworlds that the Royal Families of Wetpr were somehow linked to The Great Ruler in ways that other men were not. These rumors brought both fear and grandiose ideas of riches and power to the worlds of darkness.

Roch had not seen through Demetries' disguise and still thought he was in the company of his loyal caption, Jonas. Demetries was ecstatic when Roch sent him after the Sanuri. A demon that killed the Sanuri would be held in the highest of esteem and honor by all of the dark worlds. And this assignment also gave Demetries access to the Royal Family of Wetpr; perhaps their secret would be exposed.

The following evening, Marie served dinner to the Sanuri, Sudfad and his sons in the King's study so the men could continue their nightly discussion without interruption. As Marie was setting the table the Sanuri turned to her and asked, "Marie I hope Petra is not in your way?"

"No My Lord no, a fine boy he is and a hearty appetite; he is in the kitchen now with the girls," said Marie as she put platters of food on the table. "The Queen and Laurel are going through the Princes' old clothing trying to find one of the military uniforms the boys used to wear for events. Queen Renya thinks Petra should be dressed like the other boys." All the men smiled at this comment.

"Gentlemen let us take a break and enjoy this fine meal The Great Ruler has provided," said the Sanuri.

As they ate, Raul said to his father, "Simon and I have been talking and we just can't believe that you and Mother were able to hide all the experiences you had being the Keepers of the Scrolls, from us."

"We had to keep all of this from you, for one thing children cannot be trusted to keep a secret but most importantly we didn't want you living in fear."

"I must remind you," said the Sanuri. "They were forbidden to tell you just as you are forbidden from telling your sons until the appointed time. This role is one that must be earned and prior knowledge could influence the life choices that are made."

"Sanuri just how much danger is our family in because of this responsibility?" Simon asked.

"That can vary. You not only protect holy items that are greatly coveted by others but there are some who see your family as obstacles to their plans. But these threats have been the same for every generation."

After the meeting, Raul and Simon stepped into the hallway, leaving Matthew with Sudfad and the Sanuri. "Vitomas is getting suspicious that something is wrong," said Raul.

"As is Annabelle," added Simon, "I will admit I am really worried about the girls." Raul motioned for Simon to stop talking because Vitomas was coming towards them.

"Oh there you two are," said Vitomas as she ran up to Raul, stood on her toes and kissed him on the cheek. Vitomas lowered her weight to her heels and looked at both Simon and Raul. "There is something wrong," she said with concern.

"We are just tired," said Raul as he put his arms around Vitomas and kissed her on the forehead. "Let's take a walk in the garden," suggested Raul and took Vitomas' hand.

"Where is Annabelle?" asked Simon.

"She is in the kitchen with Laurel, they are altering clothing for Petra," replied Vitomas.

When Simon opened the door to the kitchen he saw Petra standing on a wooden stool with Laurel and Annabelle standing around him.

"Hold still," said Laurel to Petra as Simon walked softly into the room.

Simon put both of his arms around Annabelle's waist and hugged her. Annabelle quickly turned around and kissed Simon on the lips. "That's my old uniform," said Simon laughing.

"All of our boys will be dressed the same for the wedding," said Laurel with a smile.

"I am Simon," said Simon as he extended his hand to Petra. Although they had seen each other all week, this was the first time they talked. Petra tried to shake Simon's hand while still standing perfectly straight. "Annabelle and I are getting married."

"I know, she talks about you all the time," replied Petra.

"Perhaps later you can tell me what she says," said Simon with a grin.

"It is all good," said Annabelle with a tilt of her head.

"The Sanuri has told us about you," said Simon as he tousled Petra's red hair. "This brave little soldier saved hundreds of Shettee refugees and a priest from the Hutas," Simon said proudly but regretted his words as soon as they were said because Petra looked like he was going to cry.

"Simon why don't you take your bride for a walk in the gardens," said Laurel as she put down a box of pins.

As soon as Simon and Annabelle left the kitchen, Laurel looked at Petra and said soothingly, "Do you want to tell me about it?" A few minutes later Renya walked into the kitchen and saw Petra and Laurel hugging. Petra was crying on her shoulder. Laurel looked at Renya with tears in her eyes.

Four of the Taperian soldiers who were assigned to gather information from citizens of Salar were riding from the city back to their campsite. They had spent the entire day in taverns talking with patrons and all were quite drunk.

"I'm telling you, Jonas used to have blue eyes," said Dixon as he slurred his words. "Now they are black as night. Don't you think that is damn peculiar?"

"I think you're drunk," responded James with a loud laugh. The other two soldiers laughed also.

"Look for yourself," Dixon said defensively. "In fact let's put some money on it. I will bet a twenty dollar gold piece that his eyes are black as night."

"Well, that doesn't prove anything if we can't remember if that was always the color of his eyes," James said.

"Ok then," Dixon said. "Ask some of the other men and if anyone can remember what Jonas' eyes used to look like the wager is on."

With Jonas gone, Cerephus spent all of his time with Roch. Cerephus did not understand the change in the relationship between Roch and Jonas but he felt threatened by it. Cerephus joined Roch's army when Roch first became king. Cerephus worked hard to gain the trust of Roch and coveted his unquestioned access to the King, something the other generals did not enjoy.

Cerephus had become incredibly wealthy in Roch's employment but like Roch, Cerephus' thirst for riches was never satiated. Cerephus had no knowledge of Roch's evil destiny. Cerephus was not one of the spies of the Insidiae nor did Cerephus even know that group existed. Cerephus had his own plans for Roch.

Cerephus encouraged Roch to go on dangerous missions and quests for treasure because not only did this put Roch in peril but Roch always ordered Cerephus to run the kingdom in his absence. This gave Cerephus unquestioned freedom within the castle and great power over the other men. Behind Roch's back Cerephus had been recruiting soldiers for his own personal army; the army he would need to overthrow the King.

"It's about time you got here," Jonas barked as Dixon, James and the others rode into camp. "I was beginning to think there was some kind of trouble." Jonas stomped up to the four men as they dismounted their horses. "You all smell like whiskey, are you drunk?"

"A little," James replied with a grin.

"Well, I hope none of you did anything stupid that will jeopardize this job," Jonas yelled.

Although the four men were listening to Jonas they were all staring into his eyes and looking at him suspiciously.

"What the hell are you all looking at?" Jonas roared.

The other sixteen men were all sitting around campfires and watching the exchange between Jonas and the four riders.

"We were all talking about how differently you have been acting Jonas and some of us noticed that you look different too," Dixon said seriously. "We are wondering what is going on here."

"You're drunk!" Jonas yelled.

"Have any of you other fellas noticed a big difference in Jonas?" James yelled to the men who were watching them. Almost every one of the men said or yelled that they had.

Dixon stepped closer to Jonas. "Does anyone remember that Jonas used to have blue eyes now they are black as night," Dixon yelled to the crowd.

"So what the hell is going on Jonas," yelled Sanders as he stood up from the fire. "A lot of us noticed it's like you are a totally different person."

Jonas was quiet for a moment; he stepped back and repositioned himself so he was facing all twenty of the men. "You should be careful what you ask for?" Jonas said with a smile and a tone of voice that made all of the men realize something was very wrong. "I will say you aren't as stupid as I took you all for." Jonas continued, then laughed. "You're right, I am not Jonas," Demetries said and with these words he exposed another false appearance to them.

"What the hell!" yelled James as he pulled out his sword.

"What are you?" yelled another man.

"I am a demon, a demon that can make you all very rich," Demetries said. "Now lower your weapons, they are useless against me." A lie that Demetries said with such conviction that the men lowered their weapons. "Roch sent us here to kidnap a holy man. But we are at the threshold of the castle of the richest King in all of Opots; a King who will be distracted by the weddings of his two sons. I say we take advantage of the situation and line our pockets. What do you say boys?"

"We're listening," said Saunders.

By night's end the demon Demetries had seduced this group of murderous thieves to pledge their allegiance to him for the promise of gold. So consumed were these men with their thoughts of riches that not one of them asked Demetries how or even why he had been wearing the body of Jonas. Demetries chuckled to himself because he was always amazed at how easy it all was.

Early the next morning Annabelle and Vitomas were in Annabelle's chambers with the dressmakers who were putting the finishing touches on the wedding dresses. The women chose very different designs.

Annabelle's dress had a high waist that come just under her breasts, with a long skirt that skimmed her body and long sleeves. The neckline was slightly off her shoulders. Vitomas' dress had a rounded neck and a form fitting bodice that opened up into a full skirt at her hips. Her sleeves were long and scarf-like. Both dresses were adorned with hundreds of tiny pearls and exquisite stitchery.

There was a knock on the door then Renya walked into the room. Renya started to cry when she saw Annabelle and Vitomas in their dresses. "Oh my, I cannot start crying already," said Renya pulling a lace handkerchief from her sleeve. Both Vitomas and Annabelle ran to Renya and put their arms around her.

"I know I told you before how much I always wanted daughters, now The Great Ruler has answered my prayers," cried Renya. Both Annabelle and Vitomas started to cry also. After a few moments Renya composed herself and said to the dressmakers,

"I need to steal the girls for a few minutes, they will be right back."

Renya took each girl's hand and led them out of the room, "All the men are out of the castle so don't worry about them seeing you." Renya led the women to her personal chambers; neither Vitomas nor Annabelle had been asked into these rooms before. Laurel entered the room carrying a gown. Renya smiled and said, "This is going to be so much fun. Laurel show the girls your dress." Laurel held up a light pink lace gown decorated with pearls.

"Oh Mother that will look wonderful on you," exclaimed Annabelle. Renya went to her closet and brought out a deep purple velvet dress decorated with strands of gold.

"Renya that is so beautiful," said Vitomas as all three women admired it.

"There is one more thing," said Renya smiling. "Turn around girls." When they turned around Laurel put a beautiful long veil over each of the bride's heads. "Renya and I made these for you ourselves," said Laurel as she smiled lovingly.

"They are so beautiful," said Annabelle and hugged her mother. Vitomas was so overwhelmed she could only cry as she hugged Renya. After the women composed themselves, Renya walked over to a side table that held a silver tray with four glasses of wine; she handed each woman a glass.

"I know I sound like an old sentimental woman but for so many years Sudfad was gone in the military leaving me home with two young boys. Then as the boys grew they had their own interests and adventures to pursue and while I kept busy with my duties I will admit I was quite lonely at times."

Renya paused, "I so often wished I had a bigger family and now that you are all here I feel like it is an answer to my prayers. You girls will never know how happy Sudfad and I are that you chose to live in the castle and to raise your families here." As Renya spoke tears filled the eyes of the other women. "And my dear friend Laurel, although I had not met you before you brought my son home; I feel like I have known you my entire life." Renya raised her glass of wine, "To family, may our bonds never be broken."

After each woman took a sip of their wine, Renya continued. "Now just one more thing. Every bride must have something borrowed on her wedding day. Laurel why don't you go first." Laurel pulled a folded handkerchief out of her pocket. She slowly unfolded the blue silk material as if she was afraid it would tear. When Laurel unfolded the last corner, a golden chain was exposed. Laurel picked up the chain and handed it to Annabelle. "This locket belonged to my mother, inside is a swatch of my baby hair."

"Mother it is beautiful," said Annabelle as she admired the delicate engraving on the locket and the fine chain. "Thank you so much," said Annabelle as she put her arms around her mother and kissed her on the cheek.

"And for you Vitomas, this tiny brooch belonged to my mother," said Renya as she pinned a delicate pearl and diamond pin to the front of Vitomas' wedding dress.

"I don't know what to say," said Vitomas as she hugged Renya and kissed her on the cheek. Then Vitomas took a step back and held onto Renya's hand with her right hand and took Laurel's hand with her left. "I know you must think that I am awfully silly because it seems like I am crying all of the time but in truth I have never experienced such a loving family as I have with you. Renya I too longed for a big family and prayed over and over that I would someday escape Roch's castle and find my parents."

"After so many years I will admit I lost all hope until I met Raul. And I just feel so overwhelmed because not only have I found the love of my life but the family I always dreamed about." Renya and Laurel took turns hugging Vitomas and Annabelle.

Annabelle whispered into Vitomas' ear. Then both women turned and looked at Renya and Laurel, then at each other. Vitomas smiled and said, "Yes, let's do it now."

"Both of you please stay right here," said Annabelle. "In fact turn your backs to the door. Vitomas and I will be back in just a moment." The two women giggled as they hurried down the hallway to Vitomas' chambers.

When the women returned to Renya's chambers, Laurel and Renya could hear all manner of bustling behind them. "You can turn around now," said Annabelle with a large grin on her face.

489

"Vitomas and I wanted to do something for Renya and Sudfad and for you Mother and Father for all you have done for us. But Renya we found it so difficult to try to decide what to give people who have everything."

"So we asked Raul and Simon," said Vitomas. "And to our surprise they came up with the perfect answer and gave us the money to pay for everything. They told us we could surprise you but that we had to tell Sudfad what we were doing. So we really hope you like it." Vitomas handed Renya a small white envelope with gold trim, while Annabelle handed her mother a similar envelope.

Both Vitomas and Annabelle smiled as they watched Renya and Laurel open the envelopes. Inside each envelope was a beautifully decorated invitation to a party to be held at the castle the following night. Both women cried when they read the last line of the invitation. *The party is being held to celebrate our wonderful parents, please bring nothing but your love.*

"Before you say anything," said Annabelle "Close your eyes."

"You can open them now," said Vitomas, a few moments later as she handed a silk black gown to Renya. "Sudfad picked this out."

"And Mother I hate to tell you this but Sudfad picked your dress out also, Father isn't very good at that sort of thing," said Annabelle as all the women laughed. Annabelle handed her mother a deep purple silk dress with lace trim. "We have shoes for you also," Annabelle added. "Sudfad bought Father a wonderful suit to wear and before either of you say anything. Marie, Simon and Raul have helped with everything. The invitations, the food and the flowers you don't need to do anything but relax and enjoy your party."

"And we hope you don't think this is inappropriate but we all bought Marie a new dress for the wedding. Raul and Simon said she helped to raise them and we just love her. Raul told Marie she would be a guest at the party and the wedding but Marie said she would wear the dress but no one was taking over her kitchen," Vitomas said and all of the women smiled.

"Well, now it is I who am so overwhelmed that I don't know what to say," said Renya with her voice quivering. Laurel stared at the two young women and smiled.

"We just want to show you how much we all appreciate everything you do," said Vitomas. "Raul told me that he and Simon are not very good at telling you and Sudfad how they feel, so please know how much they appreciate you also."

Chapter XXXI
Blood Ring

Pravis and some of his men watched the castle for days. At times they would follow some of the members of the Royal Family as they did errands. Pravis wondered about the young soldier who now seemed to be the constant companion of the Princes of Wetpr. Pravis knew one of Sudfad's sons was adopted, if Sudfad adopted others that would significantly affect the plans of the Insidiae and perhaps hasten the prophecy of The Severn Sons.

The increased activity around the castle, as the Princes and Princesses prepared for the party for their parents; did not go unnoticed by Pravis and by others. As Pravis continued to spy on the Royal Family he began to realize that he and his men were not alone. Pravis sent six of his best men to follow the new intruders. No sooner had his men left, when Pravis heard a familiar voice behind him.

"Well, it's not every day one sees a high priest lurking in the bushes; is this some new act of humility?"

Pravis swung around, "Demetries what are you doing here? You are supposed to be watching Roch."

"Roch sent me here," replied Demetries with a grin. "Aren't you even going to comment on the new look?"

"Meekos told me you had taken over someone's body, who are you supposed to be anyways?"

"My name now is Jonas and I am becoming Roch's second in command," Demetries replied. "So Pravis tell me why you are here?"

"To kill the Princes."

"Princes, I thought Sudfad only had one son?"

"He adopted a second son and I am getting worried there may be a third."

"So do you and your handful of men plan to storm the castle?" Demetries asked mockingly.

"No I plan to kill them after their wedding ceremonies when they are riding through the streets," Pravis answered with annoyance. "Is that why Roch sent you here?"

"I don't understand what you mean?"

"Well, both of the brides used to live in Roch's castle, one was his queen and the other her servant."

"You mean Vitomas and Annabelle are here?" Demetries started to laugh. "This couldn't be better if I planned it."

"Well, why are you here then?" demanded Pravis.

"Roch ordered me to bring him the Sanuri of Tabrul."

"Are you joking, does Roch have any idea who he is?"

"Roch thinks the Sanuri is a holy man who can translate one of the maps that Sporos gave to the Hutas."

"You will never be able to abduct the Sanuri; he will recognize your true form immediately."

"I don't have any intentions of capturing him; I plan to kill him."

"Why Annabelle I do believe that we have the three most handsome men in all of Opots standing before us," said Vitomas as Raul, Simon and Matthew entered the Great Hall of the castle. Annabelle was putting the finishing touches on a centerpiece for one of the tables. She turned around and smiled. "I must say I have never seen you look so handsome, why you took my breath away."

"Honey which one of us were you talking about?" asked Simon with a grin as he kissed Annabelle on the cheek.

"I was speaking to all of you, my dear," Annabelle replied with a coy smile. "Matthew; Simon and Raul said they invited a number of single women to the party for you to meet," Annabelle added.

"I do appreciate the gesture but I would still like to dance with your wives," Matthew said with a grin to Raul and Simon.

"Just don't steal our girls away," said Raul and laughed. Vitomas kissed Raul on the cheek, "You will never have to worry about that," she said softly.

"Both of you girls look beautiful," said Simon with admiration. "Raul we will have to have balls more often just so they can wear the gowns we bought them."

"Matthew before you say anything, yes our husbands picked out our dresses; which is why they are a little tight," Annabelle said with a laugh.

"I hadn't noticed," said Matthew with a broad grin.

"We have some business to take care of," Raul said. "We will be back soon."

"But Honey the guests should be arriving any minute," said Vitomas.

"I am sure the two of you can charm them until we return," said Simon. "Did Raul tell you that the King and Queen have to make an entrance so they won't come down until a number of the guests are here?"

"I am getting nervous," said Annabelle.

"Honey you will be just fine," Simon said and kissed the top of Annabelle's head. "We will be back in a few minutes."

"Do the girls know?" Matthew asked as the three young princes entered Sudfad's study.

"No and we have no intention of telling them," replied Raul.

"Don't you think they can handle it?"

"It's not that Matthew," continued Raul. "This is the girl's very first ball, they are so excited and they wanted desperately to do something for Mother and Father. Simon and I just want them to enjoy themselves."

"Actually Matthew when you get to know our wives you will be amazed at what they have lived through and how strong they really are," said Simon. "As children they were taken as captives by King Roch, Vitomas suffered considerably more than Annabelle but they both had horrible lives. Now Raul and I just seem to want to protect them from everything."

"I have heard many stories about Roch and not one of them was good," Matthew replied.

"Changing the subject," Raul said as he pulled out a diagram of the castle. "We should review this plan again before the guests arrive."

Three trumpets were sounded. "All stand for King Sudfad and Queen Renya," announced a captain in the Royal Wetpr Army. Two hundred and fifty-five guests stood up in silence as the King and Queen of Wetpr made their entrance into the ballroom. Renya dressed in a black silk gown adorned with diamonds and Sudfad in his dress military uniform made a striking couple.

Behind them walked Alexander in a black suit and Laurel wearing a deep purple dress. The room remained silent as the two couples walked up to the head table in the dining area, then all four turned and faced their guests. Raul and Vitomas and Simon and Annabelle joined their parents.

"It is with great honor that we welcome you to join us in this celebration," said Raul to the crowd. "You know my parents as the King and Queen of this kingdom, but this night, we are not honoring them for their leadership and dedication to the peoples of Wetpr and we are not honoring King Sudfad for his keen abilities as the military leader of this kingdom. Tonight our family is honoring them as loving parents and inspirations to us all. With that I would like to introduce the woman I will be marrying next week, Vitomas." Raul put his arm around Vitomas' shoulders as he said these words and the guests applauded.

"But this night is not just to celebrate our parents," Simon said. "We are also celebrating the parents of my intended bride; Alexander and Laurel. Both of whom took care of King Sudfad when he was a small child."

"King Sudfad and Queen Renya and Alexander and Laurel have overwhelmed us with their love, generosity and understanding and have shown us what we should aspire to. Now I would like you to meet Annabelle, the woman I will marry next week." Simon put his arm around Annabelle and kissed her on the cheek. The room was filled with loud applause.

"Before the King addresses you, Simon and I wanted to add one more thing; it was through the eyes of our loving wives that we realized how truly blessed we are and what we owe to our parents. And for those of you who have known Simon and I since we were boys you know that we tested their patience greatly," When Raul said this the guests roared with laughter.

"What Raul is trying to say," Simon said smiling. "Is that since it took us so long to thank them, we decided to get them some additional gifts. I am going to ask all of you in this room to please move so that we can open a pathway from the main door."

The crowd moved and Simon motioned for the two soldiers to enter the room. The first soldier was leading a beautiful stallion that was a rare golden color with a white mane. The horse held its head with pride as it was presented to Sudfad. "Father, in the words of our wives, a horse befitting a king," Simon said as King Sudfad was handed the reins.

"He is exquisite," said Sudfad in awe. "Thank you my children."

"Alexander since you and Father enjoy your rides together, we thought you would like your own horse," said Simon as the second soldier handed Alexander the reins to a beautiful brown stallion with a white star on its forehead.

"I don't even know what to say," said Alexander as he admired his horse. "Thank you, thank you so much."

Simon nodded to the two soldiers who grasped the reins of the horses and walked them out of the ball room.

"Now Mother and Laurel would you please step forward?" asked Raul with a smile.

Raul nodded towards the main door of the ballroom and two soldiers walked up to Raul and Simon. One soldier handed Raul a long fur coat made from the wild engas cat that inhabits the Vandrew Mountain Range in the southern Kingdoms of Ryed and Stordt. Raul helped Renya put the coat on.

"This is so beautiful," said Renya with tears in her eyes.

Simon took a long fur coat from the second soldier and helped Laurel put it on. This coat was made from the terbot bear that roams in the northern regions of the continent. Laurel was crying and barely able to speak.

"I am so overwhelmed," Laurel whispered. As the guests applauded Vitomas whispered into the King's ear.

Raul and Simon each walked back and stood beside their intended wives as Sudfad walked forward. "I must tell you that my two daughters-in-law are in shock. I am told that Raul and Simon picked out these gifts themselves." Sudfad said smiling and the guests laughed.

"On behalf of us all I would like to welcome you to this celebration of family. So this seems like the appropriate time to introduce you to two new members of our family. Renya and I have adopted two more sons." Matthew and Petra walked up to the King. Matthew was holding Petra's hand as Petra was incredibly frightened by the crowd.

"Our family is proud to introduce you to Matthew and Petra," Sudfad said. "Two noble and fine young men, who will serve our kingdom proudly." The crowd applauded loudly.

"Please," said Sudfad after several minutes of applause. "The music will resume momentarily. Please enjoy yourselves." As Sudfad was talking he noticed that the Sanuri was standing in the doorway of the Great Hall. When the Sanuri realized he had caught the King's attention he nodded to Sudfad, who left the stage and walked over to the Sanuri, the two men then walked to Sudfad's study.

"I just spoke with Nica," said the Sanuri in a low voice. "He said the same men that have been watching the castle and following you are still staying in Salar. The Enrops have identified the buildings they see these men enter and I have indicated them on this map." Sudfad was studying the various maps that had been laid out on the large table in his study.

"Sudfad I believe these are the same men that I saw in my visions," the Sanuri said. "But Nica said that over the past few days, the Enrops have spotted a second group of men, about twenty in all watching the castle and these men are camping outside of Salar."

"Do you believe these two groups to be separate?"

"My intuition tells me yes but I have no proof at this point. But I can tell you that the second group contains a demon."

"A demon," sputtered Sudfad. "How can the Enrops identify a demon?"

"Much of creation can see the light and darkness in beings," explained the Sanuri.

"So do you want to make any changes to our plans?" asked Sudfad.

"Keep the plans as they are for the first group of terrorists we have identified. The demon and his men are mine," replied the Sanuri. "Sudfad you should return to your party. And enjoy yourself."

"Matthew you are a wonderful dancer," said Vitomas as they glided across the dance floor.

"So are you."

"Annabelle and I never danced until we came here. We have been taking lessons so we can dance at our weddings."

"Well, you certainly are a fast learner. Look over there," Matthew said with a grin, as he tilted his head towards Petra who was trying to dance with a girl about his age.

"Aren't they cute?" said Vitomas. "I felt so sorry for him; he looked like he was terrified getting up in front of the guests."

"I know, I thought I was going to have to carry him for a moment," Matthew said.

"Do you know his story?"

"Yes and I will admit I was amazed," said Matthew. "He will make a fine warrior some day."

As Vitomas looked at Matthew a sweet smile came across her face. "Those are the exact words that Raul and Simon said. Matthew the three of you act like you have been together all of your lives."

"As strange as it may sound I feel like they have been my brothers all of my life. I wish we could have gotten to know each other as kids."

"I have heard so many stories about how wild and unruly Raul and Simon were, I don't know if the kingdom would have been ready to add you to the mix also," said Vitomas and laughed.

"Vitomas; Raul and Simon have told me a little about what you and Annabelle went through and I just want to say that I can't believe it because you seem so normal."

"Why, Matthew I do think that is the nicest thing you have ever said to me," replied Vitomas with a flirtatious smile.

Matthew grinned, "Ok that didn't come out the way I meant it. It is my experience that people who have suffered like you two have are usually filled with fear and anger and want nothing but vengeance. But both of you are so sweet and kind; I truly admire the way you have risen above your past."

Vitomas looked seriously at Matthew before she spoke. "There are still scars. You are family so I suppose I can tell you. I still have awful nightmares. In fact, that is why Raul moved into my chambers before the wedding. The only time I feel really safe is when I am with him."

Matthew stared into Vitomas' eyes as if searching for an answer. "I cannot even imagine what that monster did to you girls," he said angrily. Vitomas was surprised at how emotional Matthew suddenly appeared. Then as he calmed himself Matthew added. "You are right, we are family and I would hope that if any of you ever needed anything you would come to me."

The music stopped as Matthew was speaking. Suddenly Matthew and Vitomas heard their names being called. They looked towards the main door of the ballroom and saw Renya standing with two men in priest's robes. Renya was motioning for Matthew and Vitomas to join her. "Matthew and Vitomas I would like you to meet Padre Octavos. He runs the orphanage in Salar," introduced Renya. "And this is his guest High Priest Pravis from the monastery at Malga."

"The Queen is very good to us," said Padre Octavos as he shook hands with Matthew. Then he looked at Vitomas and said, "Perhaps you could join the Queen on one of her visits, the children love her so."

Vitomas looked at Renya with surprise. "I didn't know you helped at an orphanage. I would love to go with you and I bet Annabelle would too." Renya smiled.

"Good it is settled then," said Padre Octavos persuasively.

"I am sorry but I did not catch your name," said Matthew as he extended his hand to Pravis.

"He is High Priest Pravis from Malga. I must say what an unexpected honor to have a High Priest suddenly show up at my door," Padre Octavos said with pride.

While Matthew and Pravis where shaking hands, Vitomas gasped loudly when she saw the ring Pravis was wearing; an extremely large ruby stone in a silver setting.

"Vitomas what is it, you look as if you have seen a ghost?" asked Renya.

"I have seen that ring before," whispered Vitomas as she stared at Pravis.

"I am certain you are mistaken, my child, it is very old and unique in design," said Pravis.

"Roch wears that same ring," said Vitomas and I am not mistaken as I have borne the print of that ring on my skin after many beatings."

Matthew maintained his grasp on Pravis' hand and examined the ring. Matthew's demeanor became less relaxed. "My sister Juleta wears that same ring also."

Pravis pulled his hand from Matthew's grasp and said nervously, "Well, I must be mistaken about this design being unique."

"I don't mean to be rude but Matthew was just going to help me carry in more wine," said Vitomas. "It was very nice to meet you." Vitomas grabbed Matthew's arm and started walking towards the hallway.

"Matthew we must find Raul and Simon quickly."

"Why, what is wrong Vitomas?"

"For years Roch has sent his men to spy on Sudfad's family and the strength of his army. I fear that man is a spy. Did you notice how nervous he got when we talked about the ring? Matthew, Roch does not know that Annabelle and I are here and he doesn't know that Raul is alive."

Matthew grabbed Vitomas' hand and they hurried to the front door of the castle where both Simon and Raul were standing. "Is something the matter?" Raul asked when he saw the look on Vitomas' face.

"There is a man dressed as a high priest who is talking with Renya. He is wearing the same ring that Roch and Juleta wear. He became nervous when we talked about the ring. Raul I think he is one of Roch's spies," said Vitomas excitedly.

"Padre Octavos said the high priest suddenly showed up at his door so Padre Octavos brought him here as a guest," Matthew added.

Raul looked at Matthew, "Please take care of the girls while Simon and I talk to this man." Then Raul kissed Vitomas on the forehead and said, "You and Annabelle stay with Matthew until Simon and I return. And don't worry; everything will be alright."

"Where is Annabelle?" asked Simon with concern.

"She is sitting at the head table talking with her parents. Don't worry I will take care of them," said Matthew. "Renya and the priests are standing just inside the main door."

Matthew looked at Vitomas, "You know you are going to have to act as if nothing is wrong when we go back in there."

"I know, just give me a moment." Vitomas took a deep breath then took Matthew's arm. "I am ready." The two entered the ball room through a side door and walked to the head table to join Annabelle and her parents.

"Matthew he is gone," whispered Vitomas as they saw Raul and Simon speaking with Renya and Padre Octavos. Vitomas and Matthew watched as Raul and Simon started to search the room.

Pravis exited the castle by walking through one of the doors that led out to the royal gardens. As soon as Pravis slipped into the darkness of the night he began to run. Pravis knew there were soldiers stationed in front of the castle because he walked past them when he entered with Padre Octavos. Pravis ran around the castle towards the back; he planned to enter the wooded area then climb over the stone wall that surrounded the castle grounds.

Pravis' chest heaved as he tried to breath; he could not remember the last time he ran. Pravis fell twice, tripping over fallen branches inside of the wooded area. There was little moonlight, but enough for him to see the darkness of the huge stone wall looming before him. Pravis was filled with a sense of exhilaration as he reached the base of the wall. He felt the stones, searching for an outcropping to grasp onto. The ringing in his ears sounded like drums to him; Pravis was still gasping for breath as he started to hoist himself up the wall.

No sooner had Pravis started his ascent when he could feel many hands grabbing his feet and legs and pulling him downwards. He heard no voices. The last thing Pravis remembered was his body hitting the ground with great force.

Both Matthew and Vitomas searched the huge ballroom with their eyes, looking for Pravis. Vitomas leaned forward and whispered into Matthew's ear. "Please don't tell Annabelle about this yet, let her enjoy the evening." Matthew looked at Vitomas and smiled. "I was not planning to," he said as he continued to survey the room.

"Matthew why do you think your sister would wear the same ring as Roch?" asked Vitomas in a lowered voice.

"I really don't know and it does concern me."

Matthew please don't get angry at what I am to tell you," said Vitomas. "But Raul told us that he worried about your safety because he felt Juleta was almost a female version of Roch." Matthew turned and stared at Vitomas but before he could speak, Matthew heard Annabelle talking.

"Well, the two of you certainly seem cozy," teased Annabelle.

"My Lady," said Matthew with a charming smile. "Vitomas simply feels sorry for me because you will not pay me any attention."

When Pravis awoke he did not know where he was. All he could see was darkness. Pravis felt a blinding pain in his head. When he tried to move his hand to touch his head; Pravis realized his arms were shackled to a wall. He quickly tried to move his legs and heard the chains rattle in the darkness. Pravis' memories returned, flooding his thoughts. Then he suddenly became filled with fear. Pravis did not move or even breathe, he was not sure if he was alone.

"It is about time you asked me to dance," Vitomas said teasingly as Raul took her hand and pulled her onto the dance floor.

"We found him," Raul whispered into her ear. "He is in the dungeons." Raul could feel Vitomas' body relax with the news.

"Did you speak with him? Did Roch send him?"

"Honey, the soldiers got him and by time Simon and I saw him; the man was unconscious; we will speak with him later."

"But what if there are more spies?" Vitomas asked fearfully.

"Then we will capture them also," Raul reassured her. "Honey, Simon and I never wanted to worry you girls but we have prepared for intruders. We always do when there is any type of event at the castle."

Vitomas searched Raul's face. "You think Roch may have heard about our wedding, don't you?"

"That certainly is a possibility, my dear. Now please promise me you won't worry anymore and just enjoy the evening." Raul pulled Vitomas closer to him and whispered, "Did I tell you how beautiful you look tonight?"

"Pass another jug over here," said Demetries as he and his men sat around a large fire drinking and laughing.

"I hear you are looking for me," said the Sanuri as he stepped out of the darkness towards the fire. Several of the men jumped to their feet. "Stay where you are," ordered the Sanuri with a voice of authority.

"Yes, stay back; he is mine," said Demetries as he slowly stood up with a sadistic grin on his face.

"The men you left at the castle are waiting for you in hell, Demetries," said the Sanuri loudly. He heard some of the men whisper, "Who is Demetries?" As Demetries had not told the men his real name.

"Did you kill them?" asked Demetries still grinning.

"I did not but the castle guards were not as merciful."

"I have been waiting a very long time for this," Demetries sneered. "You took my friend from me."

"If you mean Sporos I will gladly take you to him."

Demetries started to lift his arms and mumble. Suddenly he fell to the ground screaming and writhing in pain; simultaneously a light of such brilliance that it blinded the men; enveloped the campsite. The earth began to shake violently and a wind of great proportions roared through the camp, uprooting trees that collapsed around the men. Some of Roch's men were yelling and running; others stood motionless holding their swords and looking at Demetries and the Sanuri.

"Leave this place now and never return," commanded the Sanuri to the men. "And I will spare you." His voice thundered through the noise of the storm. All of Roch's men ran to their horses in such a panic that many of them left their belongings behind, even their saddles.

"Demetries you have yet a role to play in this world. But you will never wear the mask of a human again. From this night forward every creature in every world will see you for what you are; the filth deposited in the regions of hell."

Demetries' screams were heard by Roch's men as they quickly rode into the night.

"What is the significance of this ring?" demanded Matthew as he grabbed Pravis' face.

"It is just a ring My Lord."

"If it is just a ring, then tell me how does a high priest come to wear the same ring as royalty?" asked Matthew.

"I do not know the answer to that question," replied Pravis as sweat poured down his face.

"Then let me rephrase it. How does a holy man wear the same ring as those who are known to be evil?"

Pravis paused, then again said, "I do not know."

505

Long after the celebration had ended and the guests had left, Sudfad and the Sanuri stood in the hallway of the dungeons; listening to Matthew question Pravis. "I believe him to be a high priest at the monastery at Malga," said the Sanuri. "And that gives me great cause for concern. The Enrops said they saw him talking with the demon. Sudfad tell Matthew to stop questioning him. Keep Pravis locked up until after the weddings then let him go, and the Enrops will follow him to see who he reports to."

Chapter XXXII
Clarity

Roch jumped up in his bed awakened by a loud and commanding voice. "You feeble man, you would demand my audience," yelled the voice. "Who do you think you are?"

Roch looked around his room in horror when suddenly a figure of a man appeared against the wall across from Roch's bed. The figure appeared almost transparent at first but as it took form Roch saw a tall man with a black beard and mustache and black shoulder length hair with gray streaks. The man was wearing a white priest's robe. Roch could not believe his eyes. Roch shook his head, thinking he was dreaming but the figure of the man was becoming more lifelike by the moment.

"Who are you?" demanded Roch.

"Who am I?" yelled the voice with authority. "Who are you to send demons to me?"

"I demand you tell me your name," growled Roch as he jumped out of bed angrily.

"I do not bow to darkness," yelled the voice.

Roch took a step towards the apparition; the figure raised its hand from across the room and Roch was knocked to the ground with great force. Surprised Roch jumped back to his feet and looked at the figure, trying to size up his opponent. After a moment of clarity Roch exclaimed with amazement, "You are the Sanuri."

"And you are the king who murdered his parents."

"How do you know that?" demanded Roch.

"The Great Ruler sees all; you cannot hide from the light."

"I am not hiding," yelled Roch angrily

"And yet you sit in this dark castle, your greed and hatred consuming you," the Sanuri said mockingly. "You have destroyed every gift The Great Ruler has sent to you and you mock Him by calling to demons."

"I don't know what you are talking about," yelled Roch defiantly.

The figure moved closer to Roch. "This test is of choices, my murderous king; and so far you have made all the wrong choices but you can still be saved."

"Saved from what?" replied Roch mockingly.

"Beware the path you are on and the company that you keep. Listen to my words and dwell upon them for I was sent here to deliver them for your sake." The voice thundered so loudly in the room that Roch covered his ears. "But I too have a message for you. All of heaven knows the hatred in your heart for your brother and his family. I will tell you this but once; they are protected." With these words the figure disappeared.

Roch stood motionless for several minutes; not believing what he saw or heard then he quickly went to his war room and poured himself a large glass of whiskey.

With less than a week before the royal weddings, guests were starting to arrive. Those who traveled great distances came early so they could settle in and be rested before the ceremonies. Renya never stopped moving as she oversaw all the preparations for both the guests and the ceremony itself. All of the extra staff that Renya hired were under suspicion from Sudfad and his sons. Enrops were assigned to follow the staff and other workers who entered the castle grounds to determine if they were collaborating with the terrorists.

"There will be terrorists inside of the castle, you can rest assured," said the Sanuri.

"Can we not stop that?" asked Matthew as he sat with the other men in Sudfad's study.

"Actually I would prefer that we identify them and watch them," the Sanuri answered. "The terrorists who come to our doors are just the foot soldiers. We must determine who is giving the orders."

"And all these people are trying to attack us because we are the Keepers of the Scrolls?" asked Simon with a dubious look on his face.

The Sanuri looked at Sudfad then at Simon, Raul and Matthew who sat across from him at the large table in the King's study. "There is so much more about your roles and responsibilities that must be explained to the three of you. But at Sudfad's request I was planning to wait until after the weddings."

"I intend on staying here for several months after the ceremonies so I can teach you the many things you need to know. Yet I do not want to insult you by not answering your questions. Underneath this very study is a secret vault which contains many of the holy gifts of The Great Ruler."

"What!" exclaimed Raul. "How could we not know this?"

"You were not meant to know about it until the proper time. It has existed since your first ancestor made the covenant with The Great Ruler to be the Keeper of the Scrolls. Over time other items have been hidden in this vault also. They will be returned to The Great Ruler's children when they can use them wisely," explained the Sanuri.

"Can we see it now?" Simon asked.

"Yes but first I want to tell you a few more things. These gifts are coveted by many and need to be protected. For generations the sons of evil have tried to find this vault and some do suspect your family has knowledge of it," the Sanuri added.

"Sons, over the years I have stopped several attempts of armed men storming the castle in search of this vault," said Sudfad.

"Father I just cannot believe that all of this has gone on with Simon and me living under this roof and we never suspected. How can that be?" asked Raul with frustration.

"I kept it from you the same way you will keep it from your children until the time is right," Sudfad said.

"You have had enemies your entire lives that you did not realize," the Sanuri said.

"And there is more. There is an ancient prophecy that has been passed down from generation to generation since the time of the Great Separation; when The Great Ruler's children chose to leave Him and His teachings. It is called the Prophecy of The Seven Sons. It describes a holy family of warriors that do battle with the dark lords and the demons. According to this prophecy the holy warriors conquer battle after battle and do irreparable damage to the powers of darkness."

The Sanuri continued, "The prophecy does not indicate the exact linage of The Seven Sons, meaning it could be a variety of family members as opposed to seven sons of one father. Or perhaps it could mean seven sons of The Great Ruler. As you know I have walked in your world for hundreds of years. I am seeing things now that I have never before witnessed. It is the belief of this old man that all of you in this room will have a role in fulfilling this prophecy."

The room was completely silent as all of the men tried to comprehend the power of the Sanuri's words. "Trust me when I tell you that the sons of darkness are well aware of this prophecy also and some of them may suspect the roles you will play."

"So you think this prophecy will fall on the shoulders of my sons?" asked Sudfad.

"Sudfad in my heart I believe you too are counted as a son," replied the Sanuri.

"But there are not seven of us, so does that mean our future children could be part of this?" Simon asked.

"Perhaps, I do not have all of the answers yet," said the Sanuri. "But I can tell you that when it is time for the fulfillment of the prophecy there will be seven."

Matthew was staring intently at the Sanuri as he spoke. "Since Sudfad's family has welcomed me into their home, every single one of them described you, Sanuri, as part of the family. Is it possible you are one of The Seven Sons?"

"My son anything is possible," replied the Sanuri.

While the Sanuri was speaking, Sudfad pulled several lanterns off from a shelf and lit them. "Your father is ready to take you to the vault," the Sanuri said. All of the sons stood up and walked towards Sudfad; who handed them each a lantern. Sudfad walked towards the wall that contained the door to the study. Other than the door that entire wall was covered with built-in book shelves. "Matthew put your hand behind that large black book," Sudfad said as he pointed to a particular book on one of the shelves. "Now lift the lever that is behind it."

Suddenly the wall to the left of Sudfad moved; exposing a dark stair case. "I'll go first," said Sudfad as he started down the stairway, holding his lantern high to light the way. They walked down seven flights of stone steps. At the bottom of the steps were six doors the seventh door which was to the vault was concealed.

The Sanuri pressed his hand against a portion of wall and it started to move, revealing a huge wooden and metal door. Sudfad took a large and very old key from his pocket and unlocked the door. The Sanuri was the first to enter the vault.

"Behold the scrolls which you protect," said the Sanuri as he held his lantern high in the air.

As the room became illuminated by all of their lanterns, the men saw a huge table in the middle of the room which was surrounded with chairs. A very large desk set against the rear wall and thick carpets covered the floor. Huge wooden shelves covered every inch of wall space.

"This looks a little like your study," commented Simon.

"Yes your mother wanted to make it more comfortable," said Sudfad as he grabbed a heavy bound book off from one of the shelves. Sudfad wiped dust from the cover of the book and placed it on the table. "This book contains information on all of the items in here," said Sudfad.

"What are all of these things?" asked Raul.

"There are holy relics in here such as the scrolls and historical treasures that are being protected," said the Sanuri. "Centuries of wars destroyed many irreplaceable things in this world; we are attempting to preserve some of them until a time that it is safe to bring them out."

"The true location of this room has always been known only to me and certain members of your family and of course The Great Ruler," explained the Sanuri. "Remember I told you that many beings of darkness have suspected that your family may be the Keepers of the Scrolls, so everyone you tell about this vault you are putting into peril."

"But you said Mother knew," said Raul.

"You know your mother, do you think I would be able to keep this from her?" asked Sudfad.

"There are four of you now but your father, as his father before him, chose to tell their wives and to obtain their help; which was wise," the Sanuri said. "I know you want to protect your wives but you will tell them and they will be of great value to you."

The Sanuri and Sudfad saw the looks on Simon's and Raul's faces. "Remember I told you once that The Great Ruler had picked the perfect wives for you; it is true and just as Sudfad and Renya have worked together to protect these holy treasures so will you and your wives."

"We also want to protect our families," said Raul.

"I understand," said the Sanuri.

"When should we tell them?" asked Simon.

"I will be staying with you for a while after the ceremonies; I can help you explain your responsibilities to them," the Sanuri said. "But now I want to explain this room to you." The Sanuri motioned for them all to be seated at the table.

When Pravis did not return to his men after two days, Jarrod the second in command took over as leader. Pravis had not shared with any of his men that he was going to try and gain entrance to the castle during the grand ball; so Jarrod sent men out to search for Pravis. They searched the city and the areas around the castle; in frustration they started to search the areas outside of the City of Salar.

"We found signs that a number of men had abandoned their campsite quickly," Tomas explained to Jarrod.

"Something must have frightened them because they left many of their belongings behind."

"Where was this camp?" Jarrod asked.

"Just west of the city, not far from the castle grounds," Tomas answered. "There were no signs of battle or footprints of man or beast leading up to the camp; but there were trees torn out of the earth and scattered like kindling, I have never seen anything like it."

"Do you think these were Roch's men?"

"Yes, because we have not seen them in several days," Tomas answered.

"This is most unusual," Jarrod said almost to himself. "Pravis and Roch's men all disappear. Like it or not I am going to have to tell High Priest Meekos about this."

"Jarrod you saw Roch's men; did any of them strike you as men who would frighten easily?" Tomas asked.

"What are you getting at?"

"It is all so odd; do you think there are some magics at work here?"

"If there are, they are no match for our dark lords," Jarrod said as he started to write a message for Meekos.

"Vitomas, Vitomas," called Annabelle as she opened the door and ran inside of Vitomas' chambers. Vitomas was sitting on the balcony and quickly ran into her bedroom when she saw Annabelle.

"Annabelle what is the matter? Is something wrong?"

Annabelle smiled, "You will never guess who just arrived." Annabelle did not give Vitomas time to respond. "Matthew's family is here, including his sister Juleta."

"Oh, I have been dying to see what she is like," Vitomas said sternly.

"Now remember Annabelle, Juleta could be some type of spy because she wears the same ring as Roch; so we have to watch her." Both young women hurried to the main entrance of the castle. They saw a large pile of suitcases in the front foyer and heard voices coming from the parlor.

"Girls, good you are here. I want you to meet my brother Mathas and his family," said Renya when she saw Vitomas and Annabelle in the doorway of the parlor. Mathas was a large, handsome man with straight brown hair and blue eyes. His wife Rosa; was petite with brown skin and long straight black hair.

"You certainly can tell you are Matthew's father," said Vitomas after she curtsied to the King and Queen. "He looks exactly like you."

"Oh I hate formalities when it comes to family," said Queen Rosa with outstretched arms. "Come here and give me a hug." Both Vitomas and Annabelle hugged Rosa then they stepped back but she continued to grasp their hands for a moment. "Renya I must say your sons have chosen well," said Rosa warmly. "These girls are beautiful."

"And they are as wonderful as they are beautiful," said Renya with a proud smile.

Suddenly everyone heard a noise that sounded like a loud grunt. They turned to see Juleta standing near the door with a disgusted look on her face. Juleta was a handsome woman, tall and thin with long straight black hair.

"This is our daughter Juleta," said King Mathas. "Juleta come here and meet your family." Juleta walked towards them slowly, staring at each person as if she was trying to read their minds. Vitomas quickly walked up to Juleta before she reached the group and grasped Juleta's hand. "Juleta, I have heard so much about you. I am so very honored to finally meet you," said Vitomas as she stared aggressively into Juleta's brown eyes, an action that Juleta did not take graciously.

The two women stared at each other as if trying to read each other's thoughts. Then Vitomas looked at Juleta's hand which she was holding. "Why Annabelle look at this ring," Vitomas said sarcastically. Annabelle walked up to Juleta and stared at her as boldly as Vitomas.

"Where ever did you get it?" asked Annabelle sweetly.

"It was made for me," replied Juleta suspiciously. "It is one of a kind."

"Really," said Vitomas pleasantly but she did not let go of Juleta's hand. "Because King Roch wears that same ring as did an intruder in our castle the other night."

Juleta quickly pulled back her hand and said, "I am sure you are mistaken."

"No we are not," said Annabelle sternly as she stared at Juleta. The room was silent for a few moments as everyone looked at Juleta.

"Are we interrupting?" asked Matthew with a broad grin on his face. Matthew was holding his little sister Margarit. Raul and Simon were standing behind Matthew smiling.

"Boys, how long have you been standing there?" Renya asked.

"Long enough," replied Matthew as he walked into the room. "Vitomas and Annabelle I would like you to meet the apple of my eye, my baby sister Margarit." Margarit was a beautiful girl of ten with long reddish brown hair and large brown eyes. Vitomas and Annabelle each kissed Margarit on the cheek.

"Margarit I want you to meet the two girls who have stolen my heart but unfortunately for me they are marrying Raul and Simon." Matthew put Margarit down.

"Which one of you is marrying Raul?" Margarit asked.

"I am," replied Vitomas with a smile.

"I have a confession to tell you; after Raul stayed with us I wanted him to marry me," the little girl said seriously. Everyone in the room broke into laughter except for Juleta who stared maliciously at Annabelle and Vitomas.

"Why Juleta, the look on your face," teased Matthew. "Did you want to marry Raul too?"

"No," snapped Juleta. "Could someone please show me to my room?"

"Oh course," said Sudfad, who was as suspicious of Juleta as the rest of the family. "Renya which chambers did you reserve for Mathas and his family?"

"Mathas, Rosa and Margarit have the chambers to the right of the Sanuri's room and Juleta has the chambers to the left of his room."

"A fine choice," replied Sudfad with a knowing smile. "Simon, would you please ask the guards in the hallway to carry the suitcases?"

Renya took Margarit's hand. "We have another son named Petra. I will get him from his studies and perhaps the two of you can play."

"Another son?" asked Mathas.

"Yes we recently adopted him," said Renya. "A sweet boy and wait until you hear his story." After Mathas and his family and Renya left the room; Raul, Simon, Matthew and Sudfad all walked closer to Vitomas and Annabelle.

"Raul and Simon may I give your wives a kiss?" Matthew asked with a grin.

"Of course," said Raul as Simon nodded. Matthew kissed both Vitomas and Annabelle on their cheeks.

"Did you see the look on Juleta's face when you were confronting her? She is not used to that at all. Here I was worried about how she would treat the two of you but I see you can handle yourselves," Matthew said still grinning.

"I am sorry if we were rude," Vitomas said as she looked at Raul. "But when I look at her all I see is a threat to this family. Did you watch her eyes when we were asking her about the ring? She was lying to us."

"There is something evil about her," Annabelle said. "Vitomas and I already decided that we were going to keep an eye on her."

"Well sons," Sudfad said while smiling proudly. "Apparently The Great Ruler did send you the perfect wives. I am realizing how very much Vitomas and Annabelle are like Renya."

The following morning when Simon entered Sudfad's study. Sudfad, Raul, Matthew and the Sanuri were already seated and drinking coffee.

"I am sorry I am late," Simon apologized. "The girls wanted to talk with me before this meeting." Simon handed each man a piece of paper. "Annabelle drew some sketches of the ring that Juleta, Roch and that intruder wear. She and Vitomas have errands in the city today and they plan on taking these drawings to Andrew our jeweler to see if he can provide any information. The girls didn't know if any of you would want copies of the drawings."

"I will say Annabelle is a talented artist," said the Sanuri as he examined the sketches. "May I have another, Simon? I want to send one to my friends at the monastery in Malga. They have access to an incredible library of ancient texts there; perhaps they can find information for us."

"Matthew do you have any idea when Juleta got the ring?" Sudfad asked.

Matthew replied, "No, Juleta feels that the family is beneath her and shuns us."

"Perhaps she just doesn't want any of you to know what she is up to," said the Sanuri as he filled his pipe. "I learned long ago that there are no such things as coincidences. The fact that these three people wear the same ring after The Great Ruler has sent me numerous visions about terrorists threatening your family and The Holy Scrolls is something I believe we need to investigate."

"Simon, when the girls return from Salar would you ask Annabelle if she can sketch pictures of Roch, Juleta and High Priest Pravis. I believe we should start compiling a file. I cannot put my finger on it, but I believe this ring is an important clue to something."

"I don't really want to take her to the dungeons," Simon stated.

"Father are there any of the cottages on our land that are not being used by guests?" Raul asked.

"I think that old hunting lodge you boys used to play in is empty," Sudfad said. "Renya keeps telling me to burn it down, so I doubt she has guests staying there."

"Matthew after breakfast why don't you come with me and we can check that lodge out," Raul said. "Simon why don't you go in town with the girls. They are eager to help but showing that picture around may be a dangerous proposition."

"Don't you send soldiers with the girls?" Sudfad asked.

Simon and Raul both looked at each other and smiled. "The girls really don't like having the soldiers with them because they like to talk with the people in the city. The soldiers have complained that a couple of times the girls have escaped from them," Raul said.

"You mean to tell me that those two young girls have out-smarted our soldiers," Sudfad said as he found the idea humorous.

"Apparently more than once," Simon replied.

"Boys, while this is funny, you need to impress on them that it is also very dangerous for them to do this," added Sudfad. "Especially now."

"I would just like to say something here if I may," said the Sanuri as he again lit his pipe. "While Vitomas and Annabelle are young, they grew up in horror and learned to survive by following their instincts. I would not be so eager to dismiss things they may bring to you."

"I don't believe we have," Simon said.

"I did not say you did," said the Sanuri. "But these old bones are telling me there is a story before us that is just beginning to unfold."

Demetries screamed with rage as he wandered in the woods near the castle grounds in Wetpr. He cursed the Sanuri over and over for foiling his plans. Two days Demetries wandered aimlessly screaming and cursing, so consumed was he with anger and hatred. Roch's men had all abandoned him; some because they feared the power of the Sanuri and the rest ran in terror when they saw the true face of the demon exposed.

Demetries had taken over Jonas' dead body but the Sanuri had caused the illusion of the body to melt away, exposing the demon beneath. Demetries knew that it was too early for Roch to discover why Demetries had been sent to him. Demetries had to figure out a plan to fool Roch into keeping him as a confident and advisor until the time was right.

The night of the second day, Demetries built a fire for warmth from the cold night air. As he sat before the fire, Demetries heard his name called. Demetries turned around and saw no one in the darkness; then he looked into the fire and saw the face of his friend and mentor.

"Sporos," Demetries cried out loud. Demetries was elated to see the face of his friend. But soon Demetries realized that Sporos' face looked like it was in agony. Sporos was speaking but Demetries could not hear his words. The vision of Sporos remained unchanged in the fire. Demetries stared at it, trying to understand the message.

"Damn that Sanuri, may all the demons in hell torture him," spat Demetries. "He puts you in a cage," Demetries said to the image of Sporos. "And does this to me." After a moment a malicious smile worked its way across the rancid face of the demon. "All the demons in hell, of course why didn't I think of this before?" Demetries thought to himself. "I need to find Nestor and we will give the Sanuri and those kings a party they will never forget."

Chapter XXXIII
Inheritance

"Simon should be here shortly with the girls," Raul said as he handed glasses of whiskey to Sudfad, Matthew and the Sanuri who were all seated in Sudfad's study. Within minutes they heard laughter in the hallway then the door opened. Simon walked into the room with his arm around the shoulders of both Annabelle and Vitomas. Vitomas sat down next to Raul and kissed him. As Simon and Annabelle were sitting down Matthew said with a grin, "Remember Brother I am next in line."

Simon laughed and replied, "Yes but we are still working out the details."

"What is he talking about?" Annabelle asked. Raul, Simon and Matthew all sat in silence.

Sudfad looked at Raul and Simon. "You mean you haven't explained it to them?"

Raul looked at Sudfad and replied, "We aren't even married yet; we weren't going to tell them they have other suitors."

"Raul what are you all talking about?" asked Vitomas with a serious look on her face.

Raul looked at Sudfad, "Father do you want to explain it to them?"

Sudfad leaned back in his chair and got a broad grin on his face, "Oh no my sons, I think you are quite capable of this." Then Sudfad looked at the Sanuri and winked.

"Ok I don't like the sound of this, please explain what you are all talking about," Vitomas said.

Raul and Simon looked at each other and Simon was the first to speak, "By our laws men may have more than one wife and women may have more than one husband although that is less common." Simon paused.

"Simon now I am getting worried, what are you talking about?" asked Annabelle. "Do you want to take another wife?"

"Please, just let us explain the laws to you. There is also another law about wife inheritance; have you ever heard of that term?" Simon asked. Both Vitomas and Annabelle said, 'No'. By our laws if a husband dies it is the responsibility of his father to find another husband for the widow unless the first husband has already chosen one."

"What!" said Annabelle loudly. "I don't understand."

Raul started to explain, "Say I die in battle, it is Sudfad's responsibility to find another husband for Vitomas unless I already had one picked out."

"Why would you pick out our next husbands?" Vitomas asked.

"To make sure you have someone who will treat you like I would want you treated and to raise my children the way I want them raised. And in Simon's and my case, we want both of you to be with someone who could protect you from Roch and his men."

"First of all the thought of something happening to either of you is very upsetting," Vitomas said. "Honestly I don't think I would want to marry again. Are you telling us we have to marry?"

Raul put his arm around Vitomas. "Honey would you really want to live alone? And the Sanuri said we will have lots of children, they will need a father."

"But what if no one wants to marry us?" Annabelle said with her voice shaking.

"Are you kidding," Matthew said. "Besides the fact that both of you are extraordinarily beautiful women with incredible personalities; you are part of one of the wealthiest families in all of Opots and your children are heirs to the throne. Men will be beating down the doors for you."

"Raul, is he telling the truth?" Vitomas said with a frightened look on her face.

"Yes and I am not saying this would be the case if Father picked your husband, but a lot of royal marriages are made for political reasons."

"Both of you girls look so scared," Simon said as he put his arm around Annabelle. "Originally I had chosen Raul to be your next husband and he chose me."

"Raul, you know I love you but as a brother I never thought about you as a husband," Annabelle gasped.

"There is more to this," Raul said. "Say if I died and Sudfad chose another husband for Vitomas, chances are he would be of royalty from another kingdom. Which means Vitomas and the children would have to leave here and move to another area, perhaps never seeing any of you again."

"Can you girls imagine being separated? And Mother and Father certainly don't want to lose either one of you or the grandchildren. And the chances are great that whoever you marry will have other wives. At least you two girls love each other and know you can live together."

"You know this is really the last thing that I want to talk about before our wedding and I don't know whether to feel scared or angry. First of all you tell us we have no choice in the matter then you make these decisions for us without talking to us." Vitomas said.

"We didn't say you had no choice in the matter," Simon said.

"Well, you certainly made it sound that way," Annabelle said. "And Simon what did you mean when you said originally you had chosen Raul as my husband?"

"Matthew has requested to be considered for the inheritance also," Raul said. Both women looked at Matthew.

"For which one of us?" Annabelle asked.

"For both of you," Matthew said.

"Both of us!" Vitomas exclaimed. "Matthew I don't mean to insult you but I really do not understand any of this."

"If Simon and I are both killed we have chosen Matthew as the next husband for both of you," Raul said.

Everyone was silent for a few moments then Annabelle turned to Matthew and said in a sarcastic tone, "Oh, Matthew do you really think you could handle both of us?"

"I am certainly willing to try," he replied with a grin.

"Raul are you saying that if Simon dies I have to marry again but my choices will be either you or Matthew or both of you?" Annabelle asked with confusion.

"Yes, exactly."

"I'm not sure why but this is making me very angry," Vitomas said. "So next you will just tell us out of the blue that you picked the stable boy for our husband. How can you make these decisions for us Raul? Neither of you act controlling but this certainly seems that way."

Raul could see that both Vitomas and Annabelle were becoming very angry. Just as Raul was about to speak Vitomas turned to Simon and Matthew. "I don't mean to insult either one of you, I am sure you both would be wonderful husbands it is just that this is all so strange to me and I don't like the fact that we weren't even asked," Vitomas said as tears started to well in her eyes.

Raul tried to put his arm around Vitomas again but she pulled away. "You are right we should have talked this over with you but we thought you would be very pleased with our choices," Raul said. Both Vitomas and Annabelle glared at Raul.

"Vitomas do you remember that first night when you and I sat up all night with Simon? You wanted me to tell you about my family and when I told you about Simon you said that you could not believe he was adopted because he had all the same characteristics that you loved in me."

"Yes," Vitomas whispered.

Raul turned to Annabelle. "And how many times have you told me you can't believe how much Simon and I are alike?"

"Many times," Annabelle said.

"And both you girls keep telling us how much Matthew is like us," Simon said. "We wanted to pick out husbands who would make you happy and who you could fall in love with."

"Vitomas, if you were not in love with me do you think you could fall in love with either Simon or Matthew?" Raul asked.

"Yes," Vitomas said as she looked at both of the men. "Very easily."

"Annabelle you have the same question," Raul said.

"Raul I think of you as a brother but that might be because I know how much Vitomas loves you. But putting it the way you just did, I would say yes also."

"Vitomas you have told me that you think both Simon and Matthew are very attractive," Raul said.

"Now this is getting embarrassing," Vitomas said and blushed.

Raul looked at Annabelle who said, "Yes Raul I think you and Matthew are very handsome men."

"Honey I am just bringing these things up to show you why we made the decisions that we did. Neither Simon nor I meant to hurt either one of you," Raul explained.

"Girls, I probably shouldn't interfere," said the Sanuri. "But you do realize that the boys are doing this because they love you so much they want to make sure you are well cared for even if something happens to them. They aren't making these arrangements to be cruel or controlling. Hopefully they both will live long lives but if they don't, you will probably be quite comforted that they made these arrangements for you." Both the women listened intently to the Sanuri as he spoke then they sat in silence for a few minutes.

"I think we are beginning to understand that," Annabelle said. "This was a shock to both of us. But I have a question. Raul or Matthew why would you want to marry me?"

"What do you mean?" Matthew asked, surprised by her question.

"Would you be marrying me out of a sense of loyalty to Simon or because you could care for me?" Annabelle asked. "And I am sure Vitomas is thinking the same thing. I don't think either of us would ever want to get into a loveless marriage."

Raul, Simon and Matthew all stared at Annabelle in disbelief at her question. Matthew looked at Raul and Simon and said, "I'll go first." Then he looked at Annabelle and Vitomas, "I keep telling you girls that you stole my heart and I mean it. If you weren't marrying Raul and Simon I would be working hard to get both of you to marry me. I have never had feelings like this for one girl and now I have feelings for both of you and you're engaged to two of the men I admire most."

"Matthew we thought you were just kidding," Vitomas said in shock.

"I'm not sure I can explain this without making you both mad," Raul said. "You know how the two of you keep saying that Simon and I are like two sides of the same coin, well, so are you two. You are both so much alike that it would be difficult to be attracted to one of you and not the other. Does that make any sense at all?"

"Actually it does," Vitomas said. "It's like what I said about you and Simon."

"So Annabelle the answer to your question is that Matthew and I could easily fall in love with you," Raul said.

Vitomas turned and looked at Simon, although she was afraid to ask the question. "Vitomas when I was injured you took care of me with such love and compassion that at times I felt like you were my wife," Simon said. "I could easily fall in love with you."

"And there is something else that is so obvious and no one has mentioned. You and Annabelle survived and thrived because of each other when you were captives. Now that you are safe you still have that bond. Annabelle was going crazy until we brought you home. How do you two think you would react if one of you married someone else and moved away?"

"Both of you girls look so scared," Sudfad said gently. "You could feel flattered that three handsome princes would like to be your husbands."

525

"I know," said Annabelle. "Can we please change the subject this is making my head spin?" Annabelle paused for several moments then said, "All this talk almost made me forget why we came here." Annabelle handed a journal to Sudfad. "I can draw more if these pictures are not to your liking." Sudfad opened up the journal and saw detailed sketches of Roch, Pravis and Juleta. There were also more sketches of the rings.

"You really are talented," Sudfad said as he handed the drawings to the Sanuri, who in turned handed them around the room.

"Girls I asked that you attend this meeting and it wasn't to talk about your husbands dying so I apologize that both of you are so distressed now," said the Sanuri. "I wanted to ask you some questions. Both of you strike me as being very observant. I want you to think back to all those years you lived in Roch's castle. Did you ever see anyone else wear one of these rings?"

Both Annabelle and Vitomas thought about the question before answering. "No," said Vitomas. "Although Roch and his men plundered many cities and villages and took chests of jewels. But I do not recall anyone but Roch wear that ring. His ring was large like the one Pravis wears; Juleta's is made smaller for her hand."

"Do you ever remember any high priests coming to the castle or Roch speaking of any?"

"Why no," replied Annabelle. "Roch had his men kill all of the holy men in the kingdom and he bragged about it often."

"I don't think Pravis is really a high priest, I believe it to be a disguise. Some men may have come to the castle, perhaps even Roch's own men who pretended to be priests."

"Sanuri, perhaps you don't want to believe that another priest could have been conquered by darkness," Sudfad said.

"Perhaps you are right, old friend," said the Sanuri sadly.

"Roch's castle was always filled with men, scary, horrible men; and especially when they were drinking we would try to hide from them," said Annabelle.

"I am sure everything was unusual there, but if you recall anything that was particularly odd, please let us know," the Sanuri said.

"What do you mean by odd?" asked Vitomas.

"Oh any variety of things," said the Sanuri. "For example did Roch use ravens as messenger birds?"

"Ravens?" asked Annabelle. "Why we just..." Annabelle stopped talking in mid-sentence and turned to Matthew. "Matthew please don't hate us but Vitomas and I really have bad feelings about your sister Juleta, so we have been following her."

"Honey I could never hate either of you," said Matthew. "But are you going to tell me you saw Juleta using a raven as a messenger?"

"Yes," replied Annabelle.

"Where did you see this?" asked Sudfad.

"Yesterday morning in the gardens in the very back of the castle," answered Vitomas. "She was standing in the garden and a raven came to her. Juleta took something from its beak and the bird flew away. Sudfad what does that mean?"

"I won't lie to you dear," said Sudfad. "Dark lords use ravens as messengers."

Suddenly Vitomas' eyes grew wide. "Annabelle there is more going on here than they are telling us," Vitomas said. "All of this talk about what will happen to us if our husbands die at the same time we have Pravis and Juleta here, wearing Roch's ring. And now you say she is a dark lord." Vitomas looked at Raul.

"And all of the extra soldiers on duty; you're expecting Roch to attack us during the wedding aren't you?" No one in the room spoke, they all stared at Vitomas trying to figure out what to say. Finally Sudfad broke the silence.

"The Sanuri has had some visions and we also intercepted some messages that make us suspect someone is planning on attacking us."

"Is that why the Enrops are following all the guests and workers?" Annabelle asked.

The Sanuri smiled proudly, "Raul and Simon your wives are as brilliant as they are beautiful."

"And why didn't you tell me?" asked Vitomas angrily and slapped Raul's arm.

"Honey we didn't want to spoil the wedding for you girls. Mother told us that every girl dreams about her wedding day and warned us not to ruin it for you," Raul said with a grin. "And she doesn't even know about any of this."

Annabelle and Vitomas both gave each other a knowing look, then Annabelle spoke. "You are all going to be so angry with us. Sudfad you and Renya are the most wonderful people and you treat us as your daughters. We understand the positions we are assuming in this family and the responsibilities that come with them. But honestly Vitomas and I never wanted to have large, grand weddings."

"We are both finding ourselves quite overwhelmed by so many of the wedding plans. I guess I am trying to say that we feel like the ceremonies are more for the people of Wetpr than they are for us. Don't worry about telling us things and ruining the weddings for us because we really don't want these big weddings."

"Is that how you feel also?" Raul asked Vitomas.

"Yes, are you angry?"

"No," Raul said gently. "If you and I could have planned our wedding what would you have wanted?"

Without hesitation Vitomas said, "Oh Raul, I would love to be married in one of the castle gardens with just family and friends around."

"Honey what kind of wedding did you want?" Simon asked Annabelle.

"The same as Vitomas, we both wanted something simple and out in nature." Simon and Raul looked at each other, both smiling and shaking their heads.

"You are mad at us, aren't you?" asked Vitomas.

"Not at all Honey, if Simon and I could have chosen the weddings we wanted we would have said the same things you did."

"Really?"

"Yes, a simple ceremony in a garden or the woods with just family and friends."

Suddenly Simon's face broke into a smile. "Sanuri would you mind performing two wedding ceremonies?"

"Mathas you really have to talk to that girl," said Rosa anxiously. "She just stomps around here like she is mad at the world and she has been so unbelievably rude to everyone."

Mathas put down his cup of coffee. He and Rosa had been enjoying the morning sunlight as they sat at a small table in the garden outside of their chambers in the castle at Wetpr. "My dear, Juleta is always like that; did you really think she would change just because we are visiting Renya and Sudfad?"

"Actually I think she is behaving worse than usual. And how she treats Vitomas and Raul and Annabelle and Simon is scandalous. I will not have it Mathas. We so rarely get to visit your family and everyone is so friendly and loving here, except for our daughter. She is just an embarrassment to the family," Rosa said angrily.

"I agree my dear but she is a grown woman. I doubt if we can change her now."

"No, but you could talk to her and tell her to act civilized for just a few days, it would not kill her. Honestly I think she is jealous of those girls that is why she is so mean to them. If Juleta didn't scare off all of her suitors she might have a husband of her own. She is beautiful but no one can stand to be around her."

Mathas smiled. "Vitomas and Annabelle more than hold their own with her and I think it angers Juleta; she is so used to intimidating people. Honey I promise I will speak with Juleta, but I do have to go now, Sudfad wanted to meet with me."

"Curse them both," spat Juleta as she moved from her hiding spot in the garden, where she had been listening to her parent's conversation. "Well, my dear Mother and Father, when I take over the kingdom neither of you will be around long enough to be embarrassed by me," Juleta said to herself as she returned to her chambers. Juleta was so filled with rage that she kicked her bed post, then a chair and a dresser. Clenching her fists she ran around her chambers uttering curses and talking to herself.

"Everyone thinks those two little bitches are so perfect, all the damn men are in love with them," ranted Juleta as she started to throw her clothing around the room. Suddenly Juleta stopped and a smile crossed her face. "Perhaps I should give them a little taste of what a dark lord can do."

Hundreds of years before the Great Separation, the demons dwelled in obscurity in the various hell regions. Some of them were quite unaware of the other worlds that existed outside of their own. But a group of the Old Ones, the demons that existed in darkness before time itself, knew of the other worlds. Worlds they could overpower, worlds of victims just ripe for the taking. The Old Ones conspired to contact these worlds. They called out to mankind and it was not long before mankind was answering the calls and inviting the demons in.

The Old Ones were pleasantly surprised at how eager much of mankind was to have darkness in their worlds, some men and women rose above the rest in their adoration of the Old Ones. In the worlds of humans these people chose to emulate the kings of darkness as much as possible, so they created a secret society called The Insidiae, the conspirators. Just as the Old Ones, this group of humans sought to conspire against the worlds of man and even The Great Ruler Himself.

This insidious group grew in great proportions as the demons promised the humans earthly wealth and power for their allegiance and for their souls. But as anyone who is consumed with darkness, the members of the Insidiae trusted no one, not even themselves. They saw traitors in every shadow and often concealed their faces and identities when they met with other members of their groups.

The one object that allowed members of the Recupero Sect of the Insidiae to recognize each other were the Blood Rings that they wore. Large red rubies set in ornate silver bands. The engraved decorations on the bands of the rings were actually ancient symbols of the Old Ones. These rings symbolized the inheritance these demon worshipers would receive for their allegiance to darkness.

"Mathas I am so pleased you could join us," said Sudfad pleasantly as he held the door open to his study.

"I didn't realize this was a meeting," replied Mathas as he looked at Matthew, Raul, Simon and the Sanuri who were all seated around the large table in the study.

"There are a couple of things we need to discuss and I don't want to upset the women," Sudfad said as he took his seat.

"What sort of things?" asked Mathas.

"Without going into all the long details we have reason to believe there may be an attack on our family during the wedding ceremonies. Now we have been making great preparations for such an event but we thought it only fair to tell you and your men."

"I am glad you did Sudfad. You must know that my soldiers are at your command under these circumstances. Who do you suspect?"

"Father we have identified two separate groups that have sent spies to the castle, some of the men work for King Roch and the others, we have yet to find out who their leader is," Matthew explained.

"Two groups, that is interesting," said Mathas.

"From our information," continued Sudfad. "We believe there are plans to attack the couples as they ride in their carriages through the streets of Salar and this attack may be in addition to an attack on the castle itself. I am sorry to put you and your family in harm's way."

"Sudfad this will not be the first battle I have fought," Mathas said. "But I will need to put extra security around the women."

"Thank you for standing with us," Sudfad said.

"By The Great Ruler we are all family," Mathas replied.

"And on that note there are some other things we need to discuss," Sudfad continued. "Matthew has become such a beloved member of our family that I have officially adopted him also. Which means he is now included in my inheritance as well as yours."

"Why Sudfad, that is so generous of you," Mathas said and turned to Matthew. "Son I hope you realize what an honor this is for you. As usual son, you make me proud."

"Thank you Father and I hope this does not upset you," Matthew said. "But I feel like I grew up in this family and am honored to be considered a part of it also."

"There is one more thing," Sudfad said when Matthew interrupted him.

"Sudfad perhaps this is something I should tell Father."

Matthew moved to a chair closer to Mathas, "Father you know how much I love and respect you as does everyone in this room; but I am about to tell you some things that may break your heart."

"Matthew what on earth are you talking about?" Mathas asked.

"All of us, including the Sanuri have been monitoring the threats against Sudfad's family. We have proof that some dark lords are involved although we do not know why. Father one thing I have learned since I have been here is how the dark lords communicate with others, they use ravens as messengers."

Mathas' face turned white, "Matthew certainly you are not saying Juleta is a dark lord?"

"Father you and I have both seen her use ravens in such a manner and there is more," Matthew explained.

"We caught a spy inside the castle who wears the same unique ring as Juleta; the same ring that King Roch wears. Although we do not know the meaning of the rings we do not believe these are mere coincidences." Mathas stared at Matthew without speaking.

"Mathas," said the Sanuri. "You know we would not come to you with these things unless we had grave concerns. Before your visit here, it has been some time since you and I spoke. I know what a good man you are and you have always had a keen awareness of what is going on in your kingdom. In your heart you must have suspicions as to what is going on in your family."

"Rosa and I had words about Juleta just before I came here. She has such a darkness to her soul that my other children do not have," Mathas said sadly. "I do not want to believe what you say, yet I know all of you as men of honor and I know you would not lie to me about such matters."

"Father the reason we are telling you is not to hurt you," Matthew said softly. "But so you can better protect the family from Juleta. She has never concealed the fact that she is the first born and greatly desires the throne."

"And I have never concealed the fact that you are my first son and you will inherit the throne."

"So that we all understand," the Sanuri said. "Mathas you and Matthew are the only people who are standing between Juleta and what she most desires."

"Do you think these attacks are directed towards Matthew and me?"

"We know that Roch has long desired to kill Sudfad and his family, we just don't know if he has learned that Vitomas and Annabelle are here; which would give him greater cause to attack. But as Matthew said, we did catch an intruder who also wears the same ring as Juleta. It is possible that your family as well as Sudfad's are targets," explained the Sanuri.

Chapter XXXIV
Until Death Do We Part

Demetries sat inside a circle of thirteen large stones. He had painted his face with the blood of an engor, which he caught in a trap. The trees were filled with engors that were screaming at Demetries for killing their kind. Demetries had hallowed out a small piece of wood so he could use it as a ceremonial bowl. The bowl was filled with the blood of the engor; the price to be paid for summoning a demon.

As Demetries chanted he poured small amounts of the blood on top of each of the thirteen stones. Then he poured a little on top of his head. Demetries sat back down inside of the circle and drank from the bowl. Although it was early morning a darkness came over the place where Demetries was sitting. The earth began to shake slightly. Demetries now stood up and chanted louder in the ancient tongue of the Old Ones.

When the wind started to pick up Demetries screamed out, "I call forth Nestor." The wind increased in strength as a form started to take shape in front of Demetries. As the form appeared more solid the wind decreased, until Nestor stood before Demetries.

"You always did have a flare for the dramatic," Demetries said as he walked forward and grasped Nestor's hand.

"Old friend it is good to see you," Nestor said. "Is it true you are on a special mission for Omnibus?"

"Yes but that is not why I called you," Demetries replied. "The Kings of Wetpr will be married in three days. I want to kill them and the Sanuri during the ceremonies."

"Killing the Sanuri; that is not an easy task, which you know."

"He has banished Sporos to the regions of The Abyss. And not only has he taken my human form from me but he has cursed me so I will never be able to hide my true identity from mankind again," Demetries said angrily. "If I cannot complete my mission because Roch understands who I am, the punishment from Omnibus will be an eternal horror."

"Do not take lightly the punishments that the Sanuri can call forth as an emissary of The Great Ruler, my friend."

"I fear Omnibus more."

"What is it that you want from me Demetries?"

"I need an army to attack the castle."

"Demons?"

"Whatever you can provide on such short notice."

"I can get you what you want but you know the price will be very high," said Nestor.

"Have you raised your rates?" asked Demetries with a grin.

"No. If I bring you humans, they have no conception of what the Sanuri can do to them; they will accept a fair price. But demons on the other hand are another matter; they will know they risk eternal punishment."

"I have access to King Roch's fortunes. Bring me who you can and I will pay them handsomely."

"Oh Annabelle I am so nervous," said Vitomas as she hurried around the west wing of the castle. Simon and Raul decided to hold the small intimate weddings in the castle gardens just outside of the west wing, where Raul and Vitomas would live after they were married. The west wing was the farthest away from the chambers where the wedding guests were staying.

"I know," said Annabelle as she styled her long curly black hair. "I thought this was such a wonderful idea that Simon had last night. But why did the men want to have the weddings so early in the morning?"

"Because it doesn't take them as long to get ready," said Vitomas anxiously. "They have no idea what we have to go through."

"I thought Renya would be mad when we told her but she is so understanding," Annabelle said.

They heard a knock at the door, then Matthew's voice, "I am just checking, do either of you need anything?"

"Matthew it is bad luck for you to see us before the wedding," Annabelle called out.

"It is only bad luck for your husbands to see you before the wedding, I am not that fortunate yet."

"He is right," said Vitomas as she opened the door and let Matthew into the master bedroom. "We could use some help, if you don't mind buttoning the backs of our dresses."

"Whatever I can do," Matthew said smiling. "We have the chairs set up and a small table for refreshments. I just checked with Raul and Simon and they are almost dressed." While Matthew was talking Vitomas left the room to put on her wedding dress. When Vitomas returned to the master bedroom both Annabelle and Matthew stared at her.

"You look so beautiful Vitomas, I hope my dress fits me as well," Annabelle said as she put the finishing touches on her hair.

"You took my breath away," said Matthew as he walked towards Vitomas. She turned around so Matthew could button her dress. "By The Great Ruler there must be over one hundred small buttons back here!" he exclaimed.

"There are one hundred and thirty six buttons and Annabelle's dress has more."

"My you boys look nice," said Marie as Simon and Raul walked into the kitchen.

"Marie what are you doing still working?" asked Raul as he saw she was frosting a cake. "Let someone else finish that, you have a wedding to go to."

"It will be just a moment boys."

Raul and Simon looked at each other then they both walked over to Marie and standing on either side of her, they picked her up and started to walk towards the kitchen door.

"You two are crazy," Marie said as she was laughing. "But I can't go out there looking like this; I have to put on that beautiful dress you bought me."

Raul and Simon set Marie back on the floor. Laughing, Marie hurried towards her chambers. With a grin Simon called after her, "Marie the girls said they wouldn't marry us unless you were there and if you make us miss our weddings, you will be stuck with us until we are old and gray."

"Oh you Simon, the things that come out of your mouth," Marie said as she hurried her portly frame down the hallway."

The Sanuri stood in the garden in front of a large fish pond that was surrounded with flowering bushes. There was a stone path that led to the pond, a path the wedding couples would walk down. Renya and Laurel walked into the garden hand in hand.

"You two are absolutely beautiful," said the Sanuri.

"Oh," said Renya between sniffles. "Can you believe it; we both have already started crying?"

"Well, you cannot tell," said the Sanuri as he helped them into their chairs.

"The girls thought we would be mad," Renya said to the Sanuri. "But actually Laurel and I both think this is rather romantic."

"My Lady, where would you like us to stand?" asked one of Marie's younger sisters. Marie arranged for two of her sisters to play the flute and violin for the ceremonies." Renya got up and walked the girls around the garden until she found a spot she thought was suitable.

"That music is quite lovely," said Laurel as Renya returned to her seat.

Raul and Simon walked from the castle towards the Sanuri. They stopped to kiss Renya and Laurel before they took their places for the ceremonies. Both men were wearing the formal dress uniforms of the Wetprian Army.

The uniforms were black with scarlet stripes down the sides of the legs and scarlet sashes that were worn across the chests. The top front sections of both military jackets were adorned with even rows of medals.

Matthew walked down the stone path and stopped to kiss Renya and Laurel on their cheeks. "Matthew I haven't seen you in that uniform before, you look so handsome," Renya said as she squeezed his hand.

"Why thank you My Lady," Matthew said with a smile then walked up to Raul and Simon.

"Did you remember the rings?" Simon asked.

"Oh yes," replied Matthew. "And the two of you owe me a bottle of whiskey. Between your two brides I just buttoned two hundred and eighty-four small buttons." Both Raul and Simon laughed.

"I think we owe you more than one bottle," Raul said.

"Wait until you see them," Matthew said. "You both are lucky men."

In less than a minute the music changed. Raul, Simon and Matthew all looked towards the castle. The stone path was too narrow for both brides to be escorted side by side; so Sudfad walked with Vitomas down the path first. Alexander escorted Annabelle a short distance behind. Matthew looked over at Raul and Simon and smiled when he saw the looks of adoration and love on their faces as they watched their brides walking towards them.

The Sanuri too, smiled when he saw the two princess brides. But as he gazed upon them a fleeting vision came before him. The Sanuri looked up and saw a flock of ravens circling overhead. He quickly looked around but did not see any other threats. When the Sanuri looked up again he saw Nica leading a flock of Enrops towards the ravens. "Thank you," whispered the Sanuri.

The Sanuri waited until each bride had been handed over to her groom, before he began to speak. "At the request of the two beautiful couples standing before us, this ceremony will be short and simple," the Sanuri said.

538

"The Great Ruler has brought these two young couples together and only he knows the paths they will take. May the presence of The Great Ruler engulf this holy family. May they be blessed with love eternal and may their love spring forth great multitudes of children. Raul and Vitomas and Simon and Annabelle do you promise to follow the path that The Great Ruler sets before you, especially at times when you cannot see where it goes?"

Both couples answered, "We do."

"Do you promise to love each other through all times and all adversities?"

Both couples answered "We do."

"And finally do you promise to honor the covenants of this family?"

"We do."

Suddenly thousands of white flower petals started to rain down on the wedding ceremony.

"Why, where are these coming from?" asked Renya as she looked into the sky. The petals fell softly on the two couples as they kissed for the first time as man and wife. The petals covered the ground like snowflakes, giving off a heavenly aroma.

The Sanuri looked up and saw that the ravens were gone. He searched the landscape with his eyes for signs of the dark lord who had sent the ravens to destroy the wedding ceremonies. Soon loud screams were heard coming from behind a large tree near to where the newlyweds were standing.

Loud, painful screams filled the air. All the men started to run towards the tree but the Sanuri stopped them. Within moments they saw Juleta leave her hiding place and run towards the castle screaming as large boils formed everywhere one of the floating flower petals touched her skin.

"Where have you been?" snapped Demetries irritably.

"My work does take time Brother," replied Nestor. "I am a broker with a reputation to live up to. You want a product and I provide you with the best available, that is why my services are so expensive."

"Ok, ok," snapped Demetries. "I didn't mean to offend you; it is just that time is short."

"I understand," said Nestor smiling. "Now aren't you going to ask me what I found for you?"

Demetries stopped pacing and stared at Nestor. "Is it good?"

"Oh yes you will be very pleased but it will cost you."

"I got you five hundred Timbar. That is if you can afford to pay for them."

"Timbar?" Demetries was not familiar with the name.

"You may be more familiar with their common name, Ghost Dragons."

"Ghost Dragons, I thought they were a myth," said Demetries.

"No, they are a weapon used by the Old Ones," replied Nestor. "They are black and fly. If you have them attack at night, their prey cannot see them until the Ghost Dragons are on top of them; thus the name. They are about half the size of a human man but insatiable in their lust for blood. They don't use weapons because they tear their prey apart with their claws and teeth."

"Can they be killed by humans?"

"Yes, but that rarely happens because the Ghost Dragons are so fast and powerful."

"How much for their services?"

"They demand three chests of gold, half now and half when the attack is over," said Nestor. "And I want a chest of jewels."

"I can get these things but not before the wedding," spat Demetries.

"That is the deal, take it or leave it."

After the ceremony, the royal couples gave a toast then hugged and kissed the family in attendance; then they quickly returned to the west wing. They did not want any of the guests to know about the wedding in the garden. Simon, Annabelle, Raul, Vitomas and Matthew all walked hand in hand back to the castle.

"Thank you for giving us the wedding we really wanted," said Annabelle as she hugged Simon's arm.

"As it turns out it is the wedding Simon and I wanted also," said Raul and kissed Vitomas' hand. "First we have a toast in the parlor, then we have some surprises." After Simon had poured everyone a glass of fine wine Raul held his glass up first and said, "To family, may our bonds never be broken." Everyone repeated the toast and drank from their glasses.

"What do you suppose happened to Juleta out there?" asked Annabelle.

"I don't know," said Simon. "But I suspect that may have been our wedding gift from the Sanuri."

"Well, I should leave you newlyweds alone," said Matthew as he put his glass on top of the small table.

"Oh no you don't," said Vitomas with a smile and quickly grabbed one of Matthew's arms. Within moments Annabelle grasped his other arm.

"What is going on?" asked Matthew with a grin.

"Follow us," said Raul as he and Simon started to walk through the west wing. They walked down several long hallways before Raul and Simon stopped in front of a large wooden door. "Since we are all moving out of the central wing we didn't want you to feel left behind," said Raul as he opened the door. Annabelle and Vitomas escorted Matthew into the chambers.

"This is for you to live in as long as you want," said Simon with a proud smile.

"Raul and Simon did this all themselves," said Vitomas. "They had these chambers designed for you. Chambers befitting a king." Matthew's eyes grew wide and he was silent as they led him through the rooms.

"And you have your own study," said Raul as he opened a door.

Simon walked inside of the study and opened a second door revealing a small room filled with weapons. "Complete with a weapons room," Simon said.

"I don't know what to say," Matthew stumbled over his words. "I cannot believe this. You even have books on the shelves."

"We tried to put you as far from the nursery area as possible," Vitomas said as she squeezed Matthew's hand.

"And there is a private entrance for when you entertain all of your lady friends," Annabelle said with a grin.

"I do believe I am with my two favorite lady friends," Matthew said and kissed each of their hands. They finished the tour by ending up in the master bedroom, which had doors that led to a private garden.

"Now this is our surprise," said Annabelle as she opened the doors to the garden. There was a small table decorated with a white cloth and white candles in the middle of courtyard. The table contained plates of berries, cheeses and breads. There were glasses, a bottle of fine whiskey and two bottles of wine on the table.

"Where did Vitomas go?" asked Raul as he suddenly realized she had disappeared.

"She will be here shortly," said Annabelle who could not stop smiling.

"I really don't know what to say," said Matthew with his voice shaking from emotion.

"Well, you don't' have to live here," said Raul with a grin. "You can stay in your other chambers if you like."

"Of course I want to live here," Matthew said. "But this isn't chambers this is a home." Matthew was visibly touched by the generous gift from his cousins.

Vitomas walked into the garden carrying a large basket. She took three boxes out of the basket, handing one to each man.

"What is this?" asked Raul.

"Well Honey, open it up and see," said Vitomas.

Each man opened their box and found a finely crafted dagger. The hilts of each dagger were decorated with a golden emblem of the Royal Family of Wetpr on one side and their name written in gold on the other side. The royal emblem also contained inset precious stones.

"Your mother told us where you get your weapons made. So we went there and Sorenson designed these for you. He promised us they would be something you could use and not just a decoration," Annabelle said.

"Honey they are beautiful," said Simon as he felt the weight and balance of his weapon.

"We had one made for every man in the family, including the Sanuri," said Vitomas. "We thought those gifts could be from all of us. So we can give them now or wait until after the big wedding, whatever you would like to do."

"Of course Petra is too little to have his now so we will give it to Renya," added Annabelle.

"And this is what we got for Renya and Laurel," said Vitomas as she pulled two boxes out of the basket and opened them. Both boxes contained sets of hair combs. Each comb was decorated with gold and jewels.

"You did well," said Raul as he hugged and kissed Vitomas. Simon hugged and kissed Annabelle and Matthew kissed both women on their cheeks.

"Well Brother," said Simon smiling. "Are we going to let the girls outdo us?"

543

"I think not," said Raul with a grin. "Follow us; we also hid something in Matthew's chambers." Raul walked into the master bedroom and opened the door to a small room. Sitting on the floor of this room were two different designs of traveling cases.

"I don't understand," said Annabelle.

"Honey, both of you open the smallest bags first," Simon said.

There were three medium sized bags and a small bag of each design setting in a group. The women each grabbed a small bag.

"This is so heavy," Annabelle said before she opened her bag.

"Raul, this is filled with gold coins," said Vitomas in amazement.

"Yes it is," Raul said smiling and gave her a hug.

"Since the two of you have never really been any place," Simon said. "The four of us are going to do a little traveling after the big weddings. Raul is going to take us to see some of the sights he discovered during his travels."

Both women squealed with delight and hugged their husbands. "Before we leave, take some of that money and buy good boots and some clothing appropriate for the outdoors. There are some waterfalls I want to show you that you will never believe," Raul said.

"And Matthew has offered to act in our place and to help Father while we are gone," Simon said.

"There you are," said Padre Bartholomew with relief when he found Padre Thomas mediating in the eastern gardens of the monastery.

"What is it my friend?" asked Padre Thomas as he looked up at Padre Bartholomew.

Padre Bartholomew knelt down near Padre Thomas and whispered, "The Enrops just brought a letter from the Sanuri. They said it is of great importance and should only be opened where no other eyes can see."

"Please help me up," said Padre Thomas as he tried to stand up. "Let's go to the Hall of Antiquities."

The two old priests moved quickly through the halls of the great monastery until they arrived at the massive doors to the Hall of Antiquities. Padre Thomas pulled a large ring of keys from his pocket and unlocked the seven locks on each of the two doors. Once they entered the hall, both priests lit enough candles to cast light on the large table they took seats at.

Padre Bartholomew pulled a large envelope from an interior pocket of his robe. The back of the envelope contained the wax seal of the Royal Family of Wetpr. He took several sheets of folded paper from the envelope and handed them to Padre Thomas. These sheets contained drawings which Padre Thomas studied as Padre Bartholomew read the letter out loud.

My dear friends, I hope this letter finds you safe and well. Some unusual things have occurred at the castle at Wetpr and I ask for any help you can give. On the night of a grand ball at the castle a man acted suspiciously and later ran from the ball and tried to escape the soldiers. There is a drawing of this man included in this letter; he stated his name was High Priest Pravis from the monastery at Malga. While I am aware there is a priest of that name at your monastery I have never seen him.

Please send me word if that is his true identity. Pravis ran from the castle when Princess Vitomas recognized a ring that he was wearing as identical to a ring that King Roch wears. Princess Juleta, from the Kingdom of Lentz is also at the castle and is wearing an identical ring. Juleta is an evil person, who I suspect as being a dark lord since she uses ravens as messengers. Pictures of the rings are in this letter. Please let me know any information that you can find about them. And please use the utmost discretion in these matters.

Sanuri

"The Great Ruler be with us," said Padre Thomas as he spread the drawings out on the table before them.

"High Priests Meekos and Tenebrae also wear those same rings," gasped Padre Bartholomew. The two old priests looked at each other as they tried to comprehend the enormity of the secret that was slowly unfolding before them.

Chapter XXXV
Exposed

Raul, Simon and Matthew were seated in Sudfad's study with Sudfad and the Sanuri for their morning meeting.

"We decided not to use two small bocas but one larger one instead," explained Raul. "The girls will sit in between Simon and me. We will have weapons in the boca and Simon had shields shined and hung on the outside of the boca."

"We will have twelve soldiers riding in front of the boca and twelve behind it. Matthew will be riding behind, if anything happens to Raul or me he will be responsible for protecting the girls," Simon added. "Father that leaves you to command the troops at the castle until we return."

"The Enrops are going to assist us," said the Sanuri. "If it works as I hope, the Enrops will spot trouble along the route before you get there. Then I can warn you about what is ahead."

"Then will we send troops?" asked Raul.

"Actually, I was planning on having the Enrops attack any small groups or individuals."

"The Enrops attack?" questioned Sudfad.

"They are our allies in this unholy war," the Sanuri said. "And they are extremely powerful creatures, those becks and claws can do a great deal of damage."

All the men jumped to their feet when the door suddenly burst open. Renya stormed into the room and slammed the door shut behind her. "Sudfad I demand to know what is going on."

"Honey, take a seat and I will explain," said Sudfad soothingly.

"I will not," yelled Renya angrily. "I just overheard the girls talking about precautions the boys are taking because of threats against this family. Sudfad you and I have fought side by side, you have no right to keep these things from me."

Raul, Simon and Matthew all looked at Renya then at each other then back at Renya. They had never seen Renya this angry before and it was the first time they heard that Renya had fought side by side with Sudfad.

"Honey I did not tell you because I know how important these weddings are to you, and for once I wanted you to be able to enjoy your family like a normal woman."

"I stopped being a normal woman when I married you and vowed to uphold the covenants," said Renya as she walked towards Sudfad. "Now I demand that you tell me what is going on."

"Renya, I suggested to Sudfad that he not tell you about this," the Sanuri said. "Before I came here I had a series of visions in which I saw the newly married couples riding down the streets of Salar. In every vision there were threatening eyes appearing in the crowds and windows along the streets. I felt an overwhelming sense of danger for your children during each of these visions."

"Sanuri you have no right to keep these things from me either. Did you recognize the threats in those visions?"

"I did not."

"Mother," was the only word Raul got out before Renya interrupted him. Renya spun around and faced her three sons.

"Raul, this is between your father and me," Renya snapped.

"The boy was going to tell you about the precautions we have taken but my dear there is more," Sudfad said as he removed something from his desk drawer and walked towards Renya. "Some days ago Enrops were sent by The Lion to intercept a flock of ravens that were leaving Salar. The Enrops destroyed the ravens and brought us the message they were carrying." Sudfad handed the note to his wife.

"And do you know who this note was intended for?" asked Renya after she read it.

"No."

547

"Did Juleta send it? I know you suspect her of being a dark lord," Renya asked.

"It was intercepted before her arrival here," Sudfad explained.

"So we have another dark lord near our home," Renya's voice was filled with anger. "Did she have anything to do with this?"

"I don't know," Sudfad said.

"Why not?" demanded Renya.

"Because we didn't ask her," said the Sanuri with a grin.

"What?" shrieked Renya, as she charged past Sudfad and entered the weapons room. "It is bad enough that we have a dark lord under our roof but I will not have her threatening this family Sudfad." Renya walked out of the weapons room with a dagger in the sash of her dress and a sword in her hand. "I will get to the bottom of this," Renya said as she marched towards the door.

"Mother what are you doing?" Simon asked.

Renya swung around and faced her three sons again. "None of you will fight with a woman but I will not make that same claim." Then she turned and marched out of the study.

"Does she know how to use that sword?" Matthew asked.

"As well as I do," responded Sudfad as he hurried out of the study to catch up with Renya.

The Sanuri stood up. "Now you boys will finally get to see your mother for the warrior she really is. Well come on, what are you waiting for?"

Screams, screams of horror, screams of pain filled the caverns below the River Nebu near the castle of King Roch. The Taperian soldier who was hung by his arms from a stone wall; once again lost consciousness.

One of the Huta warriors, a monster of a man named Derlock, threw a bucket of cold water on the soldier; bringing him back to consciousness. Then the other two Hutas continued to slice pieces of the soldier's skin from his body. A fourth Huta ran into the underground chamber and handed Derlock a small piece of paper.

"It is from the Master, a raven brought it," said Toomback. "The ravens are waiting.

An evil grin slowly came across Derlock's face as he read the note. He turned to the two Hutas who were torturing the soldier, "Kill him, we have work to do."

Derlock walked over to the dying soldier and stuck a writing instrument into one of his wounds. With the blood of the soldier, Derlock wrote a few words on the note and handed it back to Toomback. "Give this to the ravens and tell them that we will not disappoint Demetries. Then wake the men, we're going to attack Roch's castle."

Renya burst into Juleta's chambers and marched into the bedroom where she found Juleta lying in bed, moaning because of the hundreds of painful boils that covered her body. Matthew was the last to enter Juleta's chambers and he locked the door behind him.

"I know what you are," said Renya sternly as she walked towards Juleta.

Juleta quickly sat up and a look came over her face that startled Raul, Simon and Matthew. "That is the true face of evil you are seeing," explained the Sanuri. Renya kept walking towards Juleta, unscathed by the fact that Juleta was now in a crouching position and hissing at her. Before Juleta could jump at Renya, Renya quickly thrust the tip of her sword against Juleta's throat. Smoke began to rise from the area where the sword touched Juleta's skin.

"These are not normal weapons by dear little demon," Renya spat. "These weapons have been blessed by The Great Ruler Himself. Now I am going to ask you some questions and you will give me the answers I seek or the pain I will inflict will send you back to the hell regions."

Juleta sat on the bed on her haunches like an animal. She hissed at Renya, then looked around the room at the others. Matthew stood in horror as he watched the scene. Matthew did not recognize his own sister, the monster before him had dissolved Juleta's image. Becoming impatient Renya stepped forward and placed the side of the sword against Juleta's right arm. Juleta screamed in pain as the sword burned through her skin. "Are you going to answer my questions?" Renya demanded.

"Yes," said Juleta in a voice that sounded more as a man's than her own.

"Were you sent here to harm this family?"

"No, I was not," replied Juleta.

Renya moved towards her again. And Juleta said, "Truthfully I was not. Father brought me here for the celebrations. I tried to attack the small wedding because I hate those girls. That was my idea and mine alone but he stopped me," Juleta said with contempt as she looked at the Sanuri.

"It was not I who stopped you, The Great Ruler was watching over this family."

"What is she talking about?" asked Raul.

"I will tell you later," replied the Sanuri.

"Then who is planning an attack during the wedding ceremonies if it is not you?" Renya demanded.

A smile came across Juleta's face. "You have many enemies and there are many eyes in the darkness that watch you."

"You are not telling us anything that we do not already know," replied Renya sternly. "Now I ask you again, who?" Renya touched Juleta again with the sword. And Juleta screamed. The Sanuri stepped towards Juleta and she covered her eyes from the light that surrounded him.

"Demon I order you to tell us," said the Sanuri in a commanding voice.

Juleta started to choke; she grabbed her throat trying to stop the words from coming forth. "The Insidiae have you marked for death."

"Who are the Insidiae?" Simon asked.

"They are a group of humans who have sold themselves to the demons. They call themselves the Insidiae, the conspirators. They conspire against all that is good, even The Great Ruler Himself," said the Sanuri.

"Why?" demanded Renya.

"Because there are many who believe you stand in their way and there are others who believe your family is the one told of in The Prophesy of The Seven Sons."

"Tell us of the plans to attack."

Once again Juleta started to choke before she spoke, "I truly know nothing of the plans to attack. I don't even know if the Insidiae are involved. But believe me when I say, if I would have known about the plans I would have joined them."

"There is more or you would not have choked on your words," said the Sanuri. "Tell us what you are not saying."

"I truly don't know about any plans to attack your family during the wedding ceremonies."

"Are you a member of the Insidiae?" Sudfad asked sternly.

"Yes."

"Tell us who the others are?" Renya said.

"I cannot," said Juleta as she grabbed her throat. "We are a secret society. That is the beauty of it; we conceal our identities even from each other."

"Then how do you recognize each other?" demanded Sudfad.

"The rings," stated the Sanuri.

"Good guess," said Juleta with a mocking laugh. "But not all the Insidiae wear the same rings."

"Then I order you to tell us the meaning of those rings," the Sanuri shouted.

Juleta writhed around on top of the bed, grasping her throat before she said, "These rings are worn by those of us who are loyal to Omnibus."

"Who is Omnibus?" asked Matthew.

"An ancient demon that was imprisoned in The Great Abyss centuries ago," the Sanuri replied to Matthew then turned back to Juleta. "Tell us all you know of the plans to attack this family."

Juleta hissed at the Sanuri, "I know nothing; I have already told you that."

The Sanuri stared at Juleta, then stepped closer to her and stared into her eyes. "It is the way we are wording the questions," the Sanuri said to the group then he said to Juleta. "Tell us what you know about plans to attack Mathas and his family."

Matthew stood in horror, not wanting to hear his sister's words. The face of Juleta changed again and then a different voice spoke. "You always were a worthy opponent," said the voice sarcastically. "Juleta called to us to help her gain the throne of Lentz and we answered; but of course you know we always do."

"Who am I speaking with?" demanded the Sanuri.

"What, you do not recognize my voice; I must say I am hurt."

"Stolas," spat the Sanuri.

"Release us!" demanded Stolas.

"When we have the answers that we seek," the Sanuri replied.

"Then I am forced to release the girl, there will be severe consequences for her because of the information she had given you," Stolas warned. Then Juleta turned and stared at Matthew but the voice that spoke was still that of Stolas. "Matthew, the Sanuri thinks that he saved you by bringing you into this family. But he actually signed for your death." Suddenly Juleta screamed and collapsed onto the bed. As she lay there unconscious they saw the boils disappearing from her skin.

"Who is Stolas?" Sudfad asked.

"He is a high prince of the Barkayas hell dimension," replied the Sanuri.

Renya turned and looked at Sudfad. "Well, we still don't have the answers we need. Do the girls know about this?"

"Only that there are threats," Raul said.

"Sanuri as soon as the wedding ceremonies are complete, you need to seat down with all of the children and explain the lives they have now assumed. And please do it before their travels," Renya said, then she turned to Sudfad. "And Sudfad I think it is about time you taught the boys how to deal with demons, it isn't as if there haven't been any sneaking around the castle."

Renya turned and looked at Raul, Simon and Matthew, who all stared at her with awe. "Well!" Renya said angrily as she expected the boys to complain about her behavior.

"Mother we have never seen this side of you, you were incredible," said Raul as he stepped forward and kissed his mother on the cheek. Simon walked forward, followed by Matthew and they all kissed Renya.

"Boys I am going to tell you some things you do not want to hear," Renya said. "When you brought the girls home, Sudfad and I watched them not only to make sure they would make proper queens but to determine if they had what it took to be married to the Keepers of the Scrolls. And we decided they do."

"But all three of you look at those girls like you look at me. You cannot see past our roles as wives and mothers. I too, swore an oath to The Great Ruler to uphold the ancient covenants, but I think it was my role in trying to protect the family that brought out the true warrior in me."

"I saw Vitomas and Annabelle when they challenged Juleta and Pravis. They are as protective of this family as I am. You must allow them to be themselves. Sudfad was gone a great deal and Raul there were times when I defended the castle and you." Raul looked at Sudfad, who nodded in agreement.

"Granted there are more of us now," continued Renya. "But mark my words those girls will be put into positions where they have to protect others. Simon are you still giving Annabelle lessons in how to use a sword?"

"Yes," said Simon, as Matthew turned quickly and stared at him.

"Good, I suggest you continue and teach her how to use other weapons also. And Raul, you are so afraid that something is going to hurt Vitomas again, she is a strong girl. Do not put her in a cage. Teach Vitomas what she needs to be your wife now."

One Huta warrior climbed on top of the wall surrounding Roch's castle and grabbed one of the Taperian soldiers who was standing guard. While the Huta fought with the soldier a second Huta warrior ran up behind the soldier and cut his throat. The Hutas let the soldier's body drop and sneaked up to another soldier who was standing guard a couple of hundred feet away.

When all of the soldiers along the top of the wall had been killed; Derlock led another group of thirty Hutas through a secret tunnel that went under the wall and into the lower regions of the castle.

The door leading into the tunnel was well hidden by vines. Derlock would never have known of its presence had Demetries not given him directions in his note. The hinges of the great door were long unaccustomed to moving and squeaked loudly as the Hutas pried the door open.

The two Hutas who were carrying lit torches led the way down the long and narrow corridor they found behind the door. Derlock was third in line. The corridor was filled with spider webs and hordes of rats ran before the feet of the Hutas; it had been a long time since a human had invaded their space.

Finally the long corridor split into three directions. Following Demetries orders they followed the hallway to the left. Several minutes passed before they took another left and then a right. The corridor ran the length of the castle; but about half way through the corridor they came upon a door with two sleeping Taperian soldiers sitting on either side of it. Neither of those soldiers ever awoke again.

Derlock and his men entered the guarded room. Their torches illuminated the years of plunder that Roch had been hording. Chests upon chests of gold, silver and precious jewels were piled upon each other. The room was filled with treasures of all kinds. Narrow pathways wound around the enormous piles of riches. Derlock directed his men to take the chests of treasures that Demetries had ordered.

As they were leaving the room, Derlock spied a ring with an unusual inscription. The ring held a huge emerald stone set in gold. Derlock took the ring for his own; an act he would later regret.

Pravis paced back and forth in his small dimly lit cell. It had been two days since the Princes took him to that cabin and had Annabelle draw his picture. Pravis was not sure what the Sanuri was up to, but he was sure the Sanuri was behind that. Pravis had a tiny window in his cell that had two iron beams running through it to prevent escape. Day after day Pravis called to ravens but none came.

"I have to warn Meekos," Pravis kept saying over and over to himself.

Pravis paced the stone floor, wringing his hands and trying to figure out a way to inform Meekos that the plans may have been compromised. Pravis stopped abruptly. "I could die down here and no one would ever know," he thought. The sweat started to run down Pravis' body as his own fears took control.

A clinking sound suddenly disturbed the silence. A soldier walked up to the door to Pravis' cell and slid a plate of food under it. "That's it," Pravis thought. "I will have to escape." Pravis ran to the door and yelled out, "Sir, what day is this?" The soldier did not answer. "Tell me, is it the day of the royal weddings?"

"The royal weddings," a prisoner yelled from another cell as he taunted Pravis. "What now, are you expecting an invitation, are ya?" Other prisoners laughed at this comment. "Mister la de da over there wants out so he can attend the royal wedding boys, now ain't that sweet," continued the prisoner.

"Shut up, just shut up," screamed Pravis.

"Mathas we are sorry to have to tell you of these things," Renya said softly. "But we were all there, we all witnessed it."

"I do not doubt you," said Mathas as he put his head into his hands to compose himself before he spoke again. "I have always known there was something terribly wrong with that girl, in a strange way this does not surprise me and yet it is so hard to think that I have lost my child to darkness."

"Father from what I saw I think you lost her a long time ago," Matthew said as he put his arm around his father's shoulders.

"Sanuri, you say the demons have left her?" asked Mathas.

"Yes, old friend but that was only so I could not force them to give us information. They will return because Juleta will call to them; that is how they came to her to begin with."

Tears ran down Mathas' cheeks as he sat in Sudfad's study. Mathas sat in silence for several moments before he spoke. "If she is without demons now, perhaps this is the time to act," Mathas said. "Sanuri I cannot kill my own daughter."

"No one is asking you to," the Sanuri said.

"Then I know what I must do," Mathas said. "Matthew pick six of the soldiers I brought with us. Give them each a small bag of gold coins. Tell them to saddle their mounts, they will be escorting Juleta from this kingdom then they are to return to us here."

Mathas looked at Raul and Simon. "After Matthew returns bring Juleta before me, in shackles if you have to and have someone pack her things. She will be leaving as soon as I am done talking to her." Both Raul and Simon left the room. "Renya and Sudfad, I am so sorry to bring a monster into your home. But I beg of you please help me explain all of this to Rosa."

"Of course we will," said Renya as she hugged her brother tightly.

556

Several minutes passed before Matthew returned to the study. "It is as you wish Father; the men are waiting outside. Raul said we could have a small boca for Juleta and her things. That too, is waiting in front of the castle."

Raul and Simon opened the door to the study and escorted Juleta into the room. She did not resist them. Juleta walked up to Mathas and stared at him challengingly. "Well Father, I guess you have heard," she said mockingly.

"I am no longer your father," Mathas said sternly. "From this day forward you are no longer part of our family. You have no claim to the inheritance or to the throne. You are banned from ever entering the Kingdom of Lentz. If you defy this order you will be punished by death. Do you understand me?"

Juleta looked shocked for a moment. "But where will I go?"

"You choose to consort with demons, perhaps you should live among them," replied Mathas.

"You will not stay here either" Sudfad said sternly. "You are no longer a member of this family; you gave up your claims and rights among us when you planned to overthrow your father. You are banned from the Kingdom of Wetpr."

"Will you punish me with death also?" Juleta asked mockingly.

"As much as it breaks my heart to say so, yes," replied Sudfad.

"Your belongings are being put into a boca as we speak. There are six soldiers ready to escort you from this kingdom. Do not return," Mathas said. Then as an afterthought Mathas turned to Matthew, "Matthew throw her a bag of gold coins." Matthew took a small bag from his pocket and walked up to Juleta and put it into her hand.

"This is as much of an inheritance as you will ever get from me," Mathas said with disgust. "Take her from my sight." With those words Raul and Simon started to escort Juleta from Sudfad's study but she turned and ran back towards her father. Juleta only made it a few steps before Simon and Raul had tight grasps on her arms and were dragging her from the room.

"I curse you, I curse you all," screamed Juleta as she was dragged to the boca.

"I feel sorry for those soldiers," said Raul as he and Simon returned to the study.

"I noticed that Enrops were following them," Simon said.

"Yes to make sure they leave the kingdom," Sudfad said.

"Matthew, you should know that when the demon Stolas was talking to you before, he was trying to create chaos," explained the Sanuri. "Demons feed off from the fear of humans."

"Are you telling the truth?" Matthew asked.

"Yes, one of the best ways a human can conquer a demon is not to feed it. If you can face a demon without fear, that demon has no chance of survival."

"It certainly took you long enough," Demetries yelled with anger when Derlock and the band of Hutas rode into his camp. The Hutas dismounted from their horses and bowed before Demetries. "We are sorry if we offended you Master," said Derlock. "We came as quickly as we could."

"Did you bring the treasure?"

"Yes, we found it exactly where you said it would be." Derlock turned and motioned for several of the warriors to bring over the chests. Once the chests were placed on the ground, Derlock opened each one to show Demetries what they contained.

"You have done well," said Demetries.

"Thank you Master."

"After you and your men take care of your horses, gather around the fire and I will tell you of my plans. For tomorrow we will attack the castle of the Royal Family of Wetpr."

"What is going on here?" screamed Pravis with frustration. Every attempt that Pravis made to call forth a demon or a raven had failed. "My magics are useless in here," Pravis thought to himself. "What kind of curse has the Sanuri placed upon me?" Then Pravis thought of his ring. He took off his blood ring and set it in the middle of the floor of his small cell.

Pravis started to chant in the ancient language of the Old Ones. He took a small piece of stone from the floor and cut himself until he could produce a few drops of blood to cover the ring. Pravis chanted for over an hour but this too, failed. Frustrated and angry Pravis put his ring back on his finger and stood up. He started his routine of pacing back and forth when he suddenly became extremely fatigued. Overwhelmed with tiredness, Pravis lay down on his cot.

"There is a special place in hell for men who claim to be holy yet defy The Great Ruler and call to demons," said a loud and commanding voice.

Pravis quickly sat up and looked around his cell. "Who is there?" he called. There was no answer. "I must have been dreaming," thought Pravis as he shook his head and lay back down.

"You have defied The Great Ruler and the holy oath that you swore to become a priest; there will be no mercy for you unless you change your ways."

Again Pravis sat up in bed but this time his heart was seized with fear when he opened his eyes. "Who are you?" asked Pravis with his voice shaking.

"You claim to be a holy man and yet you do not recognize an emissary of The Great Ruler," said the large male lion that was standing in the center of the cell.

"I have heard of you," Pravis said in a whisper.

"And I too have heard of you," replied The Lion. "I have been watching you for some time and I do not like what I see." The Lion walked closer to Pravis. "It is beyond my understanding how any creature can turn from The Great Ruler and worship demons. But that was your choice."

559

"The fact that you commit these atrocities under the cloak of holiness is a sin of incredible proportion. The Great Ruler weeps for the man you have become. I am not The Great Ruler. I will give you this message but once. Ask The Great Ruler to forgive you and change your ways. Stop the evil you are plotting, you will never succeed with your plans."

Pravis sat on his bed shaking with fear. The Lion emitted a presence of such great power that Pravis felt as if he was being pressed against the stone wall of his cell. Pravis did not utter a sound while The Lion was speaking. Then suddenly The Lion was gone. Pravis was afraid to move and sat in the same position until he eventually fell asleep.

The next morning Pravis was awakened by the sounds of trumpets. He jumped out of bed. "The weddings," Pravis said out loud.

Chapter XXXVI
The Time of Kings

The Sanuri stood under an archway adorned with white roses, in the presence of thousands of people attending the royal weddings. Two steps lower than the Sanuri stood Raul to the right and Simon to the left; both men wearing the dress uniform of the Wetprian Military. Hundreds of seats of various types had been placed on the castle lawn for spectators as well as the hundreds of guests. Renya and Laurel sat in the front seats with Petra who was also dressed in a miniature version of the black and scarlet military uniform.

A long red carpet ran down the middle of the seating area leading to the altar. Thousands of excited voices outside of the castle grounds formed a low buzzing sound that competed with the sound of the trumpets. Soldiers in perfect uniforms either stood at attention on the grounds or sat on horseback, many of them carried flags.

Finally the trumpets stopped, the signal that the weddings were about to begin; and the City of Salar fell silent. Simultaneously Alexander escorted Annabelle down the long red carpet as King Sudfad escorted Vitomas; on cue musicians started playing harps and violins.

The brides carried identical bouquets of white and red roses. As they walked closer to the waiting grooms King Sudfad smiled when he saw the looks on the faces of his sons. Matthew was not up at the altar for this ceremony instead he stood in the rear, watching for any sign of attack.

Renya and Laurel started to cry when they saw the young brides. The guests sitting next to the aisle were throwing roses down on the carpet ahead of the brides. Proudly King Sudfad and Alexander officially handed the brides to their waiting grooms.

Both couples stood before the Sanuri as he sang in the ancient language. When the Sanuri finished singing he turned and lit three large white candles. He held up one of the candles and chanted the praises of The Great Ruler for uniting the two couples. After putting the candle back into its holder on the altar, the Sanuri turned to Raul and Vitomas.

"Raul and Vitomas do you promise to honor all your days this gift of marriage that The Great Ruler has given you?"

Holding hands and staring into each other's eyes Raul and Vitomas each answered, "I do."

Then the Sanuri turned to Simon and Annabelle and asked," Simon and Annabelle do you promise to honor all your days this gift of marriage that The Great Ruler has given you?"

Simon squeezed Annabelle's hands and tears of joy ran down her cheeks as they both answered, "I do."

"You may all kneel," said the Sanuri to the two couples. "Love is the greatest of all the gifts The Great Ruler has given us. There is nothing made by man that can compare, nor will there ever be. These two young couples have been blessed with this gift. A gift that will carry them forward into the challenges of raising families. A gift that will carry them forward into the challenges and responsibilities of uniting and leading a great kingdom. A gift they have sworn to carry forward as they honor the covenants made with The Great Ruler."

"Raul and Vitomas do you promise to follow where The Great Ruler leads, no matter how dark the way?"

"We do."

"Simon and Annabelle do you promise to follow where The Great Ruler leads, no matter how dark the way?"

"We do."

"Then as you have surrendered your lives to The Great Ruler so shall He bless you and your family all your days," said the Sanuri with arms uplifted. The two couples stood up and kissed and hundreds of white doves were released into the air. Cheers rang throughout the city. The couples walked down the red carpet to their waiting boca that was drawn by six white horses. Each horse had a wreath of red and white roses around its neck.

When they reached the boca Simon and Raul lifted their brides up into the seats, then took their places so that both brides were sitting in between the two grooms. Twelve soldiers riding twelve black stallions rode in front of the royal boca. While twelve soldiers riding twelve black stallions rode closely behind the boca.

Once the boca started moving rows of additional soldiers on horseback fell in behind it. Two soldiers sat in the front seat of the boca, one of whom was driving the team of horses. As they rode through the crowded streets people cheered and threw flowers at the young couples.

Matthew rode on horseback at the rear of the boca. He searched the faces in the crowd uneasily. The hair on the back of Matthew's neck was standing up and he had an overpowering feeling that something was wrong, terribly wrong.

The Sanuri walked up to Sudfad as the couples were getting into the boca. "The men are all in place," said Sudfad without looking at the Sanuri. "How is it again that you are going to watch over the route and the castle?"

"The Enrops will be my eyes," replied the Sanuri. "I will see what they see."

"I don't understand that at all," said Sudfad with a shake of his head. "But knowing you it will work."

"Take the family members into the castle," the Sanuri said.

"Renya is already escorting them to the Great Hall. We have the tables of refreshments set up and musicians," said Sudfad. "Hopefully they will not realize what is going on."

"Mathas and his men?"

"They are stationed at the rear of the castle."

"Sudfad, I had told you that in my visions I saw terrorists inside of your castle. Just because Juleta is gone; does not mean there aren't others."

563

The royal couples waved and smiled to the adoring crowds but Raul and Simon were ever vigilant. Their eyes constantly moving, Raul and Simon searched the roof tops and faces in the crowds for the terrorists.

The crowds were so large that there was no room to stand in the streets; people were hanging out of windows and doorways to get a glimpse of the royal couples. Raul and Simon each looked back at Matthew who signaled to them that something was not right. They too felt the eerie sensation of impending doom.

Then as one, Matthew, Raul and Simon heard the Sanuri's voice although he was not with them, "Tell the driver to turn left." Raul and Simon looked at each other in surprise then they turned and looked at Matthew; he nodded that he too had heard the voice. Vitomas and Annabelle were focused on the crowds and appeared not to have heard it.

Simon quickly leaned forward and told the driver to turn left. As the boca turned the corner the three Princes turned and looked to their rear; they saw the sky darken with Enrops descending into the crowd. By turning the corner, the Princes' changed the route they would take through Salar.

"Tell the driver to slow down," said the Sanuri's voice. Simon was the closest to the driver and leaned forward with the message. "Listen to me very carefully there are two who are with you who are not your soldiers, they are the two in the front seat of the boca. We have found the two soldiers they killed. In a few moments you will be in front of several large tables of refreshments; have the driver stop and all of you get out of the boca and raise a toast to the crowd, I will do the rest. Matthew you stay with the wedding party."

When Simon told the driver to stop he started to protest but followed the Prince's orders. Raul and Simon quickly took their brides off the boca and literally carried them to the tables. Simon poured glasses of wine as Raul made a toast to the cheering crowds. Suddenly a loud clap of thunder roared through the clear blue skies startling the horses. Several of the black stallions moved out of formation as their riders tried to calm them. The six white horses pulling the boca started to run wildly, without the stallions to block them, the team of horses ran down the street uncontrollably.

The crowd quickly moved out of the way of the runaway team of horses. While a team of horses running wildly through the streets would normally gain attention; the crowd was focused on the royal couples.

The people of Salar felt honored that the royal couples were standing among them and toasting them. After the toasts the newlyweds talked and laughed with people in the crowd until a group of soldiers returned with the boca.

The boca and the horses appeared unaffected but the two men who had been posing as soldiers were missing. Raul motioned for one of the returning soldiers to speak with him away from the brides. "My Lord, we found the boca stopped and the two men lying on the ground dead," said the soldier. Then in a hushed voice he continued, "My Lord when we turned them over they were not our men."

"Thank you," said Raul and returned to Simon and Matthew with the news. Vitomas and Annabelle were receiving flowers and hugs from children and women in the crowd and did not notice that their husbands were distracted.

Suddenly Simon saw a flock of Enrops flying into an open window that was about one hundred yards down the roadway and across the street; the boca would have passed that window had the Sanuri not stopped them. They heard the Sanuri's voice again, "You are safe where you are, I will tell you when you can return to the boca."

After a few minutes the Sanuri's voice returned. "Get into the boca and continue your ride for five blocks then turn around and return to the castle." Simon and Raul followed the Sanuri's instructions; just as the boca was pulling up to the castle gates the Sanuri said, "Come directly into the castle take your wives to the Great Hall where Renya and Laurel will distract them; then go to your father's study. Matthew position your men around the interior of the wall surrounding the castle then join them in Sudfad's study."

When the boca entered the royal courtyard, both Simon and Raul noticed there were no guests outside and some of the chairs were overturned. They quickly walked into the Great Hall which was filled with guests and music. Renya and Laurel were waiting for them at the entrance.

Laurel grabbed both of the young brides and said, "You must see the cakes that were prepared."

Renya looked at her sons and said, "Go to your father."

"Is he hurt?" asked Simon.

"No but you must go," replied Renya.

As Raul and Simon walked quickly to the study they noticed guards by the doors and archers by the windows. When they entered the study they saw Sudfad showing the Sanuri a map of the royal grounds.

"You are alright Father?" asked Raul.

"Yes but as soon as the boca left, the Enrops saw men with weapons mixed in with the guests who attended the ceremony."

"Was anyone hurt?" asked Simon.

"Only the intruders. I believe those were with the same group of men who were lying in wait for you in the city." replied the Sanuri. "These old bones are telling me this battle is not over." Raul and Simon walked into the weapons room; they each grabbed shields, swords, daggers and battle axes.

"Raul you are in charge of the north and west wings," ordered Sudfad. "Simon you have the south and east wings. When Matthew comes I will have him take a detail of men to the roof. I will be in charge of the central wing."

"Boys as I told your father, there may be terrorists inside of these walls; do not let your defenses down," warned the Sanuri.

The sun was just starting to set when the Sanuri walked onto the roof of the castle. He found Matthew standing on the highest peak of the roof while dozens of soldiers stood watch from behind the stone wall that surrounded the top of the castle.

"Come down my son and take a break," called the Sanuri. "Have some food and drink."

Matthew jumped down and landed on his feet next to the Sanuri. "Have Raul and Simon taken breaks?"

The Sanuri smiled. "They did, they each gave a toast and had a dance with their brides. Now it is your turn."

"And the guests, do they suspect anything?"

"They don't seem to, but remember they have Sudfad and Renya to keep them distracted."

"Sanuri it is just too quiet, I don't like it," said Matthew. "I feel like we are being watched."

"We are," replied the Sanuri. "I just don't know who is watching us yet. And Matthew these threats may be directed at you and your father as well as Sudfad's family."

Matthew was just starting to descend down the stone steps from the roof when he heard the sound of the Horn of Shana; it was the signal that the Army of Lentz used to announce danger. "Hutas, Hutas" was called out by the soldiers fighting alongside King Mathas. The Sanuri stopped Matthew from running down the stairs to help his father. "Matthew stay at your post, this will not be the only attack we have tonight," said the Sanuri as he ran down the steps towards the battle.

Sudfad told Renya about the attack as he left the Great Hall to join in the battle against the Hutas. Smiling and gracious as ever, Renya walked through the crowded hall until she found the brides. Renya took Vitomas and Annabelle by the hand and escorted them into the hallway.

"My darling daughters, I hate to do this to you on your wedding day but it is time you learned what it is to be queen. Follow me." Renya led both of the women into Sudfad's study and then into the weapons room.

"Hutas are attacking the castle as we speak and the men feel there will be other attacks during the night. You must not let the guests know what is happening." As Renya spoke she handed each of the women a dagger. "Hide these someplace in your dresses where you can grab them quickly."

"If you do not know how to use them, you will learn fast if the Hutas make it into the castle." Both women grabbed their daggers without hesitation or questions. "Annabelle, I am told you know how to use a sword," Renya said as she was grabbing weapons.

"Yes Renya."

"Vitomas what weapons can you use?"

"Renya I have seen most of these weapons used before," said Vitomas as she picked up a sword and a small battle axe. "And I have seen those demons attack before, they show no mercy."

"Girls I am proud of you; you truly are our daughters. Now remember you are protecting the family and all you hold precious in this world. At times like this your fear must not take over." Renya walked to a closet and pulled out several blankets.

"Why do you have bedding in here?" asked Annabelle.

"Because during times of great conflict, Sudfad and sometimes others would sleep in here," Renya said. "Now wrap these blankets around the weapons you have chosen and we will hide them near the servants entrance to the Great Hall."

"What about Raul and Simon?" Vitomas asked.

"Honey I think all of our husbands are fighting as we speak," Renya replied as she ushered the women into the hallway.

As soon as the Sanuri reached the rear of the castle, a flaming arrow flew past his right ear. The groans and screams of combat filled the air. The Sanuri spotted Mathas doing battle with two Huta warriors. As the Sanuri ran to help the King the Sanuri slid and almost fell in a large pool of blood that had formed in a lower area of the ground. Near the pool lay two of Mathas' soldiers with their throats cut.

Raul too was fighting his way towards Mathas. A powerful combatant, Raul was trained in welding weapons with both of his arms. A blow with Raul's battle axe crushed the skull of a Huta warrior while his sword pierced the heart of another.

The Hutas were outnumbered but they did not believe in retreat. Every Huta hoped to die in the glory of battle. The Sanuri reached Mathas first and thrust his sword through the Huta who was about to stab Mathas in the back. The momentary distraction caused by the Sanuri gave Mathas the edge that he needed to weld a deadly blow with his battle axe to the other Huta. A huge man and experienced warrior, Mathas fought with a battle axe in his left hand and a sword in his right.

"Raul!" yelled Mathas as he saw three Hutas attack his nephew. The Hutas had knocked Raul to the ground but instead of landing on his stomach, Raul curled his body and rolled forward, narrowly escaping a sword that was thrust at him. Raul jumped back up to his feet as one of the Hutas welded a battle axe at him. Raul did not have his shield so he quickly sucked his chest in and jumped backwards, avoiding the blow.

Mathas hit one of the Hutas in the chest with his battle axe. The powerful blow caused the Huta to fall to his knees. Mathas stabbed the Huta through the chest with his sword as the man was going down. Mathas quickly turned to see the Sanuri kick one of the Hutas in the side of the knee; the man screamed in pain and doubled over. The Sanuri thrust his sword into the back of the Huta's head.

"Something is not right here," the Sanuri screamed above the din. "This was not a battle it was a distraction." As the soldiers of Wetpr and Lentz killed the last of the Hutas, Mathas, Raul and the Sanuri ran back towards the castle. Before they reached the door, Mathas pushed both Raul and the Sanuri aside as the body of a soldier fell from the roof. For just a moment, they looked at the body of a young man who had his throat torn open, then they ran as fast as they could towards the stone steps that led to the roof.

Sudfad was running from the Great Hall to the rear of the castle when he heard screams coming from the roof, turning Sudfad ran up the many levels of stone steps with his sword in his hand. Sudfad's age was balanced by the adrenaline pumping through his body. Quickly he sped up the steps and onto the roof. Sudfad was not prepared for the scene before his eyes. Creatures the likes of which Sudfad had never seen before were flying in the air, circling the roof of the castle and attacking his men.

The full moon was rising, lighting the battlefields so the thick black outlines of the Ghost Dragons could be seen. Sudfad heard a scream coming from his right. He turned and saw one of the black creatures grab a soldier and start to fly away with him. Out of nowhere Matthew appeared and jumped up as the Ghost Dragon was starting to fly. Matthew cut the tail off the Ghost Dragon with one powerful slice of his sword. The dragon screamed in pain and began to thrash around wildly, dropping the soldier to the roof top.

Matthew ran up to the creature to pull the soldier to safety as Sudfad was running towards them. Sudfad distracted the dragon as Matthew dragged the injured soldier a few feet away. Then Sudfad and Matthew both approached the injured dragon. The creature reared up as to strike and Sudfad thrust his sword deep inside the heart of the creature. Meanwhile Matthew jumped on the back of the dragon and drove his sword into its brain.

No sooner had Simon heard screams coming from the roof, then a Huta spear grazed his left leg. A war cry screamed by dozens of Huta warriors rang out in the night as they ran towards the castle. Simon watched the advancing Hutas until they came within several hundred feet of his men, then Simon ordered the archers to "Release!" Dozens of arrows soared through the crisp night air. Thuds could be heard as the arrows landed in their targets.

"Release!" yelled Simon again. The first row of archers got down on one knee as a second row stood behind them and released their arrows. "Release!" Simon yelled. The ranks of Hutas were falling before the barrage of arrows. "Release!" Simon ordered a fourth time. "Something is wrong here," Simon thought. "This is too easy." Then he saw the shadows of the Ghost Dragons.

"Ghost Dragons," uttered the Sanuri in disbelief when he, Mathas and Raul reached the roof. "Raul," screamed the Sanuri. "Order your men to retreat inside of the castle, these are demons."

570

The circling dragons screamed in a high pitch that momentarily disoriented the soldiers. Mathas, Raul and the Sanuri split up; each running to help the fighting soldiers off from the roof top. Suddenly Mathas was flung to the ground; he could feel a sharp pain in his sides as one of the Ghost Dragons tried to pick him up.

Raul jumped onto the back of the creature and climbed his way towards the head as the dragon tried to throw Raul off. Raul grabbed the hair on the top of the creature's head and pulled the head backwards exposing the neck. Then Raul cut the Ghost Dragon's throat. The Sanuri ordered two of the soldiers to carry Mathas into the castle.

"These demons can be killed," Raul yelled.

"Yes but look, there are hundreds of them," yelled the Sanuri. "Get all of your men inside of the castle."

The grounds before them were littered with the bodies of dead Huta warriors. But the horror had just begun. Suddenly dozens of winged creatures were landing on top of the Huta warriors. Creatures that Simon and his men had never seen before.

"Release!" yelled Simon, a second and a third time but the arrows did little to stop the advancing Ghost Dragons. As the creatures got closer, Simon gave the command and he and his troops charged the beasts from hell. Fighting from a ground position the dragons were not as powerful as they were in the air. The battle was fierce but the soldiers of Wetpr would not back down.

Simon heard a bloodcurdling scream and saw one of his men on the ground with a Ghost Dragon on top of him. The dragon was tearing the soldier's heart out. Simon ran up to the creature and with one powerful blow of his sword, Simon sliced the dragon's claw off. The dragon screamed and lunged at Simon. Simon thrust his sword through the creature's throat. No sooner had Simon dislodged his sword then another Ghost Dragon grabbed him from behind.

Simon felt searing pain as the dragon impaled his claws into Simon's back. Simon quickly dropped to the ground and threw his body to the left, freeing himself from the hold of the creature. Two soldiers ran towards Simon as he faced the beast. The dragon lunged at Simon, who stabbed it in the chest with his sword. The Ghost Dragon reeled backwards as a soldier jumped on its back and thrust his sword into the dragon's brain.

Marie screamed when she turned and saw a Huta warrior coming towards her. Vitomas ran into the kitchen and saw the warrior just feet away from Marie. The warrior looked at Vitomas when she entered the room but not seeing Vitomas as a threat the Huta returned his focus to Marie; advancing towards her with a large knife in his hand.

"Annabelle!" screamed Vitomas as she ran to the hearth and grabbed a kettle of boiling water. Vitomas ran screaming towards the Huta warrior; as she was trying to draw his attention away from Marie. When the warrior looked at Vitomas she threw the boiling water into his face.

The warrior yelled as he was burned and momentarily blinded. Vitomas started hitting the warrior over the head with the heavy pot. He fell to his knees then to the ground. Vitomas turned to run from the kitchen when the warrior grabbed her ankle, tripping her. Vitomas hit the floor hard, falling on her face and stomach.

Instinctively Vitomas rolled onto her back as the Huta was climbing on top of her. Vitomas tried to grab for her dagger but the Huta grabbed both of her wrists and pinned them against the floor. Fear consumed Vitomas as she stared into the eyes of her attacker.

Suddenly blood started to drip out of his mouth and onto Vitomas' wedding dress. The Huta's grasp on her wrists weakened as he fell forward, landing on top of her. Vitomas screamed and pushed the dead body off from her. Renya reached down and helped Vitomas to stand up. "Are you alright?" Renya asked.

"Yes, well, I think so," said Vitomas as her knees grew weak, now that the impact of what had happened was catching up with her.

Renya pulled her sword out of the Huta's back and said, "Help me block this door."

Raul ran around the roof of the castle yelling for his men to retreat. The shrill screams of the Ghost Dragons and the flapping of their wings made a tremendous noise, preventing the soldiers from hearing Raul's commands. Raul grabbed one soldier and told him to go down the stairs and tell the soldiers in the back of the castle to retreat. Raul grabbed another soldier by the arm and as Raul was ordering the man to tell Simon and his men to retreat a dragon flew over Raul's head and knocked him forward.

Raul fell over the wall that surrounded the roof. The soldier jumped forward and grabbed Raul's arm. The soldier screamed for help as the dragon circled over his head, threatening both him and Raul. Sudfad and the Sanuri were fighting side by side when they heard the screams, they both ran towards the soldier.

Raul grasped the soldiers arm with his right hand. The dragon had torn a hole in Raul's left shoulder and blood was running down his left arm and onto his hand, making it difficult for him to grasp the stone wall. Sudfad and the Sanuri reached the soldier almost simultaneously. When Sudfad saw that it was Raul hanging over the side of the castle he yelled, "Son, we are here. Hold still and we will pull you up." The three men pulled Raul to safety.

"Sudfad get your family and your men inside of the castle, now!" ordered the Sanuri.

"What about you?" Sudfad asked.

"I still have work to do."

No sooner had a soldier plunged his sword into the head of a Ghost Dragon, when another flew up and grabbed the soldier with its claws. Simon jumped on top of the dragon as it was starting to fly upwards with the soldier.

Simon hung onto the beast with his left hand and hacked at one of the dragon's wings with the sword in his right hand. After three strikes with the sword, the dragon was seriously injured. Simon started to plunge his sword into the body of the dragon, strike after strike took its toll and the beast dropped the soldier it had been carrying.

Simon jumped off from the dragon and ran towards the wounded soldier who was lying in a mangled heap on the ground. Simon rolled the soldier onto his back and cradled the man's head in his arm. Blood was gushing from several of the young soldier's wounds.

"I am sorry My Lord," said the young man as blood gurgled out of his mouth.

"You have nothing to be sorry for," whispered Simon. "You fought valiantly, you fought with honor."

The young soldier of Wetpr tried to raise his bloody hand. Simon grasped the hand and felt the life force leave the young man. So many battles and the deaths still tore at his heart. Simon looked up as another soldier ran towards him. "My Lord, the King has ordered us to retreat inside of the castle."

Annabelle ran into the kitchen with the weapons as Renya and Vitomas pushed a heavy table in front of the kitchen door that opened to the exterior of the castle. Both of the women turned and looked at Annabelle when she entered the room. "Look out!" screamed Annabelle as she ran towards the women.

Renya heard glass breaking and suddenly her head jerked backwards. A large Huta warrior had thrust his left arm through the window and grabbed Renya by the hair. He held a knife in his right hand. Annabelle dropped all of the weapons onto the floor except for a sword.

Annabelle wielded the sword with all of her might and sliced deeply into the forearm of the Huta; who screamed in pain and pulled his arm back. But incredibly, the Huta immediately thrust his right arm through the window and grabbed Renya again.

"Renya pull forward," yelled Vitomas as she picked up a small battle axe. "Annabelle help pull him in." Annabelle and Renya pulled the Huta warrior towards them. As soon as the Huta's head came through the window, Vitomas used both of her arms and the strength of her body to impale the axe into his head; killing the Huta instantly. When the man dropped forward his fist opened, dropping a large handful of Renya's hair onto the floor. Marie had run out of the kitchen after Renya killed the first Huta warrior, now she ran back in.

"On my," Marie gasped with a shudder as she was momentarily distracted by the sight of the dead Huta draped over the window sill. "My Ladies, the men are coming in and all the Princes are hurt." All four women ran out of the kitchen.

The Sanuri stood on top of the roof. All of the soldiers had taken shelter inside of the castle. He looked to his right and saw a flock of Enrops attacking a Ghost Dragon; the Sanuri called to the Enrops and told them to go inside also. The Sanuri held both of his arms upward and looked towards the heavens, "Oh Great Ruler, I beseech you, please protect this family and all who dwell here from these creatures of hell."

"Well, Sanuri it looks like you are all alone." The Sanuri recognized the voice as that of the demon Stolas. The Sanuri saw that he was now surrounded by Ghost Dragons who had landed on the roof of the castle. Stolas was speaking through the dragon that stood directly in front of the Sanuri. "Where are all those humans you are always protecting? Did they leave you?" Stolas asked mockingly.

"Stolas; have you not learned by now that I am never alone?" replied the Sanuri confidently. The dragon that was speaking took a step towards the Sanuri, then stopped as a sound filled the night. A sound so loud that it shook the earth, a sound so loud that it shook the castle; a single lion roared. Suddenly lightning bolts shot from the heavens and struck dozens of the Ghost Dragons. Instead of retreating the army of Ghost Dragons flew chaotically as they searched for the powerful Angel who had just declared war on them.

"And you accuse me of parlor tricks," Stolas said sarcastically. "Is this really all you have Sanuri?"

A wind of tremendous proportions came upon them blowing the Ghost Dragons out of the sky. Huge trees were uprooted by the twisting motion of the winds. Debris of all manner was sucked into the giant funnel clouds that were forming and tearing across the land. Demetries, Derlock and a handful of Huta warriors ran for their lives as they saw the Ghost Dragons being sucked into the funnel clouds.

Sudfad had ordered that all of the wounded soldiers should be taken to the Great Hall. Several soldiers were helping Raul, Simon and Matthew towards that area when the women ran up to them. Both Vitomas and Annabelle started to cry when they saw their blood soaked husbands.

"Are you alright?" yelled Raul fearfully when he saw Vitomas come towards him. Her wedding dress was soaked with blood. Vitomas had blood spattered on her face and she was still holding the bloody battle axe. Annabelle and Renya were behind Vitomas and they too were covered in blood.

"Annabelle," gasped Simon. "Mother."

"We are alright," Vitomas said as she kissed Raul, "It's not our blood." Vitomas quickly looked at Raul's wounds, then at Matthew's while Annabelle was examining Simon's wounds. "Please take them to the west wing," Vitomas said to the soldiers. "We will take care of them."

"Wait," said Simon who was still hugging Annabelle. "What happened to you?"

"We can tell you about it later," Annabelle said. "We need to take care of your wounds."

"I'll tell you," Marie said with great pride. "Vitomas saved me from a Huta that was coming at me with a knife. When he got her down on the floor, your mother ran a sword through the devil. Then another one of those demons grabbed your mother and the girls killed him. I have two dead bodies in my kitchen." The three Princes looked at each other in disbelief. When suddenly two soldiers walked up to the group carrying Mathas.

"Father," yelled Matthew.

"I'm alright son," Mathas said weakly.

"Well, you don't look alright," Renya said as she started to examine his wounds.

Sudfad came down the hallway helping a wounded soldier to walk. Sudfad stopped abruptly when he saw his entire family covered in blood.

"We are alright dear," said Renya. "It's the men who are hurt. We need to get them to the physicians."

"Here, you hold him steady," said Sudfad to an uninjured soldier, about the man Sudfad had been helping. Then Sudfad grabbed Renya's hand and they walked through the main doors of the Great Hall.

"Attention!" yelled Sudfad. "Stop the music!" People started to gasp when they turned and saw their King and Queen covered in blood. "You are safe. But the castle was attacked. I have many wounded soldiers who need help. Please everyone move the tables to the sides of the room so we can make space for the men who have been protecting you this night. I assume the physicians are still here?"

Philip the physician to the Royal Family and three physicians from Salar were in the Great Hall with their families. All of the physicians ran forward, yelling orders at their wives and children to help. Marie grabbed a couple of the extra staff members, who had been hired to help with the wedding. She gave them duties of retrieving blankets, bandages and hot water. "I'll need someone to move those dead demons out of my kitchen," Marie yelled. Sudfad motioned for a couple of soldiers to go to the kitchen.

"Bring the boys in here," Sudfad ordered the soldiers who were helping the wounded princes.

"No Father," said Raul. "Take care of the men first. The girls can take care of us."

"Unfortunately we are getting enough practice," said Annabelle as they walked towards the west wing.

"Where is the Sanuri?" asked Renya as she and Sudfad helped Mathas into the Great Hall.

"The last I saw him, he was on the roof," Sudfad said. "He told us all to leave."

"Were there Hutas on the roof?"

"No some type of demon dragons."

"What!" exclaimed Renya. "And you left him alone?"

"Thank you," Vitomas said to the soldiers as they helped the wounded princes into chairs around the kitchen table. "Before you go, would you be kind enough to move two beds from one of the guest rooms into that room over there?" Vitomas pointed to a large guest room off from the kitchen. "I want all three of them in one room so we can watch them."

Annabelle put a large kettle of water on the hearth, then ran to a cupboard and grabbed towels and cloths. Vitomas walked into the kitchen with a large basket containing bandages, scissors and three bottles of whiskey. Vitomas put the basket on the table and handed a bottle to each of the Princes. "You better drink this." Both Annabelle and Vitomas moved quickly, cutting off the men's jackets and pressing towels against the bleeding wounds.

"You're going to have to burn the wounds to stop the bleeding," Raul said to Vitomas. "Do you think you can do that?"

"I will have to," Vitomas said with tears in her eyes. "It was just so awful that time you did it to Simon."

"Honey we will help you through this," Raul said. "Get several knives and put them on the fire."

"Can we use these?" asked Annabelle as she pulled one of the daggers from her dress. "Your mother gave us them."

"You're going to need something wider," Simon said. "Maybe just heat up our swords." Annabelle put the swords on the fire and brought the hot water back to the table. The Princes drank their whiskey as Vitomas and Annabelle washed their wounds. "I think we are going to have to burn Matthew's first," said Vitomas as she examined the large wound in his side. I can't slow down the bleeding."

"Matthew are you alright?" asked Annabelle fearfully as she caught Matthew as he was falling off the chair.

"Annabelle hold him," yelled Vitomas as she ran to the hearth to grab a sword. "Oh Raul," Vitomas cried.

"Honey you fought with Hutas tonight, you can do this."

Tears ran down Vitomas' face as she placed the searing sword against Matthew's bleeding wound. Matthew screamed and lost consciousness. "Help us," Annabelle screamed loudly and the soldiers who were moving beds ran into the kitchen.

"Hold him so we can burn his wounds," Annabelle cried as she moved so the soldiers could take hold of Matthew. "I think you are going to have to help us put them all in bed too," Annabelle continued to say to the soldiers as Vitomas burned another of Matthew's wounds. The kitchen was filled with the stench of burning flesh as Annabelle and Vitomas cauterized the worst of the men's wounds.

All three of the Princes lost consciousness as their wounds were cauterized. The soldiers carried Raul, Simon and Matthew and put them into the beds in the large guest room. Annabelle turned to one of the soldiers, "Would you ask one of the physicians for some of their special thread and needles? We are going to have to stitch some of these wounds."

"Yes My Lady," said the soldier before he turned and left the bedroom.

"Do you know how to sew the stitches?" Vitomas asked.

"Yes, Gala showed me once."

Chapter XXXVII
Revelations

The Sanuri remained unscathed as the funnel clouds of wind carried the Ghost Dragons back to hell. "Thank you," he said to the heavens after the winds had calmed and the lightening stopped. "Bless these souls," prayed the Sanuri as he looked at the dead bodies scattered around the roof top. With a saddened heart, he walked to the stone steps that led downward into the castle.

But before the Sanuri started his descent, a vision flashed before his eyes. In the vision the Sanuri saw Demetries, Derlock and a small band of Hutas running away from the castle. Suddenly the Sanuri felt a presence of great power behind him. Smiling the Sanuri turned around.

"Thank you my friend," said the Sanuri. "Your help was most appreciated."

"You could have asked for help a little sooner," The Lion responded.

"Yes and I should have. But please explain to me how the Ghost Dragons came here. I thought their kind had been wiped out."

"Ancient dark magics created them," replied The Lion. "Magics only the oldest of demons would know. There was great darkness behind this attack tonight. The demons and dark lords are joining forces. They have heard that Sudfad adopted two more sons which makes them fear that this family will fulfill The Prophesy of The Seven Sons."

"Will it?"

"You have earned the right to know now," said The Lion. "Yes and you Sanuri are one of the sons."

"Are Raul, Simon, Matthew, Sudfad, Petra and me six of the seven?"

"Yes but all of the sons are not yet ready. Before they can fulfill their destinies each of them has to be attacked by a great darkness and they have to conquer it. And they will have to conquer it without your help, no matter how badly you want to intervene. By conquering their darkness they will expand the boundaries of their existence. You remember; you walked the trail of tears."

"And the seventh son?"

"He is battling with great darkness and has been for some time. You will know him when you see him for he will be wearing the scars from the demons. He will emerge from the fire a mighty warrior and his knowledge of the demons will help to bring them down."

The Lion started to walk away but stopped and turned back to the Sanuri. "You have not heard the last of Juleta. Her fury has no boundaries and she has been calling to demons since she left this castle. Juleta will bring great darkness to this world unless you stop her. Also, the Princes will now need to heal before they can take their wives traveling. This delay in their plans will ultimately save their lives. Please advise them that they should travel in the company of soldiers."

Raul was the first to regain consciousness. He smiled when he looked around the guest room which now contained three beds, all lined up side by side. Next to each bed was a small table. Each table had a pitcher of water, a bottle of whiskey and two glasses.

Two stuffed chairs had been placed against the wall, facing the beds. All of the other furniture had been moved out of the room. Raul looked over at Simon, who was lying in the bed to his left and groaning. Matthew was in the bed to the left of Simon, the bed closest to the door.

Suddenly voices could be heard coming from the direction of the parlor. As the voices grew louder, Raul recognized two of the voices as belonging to his mother and father. Renya, Sudfad, Rosa, Margarit and the Court Physician all walked into the guest room that housed the three wounded princes. Margarit ran to Matthew's bed and jumped on it before Rosa could stop her.

Matthew awoke as Margarit was stroking his hair with tears running down her face. Hearing the voices, both Annabelle and Vitomas ran to Renya and put their arms around her. The horror that they had shared only strengthened the bonds between the three women.

"Renya we had to burn their wounds," Vitomas said as she was still visibly upset from the ordeal.

"And I am sure you did just fine," Renya said warmly as she hugged both of her daughters. Simon awoke when the physician was examining his wounds. Raul could sit up without assistance but both Simon and Matthew needed help, which was given by everyone in the room.

"How is Father?" asked Matthew as he sat in bed with his arm around his little sister. Rosa sat down at the foot of his bed.

"The physicians said he will be alright," said Rosa. "They said he bled so much it appeared his wounds were worse than they were. But he will be confined to bed for at least a week, so we will be staying here longer than we originally planned." Rosa turned and gave Sudfad and Renya a warm smile. "Of course Renya and Sudfad are making us feel as if we belong here."

"Mother where were you and Margarit during the battle?" Matthew asked.

"Renya made me take Margarit upstairs. She had us hide in a room with Laurel and Petra," said Rosa. "We were all scared but just fine."

Raul said smiling. "Vitomas Honey, why don't you bring some wine in here, I think everyone could use a drink?" As Vitomas left for the kitchen, Sudfad walked up to one of the small tables and poured himself a glass of whiskey; he then filled the glasses of each of the Princes. Vitomas carried a tray containing glasses and a bottle of wine into the bedroom; when everyone had a full glass; Sudfad held up his glass and said, "To family, may our bonds never be broken."

"I am glad to see you girls changed out of those bloody dresses," Raul said. When he saw the looks of sadness on Annabelle's and Vitomas' faces Raul added. "I know you two talked about saving them for our daughters, so Simon and I will have two more made for you if you want."

"Really?" asked Annabelle with a big smile.

Vitomas kissed Raul on the forehead, "I think we would like that dear."

Philip the Court Physician examined Simon, Raul and finished by examining Matthew; then Philip turned and poured himself a glass of whiskey. "I must say you girls do fine work. I couldn't have done better myself. Here is something that will help with the pain," said Philip as he handed Annabelle a packet of powder. "Mix two spoonful's in a small glass of water. It is very potent so it will make them sleep. But don't give it to them if they have been drinking."

"I think I might prefer the whiskey," said Simon. Annabelle was sitting on the bed next to Simon and squeezed his hand.

"How come you only brought two chairs in here instead of three?" asked Raul.

"The chairs are for us," said Annabelle. "We are going to sleep in them, so we can keep an eye on all of you."

"There is room in the beds," Simon said. Annabelle gave him an incredulous look then looked at Vitomas who said. "As injured as the two of you are, we would only cause you more pain if we were moving next to you in bed. We will be just fine in these chairs."

"You're wives are right," said Philip.

As Philip started to leave the room Rosa said, "Wait we will walk with you, I should be getting Margarit to bed." Rosa turned and kissed Matthew on the cheek. Margarit had her arms around Matthew's neck and was kissing his face. "Honey you have to let Matthew get some sleep now so he will heal," Rosa said.

"I will be back in the morning," Margarit said as she reluctantly got off his bed. Matthew smiled as he watched his mother and sister walk out of the room. As soon as they left, the demeanor of the Princes turned to business.

"What happened to the dragons and Hutas?" Raul asked. "The last I saw of the Sanuri he was ordering all of us into the castle."

"He said he called for help and The Lion came," Sudfad answered. "The Lion caused a great storm to overtake the battlefield. Lightning bolts shot through the sky, striking many of the dragons. Then winds like we have never seen before came upon us. The winds were so strong they started to whirl as huge funnels and they sucked all of the dragons and Hutas into them, and then disappeared."

The three wounded princes all looked at Sudfad in disbelief. "I really wish I could have seen that," Simon said.

"And the men?" Raul asked.

"We lost twenty-three," Sudfad said sadly. "But many are wounded; I don't have a count yet."

"Speaking of your men," said Annabelle. "I don't know the names of the soldiers who helped us with Simon, Raul and Matthew but they were very kind and a great help to us. Could we get them sometime in appreciation?"

"Yes dear," said Simon as he kissed his wife's hand.

"Now that Margarit is gone, I want to hear about what happened to you and the girls, Mother," Raul said in a demanding voice.

"Raul don't talk to your mother in that tone of voice, she was wonderful. You would have been proud to see how calm and in charge she was of everything," Vitomas snapped.

Raul smiled, "Vitomas that is the first time you have yelled at me."

"I doubt if it will be the last," Simon said sarcastically.

584

Matthew started to laugh then winced in pain. "Oh don't make me laugh," he groaned.

"I am sorry; it is just seeing you and the girls; covered in blood was far worse than facing those devil creatures," Raul said.

"I understand," said Renya. "But I also told you not to underestimate your wives." Renya turned to Vitomas and Annabelle. "This family has more duties and responsibilities than you are aware of. The Sanuri and your husbands will be explaining them all to you very soon." Renya turned back to Raul, "Actually I think you should have Vitomas explain the first attack to you."

Vitomas was sitting on the edge of Raul's bed, holding his hand. "Your mother told us that the castle was being attacked and took us to Sudfad's weapons room. We all chose weapons and hid the daggers in our dresses and wrapped the larger weapons in blankets because we didn't want to let the guests know about the attack. Annabelle and I had just finished hiding the weapons near the servant's entrance to the Great Hall when I heard a scream and ran into the kitchen."

"Marie was backed up against the wall and a Huta was coming towards her with a knife," Vitomas continued. "I screamed for Annabelle because I didn't have any weapons other than the dagger. I grabbed a pot of boiling water and threw it in the Huta's face then I started hitting him over the head with the pot."

"The Huta fell to the ground and I turned to run but he grabbed my ankle. I tripped and fell on the floor. He got on top of me and pinned my arms so I couldn't grab the dagger, then he just sat on top of me looking at me for a moment. The next thing I know, blood is running out of his mouth and he fell on top of me. Renya had run her sword through him. Then Renya helped me up and said we should block the door."

All of the men were quiet as Vitomas talked. Raul could feel the blood drain from his face as he listened to how close his wife and mother came to being killed. "Vitomas, this is difficult for me to listen to," Raul said as he squeezed her hand. "I feel proud and terrified at the same time but I do have a question. With all of the soldiers in the castle why did you yell for Annabelle?"

"I wanted her to bring the weapons."

"Honey if something like this ever happens again, please call for the soldiers," Raul said.

"It would not have done any good if she had," Renya said. "They were all doing battle."

"Renya and Vitomas were pushing a large table in front of the kitchen outside door when I ran in with the weapons," Annabelle explained. "Both Renya and Vitomas looked at me when I ran into the room; it was then that I saw him."

"Another Huta broke the window with his arm and grabbed Renya by the hair. I ran up and dropped all of the weapons except for the sword. Simon I did just like you taught me, I brought it down with all my weight and cut his arm to the bone." Simon stroked Annabelle's hair as she spoke, he could feel the fear rising in his chest.

"He screamed," continued Annabelle. "We thought he would leave but in a second he thrust his other arm in the window and grabbed Renya again. Vitomas picked up the battle axe and told both of us to pull the Huta forward. When his head came towards her, Vitomas hit him with the axe and killed him." Everyone in the room sat in silence for a few moments.

"Sons, I know what you are feeling," Sudfad said as he held his wife's hand. "I would rather face a hundred enemies than to think of my wife facing one. I think we should all thank The Great Ruler that none of them were harmed."

When Simon finally spoke, his voice was soft. "You all seem to be handling this well right now and I think that is because there is still so much going on. But at some point the horror of what happened to you will catch up to you. Don't be surprised if you cry for a couple of days."

Simon looked at Raul then at Matthew before he continued. "All of the men in this room have killed enemies and we have watched our own men die. Taking someone's life should never be easy and don't ever wish that it becomes easy because only monsters like Roch can kill without feeling some type of sadness or remorse."

Chapter XXXVIII
Demon's Wake

"I don't understand how this could have happened," screamed Meekos. "Pravis I send you on a simple mission and you come back and tell me this story. Do you even know what happened to our men?"

"No, I looked for them when I got out of the dungeon and found no one. I thought perhaps they had returned here," explained Pravis.

"Well, they did not," screamed Meekos. "If you would have kept me informed of your whereabouts perhaps I could have helped you."

"Meekos I sent several messages to you; are you saying you did not receive them?"

"Messages?" Meekos said with a look of concern moving across his face. "Pravis I never received any of your messages. That is why I started out towards Wetpr myself. How we missed each other along the road I will never understand." The two men stared at each other in silence for a few moments.

"Pravis something is not right here. Now please tell me your story again and do not leave out any details."

Pravis stared at Meekos in silence. Soon sweat started to run down Pravis' face. "There is something I did not tell you Meekos. I had a visitor while I was in the dungeon. The Lion, he appeared in my cell."

"What lion?" asked Meekos with annoyance. "What are you talking about?"

"The Lion, the one we have heard of; the emissary of The Great Ruler," Pravis said. "He is real, he does exist."

"The Lion, are you sure you weren't dreaming?"

"No, I was not. He said there is a special place in hell for us and that we would never succeed with our plans."

Meekos stared at Pravis for a moment. "I think it is time we contacted the Old Ones."

Demetries was still assuming the identity of Jonas when he returned to the Kingdom of Stordt and walked into Roch's war room as Roch was eating breakfast.

"I was wondering when you were going to return, you have been gone for weeks," Roch said without looking up. When Jonas did not respond Roch looked at him and yelled, "What the hell happened to you, were you in battle?"

Jonas sat down at the table, his entire body was black and purple with bruises; his face and body were covered with open, running sores and boils. "I tried to bring you the Sanuri as you ordered My Lord," said Jonas through a mouth filled with sores and lesions

Roch sat back in his chair and stared at Jonas for several moments before speaking. I can understand the bruises but in all my days I have never seen anyone in your condition before. What happened to you?"

Jonas had expected this question. He was not yet ready to reveal his true identity to Roch. "The Sanuri put a curse upon me."

"You are sure it is a curse and not a disease that you can give to others? Because you look awful."

"It is a curse," snapped Jonas. "Forgive my shortness My Lord, but it is a very painful curse."

"Well, the Sanuri has been busy. He was here. The Sanuri came here one night," said Roch.

Jonas gave Roch a look that made the hair on the back of Roch's neck rise. "What do you mean the Sanuri was here?" Jonas growled.

"He appeared out of nowhere and said I had sent demons to him."

Jonas stared at Roch for a moment then smiled and walked out of the war room.

When Sudfad opened the door to his study he saw the Sanuri looking out of the window behind Sudfad's desk. "Sorry I am late," Sudfad apologized. "I stopped to see the boys first."

"I have only been here a few minutes," said the Sanuri. "How are they doing?"

A broad smile worked its way across Sudfad's face. "Actually I believe they are in better shape than they let on." Sudfad said with a laugh. "They have all of the women in the castle attending to them and Marie makes them special deserts every day. Vitomas and Annabelle are waiting on them constantly. I rather think they are enjoying it."

The Sanuri too smiled, "Let them have their little indulgences. Actually I was going to speak with them today. I want to ask the boys if they want to be present when I explain the roles of Keeper of the Scrolls to Annabelle and Vitomas."

"I bet they will," Sudfad replied. "You could always take the lessons to them. You would have a captive audience so to speak," Sudfad said with a laugh.

"That my friend is an excellent idea. But before I forget; I came here to give you some news," the Sanuri said. "As you know a week after the wedding, we released Pravis from the dungeons. Enrops have been watching him ever since. When Pravis was released he went to Salar and to the very buildings where we had found terrorists. Pravis stayed in Salar for several days. I am sure he was gathering information about what happened during the ceremonies."

"Then he started to ride southward. This morning an Enrop told me that Pravis rode straight to the monastery at Malga without making any other stops except to camp at night."

"So whoever sent him, knows his mission did not succeed," said Sudfad thoughtfully. "Which means we may need to prepare for another battle."

"Sudfad this all breaks my heart. It is inconceivable to me how anyone at all; much less priests who have entered into a covenant with The Great Ruler can allow themselves to be seduced by demons. What in their beings causes them to make such choices?"

"We know that Pravis is a member of the Insidiae and we suspect that Meekos is either a dark lord or also a member of the Insidiae or both. But what we don't know is if they are really priests or imposters who have infiltrated the church."

"The last two nights I have written down all that we know and all that we suspect about Pravis and Meekos. This morning I sent those documents to High Priest Raphael, a leader of the Patronus and asked him to start an investigation."

"I am somewhat familiar with the Patronus," stated Sudfad. "But perhaps you could explain their organization to me."

"Most people are not familiar with them at all," replied the Sanuri. "That word in the old language means 'protectors'. They are an old and rather secretive army of men who are the protectors of the Church. They work on behalf of The Great Ruler. They are pious and good men."

Sudfad watched the Sanuri for a few moments as the Sanuri again turned to look out of the window. "Sanuri this is probably not my business," Sudfad said sincerely. "But I don't always understand, well, why there are some shall we say situations that you can get involved with and others that you leave to men. I would have thought that you would be leading the investigation into Meekos and Pravis."

"My friend your question is infinitely more complex than you realize," the Sanuri said. "And I will admit sometimes I do not understand either. There are times that I would ask The Great Ruler to allow me to destroy all of the demons and to take all of the darkness from this world. But that is not my role here. I too am a man and I learn something every day that I am here."

"People are tested and need to grow to transcend their darkness. While I do not always understand these tests or the reasons that some people are in this world, I am told that everyone has a role to play and I must respect that. I cannot learn their lessons for them. Although I wanted to lead the investigation into those priests I was told to turn it over to High Priest Raphael. And I feel fine with that. Raphael is an exceptional man, a faithful servant and a fearless warrior. Not unlike you my friend," the Sanuri said.

Demetries walked into the dark dampness of a cave under the River Nebu. As soon as he entered the cavern he heard movement and quickly grabbed his sword; Demetries continued walking down a long corridor until he entered a large chamber that was lit by multiple fires.

As Demetries entered the chamber, one hundred Huta warriors stopped and stared at him. Demetries slowly pulled his dark hood back revealing his boil infested face. The Hutas instantly bowed before him.

"We have been waiting for you Master," Derlock said as he straightened himself up from his bow.

"So far it appears we will continue with our plans," Demetries said. "You will need to prepare the chambers for the sacrifices."

"Father are you sure you are fit to travel?" Matthew asked. Mathas and Rosa were seated in chairs next to Matthew's bed. Margarite sat on the bed with her arms around Matthew's neck.

"My wounds were not as severe as yours my son, I need to get back to my kingdom."

"I understand Father."

"We don't want to leave you behind but you are well taken care of here," Rosa said smiling as Annabelle brought a tray into the room and set it on the table next to Matthew's bed. She poured four glasses of milk from a pitcher, handing them each a glass. Then Annabelle passed around a large plate of freshly baked cookies. Annabelle stoked Matthew's hair and leaned down and kissed Margarite on top of her head.

Matthew squeezed Annabelle's hand, "Thank you. Where are Raul and Simon? I thought you and Vitomas were taking them out for a walk."

"They are sitting in the garden, enjoying the sunshine," Annabelle replied.

"My family is leaving and would like to say goodbye to them."

"Oh, I can bring them in."

"No, no dear, don't worry about it," said Mathas. "We will go out to the garden before we leave."

"Well, let me say goodbye," said Annabelle as she gave each one of them a hug and kiss before she left the room.

"I like Annabelle and Vitomas," Margarite said as she was shoving a cookie into her mouth.

"Apparently so does your brother," Rosa said smiling.

"Sudfad told us that you requested consideration for inheriting the girls if something happens to Raul and Simon," Mathas said. "I must say it took us by surprise."

"Sorry Father and Mother, I should have told you first," Matthew said. "But why does it surprise you so?"

"Son, you have never once talked about marriage and now you have requested to inherit two wives," said Mathas.

"What your father is trying to say," Rosa explained. "Is that although we never want to think of either Raul or Simon dying, we both approve of Vitomas and Annabelle as wives for you."

"Thank you," Matthew said. "I will admit it is just my luck that I finally find not one but two girls who steal my heart and they are married to my cousins," Matthew laughed at the irony of the situation.

"Son, promise us one thing," Rosa said as she leaned forward and took Matthew's hand. "Please don't waste your life waiting around for these girls. You can certainly marry, then later if something happens to Raul or Simon you may take their wives also."

Demetries stood before one of the great fires in the cave under the River Nebu. He danced before the flames and cursed the Sanuri. Demetries grabbed a dagger from his belt and cut the inside of his left hand and dripped blood into the fire. Then Demetries shook his hand as he danced and sprayed blood droplets on the walls of the cave. Demetries stopped dancing when he had completed an entire circle around the fire and smeared blood on his face and forearms.

"Sporos, Sporos come forth, My Master, my friend. Come forth and destroy the Sanuri," Demetries screamed into the flames. "Destroy the man who imprisoned you. Destroy the man who has cursed me. Destroy all who stand in the way of our plans."

The Huta warriors stood in a large circle around Demetries, singing and screaming; agitating themselves into a trance-like state. "Sporos my brother, My Lord help me to find you," screamed Demetries.

Suddenly great billows of ash rose high into the air and the face of Sporos screaming in The Abyss, appeared in the fire. When the Huta warriors saw this, they all bowed and faced the ground. "How do I get to you?" Demetries called into the fire. Then the face of Sporos was gone.

The Sanuri, Sudfad, Renya, Laurel, Alexander, Petra and Marie all stood in the front courtyard as hundreds of Enrops landed on the ground. Nica, the leader of the flock, walked towards King Sudfad.

"I want to thank you for saving my family," Sudfad said.

"You are most welcome," replied Nica.

"You and your tribe will always have a home at this castle and in the Kingdom of Wetpr as long as my family reigns." Sudfad continued, "Wetpr is a large kingdom and has been blessed with great abundance I think you will be comfortable here."

"In return for your graciousness we will be eyes where you cannot see," replied Nica with dignity. "My brethren and I make this pledge to you and your family as long as you walk in this world."

King Sudfad bowed and said, "Thank you."

When the small ceremony was completed, Petra ran up to Nica and asked, "Can you play now?"

Demetries, still in the guise of Jonas joined Roch in the war room. Roch handed Jonas a glass of whiskey.

"Do you feel as bad as you look?" asked Roch seriously as he was repulsed by the open sores and boils that covered Jonas.

"Yes My Lord and I know I am hideous to look at; but there is something of great importance that I failed to tell you at our last meeting," said Jonas with insincere reverence. "And I am most sorry but it is difficult to tell you."

"What is it?" asked Roch as he sat down behind his desk, deliberately putting distance between him and Jonas.

"I never told you where I found the Sanuri."

"Go on," said Roch with growing apprehension.

"I found him at your brother's castle in Wetpr," said Jonas.

"Why was he there?"

"To officiate at the weddings of both of the King's sons," Jonas said with inward delight.

"You don't know what you are talking about," yelled Roch. "Sudfad has just the adopted son; I had Raul killed."

"My Lord, Raul is very much alive," Jonas paused to let Roch dwell on the meaning of this information.

Suddenly Roch's eyes widened and he jumped out of his seat. "Jonas who did Raul marry?"

Jonas was trying to savor the moment. "Vitomas, My Lord, Vitomas."

Roch picked up the chair he had been sitting on and threw it against the wall, smashing it to pieces. Then Roch started to pick items off his desk and throw them against the walls of the war room as he screamed with rage. Roch kicked his desk with such force that he broke one of the legs. Then Roch stopped all movement; Roch turned and looked at Jonas with a presence of such insanity that the demon took pause. "Tell me Jonas, who did the other son marry, was it Annabelle?"

"Yes, My Lord," Jonas said while trying not to grin.

"Those two bitches," screamed Roch as he pounded the top of his desk with both of his fists. "They tricked me, they all tricked me. I'm going to kill them, Sudfad and the whole lot. I'm going to teach them all a lesson; no one steals from me and gets away with it!"

Roch ran to the door of the war room and flung it open, "Sophie get in here!" Roch screamed loudly. "Cerephus, someone get Cerephus!"

"Yes My Lord," yelled a soldier who then ran out of the castle to look for Cerephus.

Sophie was breathing so heavily from running she could not speak when she first entered the war room. Roch grabbed her by the arm and shook Sophie roughly. "Sophie, Raul is alive and married to Vitomas and Annabelle just married Sudfad's other son. Did you know of any of this?" Roch screamed.

"My Lord that cannot be, why I saw the body myself and so did the physician," Sophie said fearfully. "Your information must be wrong."

Blinded by his rage, Roch now swung around and walked towards Jonas. "Jonas what happened to you?" gasped Sophie.

But before Jonas could answer her question, Roch grabbed him by the throat squeezing tightly. "Jonas are you sure of this information?" Roch demanded.

The demon Demetries was a much more powerful being than Roch. Demetries despised Roch and was filled with rage when Roch grabbed him. In that instant Sophie could see from Demetries' eyes that he was going to reveal his true identity; something she had to stop from happening.

"My Lord, My Lord you are choking him, he cannot answer you," Sophie screamed as she ran up to the two men. "Please My Lord, release him." Roch let go of Jonas's throat and took a couple of steps backwards. Jonas stared at Roch with hatred in his eyes.

"What is going on here?" demanded Cerephus as he entered the war room. Cerephus could see he had interrupted something. Cerephus stopped abruptly when he saw Jonas.

"I sent Jonas after the Sanuri, he came back looking like this and told me that Sudfad's son is alive and married to Vitomas and Annabelle married the other son."

"But that is impossible; I saw the boy's body myself. He was dead I tell you," Cerephus said.

"If you don't believe me just send some men into Wetpr. The Princes were married in a double ceremony and King Sudfad opened up the celebration to all his people like he always does. Or if you can hold yourself from attacking me, you could just read this," Jonas said angrily as he pulled a wedding invitation out of his shirt pocket and handed it to Roch.

Roch grabbed the invitation from Jonas' hand, his face turned bright red as he read it. "Does this look like the bastard is dead?" screamed Roch as he threw the invitation at Cerephus. "They tricked all of you, I don't know how they did it but they played you all for fools!"

Roch turned his back on them and walked over to the window in his study. He stared out the window for several minutes without speaking. Then he turned and looked at Cerephus with disgust. "Cerephus you have never let me down before, I should kill you."

596

"But you have been loyal to me for many years so I will give you one more chance; prepare the men, tomorrow we ride for Wetpr."

That same evening Raul, Simon and Matthew were all sitting up in their beds in the large guest room. Vitomas and Annabelle were each sitting on the beds of their husbands as they all listened intently to the Sanuri speak. After about an hour of instruction, Sudfad and Renya entered the room and sat in a couple of the extra chairs that had been placed in the room for visitors.

"I asked Sudfad and Renya to join us tonight as there are some things I must share with them also," said the Sanuri.

"First I want to say that I have very much enjoyed spending so much time with all of you the last few weeks. As I expected you are all excellent students. And as for both of you; Vitomas and Annabelle I don't know if the family has told you how proud they are for the courage and faith you have shown in your eagerness to accept your roles as Keeper of the Scrolls."

"Your husbands, as always, are fearful for your safety but after the battle that took place here I do believe they have seen a different side of you and Renya," the Sanuri said. "I am told you plan to start your travels in a couple of weeks, is that true?"

"Yes, we plan to visit Mathas and Rosa first, then I am taking them eastward to the shores of the Sea of Grevtd. We will travel southward along the coastline for a while, probably ending up in Port Friada," Raul said. "There are so many things I want to show them."

"And how do you plan to travel?" the Sanuri asked.

"A carriage for the girls and extra horses."

"Are you having soldiers escort you?"

Raul stared at the Sanuri. "Sanuri I know you, you would not be asking these questions unless there was a reason."

"The night of the battle, after I told you to get all of your men inside of the castle, The Great Ruler sent me help," explained the Sanuri. "The Lion came to our assistance. When our attackers had been defeated The Lion walked up to me. The reason I have asked Sudfad and Renya to join us, is so all of you could hear his words." Everyone in the room sat in silence staring at the Sanuri.

"He told me that we are the family of The Seven Sons that the ancient prophesy speaks of. Matthew was right, I too am considered one of the sons, as is Petra. Sudfad with you, Raul, Simon and Matthew we are six. He told me that not all of us are ready to fulfill the roles described in the prophesy yet. The Lion said that each of the sons would have to be attacked by a great darkness and would have to overcome that darkness before they are ready to fulfill their destinies."

"The Lion said the seventh son is battling darkness and has been for some time. The Lion also said we will know the seventh son when we see him because he will bear the scars from the demons and that his knowledge of the demons will help to defeat them."

"Sanuri what exactly is The Prophesy of The Seven Sons?" asked Annabelle.

"It is a prophesy as old as time in this world. It tells of Seven Sons of light, who conquer the demons of the night."

"Is this part of being Keepers of the Scrolls?" Vitomas asked.

"My dear, I honestly don't know yet," replied the Sanuri.

"Did he give you any more information about the seventh son?" Sudfad asked.

"No, only that he would be powerful," replied the Sanuri. "But he did send a message for Raul and Simon. The Lion said that you had to postpone your travels because of your injuries and this ultimately saved your lives. I am to tell you to take soldiers with you on your journey."

"Is it safe to take our wives?" Simon asked with concern.

"Follow his instructions and you will be fine," the Sanuri said. "You have many enemies but you cannot live your lives in fear."

Chapter XXXIX
Allies

Cerephus left the war room as soon as he received his orders to prepare the troops for war. Sophie and Jonas followed Cerephus as no one wanted to be near Roch. As soon as they were out of Roch's sight, Sophie grabbed Jonas and dragged him down a deserted hallway. When Sophie was convinced they were alone she stopped and turned to the demon.

"You had better find a way to stop this war Demetries. If Roch is killed our mission will fail and the wrath of Omnibus will be upon you," Sophie said angrily. "I'm going to send a message to Meekos."

"No, wait, I will think of something," Jonas said. "I might have to reveal who I am to stop him."

"That is up to you," Sophie said. "As long as you don't tell him about the mission. Tell him anything he will believe and tempt him with treasure that always distracts Roch from other things."

"I am sure you will be quite happy here, My Lady. The former owner died of old age. He had no family so as you can see the castle is completely furnished. I will admit it does need a good cleaning though," said George, an Advisor to King Fahra of Zorta.

"Thank you George, this is perfect," said Juleta as she pulled back the drapes to the windows in the parlor. "I will need some staff."

"Of course My Lady; across the river is the Village of Toman, I am sure you can find many people to hire there," George replied.

Juleta turned around and gave George a flirtatious smile. "George you have been so gracious I wonder if I might impose on your generosity."

"My Lady anything."

"The day is young, would you mind accompanying me to Toman and helping me to hire some staff and some men?"

"I would be honored, My Lady. You will need to fill the cupboards here also; there is no food or drink in the castle."

Juleta smiled sweetly as she took George's arm and the two of them walked towards the front door of the castle. George, a man more than twice Juleta's age was more than flattered at the attention she paid to him. "Why George, I just don't know what I would do without you. You have been so incredibly helpful." Juleta purred.

"My Lady, I know it is none of my business but I don't understand how your father has permitted you to travel so far from home and now you plan to live in Zorta. A woman as young and beautiful as you are should have protection; there are many dangers to be aware of. How can your father allow you to be alone?"

"George I don't want to speak of it. My father is such a monster," said Juleta as she covered her face with her hands and pretended to cry. George put his arm around Juleta's shoulders to console her.

"I have only heard good things about King Mathas but he must be a monster if he abandons such a sweet and fragile thing as you. Now, now don't you cry; I will take care of you."

After talking with Sophie, Jonas walked back into the war room and boldly poured himself a glass of whiskey, then he sat down on a chair by the table and stared at Roch. "Roch you're a fool if you think you can attack Wetpr on a whim and win," Jonas said challengingly.

"Jonas what are you saying?" demanded Roch.

"You heard me and you know I speak the truth," Jonas said. "I just returned from Wetpr; that castle as well as the kingdom is heavily fortified and they are waiting for you to attack. You would be walking into a trap. Don't you think they know you would hear about the weddings?"

Cerephus entered the room and poured himself a drink as Jonas was talking. "I don't like the tone of voice you are using but you may have a point," Roch said. "Don't forget I am your King."

"You aren't my King and you never have been," Jonas said sarcastically. "You're nothing but a pompous, self-absorbed excuse for a man and you disgust me."

Roch charged at Jonas as he was speaking; Roch's anger overruling the pain of his broken ankle. But now the ancient demon was no longer playing a role. Demetries held up his hand and mumbled and Roch was lifted off the floor and thrown against the far wall of the war room.

Roch fell to the floor then started to scream in pain as he felt like hot swords were being thrust into his body. Cerephus grabbed his sword and took one step towards Jonas who held up his hand and said, "Cerephus this is not your fight." Cerephus stopped abruptly and watched the scene with horror.

"Had enough my King?" Jonas asked sarcastically.

"Jonas I don't know what you are doing but stop it," Roch screamed.

"I am not Jonas, he died from a head wound inflicted by a Huta warrior; remember you cared for him Roch," said Demetries.

"I do not understand," said Cerephus fearfully.

"I took over Jonas' body; after all he had no use for it anymore," said Demetries as he stared at Roch, who was now standing up. Both Roch and Cerephus glared at Demetries but neither of them spoke. Demetries started to laugh, "What nothing to say? I will admit that I don't often get to see fear on the faces of two such murderous men as you. That seer tried to warn you but Roch you are just too arrogant to listen to anyone."

Roch was quiet as he remembered the words of Miranda. "How did she know who you were?" Roch asked.

"Well this is where it gets complicated," Demetries replied. "Jonas was still alive but barely so I was sharing his body. She didn't realize who I was at first."

"You're a demon," Roch said accusingly. "The Sanuri said I sent him demons."

601

"Well you aren't so stupid after all," Demetries said as he sat down on his chair.

"A demon," uttered Cerephus in astonishment.

"Oh please don't act so self-righteous; the two of you have been called demons your entire lives," Demetries said mockingly. "And besides you both call to us all of the time and yet you are surprised when we answer?"

"What do you want?" Roch demanded. "Why are you here?"

"First of all you stop treating me like I am the hired help Roch," Demetries said. "And second, I came to do some business."

"Really," Roch said as a smile crossed his face. Roch grabbed his glass and a bottle of whiskey and sat down at the table with Demetries. "So tell me, what did you say your name was?"

"I didn't, you can call me Demetries."

"Demetries so what kind of business are you interested in?" Roch asked.

Juleta was standing in front of one of the large windows in the parlor. She never tired of looking upon the River Toba that bordered the west side of the castle.

The river ran from the Phonicha Ocean which was the northern border of both the Kingdoms of Wetpr and Lentz, southward until it reached the Inlet of the Sea of Grevtd at Port Friada. Birds of all kinds as well as other wildlife were drawn to the waters. Juleta enjoyed watching the creatures and the fish that occasionally jumped into the air; their movements seemed to mesmerize her and to take her to another time in her life.

"My Lady," said Selen the housekeeper as she walked into the parlor. "You have a visitor."

"Who is it?" Juleta asked without turning around.

"He said his name is Thaos and that you sent for him, My Lady."

602

"Yes, show him in," said Juleta as she turned and faced the door to the parlor. A handsome, muscular young man with dark curly hair entered the room. He was completely dressed in black leather with a black eye patch over his left eye. Juleta paused for a moment as she was quite struck by the attractiveness of this man. "Selen please close the door, so we can speak in private," Juleta said as she motioned for Thaos to take a seat. "I have heard a great deal about you," Juleta said flirtatiously as she sat in a chair across from Thaos.

"And I have heard about you," Thaos said as he sized up Juleta.

"You are a man with many talents," Juleta said with a coy smile.

"And you are a woman with many enemies and great ambition," Thaos replied impassionedly.

Juleta stared at Thaos; she was shocked by his words and demeanor. Then a sly smile came across her face. "Well I see we understand each other so I won't beat around the bush. I need your services and I pay well."

"I am listening," replied Thaos.

"I want to sit on the throne of Lentz and I will need a powerful army."

"I have heard that you are a dark lord; can't you just conjure up an army?" Thaos asked mockingly.

"Well I see you have found out a great deal about me."

"I like to know who I am doing business with."

"So tell me Thaos what have you heard about me?"

Thaos stared coldly at Juleta and replied, "I have heard that you are a spoiled, rich girl with a heart as black as night. You have been banned from your homeland and the Kingdom of Wetpr for treason against your father and for being a dark lord." Juleta's face betrayed her anger. "Did I leave anything out My Lady?" Thaos asked in a sarcastic tone.

"And where did you hear these things?" demanded Juleta.

"News travels quickly when a princess is kicked out of her home," Thaos said. "You are the talk of many cities and villages."

"Thaos are you telling me the truth?"

"Why would I lie about it?"

"Because if what you say is true I will have to delay my plans for a while," Juleta said angrily.

Several weeks later the Sanuri was preparing to leave the castle in Wetpr in the early morning hours. "Sanuri do you have to leave so soon?" asked Petra as he helped the Sanuri put the last of his belongings into the boca.

"My dear boy," replied the Sanuri with a laugh. "I have been here for months; I am sure I wore out my welcome long ago."

"You never wear out your welcome here," said Sudfad as he, Renya and Matthew walked up to the boca.

"Sanuri this is your home; always remember that," said Renya.

The Sanuri walked up to Renya and grasped both of her hands with his. "Thank you my dear and I will return for the christenings."

"Christenings!" said Renya with excitement.

"I told you The Great Ruler would bless you with many grandchildren," the Sanuri said with a smile and a wink. "I will return in a year or less."

"Sudfad did you hear that?" asked Renya. "We will have grandchildren soon." Sudfad smiled and put his arm around Renya's shoulders.

"Sanuri where will you go?" Sudfad asked.

"I have much work to do. The Great Ruler has sent me visions of the places I need to go," said the Sanuri, then he turned and walked up to Matthew. "Speaking of visions; The Great Ruler has given you a powerful gift Matthew, do not discard the visions that he sends to you for they are messages."

The Sanuri walked back to Sudfad and shook his hand, "My dear friend, take care of this family for there are always demons at your door."

Petra and Renya cried as they watched the boca drive away from the castle. "Come on you two," said Sudfad lovingly as he put his arms around both of them. The four turned and walked towards the castle.

"Matthew, after breakfast I need to discuss some business with you," Sudfad said.

"Sudfad I can tell from your voice it is something serious," Renya said. "What is the matter?"

"Petra run in and tell Marie we are ready for breakfast," Sudfad said. When Petra entered the castle, Sudfad turned and looked at Matthew and Renya. "I have heard there is an army of barbarians gathering in Zorta. I sent Enrops out to warn Raul and Simon."

"What have you heard about this army?" asked Matthew. "Who is paying it?"

"I don't know, all I have heard is that it is led by a man named Thaos."

"So this is where Archetenus was taking you," said Annabelle as the two women bought gifts in a large store in Port Friada. "Do you think he is here?"

"I have been wondering about that," Vitomas replied. "Raul hasn't said anything but I believe he has been thinking about Archetenus too. I so hope we don't run into him." While Vitomas spoke she was walking between tables of goods. "Look at these shawls Annabelle they are made of silk, in colors I have never seen before, I think we should get some for gifts." As Annabelle walked towards Vitomas and the table of shawls, Vitomas noticed a man in the store watching them.

"Annabelle, have you noticed that man who is staring at us?" Vitomas whispered.

"You mean the man in black?" asked Annabelle without turning around towards the man. "He is very handsome, yes I did notice him."

"He was in the last store we were in also and he does not seem to be buying anything."

"Do you think he is following us?" Annabelle asked. "That would be very bold since the soldiers are waiting for us outside."

"I don't know," answered Vitomas. "Let's get our gifts and see if he follows us to the next store."

Every morning King Mathas met with General Claudius and General Fahron. Not only were these seasoned warriors the King's closest friends but they helped him rule the kingdom. King Mathas was a man of wisdom. He had seen the ruin of many kingdoms after the king was killed, so Mathas distributed many of his responsibilities to these two generals, hoping that the kingdom would remain stable if something were to happen to him.

"Mathas we have found another six soldiers dead and their uniforms stripped of them," said Fahron as he entered Mathas' study.

King Mathas pounded his large fist on his desk. "Fahron, that is twenty this week."

"I know My Lord and it appears they are being killed for their uniforms," Claudius said as he poured himself a cup of coffee and sat down at their meeting table. "You know this means we may have spies among us."

"My friends we will need to put guards around our families," Mathas said sadly. "There are things that I need to tell you, things I should have told you weeks ago."

"Mathas ever since you returned from Wetpr you look as if you are carrying the weight of the world upon your shoulders," Fahron commented. "And it has not gone unnoticed that Juleta did not return with you."

"We have been hearing many stories about her," Claudius said. "Stories we do not want to believe."

"I should have told you first," Mathas said with tears in his eyes. "It was not deception that prevented me from telling you but rather a father's broken heart."

"My Ladies, can you carry all of these packages?" asked the store clerk as he added to the pile that Annabelle was holding. "Should I call to the soldiers to help you?"

"No, no," laughed Annabelle, "We have them." The two princesses turned from the counter and started to walk towards the door of the store; when a package fell from the stack that Annabelle was carrying. As she tried to catch it, Annabelle unbalanced the other packages and they all fell to the floor. Annabelle and Vitomas both started to laugh. Before Annabelle could bend down to pick up the packages the man in black quickly came up to her.

"Allow me My Lady," said the man as he knelt down and picked up the spilled packages. "I can carry these to your carriage," he said as he stood up, towering over both of the women.

"Thank you," said Annabelle sweetly.

"My Lord, you have been watching us for some time," said Vitomas. "May I ask why?"

The man smiled broadly, showing perfect white teeth and dimples. "Actually My Lady I have been staring at the two of you for some time. I apologize if my bold behavior offended you; but I have never before seen two such beautiful women. I find I cannot take my eyes off from you." Both Vitomas and Annabelle blushed and smiled at his words. Seeing he had won over the Princesses the man continued. "May I ask what all these packages are for?"

"We are returning home tomorrow," said Annabelle. "So we are buying gifts."

"And where would home be?"

"Wetpr," replied Annabelle.

"Ah, such a distance you two have traveled."

"We are not alone," said Vitomas still suspicious of the charming young man. "Our husbands have taken us travelling as wedding gifts."

The man feigned a look of sadness. "Alas my heart is broken; but I should have known that two such extraordinarily beautiful women as you would be taken. Might I ask where your husbands are?"

"I'll bet the girls are buying out the city," laughed Raul as he and Simon walked across the dirt road towards their soldiers, who were standing guard outside of a large store.

"We will have to do this again," said Simon. "Everything seems even more exciting when you see it through the eyes of the girls."

"Well another trip might have to wait awhile Brother," Raul said with a proud smile. "Vitomas didn't want me to say anything yet but she thinks she is pregnant." Simon turned around and slapped Raul on the shoulder. "Congratulations, I hope I can say that soon," Simon said happily. The two men continued walking towards the store. As they got closer they could see into the store through the large front window.

"Who is that the girls are talking to?" Raul asked as both men quickened their pace.

The soldiers stood outside of the store facing the street. "My Lords," said both of the soldiers as Simon and Raul quickly walked past them.

"Speaking of our husbands, here they are now," Vitomas said. Then she looked at the man in black, "I am sorry My Lord I did not get your name."

"Thaos," said the man as he handed Annabelle her stack of packages.

"Thaos this is my husband Raul and Annabelle's husband Simon. When Raul and Simon heard the man's name they both instinctively stood in front of their wives.

608

"Simon, what are you doing?" Annabelle asked indignantly.

"Annabelle, Vitomas are you alright?" Simon asked without taking his eyes off from Thaos.

"Honey we are both just fine, this gentleman helped me pick up my packages," Annabelle said.

"Raul, he has been a perfect gentleman, what is going on?" asked Vitomas.

Ignoring his wife's question Raul spoke to the man, "Are you the same Thaos who is gathering an army of barbarians in Zorta?"

"I think barbarians is such a strong word," Thaos said mockingly. "I prefer to describe them as men with similar skills." Thaos did not wavier in his gaze or stance as he faced the two powerful princes.

"Why are you here and why are you talking to our wives?" Raul demanded.

Once again Thaos smiled broadly. "Raul, Simon I am not your enemy," he said in a smug manner. "But I work for one who is. I make a habit of trying to find out everything about the people who employ me, their habits, their fears, what motivates them. My current employer is motivated by a great deal of hatred and ambition. She hates your family and your wives in particular."

"Juleta," Raul said.

"And I will admit now that I have met all of you I can see why," Thaos said grinning.

"And what is that supposed to mean," growled Simon as he stepped towards Thaos.

"Now Simon that actually was a compliment," said Thaos as he enjoyed taunting the Princes. "Here you have two beautiful and charming princesses married and obviously in love with two rich and handsome princes. You are everything that Juleta covets. Except of course for her father's throne."

Raul stared at Thaos as he spoke, trying to size him up. "Tell me Thaos, do you also find out everything you can about those you intend to attack?"

"When the opponents are worthy adversaries I do," Thaos said with a grin.

"Thaos your fight is with us, you leave our wives out of it," Raul said. Thaos did not respond.

"Thaos, a man of your profession does not offer up the information you have given us," Simon said suspiciously. "Why have you warned us about Juleta?"

"Let's just say it is my wedding gift to you; do not expect another," Thaos bowed before them. "My Ladies it truly was a pleasure to meet you." Thaos turned and swaggered as he walked out of the door. Both Raul and Simon watched as Thaos walked down the busy street before they turned to their wives.

"What did he say to you?" Simon asked.

"Well, nothing really," replied Vitomas. "He had been watching us in a couple of stores, when I asked him why he said it was because he thought we were beautiful. He was very charming. He mostly asked us questions."

Raul and Simon both looked at each other then back to their wives. "And what did you tell him?" asked Raul.

"It was me, I am sorry, I didn't know," said Annabelle.

"Honey what did you tell him?" Simon asked.

"I told him about the wonderful trip we have taken and that we are headed back to Wetpr tomorrow."

"Did you tell him what route we are taking?" Raul asked

"No, oh I am so sorry," cried Annabelle.

"It's alright Honey," said Simon as he put his arm around her shoulders.

"I didn't see any of his men on the streets, which means they must be waiting outside of the city," Raul said. "We are going to have to change our plans."

The horses snorted; their breath visible in the cold night air. Juleta's men gathered on a ridge looking down at the Village of Isador in the northern regions of the Kingdom of Lentz. Isador lay just within the lands of the Valdore Tribe. A tribe led by a warlord named Usman.

"Remember what the witch ordered," Lazo said to his men. "Leave some survivors so they can recognize these uniforms. Let's go." Lazo led the charge on the small village. The sleeping villagers were unaware of the horror that was upon them; there were no sentries to warn them for the villagers had never had need of sentries before. The villagers slept as Lazo and his men raced towards them. The villagers slept as the invaders shot flaming arrows into the thatched roofs of their tiny homes. The villagers slept as the demons came to their doors.

Chapter XXXL
Cursed

"What are those old fools doing now?" Meekos asked sarcastically as he stood in a window of the monastery at Malga with High Priest Tenebrae and High Priest Pravis. The three high priests were watching Padre Bartholomew and Padre Thomas walk towards one of the back gardens.

"Why would they want to go to the garden this late in the day?" Tenebrae asked. "The sun is almost down."

"They have been sneaking around here for weeks," Meekos growled. "Pravis dress some of our men in priest frocks and have them follow those two; I know they are up to something."

"Are you sure those two old men are worth our energy?" Pravis asked disdainfully. "I mean how can they really be a threat to us?"

"They are friends with the Sanuri and that makes them threats to us," Meekos replied. "Besides I don't believe either of them are as stupid as they act. For all we know they could be spies sent to watch us."

"Meekos you are getting paranoid," Tenebrae scoffed. "If the Sanuri had any idea of what we were doing he would be here in a heartbeat to try and stop us. You're seeing shadows where there aren't any."

"Perhaps you are right," Meekos said. "But I am not going to take any chances, not with the time of the ascension so close at hand."

"Well, they didn't stay in the garden long, they are already coming back," Pravis said.

"Yes I can see that," snapped Meekos. "Notice neither of them are carrying plants or gardening tools. Why would they spend a few minutes in the back garden at this time of night unless they were somehow passing information or burying something? First thing in the morning we are going to take a walk in that garden," Meekos said sternly. "Pravis contact our men tonight and have them start following those priests tomorrow."

"If you don't tell Meekos I will," Sophie threatened Demetries.

"I am doing my job," Demetries said. "I'm watching Roch and so far keeping him alive."

"But the fact that Roch now knows you are a demon is something that Meekos should be aware of," Sophie continued.

"Why?" Demetries asked.

"You aren't afraid of telling him are you?"

"I fear no man."

"That may be the case but you fear the Old Ones and if you cause problems for the ascension you will have a great deal to fear."

Archetenus was sitting in the Ghost Ship Tavern playing cards with five other men. Since arriving in Port Friada, Archetenus spent a great deal of his time in taverns. The Ghost Ship Tavern was close to the ship yard and had a reputation for being one of the most dangerous taverns in the city. A reputation that drew Archetenus as it did others of his kind.

Killings were a nightly occurrence that barely disrupted the regular tavern patrons. The bartenders usually just tossed the dead bodies into the street and resumed their business. The wooden floor of the tavern was reddish brown from all the blood that had soaked into it over the years.

Archetenus had spent so many years planning his life around the fantasy that he created with Vitomas that now he felt loss. Although Archetenus liked not taking orders from anyone; he was bored with his life.

Archetenus had not called to Miranda or spoken to her since his arrival in Port Friada. He was staying in a small and dirty hotel room near the ship yard. Although he could afford much nicer accommodations, Archetenus felt comfortable in this section of the city.

This night as all of the others, the patrons of the Ghost Ship were loud and drunk. Although Archetenus appeared to be concentrating on his hand of cards, nothing in the tavern eluded his notice. Archetenus liked to drink whiskey but he was still paranoid about the curse that the witch had placed upon him. Archetenus suspected, and rightfully so, that he was still being hunted by demons and possibly Roch's men.

The Ghost Ship Tavern was small and crowded. The tables were set close together which often led to fights as men accused each other of cheating at cards. Archetenus watched as Rex, one of the regular patrons joined the card game at the next table.

Rex was a small and skinny man with red hair and exceptionally white skin. Rex was unassuming, the type of person no one would notice in a crowd and this was his value. Rex was not only the most notorious pickpocket in Port Friada but he knew everything that went on in the city. Rex was the man you went to if you wanted information or a connection.

"Well boys," Rex said with a smile to the three men he had joined at cards. "You will never guess what I saw today."

"Don't really care," growled a man nicknamed Smoking Joe. "Just shut up and play."

"Let him talk," said another man at the table, who told everyone his name was Black Jack but no one ever believed him.

"I saw real royalty today," Rex continued. "I saw the Princes of Wetpr and their new brides."

"I told you to shut the hell up," Smoking Joe said in a low growl.

"Let him talk," said Archetenus loudly. "This I want to hear."

Rex turned to Archetenus, glad to have an audience. "This morning I was standing around Endevor Street; that's the street with all of the banks and fancy stores. And I saw, I don't know, maybe thirty soldiers, on horseback, stop in front of the Excelsor Hotel. You know that is the most expensive hotel in the city. I have made a lot of money from the guests there."

"I don't care about that, just tell me about the Princes of Wetpr," Archetenus said with annoyance.

"Well," continued Rex. "Pretty soon this real fancy carriage pulls up in front of the hotel too and it's being driven by two more soldiers. So I mosey over to the hotel and get me a seat in the lobby. Me and another guy were just sitting there watching soldiers carrying packages from the upstairs to the carriage. I turned to the guy and asked him if he knew why the soldiers were there. Well he tells me that both of the Princes from Wetpr just got married and they are travelling with their brides."

Archetenus could feel the anger rising within him. "Did you see them?"

"Hell ya."

"Describe them to me," Archetenus demanded.

Rex gave Archetenus a scrutinizing look as he was wondering why Archetenus was getting so angry. "Well these two couples walk down the stairs into the lobby. Both the guys were big men, look like fighters. One had black hair and the other had blonde. Well the one with the black hair had a beautiful blonde woman hanging on his arm. And the other guy had an equally beautiful woman holding his hand, she had black hair. Tell me do you know them?"

"Yes," growled Archetenus who was feeling like Vitomas and her prince were flaunting their marriage in front of him. "Are they still in Port Friada?"

"No, they were leaving, that's why the soldiers were packing all those bags," Rex said. "The guy I was talking to said they'd been here for a week."

Noreen lay in bed wide awake. Henry was snoring beside her. The whiskey on his breath made her nauseous. Noreen and Henry had been together since they both were sixteen; she thought he was her best friend as well as the love of her life. Now Noreen lay awake every night trying to figure out what was happening to their lives.

Henry was so excited when Noreen got pregnant but as the time grew closer to Jacob's birth; Henry started changing. At first he was less attentive to Noreen. Then it seemed like Henry was angry all of the time. After that he started to leave for days at a time. Henry would go to nearby towns and villages to play cards and, and, Noreen didn't want to think of what else he might be doing.

Noreen hated it when Henry left her alone. Their closest neighbor was over ten miles away and Noreen would get so lonely. Noreen hoped that Henry would change, would get back to his old self after the baby was born, but Henry's behavior became worse. Henry wanted nothing to do with Jacob; he wouldn't even hold his son.

"Is it my imagination?" thought Noreen. "Or has he gotten worse since we got that ring? Henry had been neglectful to her before but now." The tears ran down Noreen's swollen and bruised face.

After Rex finished his story, Archetenus bought two bottles of whiskey and walked out of the Ghost Ship Tavern. Archetenus drank from one of the bottles as he walked the five blocks to the Sea's End Hotel where he was staying. When Archetenus entered the lobby he heard yelling and glass breaking. Then he saw the desk clerk and another man who he did not recognize dragging a man down the steps, through the lobby then they threw him into the street.

"You're never allowed in here again!" yelled the desk clerk. Then he wiped his bloody hands on his pants and walked back to his post behind the desk in the lobby. Archetenus never said a word; he just turned and walked up the stairs to his room which was on the second floor. As was his routine, Archetenus searched his small room as soon as he entered it.

Archetenus hid his money under some loose floorboards that were concealed by a large filthy and tattered carpet. Once he was satisfied that no one had been in his room Archetenus threw himself on the bed and opened the second bottle of whiskey. He drank half of this bottle down with a couple of gulps.

"What the hell were they thinking coming here? Of all the places in Opots they come to Port Friada when they know I am here," thought Archetenus. "Was that damn prince trying to rub my face in it? He's married to my woman. I should kill them, kill them all."

Archetenus took two more large gulps of whiskey and his eyes started to close. He lay on the bed mumbling to himself; fighting the sleep that was taking over his body. Suddenly Archetenus' eyes popped open. The thought that entered his mind made his adrenaline surge through him. "What if Vitomas wanted to come here to see me?"

"Meekos what is it that you summon us in the middle of the night?" demanded Tenebrae as he entered the parlor in Meekos chambers. As the Senior High Priest of the monastery, Meekos had lavish chambers that were extravagantly furnished. Pravis was already sitting in a chair across from Meekos, in front of the hearth.

"Sit down," grumbled Meekos. "Obviously I wouldn't wake you unless it was important. Pour yourself a drink."

Meekos waited until Tenebrae got his drink and sat down before he spoke again. "I got this letter from Sophie and there are numerous disturbing things here." Meekos handed the letter to Pravis but kept talking as Pravis read. "First she wants to know why I have not responded to her letter about Roch losing his blood ring. A message that I never received."

"Then Sophie goes on to say that Roch sent Demetries, who was still in disguise, to kidnap the Sanuri. When Demetries finally returned to Roch's castle he had lost all his men, he was incredibly battered and the Sanuri put a curse on Demetries so he can never hide his true appearance again. Sophie said that Demetries admitted to Roch that he is a demon but did not tell Roch about the mission."

High Priest Tenebrae had not yet read the letter. "Well isn't Roch suspicious now?"

"Apparently Demetries appealed to Roch's greed and the two have become business partners of sorts. Sophie said Demetries is still performing the duties I have paid him to do. But Sophie has never liked Demetries and now questions why he would not tell me this information himself. And frankly I question it too."

High Priest Pravis read the letter and handed it to Tenebrae. "Meekos," Pravis said angrily. "You basically told me that I was a paranoid fool when I voiced concerns about the Sanuri. You said the stories we have heard about the Sanuri were mere stories. Well, you failed to tell us everything in that letter or did you miss the part where Sophie says that the Sanuri fought an army of Ghost Dragons and won?"

Meekos was not used to his underlings speaking to him in such a fashion but he knew that Pravis was right. "I don't appreciate your tone of voice," Meekos said irritably. "But Pravis you are right; I underestimated him."

"I'm not angry that you underestimated the Sanuri," Pravis continued. "I'm sick of you treating Tenebrae and me like we are fools. I am not a stupid man when I tell you something listen to me!"

"When you two are done quarreling shall we talk about Roch's missing ring?" Tenebrae asked with annoyance. "Sophie asks some very good questions here and honestly I don't know the answers to them. Do either of you?" Both Meekos and Pravis looked at Tenebrae without speaking. "Well instead of fighting among ourselves perhaps we should be finding the answers to these questions," Tenebrae continued.

"I don't know if Roch losing that ring will affect the ascension because Roch has become so evil that he has a connection to the Old Ones without it," Meekos said. "That ring was the original and the only one which contained the blood of Omnibus. All the rest of the blood rings are mere copies of that one. But because that ring is connected to Omnibus, the ring itself will call to demons."

"What do you mean?" asked Tenebrae.

"I mean it will literally call to demons, so it shouldn't be that hard to find," Meekos said. "We will have to find a spell that will allow us to hear the ring calling."

"And what do we do if a demon gets to it before we do?" Pravis asked.

"We'll have to figure that out if it happens," Meekos snapped.

"And if a human has it?" Tenebrae asked. "Will he become bonded to Omnibus?"

"He might," Meekos said. "But I would really doubt that he would live that long. I am sure demons are already answering its call."

Matthew jumped out of bed. He stood in his bedroom wet from sweat and shaking. When Matthew realized he had been dreaming he calmed a little. Matthew walked across the room and poured himself a glass of water. "I have never had a dream seem so real," Matthew thought as he walked over to the window and opened it. The cool night air felt refreshing as he gazed upon the moonlit garden.

Matthew remembered every detail of his dream vividly. His father was riding when the horse reared up and threw Mathas to the ground. The ground was covered with snakes, snakes such as Matthew had never seen before. The horse, wild with fear, tripped and fell on top of Mathas. Suddenly Matthew remembered the words of the Sanuri that his visions were messages from The Great Ruler.

"I must go to Father," Matthew said out loud as he quickly turned to pack his belongings.

The blood turned into roses

The pain, it fell away

As the Angels carried souls

Off that battlefield that day

Walking With Angels © 2009

By

Sandra J Yearman

Glossary of Characters

Aaryan: a male Grand Master of the Insidiae

Abaddon: an ancient demon/one of the Old Ones

Abella: daughter of Prince Lakin and Princess Zada/Ruala

Abigail: sister of Marie/ nurse for grandchildren of King Sudfad

Adi: son of Elen and Batya/ Ruala

Adrone: youngest son of Joshua and Iris/younger brother of Vivian/Clan of Gesmal

Adwell: Prince/ son of King Zachariah and Queen Noella of New Samona/husband of Nada/father of Misha/ Adwell was killed in battle leaving Nada to raise ten children/Ruala/

Ael: an ancient demon/ one of the Old Ones

Ahriman: an ancient demon/ one of the Old Ones

Akasha: former king of Ryed/grandfather of Nehmota

Alexander: former servant of King Roch's parents/ father of Annabelle

Alexander: one of the twin sons of Simon and Annabelle

Alexandras: King of Wetpr/brother of Jaretta/uncle of Sudfad and Roch

Alexas Rose: daughter of Matthew and Angelina

Alexis: son of Usman, the leader of the Valdore Tribe

Alice: and her husband find Jorge near death in Nora

Ana: Princess/daughter of Zeman and Oda/niece of King Manu of New Samona/Ruala

Anda: one of Chief Romogi's three wives/Huta

Andres: Princess of Ryed/daughter of Oren and Astrel/ has twin sister Jorga

Andrew: jeweler in Salar

Andrus: father of Rabi/Ruala

Angelina: daughter of Sorren, Chief of the Nordes Tribe/female warrior

Annabar: daughter of King Sharonne

Annabelle: handmaid and best friend to Queen Vitomas of the Kingdom of Stordt

Anthony: one of the twin sons of Simon and Annabelle

Arca: Enrop leader who protects King Mathas' family

Archetenus The Brave: Captain in the Taperian Army

Arianna: daughter of Simon and Annabelle

Ariel: daughter of Raul and Vitomas

Armstrong: soldier and scout in the army of Wetpr

Arthur Marcus: father of Hannah

Asher: male Ruala warrior

Asmodeus: an ancient demon/ one of the Old Ones

Astrel: former princess of Ryed/daughter of Akasha and Norah

Atomos: Elder of the Centras and Keeper of the Box of Itifer

Augustus Endleson: a wealthy businessman who owned part of the City of Nora

Baal: an ancient demon/ one of the Old Ones

Babu: Enrop

Bac: male Ruala warrior

Bachnenus: warrior guarding refugees/Shettee

Bali: Enrop leader of the flock that does battle at Juleta's castle

Balin: Prince of Norkv/son of Thaddius and Omara/grandson of Benjeman and Esther

Banacus: General in the army of King Tobias of Puntd

Banaka: a female Grand Master of the Insidiae

Barak: Prince of Norkv/grandson of Benjeman and Esther

Barak: Prince/son of King Neputa and Queen Tiara/Shettee

Barid: Prince of Ogg

Barid: Prince of Ryed/son of Nehmota and Vasart

Bastra: Huta captain

Batya: wife of Elen/Ruala

Beatrice Endleson: wife of Augustus

Becca: Princess of Norkv/daughter of Thaddius and Omara/granddaughter of Benjeman and Esther

Behtay: Princess/daughter of Segal and Cahina/niece of King Manu of New Samona/Ruala

Bekka: female Ruala warrior

Bella: wife of Claudius and mother of Stephan

Benedict: Prince of Norkv/son of Benjeman and Esther

Benjeman: vicious rebel leader who overthrew the government of Samona

Bentra: an ancient demon/ one of the Old Ones

Berta: Queen of Stordt/wife of Micha/grandmother of Roch and Sudfad

Bertha: an elderly woman from Nora

Betty: a woman from Nora

Betu: male Ruala warrior

Black Jack: a regular patron at the Ghost Ship Tavern in Port Friada

Brik: son of Prince Lakin and Princess Zada /Ruala

Brina: Princess of Norkv/daughter of Valor and Cai/granddaughter of Benjeman and Esther

Cabal: son of Karzman and Nadia

Cacu: Enrop leader that joined Raul and Simon on a mission

Cade: son of King Pergo and Queen Vinus/ Kingdom of Gandt

Cadi: daughter of Prince Hadar and Princess Paj/ granddaughter of Manu/Ruala

Cael: Shettee boy who is adopted by Thedes and Ibula

Cahina: Princess/ married to Segal son of King Zachariah and Queen Noella of New Samona/Ruala

Cai: Princess of Norkv/wife of Valor who was the son of Benjeman and Esther

Calen: male Ruala warrior/cousin of Luca/son of Maxwell and Emeral/

Calla: female Ruala warrior

Calvin: a desk clerk at The Captain's Retreat Hotel in Port Friada

Campbell: one of the spies at the Castle at Wetpr

Canton: Cisero's second in command

Cara: Princess of Ogg

Carlsman: a Lieutenant in the Army of Lentz

Carson Dormors: a wealthy landowner in the Kingdom of Ganz

Carston: member of the governing body of Nora

Casey: male Ruala warrior/father of Melanie/husband of Tasha

Cassandra: daughter of King Friada and Queen Marla of the Kingdom of Ganz

Cassandra: female Ruala warrior

Cedrick Teivel: a ruthless, powerful man in the Kingdom of Ryed

Celo: Prince of Ryed/son of Oren and Astrel

Cere: daughter of Tristt/Shettee

Cerephus: General in the Taperian Army

Cerey: orphan girl/sister of Nicholas

Ceria: Princess/daughter of Gunnel and Uma/niece of King Manu of New Samona/ sister of Elan/Ruala

Chaez: son of Fahron

Chaladrone: an ancient demon/ one of the Old Ones

Chalta: daughter of King Pergo and Queen Vinus/ Kingdom of Gandt

Chance: works with the Patronus

Charlene: a woman from Nora

Charles: hired farmhand of Arthur Marcus

Chief Romogi: leader of the Hutas/ Kingdom of Marba

Christopher: six year old boy who Luca saves from the Hutas/brother of Lila

Ciao: female Ruala warrior

Cisero: a member of the Insidiae

Clair: a woman from Nora

Claudius: General in the Army of Lentz

Cleo: a man who works for Cicero/a vessel

Cobren: Prince of Norkv/son of Grace and Makalo/Grandson of Benjeman and Esther

Compro: Taperian soldier injured at Wall of Dorath

Corwin: son of King Fahra and Queen Sitha of Zorta

Crater: a soldier in the army of Wetpr

Crispus: a guard at King Roch's castle

Dack: male Ruala warrior

Dacron: former prince of Ryed/is murdered by his younger brother Nehmota for the throne

Dael: an ancient demon/ one of the Old Ones

Dagon: a male Ruala warrior

Dagor: son of King Fahra and Queen Sitha of Zorta

Dai: son of Gael, grandson of Manu/Ruala

Damas: an ancient demon/ one of the Old Ones

Danar: a man created to be a vessel for demons

Daniel: an emissary of The Great Ruler who takes on the disguise of a human man

Danilla: mother of King Mathas

Darius: Prince of Samona/son of Thomas and Rewel/brother of Varden

Delilah: wife of Dieter

Delilia: Queen of New Samona/mother of Ibula, Lakin, Gael and Hadar/ wife of King Manu/Ruala

Demanko: a demon

Demetries: a demon

Denise Froush: wife of Martin who is a wealthy ship builder in Port Friada

Denks: a soldier in the army of Wetpr

Denton: one of the spies at the Castle in Wetpr

Derek: friend of Thaos

Derlock: Huta warrior

Dieter: member of the Insidiae

Dion: Princess of Samona/wife of Yorggi who was the son of Thomas and Rewel/brother of Varden

Dixon: a Taperian soldier

Dominic Petlov: was the senior High Priest at the monastery at Malga before he was murdered

Dorme: Prince of Ogg

Doros: works for High Priest Meekos

Douma: King of Ogg

Duncan: Chief of the Clan of Gesmal in Ryed/ husband of Liza

Duran: father of Nikki/Nordes Tribe

Edith: wife of Lloyd a banker in Nora

Elan: male Ruala warrior/son of Gunnel and Uma/

Eldridge: works with the Patronus

Elen: son of Andrus and Naomi/ brother of Rabi/ Ruala

Elexas: a female Nordes warrior

Elsa: female Ruala warrior/mother of Mia/wife of Tyron

Emeral: mother of Calen/Ruala

Emeric: a male Grand Master of the Insidiae

Emmet: worker for Gabriel

Emon: a male Grand Master of the Insidiae

Erebus: sorcerer from Ryed

Esser: Prince/son of Segal and Cahina/nephew of King Manu of New Samona/Ruala

Esteban: a member of the Insidiae

Esther: Queen of New Norkv/wife of rebel leader Benjeman

Fabron: Prince of Ogg

Fadil: a male Grand Master of the Insidiae

Fahra: King of Zorta

Fahron: General in the Army of Lentz

Fala: female Ruala warrior

Farnsworth: General in charge of building Fort Serpha in Wetpr

Fatima: Prince of Ryed/ son of Oren and Astrel

Fatronas: an ancient demon/one of the Old Ones

Fengu: Enrop leader who helps Gabriel and his group against Omnibus

Ferguson: a Sergeant in the Army of Lentz

Fraisier: a businessman and member of the Insidiae in Nora

Friada: King of the Kingdom of Ganz

Gabriella: sister of Marie/nurse to grandchildren of King Sudfad

Gad: male Ruala warrior

Gael: Prince/son of King Manu and Queen Delilia/Ruala

Gala: a healer from the Kingdom of Stordt

Galen: male Nordes warrior

Geoff: Prince of Lentz/son of Princess Isabella and Captain Josef

Geoff: Prince of Norkv/son of Benedict and Sasaha/grandson of Benjeman and Esther

George: an advisor for King Fahra of Zorta

George: middle son of Chief Duncan and Liza of the Clan of Gesmal in Ryed

Gita: wife of Hadi/ Ruala

Gladys: member of Nordes Tribe/ mother of Nikki

Glenda: great, great, great grandmother of Gala/ a healer from the Kingdom of Stordt

Grace: Princess of New Norkv/daughter of Benjeman and Esther

Gracie: cook for the Arthur Marcus family

Grady: worker for Gabriel

Great Ruler: God

628

Gregory Bancar: a wealthy landowner in the Kingdom of Wetpr and member of the Insidiae

Gunnel: Prince/ son of King Zachariah and Queen Noella of New Samona/husband of Uma/father of Elan/Ruala

Hadar: Prince/son of King Manu and Queen Delilia/Ruala

Hadi: son of Andrus and Naomi/brother of Rabi/Ruala

Hadu: female Ruala warrior

Hamon: one of the members of the Nordes Tribe who was injured in an attack at Snakes Crossing

Hamond: General of the Taperian Army who declares himself king

Hanger: one of the spies at the Castle at Wetpr

Hannah: physician in Nora/ Roch murdered her sister

Harold: owner of the general store in Nora

Harriet Marcus: mother of Hannah and Laurabelle/wife of Arthur

Hatus: General in the Army of Lentz/on loan to Sudfad

Hector: fighter hired by Juleta

Hector: Prince of Samona/son of Varden

Henry: and his wife Alice find Jorge in Nora

Henry: husband of Noreen/father of Jacob

Hermanas: second in command to Archetenus at Wall of Dorath

High Priest Aaron: member of the Patronus

High Priest Amos: a member of the Patronus

High Priest Barnabas: most Senior High Priest of the monastery at Leven

High Priest Caleb: member of the Patronus

High Priest Ephraim: a member of the Patronus

High Priest Gabriel: member of the Patronus/demon hunter

High Priest Gideon: a member of the Patronus

High Priest Gregory: member of the Patronus

High Priest Joseph: member of the Patronus, in charge of the Cicero Headquarters

High Priest Josiah: member of the Patronus

High Priest Meekos: priest at the monastery at Malga

High Priest Nicholas: most Senior High Priest of the monastery at Philiste and most Senior High Priest of the Patronus

High Priest Paulas: member of the Patronus

High Priest Phanuel: member of the Patronus

High Priest Philetus: member of the Patronus in charge of Malga Headquarters

High Priest Pravis: priest at the monastery at Malga

High Priest Raphael: a leader of the Patronus

High Priest Rueben: member of the Patronus in charge of Nora Headquarters

High Priest Silas: a member of the Patronus

High Priest Tenebrae: priest at the monastery at Malga

High Priest Timothy: was murdered by Meekos, Pravis and Tenebrae

High Priest Tyrus: a member of the Patronus

High Priest Uriel: member of the Patronus

High Priest Vincent: assigned to the monastery at Malga before he was murdered

High Priest Zophar: priest at monastery at Malga/ trained as a healer

Hores: son of Chief Romogi and Anda, Kingdom of Marba/Huta

Horta: Prince/son of Gunnel and Uma/nephew of King Manu of New Samona/brother of Elan/Ruala

Hunter: Prince of Samona/son of Varden

Ian: husband of Mia/ brother-in-law of Calen/ Ruala

Ibula: warrior princess and healer of the Ruala Tribe/daughter of King Manu and Queen Delilia/

Iden: warrior guarding refugees/Shettee

Igor: brother of King Sharonne

Imad: a male Grand Master of the Insidiae

Ina: daughter of Mia and Ian/ Ruala

Ingr: female warrior of Nordes Tribe

Inon: one of Cisero's men/a vessel

Ipos: an ancient demon/ one of the Old Ones

Iris: mother of Vivian/wife of Joshua/Clan of Gesmal in Ryed

Irit: daughter of Hadi and Gita/ Ruala

Isabella: Princes of Lentz, sister of Mathas, Renya and Tasha, married to Captain Josef

Isadore: wife of Fahron

Isla: female warrior of Nordes Tribe

Isla: daughter of Prince Lakin and Princess Zada/Ruala

Ivan: youngest son of Chief Duncan and Liza of the Clan of Gesmal in Ryed

Jace: husband of Oda/ brother-in-law of Calen/Ruala

Jack: member of governing body of Nora

Jackson: a private in the Army of Lentz

Jacob: boy who Angelina found in the woods

Jacot: son of Prince Lakin and Princess Zada/ grandson of King Manu/Ruala

Jaden: Sergeant in the Army of Lentz

Jago: son of Elen and Batya/ Ruala

Jake: works for Talverson Transport Company in Port Friada

Jakiv: Prince/son of Segal and Cahina/nephew of King Manu of New Samona/Ruala

Jama: Enrop leader who protects Chief Sorren's family

James: Taperian soldier

Janja: Princess/daughter of Gunnel and Uma/niece of King Manu of New Samona/ sister of Elan/Ruala

Jared: hired fighter

Jaretta: King of Stordt/husband of Queen Lillian/ father of Roch and Sudfad

Jarrod: works for Pravis/leads attack on castle in Wetpr

Jasper: Prince of Lentz/son of Princess Isabella and Captain Josef

Jatu: Enrop leader who protects Fahron's family

Jeb: friend of Thaos

Jeb: one of Cisero's men

Jela: Queen of Samona/wife of Varden

Jeremy: cousin of Andrew the jeweler in Salar

Jerik: a male Grand Master of the Insidiae

Jess: a soldier of Wetpr

Jillian: Queen of Ogg/wife of King Douma

Jinn: an ancient demon/ one of the Old Ones

Joao: male Ruala warrior

Jonas: Captain in the Taperian Army

Jorga: Princess of Ryed/daughter of Oren and Astrel/ has twin sister Andres

Jorge: a cook who is kidnapped from Endleson Hotel in Nora

Josef: Captain in the Lentz military/ married to Princess Isabella, sister of King Mathas

Joshua: father of Vivian/husband of Iris/Clan of Gesmal in Ryed

Juleta: cousin to Raul and Simon/daughter and oldest child of King Mathas and Queen Rosa

Kadin: a member of Valdore Tribe

Kagen: a man who kidnaps and exploits children

Karta: male Ruala warrior

Karzman: leader of Kozach Tribe/ stepfather of Michael

Kasper: Prince/son of Zeman and Oda/nephew of King Manu of New Samona/Ruala

Kata: Princess/daughter of Gunnel and Uma/niece of King Manu of New Samona/ sister of Elan/Ruala

Khryriss: an ancient demon/ one of the Old Ones

Kiana: Princess/daughter of Gunnel and Uma/niece of King Manu of New Samona/ sister of Elan/Ruala

Klass: Lieutenant in the Wetprian Army

Koby: male Ruala warrior

Koh: son of Prince Gael and Princess Mada/grandson of King Manu/Ruala

Kora: Princess/ married to Raphael son of King Zachariah and Queen Noella of New Samona/ mother of Luca/ Raphael and Kora were killed in battle when Luca was a small boy/Ruala

Korth: son of Tristt/Shettee

Kraus: hired fighter and intended vessel, works for Dieter

Kretcher: Commanding General of Fort Polta in Wetpr

Krister: Princess of Samoan/daughter of Thomas and Rewel

Kyra: young sister of Marie/ friend of Petra

Laban: Prince of Samona/son of Yorggi and Dion/grandson of Thomas and Rewel

Lael: daughter of Nina and Rhea/ Ruala

Lakin: Prince/son of King Manu and Queen Delilia/husband of Zada/Ruala

Lala: Princess/daughter of Adwell and Nada/niece of King Manu of New Samona/ sister of Misha/Ruala

Lana: female warrior of the Nordes Tribe

Lana: Princess/daughter of Segal and Cahina/niece of King Manu of New Samona/Ruala

Lani: daughter of Mia and Ian/Ruala

Lara: one of Usman's wives

Larson: a fighter hired by Juleta

Laurabelle: Hannah's sister who was murdered by Roch

Laurel: Annabelle's mother and former servant of King Roch's parents

Lazo: fighter hired by Juleta

Lea: Princess/daughter of Adwell and Nada/niece of King Manu of New Samona/ sister of Misha/Ruala

Leo: Prince of Samona/son of Darius and Rebek/grandson of Thomas and Rewel

Lila: seventeen year old girl who Luca saves from the Hutas/sister of Christopher

Lilian: female warrior of the Nordes Tribe

Lillian: Queen of Stordt/wife of Jaretta/ mother of Roch and Sudfad

Lily: daughter of Calen and Natasha/Ruala and human

Liza: wife of Duncan the Chief of the Clan of Gesmal in Ryed

Lloyd: banker in Nora

Loftus: Commanding General of Fort Styls

Loni: daughter of King Friada and Queen Marla of the Kingdom of Ganz

Louie: works for Talverson Transport Company in Port Friada

Luca: male Ruala warrior

Lucifer: an ancient demon/ one of the Old Ones

Luque: Prince/son of Segal and Cahina/nephew of King Manu of New Samona/Ruala

Mab: a female Grand Master of the Insidiae

Mabon: warrior guarding refugees/Shettee

Mada: Princess /wife of Prince Gael/Ruala

Madam Bular: owner of a dress shop in Port Friada

Maggie: elderly store owner in Salar

Mahon: son of King Neputa

Makalo: Prince of Norkv/husband of Grace who was the daughter of Benjeman and Esther

Malana: daughter of King Neputa

Mali: Princess of Norkv/daughter of Makalo and Grace/granddaughter of Benjeman and Esther

Maligma: an ancient demon/ one of the Old Ones

Malik: member of the Insidiae

Malus: sorcerer from Ryed

Mandrake: Taperian soldier

Manu: King of New Samona/The Chief of the Grand Council made up of Rualas and Shettees/ father of Ibula, Lakin, Gael and Hadar/husband of Delilia

Marcia: friend of Hannah's/ Roch's men murdered her family

Marcus Stephan: son of Stephan and Ingr

Margarit: daughter of King Mathas and Queen Rosa of the Kingdom of Lentz/ cousin of Raul and Simon

Margolia: girl from Nora who was sacrificed to a demon

Marie: a cook for King Sudfad and Queen Renya

Markus: a soldier in the Army of Wetpr

Marla: High Priest Meekos' housekeeper

Marla: Queen of the Kingdom of Ganz

Martha: a cook for Cerephus

Martin Froush: wealthy ship builder in Port Friada/husband of Denise

Mary: Jared's young wife who was brutally murdered by Hutas

Mata: Igor's wife

Mateo: Chief Healer of the Ruala Tribe

Mathas: King of Lentz/ brother to Queen Renya

Matilda: one of Usman's wives

Matthew: son of King Mathas and Queen Rosa of the Kingdom of Lentz/ cousin of Raul and Simon

Maxwell: father of Calen/ Ruala

Maxwell: infant son of Nina and Rhea/grandson of elder Maxwell/Ruala

Melanie: female Ruala warrior/daughter of Casey and Tasha

Melina: mother of Thaos

Melinda: grandmother of Misha

Mia: daughter of Maxwell and Emeral/ Ruala

Mia: female Ruala warrior/daughter of Tyron and Elsa

Mica: Princess of Norkv/daughter of Benedict and Sasaha/granddaughter of Benjeman and Esther

Micha: oldest son of Joshua and Iris/older brother of Vivian/Clan of Gesmal

Micha: son of King Sharonne/ grandfather of Sudfad and Roch

Michael: ancient king of Wetpr/father of Queen Sumona

Miranda: emissary of The Great Ruler who takes on the disguise of a human seer

Miriam: a friend of Hannah's/works at Endleson Hotel in Nora

Misha: male Ruala warrior/lieutenant

Molach: a member of the Insidiae

Moloch: an ancient demon/one of the Old Ones

Morris: member of governing body of Nora

Myla: wife of the owner of the Dragons Inn in Salar

Naal: warrior guarding refugees/Shettee

Nabi: male Ruala warrior

Nada: Princess/ married to Adwell son of King Zachariah and Queen Noella of New Samona/ mother of Misha/ Adwell was killed in battle leaving Nada to raise ten children/Ruala

Nadia: wife of Karzman

Naomi: mother of Rabi/ Ruala

Napo: Enrop leader who protects Claudius' family

Natasha: sister of High Priest Gabriel

Nathaniel: Sorren's oldest son/ Nordes Tribe

Nebula: son of Chief Romogi and Anda/ Kingdom of Marba/Huta

Nehmota: King of Ryed

Neputa: leader of the Shettee Tribe when it was conquered by the Hutas

Nestor: a demon that specializes in procuring things for a price

Nica: Enrop leader who protects Sudfad's family

Nicholas: orphan boy /brother of Cerey

Nicolas: Prince of Puntd/son of King Tobias and Queen Tasha

Nieatzae: an ancient demon/ one of the Old Ones

Nikki: female warrior of Nordes Tribe

Nina: daughter of Maxwell and Emeral/Ruala

Nina: youngest daughter of Karzman and Nadia

Nita: Princess/daughter of Adwell and Nada/niece of King Manu of New Samona/ sister of Misha/has twin brother Waed/Ruala

Nobel: former prince of Ryed/son of Akasha and Norah/father of Nehmota

Noella: the first Queen of New Samona/wife of King Zachariah/mother of seven sons/Ruala

Norah: former queen of Ryed/grandmother of Nehmota

Noreen: mother of Jacob/ wife of Henry

Norris: hired fighter and intended vessel, works for Dieter

Nyla: oldest daughter of Karzman and Nadia

Oda: daughter of Maxwell and Emeral/ Ruala

Oda: Princess/ married to Zeman son of King Zachariah and Queen Noella of New Samona/Ruala

Odam: male Ruala warrior

Odell: one of the spies at the Castle at Wetpr

Omar: Prince/son of Zeman and Oda/nephew of King Manu of New Samona/Ruala

Omara: Queen of Norkv/wife of Thaddius who was son of Benjeman and Esther

Omnibus: an ancient demon/ one of the Old Ones

Omoria: former queen of Ryed/wife of Nobel/mother of Nehmota

Opago: an ancient demon/ one of the Old Ones

Oren: former prince of Gandt who marries princess Astrel of Ryed

Ottillia: Princess of Lenz/daughter of Princess Isabella and Captain Josef

Padre Augustus: a member of the Patronus

Padre Bartholomew: survives the massacre at the monastery at Avaide

Padre Cornelius: a member of the Patronus

Padre Darius: a member of the Patronus

Padre Dibon: a priest at the monastery at Malga

Padre Dominick: priest at monastery at Malga

Padre Edgar: member of the Patronus

Padre Edward: a member of the Patronus

Padre Francis: priest at monastery at Malga

Padre Joram: member of the Patronus

Padre Lucas: a member of the Patronus

Padre Octavos: runs orphanage in Salar

Padre Philip: a member of the Patronus

Padre Philip: a priest at the monastery at Malga

Padre Simpson: priest at the monastery at Malga

Padre Sorben: a member of the Patronus

Padre Stephens: priest at monastery at Malga

Padre Thomas: priest at the monastery at Malga

Padre Tobias: a member of the Patronus

Padre Xavier: priest at monastery at Malga

Paj: Princess/wife of Prince Hadar/Ruala

Pata: daughter of Chief Romogi and Trina/Huta

Paul: third son of Joshua and Iris/younger brother of Vivian/Clan of Gesmal

Paulas: Sergeant under Archetenus in Taperian Army

Paulas: a man who works for Cicero/a vessel

Paullo: works for High Priest Meekos

Pearl: eldest daughter of King Tobias and Queen Tasha of Puntd

Pergo: King of the Kingdom of Gandt

Peter: Sorren's second son/Nordes Tribe

Peters: member of the governing body of Nora

Petorus: an ancient demon/one of the Old Ones

Petra: peasant boy from Ort who saves Padre Bartholomew

Philip: Prince of Puntd/ son of King Tobias and Queen Tasha

Phillip: Court Physician to the Royal Family of Wetpr

Polgate: one of the men who kidnapped Petra

Potomas: warrior guarding refugees/Shettee

Powell: a lieutenant in the Military of Lentz/stationed at Fahron's castle

Prescott: a hired killer

Rabi: male Ruala warrior

Radnor: a male Grand Master of the Insidiae

Rael: Prince of old Samona/husband of Krister who was the daughter of Thomas and Rewel

Rahi: a female Grand Master of the Insidiae

Rakio: Prince/son of Adwell and Nada/nephew of King Manu of New Samona/brother of Misha/Ruala

Rako: a male Ruala warrior

Raphael: Prince/ son of King Zachariah and Queen Noella of New Samona/husband of Kora/Ruala/father of Luca/ Raphael and Kora were killed in battle when Luca was a small boy/Ruala

Ratri: male Ruala warrior

Raul: Prince/son of King Sudfad and Queen Renya of the Kingdom of Wetpr

Raum: an ancient demon/ one of the Old Ones

Rebek: Princess of Samona/wife of Darius, who was the son of Thomas and Rewel

Renya: Queen of Wetpr/ wife of Sudfad

Rewel: Queen of Samona/wife of Thomas/mother of Varden

Rex: a notorious pick pocket in Port Friada

Rhea: husband of Nina/ brother-in-law of Calen/ Ruala

Riftca: male Ruala warrior

Roch: King of the Kingdom of Stordt/brother of King Sudfad

Rogers: one of the men who kidnapped Petra

Rolif: son of Chief Romogi and Silva/ Kingdom of Marba/Huta

Romale: member of the Insidiae

Romos: an elder of the Centras

Rosa: Queen of Lentz/wife of King Mathas

Rosalie: a dressmaker in Nora/wife of Peters

Ryan: grandson of Jeb/friend of Thaos

Sabot: member of the Insidiae

Sahil: a male Ruala warrior

Samara: wife of Tristt/Shettee

Samat: son of Chief Romogi and Silva/ Kingdom of Marba/Huta

Samos: Prince of Norkv/son of Thaddius

Sampson: oldest son of Chief Duncan and Liza of the Clan of Gesmal in Ryed

Sampson: Sergeant in the Taperian Army

Samuel: a high priest at the monastery at Malga who was murdered

Samuel: Prince of the original Samona/grandson of Thomas and Rewel

Samuel: second son of Raul and Vitomas

Sanuri: a holy man/emissary of The Great Ruler/warrior

Sar: an Enrop

Sar: male Ruala warrior

Sara: daughter of Usman

Sarah: baby granddaughter of Mathas and Rosa

Sarah: housekeeper for Claudius and Bella

Saran: daughter of Karzman and Nadia

Sasaha: Princess of the original Samona/granddaughter of Thomas and Rewel

Sasha: female warrior of the Nordes Tribe/wife of Galen

Satan: an ancient demon/ one of the Old Ones

Saunders: a Taperian soldier

Schroeder: man who works for Insidiae leader Dieter

Segal: Prince/ son of King Zachariah and Queen Noella of New Samona/husband of Cahina/Ruala

Seguna: former princess of Ryed/daughter of Akasha and Norah/ committed suicide

Selen: house keeper for Juleta

Shara: wife of Sorren/Nordes Tribe

Sharonne: King of Stordt; great, great, grandfather of King Roch and King Sudfad

Shon: son of King Fahra and Queen Sitha

Shone: Princess/daughter of Zeman and Oda/niece of King Manu of New Samona/Ruala

Sicily Bella: daughter of Stephan and Ingr

Sila: Princess of Ogg

Silva: one of Chief Romogi's three wives/Huta

Simmons: Commanding General of Fort Nir

Simon: adopted son of King Sudfad and Queen Renya of the Kingdom of Wetpr

Sinclair: King of Lentz/father of King Mathas

Sirius: works for High Priest Meekos

Sitha: Queen of Zorta

Smoking Joe: a regular patron at the Ghost Ship Tavern

Sonja: female warrior of the Nordes Tribe

Sophie: cook and servant of King Roch

Sorren: leader of the Nordes Tribe

Sporos: priest turned demon

Stephan: Captain in Army of Lentz/son of Claudius and Bella

Stiller: a fighter hired by Juleta

Stolas: an ancient demon/one of the Old Ones

Stone: hired fighter and intended vessel, works for Dieter

Sudfad: King of the Kingdom of Wetpr and brother to King Roch of Stordt

Sudfad: little Sudfad is grandson of King Sudfad

Sumona: Queen of Wetpr/wife of Alexandras/aunt of Roch and Sudfad

Syrius: a Bakken hired by Juleta

Tabeth: daughter of Fahron

Tabith: son of Tristt/Shettee

Tabitha: Princess of Lentz/daughter of Princess Isabella and Captain Josef of Lentz

Tadeo: Prince/son of Adwell and Nada/nephew of King Manu of New Samona/brother of Misha/Ruala

Tafer: a warlord who drove the Hutas out of the Kingdom of Norkv after years of wars and rebellions

Tahira: Princess of Samona/granddaughter of Thomas and Rewel

Tahira: a female Grand Master of the Insidiae

Tal: son of Oda and Jace/ Ruala

Talmai: Shettee boy who Thedes and Ibula adopt

Tambor: male Ruala warrior

Tamour: General in the Army of Lentz/on loan to Sudfad

Tanner: a Sergeant in the Army of Lentz

Tapster: a demon who works for Meekos

Tarig: a lieutenant in the Huta army

Tarin: son of King Neputa and Queen Tiara/Shettee

Taron: Prince/son of Adwell and Nada/nephew of King Manu of New Samona/brother of Misha/Ruala

Tasha: Queen of Puntd/ married to Tobias/ sister of Renya and Mathas

Tasha: female Ruala warrior/mother of Melanie/wife of Casey

Tate: a Lieutenant in the Wetprian Army

Tavin: son of Prince Lakin and Princess Zada/Ruala

Tega: housekeeper for the cabins of the captains of the Taperian Army

Tegman: soldier of Wetpr

Temark: villager of Neva

Thadddius: Prince of the new Kingdom of Norkv/son of Benjeman

Thaddies: member of Nordes Tribe/ father of Ingr

Thanatoes: an ancient demon/ one of the Old Ones

Thaos: a hired fighter

Thatcher: Prince/son of Zeman and Oda/nephew of King Manu of New Samona/Ruala

Thatus: Taperian soldier

The Lion: emissary of The Great Ruler who takes on the appearance of a lion when he is in the world of man

Thedes: warrior guarding refugees/Shettee

Thomas: King of the original Kingdom of Samona/father of Varden

Thomas: second son of Joshua and Iris/older brother of Vivian/Clan of Gesmal

Thomas: the young husband of Zoya who was murdered in Taperia

Thompson: Wetprian soldier

Thronson: one of Meekos hired killers

Tiara: Queen of Shettee Tribe when it was conquered by Hutas/wife of Neputa

Timothy: son of Fahron

Tito: member of Valdore Tribe

Titus Derek: son of Thaos and Nikki

Titus: a lieutenant in the Taperian Army

Tobart: a member of the Nordes Tribe

Tobias: King of Puntd.

Tomas: works for High Priest Pravis

Tome: a businessman and member of the Insidiae in Nora

Tomi: son of Usman the leader of the Valdore Tribe

Toomback: Huta warrior

Torance: father of Thaos

Torin: oldest son of Karzman and Nadia

Tratz: one of the men who kidnapped Petra

Travor: Taperian warrior who was injured at the Wall of Dorath

Tresdore: son of King Sharonne

Trevor: Prince/son of Zeman and Oda/nephew of King Manu of New Samona/Ruala

Tria: daughter of Oda and Jace/Ruala

Trina: one of Chief Romogi's three wives/Huta

Trina: Princess/daughter of Zeman and Oda/niece of King Manu of New Samona/Ruala

Trist: a male Ruala warrior

Tristt the Horrible: Shettee warrior

Tye: Prince of Norkv/son of Princess Grace and Prince Makalo

Tyron: male Ruala warrior/father of Mia/husband of Elsa

Tyson: Wetprian soldier

Ulger: a demon

Uma: Princess/ married to Gunnel son of King Zachariah and Queen Noella of New Samona/mother of Elan/Ruala

Umar: Prince/son of Adwell and Nada/nephew of King Manu of New Samona/brother of Misha/Ruala

Uri: son of Nina and Rhea/ Ruala

Usman: leader of the Valdore Tribe

Valor: Prince of the new Kingdom of Norkv/son of Benjeman and Esther

Vandrew: Petra's male tutor

Vania: Princess of Samona/daughter of Yorggi and Dion/granddaughter of Thomas and Rewel

Varden: last king of Samona/he and his family were murdered by rebels

Vardin: one of the men who kidnapped Petra

Vasart: Queen of Ryed/ wife of Nehmota

Vinca: Queen of Stordt, wife of Sharonne

Vincent: Prince of Ryed/son of Nehmota and Vasart

Vinus: Queen of the Kingdom of Gandt

Vitomas: Queen of Stordt

Vivian: a demon hunter from the Clan of Gesmal

Voltar: Prince of Samona/son of Darius and Rebek/grandson of Thomas and Rewel/later becomes King of Wetpr

Waed: Prince/son of Adwell and Nada/nephew of King Manu of New Samona/brother of Misha/has twin sister Nita/Ruala

Wallis: member of governing body of Nora

Wilard: Captain at Fort Polta

Willis: son of King Pergo and Queen Vinus/ Kingdom of Gandt

Xeni: a female Grand Master of the Insidiae

Yara: daughter of Nina and Rhea/Ruala

Yorggi: Prince of Samona/son of Thomas and Rewel/brother of Varden

Yori: son of Usman the leader of the Valdore Tribe

Yuri: Prince/son of Adwell and Nada/nephew of King Manu of New Samona/brother of Misha/Ruala

Zac: one of the men who kidnapped Petra

Zachariah: first King of New Samona/husband of Queen Noella/father of seven sons/Ruala

Zada: Princess/wife of Prince Lakin/Ruala

Zadok: a male Grand Master of the Insidiae

Zede: an ancient demon/ one of the Old Ones

Zehmann: an ancient demon/ one of the Old Ones

Zeman: Prince/ son of King Zachariah and Queen Noella of New Samona/husband of Oda/Ruala

Zorda: Taperian soldier injured in battle at the Wall of Dorath

Zoya: a seer from Taperia

Glossary of Terms

Aboultis: the calling cards of demons

Abyss: a vast void used to imprison demons

Acura: the whispering shadows/are in the inner circle of demons that directly serve the Old Ones

Amark: ancient language of The Great Ruler

Amulth: means filth in the language of demons/these monsters are made out of the waste of tortured souls from the hell dimensions

Anewa: one of seven continents in the World of Nunc

Aplewort: an herb when mixed with water purges poisons from a body

Asherane: ancient tribe that lived in the northern regions of the Kingdom of Lentz

Astras: the ancient underground city of the Centras

Beltrad: a species of lower level demons

Blood rings: Large red rubies set in silver with markings of the Old Ones

Boca: a covered wagon pulled by horses

Box of Itifer: a gift to the world of man from The Great Ruler; this gift affects the balance of creation

Bozie: a game of skill played by the Nordes Tribe

Cava plant: a poisonous plant that grows freely near bodies of water

Centras: ancient race of creatures who have the responsibility of protecting the Holy Box of Itifer

Chalice of Ascension: a gift from The Great Ruler, this gift contains unimaginable powers

Cicero College: in Wetpr, outside of Salar, where Raul, Simon and Hannah attended college

Clan of Gesmal: a tribe of demon hunters who live in the southern region of the Kingdom of Ryed

Crystal pillars: in the Ice Caves of Mordv/are blessed by The Great Ruler and filled with spiritual life force

Czarsta: one of seven continents in the World of Nunc

Demalogs: an inferior species of demons

Demosa: a slow acting poison from the cava plant

Diamond of Cazo: a gift from The Great Ruler, this gift can unleash powers from the center of the world

Durisks: large demonic birds/their elongated beaks contain rows of fangs

Engas: a wild cat that inhabits the Vandrew Mountains

Engor: a small pack animal that lives in trees

Enrop: a large species of bird that can speak many human languages

Farduth: a Shettee necklace that symbolizes a male has completed his rite of passage to become a warrior

Gafet: an ancient Shettee weapon

Gants: large apelike creatures/Watchers of the Caves of Muldun

Gate of Isula: the only opening in the great Wall of Dorath

Gefrey Games: games of sport where men fight each other and great beasts to the death

Grand Masters: the first people to call to the demons and invite them into this world

Great Ruler: God

Hall of Antiquities: a giant hall located in the monastery at Malga/ a sanctuary for holy items and manuscripts

Hall of Light: the Great Hall in the Ice Caves of Mordv

Hengers: giant blue eagles/ birds of war

Highland Pass: the only passage through the Rosu Mountain Range

Holy Scrolls: gifts given to each kingdom by The Great Ruler, these gifts contain powers, wisdom and immortality

Holy Vault: a secret vault under the King's study in the castle in Wetpr designed to protect holy objects

Horn of Asher: a horn used by the Patronus warrior priests to signal each other

Horn of Cass: a horn used by the Wetprian soldiers to signal each other

Horn of Cornwell: a horn used by Dieter's men to signal each other

Horn of Eel: a horn used by the Ruala warriors to communicate with each other

Horn of Esker: a horn used by the Valdore Tribe to communicate with each other

Horn of Ire: a horn carried by the Taperian soldiers to communicate with each other

Horn of Shana: a horn carried by the soldiers of Lentz to communicate with each other

Horn of Tula: a horn used by the members of the Nordes Tribe for communication

Horn of Vamont: a horn used by the Kozach Tribe for communication

Horn of Xepoltr: a horn used by the Shettee warriors to communicate

Huta: a race of humans that is driven by hatred and ideas of racial superiority who live in the Kingdom of Marba

Insidiae: means conspirators/a highly organized secret group of humans who have sold their souls to demons

Jacar: giant leech-like creatures

Jacept Plant: a plant that a powerful poison is made from

Kafer: a small crescent shaped knife carried by the Beltrad

Keepers of the Scrolls: the Royal Family of the Kingdom of Wetpr entered into a covenant with The Great Ruler to protect his gifts until a time when they can be safely given back to the world of man

Kozach: a tribe that lives in the far north central regions of the Kingdom of Wetpr

Lamsman: an ankle bracelet worn by Venatores/stones in the bracelet signify great feats they had to accomplish to become a demon hunter

Linges plant: a plant that grows in damp, swampy regions in Opots/the white berries are used to make the drug Melanwhop

Mark of Satan: a coiled red snake with green eyes and a yellow tongue

Matu potage: a food staple of the Shettee Tribe

Mayka: one of seven continents in the World of Nunc

Melanwhop: a drug made from the linges plant, causes lethargy and apathy

Mordov: the special place in hell for hypocrites

Motfer: the land of the dead

Nefandus: a secret sect within the Insidiae

Nordes: a tribe of fiercely trained warriors who live in the northern region of the Kingdom of Lentz

Nunc: the world where this story takes place

Old Ones: the original demons that came to the World of Nunc

Opatu bread: a food staple of the Shettee Tribe

Opots: one of seven continents in the World of Nunc

Oran: a tobisk that is filled with a mixture of ramni oil, buruto powder and meno salts, designed to explode on impact

Patronus: an elite group of men who serve as the protectors of the church

Porto: one of seven continents in the World of Nunc

Prostras: an ancient tribe that once inhabited the Ice Caves of Mordv

Raftifa: ancient bat-like creatures that devour human flesh

Ravens: messengers used by the dark lords

Recupero: a sect within the Insidiae that worships the demon Omnibus

Rogetts: a tribe of humans that have digressed into murderous mutant monsters

Rualas: an ancient tribe of warriors said to be half human and half bird

Salszar: one of seven continents in the World of Nunc

Salts of Envoy: a sleeping potion

Scio: a crystal ball

Scroll of Imari: a gift of The Great Ruler, a scroll that unleashes the power of the Box of Itifer

Seal of Natun: a gift from the Holy Ruler that can open doors to other worlds

Serpents of Satan: can only be called forth by dark lords and demons, large red snakes with green eyes and yellow tongues

Seven Sons Prophesy: an ancient prophesy about seven sons who stand up against the demons and dark lords

Shesone: an ancient fighting style of the Shettee Tribe

Shettee: an ancient tribe of warriors said to be half human and half lion

Solv: a specific prison within the Abyss

Song of the Second Son: an ancient prophesy about an evil that is passed between second sons of a family resulting in a monster that brings terror and darkness to the world of man

Sundra Templer: a gift from The Great Ruler that was stolen by dark lords/an orb with extraordinary powers that can be used in multiple ways such as transporting humans through other worlds

Tabutu: an ancient form of fighting developed by the Asherane Tribe of the Kingdom of Lentz

Talisman: an object with magical or supernatural meaning

Talmuth: giant red dragon-like creatures

Tangers: large wild, grazing animals that travel in herds

Tansof: one of seven continents in the World of Nunc

Telgras: a hell beast that looks like it is half wolf and half panther

Teragon: death terror/a monster created as a result of diabolical acts

Terbot bear: a bear that roams in the northern regions of the Continent of Opots

Tervator: fourteen foot monster that walks like a man with long dark hair over its entire body and bull-like horns protruding from its head

Texts of Semalia: ancient texts about demonic language and rituals

The Celebration of Days: an annual celebration of the Centras

The Hall of Understanding: the building in Astras where the history of the Centras is documented in drawings

The Hunters: another name for the Shettee Tribe

The Lion: a very powerful messenger of The Great Ruler assumes the form of a lion when he walks in the worlds of man

The thirteenth color: not seen in the world of man it is the color of horror/hell

Timbar: ghost dragons/ demons that can fly

Tinchure water: an herbal pain remedy used by the Nordes Tribe

Tincture of the Redeti Plant: Hutas dip the tips of their weapons in this insect infested liquid. The insects lay eggs inside of the victim. When the eggs are mature and hatch, two inch worm-like creatures are produced and will eat the organs of the victim causing a long and painful death

Tobisks: sphere shaped objects, metal and hollow inside that are designed to be launched from a Trebuchet

Trebuchets: wooden machines used to catapult objects

Tygrus: a ship that docked in Port Friada

Unholy altar: altar used to worship demons

Valdees: the tribe that lives in the underwater Kingdom of Ogg

Valdore: a tribe of merciless separatists who live in the extreme northern regions of the Kingdom of Lentz

Venator: means hunter in the old language

Venom of the Atha serpent: one of the poisons that Hutas put on their arrows

Vessel of Darkness: a human created from darkness to hold the essence of a powerful demon

Wall of Dorath: a giant wall that separates the Kingdoms of Norkv and Xepoltr from the Kingdom of Marba

Willimonns: small furry creatures that are hunted for food and sport

Xelope: the oneness of spirit with all that lives

Zendoti: demons that are distinguished by the geometrically shaped tuffs of hair that protrude from their heads

Glossary of Maps

The maps are displayed in order of relevance

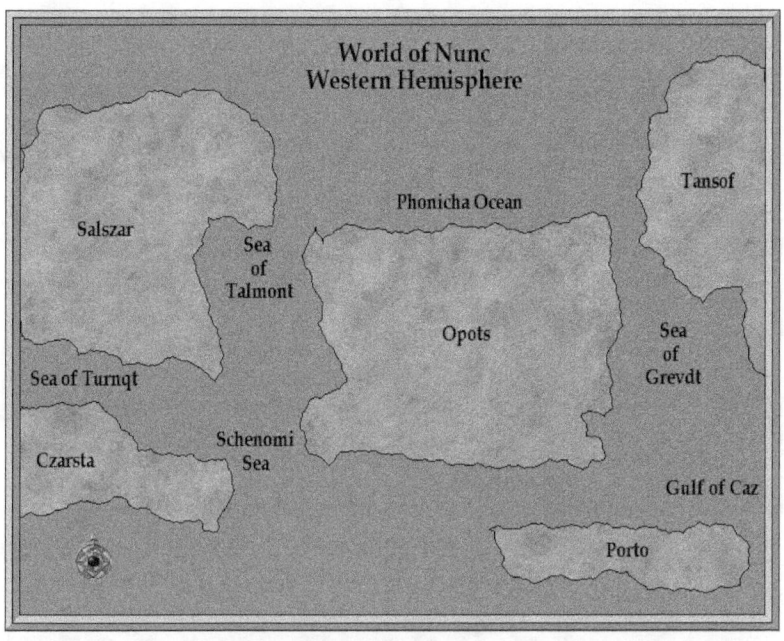

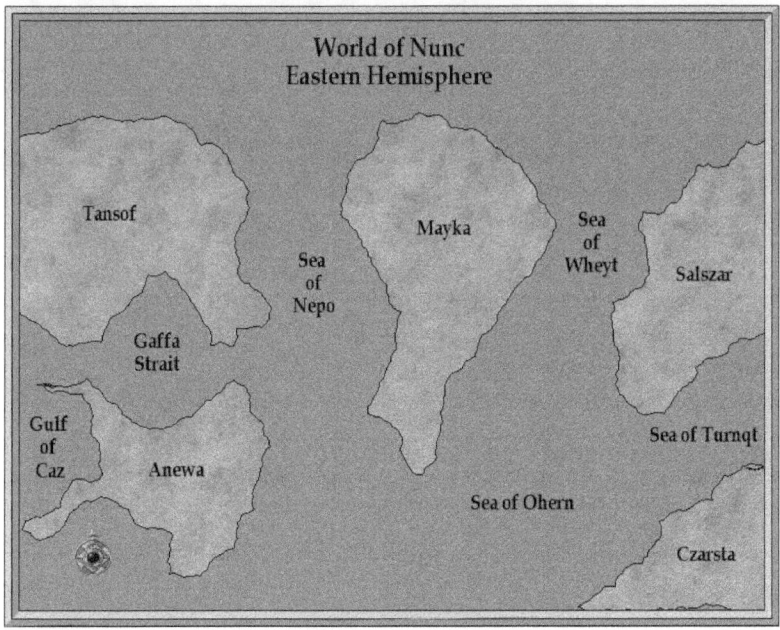

Continent of Opots

658

Western Stordt

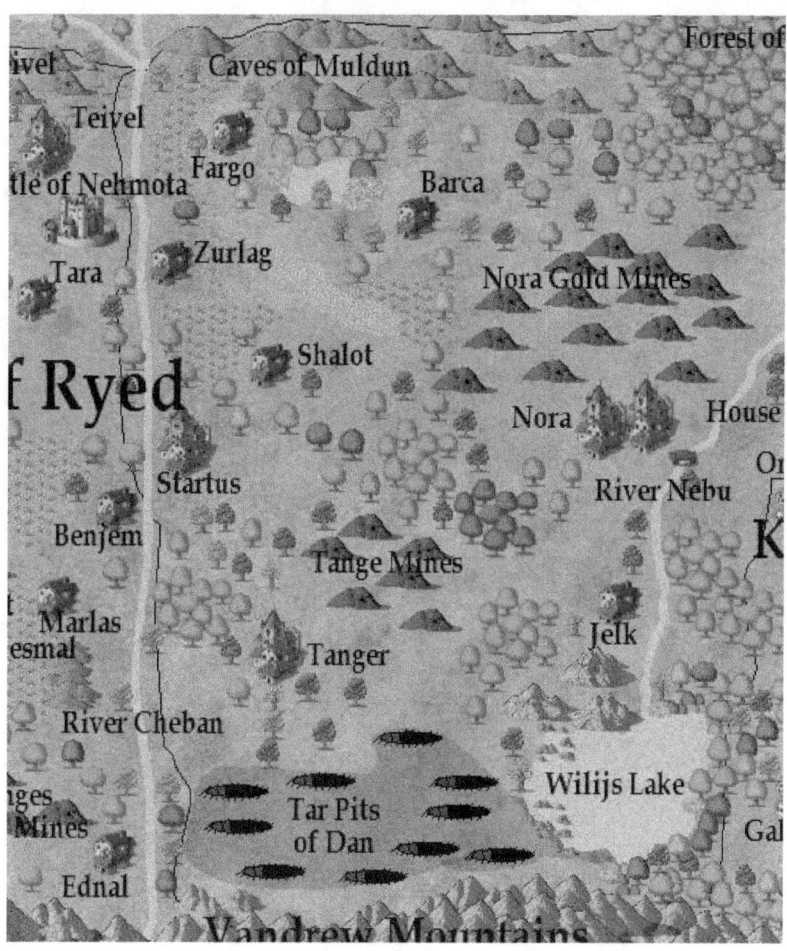

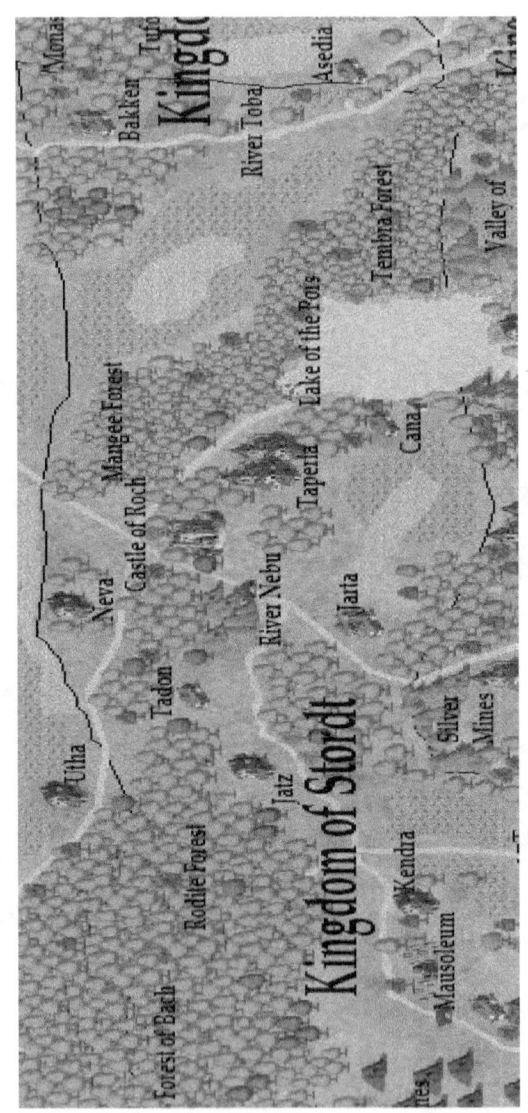

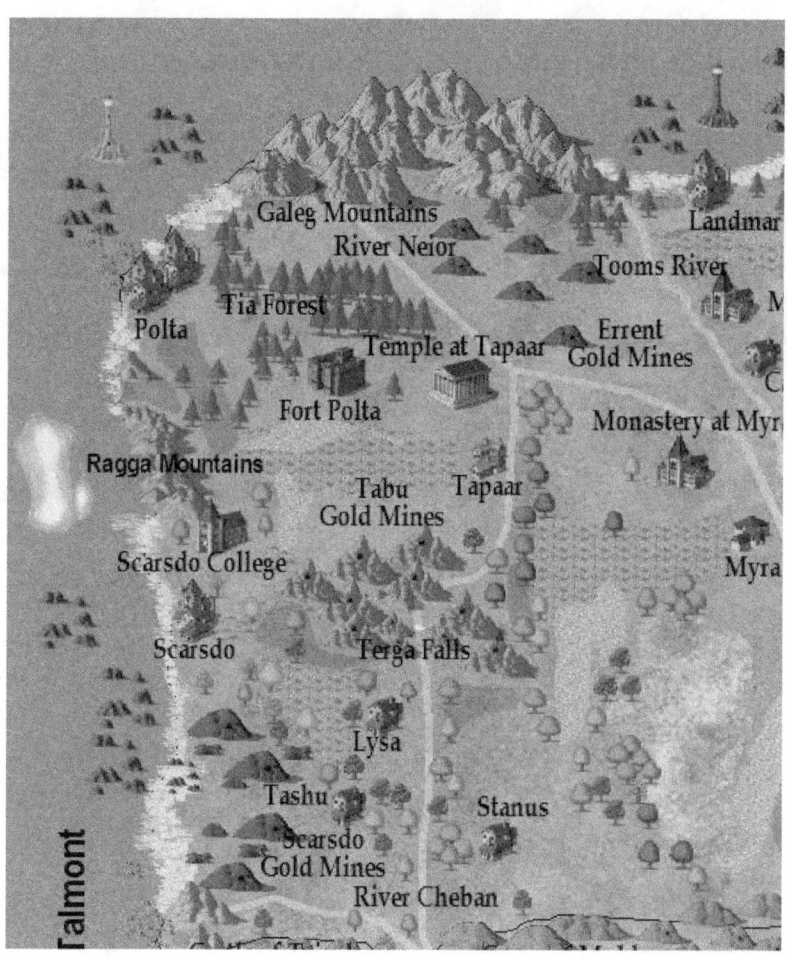

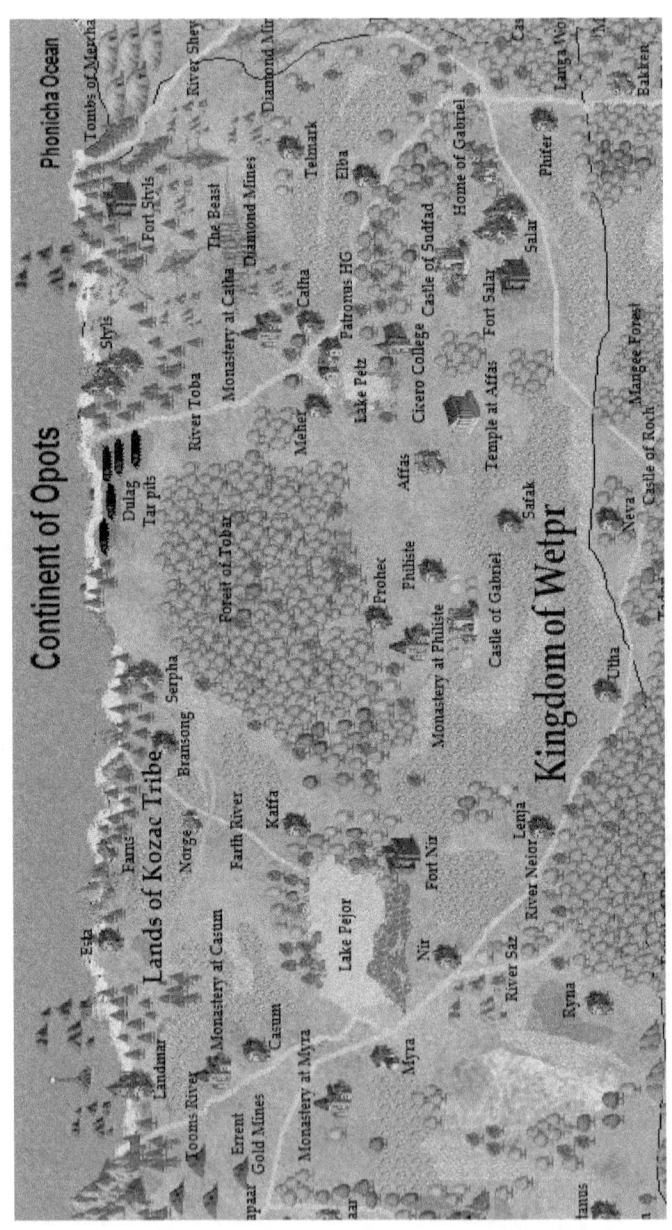

663

Marba

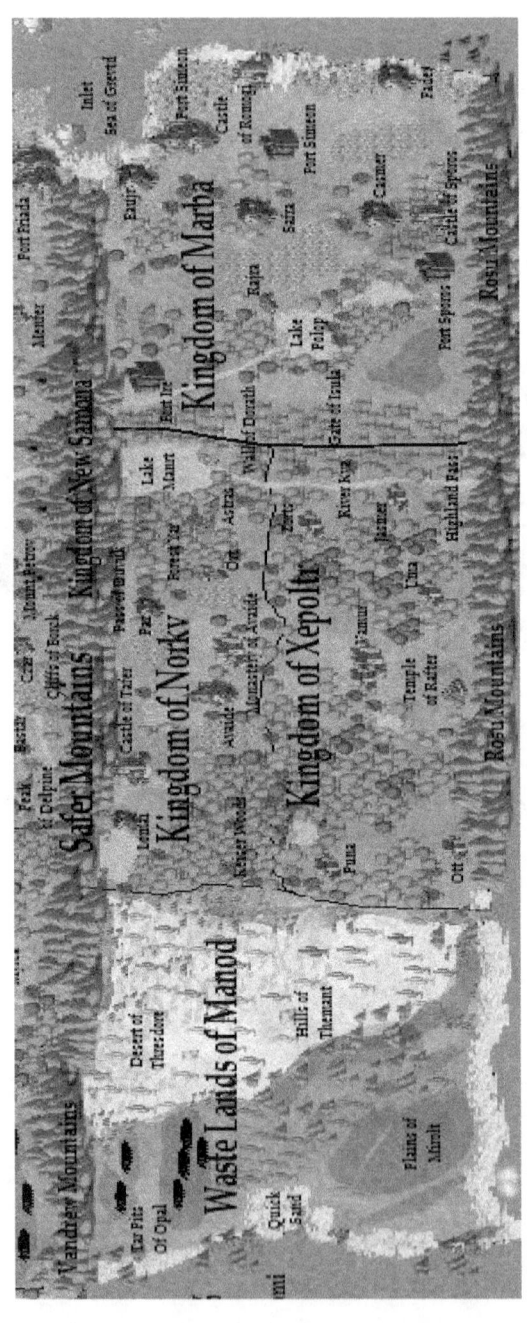

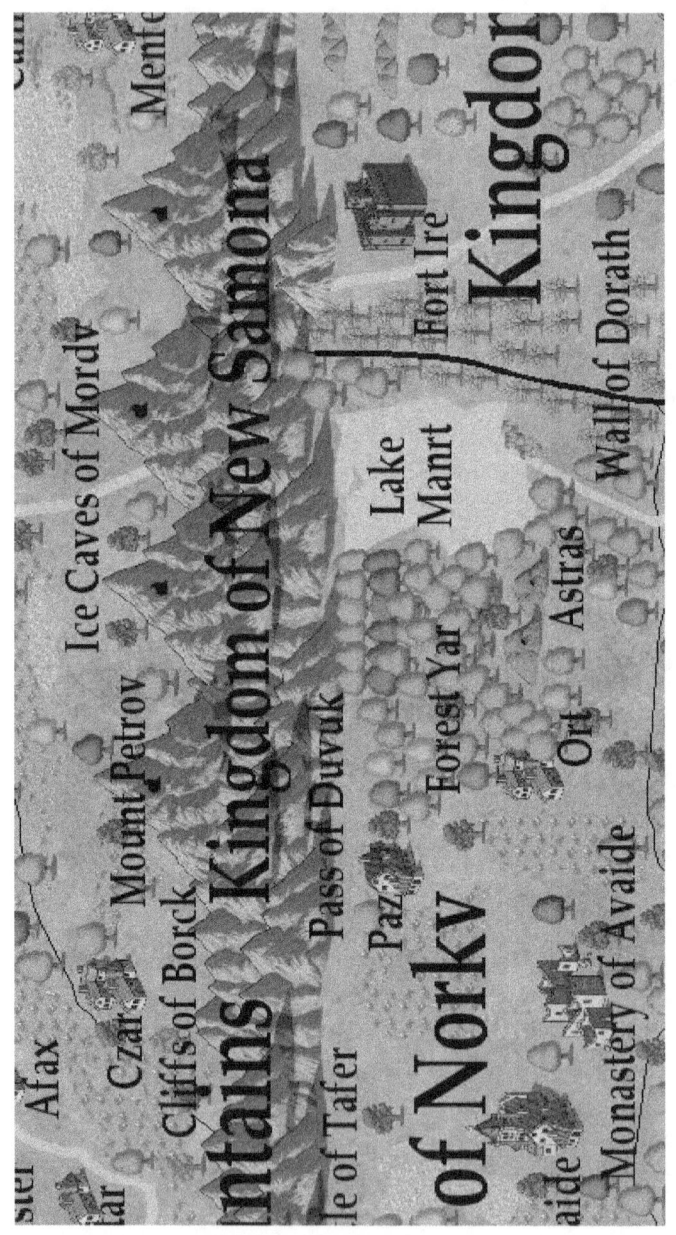

www.ingramcontent.com/pod-product-compliance
Lightning Source LLC
Chambersburg PA
CBHW052339020726
47503CB00001B/25